LIFE OF THE PARTY

christine anderson

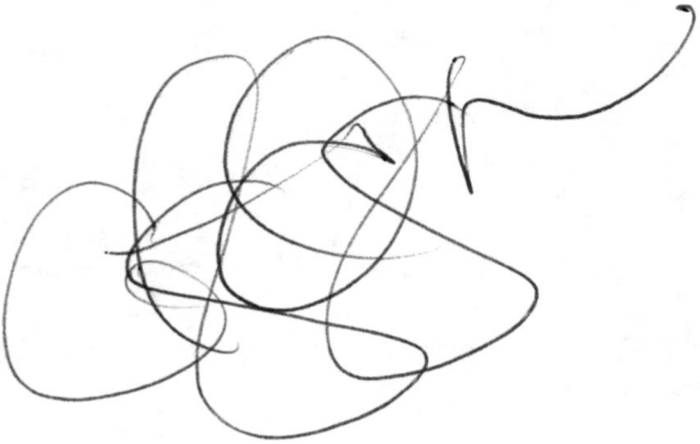

iUniverse, Inc.
Bloomington

Life of the Party

iUniverse books may be ordered through booksellers or by contacting:

iUniverse
1663 Liberty Drive
Bloomington, IN 47403
www.iuniverse.com
1-800-Authors (1-800-288-4677)

ISBN: 978-1-4502-7181-3 (pbk)
ISBN: 978-1-4502-7182-0 (cloth)
ISBN: 978-1-4502-7183-7 (ebk)

Library of Congress Control Number: 2010916420

Printed in the United States of America

iUniverse rev. date: 11/18/10

For the one who will always love me,
even though I will never deserve it

The world can be a dangerous place.
I dove headfirst into that world; one I knew
nothing about, but with the arrogance of
youth assumed some control over.
I almost drowned.
I would've drowned, had he not saved me.

This is my story ….

CHAPTER 1

On the morning that this story begins, my father was peering at me over his newspaper, watching in disgust as I sprinkled yet another spoonful of sugar on my grapefruit.

"I think that defeats the purpose, Mac." He grinned. The look I gave him was as sour as the fruit.

"It's gross." I replied.

"Mac." My mom frowned as she bustled about the kitchen. "You'll give yourself a cavity. What's the matter? You always liked grapefruit."

I had no answer for this, stabbing at the poor fruit with my spoon instead. Mom shook her head and yawned. She had just walked in the door from another nightshift at the hospital and was probably in no mood to deal with me. She poured herself a coffee instead.

I pushed the fruit aside as my father shook his head and returned to his paper. My black nail polish was chipping. I sat back and picked at it.

"You know Mac; it's supposed to be a really hot day," Mom eyed my hoodie, "maybe you want to wear something lighter. What about the skirt I got you?"

"I don't do skirts, mom. You knew that when you bought it for me." Of course she did, but the fact that I didn't dress up all pretty for school bothered her. She felt inclined to leave these none too subtle hints upon my bed from time to time, skirts and trendy shoes and button up blouses. They all became smunched into a pile in the back of my closet, which really isn't saying much because even my preferred clothes ultimately ended up that way. It's not that I don't care about my appearance, I'm not a grunge or anything, but I'm not into the valedictorian-wear my mom feels is necessary. My typical outfit involved blue jeans, some sweet t-shirt, a hoodie, and any kind of dark skater shoes that made my size nine feet look at least two sizes smaller. Today I was wearing my favourite shirt, a dark blue Three Stones sweater with orange cuffs on the sleeve and a flaming fireball emblazoned on the front. I knew she hated it.

"I'm wearing a shirt." I informed her. She sighed and nodded curtly, yawning into her cupped palm.

"So, Mac." My father set his paper down. "How goes the job search?"

I scoffed and rolled my eyes. "This again?"

"Yes, this again. You're seventeen years old with no plans for higher education. You can live here, that's fine, but not for free. You're plenty old enough to get a job. When Marcy was your age—"

"I'm well aware of Marcy's fantasticness, thank you." I interrupted him. I turned my focus from him to the ends of my long, curly dark hair, pretending to look for split ends. I hoped he'd get my hint. He didn't.

"Well, fine. I've leaving town until Saturday. When I get back, I'd like to have some answers. Maybe you could get a job at the hospital. Are they still hiring, Deb?"

"Oh, there's always work." Mom perked up. "You may have to Candy-Stripe at first, but that always looks good on a resume. Do you want me to speak to Doug for you, Mackenzie?"

I looked at their hopeful faces incredulously. There was no way in hell I'd volunteer to clean up after a bunch of sick people. "Uh … we'll see." I answered. I was saved then by the loud, off key baap of a car horn out front.

"Oh, Riley's here." I said with relief. "I gotta go."

Mom made her face then, almost on cue, the face that makes its appearance whenever Riley's name is mentioned. It's not that she hates him exactly, but she feels I could do with better friends, a bunch of girl friends preferably. Also, she considers Riley the boy from the "wrong side of the tracks." I like to remind her from time to time that Riley and I only met because we lived next door to each other for years while my mom was still in school, before my parents became "established." Apparently she forgets that, and the fact that she and Riley's mother used to be very, very good friends. Until we moved into a new house in a new neighbourhood, that is.

I rolled my eyes at her and waved absently to my father.

"Alright, bye." Nothing annoyed me more than "the face." I grabbed the books that I brought home last Friday, and hadn't touched since, on my way out the door.

Riley's car was a sight. It was giant, purple and rusty, with red velour upholstery and a beaten up dashboard, but it was my chariot to freedom. My first sincere smile of the day was given for his benefit as I hastened happily towards his car.

"Hey man." I sank into the front seat beside him.

"Hey." He said warmly. He sat back in the seat and gazed at me for a minute.

"What?" I asked abruptly.

"Nothing." He decided, pulling the car into the road. I shrugged and lit my cigarette, taking that first precious drag and blowing the smoke satisfyingly out the window. I felt the tension melt away.

"So," he sounded nervous. "That was some party, hey?"

"Oh, yeah." I groaned. "I felt so sick yesterday."

"Is that why you didn't call?"

"I guess so. Why, did I say I would?"

"Yeah."

"Oh, sorry."

"No problem."

We rode in silence for a moment, and I gazed at Riley through the corner of my eye. He was acting very strange. I had known the guy since we were in kindergarten, and such a close relationship enabled me to know instantly when something was amiss. He was without a doubt my best friend in the whole world, better than any girlfriend I'd ever had, someone who really understood me and didn't judge me and someone I could have tons of fun with without having to worry about the petty, trivial shit that accompanies most high school relationships. We were totally accepting of each other, no matter what.

Riley looked different today. His hair was dark, short, messy curls, but today I detected some kind of styling product in it. He was wearing his good Darkstar shirt too, the one he usually saved for going out on the weekends. I leaned closer and took a whiff, inhaling the deep scent of men's cologne.

"… Mmm. You smell good today, Ry. Alright, who's the girl?" I smiled conspiratorially. He was too easy to figure out.

"What do you mean?"

"Come on, tell me. Who's the girl you're so dolled up for?"

"Um … I don't know … Mac, how much did you have to drink the other night?"

"Ohhhh …." I groaned again. "So much. Too much. I can remember up until the Quaalude and then it's all just a black patch in my memory." I laughed. "Why, did you hook up with someone? Oh, I'm so pissed I can't remember. Don't make me guess, just tell me who it was."

"It was … it was nobody." He mumbled. "No one you know."

"Oh really? Was she hot?"

"Yeah, she was."

"Really? Oh …." I laughed and groaned. "Who brings 'ludes to a party anyway? This isn't nineteen seventy-four and we're not in California."

"You need to be careful with that shit." Riley warned as he turned a corner. "Mixing that stuff with alcohol can mess you up."

"Right, like you can talk." I accused. "Mr. E. I'm surprised your heart still works."

"Not only does it work, my heart could out-beat your heart any day."

I laughed with him and sunk back into the seat, glad that he had relaxed.

"So, are you going to introduce me to her then?"

"No, I'm not."

"What?" I pretended to be upset. "Why not?"

"You know why, Mac." Riley shook his head and shot me a sideways glare. It was true, I did know why. Something seemed to come over me every time Riley had a girlfriend … not exactly jealousy but … possession almost. I've tried to be a good supportive friend and accept his new relationships, but I can't help myself. As soon as he and his girl of choice become "official," I panic at the thought of losing my best friend to the claws of a she-devil that will occupy all his time and energy. My fear is that one day he will become so enamoured with one of these girls that I'll be out of the picture indefinitely. And it's not like I want him for myself; Riley is like my brother. But I don't want him with anyone else either.

Super selfish, yep, that's me. I looked over at Riley and smiled. He was good looking; I couldn't blame the girls for wanting him. And he was special, to me anyway. He was loyal and caring, one of the good ones. I guess I knew it was only a matter of time before he did meet someone that replaced me as the #1 female in his life—next to his mom of course—but I wanted to avoid that for as long as possible.

I shrugged and changed the subject. "Man, Mitch won't get over this whole job kick he's on." I complained. "I'm supposed to make up my mind by Sunday when he gets back. They actually mentioned me taking a job at the hospital. Could you imagine?" I scoffed.

"Why don't you sell insurance like your dad?" Riley joked.

"Yeah. That'll be the day." I rolled my eyes. "Do you think he has a bunch of affairs when he travels? He's gone nearly every week."

"You're reaching, Zee. Your parents have the perfect marriage and you know it."

I shrugged again.

"You could get a job at the restaurant." Riley offered. "They're always hiring there."

I laughed outright. "Yeah, okay. The only place worse than the hospital would be a restaurant. I don't know how you do it. Customer service? No thanks."

"What do you want to do then?"

"I don't know." I flicked my cigarette out the window. "Be a bum? Laze around?"

Riley laughed. "But how would you support all your habits?"

"Well, my dear, that's what I have you for." I batted my eyes at him charmingly.

Riley smirked and pulled into the student parking lot. I groaned automatically, eyeing the ominous red brick school building with much disdain.

"Two more months, right?"

"Two more months, yep." He nodded. "Then we're done forever."

"I can't wait."

"I know." He turned off the ignition. "Two months until sweet, sweet freedom."

Sweet, sweet freedom. I thought of this mid-math class, smiling in anticipation of the thought. The teacher was droning on and on about quadrants or something or other, and I half-listened with my head curled into my arms, doodling randomly on the loose-leaf pages in my binder. Mr. Lemmon noticed my disregard for his teaching; I know he did, but he'd given up trying. I could always sense the disappointment that emanated from my teachers whenever their gaze came to rest upon me. I think for a moment they picture the freshman I had once been, chubby and fresh faced, dressed in the pretty clothes her mother bought, eager and willing, hand raised needle-straight in the air whenever a question was posed. Just another Marcy in the making. Now, their heads shake sadly at what might have been and their eyes roam past me, on towards someone who might actually live up to their potential. Not that this bothers me. It took years to convince them I wasn't anything special and unworthy of the effort. Now we'd finally reached an understanding—they leave me alone for the most part and I try not to fail their exams. No more honour roll hopes here, only the bare minimum of effort.

I'm not sure what happened to me. There's no defining moment in my life that separates the good girl I used to be from what I've become. It was like a gradual transformation, and one day I realized that I just didn't care anymore. I started living to please myself instead of everybody else, and realized there's more to life than school and studying and going to college to get a good job and make the most money possible. There's fun, friends … life outside of how we're told to live. Basically, I just started rebelling.

And I've loved every minute of it.

"Quit hogging that, jerk." I slapped Riley playfully on the arm and stole the joint from his outstretched fingers. "Puff, puff, pass … ring a bell?" Riley laughed and coughed as the smoke poured from his mouth.

"I'll ring your bell." He promised. I giggled at his empty threat, feeling a heaviness settle into my eyes, a giddiness creep into my belly. I leaned back against the windshield of his car, inhaling deeply and staring into the cerulean blue summer sky. School was out for the weekend, and to celebrate as we always did Riley and I drove to the outskirts of town, parking in an old abandoned farmyard littered with crumbling barn-wood buildings, tucked well out of the way down a lone dirt road.

We lay on the hood of his car, basking in the warm sun, listening to Dr. Dre through the car speakers and getting as high as we could.

"So," I exhaled the thick smoke, wincing to keep from coughing. "What's up for tonight? What do you want to do?"

"I don't know." Riley took the joint from my fingers as I got to work rolling another. "Ben's parents are gone for the weekend. We could head over there."

I thought about that a moment and shrugged. "We do that every weekend. Its fun, don't get me wrong, but I'm in the mood for something else."

"What, you don't want to get high and watch *Half Baked* again?"

"Please, I could recite that movie by heart." I giggled. "What else could we do?"

"Not much to do, here."

"Yeah." I agreed. The town we lived in was the largest in the district, but still painfully rural. There were no theatres, no malls, and no pool halls. Until we turned eighteen, the most exciting activity to be had was the small bowling alley that offered Glow Bowling every Saturday night. It was fun for a while, but now mostly inhabited by fifteen and sixteen year olds trying weed for the first time.

"I wish we were eighteen." I complained. There were an abundance of clubs, pubs and bars in our little city, but none of them could be enjoyed by either of us for months, a time we were eagerly anticipating.

"I know. Only three more months for me, but you've got all summer." Riley puffed thoughtfully. "But, you know, a guy I work with is playing at the Aurora. He's got an in with the bouncers, I bet if I called him we could get in."

"Really? What do you mean playing? Like the jazz flute or what?"

Riley laughed. "No. Like his band is playing. Rock music. It'd be something different."

"Really? I've never been to a club before." I giggled excitedly. "Can we go? Do you want to?"

Riley smiled and whipped open his phone. He slid off the hood and dialled, pacing through the tall grass along the length of the car, talking and laughing and saying, "Dude" every other word. I rolled my eyes and laughed.

"Are we good?" I asked when finally he hung up.

"Golden. I just talked to my buddy." He slid back onto the hood. "Do you want something, for tonight?"

This was where Riley's wrong side of the trackiness came in handy. He had connections, and he could get any drug at anytime, whatever he wanted. I bit my lip and thought.

"I don't know. What are you getting?"

"Uh … I was thinking of getting some mush maybe. Get my zoom on. Want?"

"No." I shook my head. "No thanks. Maybe … maybe I'll try some E."

"E? Are you sure? You've never had it before."

"Yeah. I don't know, it looks like fun. And you take it like … with every meal. It can't be that bad."

"It definitely doesn't feel bad." He admitted. "Alrighty then. Your wish is my command." He flipped his phone open again and hopped back off the car. I didn't mind his attention deficit too much as this left the remainder of the joint to me. I took my time smoking it, feeling my eyes redden and my tongue turn pasty. I watched Riley while he hung up his phone and dialled again, calling the rest of our friends to extend the invite. They were all in, it seemed, and I eavesdropped on the plans to meet them at the Aurora at nine o'clock.

"Get a table, have some drinks." Riley explained to me, hanging up his phone one last time.

"Sounds good to me … dude." I laughed, thoroughly, impossibly stoned by then. He laughed at me, which only caused me to laugh harder, and so on, until we were both giggling soundlessly and ridiculously. It was one of those moments where everything is right in the world. The grasshoppers sung lazily around us, hidden in the unkempt prairie grass that shimmered blue and green in the gentle breeze. We were young, high, happy, and laying beneath a perfect blue sky with the sun hot above. The air nearly hummed with anticipation, the realization that endless possibilities lay ahead of us, each of them offering nothing but freedom, excitement and abundant happiness. I grinned, lit a cigarette, and shut my eyes.

I would take all they had to offer.

CHAPTER 2

"Come on Mackenzie." Riley grasped my hand tightly and led me through the jostling crowd crammed into the Aurora. I followed him, a little overwhelmed by the bombarding stimulation. Random neon beer signs hung on the fabric walls, which were nearly shaking in time with the explosive bass pumping from the speakers. A thick haze of smoke hung suspended in the air, circulated only by the movement of the people that had to push to get around one another. Cigarette butts littered the floor, which was in parts sticky, in other parts wet and slimy. High pedestal tables lined the central dance floor and the walls were bordered with ripped vinyl booths. Everywhere there were people, some disgustingly drunk, others just to the rowdy point, still others looking around timidly as they sipped their water … obvious designated drivers. Riley squeezed us through this crush until we finally made it to the booth table where our friends had already congregated.

"Hello boys." I smiled as we approached. They shoved over to make room, Ben, Jacob, Toby and some random girl I'd never met. I nodded at her and sat down, a little disappointed she was there. I loved being the only girl in a crowd of guys. They were all my closest friends, nothing sexual at all, but it made me feel special to be one in their crowd. I loved guys. Girls were so hormonal, so emotional and petty. Never had one of my guy friends given me the silent treatment or spread a rumour behind my back. I could trust them completely.

"Hey, this is Charlie," Ben introduced. I swept my eyes over her quickly and decided I didn't like her. She was blond and thin and pretty and had a cool name. I smiled briefly and took off my jacket, feeling the need to expose some more skin, just to even things up. I'd never been comfortable in tiny little halter-tops like the one Charlie was wearing, but my black *Cry-Baby* t-shirt was a child's size, hugging me in just the right places, showing a decent amount of my flat stomach and a newly acquired bellybutton ring. My jeans hung low on the hip, silver hoops hung from my ears and I had applied plenty of dark eyeliner and lip-gloss. My long hair was up in a high, messy ponytail due to hairspray and plenty of backcombing. I looked good, at least; I felt like I did.

"What's up, what's up?" Toby grinned, compliments of the mushrooms he and Riley had taken earlier. His pupils were large and dark in the dim light.

"Not much. How are you doing now, my friend?" I asked knowingly.

"Hooo … whoa …." He shook his head of unruly dark hair. "Good. I'm good."

"How about you, Jacob?"

"Better now. You're looking hot, Mac." He nodded. I smiled my gratitude. Another reason I liked guys better.

"You are." I winked slyly at him. Then Riley slid onto the seat next to me, settling himself in before he slipped something into my hand.

"Here. After you take it, drink only water. Understand?"

"Oh. Okay." I nodded, like a child taking instruction from a parent. I felt the small round pill in my palm and excitement surged in my stomach. This was going to be the best night ever. It was early for a bar to be so packed, bespeaking of the band's fame, and the crowd was loud and unruly, here to party. The music blared over the speakers—some fast, synthesised dance song that only added to my stimulation. I watched the people coming and going, ordered a rye and Coke from the waitress and just took in the scene, a huge grin upon my face, happy to be there partying with my friends.

Riley glared at me as the waitress shoved a jug in my direction, his brown eyes lost in the immense width of his pupil. He watched me take a drink.

"I told you no booze." He demanded.

"But I haven't taken it yet." I had to yell to be heard.

"Take it now. No more of these." He grabbed the drink from my hand and replaced it with a glass of water. I hesitated a moment, as I always did before taking anything illicit and mind-altering. For some reason I had to weigh the consequences, but even if they were potentially severe, inevitably I would take whatever it was. I was seventeen, and invincible, and ready for a good time, eager and willing to experience everything life had to offer. I smiled at Riley and shrugged, popping the ecstasy into my mouth and tasting the chemically chalk before washing it down with a big gulp of water. I opened my mouth wide, showing him it was all gone. He grinned at me, and then leaned in to whisper.

"Don't go anywhere without telling me. Okay?"

"Okay." I agreed. It touched me when Riley was like this, when he took care of me. I smiled warmly at him. "You either."

He nodded and drank from my rye. To me it seemed that the crowd was reaching a fevered pitch, but as time went on, it all became a blur. I was aware of myself, unconsciously chain smoking, grinning from ear to ear in my comfortable seat at the back of the table. The music was pumping, into my soul it seemed, the lights beckoned me, the rhythm washed over me. I felt gloriously, deliriously happy, like there was a pent-up energy within me that needed to be expelled and could only do so in the form of radiating euphoria.

"How you feeling, Mac?" Riley leaned over to me once. I looked at him and smiled with all the love in my heart.

"I love you Riley. I love you." I professed emphatically. He looked surprised at first, but then after a moment he laughed sheepishly.

"Yeah. E will do that to you."

He was right. I think I even told Charlie I loved her at least once. But I did—at that moment I loved each and every person near me with all my heart. Everything was perfect, the lights, the music, the people surrounding me, the dance floor ....

"Riley, let's dance." I decided suddenly. It was the best idea I'd ever had, or so it felt.

"Zee, I don't really ...."

"No, come on." I stood and grasped his hand, forcing him to follow me. The crowd was no longer overwhelming as I shoved our way through, reaching at last the cramped little dance space with the coloured block floor. I stared at the changing colours in awe until Riley shook me out of my trance. Laughing we started to dance, closely, compelled by the tight crowd to move even closer together. Papa Roach rocked over the speakers, and as we danced, I shut my eyes, felt the music, felt the heat from the people around me. My hips swayed, my arms rose in the air, my hair hung damp around my face. Eventually I opened my eyes, and Riley was stock-still, staring at me. I couldn't discern the look on his face, and it nearly alarmed me to sobriety.

"You okay, Ry?"

"Yeah, I just … I need … I can't wait, Mackenzie … I have to talk to you."

I shut my eyes again, I couldn't help it. It felt so good to dance, so freeing.

"Can we talk later, Riley?"

"No. Mac—" He was interrupted then by the sudden cheering of the crowd. The music was cut, and the change in pace startled me aware again. The band had taken their place on the stage and try as he might, Riley could not be heard over the excited throng pressing their way to the front.

"Come with me." He mouthed, grabbing my hand and pulling me along with him. I complied happily as we weaved our way through the people, but when the band started playing it became nearly impossible for us to move. I could tell Riley was agitated as he ran his hands through his dark hair. I stopped and lit a smoke, meaning to offer it to him as a means to calm him down—he was on mushrooms after all, and it was crowded—but when I looked up then I forgot everyone and everything around me.

He was so beautiful. And it wasn't just the E talking. I actually heard myself gasp at the sight of him. His jeans were ripped and tightly hugged his thighs, spread apart below a sleek red guitar. Deft fingers skimmed across the strings, strumming, picking, changing chords. His hands were tanned and dark; his arms tattooed and muscled, his torso covered by a dark black t-shirt, tight enough to hint at the firm chest beneath. His hair was dark and short and messy, his cheeks stubbled and tan, his face passionate as he crooned into the microphone. He was the hottest guy I had ever seen. Not in a pretty boy way, but in a motorbike riding, bad boy kind of way. It wasn't just that he had model looks or anything; it was the way his face contorted as he screamed into the mike, the unbridled passion with which he sang.

I had to have him. My eyes remained upon his form even as Riley continued to drag me through the crowd. I allowed him to pull me back to our table, but would go no further, refusing to do anything but watch my dream man sing.

"Who is that Riley?" I asked, transfixed.

"Who?"

"The singer."

Riley looked up, then back at me quickly, his face showing alarm. "Why?"

"Because I want to know."

He sighed. "That's Grey. That's the guy I work with."

"Grey." I repeated in a breathless whisper. "Like the color grey?"

"I don't know. Can we go Mac? I need to talk to you."

"Can you introduce me to him?"

"What? Sure—whatever—just … just hold on …." Riley searched through his pockets until he located his vibrating cell phone. He held up his hand.

"I have to take this. I'll be right back." His tall form disappeared then, through the crowd in the direction of the exit. I turned my full attention back to the gorgeous man onstage, realizing as I did so that many other females felt the same way. Some were practically salivating as they stared, others were debating taking their shirts off, I could tell. Though their music was actually good, I suddenly understood why the band Serpentine had such a good turn out.

I sat down at the table, lights dancing before my eyes. The ecstasy was a good, good thing. I leant against Toby, trying to seem aloof and casual even though my eyes were glued to Grey—watching—memorizing every move he made. The boys around me were rowdy and entertaining, so I sat back and laughed with them, perfectly satisfied gazing at my dream man as he screamed into the microphone. The fact that so many women wanted him only made me want him more.

"You okay, Mac?" Toby wondered.

"Yeah, I'm good." I smiled. "You?"

"Whoooh. I'm good, but man, these mushrooms are intense."

"Oh yeah? In a bad way?"

"No. Good, in a good way."

"Okay." I leaned back against him. "Good."

We sat and watched and laughed until the band's set had ended. I blinked in disappointment as the lights dimmed and they made their way off stage. Only then did Riley return. He looked slightly pale, his face wore a sheen of sweat and his eyes darted rapidly. I sat up as he approached.

"You okay Ry?" I wondered. He didn't look okay. "What took you so long?"

"Oh, nothing. Yeah, I'm good, I'm good. Some guys called and needed some stuff." He explained, sitting next to me. I could practically feel the heat radiating from his body. He sniffed and wiped at his nose.

"What stuff, Ry? You don't look so good." I didn't need him to answer. I had my suspicions.

"Nothing." He answered tersely.

"Okay … well, do you want to talk or what?"

"Yeah." Riley cleared his throat. "Let's go—oh, hey man, how's it going?" He asked then, going through the motions of an elaborate handshake with whoever stood next to him. "Here, have a seat."

Then strong arms were rested on the tabletop beside, leather-studded bracelets upon the wrist, a beer in the hand. To my delight, the owner of those limbs was none other than Grey, who proved even handsomer up close. His eyes were dark blue and fathomless and his lips were full and brooding. Cool and detached, as if he were completely indifferent to what was going on around him, even his smile was apathetic, guarded almost. I leaned forward with rapt attention.

"Sorry man, I missed most of your show. But what I heard was good." Riley apologized. Grey nodded.

"I heard it all. And it was awesome." I interjected, throwing Grey an inviting smile. He glanced briefly at me and shrugged, turning his attention back to Riley.

"Something tells me you're responsible for the blackness of her eyes." Grey chuckled slightly and tilted his beer against his lips.

"Yeah." Riley muttered.

"It explains why I liked your band so much, anyway," I was blatantly eavesdropping, but shamelessly holding out my hand to him. "Forgive Riley's rudeness. I'm Mackenzie."

"Mackenzie." Grey hesitated a moment, then grasped my hand in his. The contact was brief, but his palm was warm, his touch electrifying. "Grey."

"Grey." I repeated slowly. Never had I been so attracted to someone. He was strong and rugged and rough, a total man in every sense of the word. Suddenly I wanted to know everything there was to know about him, and I wanted him to know me … to know every part of me. If there was such a thing as love at first sight, I think it happened to me right then.

"Why don't you come join me in the VIP? I've got …." Grey's voice became inaudible then as he spoke with Riley. I leaned forward but could not make out the rest of their conversation, which meant they were talking about drugs. Drugs or some girl. I frowned at that thought.

"Well, actually, we were about to …." Riley sat back and turned to me. His face was completely pale now. "We were just about to leave."

"Oh, no. We can stay. I'd love to stay, wouldn't you?" I smiled hopefully at my friend. "Ry, we can talk later, can't we? Come on, VIP!"

Riley didn't answer for a moment, just looked at me—his eyes wide, his expression wary. He looked sweaty and worried about something. Then he shook his head.

"You know what? Forget about it." He stood and slapped Grey on the shoulder. "Take care of her, Grey. I'm out of here."

"Wait, Ry!" I exclaimed, and he paused—his eyes cold, his face tense. "You're not leaving? Stay and hang out."

"No." He avoided my eye contact. "I'm going to go. Stay. Have fun."

"But …." I tried to protest, but he was already gone, swallowed up by the crowd. I turned to Grey in disbelief.

"I don't know what's up with him. It's not like him at all. Do you know?"

"Nah." Grey shook his head nonchalantly and peeled the label off his beer bottle. "He looked kinda twitchy. Maybe a bad trip."

"Do you think he'll be okay? Should I go with him?"

Grey shrugged noncommittally.

I frowned in doubt as Toby tapped me on the shoulder.

"Mac, I guess we're heading out. Coming?" He asked.

I was torn. I desperately wanted to go to the VIP with Grey—even though I wasn't really invited or sure he wanted me there—but Riley was acting so strange, almost like he was angry at me. Maybe it was just the mushrooms he took, and if so, there wasn't much I could do for him. I bit my lip indecisively.

Grey chugged the rest of his beer and set it down, making like he was about to leave. I panicked.

"If I stay, can I come with you?" I heard myself asking. Deep down I felt foolish asking a perfect stranger, especially one as hot as him, to hang out with me. I felt like I was twelve years old, and yet, I really didn't care. Anything that bought me more time with Grey was worth it.

"Suit yourself," was his reply.

"Okay, Toby, I'm going to stay." I decided excitedly. I stood up and gathered my things. "Have fun okay. I'll call you."

"Are … are you sure Mac?" he eyed me and Grey doubtfully. "Are you okay?"

"Yeah, I'm good. I'm great actually. Will you watch Riley for me though? He's acting kind of strange."

"Sure thing, but—"

"'Kay, bye Toby! I have my cell!" I waved and turned hastily to follow Grey, whose muscular form was already heading towards the back of the club. I didn't want him to see me running after him, so I tried ever so casually to make up the distance between us while seeming as aloof as he did. Finally I found myself right behind him, pressed against him at times when the crowd surged. At one point when I fell behind, he noticed and grabbed my hand so we wouldn't be separated. I nearly swooned at the strength of his hand, possibly one of the most thrilling moments of my life.

The VIP room was really just an extension of the club, it had the same fabric walls and faded carpet, but the lights were even dimmer and there was actually space to move around. A number of people had already gathered, congregated around the various band members who looked up as we entered. Grey was greeted with cheers and handshakes and shouting, and someone handed us each a beer. Briefly I remembered Riley's warning not to drink, even as I popped the cap off and took a swig.

I'm not sure when it happened—maybe when I was fumbling with my beer bottle—but when I looked up Grey had disappeared. I frowned and looked nervously for him through the crowd of groupies and other hangers-on, but he was nowhere to be seen. Awkwardly I stood trying to seem like I fit in, but when no one gave me so much as a smile, I made my way to a couch at the back of the room and sat by myself. I could feel the embarrassed heat in my cheeks as I lit a smoke and decided to leave and find the guys once it was finished.

But my resolve was like my cigarette—up in smoke—when Grey was suddenly present again, mixing with the others in the main part of the room. I don't know where he had come from, but he looked more relaxed now, almost jovial at times. I sat and watched him, lighting another smoke so I'd look occupied, pretending to be interested in anything but him. His friends gathered around him, hanging on his every word, laughing at his one-liners and witty replies. The loud bursts of mirth from among the crowd quickly snared the attention of the rest of the room, and all other conversations hung in the air as people turned and craned their heads, hoping to get in on the joke. This was a completely different Grey from the one I met earlier, popular and lively instead of brooding and dispassionate.

I think by that point my eyes were in the shape of hearts, like when cartoons fall in love. I sat and tried to look as pretty as possible, willing in my heart for him to notice me but too intimidated by his crowd to do anything else about it. Gathering my courage, I stood and made my way past their rowdy group to a stool at the VIP bar. There was a better chance he'd notice me there, and then at least I wasn't some nerd sitting alone in the dark.

"Two shots of Crown." I ordered, completely disregarding Riley's warning now. I was too nervous and uncomfortable not to drink. Besides, maybe if Riley hadn't effed off for no good reason I would've had someone to talk to instead of sitting there alone, like a total tool. I paid the lady and flipped back my first shot expertly.

"I'll take that, thank you." A hand grabbed my other shot before I had a chance to take it.

"What are you doing?" I looked up at Grey with shock, only half-annoyed. The other half of me was thrilled by his very presence.

"A water for her please." He ignored me and sat down. The waitress gave him an "anything for you" look and plunked an icy glass before me.

"Thanks, but I'll take another shot." I decided.

"No she won't." He shook his head and she obliged with a smile, completely ignoring me as she headed down to the other end of the bar.

"Mackenzie, right?" He tipped back my shooter and then slammed it loudly on the bar.

"Yes."

"You shouldn't be drinking kiddo. Not when you're as high as you look."

"Ugh," I gave him a look of complete disgust. "Don't call me kiddo."

"Sorry." A smirk curled his lips, the first smile I'd ever received from him. "How old are you anyway?"

"Seventeen. Tragic, isn't it?"

"Doesn't seem to be holding you back any."

"I guess not." I shrugged. "Why, how old are you?"

"How old do you think?"

"I don't know …," I bit my lip in thought, "given the stubble … I'd say … forty-two, forty-three? Am I close?" I giggled.

"Ouch." He smirked again. "Now that's tragic."

"Okay," I laughed, "for real. How old are you?"

"Twenty-one. Old enough to know better." Grey shrugged and smiled at me, a real smile this time. I grinned right back, crazily, foolishly in love with him.

But then my cell phone rang.

"Uh, hold on one sec." I mumbled hastily, checking the number before flipping the phone open. The call was from Ben's house.

"Ken?"

"Yes?" I hoped my voice held just enough impatience. "What's up?"

"Man, you gotta get over here right away. Riley's totally freaking out."

My heart hit the bottom of my stomach. I stood up off the stool.

"What do you mean freaking out? Is he okay? What's going on?"

"I don't know. I think it's the mush. He's goin' crazy Ken; he says you're the only one that'll make him feel better."

"Shit, Ben." I sighed. "Dammit. Tell him I'll be right there. I have to walk, I don't have a ride. I'll be there soon, just, try and keep him calm."

"'Kay, hurry. Bye."

"Bye." I hung up quickly and stuffed my phone hastily in my purse. "I gotta go. Riley's having a really bad trip."

"Shit, really?"

"Yeah." I threw my coat on. "I don't even really know what to do."

"Not much you can do. Just ride it out. And no matter how much he insists, don't take him to the hospital. No one ever died from a mushroom trip."

"Thanks." I smiled at Grey regretfully. How I wished I could stay. "Bye. See you around."

"Have a good night, kiddo."

I shot him a look and shook my head, and we were smiling at each other even as I reluctantly turned to leave him.

CHAPTER 3

The pavement shone in the streetlights, wet with a recent rain. The air was chill and damp as I walked, smoking, my boots clipping loudly in the quiet. My mind was racing with the evening's events as my ears still thrummed with phantom bass. I felt like the worst friend in the world, ditching Riley when he needed me so I could swoon over a man four years older than I. But I was coming now, in the dead of night no less, to help my friend ... though most of me wished I could be back at the club, basking in Grey's voice and smile and attention instead of out walking in the cold.

I hoped Riley was all right. My experience with mushroom trips was about equal to my experience with men ... both nonexistent. I talked a big game, but when it came to relationships I had never really found anyone special enough. I'd make out a bit at parties and stuff, but I could never do the one-night-stand thing, especially when I was still a virgin. Most of the girls I knew were up into the double digits with their sexual escapades, but I couldn't fathom how they could do that, how they could be so cavalier about sex. Sure, we seem to have moved past the whole waiting for marriage thing, but shouldn't it at least mean something?

There were plenty of rumours circulating at school that conflicted with my state of virginity, which was fine with me. It made me seem more bad-ass, I guess. And to me, that was not a bad thing. But bad-ass did come with consequences some times, like Riley's trip right now.

About four blocks later, Ben's house came into view—a sprawling bungalow nestled in the back of a cul-de-sac, edged with manicured trees and expensive landscaping. Ben's parents were loaded, which worked out well for us, as they left nearly every weekend in escape to their cabin on the lake. Ben's mom even made sure the cupboards were well stocked before departing and entrusting the house to their youngest son and his rowdy friends. We really tried to keep it clean and nice for her though, because she did trust us. I really think she was quite wise about the whole thing.

"Fuck, Mac, am I glad to see you." Ben let out a waft of steamy smoke and stood from the curb as I approached him. "Its nuts in there."

"I don't know why you're so glad. I don't know what to do anymore that you would. Ugh … my feet are killing me."

"It's not me he's been asking for all night." Ben raised his eyebrows. "Were you having a good time with what's-his-name? Sorry to spoil your fun."

"It's all good." I flicked my smoke into a puddle, listening to the sizzle when it hit the water. "His name is Grey. And yes, we were having fun." I sighed. "Where's Riley? What's going on?"

"Go see for yourself. I don't know where to begin."

"Okay. Wish me luck." I headed into the house then, somewhat anxious and not sure what to expect. The upstairs was bathed in darkness, so I went downstairs into the dim light of the TV room. Riley was there, alone and slouched upon the loveseat, staring at the empty screen on the TV—the only light in the room. It tinged everything an eerie blue.

"Hey Ry. Whatcha doing sitting in the dark?" I asked. There was no answer, which kind of creeped me out. I flicked on the lamp nearest me. "Ry?"

"Shut that off!" He screamed suddenly, pointing a small toy golf club at me like it was a sword. "Wait, wait, Mackenzie, is that you?"

"Yeah, it's me. What the hell are you doing?"

"Exactly. Exactly." He nodded his head in agreement, which made no sense. His hood was pulled down past his eyes, and all I could see was the tip of his nose and his mouth, which was set in a grim line. "See, I knew you'd understand. I hoped you'd come."

"Of course I came. What's going on?"

"I just …." He pulled his hood down further. His voice was hoarse and choking. "I can't control it. I can't. The things I'm seeing … it's not right. They're not right."

"What are you seeing?" I sat down in the chair beside the lamp. "There's nothing here, Ry. Nothing but me."

"No, I can't tell you. It's too terrible. Just be here. I think I'm dying."

"I am here. And you're not dying; you're going to be okay. Remember that one party when you ate all those hot wings before they were cooked?

You swore you were dying then, but you were fine. You just gotta ride it out."

"This is slightly different than food poisoning, Mac." Riley growled at me. "I didn't see shit then."

"Oh, yes you did." I laughed, trying to lighten his mood. "That's all you saw for days."

"Mackenzie!" He shouted at me, stopping my laughter abruptly. "Don't you get it? I'm in Hell. I'm *in* Hell. I see Hell right now."

"… What?"

"It's evil. All of it is evil, and I see it now. I see it clearly now and I wish I'd known the truth before. I wish I had the chance to choose again. I'd choose differently."

"You are rambling about who-knows-what right now, Riley. Just relax. You are not going to die." I sounded more confident than I felt. "Just take it easy, think of pleasant things. In a few hours this will all be over."

"No, it won't ever be over." His said desperately, clawing at his hood and his face. "Help me, Mac. Help me."

"I don't know what to do." I admitted, slightly panicked by his plea. "Tell me what to do Ry and I'll do it, whatever you need."

He shook his head and then, pressing his hands against his face, Riley began to cry, silently sobbing into his palms. I had never in the fifteen years of our friendship seen Riley do that. Not when his dad left, not when his dog died, not even when he broke his wrist in Phys Ed. Those quiet tears scared me more than anything he ever could have said or done. I felt hollow and lost. Riley had always been my rock—the strong one, manly, emotionless. Now I didn't know what to do.

"Hey, Ry. It's okay. It's okay." I struggled to control my voice, realizing that my hysterics would do nothing to ease the situation. I spoke softly and soothingly, like my mom did when I was sick or sad, and crossed over to him. As I put my arms around his shoulders, he jerked startlingly from my touch. I could feel the heat pouring off of him.

"What can I do? Tell me what to do." I pleaded.

"I don't know. Make it stop. Pray. Pray for me."

Pray? I held his trembling form as tightly as I could. I didn't want to mention that prayer wouldn't do anything for him, minus the fact that I'd never prayed a day in my life and wasn't entirely sure how it was done. He shut his eyes then and his lips began to move silently, and I knew he was petitioning God, begging Him with all his might for this to stop.

"Please Mackenzie. Pray. Pray for me." His eyes, completely void of color in the dim light, were hauntingly desperate and filled with terror.

"Okay." I nodded, hugging him to me. "Lord …." I didn't know what to say, what to even ask for. Help Riley have a good mushroom trip? I doubted God would be into that kind of thing.

"Lord." I started. "Please save my friend Riley from Hell."

I awoke the next morning to a horrible kink in my neck. Slowly I strained to turn my head, rubbing the aching muscles with a stiff arm. Riley slept next to me, his face pale, but calm and peaceful now. He had thrown one of his arms around me during the night, and it lay heavily around my waist, warm and comforting. I was relieved that our rightful roles had been restored, and he was again taking care of me. I sighed contentedly and snuggled against him. There was no safer place in the world than Riley's arms. None I had found anyway.

I studied his face while he slept. Dark smudges lay beneath his eyes, a tribute to the horrible night we had spent. For hours we sat together, and I tried to comfort him as best I could, but there wasn't much I could do. He had to ride it out by himself, and what he went through I don't think I'll ever comprehend. He tried to keep it mostly to himself, but at times he trembled so violently I nearly thought he was having a seizure. Other times he paced the room, muttering incoherently, trapped in the utter torture of his hallucinations, at the total mercy of his mind.

But eventually, like Grey said it would, the terror faded. I felt Riley's body gradually relax, the tension unwinding as the mushrooms wore off and the delusions finally dwindled. Exhausted from the ordeal, I had passed out sitting up, unable to keep my eyes open once I knew he'd be okay. My body ached from the uncomfortable sleep in such an unusual position, but I didn't regret it. Not for Riley.

"Mmm … what time is it?" He asked then, his eyes still shut in a grimace.

"I don't know." I looked at the bright sun filtering through the Venetian blinds. "Mid-morning? Early afternoon?"

"Too early, whatever time."

"How you feeling?"

"Not good." He opened his eyes, slowly, and looked up at the roof. "Gut rot."

"I would imagine. Among other things."

"Man …." He shook his head.

"You okay?"

He hesitated. "Yeah. Let's not talk about it. I wish I'd never put you through that."

I scoffed. "Psssh. I'm fine."

"Yeah. Well, I'm sorry. I think that was the last time I'll ever do mush."

"I should hope so. I will personally kick your ass if you ever do them again."

"Deal." He smiled. "How was your first E experience?"

"Umm …." I thought. "Pretty awesome. Yeah, I definitely loved it."

"I thought you would."

"What's not to like?"

"Yeah …." He nodded, but I noticed he looked … worried almost. Like he was frowning.

"What?"

"Nothing. Sorry to ruin your night."

"No, you didn't. It was fine, really. Oh, and guess what else. You'll never guess."

"What?" He smiled.

"Do you think … could you still get me that job, at your restaurant?"

"What, really?" His eyes brightened. "That'd be awesome. They're always hiring, I'm sure it'll be no problem. Sweet. What made you change your mind?"

"Well …." I looked away, feeling a blush of heat sweep my cheeks. "That's where Grey works, right?"

Complete silence. I glanced up at Riley, but the look on his face was totally indiscernible. His eyes were flat, void of emotion, but his face seemed hard. He looked up at the ceiling again.

"Mackenzie …," he gulped, as if thinking out his words carefully. "Do you really think that Grey would be good for you? I mean, he's a decent fellow, but he's not exactly someone you bring home to mom."

"You seem to think it's that easy, like I'd even stand a chance." I scoffed.

"I think you'd be surprised."

"Okay, let's say I do. What's so bad about him? He seems to have lots of friends. And his band is doing really well, aren't they?"

"Yeah, I guess. I don't know. I don't want to bad mouth the guy, but I think you could do better."

"I think the same for you, whenever you meet someone." I admitted, meeting his deep brown eyes. "I think it's a curse of ours, Ry. We care too much about each other to be only friends, but friends are all we'll ever be. Don't you agree?"

He stared up at the ceiling, hesitating before he slowly nodded his head.

"Right. Just friends. That's all we'll ever be."

I thought about his slowly uttered words, and although I agreed with them, for some reason they bothered me. It was almost like there was a sudden separation, a mutual and silent decision we both made in that moment, to have those words come true. Ever since we'd reached adolescence the possibility had always been there, like a white noise in the background, a constant subconscious thought that flirted with our deep bond of friendship and threatened to make it more. I had always denied this hidden feeling and curiosity and I'm sure he did the same. But his words, as they rent the air, brought with them a feeling of definite, a sudden detachment in our closeness, as though certain things forever available were now forbidden to each other and forever-off limits. I wondered if he felt it too. It was a terrifying feeling, as though we had just mutually agreed to go our separate ways.

"Riley—" I tried hard to control my voice. I was searching for an easy way, any way to make this work without losing my best friend in the process. "Promise me that no matter what happens, no matter who we end up with or what we go through; promise me you'll always be there. Promise that, that you'll always love me."

He turned back to me then, and a little smile curved his lips. His dark eyes were the same, warm and comforting. But the detached feeling remained.

"You don't need me to say that, Mackenzie."

"Why?"

"Because. You know it's the truth."

CHAPTER 4

Dad was waiting for me on the front porch of our house when I slowly ambled up the sidewalk, frowning from the lack of sleep and tormented emotions. He wore the sheen of someone who had just spent the day in a plane, his suit was rumpled and his face needed shaving. He didn't look overly impressed with me.

"Is this a habit of yours? Staying out all night without telling anyone?"

"Well, hello to you too." I squinted. "No, it's not a habit. And what difference does it make? No one was here anyway."

"The difference is, you are seventeen years old and you have a curfew, which you've only broken by about, oh, twelve or thirteen odd hours."

"How do you know? Maybe I came home last night and left really early this morning. You'd never know."

He didn't answer, just looked at me hard, as if he were trying to figure me out. He sighed and rubbed a hand over his face. It was easy to beat my dad at this game. Most of the time he didn't have the patience or the energy to try and battle me.

"Well, you made it just in time." He smiled then, his voice overly chipper, his I-just-want-to-get-along-with-you-today voice. "Marcy's coming over to dinner! She just called." He grinned broadly.

"What! Wow." My sarcasm was obvious. "What are you still doing here? The fattened calf isn't going to kill itself." With that I brushed by him, rolling my eyes, and headed quickly in and up to my room before he could bother me anymore.

To my horror of horrors, my mother had laid out on my bed a neat little cardigan set, bubblegum pink, with a grey plaid skirt to go with it. I made a noise of frustration and leaned against my door until it slammed shut. Silently I repeated my mantra, only a few more months and I would be on my own, away from these people, living in sweet freedom, a life totally void of anything involving the hue bubblegum pink. I sat on my bed, purposely seating myself right upon the offending garments. I wanted a smoke, but since my mom was a doctor, she'd smell it instantly and then really be a pain in the ass.

I flopped down on my bed with a sigh, fraught with dismay at the thought of a "Marcy dinner" in my near future. Don't get me wrong, she's my sister and I do love her, but come on. For one thing, she's in med school, which my parents just rant and rave about. They brag about her to all their friends. She has this real hotshot boyfriend, a surgeon of some kind, who was all magna and summa when he graduated a few years ago, but he's nearly as old as my father, in my thinking anyway. They live in the city, in this high rise, modern blah blah ... anyway it's really swanky. To top it all off, Marcy is gorgeous, with her dark eyes and athletic build and immaculate sense of fashion and togetherness. Her jaw would have dropped in tremendous delight if offered the outfit I was currently wrinkling to the best of my ability.

I sat up suddenly and smiled to myself. I had just been gifted with the most amazing idea. I nearly laughed at myself and my genius, hopped off my bed, and eagerly got to work.

"Mackenzie! Come down to eat!" Mom called up the stairs.

"Okay, I'll be right down!" I called back, smiling in anticipation. I looked in the mirror and made a few last minute adjustments. The outfit I had just created looked pretty good in my eyes, something I would possibly wear out with the guys. The bubblegum pink top was now the owner of a great black skull that sat across my chest, actually pretty good, a credit to my old art classes and a faithful black Sharpie. The grey skirt I left basically alone, only adding a few well-placed rips—which of course had to be fixed with an overabundance of safety pins. Beneath those were some fishnets I had worn for Halloween one year, and to top it all off, I put on some heavy, old black army boots that had been hanging out in the bottom of my closet. They were Riley's from his short stint in Cadets, which his mother forced him to quit when someone stole his brand new and very expensive boots.

He had really hated that group.

After just a dab more eyeliner, I bounded happily down the stairs and into the dining room.

"Good evening," I announced. Marcy, Greg and my father looked up at me, ceasing their conversation, their eyebrows raised. My mom stopped cold in her tracks and glared at me.

"Mackenzie Anne, what have you done to your clothes?" She demanded, setting down the potatoes.

"What, this?" I asked in amazement. "I just added my own artistic flair. You should be encouraging my flair, you know."

"Do you even know how much that outfit cost? Look at it now, it's ruined."

"Well, then save yourself the trouble next time, mom. Really." I sat down at my place, very satisfied with myself. I hoped she'd get the hint. Marcy and Greg exchanged a look of disapproval, and Dad sat thoughtfully. He looked very tired.

Dinner went on, as Marcy recounted her amazing abilities in full, with Greg interjecting any excellence she may have forgotten. I sat silently through it all, pushing my food around on my plate. Marcy looked breathtaking in her white buttoned blouse and grey blazer—her dark hair, recently bobbed, pin-neat and perfectly curled at her jawbone. Her flawless skin was made-up just right so she looked gorgeous without seeming like she tried to. Greg at her side sat dapperly in a blue sweater with a white collar, and I nearly expected him to pull out a pipe and expound on theology.

But then I noticed it. How could I not before? How did my mom not see? I looked at her quickly to make sure she hadn't developed a sudden case of blindness. Now that I had seen it, it was impossible to ignore. Shining and gleaming in the dim lights of the dining room, there, upon Marcy's left hand, sat a ring of extraordinary size and carat.

"What's with the ring?" I blurted suddenly, totally interrupting their conversation. Marcy looked hard at me and then blushed into a smile, beaming as she held up her hand for my parents to see.

"I was going to announce it … properly … but, Greg asked me last night! We're getting married!" She exclaimed.

The noise my mother made then cannot even be described. It was something like a train whistle combined with the high-pitched scream of a teakettle. My ears actually cringed at the sound. She jumped up and covered her mouth and grasped Marcy in a tight hug, enthusiastically proclaiming her approval and excitement. Dad smiled broadly and clinked his wine glass against Greg's.

"Congratulations, son. It'll be an honour to have you in the family."

I just sat and watched the madness ensue. Finally, when the initial excitement settled and only brief bursts of high-pitched noises were exploding from my mother, Marcy looked over at me. She smiled.

"What do you think, Mac? Aren't you happy?" She asked cautiously. Everyone turned to watch my reaction.

"Absolutely. That's awesome. Congratulations." I held up my water glass in unenthused cheers. "Can't wait."

"And," Marcy smiled again, "we'd like you to be in the wedding."

"Me?" I was sincerely surprised. "Why?"

"'Cause silly. You're my little sister. Who better?" She reached across the table and squeezed my hand. I couldn't help but be touched by the offer, especially since I'd given Marcy nothing but attitude for the last few years. I smiled at her.

"Sure, that sounds great."

Greg chuckled. "Unfortunately for you, we're leaving the skulls out of the décor." He smirked and sipped his sherry. "Unless you would like black and white for a theme, dear?"

All those around the table laughed then, as if it were the funniest joke they'd heard in ages. Then Marcy gushed, turning to my mother and describing in full her actual theme and color choices, which she had already decided on, even though they'd been engaged for all of twenty-one hours. I sat back and sneered at Greg. What a dick. Who under the age of fifty drinks sherry with their meal anyway? And his hair. He looked like a game show host from the early eighties. Dick. I made a mental note that when—no—if—I ever got married, black and white would make a definite appearance. Oh, and Greg wouldn't be invited.

"So, Mackenzie." Dad interrupted my future revenge scheme, wiping at his mouth with his napkin and plunking it onto his plate, a motion that followed the end of all his meals. He took a drink of wine and made sure he had my attention.

"Yes?"

"Did we decide anything? About the job?"

"Oh, yes, actually, we did."

"We did?" Mom turned mid-flower discussion. "But I haven't spoken to Doug yet about—"

"Don't bother; Riley's getting me a job."

There, right on cue. The face.

"Riley? Where?" Asked the scrunch of disapproval.

"At the restaurant he works at. Um … something Wheat … Red Wheat, I think?"

Stunned silence followed. Someone scoffed, and I can't be sure, but I think it was Greg. Dick.

"What?" I asked in amazement. "What? You tell me to get a job, so I get one, and now you sit here like I just told you I'm running away with my lesbian partner or something."

"Well, Mackenzie." Dad shook his head. "This wasn't exactly what I had in mind."

"What did you have in mind? A job that I work at and pays me money? 'Cause this is one of those jobs."

"I just thought …," he trailed off.

"You sure you don't want a job at the hospital? It won't be a problem; I could call right now …."

"Mom! Stop! I don't want your damn hospital job." I got up from my seat. "You guys are friggin' impossible."

But there was a smile on my face as I strode up the stairs, back to my room.

CHAPTER 5

It smelt like hot oil and musty cloths. Like pizza sauce and spices and strong brewed coffee. Like Descaler and mop water and Italian salad dressing. I stood hesitantly at the entrance to the waitress area, overwhelmed by the pungent aromas as I waited for Sophie, who had just disappeared through a set of swinging doors into a hectic chaos beyond. She had bid me wait for her so she could "show me the ropes," her arms laden with plates on her way to the dish pit—like six plates between two arms. I wondered if I would ever be able to do that. And if I'd have to pay for the plates I broke.

As I waited I tried inconspicuously to look for Grey through the narrow glass window on the door, but all I could see was a hairy knuckled hand dumping fries into the deep fryer. I looked around the seating area instead. The Red Wheat was a typical family affair restaurant. The carpet was a faded burgundy/hunter green combination of swirls and flowers, oak woodworking framed the white sprigged wallpaper, the tables were burgundy topped and surrounded by wooden chairs with green seat pads. It was homey and comforting though—not cheap or tacky—and since most of the seats were filled with patrons, I took that as a good sign.

"Okay." Sophie re-emerged then, smiling quickly and wiping her hands on her soiled black apron. "Sorry to make you wait. I don't know why Ralph always insists the new people come during supper rush. Its really inconvenient but I suppose it's a fast way to learn …." Her speech trailed off and she was moving again, whisking around the restaurant, taking orders, clearing plates, refilling coffee. I had no choice but to follow close behind, feeling awkward and out of place while trying to seem preoccupied and knowledgeable.

Sophie didn't exactly help my discomfit. She would point at me with her pen and clarify "trainee" to all her customers, who would in turn smile sympathetically at me and nod with understanding. Between tables she would explain as we walked, talking a mile a minute about menu choices and writing orders and making the most efficient use of our time.

As we came into the waitress station there was another girl there, tall and blonde and pretty, leaning on the counter and talking to one of the cooks through the long narrow window where food orders were placed. She giggled and played with her curly hair—obviously flirting. And then I recognized her.

"Hello Charlene." Sophie frowned and Charlie straightened up. I smiled. So Charlene was her real name.

"Oh, hey Soph. Oh hey—I remember you." She smiled at me then. "From the other night, like a week ago. Mackenzie, right?"

"Yeah that's me." I nodded.

"I'm glad you two know each other." Even then Sophie didn't stop moving. She placed her order and went to the fridge to make a salad.

"Mackenzie, I need two large Pepsi's please. Charlene, you're late."

"Yeah sorry, I was like, waylaid."

"Well, table seventeen needs ketchup and table nineteen needs a refill. Are you sure that outfit is work appropriate?" Then Sophie paused, taking in Charlie's ensemble, and I looked over mid-Pepsi-pour to get a good look as well. She had on tight black Capri's and cute strappy sandals, with a white halter-top deep cut down the front. She looked really, really good, but not like a waitress. I looked down at myself, dressed in nice black pants, black skate shoes and a long sleeved striped green Henley—and felt like a Hutterite in comparison.

"What's the matter with my clothes?" Charlie asked. Sophie shook her head and raised an eyebrow.

"It's not for me to say. Let Ralph tell you if he has a problem with it." Then under her breath, she laugh-muttered, "Yeah right."

"Did Sophie explain to you about our uniforms?" Charlie laughed. Sophie shot her a look and left the waitress area, a ketchup bottle in one hand and coffeepot in the other.

"What uniforms?" I asked Sophie, following closely behind with the Pepsi's. I didn't want to be stuck alone with Charlie and forced to make polite conversation.

"We don't have any." Sophie explained. "You can wear whatever you want, tastefully, mind you. Keep in mind that whatever you wear will be ruined eventually."

I smiled. Perfect. Another use for my mom-bought wardrobe.

My luck ran out at the end of the night, when Sophie announced she was leaving us to close up, this proclamation coming just as suddenly as the rest of her actions had. She did look worn though—her thin dark hair falling loose from the severe, tight ponytail she wore at the exact center of her head, the slight smudges under her eyes making the rest of her narrow face appear even more peaked. But she smiled at me before she left.

"You did good tonight, Mackenzie. If I didn't have to be here first thing tomorrow I'd stay and teach you some more. You show promise though. Remember, only two free refills, right?"

"Right." I nodded, accepting Sophie's praise. The restaurant was obviously her life and she clearly knew what she was talking about. I wondered how old she was. And when she became a waitress. And if she had done it just to show her parents a thing or two.

"Just you and me, hey?" Charlie leaned against the counter, grinning when Sophie finally left. "Take a moment. Have a drink. Sophie's always rush, rush, rush. I don't think it's necessary."

"It was busy." I felt the need to defend the poor woman.

"Yes, it was. But it's not now. Take a load off."

I shrugged and joined her at the counter with a drink, trying to clandestinely place myself in direct view of the kitchen. I hadn't had even a second to scope out the situation back there, apart from Rory the hairy knuckled line cook and the dish-pit full of grade seveners. Now I peered through the take-out window, searching for Grey as casually as I could. He was nowhere to be seen, but I did spot Riley, hard at work ladling pizza sauce onto dough. He leaned over with concentration, his eyebrows knit and his tongue pointing out the right side of his mouth, like it always did whenever he was super focused. I wondered suddenly if he did that when making out with someone. Super random.

"Is Grey working tonight?" I asked Charlie nonchalantly, sipping my Pepsi.

"No. Off tonight." Her smile became an eye roll and then she shook her head. "Don't even tell me."

"Don't tell you what?"

"I can't believe … you started here for him, didn't you?"

"What?" I pretended to be appalled; amazed that she had seen through me so quickly. "Of course not."

"Yeah, right. Well you wouldn't be the first one, honey. This place gets more resumes than West-Jet."

"Oh?"

"Yeah. But listen; if that's all you're here for, you're wasting your time. Grey … well … I can't figure him out. I've worked here for nearly a year and he won't give me the time of day. It's the same with all the girls. Maybe he has a thing about dating where he works." She shrugged.

I translated this statement to mean that Charlie had hit on him and he'd rejected her. I nodded for her to continue.

"I don't know what else to tell you. Good luck, I guess. But take it from me, I've seen pretty much every attempt under the sun and he never goes for it."

I nodded again. "Well. Luckily, that's not what I'm here for."

"Right." Charlie smiled and nodded. "I forgot. Anyways, maybe he's gay."

I thought of Grey's stubbled face as it screamed into the microphone, of his thigh-hugging blue jeans and studded leather bracelets. No, nothing about Grey could or would ever be gay. But he would be a challenge. I kept this thought to myself, picked up a coffeepot and went out to check the customers.

There was still vacuuming to do, salad dressings to refill, the coffee machine to clean, ketchups to wipe … the list went on and on. I had no idea there was so much to a waitressing gig. By the time I plunked myself down at a table to roll the cutlery my feet ached, my legs stumbled and my eyes burned with exhaustion. Most of the kitchen crew were already out front, relaxing at the tables and drinking coffee. A thick haze of smoke hung in the air above them.

"Hey Mac." Riley left his table and joined me, his checked kitchen duds replaced by street clothes. He sat down with a sigh. "How was your first day?"

"Tired." Was all I could say. He laughed and handed me a smoke. "Here, this will make you feel better."

It did. I instantly relaxed the moment the precious burn hit my lungs. "Thanks."

"No problem. It'll get easier you know. My first day I was so overwhelmed."

"Yeah. Is it always this busy?"

"Most nights. But your tips will be worth it, trust me."

"Tips!" I totally forgot. I smiled and nearly ran back to the waitress area, despite my aching legs, for my newly decorated Styrofoam cup filled with change. I had written my name on it in big black letters, complete with a few pointy stars for company.

"Can I trust you?" I teased, handing the cup to Riley so I could resume my cutlery rolling. He shrugged and smiled back.

"I guess we'll see."

We sat in silence for a moment, both bent over the task at hand. As I took another drag of my cigarette, I suddenly realized why nearly every single person at the restaurant indulged in the delicious filthy habit. Nothing helped relax you after a tiring, busy shift like the simple pleasure of a smoke.

"Not a bad haul." Riley decided then, jumping up to exchange my small change for bills from the main till. He handed me a few twenties and a ten. I smiled in delight.

"Wow, worth it!" I declared happily. "Let's celebrate! This is more then enough for a bag. What do you say?" Weed smoke would be even more relaxing.

Riley surprised me by hesitating. He looked at my small pile of money and frowned.

"I don't know, Mac." He sighed.

"What? Why not?"

"I don't know. It's a school night."

"It's a … what?" I stared at him in stupefied shock, "… and?"

"And, I don't feel the need to be ripped all the time, alright?" Though he kept his voice low, there was no mistaking the sudden edge to it. He looked at me in frustration. "There's more to life, you know."

I was speechless. I stared at him curiously. Never since the day Riley smoked his first joint had he ever turned down weed. Free weed especially. At school, after school, on the weekends, in the evenings, at important family functions … Riley was always high. He was high so often that his mom only got suspicious when he was sober. Being high was the norm for Riley.

I frowned back at him, my night suddenly shot. The last thing I wanted to do was go home to an empty house by myself.

"What brought this on?" I wondered.

"Just …." He sighed again, like I was being difficult. "Just forget about it. Do you still need a ride?"

I shrugged. "I guess. I don't know. I don't want to go home alone." I looked at him hopefully. "Will you come with me? We can hang out, watch a movie, and I can get high while you … sit there I guess."

"There's no way I'd be around weed without smoking it."

"Well, problem solved then."

"No, Mac. That means I'm not coming. Not unless you can handle abstaining for an hour or so." He rolled his eyes and shook his head doubtfully.

"What …?" I couldn't believe the sudden one-eighty that had occurred in Riley's mind during the few short days since the weekend. I hadn't talked to him at all on Sunday and though today he'd been abnormally quiet, I was too distracted both by my first day at work and my constant Grey musings to really pay attention.

But Riley had my full attention now.

"What's with all the judgement all a sudden?" I leaned forward and stamped out my cigarette.

"No judgement … just don't try and force me to do things I don't want to do."

"But until like, three seconds ago, you did want to do these things."

"Well I don't anymore, okay. So can we just drop it?"

I stared at him a moment. "Whatever." I muttered. But I wasn't ready to drop it, not even close. There was no way I could just relax and try to shrug it off—it made me anxious. Our relationship didn't need anymore change at the moment; it needed good old repetition and routine until we were comfortable again, until we were just Riley and Mackenzie like always. The Riley and Mackenzie who got high and had fun and just were what they'd always been.

"Look, I'm sorry." Riley softened and gave me a slight smile. "It's just, it's hard enough as it is, you know?"

"What's hard, Ry?" I lit another cigarette. We were completely oblivious to the cooks and staff and the crowd around us—thinning out as they went home for the night—caught up in our own little saga.

"Can we talk about this later? I don't want to turn it into a big thing … and I know your flair for drama."

"What flair for drama?" I wondered, but Riley ignored me.

"Did you see your schedule?" I guess he considered the case closed.

I sighed. "No. I know I work tomorrow night but that's it."

"Here," he unfolded a sheet of paper for me to see. "You're on tomorrow, Friday night and Sunday afternoon. You'll probably get more shifts as you get better."

"When do you work?" I asked, taking the paper from him. I gave it a quick glance. Riley worked nearly every night I did but Saturday. Good to know. What I really wanted to see was Grey's schedule, and I realized in disappointment that he mostly worked during the day while I was in school. Stupid age! But then, not all was lost. He worked the Friday nightshift that week, right alongside me.

I smiled at the thought. "We work together every time." I announced to my friend.

Riley nodded. "I requested that. Thought I could help you out if you needed."

"Thanks Ry." I was touched.

He shrugged. "No big deal."

I sat back in my chair and studied him through the curling smoke of my cigarette. He was getting hotter every day. His dark messy hair, his warm chocolate eyes ... if he weren't my best friend in the world, he'd be awfully tempting. I felt almost ... disappointed that I couldn't feel for him that way. He was so caring too ... the way he thought of me, the way he rearranged his schedule to help me out. I sighed. It was only a matter of time before a girl threw herself at him, inevitable that he would meet someone. Then he would be spending all his time thinking of her and trying to please her instead of me. I frowned. I was selfish enough to hate the thought of him happy with someone else. Some friend I was.

"Come on." I smiled. "Can we go get high now or what?"

Riley shot me a look, shook his head, and smiled resignedly. "Mackenzie, you're going to be the death of me."

I took that as a yes. "So you're in then?" I smiled. I thought I had won.

"No. I'm not in. But I will give you a ride home."

"Oh." I was deflated. I frowned as Riley got his stuff together. A flutter of panic settled into the pit of my stomach but I tried to push it aside. He was still Riley. Weed or no weed, he was my friend, my best friend, and he always would be. Nothing could or would change that. I tried to give him a sincere smile as we walked to the car.

But the worry remained.

CHAPTER 6

We rode silently. Riley's window was rolled up, he chewed his gum compulsively. I sat with my arms crossed, dying for a cigarette, staring glumly out the window at the larger, newer homes lining my street that gradually changed to older, smaller houses as we drove towards the school.

I was irritated. Riley had decided, among everything else, to quit smoking as well. It pissed me off that I couldn't smoke in Riley's car now, something I'd done every single school morning since grade eight. He hadn't specifically forbidden it, but the way he gripped the steering wheel told me he was just as desperate for a smoke as I was. It wouldn't help anything if I lit up right now.

"What's eating you this morning?" He asked me tersely when I started biting my nails.

"You know what it is." I answered, just as icily. I sighed. "This totally sucks, Ry."

"What, now you have to go like, another ten minutes before you can smoke in the morning? Is that what sucks?"

"Yes, that, among other things." I admitted.

"Oh, I'm sorry. I totally forgot that everything's about you." Riley's voice oozed sarcasm. I realized it probably wasn't the best time for this conversation, since we were both irrationally irritated by the lack of nicotine. I fidgeted.

"Whatever. Forget it." I shook my head and resumed watching out the window. I didn't want to fight with him. I just wanted Riley, the way he was before, the way we were before. Everything was changing, too fast, slipping from my grasp quicker than I could re-grip it. And I still didn't quite understand the reasoning. Riley hadn't explained it to me yet.

"Why," I started again, keeping my voice lighter, like we were in the middle of a pleasant conversation. "Why do you need to clean up anyway? It's not like you're a junky or anything Ry, you just like to have a little fun. There's nothing wrong with that. You're young. You're allowed."

"Are you kidding me? Were you not there the other night? That is not what I consider fun." Riley turned his dark eyes to me incredulously. "I could've died, I felt like I was going to die. That trip scared me straight. I'm not even the same person anymore, I don't think the same about things, I don't feel the same. I don't even want the same things." He looked at me pointedly. "Can't you understand that? I've been given a second chance. A chance to get out while I still can. I don't want to screw it up."

I watched his hands as they turned the steering wheel and we pulled into the gravel lot at school. His knuckles were white with earnest. I marvelled again at the complete transformation that had occurred within my friend in just a few short days. I felt like I didn't even know him anymore, I had never seen this side of him before.

I stared back out the window. The significance of his words and what he meant by them made me bite my lip in concern. Riley wasn't just going through a temporary phase like I hoped. He was making a life change. He was done—done with it all, done with the partying and the drinking and the smoking and the fun. I realized too, that for once, I felt totally different from him.

I wasn't ready to be done. I loved what we did; I lived for the weekend, for our Friday afternoon farmyard tradition. To be stoned and laugh and drink. To be wild and crazy and experience everything. That's what I wanted out of life.

I tried to imagine that life without Riley. I saw no one beside me at parties … I imagined myself lonely and forlorn, sitting amidst the abandoned farm buildings with nothing but the prairie grass for company, smoking a joint. I saw myself in the passenger seat of his car, but I wasn't going anywhere, because there was no driver. Mackenzie without her Riley was just Mackenzie. And that future looked bleak.

"You're ruining everything." I blurted suddenly, rash from my grim imaginings. I didn't want that life, not without Riley. Why did he have to go and have that stupid mushroom trip? Who was I going to hang out with now?

Riley glared at me, his eyebrows raised in disbelief. "I'm ruining everything?" He stared at me a moment and scoffed. "The only thing I'm ruining is your good time. You … you don't even see that I nearly died the other night. That I was scared shitless and will never put myself in that situation again. I'm lucky and thankful to be alive and I need to change before I totally lose control and turn out just like my father …." His voice broke and he looked away from me, gripping the steering wheel again. I stared at him, speechless. He recovered quickly. "You … you have got to be the most selfish person that I have ever known. I bet you're not even upset about our friendship, but because you'll have to find another dealer. Is that right? Am I close?"

"No, that's not what I—"

"Stop it. Just stop it." He stared ahead. "If you ever cared for me, at all, even a fraction of what I feel for you, we wouldn't be having this conversation. You'd be understanding, hell; maybe you'd even be proud of me, inspired even. But no, it's all about you and your precious fun. That's what sucks."

"Riley, I—"

"You can't Riley your way out of this one." He shook his head. His arms were trembling, his hands gripped around the steering wheel with tension and anger. "Why can't … why can't you …." He trailed off, his eyes closing as if he had given up. I heard him sigh. We sat for a moment. "You know what? You want to smoke so bad Mackenzie?" He turned to me. "Find yourself another ride then."

The hinges squeaked suddenly, the car door slammed loudly and then Riley was gone, stalking across the dirt parking lot without looking back, his arms and shoulders rigid with anger. I felt tears well as I watched him walk away. I wanted to get out of the car and follow him, to yell and scream and plead my case like I normally did when we fought. But it was different this time—this time I felt utterly useless, for I knew no matter what I said or what I did, it wouldn't change anything. It wouldn't put us back the way we were.

I stayed, frozen in the passenger seat of Riley's beat up old car, totally alone, just as I had imagined only moments earlier. I started to cry. I cried because I didn't know what to do, didn't know how to stop him from leaving me. I cried because I knew, deep down, that everything Riley said about me was true. Everything he accused me of. I was selfish; I did everything for all the wrong reasons. I felt tears well up, spill over; I felt them warm on my face. I cried because I was a terrible friend. I cried because I did care for Riley, deeply, beneath it all.

And I cried because I knew that we would never be the same.

The day was horribly, hideously long. My eyes were red and puffy by the time I made it to class, which got me some attention, and though I liked that, I was still miserable. If Riley noticed he didn't say anything. With the size of our school it was inevitable to share nearly every class, as we did, but instead of our normal places, Riley chose to sit in any available chair as far away from me as possible. It hurt, and every time he did it, tears welled again. I hated having people mad at me. Well, my friends anyway. Especially Riley.

I made it through the morning, and then at lunch, I decided to mend things. To beg and grovel and do whatever it took to make him like me again. I waited by his locker, leaning impatiently. I sat on the floor. I even took out my homework for something to do while I waited. I missed three or four lunchtime cigarettes. He never came.

Finally, at the warning bell, I spotted him. A classroom door flew open—some kind of lunchtime meeting must have been going on—and students started pouring out. I never expected Riley to be there, I was just watching for something to do. But then he *was* there, laughing as if nothing was at all wrong in the world, like he hadn't just had a devastating fight with his best friend. He was laughing with a girl. My eyes opened in panic and I got to my feet, staring. They were laughing together and then seriously, she put a hand on his arm. He placed his hand on top of hers and his lips mouthed, "thank you," and then they were hugging.

I swallowed hard. Thank you for what? For the best sex ever in that classroom? For fulfilling a part of me Mackenzie never could? For becoming my new best friend? For letting me fall madly in love with you?

Had all of my fears come true today? I scrutinized the girl, critiquing her instantly, comparing our features quickly to judge how threatened I should feel. She was shorter than me, and chubbier, though her round face was pleasant. She wore jeans and a plain brown t-shirt and nondescript footwear … boots, maybe? Not a dresser, that was for sure. Her hair was a color between brown and blond, completely natural and long, straight. She wore little make-up, and I was chagrined to admit she was still pretty without it.

At least she was chubby.

I recognized her. In a school this small, it was inevitable to know everyone—or at least of them. Her name was … I couldn't remember her name, but I knew she was one of the "brainiacs." What could Riley want with her?

I shook my own dark, curly locks around my shoulders and waited for Riley to approach. I practiced my best please-don't-be-mad-at-me eyes. I watched them walk together towards me down the fluorescent-lit hall, and when he looked up and noticed me, the smile fell from his face. I gulped.

"Riley." I gave him the eyes.

"Mackenzie." He nodded. "I'll see you later, Emily." He grinned at the chubby girl.

"Sure, Riley." Her voice was all sweetness and roses. She smiled big, with adorable dimples. "See you soon."

Emily. That was her name. I shared a few classes with her, but had never really noticed her until now. I hated her instantly. I watched her walk away and wished her bodily harm.

"Don't start." Riley warned me. I spun my eyes to meet his, and gave him a soft smile. He knew me well enough to recognize the instant, unreasonable jealousy.

"No, of course not. Look, Ry, I just wanted to say sorry." I bit my lip and tried to look as contrite as possible. "I've been terrible, I know, and you're right. About everything. But I'll stop now. I'll be understanding and all the rest … I just …" I shrugged. "I can't help that I'm going to miss hanging out with you. That's what I'll miss, you know. Not the dealing or anything. Just you. You're my best friend." My voice broke on the word. At least, he used to be. The tears, so near the surface, stung me again. "I do care for you, even when I don't act it, and I don't—"

"Are you finished?" He interrupted me then, but there was a slight smile tugging hesitantly on his lips. I stopped mid-sentence and nodded dumbly.

"So dramatic." Riley sighed, opening his locker and pulling out a thick black binder. He slammed the locker door shut and closed the lock. I just watched him, anxious, biting my lip—chapped already from all this stressing. Riley was quiet, deep in thought for a moment.

"Mackenzie," when he looked up at me, his dark eyes were hard, his jaw clenched. My stomach did a little flip of panic, my body reacting in a flash of heat, sweat breaking upon my skin in worry. I forced myself to look at him, steadily, but I could feel the tears rising. My throat ached.

"Mackenzie," he started again, softening when he noticed the tears in my eyes. "I'm sorry … but I meant what I said earlier. About changing. I think … I think it would be easier if we just … if we spent some time apart …."

"What?" My eyes darted anxiously across his face. "Why? Riley I'm sorry for earlier. I'm so sorry, and I won't interfere with your new life … your new plans … I promise. I'm happy that you're doing so well, that you're so strong …." I lied, but I was desperate. "Just … please, don't say we need to be apart. Please? I don't know what I'd do without you. Not just to party with, but to be with. You know?"

"Yeah, right." He scoffed in disbelief. I grasped his hand and forced him to look at me.

"I mean it, Ry. You're my best friend. Who knows you better than I do? Who knows me better than you? Come on …," I smiled at him. "Riley and Mackenzie just like always."

He shook his head. "But it won't be just like always, Mac. I'm giving it all up for good. All of it. So you either have to accept that and me, or we can't be friends anymore. The thing is … I'm not that strong, and if you keep pressuring me to do these things, I'll do them, and I won't look back. And I don't want that. Not anymore."

I nodded. "Okay, okay that's fine. Honestly Ry, you are more important to me than just a buddy to get high with. I will miss you, 'cause you're friggin' funny when you're high, but I won't pressure you anymore." I laughed. "As long as you promise not to become one of those people."

"What people?"

"You know; the people that we hate. The ones that quit stuff and then judge the other people for doing exactly what they just quit. Don't do that to me, okay? Or I'll totally lose it on you."

Riley stared at me a moment. "That sounds fair," he chuckled, "but … wouldn't you rather give it all up, too? Wouldn't you like to live for yourself, and not just in pursuit of your next high? I mean, chasing down a few hours of conjured happiness, when you could live that way, everyday, doesn't that seem ridiculous?"

It was my turn to stare. Never in my life would I have imagined those words from Riley's mouth. I had no choice but to laugh, in stupefied shock, and shake my head.

"I wouldn't hold your breath there, my friend. Good speech though." I couldn't even imagine the same thing happening to me. "So, we have a deal, then?"

"We have a deal." Riley smiled and shook my hand, as if we had just conducted some important business. "But don't think I give up that easily. I'm not giving up on you Mackenzie, not when I know what's best for you."

I laughed again. "Good luck. You'll need it."

"Why's that?"

I thought of my desires, my youth, my plan for life which did not extend past this evening—highlighting the areas when I would be high, skipping past the areas when I would be sober, already impatient for the feel of a joint to my lips. I was young. I was not done having fun. If anything, I wanted complete, reckless amusement at any cost. I wanted danger, complete abandonment—wild, careless, excitement.

I shrugged my shoulders, but I was grinning. "I'm a lost cause." I decided.

And I was delighted to be so.

CHAPTER 7

My heightened pulse had nothing to do with the fact that I was waiting on tables, alone, for the very first time. It had nothing to do with trying to remember menu choices and prices and customer needs. I wiped my sweaty palms on my sleek black skirt and tried to breathe normally. My anxiety had nothing to do with waitressing and everything to do with him.

He was there. After all my scheming and waiting and new-jobbery, he was finally there, behind the narrow slit of a window dividing the kitchen from the waitress area. I snuck another glance at him. All I could see was the blue fabric of his bandana as he bent down at the line. Then he lifted his head, and Grey's heartbreakingly handsome face became visible, the deep tone of his skin darkened by a few days growth of stubble. His blue eyes were narrowed as he worked, his hair pulled back in the blue bandana tied round his forehead. Even in the black and white checked kitchen attire—messy with pizza sauce and who knows what else—he was gorgeous. His sleeves were rolled up, showing his dark, tanned forearms firm with muscle. The apron he wore hinted at slender hips, outlined his hard torso, and implied at the defined muscle beneath. It was all I could do not to openly drool at him, to grovel at his feet and offer him a lifetime of servitude in exchange for a smile, a touch.

I patted my hair in place, took a deep breath, and approached the window. My table wanted extra garlic bread. It was the perfect excuse to talk to him.

"Excuse me." I cleared my throat, watching him expectantly. His head barely lifted, barely acknowledged me, but just the feel of his blue eyes against my own was enough to make my heart race even faster.

"What." He looked back down at his work.

"Um … can I get some more garlic toast, for table thirteen?" I asked nicely.

He looked up at me again, a slight smile bending his perfect lips. He raised his eyebrows and then leaned in closer to me. I focused on breathing.

"See this?" Grey asked, his voice low, like velvet. He held up an order sheet.

" … Yes …." I smiled.

"Take this," his tone was condescending, "take your pen, write *one garlic toast*," he did exactly that, made sure I was watching, smartly—his eyes innocent, his voice sarcastic. "Then stab it on the puck, like so …," he demonstrated for me, taking the order sheet he had just scrawled upon and placing it roughly on the hockey-puck-nail apparatus. "And then you wait, and I go back there, and put it in the oven. And when it's done, I bring it to you. Okay?"

" … O … okay …." I stammered stupidly. Heat rushed to my cheeks in an embarrassing blush, adding to my humiliation.

"There's no need for this," he motioned with his hand to me, and then back to him. "There's no need for us to talk. Ever. Okay? Can you remember that?" He muttered something then … I heard the words "stupid" and "waitresses" and "all."

I nodded, dumb with shock, and backed away from the window, trying to put some distance between me and his sudden, unexpected scorn. I could hear him chuckling behind the counter, and at the sound, my mortification turned swiftly to anger. Clearly I remembered Grey at the club and the smiles he had given me as we laughed and talked together. But either he'd totally forgotten me and I didn't even register in his memory, or he did remember and simply didn't care. Seething, I imagined him later on, regaling his kitchen friends with the story of his sheer wit that put the new girl in her place. Grey or no Grey, I would show him. He couldn't be such a dick and get away with it.

Quickly and impetuously, I stormed back to the counter, hastily scribbled, "Screw you!" on an order sheet and stabbed it on the puck. Then I rang the bell beside it as hard as I could, the poor instrument protesting with a loud, tinny clang that instantly got Grey's attention. He swung around again from the oven, and the moment my eyes rested on his handsome, perfect face, I'd completely forgiven him and wanted to take it all back. What had I been mad about? I couldn't seem to remember. He kept his icy blue eyes upon me, a small smirk on his lips, and reached to retrieve the order. It was too late to take back the rashly worded message, and my brow furrowed with fresh worry. Surely, this would make him hate me forever.

His eyes scanned the page for what seemed like eternity. I grimaced at my own stupidity. Why couldn't I've just let it go?

Grey raised his eyebrows, and then he glanced at me. His blue eyes were … surprised? Amused? I couldn't tell. Then, he chuckled slightly, shook his head, and a smile broke over his perfect lips.

I didn't want him to see my utter relief at his reaction. With an effort to seem completely calm and in control of myself, I shook my head at him, as if the whole thing were totally immature and beneath me, and then stalked out of the waitress area. I could hear Grey chuckling again from behind the counter.

This time I didn't mind.

The night continued. It was Charlie and I, alone, again, but I actually came to find I didn't mind it. Charlie knew what she was doing, and albeit lazier than Sophie, it was actually a nice change. She was wearing a dress tonight, low-cut and white with little pink flowers on it, like the kind someone would wear to a wedding. Her high heels clicked on the brown tile floor of the waitress area. Her hair was half up, half down in blond curls, her make-up done to a tee. She looked gorgeous, and I couldn't help admiring her. If Grey didn't go for her even, what chance did I really have?

Charlie caught me staring. She smiled at me and motioned with her hand to outline her outfit. "It helps with the tips," she admitted, "you should try it. Not that you don't look good. I like your skirt."

"Thanks." I looked down at myself, at my bright pink turtleneck and black pencil skirt. My dark curls tumbled down from the loose ponytail I wore; I had comfortable, practical black skate shoes on. I smiled at Charlie, I couldn't help it. I wanted to hate her, I really did, but she was so beautiful, and so damn cool. I couldn't help but want her approval, her compliments.

"I like your style." She confessed. Her pink lips smiled at me. "Sometimes though, a little cleavage, it goes a long way."

Near the end of the night, I saw the proof. Her Styrofoam cup was loaded with change, five-dollar bills mixed into the coins. Mine was full too, but nowhere near hers. I considered her advice. It might be worth it.

Grey ignored me the rest of the night. Well, mostly. Once, we happened to look up at the same time, and our eyes met, and he gave me the most genuine smile I had ever received from him. It lasted only briefly, before he turned away and his expression resorted back to its normal, stoic appearance—but I was overjoyed. I couldn't help but feel like I had made some progress, however small. If nothing else, I'd made myself memorable, and that seemed a victory in itself.

I was painfully aware of him the entire night. I knew every move he made, every word he said, every time he left for a smoke break. A few times I debated just "happening" to go outside at the exact time he did, but I wasn't ready for that. I wasn't near brave enough. Instead I worked away, mostly silently, trying to do the best job possible so he'd notice, making my orders perfectly legible and exactly how he'd want them.

When the open light was finally shut off and the staff had gathered at the tables for coffee and cigarettes in the traditional manner, I joined Riley at his table, but I sat so Grey was in plain view. He had changed into dark jeans and a long sleeved grey shirt, his leather bracelets were back, his hair messy out of the confining bandana. The breath caught in my throat just looking at him, even from afar. The guys with him were laughing, flicking their cigarettes messily at the ashtray. I was surprised to recognize both the guitar player and the drummer from Serpentine, Grey's band.

"Hey, I didn't know they worked here too." I whispered to Riley, motioning with my eyes. He turned briefly to look over his shoulder, popping his gum as he did so.

"Who, Zack and Alex? No, they don't work here. They work at some lumberyard downtown. They're always around though, scamming free food and stuff. They're in Grey's band, and Ralph doesn't seem to mind."

"Who is this Ralph? I keep hearing about him but I've never seen him. He didn't even hire me. That Mark guy did." I nodded towards the spiky-haired blonde trying to wrestle a cash-out slip from the register. Mark was young, maybe twenty-seven or thirty, with a healthy obsession for eighties rock. Even now, Cheap Trick could be heard playing somewhere in the back of the kitchen.

"Yeah, Mark's the manager. He's a good guy. He's here like twenty-four seven too, so he does most of the hiring and scheduling and shit. Ralph's the owner but he hardly shows, mostly if there's firing to do, or in the afternoon … he likes the nightlife. Don't worry though, you'll meet him." Riley sighed and rolled his eyes. "Ralph always insists on meeting the new waitresses personally."

"What is he, some kind of perv?"

"Let's call him very bored and leave it at that." Riley chuckled. I raised my eyebrows but let it go. I was dying for a cigarette, and watching Grey and his friends smoke was not making it easier. How could Riley do it?

"Go ahead, Zee." Riley smiled. "You can smoke. I won't renege on our little contract."

"What are you, reading my mind now?" I chuckled, but reached gladly for my cigarettes.

"It's not hard to read your mind when you're so damn predictable. Go ahead."

"Is it very hard?"

"No. Don't worry about it."

"Okay." I knew Riley was lying, but I was also desperate. I tried to keep the smoke from reaching him and inhaled happily. I glanced at Grey and his band mates again over Riley's shoulder. They seemed to be planning out their next gig. I paid close attention, trying to hear the date of their next show.

"So, how'd it go anyway?" Riley wondered quietly, noticing my rapt interest in the table behind him. I shot him a puzzled look. "With Grey," he explained, "isn't that what you got this job for? So, how'd it go?"

"Well ...." I smiled, and told Riley the whole shameful "screw you" story, my voice quiet enough that we wouldn't be overheard. My friend was laughing by the end of it and he shook his head at my foolishness.

"Leave it to you, Mackenzie. Grey's a jerk to everyone here, some days worse than others—it takes a while to warm him up. Most people just accept it and try to ignore him. Not you though. You're probably the only person that has ever stood up to him." He shook his head again, and chuckled mirthlessly.

"What?"

"Nothing." Riley muttered. "I just bet you made an impression, that's all."

"I wouldn't count on it." I argued, but at the same time, I desperately hoped so. I blew my smoke out and glanced at Grey's table again. The band mates were totally immersed in conversation, a serious one, by the looks of it. I watched carefully, wishing that Grey would look at me again.

"Yeah, you made an impression. Of course you did." Riley sighed quietly in his chair. I was aware of his eyes on me, but was too busy looking at Grey to acknowledge him.

CHAPTER 8

My life was in the doldrums. I couldn't really pinpoint the exact moment it happened, but suddenly my schedule was full with work (of all things) and I was home relatively early every night, giving me ample time for homework (or it would've, had I wanted to do it). Stone sober during the day and most nights, stuck at Ben's house watching the same damn movie every weekend and basically just all out bored. Riley was pretty much non-existent these days, somehow he had drifted farther and farther from me. I saw him only in the mornings when we drove to school and the random nights we happened to work together. The rest of his time he seemed to be spending with fat Emily—or the "Christian," as I called her.

In all my spare time, I had done a little reconnaissance work on Riley's little friend, and my discoveries were unsettling to say the least. Emily ran a lunchtime group, Faith ... something ... Soldiers, maybe, I couldn't remember what it was called, but it was the very meeting that my friend Riley disappeared to every day. He thought I didn't know, and he refused to talk to me about it or her, which could only mean they were becoming serious. The thought made me nearly sick to my stomach ... I could practically watch him slipping away. I tried to keep a brave face and not nag him too much, remembering our little pact and attempting to stay positive for him. I clung to the daft hope that we'd make it through this rough patch and find a way for us to be together with our friendship still intact, somehow, uncommon interest's aside.

But I just didn't see how it would work.

I had made little to no progress with Grey either. On the days we happened to work together, which weren't very often, his moods changed so much that I was confused on the best of days. He was never openly hostile again, but he ranged between totally indifferent and nonchalant to smiling at me openly from behind the order counter. To say I was baffled was an understatement, but at least he was being generally friendly. And totally gorgeous, of course.

Sundays were probably the worst though. On Sundays, Marcy made a point of coming to our house so she and my mom could work on wedding plans, which in turn meant I had to help with wedding plans, and that Greg the dick would also be there, in his collared shirts, saying unfunny things that made my parents laugh. Sundays couldn't go by fast enough. It's hard to choke through a whole day with a fake smile on your face when trying to be enthused about something that held no interest at all.

Worse yet, with graduation approaching quickly, the warm, hazy air of summer only encouraged all manner of wild, teenage activity. Yet I was stuck … trapped in a routine that disabled me from enjoying any kind of young summertime fun. Riley and I had grand plans for this time of the year, a wicked camping trip up river somewhere, all the booze and drugs we could want. I would've been willing to go to the other parties too, held by kids we really didn't hang out with, but I didn't want to go alone.

Riley was out and Ben, Toby and Jacob weren't really willing to go either, they preferred to hang out at Ben's house and get high without having to socialize with anyone else. Not that I blamed them. I'd sat many times, for hours, while the three of them laughed—just laughed, pretty much non-stop, at who knows what. They didn't need to go out to be entertained. But I craved some craziness, some … opportunity. A little drama in my otherwise lacklustre life.

I sighed, finishing the loop on my binder that made the doodled flower complete. If something exciting didn't happen soon I was going to lose my mind. The teacher was going over materials we should study for finals, but I ignored him. The very thought of those dreaded exams bored me nearly to tears. I began work on another flower—another, larger, grander flower than the one before it. It seemed that if I wanted something to happen, I'd have to do it myself. And I was just on the verge of crazy enough, to be brave enough, to make it happen.

I had my plan in action the moment the bell rang. I nearly sprinted down the hall towards Riley's locker, smiling victoriously when I beat him there, and turned to wait. Kids rushed by me on their way to the cafeteria or to the parking lot and their awaiting cars, some pushed through the nearby doors to begin the walk uptown to the closest convenience store. I spotted Riley coming down the hallway, but the smile fell off my face when

I saw Emily close beside. The people had to move around them instead of barging through the middle, because to my horrified eyes, Riley's hand was wrapped tightly in Emily's, their fingers as intertwined as their eyes seemed to be, completely oblivious to all those around them. Completely oblivious to me.

I felt like I couldn't breathe. Like I had been kicked in the guts, like I had been horribly, brutally betrayed. I took a breath to steady myself, to try and talk some rationalization into my befuddled brain. Riley wasn't mine, I had never claimed him in that way. So why did I hate, with every part of me, the fact that he was holding Emily's hand? I couldn't answer that question. I just hated it. I fought the urge to run over and tear his hand from hers and make him look at me. Maybe that would snap some sense into him.

I can't imagine what my expression must have been. Riley did look up eventually—it was inevitable as they came closer—and when he saw me his face became alarmed. But his hand was still tight around hers.

"Mac? Are you okay? Did someone die or something?" He asked.

"… No … no—" I choked out. My throat seemed to have closed. I shook my head instead of trying to talk.

"What's up then? Oh, hey, you know Emily, right?" Riley looked down at the chubby girl and I saw it then … how his dark chocolate eyes warmed, how his face seemed to beam at the sound of her name on his lips. He loved her. I knew he did. I wanted to cry, right there in front of them. How did this happen? How did I let this happen? I felt the panicky tears start climbing up my throat, and I gulped to hold them in.

"Yeah, sure," I barely looked at her, "hey, Ry, do you think I could talk to you for a minute?" My voice was a raspy whisper.

"Yeah, of course. I'll just be a minute, okay Em?" He smiled again at her. "Save me a seat?" She nodded submissively and grinned.

"Sure. Just don't be late, okay? Bye Mackenzie, nice to see you."

I gave her a tight smile. It was probably more like a grimace, but at least I tried. Emily galumphed off down the hallway and I let my breath out, the tears held at bay for the moment.

"So, are you okay or what? You look kind of terrible." Riley smiled, opening his locker to exchange books. "Late night or something? Can't say I miss that. You're looking at a full eight, every night. I've never felt better."

"That's really great, Ry." I tried to be enthused, tried to seem light-hearted. It all sounded wooden to me. "Um … so, I was just wondering, well, I was hoping that we could hang out sometime soon ... just me and you." I looked up at him hopefully. Emily was definitely not invited.

"Sure ... yeah of course. Um ...." Riley thought it over. I frowned impatiently. When did this become so awkward? Hanging out with Riley used to be as natural as breathing, and now we had to watch ourselves, had to keep things from each other, had to think things through before saying them.

"I'm just trying to figure ... this week is crazy, when I'm not working I've got to get my studying done, what with the camping trip this weekend ...."

"What camping trip?" I interrupted suddenly. A faint hope that he had planned our trip in secret, to surprise me, glimmered briefly.

"Oh, yeah, we're heading to Moose Lake this weekend, Emily and her family and I, kind of a pre-grad celebration thing."

"What?" My hope died, snuffed out with barely a fight. I couldn't believe my ears. Anger and injustice began to mix with my panic and worry, roiling together just below the surface. "You're going on *our* camping trip? With the Christian?" I said her nickname with as much disdain as I could muster.

"What?" Riley chuckled, but the sound was dangerous. "What did you call her?"

I didn't answer. I just stared at him in disbelief, and I could feel my tears welling. My sight became blurry, my voice wobbly. My throat burned.

"I can't believe you." I managed.

"What's the big deal?" He asked with concern, his own anger forgotten as soon as he saw me crying. It worked like a charm, every time.

"I don't know. I suppose you've probably forgotten, since you're so busy with *her* all the time."

"Leave her out of it. Get to the point, I've gotta go." Riley was getting impatient. He had to go be with *her*, is what he meant.

"We were supposed to go on a camping trip, remember? Us! For pre-grad. We planned it for months. Remember?" My voice was thick.

"Well, sure ... I remember." He softened. "But, I told you Mac, I can't do those things anymore. You know I can't. I'm sorry. I know it sucks."

I frowned, and crossed my arms around the volatile mixture of emotions within me. My entire chest seemed to burn.

"Hey, Mac. Come on, don't be upset. I know ... maybe I could ask Emily if you could come with us this weekend. We could all hang out. What do you say?"

I scoffed incredulously at him. It wasn't so much his words, as ridiculous as they were. It was the fake enthusiasm I could hear in his voice. He didn't want me to go with them anymore than I wanted to go. He didn't want me with him. And that killed me.

There were no words. The tears overwhelmed and spilt down my cheeks. I shook my head and turned from him, heading blindly down the badly lit hallway, no direction in mind but out. Part of me was conscious for him, waiting to hear him call my name, waiting to hear his footsteps falling behind me. He couldn't just let me go, could he?

And when he never came, when he never followed, I had my answer. And I knew then why I hated seeing Emily's hand twined within Riley's. Because she had replaced me, just as I feared and easier than I ever could've imagined, and seeing that physical bond had been like tapping the final, inevitable nail into our coffin.

Riley and I were done.

CHAPTER 9

Our night was coming to a close. I caught a sight of my face in the decorative mirror, amazed that my eyes were still red, though the puffiness had gone down. I had gone through all the motions a waitress was expected too, but I had no enthusiasm, no patience at all for any of the people surrounding me. I just wanted to go get high, higher than I'd ever been, to have a break from the doldrums and find some numbing peace in the process. My thoughts weren't allowed to even sneak by Riley's name. It was all too close, and then I'd end up where I'd been for most of the day. Trying to hold back tears that would just inevitably break through.

"How you holding up, hon?" Charlie asked me, back in the relative safety of our waitress area, and rubbed my shoulder comfortingly. I had indulged a few details to Charlie, only because she demanded to know and wouldn't accept my allergies excuse. She knew both Riley and I, and could sympathise fairly well. Also, it felt good just to talk to someone, and she was surprisingly easy to talk to.

"I'm okay." I decided. Just minus one best friend. I took a deep, shaky breath.

"Here." She handed me the large plastic container for House dressing. "Go hide for a minute. I've got things under control out here."

"Thanks, Charlie." I nodded, glad for an excuse to drop the fake smile from my face for a few minutes. I headed through the dish-pit to the large walk-in refrigerator. It smelt in there, like oil and cheese and eggs and sour milk and whatever else happened in refrigerators. There were shelves upon shelves of cold food and sauces and supplies. I took the large, heavy, black funnel from the wall and tried to remember how Sophie had shown me to refill the dressing, having never actually done it myself before.

A large white bucket sat on the floor, the word "House" scrawled in faded black marker. Then I remembered. I sat the dressing container on the floor, taking the lid off so I could place the funnel in the top. Carefully I removed the wide lid from the heavy bucket, trying not to get covered in the thick white-green gloop in the process. By the time I had the bucket lifted and into position to pour, the funnel had tipped sideways out of the top of the dressing container and was lying on the floor upside down. Quickly I put the bucket down and retrieved the funnel, hoping I hadn't broken any health codes in the process. I placed it back in the container, where it rested precariously against the edge, and grasped the bucket again.

A curse escaped my lips when I noticed the black funnel, upside down on the floor again. Vaguely I remembered the poor woman from *The Gods Must Be Crazy Two*, trying desperately to get a rusty drink from that old rickety windmill while the monkeys kept making off with her can. Suddenly, I could sympathise with her.

I looked around for a moment, deciding to prop the funnel/container up against the wall to keep it in place. It looked like it would work, but barely had I started pouring when the funnel tipped out again, this time falling to the floor and splattering dressing everywhere. I bit my lip and cursed again, closing my eyes in frustration. Now I had a mess to clean as well. The last thing I needed.

"Damn monkeys." I breathed nonsensically. It was then I heard him chuckling. I looked up quickly in surprise and found Grey, standing there at the entrance to the fridge, his arms folded on the nearby wire shelf, his head resting on his arms, his eyes wide with amusement. He had been watching me. I felt the alarming blush rush to my cheeks. His blue eyes were dancing with laugher, even more beautiful then when they were sullen.

Normally very, painfully aware of him, I had been utterly distracted all night; even to the point where I almost forgot he was working. I smiled at him now though, pleasantly surprised, probably the first real smile of my whole day.

"Would you like some help?" He offered.

I shrugged, trying to play it cool, but then admitted, "Yes, I would. Please."

"Here. Hold the funnel." He sauntered over and picked up the pail as if it weighed nothing at all. I bent down and held the funnel upright for him. We worked in silence a moment, watching as the thick dressing poured neatly into the container.

"So what's with you tonight?" Grey asked when he was done, flipping the pail up expertly. "Cursing monkeys by yourself? You look like you've been crying all day."

"Oh … it's nothing." I stammered, and I could feel myself flush bright red. "Nothing to bore you with."

Grey shrugged, and then he smiled, sitting upon the white bucket and patting an overturned milk crate beside him. "Come on. Indulge me."

"Um …. Okay." I felt like my smile might split my face in two. I sat down beside him and tried to stay cool. Why was Grey talking to me all of a sudden? It didn't matter, as long as he was.

"So …." He was close enough for me to smell not only the scents of the kitchen, but also his own scent … a hint of men's cologne, sweet and masculine. His blue eyes were even more intense up close, so clear and beautiful. Hypnotising almost. He smirked, and motioned for me to tell my story. What was I upset about again? I couldn't seem to remember. Oh, wait … of course ….

"Um … well, Riley and I had a fight … sort of." That was barely scratching the surface of what we were going through, but I thought it'd do.

"About?"

"Well … he's kind of, done with the party life, you know, and I'm not."

"I noticed that actually. He doesn't even smoke anymore."

"I know! It's frustrating. But I've tried to be understanding."

"Are Riley and you … together? You worry about him a lot."

"No we're not together." I shook my head. "We're best friends … at least we used to be." I wanted to stop there.

"Go on." He encouraged. It was hard to think straight with Grey so near. I kept my eyes busy, cataloguing all the items on the shelves of the refrigerator, and took a deep breath.

"Well, he met this girl …." I started, but I could tell my voice was about to break, and I stopped then. I looked up at the roof and prayed that I wouldn't break down, not now, not with Grey here, actually talking to me. What a way to impress him. I cleared my throat and held it together. "Anyway, we're over. It's just … over."

The finality of my words hung in the air.

"That sucks." Grey decided. I nodded; amazed that we were having this conversation, amazed that he actually cared.

"Yeah, it does." I admitted.

"Did you tell *him* to go screw himself?"

"No." I laughed loudly, his question surprising me. "No, I didn't. Maybe I should've." I looked at Grey and grinned.

"It's amazing what a simple 'screw you' can do to a man." He chuckled. I laughed with him again, repentant.

"I'm sorry about that, I just … I didn't even think … it was just the first thing that came to me."

"Don't be sorry." Grey smiled. "I enjoyed it. Really."

"Okay. Well, I'll remember that."

"Okay." He nodded. "Mackenzie." He stood up off his bucket and stretched out a hand to me. Hesitantly, I put my palm in his, praying that my hand didn't feel sweaty or sticky or gross. He pulled me to my feet and suddenly I was very, very close to him. Closer that I'd ever been. I drew in my breath and forced myself to look at him. Forced myself to meet his gaze.

"Come out with us tonight." He grinned. His smile took my very breath away. "I promise, by the end of the night, you won't even remember what you were sad about."

I couldn't even think rationally. Grey was asking me to go out with them. Somehow I managed to keep a calm exterior, but the Mackenzie within me was doing a very childish and horribly embarrassing triple-arm-pump of exultation. I gave Grey a wide, dazzling smile.

"I'll take that as a yes." He chuckled again. "Eleven o'clock. We'll pick you up." He edged slowly out of the refrigerator.

"Great." I nodded. Grey smiled at me again as he left, only to pop his head back into the fridge when I was cleaning up my mess a moment later.

"And Mackenzie?"

"Yes?"

"Get ready. We're getting fucked up tonight."

I beamed up at him. "Perfect."

CHAPTER 10

A quick glance at the clock told me it was almost ten. Hurriedly I wiped up the waitress station, aware now as Grey worked behind the counter near me, whistling as he stacked up the ramekins, the glassware clinking together. A surge of excitement spread through me, making my stomach churn convulsively. In an hour, I'd be out with Grey. One hour.

"Hey, you almost done?" Charlie came in and surveyed my work. "Good. We don't want to be late, and we still have to get you out of those clothes."

"Out of my …?" I looked down at myself, dressed in dark pants and a turquoise blue sweater, and puzzled. Charlie giggled.

"For tonight, silly. You're coming to my house. I'm going to doll you up before we go."

"Tonight? You're coming with us?"

"Of course. You think I'd let you go with those idiots by yourself?" Charlie shook her head, her blond curls flipping around her shoulders. "Come on, let's go." She stretched her hand out to me.

I took her hand, hesitantly, and smiled, but felt disappointment leak into my chest. Had Grey asked Charlie to come? Why had he asked me then? Maybe Grey was into Charlie and just asked me along to make it seem like a group thing. I frowned, and felt stupid. There was no competition between Charlie and me. She'd win hands down.

My excitement began to drain, my night heading quickly in a downward spiral. I followed Charlie through the restaurant into the warm, fragrant air of summer night, but I lacked my previous enthusiasm. Then she smiled at me.

"Zack asked me to come along. You don't mind, do you? I just couldn't say no, I've been waiting so long …."

"No, of course I don't mind." I exclaimed suddenly, her words alleviating all my worries. My anticipation surged again, stronger than ever. Grey didn't want her! I giggled excitedly as we climbed into her car. "I can't wait. This is going to be great."

"I know!" Charlie laughed and lit a smoke. She threw her little sedan into reverse and then punched it when we were the right way around. We rolled the windows down and let the night air wash over us, racing through the empty, quiet streets. Slipknot blared through her speakers, the music lost somewhere behind us in the calm night air, the dull thumping bass of her stereo wafting down the streets.

This was it. This was living. This was exactly where I wanted to be.

We pulled up to Charlie's condo just a little after ten. She lived in a quiet, dark part of town, where the buildings were older and needed paint in a bad way. The trailer park where Riley lived was not far from us, and I glanced sadly in that direction.

"Come on, Mackenzie!" Charlie smiled and raced up a set of wood stairs, grey with age. They squeaked and groaned in protest. I turned from my sudden melancholy and followed her, taking the stairs more gingerly that she had, not trusting them with my weight. She fought with the saggy doorknob and flicked a light on once inside. I stepped into the entryway behind her and surveyed the little house.

It was older, apparent in the gold plastic trimmings and light fixtures, the odd cream coloured light-switch plates, the threadbare carpeting and cracked linoleum. But she still managed to make it cozy and welcoming—the walls repainted a warm green, candles covering nearly every available surface, blankets and pillows adorning the older, second-hand furniture. I liked it immediately.

Charlie swept in, throwing her bag on the kitchen counter, her coat on the chair in the living room, flicking on lights as she went. I followed into her small bedroom, sitting on her unmade bed as she rushed around, opening dresser drawers and rummaging through her closet.

"Do you live here by yourself?" I wondered, sitting cross-legged with the large, flat book she had just handed me, getting out my supplies so I could roll us a joint.

"No, I have a roommate. Katrina. She's got the bedroom at the end of the hall." Charlie made a face, throwing some chosen clothing on the bed beside me.

"You don't seem pleased." I noticed.

She frowned. "Katrina's kind of a pain in the ass. I'm thinking of kicking her out."

"Really? Why?"

Charlie stepped over to the CD player and pressed play. The room was instantly flooded with 311, loud. She smiled and came to sit next to me.

"Just roommate stuff. She's messy and always late with the rent."

"I like your house." I licked the joint and handed it to her.

"Thanks." Charlie lit the joint, puffing away until the end was smoking. She sucked in and held her breath. "Here."

I took it from her and inhaled deeply. Even just the taste and smell of weed smoke was relaxing to me. I smiled and handed it back to her. She took another drag, held it, and then passed the joint back to me.

"Okay, let's get to work." She piled some clothes on my lap, a pair of silvery studded blue jeans and a tiny, silver halter-top. I looked at them a moment incomprehensibly.

"Put them on, silly." She laughed and started taking off her pants. I grinned dumbly and nodded. We changed in her room—she into a long, tight, pink, sleeveless dress and I into the jeans and top. They actually fit fairly nicely. I took a glance in her full-length mirror, impressed. The silver top was a little low. It showed some good cleavage, hinting nicely at my breasts beneath, something I was unused to. The rest of the shirt flowed smoothly down my tight abdomen, barely meeting the jeans that rested snugly just off my hips.

"Hot." Charlie decided. I handed her the joint and she sat me down on the bed, pulling over a large make-up kit and starting on my face.

"No, you're hot." I argued. And she was, she could've been a runway model, her dress fit her so perfectly. Charlie shrugged, and smiled.

"Just wait until I'm done with you." She promised. I shook my head. We had less than half an hour. Not near enough time for a miracle.

I wasn't really paying attention to what Charlie was doing. I was nicely high by that point, content, happy. She began drawing around my eyes with a pencil. Her hands were soft and smelt like lotion.

"How old are you?" I asked her suddenly.

Charlie smiled. "Nineteen. You?"

"Seventeen." I admitted morosely. Everyone was older than me. "Do you think I'm too young?"

"Too young?" Charlie thought a moment. "Quit squinting. No, you're not too young for this crowd, that's for sure."

"Why?"

"Honey, if anyone gives you any flak for your age, it's only because they're jealous. They wish they still had your excuse to act the way they do."

"They wish they were still seventeen?"

Charlie nodded. "It's easier to get away with it all when you're that young. You are expected to become responsible at some point, you know." She leaned back and surveyed my face. "There, all done."

"Thanks." I got up and looked in the mirror, wishing now that I had paid attention to whatever Charlie had done. It didn't look like me, staring back at me. This girl had cheekbones and large, dark eyes—smouldering eyes—deep, full red lips. I gazed back at Charlie in surprise.

"Told you," she shrugged, and began painting her own face. I was amazed. I did look hot. Older, too. I liked that a lot.

"What should I do with my hair," I asked her, pulling my hands through the long, dark curls.

"Umm … put it into a ponytail, like you do, with some left in the front. And make the top … big." She demonstrated. I nodded and got to work. We primped and preened—Charlie shook out her blond curls, she pulled on her tight black knee-high boots and leant me some distressed silver-black heels, high and pretty with a closed toe.

I couldn't believe how good I looked. I didn't want to be vain, but couldn't help just staring at myself in the mirror. Charlie noticed and began to giggle at me. I laughed too, a mixture of weed and excitement and complete disbelief. This was going to be a great night. I lit a smoke to try and calm down my nerves.

"I think they're here." Charlie exclaimed a few moments later, as the dim noise of a car horn caught our attention. I looked at her desperately, suddenly horribly afraid and overcome by nervousness. She rolled her eyes and smiled at me.

"Relax. He's not going to know what hit him."

I let her lead us back through the house, flicking off lights as we went. We grabbed our bags and headed for the door. I prayed I wouldn't trip down the long flight of stairs in my heels and break a bone or something. My smoke was like a security blanket—it gave me something to do, made me seem preoccupied. Charlie waved in the direction of headlights and closed the door behind us.

Somehow I made it down the stairs and to the car. I felt young again, like a tagalong, trailing behind Charlie like a little sister. It made me angry at myself and I took a breath, willing myself to be brave and more confident.

"Hey." I recognized his voice before I saw him. A smile lit my face instantly, and suddenly, I wasn't nervous anymore. Suddenly, it all felt fairly natural apart from the excited, ramped up beating of my heart. Grey stood before me then, next to the opened car door, and smiled as he took in my appearance.

"Mackenzie," was all he said, but I could tell he approved. His blue eyes were darker, gleaming, his face freshly smooth from shaving. A hint of a grin curled his lips, almost a smirk, smug. He had on dark blue jeans and a tight black shirt—I could see his muscles hard against the fabric. If I have ever come close to swooning, it was then.

Grey gently pushed an errant dark curl off my shoulder, his fingers brushing my collarbone as he did so. I shivered delightfully. He held the door open and motioned for me to get in. I slid into the middle of the seat, squeezing up close to Alex—the other passenger—as Grey got in beside me. The backseat was fairly small, making for imminent body contact. His cologne wafted toward me with the whoosh of air from the car door shutting, and his thigh pressed against mine as he made himself more comfortable. I was nearly dizzy with elation.

Charlie hopped into shotgun, smiling excitedly. Zack shut her door and walked around the front of the car, getting into the drivers seat. He was good looking, about the same age as Grey with blonde, mullety hair that actually suited him. Multiple piercings hung from numerous places; a muscle shirt showed off the full sleeve of tattoos that covered his arms. Charlie smiled at him as he started the car.

We all adjusted in our close quarters. Grey rested his arm along the top of the seat, not quite hugging me, but I could feel the warmth of his skin along the back of my neck.

"Mackenzie—Alex, and Zack." Grey introduced. I smiled at them both.

"Nice to meet you."

Alex nodded. He was fairly scrawny; his face was as long as his sandy blond hair, but his smile was winning, and I could tell right away that he was a ton of fun.

"Let's get fucked up!" he shouted, "come on Zackie!" he gripped the back of Zack's seat, banging it a few times. Zack laughed and revved the engine in agreement. I didn't know what kind of car we were in, something older, with faded silver paint and blue upholstered seats. The engine sounded impressive anyway. I grinned as Zack suddenly slammed his foot on the gas and we squealed into the street.

"Music!" Alex demanded. Charlie pulled out a thick black binder full of CD's and started going through them. Meanwhile, Alex handed me a joint he had just rolled and I took a drag. Someone produced a flask and started passing it around. I took a swig, my eyes instantly watering, my mouth burning as I choked it down.

"What was that?" I asked when I recovered my breath. Grey had been watching me with amusement.

"Appleton Jamaican, one-fifty-one proof. You took it like a champ." He laughed.

"Well, I'm nothing if not a champion drinker." I joked.

Charlie put Godsmack into the CD player, and soon *Moon Baby* was deafening us through the speakers. A dizzying combination of weed and rum moved steadily around the car, passing in a ceaseless circle that included our driver. I didn't even think to be scared or worried, a far off distant lecture about getting in with a drunk driver barely occurred to me, and I easily ignored it. Obviously Zack had this under control.

"How are you feeling now?" Grey asked quietly, about an hour into our trip. He lowered his mouth wonderfully close to my ear to be heard. His breath gave me delicious shivers, my skin goose bumps.

"Amazing." I breathed.

"Just you wait." He promised. His hand played with the curls from my ponytail. I was in heaven.

"Where are we going? What are we—?"

"Just you wait," he chided. His hand moved from my hair, his fingers slowly tracing a trail down my neck, then up again. "By the way … you look amazing."

I blushed. "I do?"

"You know you do." His voice was lower, guttural. I smiled.

"Thanks." The feel of his fingers was addictive. My heart began to beat harder at his touch, however slight. I clenched my hands against my legs. He chuckled and stopped, placing his hand back against the seat, allowing me to catch my breath—but I missed his fingers the moment they lifted. I bit my lip and tried to calm myself.

Soon we could make out city lights on the horizon. Alex cheered. I laughed, fairly wasted already just from the drive in, let alone whatever was happening later. The talk and laughter was rowdy and lively inside the car. Alex and Grey were arguing about some bands I'd never heard of; Charlie was trying to regale me with a work story from the front seat. Zack would throw a few words into the band conversation. We weaved through the city traffic, the streetlamps lighting the interior of the car as we passed beneath them.

Finally we pulled into a parking lot filled with vehicles. I looked out the window in interest, but the street was fairly dark. The only thing that made sense to my poor befuddled brain was the turquoise blue, neon sign perched atop a brick building. It said "The Drink" in large green letters, with a martini angled off the side of it.

"We're going to a club?" I asked Grey excitedly. "But I'm not old enough—"

"Leave that to me. Come on." He opened the door and helped me out. As soon as I stood up, I nearly fell over. I hadn't expected to be so wasted, it took me by surprise. Grey laughed and steadied me.

"You okay?" His hands were warm on my bare arms.

"Yeah." I laughed happily. Better than okay. Great, wonderful … ecstatic.

"Come on." Grey took my hand in his and pulled me towards the entrance. Alex and Zack and Charlie were walking ahead of us. As we turned the corner, I was amazed to see the long line of people waiting to get in the club. It stretched nearly the entire block. I looked up at Grey but he didn't seem disappointed, like he hadn't anticipated a wait at all.

I soon understood why. When the two large, intimidating men at the entrance saw us coming, they immediately pulled back the rope and let us all through. Grey spoke with them briefly—I didn't hear the conversation, but I did notice that they called him Mr. Lewis. I raised my eyebrows at the VIP treatment and smiled.

"I didn't know your last name was Lewis." I kidded.

"There's a lot about me you don't know." Grey smirked. He grasped my hand again and we made our way inside. I looked around; this club was nothing like the Aurora at home. Modern and new, the décor was mostly black and white, with splashes of vibrant blues and greens and oranges in just the right places. The main floor was dedicated almost entirely to the dance floor, clear Plexiglas atop swirls of fluorescent color, surrounded by tall white and black plastic chairs. A shooter bar flanked the left side, and a large spiral staircase took up most of the right. The place was packed, the music thumped over the noisy din.

CHAPTER 11

"This way, Mr. Lewis." A server appeared from nowhere, and motioned for us to follow. "The rest of your party has already arrived."

"Great." We followed the waitress, who led us up the staircase. The top floor was full of circular tables surrounded by more tall plastic chairs; impossibly tall backed booths lined the walls, and all of them were full. The tables were made to mimic the dance floor. There was a bar for every wall but one, the back wall the server was leading us to. She pushed back a nearly indiscernible curtain that opened to reveal another staircase, this one much smaller than the first. Above us was another floor, similar to the one below. There were no single tables, only the larger, tall backed booths about twice the size of the usual. Each was up on its own platform, closed in by a curtain surrounding it.

"VIP?" I asked him.

"Nothing but." Grey laughed wryly. We ushered in through the curtain to join the people already there, seated around the back of the booth. The lights were dim, which I liked. The tabletop was like the others, clear Plexi over lights, the cushions upholstered in soft black and white vinyl. Grey introduced us before we sat.

"Mackenzie, this is Jimmy, Tom and Lucas. You may recognize them from the killer band Serpentine." Grey chuckled and made a sign in the air. The band mates cheered with a cacophony of curses. Jimmy was younger, with dark black hair in a faux hawk—he smiled at me politely. Tom and Lucas must have been brothers, though Tom looked to be in his late thirties and Lucas seemed younger, they shared the same shaggy brown hair and large, bushy eyebrows.

"Bass, keys, and our manager." Grey explained. I nodded. "And beside them are the lovely ladies Natasha, Tracy and Lori." I smiled, and waved once at them all, but the girls barely acknowledged me. I scarcely had time to look them over before we were moving to sit down, but I noticed lots of make-up, and skin, and a general expression of utter boredom.

We squeezed into the booth, Grey on one side of me, Charlie on the other. I was thankful to be past the scrutiny, to sit and relax. I lit a smoke. Grey was talking to Alex on the other side of him. I heard someone order champagne for everybody, and my eyebrows raised again. Was this how they always partied? How could they afford it?

A lady came around with hand-blown crystal flutes, filling them halfway with sparkling, honey coloured champagne. I looked around, but nobody was drinking theirs. It was like they were waiting for something.

After a few minutes Tom called us to attention. I did my best to lean over Grey without blocking Charlie's view, to better see the older man. The talk quieted around us, and Tom raised his glass in the air.

"Tonight, a celebration." He smiled around the group from his place in the middle. "Tonight, a first. I am honoured, and delighted, and proud to be a part of this ride with you all. Here's to your success, and to your futures. They're sure to be bright. Congratulations."

"Fuck yeah!" Alex shouted. Everyone cheered and then clinked their glasses together, laughing happily. I watched them in confusion. Though it was dim in the room, seemingly I was the only one completely in the dark.

"Um … congratulations for what?" I whispered to Grey. He turned to me; his blue eyes alight with happiness, the impact of them taking my breath away. He laughed loudly.

"Our band was signed." He explained. He clinked his glass against mine.

"What? That's awesome!" I exclaimed.

"Yeah. That's the idea," he chuckled, "we'll be recording soon."

"Wow. That's great … amazing even! Let's celebrate, shall we?"

"We shall." He promised. We smiled and drank the sharp, cold bubbly, watching each other. Now that the feeling of ceremony was over, we relaxed and ordered a round of more practical drinks, preparing to really celebrate. Grey lit a cigarette and passed it to me, lighting another one for himself. I drank my rye and Coke almost as soon as it came, trying quickly to maintain my buzz. Grey watched me take one last gulp, and smiled.

"That's impressive, but really not necessary."

"What? Why not?"

"Because." He grinned wickedly, looked around, and passed me a hand mirror from the other side of him. There were two smudgy lines reflected on the glass, and I could see my face looking down on them—could see the confusion, the comprehension, and then the anxiety that overtook my reflected expression. Cocaine. Grey was offering me cocaine.

"I promised you a good time, didn't I?"

My stomach did a little flip. Cocaine had always been something I avoided. I didn't really know why, but it was on the other side of the line I had drawn for myself. The stupid line. I'd never had an interest.

"If you don't want to, it's no big deal. Just pass it on." Grey spoke softly.

"No. I want to." I decided. Of course I would do it. It was no different than E or mush or weed, just another means to the desirable end. And I wanted that end. I wanted to be higher that I'd ever been before. I smiled at Grey.

"I don't know how." I giggled, ashamed.

"Just pinch your other nostril shut." He leaned in close to me, explaining under his breath. He handed me a rolled up twenty-dollar bill. "Then suck it in with this, and chase the line."

"From the mirror?"

He nodded. My heart beat convulsively in my chest, I was so nervous.

"Don't make fun of me." I pleaded. Grey laughed.

"I won't. Look, no one's even watching. Just don't blow out, whatever you do. I promise, you'll love it."

"I will?"

He nodded again. That was it for me. Sold.

I leaned over and did it the way Grey had said. I sucked in quickly and moved the bill down the line. Then I straightened up, sniffing, feeling an immediate burn within my sinuses. I sniffed and sniffed, rubbing at my septum, and pushed the mirror towards Charlie. Grey laughed and watched me.

"What do you think?" He wondered. I looked at him, and honestly felt no different. Just that my nose was on fire.

"I … I don't …." I was about to say, "feel anything," but was suddenly unable to speak. Because I did feel something. I felt amazing. I looked at Grey with wonder. My hands were shaking and I felt so good I wanted to cry. I can't even describe the euphoria that flooded over me, the total and complete joy and contentment that became mine in that instant. I was physically numb but mentally clear, completely awake and alert. Totally confident. I looked at Grey and smiled, buzzing.

"Wow … it's just so, and I never realized it was like this. Is it always like this? Did you do some? Do you feel the same? Can we do some more?" I was whispering. He laughed, hard, like I had said something outrageously hilarious. I didn't even bother worrying if he was laughing at me. How could he be? I was so awesome at that moment.

The mirror was passed around a few more times, clandestinely. Grey showed me how to pull my forehead back afterwards and inhale sharply to get better absorption. I loved it, more than anything I'd ever tried. Grey had been right.

After a few more lines, I was not content to sit anymore. I grabbed Charlie's hand and we went to the washroom, then to the shooter bar, then back to the booth, then back to the washroom, gabbing the entire time. Neither of us could talk fast enough or run out of things to say. Everything we said was so profound, so right on. My entire body was humming; I could feel my heart beating rapidly.

Then, I felt something else. In my mouth, there was a sudden, terrible, horrible taste. I made a face and put my hand over my lips, sliding back into the booth.

"How you doing, Mackenzie?" Grey noticed my grimace as I sat next to him. "Does it taste like hairspray?" He asked.

I nodded in disgust, my hand still over my mouth.

"Try to swallow it. It's just the coke. Back drip." He explained.

"Lovely."

"Want some more?"

"Yes."

Of course I did. I didn't want this feeling to ever end. Grey and I sat, almost completely by ourselves now as the others dispersed, some to go dance, some to get drinks. I leaned comfortably against him as we shared another mirror or two. His arm rested loosely around my waist, his hand warm. He smelt so good.

"Do we have to get you back anytime … curfew or anything?" He asked, his voice a deep rumble in my ear. I lit my eightieth some odd smoke and blew it out in a laugh.

"Hardly. My mom works nights, my dad's away on business. They'll never notice that I'm gone."

"Well, maybe I'll just keep you, then."

"Sounds good to me." I agreed.

I was content to sit now, with Grey beside me, but nothing could stop the uncontrollable chatter that poured from my lips. From our lips. Thankfully, Grey had done his share of cocaine too, and we talked, and talked, our words not coming fast enough for the thoughts that drove them.

We talked about work and the pain in the ass customers. About Charlie and how she was surprisingly likeable. I told him about my sister and her dick fiancé—how much my parents sucked. He let me blather on and on and listened intently the entire time. After expounding on Marcy's upcoming wedding, even describing the prissy dresses to him in finite detail, I figured it was time for me to stop talking.

"So, anyway … um, tell me about your band being signed. How did it happen? What does it mean?" I leaned forward and took a drink; my mouth was bitterly dry.

"Well," he chuckled at my ignorance, "basically, we've a contract with a record company. They put out the CD and set up a tour and do the marketing and everything. We just sit back, and make music." He grinned widely. "Which is really the best part."

"How do you do it? I mean, how do you write the songs?"

"Mostly me and Alex write them. The melodies just come to me. Sometimes, I'll wake up in the middle of the night, and I just have it, and have to get it down. Alex helps a ton, he can think of wicked parts for guitars and layering and stuff."

"That's amazing."

"I write the lyrics too. Sometimes it's hard, but most the time they just write themselves, like certain melodies were made for certain words, certain moods."

"Wait." I put my drink down and stared at Grey, baffled. "So, not only do you write the music and play the music and sing the songs, you write the lyrics too? How is that possible?"

"I don't know." He shrugged humbly. "It's just, easy for me. A lot of the time I can say things in songs that I can't say otherwise. Like an outlet, I guess."

"Wow. How long have you been playing?"

"Music had always been it for me, even when I was little. I started playing when I was … um … seven I think. It's only been guitar for me, ever, and if you think I'm crazy, Zack can play every instrument we have on stage and he's really, really good. A natural. I think he can even play the saxophone and shit."

"You guys are impressive. I can't even carry a tune and here you all are, writing your own music, singing, making your own lyrics …." A sudden idea occurred to me. I smiled in amusement.

"If you're so good, write me a song right now." I suggested. "Make me some lyrics."

"Right now?" Grey laughed. "No, no. I need music and a situation."

"Okay … I can do that. Write it to the tune of … *Twinkle, Twinkle, Little Star*, and make it about …." I looked down at my cigarette. "Smoking."

"A song about smoking. To the tune of *Twinkle, Twinkle, Little Star*?" He looked at me incredulously, but humoured me, and began humming to himself. He broke into a smile. "How does that shit even go?"

I laughed, thoroughly enjoying myself. Grey worked away for a moment, frowning in concentration as I watched him and smoked. He mumbled words aloud as he tried to place them into the song.

"Okay, okay, I think I've got it." He chuckled and cleared his throat. "Here goes. Smoking, smoking cigarette, how much better can it get? First I suck, then I blow, it gives me a healthy glow. Smoking, smoking cigarette, how much better can it get?"

I burst out laughing, clapping my hands for his impromptu performance. Grey laughed with me, his face reddening slightly.

"What'd you think?" He asked.

"I think … that was … the dirtiest song … I've ever heard …." I admitted between fits of laughter. Grey went over the words again in his head, and a smile broke over his face as he realized the implication.

"I didn't have much time." He explained. "I did the best with what I had."

"No, you did great. You did great. I just don't think I'll ever look at a cigarette the same way."

"Me either." He grinned.

"No." I shook my head seriously, clearing the laughter from my throat. "I mean it. I think that you are very talented. Soon, you'll be so famous that you won't remember the rest of us."

"I doubt that." Grey chuckled. "Some of you are pretty unforgettable." He looked at me when he said that, his blue eyes still twinkling with mirth, his lips curved handsomely. I gave him a glorious smile.

"Oh yeah?" My voice was a whisper. He nodded, and I felt his hand on my hip, hard and firm as he slowly pulled me closer towards him. My poor heart beat like a hummingbird's wings. With his other hand, dark and tan and warm, Grey tilted my chin up, pulling my face towards his until the inevitable moment—slow in coming—that our lips finally touched.

The kiss jolted me. The parts of me previously coke-numb were suddenly on fire. His lips pressed against mine, softly at first, then with growing intensity. He tasted amazing. I twisted in his arms so I was facing him, my hands lifted to the back of his neck, my fingers twirled in his hair. We kissed. We kissed as we had talked—compulsively, thoroughly, irrepressibly. I pressed myself against him, delighting in the warmth of his hands on my back, my waist … stroking my arms, my neck … tangling in my hair ….

His kiss was better than coke.

"Tell me, Mackenzie," he breathed, a few heavy moments later. I didn't answer, but opened my eyes to acknowledge him. His gaze fell to my lips.

"Who was it that made you sad earlier?" He kissed me. I frowned. I couldn't remember … it didn't matter.

"I don't know. It doesn't matter … I'm not sad anymore." I whispered. I could feel Grey's lips smile against mine. And then we were kissing again.

CHAPTER 12

The light was blinding. I groaned, and the noise made my head throb. My mouth was totally dry, my throat and sinuses raw … like someone had rubbed them with sandpaper. I rolled into a ball and put a hand to my feverish brow. I couldn't swallow.

"Here." An angel from heaven spoke, placing a cool glass of water in my hand. She chuckled. "Drink this."

I nodded weakly and tried to sit up, my eyes shut, my head throbbing anew at the change in position. I forced my shaky hand to bring the cup to my lips. The water was precious, life giving, cold and soothing. My throat and mouth worked better.

Next I tried to open my eyes. One slit at a time, allowing the harsh light to filter in slowly so they could adjust. I coughed, and my lungs felt burnt. Had I come down with some rare tropical disease in the night or something?

I panicked slightly, once my eyes were open. I was on the floor, somewhere, in a living room by the looks of things. A blanket covered me. I spotted Alex slumped over in a chair, but I didn't recognize anything else around me. Then I remembered the voice, the sweet angel from heaven.

"Charlie?" I croaked. The sound made me wince.

"How you doing hon?"

"Ugh. Not good. Where are we?"

"You're at my house, silly. Don't you remember?"

"Maybe. I don't know. I can't think straight." I lay back down. My hand hit something hard, and then I realized someone was beside me. Quickly—much too quickly for my poor head, I sat up and surveyed the man laying there.

It was Grey, of course it was Grey. I don't know who else I would've expected. His face was slack, relaxed, but beautiful in peaceful sleep. His shirt was off, allowing me a good, long glimpse of his dark chiselled chest and glorious six-pack. Multiple black tattoos covered his naked shoulders and muscled arms. A sudden thought occurred to me, and I looked down at myself beneath the blanket. I didn't know if it was relief or disappointment I felt when I realized I was fully dressed.

I'd only blacked out once that I could remember, at the party with Riley when I took all those Quaaludes. I hoped my mind would bring back all the moments I seemed to have forgotten of the previous night. It was way too good not to remember. Especially since I was waking up next to Grey now.

"What time is it?" I asked Charlie, who was bustling around her tiny kitchen. I could hear coffee brewing.

"Um … 8:24." She answered.

"Oh shit. I'm going to be late for school." I grimaced.

"So ditch. What are they going to do? You graduate in less than a month anyway."

"I know, and I totally would. I have this test though … it's kind of important."

"What time is it at?"

"Um, nine, I think. First period. Whatever time that is." I groaned again, and made the attempt to get up. It didn't go so well. I ended up back on the floor, my head in my hands. What was the point, anyway? After a few healing moments I moved again, this time placing my head on Grey's chest and resting my arm lightly on his torso. Mmm …. I felt better already.

"What about your parents, Mac? Didn't you say you'd call them in the morning?"

"Hmmm … did I? That doesn't sound like me."

"Yes, you did. Come on. You don't want them to be worried." Charlie came over and grasped my hand. "Let me help you up."

I was too weak to even protest. One moment I was totally content lying with Grey, the next I was pulled into a world of agony, bleary eyed, holding onto the counter to keep from falling over. I swayed unsteadily.

"Have some coffee." Charlie plunked a mug down in front of me.

"How are you so chipper this morning?"

"Practice. And I also did like, twenty less lines than you."

"Oh." That would explain it. "Can I borrow your phone?"

"Sure." Charlie handed me her cordless. I looked at her for the first time that morning. She seemed content and happy. Already done up for the day, of course she looked gorgeous. I surveyed her as my parents' phone rang in my ear.

"So, how'd it go?" I whispered at her. Just then, a door opening distracted me, and I saw Zack coming out of Charlie's room. That answered my question. I giggled with her, and then quieted as he approached.

"Hello? Taylor Residence." My mom finally answered the phone. I stepped away from the counter for some privacy.

"Hey, mom?"

"Mackenzie, is that you?"

"Yes, it's me. Hey, I just wanted to make sure that you remembered."

"Remembered what? You are in big trouble, young lady. Wh—"

"Ugh, see! I knew you'd forget."

"What?"

"I told you, the other day. That I'd be staying at my friend Charlie's house Wednesday night."

"Charlie? Is this some boy?"

"No, mom. My friend, Charlie, from work. Charlene?"

"Oh. Well, I don't remember this conversation."

"You never do. That's why I'm calling. I didn't want you to come home this morning and freak out 'cause I'm not there."

"Well, it's a little late for that. We talked about this, did we?"

"Yes, mom. You said it was fine."

"Huh. Well … I don't know …."

"Gotta go mom. I'll see you later."

"Okay … hey, shouldn't you be at school—"

I hung up the phone abruptly. All this talking was really making my head throb. I took a swig of coffee and it burnt all the way down. "Do I look how I feel?" I asked Charlie. She and Zack were sitting on barstools together at the counter.

Charlie grinned. "Easily fixed." I groaned at the sound of their laughter, heading to the bathroom to investigate myself. It really wasn't that bad. I fixed my eye make-up where it was smudged and threw my knotted hair into a makeshift ponytail-twist thing. My lips were chapped and swollen. They smiled at me in the mirror.

I changed out of the rumpled jeans and halter-top combination that Charlie had leant me and back into my clothes from the night before. They smelt like the fryer from work. I borrowed some of Charlie's deodorant, rubbed some toothpaste over my gums, and sprayed some mystery perfume all over myself. Nothing like a "fragrance shower" first thing in the morning.

When I came out of the bathroom, Alex was awake. He looked a little worse for wear, but was smiley and jovial as ever. He and Zack were being painfully noisy, recapping the best moments of the night. I snuck past them and headed back to Grey, not quite willing to leave him and this unreal dream, the one that somehow ended with me waking up next to him. He was somewhat conscious by the time I got there. I hadn't had a chance to really brush my teeth—I hoped I didn't have horrid morning breath or anything, but I felt like I did.

"Hey." I kept my voice low. "I've gotta go, to school."

"Alright." Grey growled, but he didn't open his eyes. I giggled slightly, totally able to sympathize with him and how he felt.

"There's water here." I handed him the cup.

"Tell those assholes to keep it down."

"Hey, assholes, keep it down!" I yelled at them, right in Grey's ear, realizing my mistake too late. I looked down repentantly. He was glaring at me with one eye open.

"Sorry. Uh … I'll just be going now." I smiled. Alex and Zack laughed at me.

"I bet he appreciated that." They joked.

I put a finger to my lips, "shhhh," but I was trying not to laugh. "Bye." I bent down, hesitantly, and kissed Grey's lips. To my joy and relief, he moved his hand to cup the back of my head and kissed me for longer.

"You work tonight?" He wondered.

"Yeah." I groaned. "I'm going to die. You?"

"Nope." He chuckled slightly, and winced. "I get to sleep all day.

"That is not fair." I groaned again.

"But it was worth it, right?"

"So worth it." I smiled. We kissed again, and then regretfully, I forced myself away from him. I didn't care about school, but I definitely didn't want to repeat the twelfth grade either. "Bye."

"See ya."

I waved to the group congregated around the counter. "'Kay, I'm off." I announced.

"Where are you going?" Zack wondered.

"I've got to walk to school."

"School? Geeze, how old are you anyway? Fifteen?"

"Something like that. I'll see you guys later." I opened the door to the painfully bright sunshine, took a healing breath, and stumble-limped down the old grey stairs. It wasn't far to my school, but it was far enough when every step was utter agony. I sighed and began my trek, lighting a smoke although my poor lungs wheezed in protest. I heard a car coming down the street, rustily, it sounded like. When it began to slow by the time it reached me, I turned to investigate. It was purple, old … beat up.

It was Riley.

"Mackenzie?"

CHAPTER 13

The passenger door opened to me, beckoning, and Riley leaned across the seat. He looked puzzled.

"Mackenzie? What are you doing here?"

"I stayed at Charlie's house last night." I pointed behind me.

"Oh. Well, get in, I'll give you a ride. Come on, we're late."

I hesitated a moment, but took him up on the offer. I was too achy and sore to protest, all of our differences aside. I threw my smoke down on the street and stiffly climbed into the car.

We stared at each other a moment once I was in. He was the same old Riley that I'd known forever, but to me, he seemed different already. Not in looks or appearance or anything ... just in him. Like he was ... peaceful, or something. He smiled hopefully at me, but the wide space of seat between us seemed to represent the status of our relationship. My expression was blank as I stared back at him. Riley sighed.

"You smell like a brewery." He wrinkled his nose. "And something else ... what, Vanilla Fields? Late night last night?"

"You could say that." Totally unconsciously, I rubbed my nose, trying to quell the dull ache that still resided within. It felt like my sinuses were completely dry, and each breath burnt them afresh. I sniffed a few times to try and get some moisture up there. It helped that I was out of the cool, morning fresh air.

I felt Riley's eyes on me then, hard. I turned to meet his gaze, sniffing and rubbing my nose again.

"What?"

"Were you doing coke last night?" His voice was low with accusation, almost threatening. The dark look in his eyes told me that he knew the truth, that somehow he'd figured it out from the mere minutes we had spent together. As odd as it was, the thought gave me hope. If he still knew me that well, there had to something left here, something of our old relationship that we could salvage.

"I gave it a try, yeah." I shrugged it off. "No big deal."

"No big deal." Riley laughed incredulously. He put the car in drive and pulled out into the street. "This coming from the girl who refuses to be in the same room as a rail. Do you remember how pissed you used to get at me when I did coke? Do you?"

"Yes." I said quietly.

"So? What changed? No, no, no …." Riley ginned sardonically. "Let me guess. You were with Grey, weren't you? And he was doing it. So you just had to try it, right?"

His perfect insight made me angry. I stuck out my chin stubbornly.

"I was with Grey, yes. But he doesn't have anything to do with it."

"Yeah, right." He scoffed. "So what, did you get coked up and then go at it all night long? Was it everything you ever dreamed it would be?" His voice was icy.

I stared. That was all I could do. My mouth hung open in shock from Riley's words. I knew he didn't mean what he said, he was just upset—but that didn't excuse him either. I shook my head angrily.

"Nice Ry. Real nice. Is that how you think of me? Does that seem like something I'd do?"

"Not you. But *he* would." He emphasised the word "he" with great disdain.

"Well, for your information, Grey was a perfect gentleman." I retorted. At least, I thought he was. I couldn't remember everything, but the fact that I was fully dressed upon waking was definitely a good sign.

"Yeah. Typically, prefect gentlemen convince minors to do cocaine with them. I forgot."

"What is your problem Riley? About a month ago, you were giving me ecstasy. You're no different than Grey. You *were* no different from Grey, anyway. Give him some slack."

"There's a major difference, here. You weren't madly in love with me then, like you are with Grey now. You wouldn't do everything I ever suggested just to try and get with me."

"What?" This arguing was making my head pound frantically. I shut my eyes and leaned back against the seat in frustration. "When did I become this gigantic slut in your mind?"

He shook his head, his jaw clenching … but then he sighed. "You didn't. You aren't. I know you're not … a slut … I'm sorry. It's just … you should see yourself around this guy, it's like you're a totally different person … totally infatuated. Of all the people in the world, he shouldn't have that kind of power over you. I just … I don't trust him."

"You don't trust him?" I opened one eye. "Why's that?"

"Because. He's going to hurt you, Mackenzie. I know his type; I know what he's like. He'll hurt you, in the end."

"Fff—" I shook my head incredulously and stared out the window at the passing houses for a moment. When I spoke at last, my voice was sad, regretful, and acidic all at the same time.

"Grey can't hurt me anymore than you have. So don't act all gallant, okay?"

"Then I have?" Riley exclaimed. He turned the car into the parking lot, the gravel crunching under his tires. The lot was bare of people. We were late. He stopped the car abruptly and threw it into park. The silence after he cut the engine was deafening. I could feel him staring at me, but I refused to look away from the window. He sighed.

"How have I hurt you?"

I crossed my arms and shook my head. He wasn't getting any hints from me.

"I know, I know." He groaned, and leaned his head against the steering wheel. "No one said this would be easy. It's not at all. There always seems to be something more to give up, something I hadn't thought of. But it's worth it. So worth it. I wish you could see …."

"What the fuck are you talking about?" I pressed my hands to my temples. My head was going to explode.

"Mackenzie … Zee … I'm sorry. I thought this would be hardest for me, to adjust to a new life, to make new friends, a new way of living. But it's not, is it?" He reached out then, hesitantly, and gently cupped my chin in his hand. Reluctantly, I turned my head for him.

"This is hard for you, because you have to make a new life too, don't you? One without me in it."

I could feel tears growing again, and the ache in my throat made me angry. I nodded curtly at his statement.

"I wish there were another way, Mackenzie. I hope one day you'll understand what I'm doing and why I have to do it. Maybe, one day, you'll even be proud of me."

I shrugged indifferently. I couldn't do this with him anymore, that much was certain. He had chosen his way, obviously, and the way he chose did not include me. It would be easier for me to accept that, to quit hanging around, wishing and hoping and waiting for him to be friends again. Suddenly I realized it wasn't about him letting go of me. I had to do the letting go. I had to let him go do whatever it was that he needed. I would miss him, dreadfully, but it was something I had to do. Something I could do.

"I don't think we should be friends anymore." The stream of words poured from my lips, quietly and quickly so I couldn't stop them. Once they were out, I turned back to the window so I couldn't see his reaction. I didn't want to know. I would imagine that my words hurt him and he'd be sad to see me go. My hand gripped the door handle.

"If you think that's what's best." He acknowledged. His voice was soft … sorry, maybe? Regretful? Hadn't he known all along that this was inevitable? I shook my head and opened the door. Riley was getting off easy here, and he knew it.

"Mackenzie?" He called to me suddenly, just as I was about to leave. I paused, taking the sudden opportunity to look him full on and memorize the sweet face of my best friend. His dark hair was unkempt, as usual; his brown eyes were wide and soft, his face endearing. I managed a smile for him, because I did love him, in my way, and he would always be a part of my heart. And I wouldn't let myself cry, even though the tears were choking.

"I have to save myself, you know?" He sounded hopeless. "But it's for you. It's all for you."

I blinked a few times, hearing his words, and my smile began to shake.

"Goodbye, Riley." I turned away then, before he could see me cry.

CHAPTER 14

"Wasn't it worth it?" Grey had asked me earlier that morning. By seven o'clock that evening, I changed my answer. No, it wasn't worth it. I felt carsick sitting totally still. Charlie set another glass of water on the table and brushed my hair back from my face.

"You know what would help?" Her voice was low, meant only for my ears. I didn't know, but whatever it was, I wanted it. I looked up into her lovely blue eyes.

"What?" The restaurant was totally dead—our supper rush had come and gone without us batting an eye, but that had been helpful, given my condition. Sophie had just gone home and Charlie and I were taking advantage of the situation, rolling cutlery at one of the tables, A.K.A sitting down before Mackenzie lost her lack of lunch.

"Here." She rose, revealing her perfect figure painted into a long sleeved, v-cut black dress, and grabbed her purse from the hooks in the corner of the station. After rummaging for a moment, she handed me a little pink and brown tin. "Go to the bathroom."

"Uh … okay." I took the tin from her, puzzled. She giggled.

"You'll know once you're there."

"Okay. Thanks." I headed slowly down the brown brick hallway, shivering at the change in temperature. The girls bathroom was totally empty, eerily quiet but for a dripping faucet along the sinks.

I opened the tin and immediately understood. There were a few things in it, rolling papers, a lighter, some roaches, a vial of cocaine …. At first I wondered how something that caused me to feel this rotten could possibly help, but then I was too excited to care. I took it all into a bathroom stall, unscrewed the vial very carefully, and placed a tiny amount of powder on the end of the scoop. Pinching closed my other nostril I took the cocaine quickly, almost expertly. After that, I did one more on the other side, just to make it even.

The feeling took me quickly, like it had last night. I sat in near instant relief, a smile flitting to my face as the good feelings spread. It worked. Headache, nausea … all of it was gone. I felt like a new woman, energized, recharged. Full of life and joy again.

A totally different person joined Charlie at the table where we'd been sitting. She noticed immediately, and laughed out loud.

"Told you."

"Wow, what a difference." I laughed with her. "How do you keep from doing it, all day, every day? It's so good!" I lowered my voice for that last part.

"I don't know … self-control I guess. The more you do it, the less you feel it. Remember that."

"Do you do it very often?" I handed her back the tin, which she quickly replaced in her purse.

"I try to keep it for special occasions," she admitted. "But sometimes it's helpful in a pinch. Like tonight."

"Wow, Charlie. I think I'm in love with you." I smiled.

"Me too, Mac." Charlie laughed, her blond curls shaking. "Now, tell me about your night …."

After the deadest shift in history, and a few more trips to the bathroom for each of us, Charlie shut the open sign off with great excitement. We lit a smoke, nearly synchronized, and laughed. The kitchen staff were out front already and we talked and joked with them, though I knew none of them well. They were all very friendly, and I thought myself to be very funny high. I'd never been overly outgoing, though not shy either—personable maybe, the most comfortable in my own clique. Cocaine gave me such courage, such confidence that I could approach complete strangers and strike up a conversation, have them laughing before the end. I loved it.

"Oh, hey, I think that's them." Charlie declared as she watched a pair of red taillights pull into the parking lot outside.

"Them?" I peered out into the dark.

"Well, him, anyway. I asked Zack to pick me up after work."

"Oh."

Charlie smiled. "Come on. Maybe there's someone here for you, too."

The thought was appealing. I nodded excitedly and grabbed my purse and coat, handing Charlie hers. We waved goodbye to the group around the tables and headed out into the warm summer night.

The faded silver car was pulled up at an angle outside the brick face of the restaurant. Music greeted us dimly from its opened windows—heavy guitars, thrashing, screaming vocals. Zack noticed us and jumped out of the driver's seat. I hung back so he and Charlie could greet properly. As I was staring off at nothing, giving the couple some privacy, the rear door of Zack's car opened and Grey stepped out. I couldn't stop the wide smile that leapt across my face at the very sight of him.

Dressed again in dark jeans, Grey was wearing a black short sleeved shirt overtop a white long sleeved. I loved the way he dressed; I loved his constant stubble and his dark tousled hair. His blue eyes met mine as I approached. I had wanted to kiss him, to run into his arms—but even with my coke-confidence, the look on Grey's face was enough to discourage me from doing so. I was a little taken aback at the hard, cold expression that he greeted me with. Awkwardly, I stood there, the smile falling slightly from my face.

"Can I talk to you a minute?" Grey wondered, his voice cool and indifferent. He shoved his hands in his pockets.

"Uh … yeah. Sure."

"Here." He motioned with his head for us to move. I watched him, dumbfounded; following as he formally grasped my arm and led me away to the edge of the parking lot.

"What's up?" I tried to keep my voice light, casual, but the expression on his face had me deeply worried. A deep spasm of dread crept into my belly—with it the feeling that I wasn't going to like whatever he had to tell me.

"Listen, Mackenzie." He started. I liked the way he always said my full name when so many people felt the need to shorten it. I shook my head at the random thought and tried to focus.

"Yes?"

"I just … I don't know. When I woke up this morning, I got to thinking about it, about our night last night, and I don't know … I kind of feel … bad."

"Bad? What for?" That was the last thing I felt when I thought of last night, the last thing I wanted him to feel.

"Well … I just, I hope I didn't give you the wrong idea." Grey stood, casual and cool, his hands in his pockets, his eyes on the dirty pavement below our feet. I stared at him in wonder.

"Wrong idea about what?" I crossed my arms, as if to shield myself from the blow of his words. I knew what was coming next.

"About us." He looked up from the pavement then, and met my eyes. His were totally blank … deep blue and gorgeous, but void of any emotion. I wondered if my eyes looked the same way, or if they were betraying me, showing the sudden hurt and deferred hope this conversation was causing. I took a breath and nodded for him to continue.

"I mean, we had some fun together, right?" Grey grinned at me.

"Yeah, oh yeah." I tried to force the same enthusiasm into my voice.

"Okay. Well, I just wanted to make sure we were on the same page. Don't get me wrong, last night was great—but …."

"No, yeah, totally." I nodded consentingly, even adding a good forced smile. "It was just fun, for sure. I get that. No big deal."

"Yeah?"

"Yeah. Of course, yeah." I smiled at him again, but my façade was dissolving rapidly. I had to get away from him before it all fell apart. "Just, uh … thanks for inviting me."

"Sure, no problem." Just then, an old, off key horn honked, startling me. Grey laughed.

"Zack is impatient." He explained, and motioned for us to return to the car. I followed along beside him, hugging myself despite the warm temperature of the air. Zack and Charlie were both inside the car already, waiting for us to get in.

"You coming? We could drop you off." He eyed me, with what I couldn't tell … dismay, indifference? It didn't matter. Clearly I wasn't invited to join them tonight.

"Um … no, I think I'll walk home, actually." I decided; spur of the moment. There was no way I could get into that car—so near to Grey—and pretend like nothing was the matter. I wanted to be by myself.

"You sure? Free lift?" He suggested. I met his eyes a moment, shook my head, and turned away. As he opened the car door to get in, I could hear Charlie's voice asking about me. I didn't hear Grey's reply as the door shut, and after a moment the silver car sped past me, burning down the street. The music floated in the air long after the car had faded from view.

It was windy, but the wind was warm. I let out a shaky breath and began to walk. I felt stupid, and exhausted … and just … used. Maybe it had been "young" of me to assume that Grey and I were now an item just because we'd made out for a while. Maybe people their age did that thing on a regular basis. But I didn't. I didn't go around throwing myself at every boy and making out with someone new every weekend. The short list of boys I had kissed all meant something to me; they had been and still were special. Especially Grey.

I pictured them in the car, passing the flask around, the music loud. What were they going to do tonight? Was he going to meet some other girl he could have fun with? I kicked at a random pop can thrown negligently on the street. I was so naïve. So stupid.

Maybe I had wanted him to like me too much. Maybe I had imagined all his special looks and soft smiles and grins for my benefit. But we'd had such a good time, we'd connected, more than I ever had with anyone else. Was that just a result of my wishful thinking as well? Was I really nothing more to him than a warm body to party with?

Whatever. My poor self was so exhausted. Even despite the cocaine that slowly crept from my system, I was totally drained … emotionally, physically. I could feel the edges of a headache looming. Our town was small enough that it only took fifteen minutes to walk practically everywhere. I spent the remainder of the time thinking of Grey and the night before and how wonderful it had all been. How good it had felt waking up to him this morning. How he had cupped my head to kiss me right when I was leaving.

How it had been much, much more than just fun to me.

CHAPTER 15

"Mackenzie … Mackenzie."

I groaned at whoever was shaking my shoulder.

"Mackenzie … wake up. You're going to be late for school." My mom spoke quietly, prodding my shoulder gently.

"No … no mom, I'm not going to school." I decided. My head still ached.

"What's the matter? Are you sick?"

"I don't feel good."

"What about classes? You have exams coming up so soon …."

"It'll be fine. I don't have any tests today."

I could practically hear her frown. "Are you sure? Hmmm …. You don't seem to have a fever …." She placed her forearm to my forehead.

"I have a crazy headache." I complained, pushing her arm away. I thought about telling her the truth. Actually mom, I've done a ton of cocaine the last few days, I just really need to sleep it off … then I should be fine.

"Can I get you something?"

"No, thanks. I just want to sleep." I snuggled back into my pillow.

"Okay, then. I'll be downstairs if you need me."

"Okay." I yawned. That was at 8:10.

At 3:23, I woke up again. I did feel better. I stretched, yawned, and thought about doing more cocaine. I spared a thought for the poor suckers just leaving school. I wondered if Riley had noticed my absence.

Then I remembered that he and his stupid Christian girlfriend were going on *our* camping trip with *her* family. My mood soured a little. I wondered how to buy cocaine … where I could get it from, some of my own. How much it cost. Surely Charlie would know.

I wondered if they had all woken up in Charlie's living room again. If Alex and Zack were animatedly talking about all the good times I missed out on. If Grey were on the living room floor with some girl, one who could lay in his arms all day because she didn't have to go to school, because she was his age. I grit my teeth and got out of bed. All this imagining wasn't helping.

I headed downstairs, still in my pyjamas. I could see my mom as I came around the corner. She hadn't noticed me. She was sitting at her desk, her back to me, her short, faded dark curls shaking slightly as she moved. A large stack of embossed wedding invitations sat before her. I watched as she stuffed an envelope, affixed a stamp, and then used a little water sponge instead of her tongue to wet the envelope glue. She sealed the envelope, looked at it crucially for a moment, then moved on to the next one, apparently satisfied.

I laughed quietly to myself, and rolled my eyes. My mother may have been one of the most frustratingly annoying people I knew, but she was also the cutest. Once upon a time, she had heard that cockroaches lay eggs in the glue of envelopes. Since that day, she had never licked a single one, relying on her faithful little sponge roller instead.

Technology moved too fast for my mother. She was terrified of the internet, convinced that all her personal information could be swiped just by hitting the Explorer button once. She yelled—no, screamed her order at the drive-thru box, and I could just imagine the poor person inside, cringing at the volume in her headset. She did the same thing on a cell phone, one finger in the opposite ear, nearly shouting into the handheld.

I was reminded of Homer Simpson, trying to order a tab from his computer. That was my dear old mom. I sprang lightly into the room and grabbed the next envelope from her hand before she could sponge roller it.

"Hey mom. Can I help?" I asked sweetly. Before she could answer, I dragged my tongue over the entire strip of glue.

"Mackenzie Anne!" My mom exclaimed. "What are you thinking? You'll get eggs in your tongue!"

I laughed at her a moment. Her sheer ludicrously was so very entertaining.

"I'm glad you think it's funny now. You won't be laughing the day you hatch a cute little baby cockroach out of your mouth." She shuddered, but a smile crept onto her lips. "You're feeling better." She observed.

"Yeah. I think I just needed to sleep."

"Probably stressed. All that studying." She smiled knowingly.

"Oh, yeah. Totally. Studying all night, all day. It's exhausting."

"Uh huh."

"So … can I help or what?"

"You really want to?" She asked, surprised.

"Sure. Why not." I pulled a chair up to the desk and she slid half the pile over to me. I looked at the invitation a moment—the sweeping calligraphy, the translucent paper edged with delicate silver embellishments. It was pretty. Fairly over the top, but pretty.

I sat with my mom the rest of the afternoon. We actually had a good time; my mom could be cool when she wasn't ragging on me for every little thing. It helped when I wasn't going out of my way to be a pain in the ass too—though I did lick every envelope by tongue, just to bug her.

When we were nearly done, I suddenly had a brilliant idea. I started touching the edge of my tongue with my fingertips, as if it were a subconscious gesture. She noticed, but didn't think anything of it, at first. I kept doing it, but progressed from just touching my tongue to kind of scraping it, as if it were itching. She watched me more carefully, but continued talking. Suddenly, after a few more moments, I sat up abruptly, made my eyes widen with horror, put my hand to my mouth and made a perfect, choking/gasping noise.

Her face went as white as a sheet. She stared at me, aghast, too petrified to even move from her chair. All her medical school training, right out the window. I couldn't help it, I tried to keep it up, but she was too funny. I collapsed in my chair, giggling, holding my sides with laughter.

"Mackenzie Anne!" She screamed at me in total shock, only when it became evident that I was, in fact, not hatching a cockroach from my mouth. I laughed harder, and her face went beet red. After a few minutes of disgraced anger, she began to laugh as well, shaking her head at her own foolishness. "That'll teach me." She muttered.

We were still laughing when the front door opened unexpectedly. Marcy came in, flushed with happiness, perfection in a black blazer and white blouse, dark pressed jeans and shiny black pointy-toe boots. My laughter subsided at the sight of her.

"Marcy!" Mom exclaimed. She got to her feet and hugged my sister enthusiastically. "We just finished up the invitations."

"You helped?" She asked me in surprise.

"Yeah." I shrugged.

"She was a great help." Mom added.

"Still in your pyjamas? It's five-thirty."

"I was sick today."

"What was so funny? When I came in you were laughing pretty hard." Marcy set her purse down and unbuttoned her jacket.

"Oh, Mackenzie made a joke. She pretended to hatch a cockroach off her tongue." Mom laughed again in remembrance.

"Nice." Marcy raised her eyebrows sarcastically. "That sounds funny. So, mom, I wanted to run some things by you …."

"I'm going back to bed." I announced quickly. "I feel my headache coming back."

"Don't you want something to eat?" Mom gazed at me with concern. "It might help. I could make us some nice pasta or something." She suggested hopefully.

I looked from her to Marcy. "No, I'm good, thanks." I decided.

"Oh, okay …." She sounded doubtful, but then her attention was diverted by a sample that Marcy held up. I took the sudden opportunity to make my escape, back to the quiet of my room.

CHAPTER 16

I was dying for a cigarette. I sat cross-legged on my bed, painting my nails to keep from biting them. I had no excuse to leave the house, and no way could I light up without my mom finding out. I blew on the black lacquer, tapping my foot impatiently. It was Friday night. I wondered what everyone was doing. I wanted to call Charlie, but I just couldn't. I didn't want them to view me as a little, annoying kid always tagging along. If they wanted to hang out with me, I'd wait for them to call.

I just may be waiting forever.

I thought about Ben and Toby and Jacob. I wondered if they were sitting in the same spots on Ben's nice leather sectional, eating handfuls of munchies and reciting the lines from *Half Baked* as it played on the big screen. Even that would be a more welcome scenario than hanging out in my bedroom all night, but I doubted my mom would let me leave since I'd been "sick" all day.

Just then—like an answer from heaven—my cell phone started to ring, lost in the bottom reaches of my purse. I fell to my knees, wet nails and all, and dug through the bag until the purple Nokia was safe in my hand. It was Charlie calling. I answered excitedly.

"Hello?"

"Hey, chicka. What's happening?"

"Um … not too much." I sat against the bed. "Just hanging out at home. Painting my nails."

"Why? It's a Friday night!"

"I know. But I stayed home from school today, so I can't really go out."

"Oh, really? Why'd you stay home?"

"I didn't feel well." I shrugged.

"Huh. Hey, what happened to you last night? Why didn't you come with us?"

"Oh …." I felt the heat rush to my cheeks. "I just wanted to walk."

"How come? What did Grey say to you?"

I groaned.

"Come on? Was it bad? I thought you two were going to be something."

"So did I." I sighed, and took her through the whole conversation that Grey and I had shared. "He just wanted to make sure I didn't think I was like, his girlfriend or something now."

"Really? That sucks."

"I know. I thought we hit it off."

"Hmmm …." Charlie paused in thought. "… Well, why don't you come out tonight? Take your mind off things?"

"Oh, I don't know …." I wanted to, I really did. But the thought of seeing Grey again made me uneasy. Still excited, but uneasy. I didn't know how I should act around him now.

"Come on. Just you and me … no boys allowed. We can have a slumber party. A tequila slumber party. And tomorrow you can come with me to see the guys play."

I laughed out loud. It sounded like a ton of fun, and the thought of seeing Grey with a microphone made it all the more enticing. "Oh, I'd love to, I really would … I don't know … I could check with my mom."

"Do it."

"I'm in my pyjamas still." I laughed again.

"That's perfect. We're having a slumber party, remember? Go talk to your mom and call me back. I'll come pick you up."

"Okay … are you sure? You wouldn't rather go out with your friends or something?"

"Mackenzie, you are my friend. Now, shut up, go talk to your mom."

"Okay, okay. Bye." I was laughing as I hung up the phone. I smiled. I couldn't believe I had ever thought badly of Charlie. She was so awesome, so cool, and really, really nice. She wasn't Riley, but was fast becoming a close second.

"Ready?"

"Ready."

"One, two, three … go!"

Quickly, without looking, breathing or smelling, I flipped up my shot glass and forced down the strong, pungent tequila in one gulp. It burned all the way down my throat. I picked up a wedge of lemon and sucked the sour juice from the yellow rind.

"Woooooh!" Charlie screamed, and filled our shot glasses again.

I giggled and clutched the counter for support. After convincing my mom that Charlie and I would spend a quiet night in front of a chick flick or two, my friend had picked me up—half-cut already—and we'd been drinking tequila ever since. We were alone at her house; she had told Zack specifically that it was girls only tonight. Charlie was still fairly dressed up from work; she wore some tight back Capri's and a red low-cut blouse. I felt kind of plain compared to her, in my jeans and white Deftone's t-shirt. But I was comfortable.

And I was drunk.

"Hit this, bitch." She pointed to the shot and clambered up onto the counter, far less than gracefully. I laughed, throwing my head back.

"Okay, but after this I need a break." I was only partially aware that I couldn't speak coherently.

"One, two … go!"

This shot burned less than the one before it, even less than its eight or nine odd predecessors. I barely sucked the lemon over my numb lips.

"K, k enough, enough." I waved my arm wildly at her. My limbs didn't seem to be connected to my body anymore. The room wavered dizzily. I grabbed a smoke and stumbled my way to the couch, flopping down heavily upon it.

"You can't hold your liquor." Charlie accused. She laughed from her perch on top of the counter and poured herself another shot.

"Can too." I stared blurrily at the TV screen. Noise was definitely coming from the box but I couldn't make out the picture. I lit my cigarette after a few unsuccessful tries and smoked quietly a moment, a bizarre perma-grin plastered to my face.

"Wooooh!" Charlie exclaimed again. I heard the sound of glass striking the counter. I smiled, even though I was already smiling.

"One day, maybe you'll be able to out drink me … maybe …." Charlie's voice floated to me from somewhere, but I couldn't really hear her anymore. I wasn't paying attention. The room started to spin. My lips went numb. My mouth started to sweat.

"Charlie …." I groaned.

"Oh, shit, here." She ran to me at the same time that I pushed myself off the chair. Her hands grasped me around the waist and she ushered me towards the bathroom as quickly as possible, but I knew I wasn't going to make it. Just as we reached the door, I fell to the ground and threw up all over myself. The smell was revolting.

"Dammit, Mackenzie. Get up." I felt Charlie yank me up to the toilet by my armpits, just in time for me to retch again. My entire body heaved. My nose burned. I could feel tears squeezing from my eyes.

"There's not much to clean up, it's all over you." She was saying. She undid my jeans and pulled them off, manipulating my slack arms to strip the shirt from me as well.

"Damn, girl. When did you last eat something? It's like, entirely clear."

"Dunno …," I mumbled. I spit into the toilet and experimented with opening my eyes. The room had stopped spinning. The floor in the bathroom was cold; it felt nice. I blinked stupidly into the bowl for a minute, then lifted my head and rested it on the seat. Charlie flushed the toilet.

"Better?" She asked, standing over me, grinning. She was holding my hair, smoothing it back with her hand.

"I think so." I nodded.

"Can you get up?"

"I'll try." Already I felt better. Less sick, but still drunk. Weakly I pushed myself up off the floor, using Charlie's hands to help me.

"Good?" She wondered, once I was standing. I nodded again.

"Okay. Go to the kitchen and get some crackers or something to eat. I'll go find you some clothes to wear and deal with … these …," she held my soiled clothes far away from her body and made a face. I giggled.

"Okay. Okay. Thanks Charlie … my love …." I leaned against the wall for support, laughing, and made my way to the kitchen as she headed in the other direction. I felt great now, happy and less spinney.

"One shot … hey! More tequila …." I sang to myself, giggling as I opened and slammed Charlie's cupboards, looking for crackers. "Two shots … hey, hey!" I did a little spin, grabbed a cigarette, lit it, and blew the smoke at the overhead light, still dancing. "Three shots, hey …."

Holy crap. I stopped dead in my tracks and stared, my jaw open in horror, my cheeks flaming a sudden, alarming red. I covered my mouth with my hand.

"How long have you been standing there?" I asked, my voice barely a squeak, full of embarrassment.

"A few minutes." Grey cleared his throat and smirked sexily at me. He had a large blue Tool hoodie on—it brought out the blue of his eyes. His hair was hidden beneath a black Spitfire hat. "Long enough to see the show. And you think I'm talented."

He was referring to my stupid little song and dance number. I put my head in my hands and laughed. "Well, we were doing tequila, and I just thought the song fit."

"Mackenzie?"

"Yes?" I looked up at him, biting my lip. He stared at me, and I watched as his eyes traced over my figure, from my calves to my face, slowly, taking in every detail. The heat returned to my cheeks.

"What?" I repeated. His glanced up at my eyes again, distracted from his study by the sound of my voice. Grey's expression was hard to read, but his blue eyes seemed … soft somehow. Like he was thinking tender thoughts.

"Um …," he smiled at me again, and then pointed downwards, motioning for me to look at myself. I grimaced. Did I have a big patch of vomit on me somewhere? But I thought Charlie had said it was clear …?

And then I realized. I gasped in renewed horror. Looking down, I had expected to see my shirt and jeans … but was greeted instead by the sight of my pink bra, the tight skin of my stomach, my belly button ring and my black VS boy shorts. I was in my bra and panties. I was in my underwear. In front of Grey. I looked up at him quickly in humiliation.

His face comforted me though. Grey was staring at me with admiration. He smiled, and looked me over again. I didn't know what to do; I was torn, wanting to both cover myself up but also wanting him to see. I hoped I looked okay. I hoped I looked skinny and pretty. I knew if I hadn't been drunk, I'd never *still* be standing there in my underwear. I would've died of embarrassment by now.

"I threw up …," was my explanation. I shrugged, and smiled at him.

"Thank goodness for that." He grinned.

"What are you … what are you doing here?" I wondered. "This was supposed to be girls only. Hence …." I waved a hand over myself and the obvious lack of clothing.

"This is what girls do at sleepovers?" he smirked again, "I'm getting invited to the next one." I giggled with him. "No. I don't know. Zack told me to meet him here after practice. He just had to go pick up some shit.

Oh, wait." He turned and looked out the window at the headlights that shone up suddenly. "Here they are now. Take this."

Quickly Grey unzipped his hoodie, revealing a plain white tee underneath, and stepped over to me. I prayed I didn't smell like tequila vomit. He held up the sweater and I turned to shove my arms through the sleeves, my skin tingling at the proximity of his body to my bare flesh. I turned around again and he slowly zipped the sweater up, his fingertips brushing me lightly as he did so, sending shivers through me. My body sang at his touch, however slight. I somehow found the courage to meet his eyes. We stood so close … the air between us was charged, thick almost. I swallowed and parted my lips ….

"Oh yeah, man. That was awesome. We're going to kick ass tomorrow." The front door slammed. We were jarred out of our moment. I stepped back from Grey and leaned behind the island for added modesty as Zack and Alex barged through the door. I took a deep, steadying breath. My cheeks were still flushed. I hoped Alex and Zack wouldn't notice.

Grey's hoodie smelt amazing. I took the opportunity while the guys greeted each other to bury my nose in the soft, warm fabric that had rested near his neck. It was warm, sweet but masculine, with the hint of cigarette smoke. I breathed deep.

"What is going on out here?" Charlie emerged into the living area, her hands on her hips, though a smile played on her lips. She laughed as Zack kissed her quickly. "I thought I told you we were having a girls night."

"Oh, yeah. We vetoed that." Zack grinned and placed a box of beer on the counter. The bottles clinked together.

"Hey Mac. Nice outfit." Alex winked at me, passing by on his way to the fridge.

"Thanks. I threw up." I mumbled in embarrassment.

"No, thank you. For the update." He laughed, tossing a lank of browny-blonde hair from his eyes. "I recognize the sweater."

"Looks good on her, don't you think?" Grey asked. He was alarmingly close again, standing just behind me. His hand trailed lightly down my arm. "Looks better off." He said quietly, for my ears only, I'm sure. I smiled.

"Mackenzie, what are you wearing?" Charlie shook her head at me. "I laid out some clothes for you in the bedroom."

"Okay, thanks." I hurried quickly out of the room.

"Yeah, thanks Charlie." Grey repeated. But his tone was sarcastic.

I took one last look in the mirror. Charlie had leant me a snug, long sleeved black t-shirt and some jeans. The pants were a little long, but I looked pretty good.

"Are the clothes okay? I thought they were a little more your style." Charlie stood behind me, handing me a cigarette. I took a drag.

"They're great, thanks."

"No problem." Her eyes were still bright with laughter—she nearly peed herself when she heard my embarrassing story with Grey. "Well, that's what you get for making me clean up your puke." She had said.

I apologized profusely, again, feeling like a total tool for throwing up all over myself and her bathroom. Like a nube who couldn't hold her alcohol. She just chuckled. "It happens to the best of us." She insisted.

When we came back out of her bedroom, the guys were doing some rails. I declined regrettably; Charlie had forbidden me from taking anything until I'd had something to eat. I honestly couldn't remember the last time I had sat down to a meal or even a snack. It was definitely before the night we'd gone clubbing. And that was at least two days ago.

"What are you doing?" Zack asked, pinching his nose and sniffing as he watched Charlie move around the kitchen.

"Making Mackenzie something to eat … she hasn't eaten in like, three days."

"What are you, anorexic?" He wondered.

"Not on purpose." I handed Grey back his sweater. I made Charlie sniff it, and then re-sniff it, just to make sure it didn't smell like vomit. She gave it the green light, but insisted on spritzing it lightly with some perfume before giving it back to him. She had sprayed some of the same on me as well.

I sat down on the couch and lit a smoke. I couldn't believe what had happened and I really didn't know how to behave around Grey now … now that'd he'd seen basically everything. And really hadn't seemed to mind. I reminded myself that it didn't mean anything. Of course Grey hadn't minded, what heterosexual guy would object to seeing a half-naked chick? He was just in it for fun. He was just in it for fun. I had to keep running the sentence over in my head. I wouldn't be the stupid, naïve seventeen year old again. I could be mature like them. I could keep my cool. I could have fun and make out with a boy without forming any kind of attachment.

Yeah right.

I knew I didn't have a hope. I knew I would be passionately in love with Grey, no matter what I told myself. He could yell at me and call me names and spit on me and kick me in the street and I would still love him. He just had that hold on me. Like Riley said … he had a "power" over me. It was true.

I watched Grey from the couch … watched the way he moved, the way he chased a rail, the way he smiled and laughed and adjusted the hat on his head. I sighed and wished fleetingly that he could feel more for me than just a passing interest. Wished he would look at me as more than someone to fool around with. But I also knew it didn't matter, not now. I would be whatever Grey would let me be.

As if he could hear my thoughts, when they were done, Grey sauntered over and joined me on the couch. His smile made me nearly melt to the cushions. Before I could react to him, Charlie came and handed me a plate of leftover pizza, steaming hot. I thanked her, but looked at the food before me feebly. I just wasn't hungry.

"Eat." She commanded, her hands on her hips. I nodded and took a bite off the end—it really didn't taste that bad but I could tell it came from work. She stayed until I had swallowed, and then apparently satisfied, went to join Zack and Alex in the kitchen. They were putting together a game of quarters.

"So, how does someone accidentally become an anorexic?" Grey wondered. He leaned forward, a beer in his hand, his face tilted towards me. I laughed and shrugged. Discreetly, I set the pizza down on the side table next to us, hoping Charlie wouldn't see.

"I don't know … I've just been, preoccupied I guess."

"Too preoccupied to eat? You're not sad again, are you? I thought we cured you of that."

"Oh, you did." I lit a cigarette and settled back comfortably. "I'm just not hungry."

"So, what happened with Riley? You two work it out?"

"Um …." I frowned. "I don't know, I guess you could say that. We decided … no, I guess I decided that we shouldn't really be friends right now …."

"Oh yeah? Because he's leaving?" Grey took a swig of his beer, his blue eyes totally innocent. I stared at him a moment, trying to make sense of his sentence.

"Because he's leaving …. Riley's leaving?" I tried to quell the panic rising in my chest. I wouldn't freak out until I knew what Grey was talking about.

"Yeah, I guess so. He came in today and gave his two-weeks notice. I guess right after graduation he's going out east with some chick to check out some college or something. I think that's what he said, maybe got some of it wrong, but I do know that he's leaving. I thought he would have told you."

"Yeah. That would have been nice." I raised my eyebrows in disbelief and looked at the popcorn-stuccoed ceiling. Riley was leaving me, for good. We had grown apart—rapidly, too rapidly to make any sense. We had agreed not to be friends. And now he was leaving me. With the Christian.

This was worse, worse than anything before it. Even though we had agreed to go our separate ways, I still knew Riley was around, I still knew that ultimately if I needed him, he would be there for me. And vice versa. It went without saying; it didn't need to be spoken. But how could that be if he wasn't here? When was he going to tell me they were leaving? *Was* he going to tell me?

I realized I wasn't going to get any answers tonight, and I wouldn't get any answers from anyone but Riley himself. I let out a sigh and buried my head in my hands.

"I'm sorry. I thought you knew." Grey said.

"No, no. It's not your fault." I straightened up and smiled weakly at him. "Just another result of me and Riley's basic dysfunction."

"Well, since he's quit, I'll probably be moving to nights. So we'll get to work together more, anyway." He shrugged and smiled. I thought about that a moment and felt a grin spread over my face. If anything could make this better, it was that fact.

"Come on, let me cheer you up." Grey motioned to the kitchen with his hand. He grinned wickedly. I laughed.

"I'm not allowed. Not until I've eaten."

"I can fix that for you." He leaned over me and took my pizza slice, now cold, and then folded it into his mouth in one bite. I laughed and watched him chew for a minute.

"Wow, that's impressive." I giggled. He mumbled something incoherently, holding up his hand for me to wait until he had swallowed. He was trying not to laugh.

"Okay." He swallowed again. "Okay. Pizza's all gone. You're allowed now."

"Wow, you did that for me? How gallant."

Grey chuckled. "Ready?" He held out his hand.

Of course I was. "Ready."

CHAPTER 17

"If Grey doesn't love you after tonight …," Charlie looked at me again, smiling in satisfaction. "Then there is something wrong with that boy."

"He's just in this for fun, Charlie. Remember?" I took a drag of my smoke and blew it out, staring at my reflection. We were in Charlie's bedroom, where she had dressed and made me up, yet again. It looked like she was improving with practice, the woman staring at me in the mirror was … hot, vivacious … stunning.

A short, sleek, long sleeved black dress hugged my frame, low-cut enough to make me a little uncomfortable, though Charlie promised results. My hair was in loose, glossy dark curls that tumbled around my shoulders and down my back, kept from my face by a thin silver headband. My make-up was phenomenal—dark, smoky eyes and almost startling red, full, pouty lips that looked like they didn't belong to my face. I wore black leather boots, high heeled with a pointy toe, which curved around my calves most becomingly.

I had to hand it to Charlie. I looked unbelievable, especially given that we hadn't really slept yet from the night before. I think I napped maybe an hour or two on the couch sometime earlier in the day … it was more of a slip into unconsciousness that I couldn't really remember. Most of it had been a happy blur of drinking and cocaine and Grey, Grey, Grey ….

We had just hung out, all night. Like friends. There'd been no more touching or kissing or making out, but the tension was still there, like there was a possibility for more. I'd wanted there to be more, had thought about nearly nothing else, but had totally loved the time with him anyway. He was so much fun to be around, so easy for me to talk to. I couldn't remember what topics we had covered or the funny things he had said. I could just picture us together on the ratty old couch, my mouth spread into a permanent grin as we laughed and talked and just … were.

The guys had left earlier that afternoon to get ready for their show. They were playing at the Aurora again, like the night I first met Grey … that fateful night not even two months ago that had ended up changing my entire life. It felt like ages and ages ago … like a totally different time. Back then, Riley and I were friends, best friends. Before Grey and I were … were what? Having fun?

"Wow, Charlie. You're amazing. Seriously. You have a beauty career ahead of you." I smiled thankfully at my friend. Charlie bowed. She looked gorgeous like usual—her shiny blonde hair was pulled into a loose pompadour, her dazzling blue top brought out the striking blue of her eyes. It didn't seem to matter how good I looked. Next to Charlie, I would always come second.

I didn't want to mind though. I didn't want to be so pettily jealous, not when Charlie was so amazingly nice to me and leant me all her clothes and took care of me the way she did. Not when—for some reason—she actually liked hanging out with me, a high school kid who wasn't even legal enough to get into bars.

"You look gorgeous." I forced myself to compliment her. "Seriously."

"Thanks, kid." She stuck her tongue out at me with a smile for my response to the word kid. "So, what should we do tonight?"

"Um …." I laughed. "I thought we were going to see the guys play."

"Not that, idiot. I mean, what should we *do*? What are you in the mood for?"

"Oh." I laughed again. I was still pretty drunk and high from our non-stop day of partying. But I was up for anything. "What are you thinking?"

"I don't know … I have some E lying around … we could do some blow …," she shrugged. "Whatever you feel like."

"You just have E lying around? Like all the time?"

"Not all the time. Sometimes."

"Really? I could hit some of that." It would really be like old times then. The first time I tried E was when we went to watch Grey's band.

"Okay." Charlie sat on her bed and rummaged around in the bedside drawer. She pulled out another tin and opened it up, revealing a bunch of different coloured pills.

"For us, tonight ... how about some Pink Dinosaur?" She picked out a pink one and handed it to me. Sure enough, there was a little dinosaur face stamped into it. I giggled.

"You too?"

"Yeah. Why not." Charlie took one for herself and placed the lid back on the tin. "Trust me, you'll like this one."

"I like them all." I admitted. We took turns sipping from a glass of water on her nightstand. The pill slid down my throat with ease. I smiled excitedly. Now all we had to do was wait for the fun to begin.

"Okay, hottie." Charlie slammed the cup down enthusiastically. "Let's go!"

"Are you okay to drive?" I wondered, laughing as we grabbed our purses.

"Who knows? Whoooo!" She threw her head back in laughter. "We'd better hurry, we want to get there before this hits and I really can't drive."

That seemed logical enough to me. We did one last mirror check and then headed out, bounding down her old squeaky steps, young and eager. The engine of her car roared to life, Slipknot blared over the speakers. We rolled the windows down and lit a smoke. The warm summer wind blew over us as Charlie gunned her little car down the streets, the headlights bouncing over the road. She looked at me and laughed; I smiled at her and threw my head back.

"Whhhooooo!" I yelled, my eyes shut. There was truly nothing better than the freedom I felt, the absolute release. Life was perfect. Charlie's smile told me she agreed.

By the time we made it to the club, the ecstasy was already taking hold. We stumbled from Charlie's car into the parking lot, giggling and smoking. She fixed a few stray curls for me; I adjusted her top a little.

"We're perfect. Let's go. Those boys will eat their hearts out." She decided.

I smiled at the thought and fell into step beside her. I felt shaky good, like a surge of adrenaline, only the adrenaline was pure excitement and joy. I grinned the entire way to the door, totally unsurprised when we were let past the rope again without having to show our I.D or having to wait at all. These new friends of mine had some good connections.

"Thanks Billy." Charlie waved at the bouncer. We were inside. And it was packed, just as it had been the first time. The stage was empty and dark, we were early.

"Come on, I told Zack to save us a table." Charlie grasped my hand. "Follow me." She started through the crowd, squeezing and elbowing her way through. There was barely room to move. The Aurora hadn't changed since last I came, still the same old carpeted walls and neon beer signs. It looked especially dated now that I'd been to the other club in the city. I decided I liked it though. It was kind of cozy, like it had a *Cheers* feel to it almost.

I noticed as we walked that men were nearly snapping their necks to look at Charlie when she passed by them. I tried not to pay attention to it, but then one of them caught my eye. He was looking at me, not at Charlie, and nodding, like he liked what he saw. To my surprise, I realized that men were actually looking at me. Well, at least some of them were. I was amazed. I'd never had that happen before, I'd never had that reaction before, not so obviously anyway. I felt great when we finally made it to our table, like a million bucks.

"Did you see all those guys checking you out?" I asked Charlie as we slid onto the tall black stools around the high round table. I lit a smoke and bit my lip.

"Me? Nice try. They were looking at you and you know it." She lit a smoke as well and looked out over the crowd. It was so loud we almost had to yell to be heard, but that was okay with me. I liked the atmosphere, the loud, rowdy partying that went on around us. Music pumped from the dance floor, some Britney Spears number. I smiled and took a drag of my smoke.

"What time are they supposed to play?" I wondered.

"Eleven." Charlie yelled. She looked at her silver Guess watch. "Ten minutes."

"I'm so excited!" I almost squealed. She laughed.

"I know, I know!"

"They're so good, you know? Like, amazing. Have they been together long?"

"A few years. I've only been on the scene for like a year, more of a groupie until just recently." She admitted.

"Until Zack?"

"Yeah, about then. We've liked each other for a long time; we just haven't done anything about it until now."

"Why?"

"I don't know. Guys can be dicks." She shrugged. "Especially when they have a ton of chicks all over them all the time. Makes it hard for them to commit."

"Do you think that's Grey's problem?" I worried suddenly. The thought hadn't occurred to me until right then, but it was a definite possibility. "Has he ever had … anyone …?"

Charlie looked at me thoughtfully for a moment, but then shook her head. "I don't know, Mackenzie. I'm trying to figure it out myself. I've only been around for a year or so, like I said, but in that entire time, I've never seen Grey with anyone. I mean, he's the lead singer of a band, so of course he's with girls, you know, but he's never been *with* anybody. He's never had a girlfriend that I know of … I just, I don't get it."

"What don't you get?" I leaned forward to hear her better.

"Grey just seems so into you. I don't know. I wouldn't believe his whole 'just for fun' thing. I've seen how he acts with girls that are 'just for fun'."

"And?"

"And …," she shrugged. "It's obvious. He doesn't sit on the couch with those girls for hours, hanging on their every word …."

"Like he did with me?"

"Yeah. Don't buy it Mackenzie. He cares more for you than that, I can tell."

"You can?"

"Yes. And you deserve more than that too. Don't forget."

"Charlie?"

"Yes?"

"I love you."

Charlie burst out laughing. She smiled at me and stamped her smoke out.

"Sounds like someone's feeling the E."

I nodded enthusiastically. "I am. I am. Aren't you?"

She laughed again. "Yes." We giggled.

"But I still love you, you know."

"Yeah, I know."

The music shut off suddenly, and still grinning, Charlie and I turned expectantly towards the stage. We could just make out the shapes of people walking around in the dim light up there. The crowd started cheering and shouting, even before the lights came up and the band was illuminated on stage. Once that happened they went crazy, the noise was deafening.

I smiled, happy that Serpentine was so popular. That had to feel good, to have people screaming for you. I wondered what was going through Grey's mind at that moment.

I recognized them all now; it was different than the first time. Alex on drums, Lucas on bass, Zack on guitar and Jimmy on keys. I let my eyes pass over them; there was really only one man I wanted to see. I needed to see. He was standing in the front center of the stage with his back to the audience. I watched him, enraptured. The band started playing, the guitars chugging the intro of the song, Zack and Lucas flanking either side of the stage. Grey stood between them, still backwards, his guitar hanging lazily from its strap. Then the music got louder, more intense, and just before it reached the crescendo Grey turned, gripped the microphone stand, and screamed into it.

The moment he started singing the crowd erupted into near mayhem. My breath caught in my throat. The sight of him up there in the spotlight, the dark blue jeans that hugged his thigh as he tapped his leg to the beat, the studded belt around his hips, the black Tool t-shirt that hugged his torso and showed off the smooth muscular biceps of his darkly tanned arms …. I felt my heart swell until it felt like bursting. I put my hand to my chest and just stared. I loved Grey, more than anybody else ever could. I loved him more than I thought I loved him before. He was perfect, in every way. He was meant for me in every way. His voice was smooth but raspy, thick and raw, silky but edged with a growl. It reminded me of copper, somehow, but that didn't make any sense. He sang and looked out over the crowd and shook his head back and forth in time. He held his guitar loosely slung across his hips, resting on his spread out legs. His fingers danced across the fret board with skill, his studded leather bracelets flashed in the stage lights. The cherry red electric guitar responded eagerly to his capable hands, resounding with the chugging wails and intricate notes that Grey's fingers demanded of it. A sexy smirk flitted across his lips.

The songs were good, but he made them better. The whole band really made the show, but I couldn't look at any of the others. My eyes were only for Grey. Charlie was standing next to her chair, at times she would jump and cheer and wave her arms in the air with the rest of the crowd. But I could merely stare—stare and fall madly, impossibly more in love with Grey at each strum of his guitar strings. My heart belonged to him and no one else.

The ecstasy was hitting me with full force. I nearly staggered with delight as waves of euphoria crashed sweetly over me. I wanted to dance and run and yell with pleasure, but instead I stood and smiled, smiled up at the man I loved, pouring into my smile all the joy that overflowed from somewhere deep inside of me. As if I was beckoning him, Grey turned suddenly, and he looked around until he found me, and then our eyes locked. His beautiful blue eyes met mine with such force that I couldn't breathe. It was as if he were seeing into my soul, his gaze was so intense, so powerful. We stared at each other, and I tried to pour into my expression everything I was feeling. How he was making me feel, what I felt for him, what I would do for him. I don't know what Grey saw there reflected in my face, but his lips curved into a smile—his sexy smirk, and then he turned away from me, singing into the mike. He hadn't missed a beat; I doubt our moment lasted as long as it felt. But I was trembling.

The rest of the set was a blur; I don't even know how much longer it lasted. I was seeing lights before my eyes and had to sit to keep from falling over. There was a cigarette non-stop between my fingers and my legs shook with pent-up energy. The ecstasy was intense, perhaps strengthened by the sheer force of my emotions. Or it could've been the steady diet of booze and blow I'd survived on for the last twenty-four hours … or maybe because I really couldn't remember the last time I'd eaten. Whatever the reason for the intensity, I just focused on Grey as much as I could, a smile still bending my lips even as my teeth chattered uncontrollably.

"Whooooo!" Charlie screamed again, turning away from the stage as the lights finally dimmed and the guys made their way off through the curtains. She faced me and smiled.

"Wasn't that wicked? Whooo!"

"Awesome." I agreed wholeheartedly. "Totally awesome." The house music started up again now that the band was done, Destiny's Child, *Survivor.* The beat made me want to dance. I tapped my feet impatiently underneath the table.

"This hitting you yet?" Charlie wondered. Her pupils were as big as saucers even in the dim lights.

"Um … I would say … yeah …." I giggled and trembled. I grit my teeth. "Are my eyes as big as yours?"

"Uh … hard to say … let me take a look at my own eyes and I'll let you know." She stuck her tongue out at me and laughed. I giggled with her, almost hysterically, totally giddy. "They are pretty huge though," she continued, "and your eyes are so dark anyway, now they look almost black."

"Really?"

"Yeah."

I laughed. "Do I look like a freak?"

"No. It's sexy. Just don't look the bouncers or bartenders right in the eyes, though. That always tips them off."

"Oh, okay." I would try to remember that.

"You wanna get a drink? I think the waitress is coming around now that the guys are done."

"Yeah. A rye-Coke." I decided. I vaguely remembered the night I had come to the Aurora with Riley, when he made me promise not to drink anything since I was on ecstasy. I shrugged the dim memory off. Riley could go screw himself. Charlie ordered our drinks and I lit a cigarette. If Riley really cared, he wouldn't be moving away forever without even telling me. He'd be here, with me, telling me not to drink.

"So what do we do now?" I wondered, as our drinks were set before us on the round black table. Charlie swept hers up immediately and took a sip.

"I feel like dancing." She decided suddenly, her eyes lit up. I nodded my head at her perfect idea.

"Me too!" I smiled excitedly and grabbed my jug of rye and Coke. "Let's go."

"Let's do it." She grinned and stood gracefully from the stool. I let her go in front since she had more experience pushing her way through the impossible maze of tightly packed people. Finally we made it, bursting into the only small open space available on the dance floor. It was ours though, and we made use of it. Charlie was a good dancer; she was a ton of fun to be with, totally confident. The smile never left my lips as we danced, and smoked, and drank our way into near oblivion.

"Here you guys are!"

"Zack!" Charlie exclaimed at the sound of his voice. She smiled and went to him, throwing her arms around his neck and kissing him enthusiastically. He chuckled in response. I wondered how much of this show was for the other girls surrounding the dance floor, kind of a personal "hands off" message from Charlie. I laughed.

"I've been looking for you everywhere." He grasped Charlie's hand and motioned for me to follow them. I nodded and took Charlie's other hand which she outstretched to me. Together the three of us wound our way through the crowded club until we made it to the VIP section in the back. It was so much different stepping through the door this time, now

I knew nearly everyone in the room except for new random groupies. I smiled at everyone I saw.

Natasha, Tracy and Lori had taken the beat up leather couch in the center of the room—they looked generally happier than they had the other night. I still didn't know who they belonged to. Tom was leaning against the wall in a thick leather coat talking to two other men about his age. He nodded at me. Lucas and Jimmy were settled at the bar with girls surrounding them on either side. They clinked some shots together and then threw them back to the delight of all the women.

I followed Charlie and Zack, but I was looking only for Grey. In my mid-alcohol-ecstasy haze I suddenly wondered if he were even real. What if I had imagined him? Really, could that much perfection really exist?

Yes, it could. I watched then as Grey and Alex stepped out of the little back room that adjoined the VIP section. I knew now—because I knew them—that they'd been doing blow back there. Like they probably had been the first night I came.

I shook my hair back and suddenly wished for a mirror. I had been dancing and sweating, I hoped my make-up hadn't melted off.

"Charlie." I whisper-hissed at her. I couldn't take my eyes off Grey. "Do I look okay?"

She turned and gave me a discreet once over. Then a smile crept over her lips. "You look fucking hot, Mackenzie. Go knock him dead."

I laughed at her. "Did I mention I love you?"

"Go." She smiled and gave me a little push. Grey and Alex were now in the center of the room, around the group of people settled on the thin leather couches and chairs. He hadn't noticed me yet, or maybe he had and was ignoring me. Either way, I didn't want to go right to him. I brushed my hair back and walked towards the bar, conscious of my tight fitting black dress, the tall leather boots that hugged my calves. I hoped Charlie had been telling the truth. I wanted to be hot; I wanted Grey to want me.

I ordered a drink, sudden butterflies in my stomach. The waitress plunked the rye and Coke before me. I thanked her and took a sip. I knew the moment I turned to look behind me that Grey and I would see each other, but the anticipation was like a drug. I took a deep breath, lit a smoke, and finally turned around, leaning my back on the bar.

It was instant. I could feel his eyes on me before I met them. Grey's gorgeous face was caught in an expression of amazement that betrayed his normal cool. His blue eyes were wide, his mouth open slightly. I delighted in his reaction and watched as his gaze swept over my body, slowly, as if he were savouring every moment. My pulse began to beat rapidly, even faster than before. I bit my lip and looked at him, met his eyes when at last they returned to my face. He had composed himself by then, his expression slipping easily back into the calm, collected Grey that he showed everyone. But it was too late; I already knew the effect I had on him. I had seen the evidence in his face.

I smiled gloriously and took a drag of my cigarette.

"Hey, Mackenzie, right? Can I have one of those?" Jimmy disrupted our moment, shouting at me from his spot just down the bar. I turned my smile to the young faux-hawked man.

"Of course." I nodded, slowly letting my eyes slip from Grey's gaze. I walked down the bar and handed Jimmy a cigarette.

"I ran out." He explained.

"Sure." I turned to look back at Grey. He had moved as well, almost mimicking my movement, so we were in the same proximity as before, just in different places in the room. Our eyes met and a slow smirk lifted the corner of his mouth. I grinned.

This continued throughout the evening. Slowly we moved around the room, finding some excuse to keep from actually meeting, staring at each other whenever we had the opportunity. It was like a bizarre dance we were doing, and though there was space between us, the heat between us was unreal. The thrill of anticipation.

Eventually, there were no more excuses, no one else to talk to, nowhere else to stand. Just Grey and I, coming slowly together as if it were the most natural movement in the world. We stopped close together, close enough that I could smell his delicious scent, could feel the heat coming off his body. We looked at each other a moment. I could barely breathe.

"Damn, girl." He looked down into my eyes and chuckled. I knew he was referring to my wide, black pupils. I shrugged without looking away. Then, wordlessly, his hand slid down my arm, from my elbow to my hand. I shivered at his touch. He took my hand in his and gently pulled me from the room.

We emerged back into the loud, rowdy part of the club. The party was still going strong. I wanted to die with happiness as Grey led me through the clubbers, his hand around mine. All the women that stared at him longingly as we passed would turn in surprise, glaring at me when they realized we were together. But I didn't care. They could all hate me, I didn't care. Because I was with Grey.

Kryptonite by Three Doors Down was playing. We found a space on the dance floor but we didn't need much room. Grey placed his hands on my hips, pulling me near. I looked up at him as we moved together. He smiled, his lips curving upon his stubbled cheeks, his tanned skin. I pressed my hands against the top of his chest, trailing them slowly down his hard torso, feeling each and every muscle defined beneath my fingertips. I bit my lip and looked up at him, into the full, scorching gaze of his deep blue eyes.

It took mere moments until we were kissing. He pulled me toward him, burying his hand into the curls at the back of my neck to bring me closer yet. I wrapped my arms around his neck, running my fingers through his hair. We moved together in time to the song, but neither of us was dancing anymore. We kissed feverishly, almost desperately, as the song played through … and the next, and the next …. His hands were on my arms, my back, my hips—scorching my skin through the thin black fabric of my dress as if I were wearing nothing at all. And suddenly I didn't want to be.

As if he could read my mind, Grey pulled away, his blue eyes smouldering. I didn't want him to stop. He took my hand again and wordlessly we left the dance floor. He led me through the crowd, impatient, almost. I didn't think to wonder where we were going, so long as we continued where we left off. Hastily, we made our way through the partiers into the VIP section, then down the hallway into the little room off the back. I wondered if anyone was staring at us, but I didn't turn to look.

The room was empty. There were a few club chairs in a circle and a round coffee table in the middle. A chalky mirror sat on the table. I took all this in with one glance as Grey shut the door behind us. As soon as the lock had been turned, Grey grasped me tightly by the hips with his strong hands and pushed me roughly towards the nearest chair. I fell back willingly, eagerly accepting his weight as it crushed down on me. I wrapped my legs around him and met his lips with just as much intensity.

His hands felt so good. His hands and his lips and just the hardness of his body as it pressed against mine. I had never felt this way before with any other boy. I had never experienced this level of lust, of complete and utter abandon. I couldn't think straight anymore, I just wanted all of me to experience all of him. I couldn't get enough. Swiftly I ripped his shirt off, delighting in the dark, hard muscle of his chest, running my hands down it. Slowly his hands moved from my hips to my waist, and I moaned at the delicious trail of heat they left upon my skin. Desperately I wanted his hands to move up. I arched my back instinctively, pressing my chest against him. Grey made a noise then, like a growl almost, and moved his hand to my breast.

The moment he touched me I knew I would have sex with him. The thought took me by surprise as I realized we were headed in that exact direction. I wanted it—I did, more than I ever had with anyone else. I'd never done it with any other boy because I'd never felt like this before. I'd never wanted someone so badly. I'd never been in love, real love, like I was with Grey. I welcomed his caresses fervently. I felt his hand on my knee, his fingers trailing fire as the slowly moved up my leg, under my skirt, up my thigh ….

"I love you. I love you Grey." I spoke the words before I realized it. They just slipped out. I'd been thinking them, and then suddenly they were on my lips, and I had said them. My eyes opened wide with shock, and I looked at Grey, curious to see how he would react.

He chuckled. "That's the ecstasy, sugar." He kissed me. I laughed as well, kissing him back, relieved that my words hadn't totally freaked him out. But the sudden pause, however brief, had been enough to clear my head a little.

I did love Grey, my words had been true, and I would give him everything. Everything, even if he had nothing to give me in return. Suddenly I needed him to know that. It was rash, impulsive and super, super stupid of me, but I desperately wanted to share with Grey everything I was feeling. And I had to act fast, before I stopped thinking altogether ….

"Wait, wait Grey." I whispered breathlessly.

"What?" His voice was husky.

"I do." I looked at him, right in the eyes. My heart hammered in my chest; I prayed I wouldn't lose courage. I placed my hands on either side of his face. "I do love you."

"No, you don't." He grinned. "That's just the drug—"

"No, it's not the drugs." I argued. "I felt this way before I took them. I love you." The more I said it, the easier it became.

He scoffed and chuckled at me. "What is this, some kind of joke?"

"No, it's not a joke." I sat up slightly. "I'm totally serious. I'm not going to play head games with you or screw you around or anything. I want to be honest with you, always."

"You love me?" Grey repeated sceptically. He eyed me warily.

"Yes. Yes, I love you. I think I have from the first moment …." I smiled and traced my finger over his lips, slightly parted and tinged red from my lipstick. I glanced up at him hopefully. Grey looked at a complete loss. His eyebrows were furrowed, his jaw was clenched—but his blue eyes were still warm. It looked like he was processing my words, going over them in his head, trying to make sense of them.

"Can I prove it to you?" I whispered. "Can I show you?" I caressed his cheek with my thumb a moment, and then pulled his face down to mine. Our lips met, and quickly the intensity between us renewed. If anything, Grey became more aggressive, almost like he was in a sudden hurry. Roughly he shoved the skirt of my dress up over my hips; his hands were hard against my skin. I didn't mind, I would do anything he wanted, but I couldn't help but wonder what he was thinking now. Was it possible that he loved me too? Did this new ardour mean that he shared my feelings? Or were his frenzied kisses simply his way of getting me to shut up?

I didn't know, but my heart beat harder as I realized what was about to happen. I was about to have sex, for the first time. With Grey. I wondered briefly if it would hurt, but quickly pushed the thought aside. It didn't matter. I put my hands to the back of his head and deepened our kiss, twining my fingers in his dark, unruly hair. He was everything I'd ever wanted.

But then, abruptly, Grey pulled away from me. His face was suddenly hard, his jaw clenched. He leaned back from me and glared—long gone was the warmth in his blue eyes. He was breathing heavily. I looked at him with utter confusion, stammering.

"What—"

"You love me." It was a statement, like an accusation, almost. I swallowed and nodded my head, slowly.

"Yes." I whispered.

Grey scoffed. He shook his head and chuckled lowly. His movements became swift and rigid as he pushed himself away from me, snatching his hands away like my flesh was poison. He grabbed his shirt from the floor and whipped it over his head, his muscled torso disappearing beneath the fabric. I could do nothing but watch him, alarmed by the sudden change in his mood, troubled by the obvious agitation with which he now regarded me. Clearly, the feelings I had professed were something Grey did not want to hear. I couldn't regret my decision to tell him, because every word was true. But I did regret the way he glared at me now. And I wished he felt the same.

"That's just too damn bad." Grey spoke. "Because you mean nothing to me." He made sure I was looking, waited until, wincing, I looked into his cold, hostile blue eyes. "You got that? Nothing." He repeated, his voice low, malicious. "I don't love you, I don't like you. I don't even care about you. You're just a piece of ass; I tried to tell you that. And I don't need this shit."

A sob escaped my throat. I didn't mean to let it happen, but the hatred in his voice wounded me deeply, piercing through the chemically induced euphoria to strike me directly in the heart. I clutched my chest and tried to stifle the swift pain of total rejection that his loathing caused. The unexpected sting that raced from my mind to my psyche, harsh and cutting, wreaking havoc on my self-esteem as my stomach flipped with panic.

Grey just looked at me now, like he was disgusted. Like I was disgusting to him. He shut his eyes and shook his head again, slowly. The chuckle that escaped his perfect lips was condescending; his voice was edged with annoyance.

"Damn teenagers." He muttered. Without another glance in my direction, he turned and stalked towards the door. It slammed loudly as he left the room and abandoned me in humiliated misery. Despite the nasty, hurtful things he had said I still wanted to call to Grey, to beg him not to go. Because I still loved him, even after all of that. I loved him, and always would, even if he never felt the same way about me. My tears overflowed and sobs I could not contain shook my body. Slowly I sat up, my vision blurred, my throat aching as I pulled my dress back in place and smoothed the fabric with the palm of my hand. My heart felt like it was bleeding, pouring sadness throughout my entire being as the pain ebbed through my veins.

CHAPTER 18

I was crushed. There was no other way to describe it. I cried myself hoarse in that mean, lonely little room, and then, since I had no other choice, forced myself to walk back through the VIP section. Rigid with humiliation and convinced that everyone was staring at my puffy red eyes and mascara streaked face, I nearly ran from the club, stumbling my way home in utter disgrace and rejection. I climbed into my bed without even washing my face or changing my clothes. The whole nights events were fresh in my mind. The moment I shut my eyes I saw Grey's beautiful face, his blue eyes hard and his lips sneering at me cruelly. I curled up on my side, tight in the blankets, and cried myself to sleep.

The next morning, when I awoke and was immediately bombarded again by the memory—the horrific, tragic ending to my night—the resulting wave of sadness actually made me … angry. The way most people get when they've been rejected by someone—horribly, brutally rejected by someone. Offended, infuriated. Hurt and resentful. All day long I hid out in my room, blaming my absence from hanging with the family on the clever guise of studying. I didn't open a book, mostly laid on my bed, stared at my roof, listened to angry music and wished for a cigarette. Furious. Every time I pictured Grey's face, I hated him a little bit more.

At least, I tried to convince myself I did.

There was no way I could show my face at Charlie's ever again, and though she called my cell phone multiple times, I didn't answer. Even though I knew she'd be understanding and sympathetic and possibly even make me feel better, I just couldn't. I didn't want to talk about it; I didn't want to admit what had happened to anyone. I just wanted to lie on my bed and focus on my anger, trying to hate Grey enough to totally forget about him, trying to persuade myself that I was much better off.

There was only one week of official classes left at school before final exams. Everyone at school the next day was abuzz with last days preparations, all our classes were devoted to diploma exam studying strategies. I sat silently in my desk, hating everyone around me and wishing that I didn't have to be at stupid school. But what else would I be doing? I didn't really have any friends anymore that I was aware of.

Ben, Toby and Jacob were officially AWOL, but I guess I couldn't blame them. In reality, I had ditched them—I always knew where to find the guys but I just hadn't bothered. Too busy with my other, more exciting plans.

Riley was in a few of my classes, and though I had planned to confront him about the whole moving away forever thing, I was just too drained. We acknowledged each other once, in third period when he had to walk down my aisle to return to his seat. He met my eyes and we nodded at each other. I wondered when, no—if, he was planning to tell me about the move. He and the Christian were now inseparable; I saw them everywhere together, not just at lunchtime meetings. She had taken my place in the passenger seat of Riley's car.

It was pretty hard not to wallow in self-pity. In the matter of a few short weeks I had managed to lose all my friends and get a broken heart in the process.

And I had to work right after school. There would be no more avoiding Charlie and trying to convince myself that the whole horrible Saturday night fiasco hadn't taken place. At least Grey wouldn't be working. That was something I definitely couldn't handle. I walked the few blocks from school to the Red Wheat, my arms crossed, dragging my feet.

Charlie was expecting me as I entered the quiet restaurant. There was one table of two up in the first section, but other than that the seats were empty. It was only four-thirty, still too early for supper rush.

"Hey, babe. How you doing?" Charlie greeted me. She looked me over and with that one glance seemed to understand that something was wrong. A sympathetic smile crossed her face. Her blonde hair had been straightened and shone down to her shoulders; her frilly white dress looked lovely. I shrugged. I knew I looked terrible; I hadn't the energy or the motivation to do anything with myself that morning. My dark curls hung limply down my back and I wore virtually no make-up.

"Come with me." She took me by the shoulders and gently ushered me towards the washroom. I allowed her to, I didn't care. The rubber stopper held the bathroom door so we could still see out front. We stood before the mirror; Charlie threw my hair up and deftly twisted it into some kind of knot. A little mascara from her purse and some deep red lipstick made a huge difference in my appearance.

"Thanks Charlie. What would I do without you?" I wondered, more to myself than to her. She was truly my only friend at the moment. I felt guilty for ignoring her calls the previous day.

"So, are you going to tell me what happened Saturday?"

"Like you don't know."

"I don't. Grey wouldn't talk about it. All I know is that you two went into that room, and then a while later Grey comes out by himself, looking totally stressed. Then you come out like, almost an hour later, obviously bawling. You run by without even telling me you're leaving and then Grey's standing there, watching you, all tense with his fists clenched. Did you guys have a fight or what?"

"No, not a fight." My eyes narrowed at the memory. "I told him I loved him; I know it was stupid, but it was the truth. And then … well," I scoffed sardonically, "let's just say he didn't share the sentiment."

"You told him you loved him?"

"Yeah." I grimaced. "Dumb, right?"

"No." Charlie decided. She shook her head. "No, not dumb. That took guts. You're brave, Mackenzie. I've felt that way about Zack for months and I still can't tell him."

"Why not?" I wondered.

"I don't know. Rejection sucks."

"Yeah, tell me about it." I sighed. Charlie fixed my cardigan and stood back to survey my outfit. It met her approval—though not mine—it was another one of my mom's purchases, a short khaki skirt and white top. I wore plain white sneakers as well.

"Mackenzie," she looked mystified. A frown crossed her lips. "I just don't get it. The way Grey looks at you …." She trailed off in thought.

"Whatever …." I shook my head regretfully. "It's nothing. It's over. Just … forget about it."

"You're right." She hugged my shoulders. "If he's too stupid to see it, you're much better off."

"Yeah." I nodded. I'd told myself that same thing hundreds of times in the last twenty-four hours. So why couldn't I believe it?

The fact I couldn't only made me madder.

"Okay, well ... you look great." She decided. "Come on. Let's just get through tonight and then we'll worry about the rest later. And here ... don't take too much, just enough to help." She handed me the little silver vial she kept in her purse and looked cautiously out the door. "Coast is clear. Go ahead."

Eagerly I unscrewed the lid and scooped up the white powder, inhaling deeply until I could feel the sweet burn hit my sinuses. I sniffed loudly and did another. It wasn't long until the racking pain and anger had faded, but still it did not cease. I felt better though, like I could handle it now. I felt confident. In control. Like maybe I didn't need Grey, like maybe I didn't even care.

But as I turned the corner around the waitress station, I spotted him. Grey. He was there, working; I could see his handsome face behind the line. Panicked, I gasped, hiding behind the wall so he couldn't see me.

"Charlie!" I whisper-hissed at my friend. "What the hell is he doing here!?"

She looked at me curiously. "What do you mean?"

"Grey! What is he doing here? He's not supposed to be working today."

"Oh ... well I guess when Riley gave his two-weeks notice, Mark told him not to worry about coming in at all. He gave Riley the time to study or something, so Grey's covering all his shifts now."

"What? Oh shit, that's right. Grey's covering for Riley now." I groaned. "I totally forgot."

"I know it sucks, Mac. Just ignore him. Just do your job and ignore him, okay?" Charlie looked towards the entrance at an incoming couple. "You can start now. Go seat that table." She handed me two menus and gave me a reassuring pat. "We'll get through this Mac. Just ignore him."

This turned out to be easier than I expected. By the time I returned from seating that table, another four had taken their place at the entry. Charlie and I were slammed within minutes, in half an hour every seat was full and a line up had begun at the door. This was unexpected for a Monday night, and we were nearly run off our feet. Luckily, I was kept busy enough that I couldn't worry about Grey except when I needed an order.

We didn't say one word to each other, he kept his head down most of the time anyway—the kitchen staff were just as hard pressed to keep up with the rush as we were. Dishes piled up in the pit, the salad dressings were out, and we ran out of soup before seven o'clock. Orders kept coming in; there were tables to wipe, coffees to refill, plates to clear. We could barely hear ourselves over the general restaurant din and the clamour of the busy kitchen.

This was when I first met Ralph. I was in the waitress station, filling up Pepsi's and getting a piece of pie out of the fridge at the same time. Multitasking was a necessity. The door from the kitchen opened just as I was shutting the fridge with my foot, and a tall, heavy, middle-aged man emerged. He was balding, with thin red hair. His face held deep wrinkles, but his thick lips revealed perfect white teeth. He wore a collared shirt and dress pants and smelled like expensive aftershave.

I looked up at him curiously. "Hello."

"Hello." He greeted politely, but his eyes worked me over, from the top of my head down to the toes of my shoes, then up again. His eyebrows rose. I wondered what that meant, but was too busy to really care. I squeezed some whipped cream onto the pie and placed a fork on its dish.

"You must be Mackenzie." He was staring at me.

"Yes." I was trying to be polite, but had many things on my mind. I couldn't remember if I had gotten table thirteen ketchup or not. I grabbed a bottle anyway, just in case.

"Ralph." He introduced, holding out his hand. I looked up at him in surprise, barely remembering in time that this man was my boss.

"Oh, hi." I floundered. I set down the ketchup so I could shake his hand. "I'm sorry; we've just been really busy. I didn't realize ...."

"Oh, no. No trouble. Just thought I'd introduce myself." He shook his head in approval and smiled. "That Mark, he sure can pick 'em."

"Uh ... thanks ...." I smiled again impatiently, not really paying attention. I had to get going. I grabbed the ketchup bottle again.

"We'll talk later. I'll be here doing some interviews to replace Riley. Let me know if you need any help." Ralph offered. I nodded in thanks and then whizzed by him, my mind already focused on the path I would take through the restaurant to make the most effective use of my time. A rule in waitressing was never to walk anywhere with empty hands. There was always something to grab and take or clean and I busied myself with exactly that. By the time I returned to the waitress area, Ralph was gone.

The rush didn't last all night, but it remained steady. We spent the rest of the evening just trying to get caught up. Charlie and I each took a turn in the bathroom with her little silver vial as well, a little pick me up to help us keep going.

It was at about nine o'clock, an hour from close, when a table of ten came in without a reservation. Charlie and I grumbled as we pushed tables together for them. There was nothing worse than a big table so close to closing after such a busy night. I made Charlie break the news to the kitchen. I wasn't in the mood to get sworn at.

To make matters worse, I had to wait on the table, and all of them were guys from my school. The majority of them were from my grade. There was nothing more awkward than waiting on people I barely knew but who still would recognize me. I handed them menus and we exchanged some polite hellos.

They were cowboys. All of them. I knew without even looking that our parking lot would be full of their diesel trucks, large and loud with some kind of ATV strapped in the box and mud splattered along the sides. Typical boys raised on a farm, heading to local colleges that offered courses in agriculture and livestock breeding. The talk around the table consisted of various ranch-hand work stories and rodeo cabarets. I rolled my eyes and kept my mouth shut, refilling their Pepsi's with regularity and serving them all the same large, greasy plates of hamburgers and French fries.

When they were finally done, I placed the black check holder in the middle of their table.

"Thanks guys." I said generically. One of the boys, his name was Brad, looked up at me and smiled.

"Uh, we didn't order that." He quipped, pointing at the check. I could tell he thought he was clever.

"Oh, well, it comes free with every meal." I smiled sweetly at him. His friends around the table cracked up at my little joke. Brad smiled in surprise and chuckled—he was still grinning at me as I left the table, trouncing over to shut the open sign off. The one and only plus to waiting on a big group was the chance of a big tip, but I wasn't going to get my hopes up. These were high school boys, after all.

Brad personally brought me the check holder when they were ready to go. It was stuffed with bills, but I figured it was rude to count the money right there in front of him. I shoved the folder into the front pocket of my apron.

"Thanks."

"You're welcome." Brad smiled. He looked over me, and his face was soft … admiring, almost. "So, tell me Mackenzie, why don't we hang out more?" He broached.

I laughed at him. "… Are you serious?"

"Yeah."

"Oh …." I cleared my throat, trying to be polite. "Uh … I guess it's just because we … hang in different crowds." I shrugged.

"Well, I think we should rectify the situation. Don't you?" He asked.

"I don't know. I don't really see how. Unless maybe … you start growing weed in your fields or something." I smiled at my ridiculous suggestion.

Brad leaned a hand against the wall, grinning widely at me. "See. Right there. You have the most adorable smile. Did you know that?"

I felt my cheeks warm. "Oh, you're just saying that."

"I am?" He chuckled. "Why?"

"I don't know." I shook my head. "Maybe you're still in awe of my amazing service or something."

"Trust me, Mackenzie," Brad leaned towards me then, his voice dropping seriously. "The service wasn't that good."

I laughed. I couldn't help it. I laughed and laughed, looking up at him in amazement, startled that he had an actually personality. It was a pleasant surprise. He laughed with me, and as he did his odd, amber coloured eyes twinkled handsomely. His wide smile was becoming in his face.

"Uh, thanks … I guess …." I giggled.

"There it is again. That smile." Brad sighed. He glanced back at his friends waiting impatiently by the front door. "I should go. But you and me, we'll hang out soon, okay?"

"Um …." I bit my lip, not sure what to say.

"Don't think about it. Just say yes."

"… Okay. Yes." I nodded, and found myself smiling at him.

His answering grin flashed charmingly across his face, and I watched him go, amazed. What was happening to me? Was I really desperate enough for a friend that I'd consider fraternizing with a cowboy? I shook my head as I rang up the bill, but I couldn't keep the smile from my face. Maybe I was going crazy or something, but it seemed like there was more to Brad than just Wrangler jeans and Roper boots. I watched the lights of his truck as he pulled out of the parking lot and felt an odd, inexplicable surge of hope.

Charlie met me in the waitress area afterwards, her tray full of dirty dishes, and handed me a crisp, green twenty-dollar bill.

"Your tip." She smiled in disbelief. "Man, what did you do for those guys, a lap dance or something?"

"Something like that." I joked in amazement. But I honestly had no idea. Maybe my service hadn't been as bad as Brad said it was … maybe my sudden wit had won him over … or maybe, he just liked me. I took the bill and stuffed it into my tip cup, which was almost overflowing from the busy evening. I stared at the heap of change, trying to approximate its worth. There must have been at least fifty-dollars in it before the twenty-dollar tip, which was exciting—a nice, unexpected bonus.

"Good night?" Ralph appeared then again from the kitchen, the door swinging shut behind him. He smiled nicely at me. "Looks like it." He pointed at my tip cup.

"Yeah. I hope so." I nodded. "It was busy enough."

"You girls did great."

"Thanks." I smiled at him again, but felt uncomfortable just standing there. He was my boss after all—I was sure he wouldn't like me to be idle. I picked up a cloth and spray bottle and started wiping down the counters. He leaned against the station and watched me as I worked. The longer he stood there the more whiskey I could smell, it overpowered even his nice cologne. I wondered how long he'd been drinking in the back.

"How'd your interviews go?" I asked politely, more to fill the awkward silence than to satisfy my curiosity. I didn't like thinking about Riley being replaced.

"Good enough, I suppose." Ralph sighed. "All in a days work."

"That's good."

"Yep." He pushed away from the counter and took a few casual steps towards me. I moved to the opposite side of the station to get out of his way, repositioning against the counter by the order window. The kitchen staff was busy in the back. I could see through the narrow slit that the rush had put them behind as well, normally they would be out front already, smoking and drinking coffee. Grey was at the line on just the other side of the window—horribly close to me—I could hear his hands as he worked on cleaning the steam table. I could see the back of his neck as he bent over his work. I tried not to stare; I didn't want him to catch me. It'd be so much easier if I could just ignore him.

I busied myself with organizing the countertops, stacking up the soup bowls and putting the coffee cups away. Ralph was still present in the station; he stood by the fridge now but continued to watch me. It was becoming fairly uncomfortable, I couldn't tell if he was there for a reason or just drunk and oblivious to the awkwardness. I hoped he wasn't critiquing my cleaning skills; I was in a rush to get it done so I could leave for the night.

"You liking it here so far?" Ralph asked suddenly. He staggered forwards and met me at the counter, his belly pushed up against my side. Startled, I looked up at him. His face was disturbingly close. He smiled down at me and the whiskey on his breath was strong, sour. I moved discreetly away from him so that our bodies weren't touching anymore.

"Yeah. It's been great." I spoke with false enthusiasm. This was getting weird. Where the hell was Charlie? I refilled the coffee container, moving just a little bit further away from Ralph as I did so.

"All the staff around here are real friendly." Ralph smiled crookedly at me, and as he spoke I noticed he moved closer. His voice lowered until he was nearly whispering in my ear. He lifted his arm and reached around my back, resting his hand on the side of my rib cage. The moment I felt the hot contact of his hand, I froze, my hands hung in the air mid-motion. His touch was heavy on my side, his thick fingers sticking to my shirt. I kept my eyes down, staring blankly at the countertop, not daring to move. This man was my boss. What did he want?

"You let me know if anyone gives you any trouble." His breath was hot against my neck. I shuddered involuntarily. His hand moved from my ribs, sliding slowly down my waist until it rested on my hip. I didn't know what to do. I stood there, hoping he would be done soon, thinking that if I ignored him long enough someone would eventually distract him. I hoped he'd take my unresponsiveness as rejection.

But my disinterest didn't seem to matter. With a chuckle, he swept his hand further down and his palm cupped my butt in a playful slap. I jerked at the touch, a surprised gasp escaped my lips and my eyes whipped upwards in shock. I found myself staring directly at Grey, his face before me on the other side of the window. He must have been watching—his expression was hard, his jaw was clenched, his lips tight. His eyes swept over my face. His gaze was full of anger as it settled on Ralph's drunken leer.

"Ralph." Grey warned. His voice was low and threatening.

"Oh, hey Grey." Ralph smiled innocently at his employee, completely casual, as if he hadn't just slapped my ass. My face burned red with discomfit. Ralph chuckled and began to whistle, stumbling past me on his way to the front. I let out a shaky sigh of relief once the heavy man was out of my space.

Grey was looking at me now. Hesitantly I lifted my eyes to him. I didn't know what to expect, how I should feel, how I should act. His blue eyes were beautiful, but his expression was impossible to read. A frown curved his lips.

"You okay?" He spoke like he regretted having to ask the question. I couldn't answer him with my voice, I nodded my head instead.

"Okay." He bent back down over his work, as if the whole ugly scene hadn't just taken place. That was it then, I guessed. I was still a little shaken, so I hid out in the waitress station until Charlie joined me. I told her the whole story, speaking in a hushed voice so that Ralph couldn't hear me from the tables out front. She sympathized with me, rolling her eyes and regaling me with her own tale of sexual inappropriateness at the thick hands of Ralph the boss. This definitely was not the first occurrence of such lewd behaviour.

We finished up our chores and counted out our tips without any further incidents, though Ralph had chosen a premium spot at the tables to watch us work. I hadn't realized our boss was such a creep, now I was thankful he stayed away from work as much as he did. Grey ignored me the rest of the night, he didn't even look my way again. He obviously didn't want to give me the wrong impression, to have me think his feelings had changed just because he stepped in once on my behalf. That's what his continued silence and utter indifference spoke to me anyway. But that was totally fine with me. I couldn't have cared less.

I was better off.

CHAPTER 19

The week dragged by. Classes were a joke at this point in the year; I don't know why my classmates still bothered to go. I only went for an excuse to get out of the house. I didn't have to work until Friday that week, so it was straight home for me every day after school, because I still wasn't brave enough to hang out at Charlie's. Not when the guys spent most of their time there. Zack and Alex probably thought I was just a big joke and I couldn't stand to imagine what Grey thought of me. I actually cracked my books at home; I was so desperate for a diversion from my tortured, obsessive memories and contemplations.

Friday morning dawned clear and bright, the morning air already warm—an indication of a brewing hot day, and the last day of official classes. I threw on some shorts and a tank top and put my hair up in a ponytail. My mood was lightened considerably by the promise of summer freedom in the air. One more week of school to plod through, and then we were done. Then I was finally free.

We had to clean out our lockers that day. It was almost fun, all the kids running amuck in the hallway, chucking out the grim reminders of old, boring lessons and graded assignments. I was going through my binders, flipping through page after page of doodled loose-leaf, looking for anything that may be worth keeping. A sudden presence caught my attention and there was Brad, the cowboy from the restaurant standing before me, smiling warmly with his hand on the hip of his tight Wrangler jeans.

I found myself smiling back at him. Brad was really cute, I'm sure all the cowgirls went crazy for him. The sleeves of his blue button-down shirt were pushed up to reveal his arms, dark brown with farmer's tan and thick with muscle. Away from the rest of his cowboy friends he looked less ordinary; I noticed the warm hazel of his unique amber eyes and the slight blond tinge to his reddish hair that I hadn't seen when he blended into the others.

"Hey Brad." I greeted him, my surprise apparent. "What's up?"

"Oh, not much."

"Come to take back your tip?" I wondered. Brad laughed, his smile revealing two dimples set in his wide apple cheeks. He shook his head.

"No, no nothing like that. I just wanted to talk to you."

"Okay." I decided to chuck out the whole binder. There was nothing salvageable in it. It fell into the trashcan with a bang.

He watched me a moment. "It's a shame, you know."

"What is?"

"That we've been going to the same school for nearly twelve years, and we've never really talked until now."

"Well," I shrugged and gave him a smile. "Better late then never, right?"

"Yeah, I guess." Brad cleared his throat. "So ... you going to pre-grad?"

"The party? No, I hadn't planned on it. I have to work tonight." And there was no way I was going to a class party on my own, without any friends. I doubted very, very much that Riley would be gracing the party with his perfect self, and who knew what the other boys were up to.

"Really? That's too bad, I wanted to take you."

"You did, did you?" I raised my eyebrows at him. It was still baffling that Brad wanted anything to do with me—I mean, I didn't know what a hock was, I thought calf roping was cruel, and I absolutely hated the movie *8 Seconds*. We couldn't have anything in common. But at the moment, it was flattering. He sincerely seemed to like me, and I needed to be liked at the moment. I needed a friend, some easy, carefree fun. And really ... what could it hurt?

"What time do you work until?" He wondered.

"About ten."

"I'll be there." Brad promised. "We're going to have some fun tonight."

I nodded. "Okay. Great." I couldn't help it, I liked that Brad wanted to spend time with me. I was actually looking forward to our night out, to the party. I was ready to blow off some steam.

I picked up another binder from the bottom of my locker, and for just a brief moment, I thought about Grey. I couldn't help that either. Deep down, I knew no matter how much fun I had with Brad, I'd be wishing he was somebody else. Because I still loved Grey, as pointless and futile as it may be, even despite all the efforts to convince myself otherwise.

But still, I could try. I would try. I smiled at Brad as he headed off down the hallway, giving him a little wave as he left, determined to have a good time that night.

"My replacement?" A voice beside me asked. I knew who it was without even looking. A frown fell on my face as I flipped my binder open.

"Hardly." I answered him. More doodles. An entire school year of doodles. I licked my finger and went through the pages.

Riley laughed. "That would be pretty unbelievable, you replacing me for a cowboy."

My mood soured. I was glad Riley found this so funny. "No more unbelievable than replacing me for a Christian. And you found a way to do that, didn't you?" I gazed up at him. He was the same old Riley, and a wave of sadness crashed over me as I looked into the familiar face, the warm dark eyes that had once brought me so much comfort, the wide smile that had laughed with me so many times before. I bit my lip.

"Are we going to do this every time we see each other? Can't we just have a conversation without getting into a fight?" He sighed and leaned against the lockers.

"What do you mean, every time we see each other? Don't you mean, the last time we see each other before you *move* in like a week?"

"Oh, you heard about that, did you?"

"Yes. I did. When were you planning on telling me?"

"I don't know. I don't know if I was."

"What? Why? Don't you think you at least owe me that much?"

"Yeah, I guess. I've just been … afraid."

"Afraid?" I looked up at him incredulously. "Afraid of what?"

"I don't want to say goodbye to you, Mackenzie." Riley explained. His voice lowered and he looked at me fondly. "I know things are screwed up right now between us. Come on, you've been my best friend for ages. I just don't want to say goodbye."

"But you're leaving Riley." My voice shook. "When people leave, they say goodbye."

"I know." He nodded quietly. "I know."

A sudden thought occurred to me. "You could stay." I grabbed his hand and looked up him, imploring. "Then you wouldn't have to say goodbye."

Riley shook his head. "But there's nothing for me here, Mac. Nothing."

"Nice." I felt the full sting of his words. "I'm glad to know you feel that way."

"No … that's … that's not what I meant, and you know it."

"Whatever." I stared up at him angrily. "Just go. Go and have a wonderful Christian life. Sing a round of *Kumbayah* for me, while you're at it."

"Ugh … you're impossible." Riley breathed. He shook his head and stepped around me, his form rigid with anger as he stalked down the hallway. Madly, I watched him a moment, but as he walked away I realized this could be the last conversation we ever had. I didn't want him to remember me this way. I didn't want to end things in anger.

"Riley!" I called to him. The hall was crowded and noisy, but somehow, he still heard. Maybe he had been expecting me to stop him.

"What?" He seemed in agony.

"Just … don't go without saying goodbye. Okay?"

Riley paused in thought. His jaw clenched in consideration. He looked at me and nodded, one small, slight nod, then continued off down the hallway.

CHAPTER 20

Work was slow. Charlie and I joked about living in opposite land, since Monday night had been so busy. A few tables were scattered about the restaurant, but the pace was easy and welcome.

Grey was there, sullen as usual behind the order window. As if to make up for his personable slip the other night he ignored me more than ever, if that were possible. I squared my shoulders and set my chin stubbornly, determined to completely disregard him as well, but I was so trained to be aware of his every move and breath and word that this proved nearly impossible. It was aggravating; he was always so close to me, but always so far away, out of my reach.

It was about eight that evening when Brad came by. I looked up in surprise from plating salads to see him at the entrance of the station, leaning on the wall and smiling at me.

"Brad? What are you doing here?" I wondered, relieved by the distraction. "It's only eight o'clock."

"I know. But I wanted to see you." He smiled, his amber eyes twinkling. He looked good in his tight jeans and button-down shirt. There was a little ring in his freshly gelled hair where his cowboy hat had been.

I blushed beneath the fondness of his gaze. "Oh … well … are you hungry?"

"Yeah, I am actually." Brad smiled. "And I guess it wouldn't hurt to have something in there, you know, to soak up all the beer."

"Probably not." I agreed. "Red Wheat burger? Two patties?"

"How well you know me."

"Go sit anywhere and I'll bring you a Pepsi." I offered. "Oh, and Brad?"

"Yes?"

"I'll try to do better, you know, service wise."

He grinned at me again, laughing. "See that you do."

With a smile, I wrote down Brad's order and stabbed it on the puck, then began to pour his Pepsi. I was discreetly aware as Grey sauntered up to the order window from somewhere in the back of the kitchen. He grabbed the sheet and stared at my scribbles a second, then threw some burger patties on the grill and dropped a basketful of frozen French fries into the vat of hot oil. I did my level best to try and ignore him, thinking about Brad and the party instead … revelling in how good it felt just to be wanted again.

Charlie came into the waitress area and replaced the coffee pot in the machine, nearly stopping in her tracks when she saw the smile on my face.

"What's happened to you?" She wondered.

"Nothing. Why?"

"I don't know. You lost your perma-frown."

"Oh, it's nothing." I shrugged. "I'm just going to this party tonight. I'm excited."

"Uh huh." She gave me a knowing look. "Are you sure that's all?"

"Yes." I insisted, brushing past her before she could see my cheeks redden. I took the salads to my table in the middle section and then brought Brad his Pepsi. He was sitting in the far corner of the restaurant, all by himself.

"So," Brad took a sip from his soda. "What do you want to drink tonight?"

"I don't know." I shrugged. "I'll just get a mickey of something."

"Like, hard alcohol?"

"Yeah."

He looked surprised. "Okay …."

"Why, is that odd?"

"No, I guess not … it's just surprising. Most girls get like, coolers or something."

"Well, I'm not most girls."

"That's for sure." Brad agreed, and the look he gave me sent all the heat back to my freshly cooled cheeks. "You like to party, don't you?"

"You could say that." I smiled coyly. More like, lived to party.

Just then, I heard the order bell dinging faintly from the kitchen. The food for my other table was up, ready, waiting to be served.

"I'll be right back, okay?" I touched Brad lightly on the arm.

"I'll be here." He joked.

Charlie was back in the station as I entered, grinning from ear to ear and shaking her head at me. Apparently she'd been watching us.

"What?" I tried to play dumb.

"Yeah right, what." She rolled her eyes. "Come on, who's the guy?"

"Oh, just some guy from school."

"Really? He's pretty cute. Are you going to the party with him?"

"Yeah." I nodded. "But it's not like that. We're just friends."

"Maybe … for now …," she stared up at Brad in the corner of the restaurant, her eyebrows raised in approval.

"Charlie, we don't have anything in common. He's a cowboy."

"So? Why does that matter?"

I rolled my eyes at her. Why indeed?

"Do you like him?"

"I don't know. I barely know him. But he's … he's not what I imagined, I guess. Like, he's funny. He's nice too … and he … I don't know … he seems to like me."

Charlie smiled at me. "I'm glad you're going out with him. I think it will be good for you."

"You do?"

"Yeah. Go out, have some fun, forget all about …," she didn't say his name, just in case he was listening, but Charlie motioned her head towards Grey.

"Yeah." I looked over at him, forgetting myself, and regretted it the moment I did. Just the sight of his face behind the line was enough to pang me, to remind me that I was only fooling myself. That I wasn't over him, not yet, no matter how much I tried to act it. I sighed, suddenly looking forward to the end of my shift so I could go and drink all my troubles away.

"You should go now." Charlie decided, as if reading my mind.

"What?"

"Go now. Go with him." She nodded her head up at Brad. "Mackenzie, it's like a graveyard in here. I can totally handle it. Go, have fun."

"What? No. I'll stay and help you close up." I insisted.

"Don't be stubborn. Just go."

"… Are you sure?"

"Mackenzie."

"Yeah?"

"Take your food out." She grinned.

"Oh, right." I shook my head sheepishly, sliding steak knives under the meat and then grabbing the plates from beneath the warmer. I took the food out to my table and gathered up their dirty salad bowls. On my way back to the dish pit, I stopped briefly at Brad's table again.

"Hey, Charlie says I can leave work early tonight." I informed him.

"Really?" His amber eyes lit up. "That's great. Do you think you could make my order to go then? I'll eat it on the way."

"Yeah, sure. I'll be like, five minutes, okay?"

"Okay." He grinned. "Mackenzie, I'm really glad you're coming with me tonight."

I thought about that a moment, and my answer was sincere. "I am too."

We smiled at each other and I made my way back to the station, excited for our evening to begin, eager to get as wasted as I could.

Grey was staring at me as I approached the order window, almost like he was impatient, like he'd been waiting for me. It took me by surprise; normally he kept his head down so it was impossible for us to talk. Hesitantly I leaned against the counter. After the weeks of nothing but silence from him, this sudden attention made me wary.

"Can I get that order to go?" I broached cautiously, aware of his eyes on my face, the heat of his stare.

"That's not what it said on the slip."

"I know. He … he changed his mind."

"Fine."

"Thanks." I backed off, figuring our conversation to be over.

"Who is this guy anyway?" Grey asked suddenly, surprising me again. He must have overheard my conversation with Charlie. His eyes were narrowed, glittering angrily. "Some cowboy? Why the hell are you going out with him?"

I blinked at him a moment, stupefied. The look on Grey's face told me he was used to having women fall all over him all the time, no matter how badly he treated them, no matter how hurt and rejected they'd been. I could tell he expected the same from me—and I'd felt that way once too, before—like it didn't matter what he said or what he did or how he behaved, I'd take whatever I could get. And though my stupid, foolish heart couldn't seem to stop loving Grey … I had enough pride, enough confidence to realize that I did deserve better. That he couldn't treat me like total garbage and just get away with it.

I met his gaze evenly, my dark eyes daring him to disagree. "That's none of your fucking business." I retorted.

Grey's face lost its hardness. He seemed struck, startled into amazement by my words, staring at me with … wonder, almost. He dropped his head briefly to put Brad's burger into a Styrofoam container, and then placed the package on the order counter. "Here." He mumbled.

I took the order and grabbed Brad's bill, stalking out of the station without another look back, like I was totally confident, totally in control. Luckily Grey couldn't hear my heart pounding a mile a minute. My hands were still shaking when Brad came and met me at the till, but I managed to smile.

"I'm just going to grab my coat and stuff." I handed him his change.

"No problem. I'll just be out in the truck. It's the one with—"

"I know which one it is." I stopped him wryly. The one with like, six tires on the back axle. I shook my head and grinned. "I'll be out in a minute."

I was nervous heading back into the station, afraid that Grey would still be there, wanting to talk or something. I wasn't sure how long I could keep up the whole "so-over-you routine." Thankfully he was nowhere to be seen. With a sigh of relief, I grabbed my purse and my light jacket from the hooks on the wall.

"Hey, I have something for you." Charlie stopped me with a whisper. She rummaged through her bag for a quick second and then put a small package in my hand. "Here, take this, you know, just in case. Don't look at it; just put it in your purse."

I did as I was told, and though I didn't know exactly what she'd given me, I had a pretty good idea. I smiled excitedly, buoyed by the thought.

"Charlie, you're the best. Seriously." I gave her a slight hug.

"Have fun tonight. I'll call you tomorrow and you can tell me all about it."

"Okay." I nodded. "I will." Donning my jacket, I waved elatedly and headed for the entrance of the restaurant. I grabbed the silver door handle and pulled, but a sudden hand over the jamb prevented the door from opening. I looked up in curious surprise.

It was Grey. He stood beside me, his arm above my shoulder so his palm could hold the door shut. I was amazed to find him standing there, in his white-checked kitchen attire, a black hat upon his head, his blue eyes steady and intense upon me. We stared at each other a moment before he spoke.

"Don't go, Mackenzie."

"What?" I blinked in disbelief. "Why not?"

"Just … because. Why are you doing this?"

No one could answer that question better than Grey. I looked up at him, baffled, lowering my voice so we wouldn't attract any attention from the few tables present.

"Why am I … are you kidding me?" It was because of him that I was searching for someone else, because he didn't want me. And now he was staring at me with such sincerity my poor confused emotions were roiling. He didn't care about me. So why did he suddenly care what I did? Who I went out with?

"You actually want to go out with this guy?" He demanded.

"Yeah, I do. He's a nice guy … and he's actually *interested* in me. He *wants* to spend time with me." I said pointedly.

Grey frowned. "I don't trust him." He decided.

"You don't trust him … okay …." I sighed and shook my head, rubbing my forehead in total bewilderment. "Grey … what the hell do you want from me?"

He hesitated a moment. "I just … I don't want you to go out with that guy."

I didn't understand it. I couldn't. Why now? Why? A week ago, this kind of concern would have made my whole day … but now I was just confused, frustrated … saddened even, by his sudden interest.

"Get out of my way." I uttered quietly, avoiding his gaze.

"Please, Mackenzie."

"No." I shook my head.

Grey dropped his hand from the door. "Fine. Go. Have fun." He muttered.

I didn't waste a second. I whipped the door open and stepped into the warm summer night, welcoming the fresh air on my heated cheeks, leaving Grey behind.

CHAPTER 21

"Ready?"

"Ready!"

"Go!"

Hurriedly I opened my beer, putting the can to my lips and trying furiously to keep up with the onslaught of liquid as it slammed down my throat. Beer dribbled down my chin and onto my sweater as I gulped it down, trying not to laugh, watching in near hysterics as Brad did the exact same thing.

When I was finished, I leaned back and laughed uproariously, enjoying the sound of the cheering around us. Brad wiped his lips on his hand and smiled at me, his grin spreading wide over his face.

"Dammit. You beat me again!" He was forced to admit. I could do nothing but laugh at him, already drunk and getting drunker by the minute as my system tried to deal with the four or five beers we'd already shot-gunned. I sat cross-legged on the hay bale next to a roaring fire, facing Brad, thoroughly enjoying myself.

He was easier to get along with than I ever could have imagined. We cruised the town for a bit before heading out to the party, going to the liquor store for some booze, heading to my house so I could change. Brad was surprisingly fun to be around, laid back and easygoing and just … funny. He really made me laugh. And though certain things would force me into moments of clarity where I realized that we were very wrong together … things like the chew ring faded into his back pocket or the Garth Brooks in his CD player, I had to admit that I was having a great time. If nothing else, I knew that Brad would make a really great friend. I was glad to have met him.

The crowd around us slowly dissipated now that the contest was over and I was declared the winner. A few of them waved at Brad as they moved on, but pointedly ignored me. Jocks, cowboys, popular girls, brainiacs … they were all there. The small percentage of the student body that actually partied—like my definition of party—were nowhere to be found in this crowd, but this group was still having fun. The girls were drinking beer and giggling; the boys dispersed in between them were talking loudly and comparing partying stories. It was lively and carefree, but it wasn't a hard party by any means.

It was funny, I'd gone to school with most these people my entire life, but I didn't know them any better than just a name to "popcorn" to when we were reading in class. Most of them had given me a look when I arrived—like, what is she doing here all of a sudden—but no one was mean or hostile or even unfriendly. It was still a little uncomfortable though. They all had their little cliques and I wasn't a part of them, which was totally fine with me. I wished I could've been there with my friends. We would have taken over a hay bale or two and smoked a bunch of weed and secretly made fun of all the people around us. In short, we would've had fun. Just like we used to.

I sighed and shook my head, trying to rid myself of the sudden nostalgia. The campfire was roaring, I could feel the heat on the skin of my shins even through my jeans.

"Seriously girl, how'd you learn to drink so much?" Brad demanded. "You had a whole mickey of rye in the truck before we even got here."

"Practice." I shrugged. "And, you know what they say. Liquor before beer, you're in the clear."

"Really?" Brad laughed. "I hadn't heard that one."

"What? That's not one of your cowboy mottos?" I teased.

"No. Unfortunately."

"You know what my favourite cowboy motto is? It's … oh, how does it go? I saw it on a shirt once. Oh, okay … If you can't ride it or rope it, take it out behind the barn and shoot it …."

"… Get the cowboy attitude … and pass the ammo." Brad finished with a grin.

I laughed out loud. "You know that one!"

"Oh yeah. It's practically famous." He laughed sheepishly. "I used to have that shirt, actually."

"Wow." I blew my smoke out in a giggle.

"How about this one? Cowboy motto: party 'till she's pretty."

"Oh, ouch." I laughed. "Does that really work?"

"Don't ask me," Brad grinned. "You were pretty before I started."

I laughed. I'm not sure if that's the reaction he was looking for, but I couldn't help myself. I was too drunk. I swayed unsteadily on the hay bale, setting my hands down on the stubble in an effort to sit straight. I grinned stupidly up at him as he leaned closer to me. The light from the fire danced over his face. Before I knew it we were kissing, and his arms were wrapped around me, and he was pulling me to him and pressing me tightly against his chest.

It wasn't terrible. Under different circumstances, I might have liked it. But even through my booze-befuddled thoughts, I knew that Brad wasn't the one I wanted. Even with his lips on mine, my thoughts were still with Grey. So when the cell phone in my purse suddenly began to ring, it was with near perfect timing, loudly creating a welcome interruption and startling us apart.

"Sorry." I pulled away from Brad so I could answer my phone. I could tell he regretted the intrusion, but he let me go and sat back on the bale, waiting.

"Hello?"

"Hey, Mac."

"Oh hey, Charlie. How's it going?" I felt like my mom all of a sudden, like I had to yell to be heard. The party was rowdy around us.

"Good, good." She answered. "Hey, where are you guys? There's nothing going on tonight … it's all kind of lame. Do you think I could come crash the party?"

"Are you kidding me? That'd be great. We're out at the Dam, have you ever been there before?"

"No. I never really went to my high school parties."

"Well, until tonight, that made two of us." I chuckled. I gave her directions as best as I could remember. "But the turn's kind of hidden," I explained, "so I'll meet you there at the entrance. Look for me, okay? Don't run me over or anything."

"Okay Mac." Charlie laughed. "I'm leaving now, I'll see you soon."

"'Kay, bye." I hung up the phone, relieved. Charlie had given me the perfect excuse to get away for a moment.

I liked Brad, I liked him a lot, but I only liked him as a friend. Somehow, I had to figure out a way to explain that to him, and hopefully salvage this new relationship in the process.

"Who was that?" Brad wondered when I hung up the phone. Already he was leaning closer to me.

"Oh, it was Charlie. She's going to come meet us, she just needed directions."

"That's nice." He kissed my neck, slowly.

"Uh … I told her I'd meet her at the entrance." I continued. "So … I should probably go … wait for her."

"I'll come with you." Brad offered quickly.

"No, it's okay. Stay; hang out with your friends. I'll be right back, I promise." I gave him a smile and gently pushed him away. He stared up at me a moment, his face falling with obvious disappointment. "Go shotgun some more beer." I joked. "You need the practice. I'll be back before you know it."

Reluctantly he let me leave, but I could still feel his eyes following me. I ambled away from the party and down the little gravel road, the warm wind blowing softly in the poplars above me, the path lit dimly by a tall, failing yard light somewhere in the middle of the campground. Drunkenly I stumbled towards the entrance, giggling every time I tripped over myself. I was happy to be alone for a moment. I really needed to clear my head.

At the front gate to the park I found an old pickup truck parked haphazardly on the grass right beside the turn off. Clumsily, I climbed up onto the tailgate in perfect view of the road to wait for Charlie. I kicked my feet and lit a cigarette and tried not to think of Grey.

Of course it was no use. I blew my smoke into the calm night air—it was cooler away from the fire, but I didn't mind it. Try as I might, I couldn't figure Grey out. He was unpredictable, volatile at times … but when he was being sweet … we were so good together. Maybe that's what hurt the most, knowing what we could've had.

I sighed. As drunk as I was, I still wanted to get wasted. And then I remembered, with a quick surge of excitement, that Charlie had packed me something sure to get the job done. It was perfect; I was alone so I seized the opportunity, digging through my purse until Charlie's cool silver vial was in my hand. Quickly I did one nostril, and then the other. The relief was almost immediate, and I smiled, thanking Charlie again in my head. I did another, and then another, until even my nerve endings felt like they were trembling. I lifted the scoop to do just one more snort, and mid-inhale, Brad was suddenly standing before me.

He swayed unsteadily, but his amber eyes were wide with surprise, as if cocaine was just some myth and legend he had never expected to come into contact with.

"Are you doing cocaine?" He chuckled in disbelief.

"No." I lied. I don't know why I lied, it was so obvious. I tucked the vial back into my purse and wiped at my nose. Suddenly I was high—like really high. I felt antsy, full of pent-up energy.

"Wow. You really are a bad-ass, aren't you?" Brad was asking.

"I don't know about that." I smiled shakily. "I just like to have fun."

Brad shook his head. "I didn't believe them … but they were right."

"Who was?"

"My friends. At the restaurant. They said you were bad, but I didn't believe them. You're way too … sweet looking."

"Well my friend, I guess looks can be deceiving."

"Yeah, I guess." He shrugged. "But … if they were right about that … maybe they were right about the other thing too."

"I think your friends gossip too much." I laughed. "Why? What else did they say?"

Brad shrugged again, taking a step towards me so that he was standing in between my legs. With a grin, he rested his hands on my knees.

"They said that you were easy." His voice was low now, amused. "They said you were a sure thing."

"They said … what?" The smile faded slowly from my face. And then, suddenly, all of it made sense. Brad's unexpected interest in me, the real reason for his sudden attraction even despite all our obvious differences. He didn't really like me; he didn't want to be my friend. He just wanted to get laid.

It stung. I blinked at him stupidly a moment, trying to recover from this shock. All night I'd been revelling in the thought of a new friend, and the whole time he'd just seen me as a means to an end. It was harsh, a brutal realization.

I crossed my arms. "Sorry to disappoint you." I glared.

"Don't be." He smiled wickedly. "You won't."

Then, suddenly, so quickly that I couldn't move to stop him, Brad grabbed me by the shoulders and tried to grasp me in a kiss. I struggled for a moment to get a grip, and then, either because I was coke-strong and angry or maybe just because he was so drunk, I pushed him off me, hard. Brad staggered backwards and fell in an unruly heap upon the ground. I slid quickly off the tailgate and ran as fast as I could for the approach way. I'd go all the way down the road until I found Charlie, if I had to.

I saw headlights approaching, but they were faint and off in the distance. I prayed they were from Charlie's car. Brad was tough, and drunk or no, I knew it wouldn't take him long to recuperate and come looking for me. I hoped my rejection had been enough to turn him off for good, but somehow, with a thrill of terror, I knew that wouldn't be the case.

It wasn't. Even as I ran away Brad caught up, silently, in a full run, and tackled me to the earth. It happened so quickly and unexpectedly that I hadn't even time to prepare myself. The full weight of him hit me running; his two-hundred pound body slammed my little frame down onto the grass. My head hit the hard, cold ground with a sickening thump, his weight crushed me.

I was aware of an odd, high pitched ringing sound as my vision slowly restored, the edges of my sight crackling white until the disruption faded, dissolving into a black sky of night that stretched above me, dotted with bright stars. My breath was harsh, gasping loud in my ears as I struggled for consciousness.

There was weight on me. I felt I couldn't breathe. Somewhere in the dim corners of my mind I could hear the jangling of my belt as it was ripped open. The noise shook me, and I realized sluggishly what was happening, what was about to happen if I couldn't stop Brad. I could feel his hot, sticky, thick hands on my skin. Weakly I lifted my arms, but there was no strength in me, the blow when he knocked me down had robbed me of any might. Feebly I tried to stop him from undoing my jeans.

There was another noise then, new and totally foreign, but near. The sound of car tires crunching on gravel, the sudden absence of engine noise as the vehicle was put in park and the motor cut off. Charlie. Charlie was there, she had come to pick me up. Charlie could help me.

"Shhh." Brad stopped suddenly, as aware of the car as I was. He pressed his heavy hand over my mouth; I breathed desperately through my nose. In the dim flicker of the yard light Brad's face looked eerie, crazy. He was breathing fast.

"Is this it?"

"It has to be it. Look at all the cars."

"But do you see her? She said she'd be at the entrance. Mackenzie?" I could hear Charlie's voice calling to me. Her shoes stepped onto the road. "Mac?"

I wanted to answer her. I needed to answer her. I tried to shriek as best I could with Brad's hand over my mouth. The noise was a muffled, strangled cry.

"Shhhh." Brad warned, pressing harder. Black spots danced before my eyes.

"I don't see her." Another voice, distinctly male. It was Zack. "Maybe she's over at the fire."

"Maybe." Charlie's voice sounded doubtful. "But she said she'd be here."

"She's probably totally wasted by now, maybe she just forgot. Come on, let's go check it out."

I could hear their shoes passing by on the gravel and knew this would be my last chance. They'd be too late to help me on their way back. I fought then, I had no strength but I fought. I squirmed and writhed and tried desperately for any way to free any part of me from Brad's deathly heavy grip. I screamed into his palm, I tried to bite his flesh. Somehow I managed to wind my hand up between his arms, to find his face. My fingers searched the contours of his head, my breath almost spent as they finally found what they were looking for. Roughly I shoved my fingertips into his eye sockets and pressed as hard as I could.

It worked. It was just enough to make him instinctively protect his face, to remove his hand from my mouth. I drew a hasty ragged breath and screamed as loudly as I was able with the few seconds that I had.

"What the hell—"

"Did you hear that?"

"What was that?"

"Mackenzie!" Charlie's voice. I screamed again as Brad's hand clamped back over my mouth. His eyes were red as they glared crazily down at me. His breath was hot and sour with beer. He grasped a handful of my hair and yanked my head back unmercifully, tears sprang in my eyes and I gasped in pain, my body slackening in submission.

"Shut up. Shut up." Brad demanded. Gone was the nice, funny, polite boy that had invited me to this party. He had transformed into some drunken, disgusting, lust-filled monster. Cautiously he looked up as the footfalls broke into a run, coming back towards us. My sight was dimming; I had no strength left at all to fight. I could only hope they would find us in time ….

And then, the crushing weight was lifted from me. My ribs ached as I sucked in a full breath; my bones throbbed in relief. I lay on the ground, completely stunned, gasping in breath after breath of the sweet night air.

"Mackenzie! Mackenzie!" I heard Charlie come running, she knelt down beside my head once she found me on the ground. "Oh my God, are you okay? Are you okay?"

"Yeah … I …." I couldn't talk. I opened my mouth but no words would come.

"It's okay, just relax. Just breathe." She did up my jeans and my belt, pulled my sweater back down over my torso. Her touch was cool and soft, gentle in comparison to Brad's rough, sticky hands.

"Brad …?"

"It's okay. He's being taken care of." I could discern the hostility in Charlie's voice. In the distance I heard cursing, and moaning, and the dull, bony crack of knuckles hitting flesh. I winced at the noise.

"Can you sit up?" Charlie wondered. Gently she put her arm beneath my neck and gingerly tried to raise me up. I wanted to cooperate, but the moment my position changed my poor head throbbed abominably. I leaned upon her slight form and shut my eyes as waves of pain racked over me.

"You're okay now. We'll go home soon, okay?"

"Okay." I whispered. I don't know how long we sat there as I wavered in and out of consciousness, but Charlie's voice suddenly loud in my ear startled me into awareness.

"Oh, hey the guys are back." She informed me. Then, her voice rose as she spoke, not to me, but to whoever was approaching. I heard their shoes crunching on the gravel. "She's okay. I think she hit her head pretty hard. Thank God we got here when we did," she told them. I lifted my head slightly from her shoulder and looked up as far as I could without straining. There were two sets of legs before us.

"Let me see." Zack bent before me. I could barely make out his face, but his nose ring glinted slightly in the dim light. Gently he felt around my face and my scalp. "It doesn't seem too bad, but we need more light to tell for sure. Can she get up?" He wondered.

"Can you get up, sweetie?" Charlie put her arm around my back. I nodded weakly and tried to find the strength to command my muscles. My arms gave out as I pushed against the ground.

"I got her." A voice, gruff but unmistakable, found my ears. I almost couldn't believe them. Before I even had a chance to react, two strong arms had wrapped around me, picking me up as if I weighed nothing, just as they had with the pail of salad dressing. There was such comfort in their strength. He pressed me close to his chest and I wrapped my stiff arms around his neck and burrowed my face into him. Grey's warm, delicious masculine scent wafted over me, and tears of relief flooded my eyes. My entire being shook. I could feel the trembling contrast against his hard steadiness.

"Shhh …," he whispered, though I hadn't made a noise. "Shhh …."

And then we were moving. He held me gingerly and closely, I could tell he was trying extra hard not to jostle me at all. I shut my eyes and listened to his heart beating against my ear. I was too shocked and stunned to comprehend much but the feel of his strong, warm arms around me and the sweet smell of his breath against my face. Nothing else could have soothed me more.

I heard car doors opening, and then Grey placed me gently upon the backseat of Charlie's car. He shut the door for me and then got in on the other side. Charlie got in the drivers and Zack had shotgun. She switched on the interior light and they turned back to look me over.

The bright, blinding light made me squint, and my head protested at the sudden bombardment to my senses. Charlie's brow was furrowed with concern as she gazed at me; Zack wore a slight frown on his face. Their worry was touching, but there was only one expression that I wanted to see. His countenance had been impossible to discern outside in the darkness, and now I looked up at Grey with cautious wonder.

His blue eyes searched my face with earnest, sweeping for injuries, his jaw tensed and his mouth set in a grim line. My heart fluttered, despite everything, at the anxiety I found reflected in his handsome face. He did care about me. He had to.

"Her pupils don't seem dilated." Zack decided. "But it's early yet."

"Maybe we should get her to the hospital." Charlie frowned doubtfully. "You never know."

"No." I shook my head. It took some effort to speak. "We can't go to the hospital. I'm okay, really. Nothing hurts but my head."

"Don't you think we should, just in case?"

"I just did a bunch of blow."

"So?"

"Her mom's a doctor." Grey explained for me. "She doesn't want her to find out."

"Oh … well … what should we do then?"

"Can I have a smoke? Where's my purse?" My hands were still trembling. I took a breath and looked for my bag.

"Here." Grey handed me one and lit the end. I inhaled deeply, the smoke burning down my raw throat. The cigarette shook in my unsteady fingers. Grey cracked the window for me.

"Let's go back to your house, Charlie." Zack suggested. "We can just watch her, and if anything gets worse, then we'll take her in."

"Really?" Charlie eyed me worriedly. "We shouldn't just take her in? They can't tell that she did coke unless they do a pee or a blood test."

"Please, Charlie. I don't want to go there." I didn't want to acknowledge what had happened, what had almost happened. I just wanted to put the whole unpleasant incident behind me. "They'll make me go to the police."

"Are you sure Mac? If anything happens to you I'll feel even more terrible."

"I'm sure. Honest. I'm fine." I lied. My very bones seemed to ache in places and I felt weak all over. "I'll be fine. Can we just forget about it, please?"

"Forget about it? Mac, he could have hurt you! He almost—"

"I know. I know." I shook my head. "But he didn't. I'm fine, really. It's no big thing."

"You're better off than he is, anyway." Zack chuckled darkly. "By the time we finished with him."

"Is he very hurt?" I wondered. I grimaced and looked up at Grey.

"He got what he deserved." Grey admitted. He looked down at the backs of his hands, bruised from the fight; his knuckles were scraped and bleeding. He shrugged. "Don't worry about that asshole."

I wasn't worried. But I was … regretful. I couldn't believe what had happened. The change that came over Brad had been … disturbing. I remembered the mad, eerie light in his eyes as he glowered over me, the aggression that drove his hands, his wet mouth hard upon my skin. I shuddered involuntarily.

Grey noticed. Wordlessly he wrapped an arm around my shoulders and drew me near, pressing me close against his hard chest. I lay against him and fought off the tears that threatened to spill, tears of trauma and tears of relief. My throat ached. Charlie switched off the interior light and started the car. We pulled out of the parking lot and onto the highway.

Grey's hands rubbed my back soothingly, his fingers stroked though my hair. He didn't let go of me once the entire trip.

CHAPTER 22

We were all a bit more subdued than normal. Zack and Charlie were at the counter island in the middle of her kitchen, playing a game of crib, dealing cards in between snorting lines. I was laying on the faded old couch in the living room, oblivious to the *South Park* episode playing on the TV; waiting for the joint I'd just smoked to help alleviate the fearsome pounding in my head. Grey was sitting in the easy chair not far from me, silent and pensive, his face tight as he stared at the television set.

I blinked slowly, seeing nothing, thinking about boys. Were they all so cruel, so callous and mean? First Riley had totally abandoned me, his best friend, with seemingly no good explanation except the sudden desire to completely change his life and leave all the old behind. So he'd left me behind, and that had hurt me, deeply. Then Brad had tricked me, preying on my vulnerability and my desperation for a friend, leading me to believe he really liked me when all he wanted was to get some at the end of the night. He'd hurt me, he'd viciously attacked me, and though my bruises would heal on the outside, inside I'd always carry the scar of his betrayal.

I shuddered at the thought. I couldn't keep from remembering the images and sounds and feelings of Brad's assault. I still smelt like campfire, and the smell reminded me sharply of the evening, of sitting by Brad and drinking and laughing and thinking about how much I liked him as a friend, how much fun we were having together.

I shut my eyes drowsily, hoping for sleep, desperate to forget it all in the relative peace of my subconscious.

"Mackenzie, Mackenzie, wake up," Grey shook me on the shoulder lightly, but it still sent a throb of pain racing down my arm. I moaned and opened my eyes, looking directly into his face, rigid with concern as he crouched before me, hovering; his blue eyes avid with worry. "Try not to go to sleep, okay? For a little longer?"

Ah, yes. And then there was Grey. Was it possible that he was the cruellest of all? How easily he'd made me love him, with his wit and his charm and his good looks and his talent. He'd trailed me along, making me believe I had a chance, making me delight in the connection I thought I'd found … the hope that we could be something together. But then he'd rejected me—brutally, and ignored me for weeks, like I truly was nothing to him. Now, the deep concern for me written in every worry line on his handsome face was the most confusing of all. The meanest thing he could have done after everything we'd been through was care. And the regret in his eyes, the anxiety in his features told me that he did, that he cared more for me than I could ever have imagined. How badly I wanted to believe it, to believe him. How badly I wanted to hope. But I couldn't, I wouldn't let myself. I'd only be setting myself up for more hurt.

And my heart couldn't handle much more.

"I want to go home." I whispered to him.

Gently, Grey brushed the hair out of my face. "You do?"

I nodded as gingerly as I could to try and spare my aches and pains. "Yes."

"I'll get Charlie to give you a ride."

"No." I protested. "I want to walk."

"I'll go with you then."

"No, you don't have—"

"I'm coming with you." He insisted. The look he gave me was stern. Resignedly, I nodded, and then painfully pulled myself up into a sitting position. His hands were warm and gentle as he helped me get to my feet.

"I'm going to take Mackenzie home," he announced to our friends.

Charlie frowned. "Are you sure that's a good idea? Mac, I don't know if you should sleep, after hitting your head so hard."

"Her pupils are fine," Zack decided then, after a studied look into my eyes. "And it's been a few hours already. If she had a concussion or something, we'd know it by now."

"How do you know all this stuff?" I wondered weakly, made a little uncomfortable by his penetrating gaze.

Zack shrugged. "For a while there, I wanted to be a paramedic. Lucky for you, hey?" He grinned. "You should be fine, but if anything changes, like you can't see or you're dizzy and throwing up and stuff, don't be an idiot. Go to the hospital."

"Thanks Zack."

Charlie gave me a hug then. "I'll talk to you tomorrow, okay? Are you really sure you're fine?"

I nodded gingerly. "Yeah. I just want to go and sleep."

"Okay." She looked pleadingly over at Grey. "Take care of her, will you?"

He nodded, and his words seemed to be weighted with meaning.

"I will."

The air was still warm outside, but I couldn't keep a shiver from running up my spine as we stepped onto the sidewalk. I wrapped my arms around myself and stared down at the ground, trying to seem oblivious—but painfully aware of the footsteps beside mine, the silent presence so close to my side. Grey and I walked quietly a few moments, listening to the wind in the trees, the sounds of our shoes on the cement. With every step the air seemed thicker with something … with nerves and frustration, with unspoken … impatience, almost.

Finally, Grey cleared his throat. He seemed uncomfortable beside me, fidgety. His jaw tensed a few times, and he opened his mouth to speak, but no words came out.

"I'm not very good at this." He suddenly blurted, running a hand through his thick mess of dark hair.

I didn't say anything, only looked over and waited for him to continue.

"I owe you an apology, Mackenzie. An explanation at the very least."

I nodded.

"I … uh …." He looked over at me. "… Does your head still hurt?"

"I'm fine."

"Are you sure? What about your—"

"I'm fine Grey." I nearly snapped.

"I'm sorry." He breathed deeply, and he looked at me again, his blue eyes full of warmth and sincerity. But then he shook his head and fell silent.

We kept walking. I thought I might lose my mind with impatience, but I kept my mouth shut. He wasn't going to get any help from me. If he had something to say to me, I wanted him to say it. I wanted to hear the words from his lips.

"We were …." He started again. "We were coming out there tonight so I could … apologize, Mackenzie … I've been terrible to you."

I had no argument for this.

"I just … I never expected to feel … I mean, when I saw you there, tonight, I almost lost it. I think I did a little. Just the thought of you hurt or sad … or … or worse … I …." He rubbed his hands over his face. "I couldn't take it. I couldn't stand the thought of you in pain … I was so angry. I wanted to tear that guy's face off …. But I was even angrier at myself."

I nodded for him to continue.

"I hate myself for hurting you, Mackenzie. When I think about what I've done … what I did to you, on purpose … it's … I don't know …." He struggled for a moment. "… I understand if you hate me."

I sighed. Was that even possible? "I don't hate you, Grey." I admitted softly.

"See? It's you, right? I thought that you were just like all the others … vain and petty and … boring. But you … I've never met anyone like you before. You've got this … this spark, or something. You're alive. But I didn't want to admit what I felt for you. I didn't even know I was capable of it … you know? I tried to convince myself otherwise."

I nodded again, trying to maintain my rigidity … but I couldn't help myself. My heart was melting, my careful façade breaking. He was saying all the things I'd ever wanted him to say, and my poor, foolish heart could do nothing but warm to him, utterly powerless, utterly defenceless. I crossed my arms in an effort to remain untouched.

Somehow we were standing on the street in front of my house already. The blocks had vanished unnoticed behind me as we walked, completely occupied by the sound of his voice, deep and low in the quiet, speaking those impossible words to me. Now we stopped and faced each other, the nearby streetlight shining softly over us, lighting our faces and casting our shadows long behind.

"Tell me why." I demanded.

"Why? You mean why … I hurt you?" Grey glowered down at the ground for a moment. "Because." He smirked sadly, "Because … you're so young. So … innocent. But not in a bad way … in a good way … like no one I've ever known before. I mean, look at you." He did just that, his eyes soft and tender as they swept my face. "You're so beautiful."

My voice was faint with amazement. "You think I'm beautiful?"

He looked up at me, into my eyes, and gave a slight nod. "But that's why I tried to … ignore what I felt. Why I tried to deny it. I mean … I could never deserve someone like you. You're young, and sweet, and you've got your whole life ahead of you, and I … I'm just some old loser trying desperately not to grow up."

"You are not a loser." I denied vehemently, grasping his arm. "Are you kidding me? I've never met anyone as talented as you. You're … amazing."

Silence descended again. Grey crossed his arms, thinking. I watched him warily, my heart pounding furiously in my chest as my secret hope pushed all the surging, hidden joy through my veins. I forced myself to hold back, barely containing my happiness, and waited, biting my lip, staring up into his face.

"I know it's wrong." Grey spoke then. "I know it's selfish. But I've never wanted anything so badly in my whole life. Not as bad as I want you." His blue eyes blazed sincerely. "I can't deny it anymore. But I've been horrible to you, so if you can't forgive me … if you never want to see me again … I understand."

I smiled. I couldn't help it, I never could. I loved him. I reached out and grasped his hand, gently, mindful of the bruised, swollen knuckles that had been battered fighting Brad. He'd fought Brad for me. For me.

"Grey, the only thing about this that could ever be wrong," I stared up into his eyes, so he'd know that I was truly serious, so he'd know that I meant every word with my whole, entire heart, "would be never seeing you again."

He seemed overwhelmed. He just stared at me, his eyes sweeping my face, and I smiled in return, a happy giggle escaping my lips. With his fingers he brushed the hair from my cheek, traced gently over my cuts and my bruises, and then lifted my chin with the palm of his hand.

"Can I kiss you?" He whispered.

I wrapped my arms around his neck, bringing us closer still.

"Please." My fingers curled into his dark, messy hair.

And when his lips touched mine, they were curved in a smile.

CHAPTER 23

I was on cloud nine. That was the only way I knew to describe it. Whenever I had a spare moment throughout the day my mind would instantly whir to that night, would go over again each and every word Grey had said, every move he had made, every look he had given me. Every kiss we had shared. My heart nearly burst. A wide, happy grin would spread over my face and I'd sigh with excitement and utter contentment.

I did this in the middle of our English exam. I just couldn't focus anymore on the reading comprehension, so instead I thought of Grey. I spent half the morning in my own little world, absently twisting a strand of hair through my fingers, dreamy and far off. When the teacher warned us there was only twenty minutes remaining, I suddenly snapped back into it and hastily finished the rest of my test, guessing on most the answers and assuming on the others. I hoped I would graduate.

But I hadn't seen him since Friday night. That was the only downer to my mood. And it wasn't likely that I'd see Grey before the weekend. All last Saturday the entire band had been in the city meeting with their new label and I hadn't been able to get away from my family at all on Sunday to see him. And now my parents had me on lockdown for the entire week since exams were happening. I wasn't even allowed to work, I was only permitted to go to school to write exams and then I was to head straight home and resume studying for the others.

I hadn't given in easily. I thought it was a little strange that my parents were suddenly exercising some discipline now, with only a week left of school. It wasn't like they cared what I did any other time—really; I hardly ever saw them besides the mandatory Sunday-family-day-Greg-and-Marcy-torture-day. I thought it was even funnier that they actually expected me to go along with their little rules. I was practically eighteen, pretty much on my own with only four more days standing between me and sweet, total, utter freedom. Why the hell would I listen to them now?

And yet, there I was, walking down the old crumbling sidewalk beneath the large, leafy poplars that lined the quiet residential street. The sun was warm as it shone through the trees; the air was sweet smelling and soft. I walked slowly, smoking, towards my home, my bag full of books and binders. I wasn't happy about it. I had put up a fight, a good fight at that, but my parents still had won. They played the whole "as long as you're under my roof" card, and then started ganging up on me, working as a "team" to ensure I knew who was boss. It was possibly the most frustrating hour of my life. I couldn't wait to be old enough, to do whatever the hell I wanted without having to listen to anyone ever again.

Just four more days. Four more days. I repeated this to myself. My father just happened to have the whole week off work, so he'd be home now, waiting for me. He had looked at my schedule, he knew when my exam was over, and he knew how long it took for me to walk home. So he would definitely know if I turned right now and headed down towards the restaurant where Grey was working instead. I sighed. As badly as I wanted to screw it all and go see Grey, it was probably smart of me to study. If I ended up having to repeat the twelfth grade I'd … well, I couldn't even think about it. I had to graduate. I had to go home now. I just hated letting my parents think they'd beat me.

"Hey Mac." My dad greeted cheerily when I finally made it home and slammed the front door. "How was your first test of the week?"

"Fine." I grumbled. I stormed past him and into the kitchen, dropping my bag loudly to the floor. He seemed oblivious to my attitude and followed me with a grin. His thinning dark hair was rumpled, a shade lighter freed from its usual gelly hair products. In place of his ever-present suit was a pair of dark blue sweatpants and an old ratty sweater. He looked relaxed and happy, clearly enjoying this unexpected time off.

"Must be exciting. Last week of school … big graduation on Saturday. I can't even remember my last week of school."

"Can't you?" I was completely disinterested as I threw a Pizza Pop into the microwave and hit start.

"No. I remember graduation though. I was stylish. Big, plaid bellbottoms. You should've seen them."

"I have seen them. In pictures."

"Oh, right." He tried again. "So, what are you studying tonight?" He wondered.

I made a face at him and crossed my arms, glaring at the floor with a shake of my head.

"Oh, stop being so dramatic." Dad chuckled. "It's one week of your life. It won't kill you to take a break from going out every night, will it?"

"Maybe." I shrugged. "I guess we'll see in the morning."

"You know, when Marcy was your age—"

"Dad." I had to stop him. There was no way I could keep myself even somewhat rational if he brought up Marcy's perfection now. I remembered her graduating year; she was the valedictorian of her class, gorgeous, popular, and athletic. I had been young back then, maybe grade eight, and chubby, with aspirations to be just like my big wonderful sister so my mom would cry because she was just so proud of me, too. How things changed. I retrieved my Pizza Pop and slammed the microwave shut. "Spare me dad, will you, please? I don't want to hear it."

Dad sighed. "Fine." I had finally succeeded in getting the annoying little grin to fall from his face. "I just think she set a pretty good example for you, you know. It wouldn't hurt to learn a little from her."

"Yeah, okay. The next time I want to get engaged to a total dick, I'll give her a call and get some advice."

"Mackenzie." Dad warned. He shook his head in disapproval. His mouth was set in a grim line.

"What!"

"Why …?" he looked at me, like he was completely baffled, and his head shook with incomprehension. "What makes you so angry all the time?"

"I'm not angry all the time. I just told you, I don't want to hear that shit."

"Watch your mouth young lady. I don't care how mad you are, you don't take that tone of voice with me." He pointed a finger. I sighed. I wasn't in the mood for round two—me versus them, at the moment.

"Whatever, sorry." I rolled my eyes. "Can I go now? I have a *lot* of studying to do." My voice dripped sarcasm.

My dad didn't answer, just nodded his head and waved me off with a rigid motion of his hand. I grabbed my plate and my bag and huffed past him through the kitchen and up the stairs to my room.

"Save me. Save me please." I complained into the phone, lying back on my bed, my legs crossed, my foot kicking the empty air.

"It can't be that bad. It's only for a few more days." Charlie laughed at my dramatics. "I remember high school, yeah, it's a complete drag. You're so close to being done though, just suck it up."

"Yeah." I twirled a lock of hair around my fingers. "So, what have you been up to?"

"Not much, just work."

"How's that? Do you miss me?" I smiled hopefully. "Has Grey … asked about me?"

"I told him what was up."

"What'd you tell him?"

"That your parents were holding you hostage and you couldn't come out. And that you had to go home right after your tests everyday. And that your exams are at the school and you're finished at 3:15."

I laughed. "Wow. Good details."

"Thanks. Oh, so, hey, did you see Brad today?"

"Yeah." I frowned. "He wouldn't look at me. He has two huge black eyes though—maybe they were hindering his vision. Like, he got the *shit* kicked out of him." I laughed, but a shudder ran through me. I hadn't forgotten the total violation of his attack. I wondered if I ever would.

"Serves him right. Stupid bastard."

"No doubt."

"I'm so glad Grey and Zack were with me. It was Grey's idea, you know, to go out there. He was so pissed at me for letting you go early, before you two could talk."

"Really?"

"Yeah. I feel really bad about it actually. I'm really sorry, I didn't realize Brad would turn out to be such an asshole, I mean, he looked so sweet."

"Of course, Charlie. Come on, there's no way you could've known. I didn't even know. He was sweet. He seemed totally harmless. This was not your fault, at all."

"Yeah, well I still feel bad."

"Don't."

Charlie sighed. "Anyway … I knew Grey liked you, all along. He just needed a push in the right direction, I guess, hey?"

"Yeah." I sighed happily. "Oh, hold on a sec." A knock on my door interrupted our conversation. "Yes?" I called. The door opened a crack and my dad's head poked through.

"Off the phone," he demanded. "You're supposed to be studying."

I rolled my eyes. "Okay."

"I mean it. Off."

"Okay, just let me say goodbye."

"You have two minutes."

"Okay!" I yelled. The door shut and I growled in frustration. "Charlie?"

"Yeah?" She was giggling.

"Did you hear that?"

"Yeah."

"What a pain in the ass." I sighed. "I've got to go."

"Have fun studying. I'll talk to you tomorrow."

"Yeah. If I'm allowed."

She laughed. "Bye Mac."

"Bye." I slammed the phone down in disgust. I restrained myself from throwing it at the door, barely. The urge was still there. I took a few deep breaths with my eyes closed. I was tense and agitated, I needed something —I craved something to take the edge off my mood. I wanted a smoke, I always did, but even if I found a way to sneak one, I doubted that would be enough. This was a deep belly craving, like my very veins were in need.

And then I remembered. I sat straight up in bed, my eyes wide at a sudden thought. Could I really do that? Here? Would I get caught? I bit my lip and looked at the door. There was no lock on my knob, my parents' policy on "no locked doors." I think it was supposed to be a metaphor or something.

I slid off the bed and retrieved my purse from the corner of my room, hidden beneath some rumpled clothing and CD wrappers. Charlie's vial was still inside it, I had forgotten to give it back to her on the weekend. Apparently she had forgotten too, or didn't care; she hadn't mentioned anything to me. I held the vial in my palm for a moment, my hand still hidden in the bag. The silver canister was cool and heavy, filled with promise. I went over the choice in my head, weighing my options. Cocaine was almost impossible to identify unless someone knew what to look for. Would my dad? For the most part I would seem completely sober to him, maybe just a little jittery. But I was going to be holed up alone in my bedroom all night. There was no way he'd notice.

Screw it. I needed to get high. I walked to the door and slid my back down it, sitting against it to stop anyone from suddenly entering before I had a chance to hide the evidence. It only took me a few minutes anyway, the lid was off and the white powder up my nose in an instant. I did a couple, then a couple more. The relief was instantaneous, beautiful. I could feel delight creep slowly through my veins, my tension melt and ease away. I sighed and screwed the lid back on, hiding the vial back in the purse and hiding the purse back beneath the clothes. I sat on the bed and tapped my foot. I turned up the music, a little Limp Bizkit. I pushed my studying stuff away and grabbed some nail polish.

Visions of Grey danced in my stuttered thoughts. I wanted to be with him so badly. I painted my toes and then did my nails. I took my two grad dress options out of the closet and stared at them, debating. I chose the black one—the one my mom hated—and put the other one away. I tried the dress on, and then paired it with some shoes.

I stood in front of the mirror, wondering what to do with my hair. I did it up, down, half up, half down. I spun. I put together an outfit for the next day. I picked up some deep red lipstick and painted my lips, staring in the mirror. I practiced some sexy smiles. I took the grad dress off and hung it up. I put some lotion on my legs. I did not study at all.

CHAPTER 24

I awoke with no idea when I crashed. My face was stuck to the opened pages of my math textbook; my body was crumpled in an impossible way upon the bed. I blinked at the sunlight that stung my eyes and pulled the textbook from my skin. I knew I hadn't studied at all, I must not have noticed the books piled on the mattress when I finally stumbled to bed. That explained why I'd just been wearing one.

A knock on the door made me jump, still on guard even though I had nothing to hide … now. I pushed the dark mess of hair back from my face.

"Yes?"

"Mackenzie, you're going to be late!" My mom's frantic voice got louder as she opened the door. She was still dressed in her Doctor's garb from the night before, and she looked dead tired. "I woke you up half an hour ago! What have you been doing?"

"I don't know, I fell back asleep." I straightened myself out; my body was stiff and sore from the awkward position. I yawned and stretched.

"There's no time for that." She checked my clock radio and the frown on her face deepened. "Get dressed; I'll give you a ride." Mom headed for the pile of clothes thrown in the corner of my room, the same pile that was currently concealing my secret stash. I panicked.

"Mom, give me a sec!" I stood from the bed. "I can get dressed on my own."

"Fine, just hurry." She snapped. "I'll be in the car. You have five minutes."

"Okay, okay." I stood in front of the pile, ready to ward her off if she suddenly wanted to gather the laundry or something. But Mom was too busy storming off to worry about it.

Luckily I already had an outfit picked out from the night before. I threw on my jeans, a red tank top and some flip-flops. My newly painted black toenails shone nicely. My hair was an absolute mess; I couldn't do anything but twist it into a bun type thing at the back of my head. I quickly lined my eyes with black and put on some mascara, grabbing a deep red lipstick to apply on the way. I brushed my teeth like lightning, grabbed my purse and my books and a black hoodie on the way out the door.

I could practically hear my mom's teeth grinding as I stepped out of the house and into the warm summer morning. I shoved all my things into the backseat of the car and hopped in the front. There was complete silence from my mother as she backed the car out of the drive and then zoomed onto the street.

"I can't believe you." She spoke in frustration.

"What, so I slept in." I shrugged. "It's no big deal."

"Tell that to your diploma exam." She shook her head. I shrugged again. I wasn't exactly prepared for my diploma exam anyway; ten minutes wouldn't really change things. I gripped the door as my mom took a corner too fast. "I can't believe you're seventeen. You act like you're twelve. Where's the responsibility?"

"Ugh …." I rolled my eyes and leaned against the window. "Did you and dad like, have a meeting or something? Did you decide to drive me crazy on purpose?"

"Me and your father," she said curtly, "are beginning to realize that we've ignored this situation for far too long."

I groaned. "So you did have a meeting."

She ignored me. "It's our fault, if there's anyone to blame. Our schedules are just so crazy; it's not that we haven't noticed … it's that we've been too tired to deal with it properly."

"Are you talking to me?" I wondered. It seemed she was having a conversation with herself. I looked at her in confusion.

"Things are going to change, Mackenzie." Mom warned. "You need discipline, and rules, and boundaries."

I scoffed. "Yeah, okay mom. I'm graduating in three days. You're going to start this all now? Don't you think you're a little late?"

The expression on her face told me she had at least considered that fact. She bit her lip. "No." Mom lied. "As long as you're living under our roof, things are going to change."

I slumped back in my seat. There were no words to voice my frustration. I shut my eyes and wished for some cocaine. And a cigarette. And to be out of the car already. Mom pulled furiously into the school parking lot.

"You come straight home after school, you hear me?" Mom threatened through a yawn. "We'll be waiting. We need to have a good talk, all three of us."

"Oh joy." I grumbled. I got out of the car and grabbed my things from the backseat, slamming the door as hard as I could. I turned my back on her without even a wave, stomping towards the school. Mom watched me for a minute; I could hear the car sitting there. When finally she pulled away, I waited until she was down the street before I dropped my stuff and took a smoke from my purse. There was no way I could go in and write a major exam without a cigarette first, especially not with the mood I was in.

My mood was even fouler by the time I finished my math exam. I had gone through the questions doggedly, struggling to make my brain work properly, but most often I'd gone with my best guess. The number closest to the one I came up with was the one I chose. My head pounded by the end as I handed in my test, and I frowned at the prospect of going home for a family meeting. Dealing with my parents was the last thing on earth I wanted to do. I walked through the empty halls of the school that echoed with absent students, and headed into the bright, sunny day totally miserable.

But then I saw him. My head was down; I didn't notice him at first. I looked up from the grey slab sidewalk and there he was, standing there, waiting for me beside an old white motorcycle that gleamed with steel. His bare, tanned arms were crossed against his chest; a sexy grin curved his lips when he noticed me. I could see my reflection in the large, dark aviator sunglasses that fit his face perfectly. My breath caught in my throat at the sight of him and I just stood there, amazed.

I wasn't sure what to expect. I hoped for the best, but also braced for the worst, just in case Grey had come to deliver another "we're still just friends, right?" speech. My heart beat nervously as I approached him, but I tried to stay positive.

"What's up?" I wondered. I hoped I looked okay; self-consciously I remembered my messy, bedraggled hair and obvious lack of make-up. Grey smiled—his lips curved into the playful smirk that I knew so well, and when he lifted his glasses, the way he looked at me, I could've been the most beautiful woman in the world. My cheeks flushed pink and I returned his smile wholeheartedly, my heart surging with relief.

Grey shrugged and motioned to the motorcycle beside him. "I thought maybe you'd like to go for a ride."

"Wow. And here I thought you'd forgotten all about me." I kidded.

"I'm afraid it's a little late for that."

My blush deepened at his words, and I flashed him a happy, bashful smile. "I didn't know you had a bike." I stepped forward to admire it, running my hand down the cold steel of the handlebars. I didn't recognize the make, but for an older model it seemed in good condition. The steel gleamed silverly and the white paint looked pristine.

"I keep telling you. There's a lot you don't know about me." Grey winked slyly. He flipped the kickstand, grasped the handlebars and straddled the machine. His black boots planted firmly to keep the bike from tipping and he looked up at me expectantly, his blue eyes shining.

"Hop on, sugar." He called with a grin. His jeans were tight over his bent knees; his white t-shirt hugged the hard torso beneath. He put his glasses back on. I smiled eagerly and let my backpack fall on the ground next to the sidewalk. Studying was just going to have to wait.

As I grasped the hard muscle of his arm and threw my leg over the seat behind him, fleetingly I imagined my parents—their arms crossed, their feet tapping impatiently as they watched the front door for my arrival home from school. They were going to have to wait as well. There was no way I would give up spending an afternoon with Grey just because my parents suddenly gave a damn.

As if reading my thoughts, he turned to me over his shoulder. "Are you going to get in trouble for this?" He wondered.

"No." I lied. "Who cares?"

He chuckled. "You ever been on a bike before?"

"No. Well, like, a pedal bike. Does that count?"

"No. This is easy though. Just lean when I lean."

"Okay."

"And Mackenzie?"

"Yeah?"

"Hold on tight."

I laughed and obliged him willingly, wrapping my arms around his waist, resting my hands on his hard abdomen. I could smell the delicious warmth of his skin and his cologne, very subtle, just enough to make me want more. I smiled happily to myself as a surge of excitement and anticipation thrilled through me.

The bike roared to life then, making me jump. I could feel Grey laughing as he slowly walked the motorbike backwards and away from the curb.

He shouted to be heard. "Ready?"

I nodded. One moment we were sitting there, the next we were moving smoothly out of the parking lot. We sped up upon reaching the street, and I clutched Grey tighter. It was a totally foreign feeling to me; I wasn't used to being so exposed. There was nothing to keep me in, nothing to protect me from the elements but his form before me.

But it didn't take long before I loved it. The wind floated over us, carrying with it the scent of Grey's cologne on the warm summer breeze. He was young, and strong, and gorgeous, sitting just before me, switching gears expertly, in total control of his vehicle. I had never been prouder to know someone, to be with someone, to have others see me with someone. I tipped my head back and let the wind brush over my face and my neck, a smile curving my lips.

The soft, gentle breeze was caressing as we rode, and as it stroked my arms and my skin I caught the promise of adventure, the desire for total exhilaration that only more speed and wind could bring. I wanted more. I pressed myself against Grey's back, my hands hugging his hard body closer to me. My lips found his ear.

"Faster." I requested. Grey didn't answer me, but the corner of his mouth curved slightly. I knew that he was smiling. "I want to go faster."

"Of course you do." Was all he said.

The bike roared onto the highway. Grey went through the gears like butter, one right after the other, revving the motorcycle until the engine growled in response. The countryside whizzed past on either side, a blur of shapes and shadows that I couldn't discern. The sun shone golden down on us, but its warmth was whipped away by the wind that rushed by, cutting through my clothes as if I were wearing nothing at all. Its bitter fingers pierced the very core of me, stealing my breath away, making my heart hammer with adrenaline. My skin erupted in icy shivers.

A smile curved my lips. This was exactly what I wanted. There was nothing around me. Nothing but the deafening wind. My hair tore free from its elastic and fell, caught by the currents, streaming behind me, whipping and tearing around my face. My smile deepened.

Thoughtlessly I took my hands from the safety of Grey's waist. I stretched them in the air beside me and then threw my head back, embracing the cold, letting it pour through me until it burned all the heat away. I felt alive.

I felt like I was flying. Like Kate Winslet in *Titanic*. In that moment, I was free. I let the wind take from me all my worries, all my cares, all my troubles. It swept them far, far away. My parents, my exams, Riley … none of it mattered. Nothing but the total freedom that I felt.

I loved it. I loved him. I hugged myself around Grey again, wrapping my arms tightly around his waist. He laughed beneath my hands. The engine revved and we went even faster. I clung to him until there was no space between us and my heart felt like it might burst with happiness. I never wanted it to end.

Eventually we had to slow, re-entering the town limits as the sun swung lazily over the horizon. Its warmth could be felt again on my frigid skin due to our leisurely pace, present in the soft, languid breeze that swept lightly over us. I was chilled right to the very marrow, my frozen fingers were stiff and numb but I smiled delightfully, renewed somehow by the invigorating ride.

As we paused at a stop sign, Grey glanced over his shoulder at me. He nearly had to yell to be heard. "Where to now?" He asked.

I bit my lip in thought. The sky was dimming around us, and there was a part of me—the quiet, easily mollified part—that knew I should go home. Knew I should deal with the inevitably already pissed off parents. But the other part of me—the louder, more dominant part—wanted fun and adventure at any cost. She wanted to stay with Grey for as long as she possibly could. Who cared how much trouble she'd be in?

I grinned. "I'll go anywhere you want to go."

"Anywhere?"

"Anywhere."

CHAPTER 25

I sniffed in deeply and welcomed the pleasant burn that started in my sinuses and slid down the back of my throat. I passed him the vial, pinching my nose shut and breathing deep.

Anywhere had turned out to be Grey's house. I was so surprised he had taken me there; I'd always wondered where he lived. His house—no, their house, he shared it with Alex and Zack—was in the older part of town. It was obviously lived in by bachelors. There was no kitchen table; a large beer-can castle took its place, apparently Alex's masterpiece. I had to sit on my hands to keep from knocking it over, the urge was so great. The living room was devoted entirely to a big screen TV and all its necessary components—sound surround, DVD towers, a large black, overstuffed sectional. There was a UFC poster on one wall surrounded by holes punched in around it. Grey said that when Zack got really ripped, he thought he was Tito Ortiz and liked to show off his skills, using poor Forrest Griffin in the poster as his target.

"This is good shit." Grey handed the vial back to me. I did another scoop and the rush of calming heat bore instantly into me. I grinned and shut my eyes a moment, savouring the sensation.

"I know." I sniffed. I felt the rush spread into my tongue, fuelling the speed of my words as my heart surged in my chest, pushing eager blood through my veins. "I did some last night when my dad was making me study but I didn't get anything done, but it was a blast. But I haven't studied for like, one of my tests yet. I've probably failed them all, which will suck when I have to come back next year and do it all over again … or maybe I just won't, who knows …." Shakily I lit a cigarette and inhaled deeply. "Anyway, how did you do in school? Were you a total brain?"

"Hardly." He laughed. "I guess I could've been, but I didn't care enough to try. I dropped out when I was in grade … ten, was it? Ten or eleven."

"You did?"

"Yes. It was the best thing I ever could have done."

"Why?"

"That's how I met Alex and Zack, when we started the band. I lived in the city and I knew I wanted to do music, so I just started going to auditions and stuff after I quit school. Most everyone thought I was too young, but Tom liked what he saw, anyway."

"Wait, you joined *their* band? I didn't know that."

"Yeah, they were called Warhorse back then. They were struggling. Not that I was the answer or anything, but we just work together really well. Everyone else was already there but Jimmy, he joined after me, a few years ago. We wrote some new stuff and changed our style a bit and, well, obviously it's worked out pretty good, so far."

"I can't believe you're signed. Like, that's a big deal, right?"

"Yeah. That's a pretty big deal."

I flicked my cigarette rapidly over the ashtray; my fingers were trembling. My heart fluttered hastily in my chest. "So, why don't I ever see Jimmy and Tom and … Lucas, right? You only see them at gigs and stuff?"

"They still live in the city. We practice and have the Aurora deal out here, so they come into town at least twice a week. It's kind of a pain in the ass, but our jam spot costs way less here than it would in the city, and the Aurora was our only real steady gig. When I first met the guys, Tom got me a job at the Red Wheat, 'cause I guess he knows Ralph pretty well, and Alex and Zack gave me a place to live. So I moved out here. It was a lot better than my city situation, anyway. "

"And what was that?"

Grey shook his head. When he lifted his blue eyes, they looked a bit sad. "Doesn't matter." He shrugged. "That was years ago."

"Oh." I nodded. Obviously he didn't want to talk about it, but I was intrigued. I took another scoop of delicious white powder and shot it up my nose. The cocaine made me blissfully numb but superbly aware. "How expensive is this stuff anyway?" I wondered suddenly. I'd have to pay Charlie back for all the dope I'd gone through.

"Depends on how much you want. Eighty bucks will last the night, typically."

"Eighteen, or eighty?"

"Eighty. Eight-zero."

"Really?" My eyes got big. I held the vial up to estimate its size. "How much would it cost to fill this up again?"

"Um … I don't know. Three, four-hundred maybe."

"What?" I laughed in surprise. "Really?"

"Roughly, yeah. Why," he chuckled, "you in deep?"

"No, well, this was Charlie's. She lent it to me last Friday and I've kind of … used it all." I looked down at the skimpy remnants that clung to the inside of the vial. "Good thing I've got tips now."

"Yeah, I'd say. That's going to be a mighty expensive habit, at the rate you're going."

I shrugged. "Girls just wanna have fun."

"Yeah. Some girls more than others." Grey studied me for a moment, and a smile broke over his lips. "Sometimes, I swear, you're like the female version of me."

"Well," I grinned. "No wonder you like me so much."

"Yeah, I guess that's one of the reasons." He laughed, and when he did, his blue eyes twinkled brightly, happily. I loved it. I loved being the cause of his happiness.

"There are more?"

"… Yeah," he relented. I was sitting cross-legged on the kitchen counter; he was leaning opposite me against the center island. With a smirk set on his perfect lips, he swaggered over and stood before me, so I only had to look up to see into his face.

The coke gave me confidence I probably never would've had otherwise. I put my hands on the hard muscle of his arms and slowly trailed my fingers down them. I met his eyes—eyes so beautifully clear and blue they would have rivalled any summer day—and smiled warmly at him, invitingly.

"And those reasons would be …?" I probed.

"Well … this is one of them …." His voice dropped low, he smiled sexily and then bent down to kiss me. His lips were soft against mine at first; I wrapped my arms around his neck and let my fingers delve into his messy, dark hair. His hands were warm on my waist, he used them to pull me close and my heart leapt happily in my chest.

His smell and taste and touch swept over me until my senses reeled with delight. I couldn't get enough of him. I would never get enough of him.

A noise occurred to me, vaguely, so focused was I on the feel of Grey's lips that I barely noticed it. It continued on, until he was the one that stopped and pulled away, staring at my purse in vexation. I followed his eyes to my bag strewn upon the counter, and suddenly the noise made sense to my befuddled brain. Without thinking—only to make it stop so that we could continue where we had left off—I snapped my cell phone up and whipped it open.

"Hello?" I answered abruptly.

"Do you have any idea what time it is? I have been calling—" I had to hold the phone away from me so the sheer volume of mom's voice wouldn't burst my eardrum.

"Shit, it's my mom." I cringed, whispering to Grey as she continued to rant and rave. He looked at my cell phone in awe. Mom had an impressive range when she needed it.

"Mom. Mom, hold on." I tried to calm her.

"If you don't walk in this door in five minutes, I'm sending your father to get you," she threatened. Which would have worked, had she known where I was. Plus, she forgot the threat of my father stopped scaring me when I was eight.

"Mom, relax. I'm on my way home now." I lied.

"Five minutes." She repeated. That was it, she hung up on me right afterwards. I sighed and flipped my phone shut in defeat.

"I should go." I frowned. Still twined around Grey's hard body, I could easily have changed my mind, hang the consequences. I rested my head on his shoulder.

"She sounded pissed." He smiled.

"That's because she is." I groaned. "Shit, Grey, what am I going to do? I'm still like, totally blitzed."

"Here, let me look at you." He sat me up and studied my face intently. With his hand he smoothed my hair, still a tangled mess from our earlier bike ride. His blue eyes were soft. "You look fine. Amazing, actually. They'll never suspect a thing."

"Are you sure?" I bit my lip nervously.

"Even if they did suspect something, what would it be? Alcohol maybe. At the very worst weed. Cocaine is not a conclusion parents jump to."

"Yeah?"

"You'll be fine." Grey kissed me again, and his lips hinted of our earlier passion, but it was over way too soon. He lifted me down from the counter. "We should go. Five minutes, remember."

"Right." I frowned and stuffed everything back into my purse. I had missed thirteen calls on my cell phone; my parents must have been trying to get a hold of me while we were out riding. I looked at the call list with dread. I was in huge trouble.

"You don't mind giving me a ride home?" I wondered as we put our shoes on at the front door.

"No. How are you supposed to get home in five minutes by walking?"

"I don't think we'll make it in five minutes riding either."

Grey grinned. "I'll take that bet."

It was exactly seven minutes later when Grey pulled up in front of my house. As I climbed off the bike he whistled lowly, studying our home in surprise. I followed his eyes and glanced up at the house, wondering what he was thinking, trying to imagine what it might look like through someone else's eyes. A sprawling two-story covered in cultured stone and fancy lighting, with a fully landscaped yard and manicured hedges—yeah, I knew what it looked like. Rich. At least, small town rich. I bit my lip. Maybe we were rich, but I didn't really think of myself that way. My parents were, I guess. I wasn't ashamed of their status or anything, but I didn't want Grey to think of me any differently. I wanted us to be on the same page, on even keel.

"Wow. What does your dad do?" He wondered.

"Oh, it's this new thing. He gets paid per the amount he annoys me." I kidded. "See, he's pretty good at it."

"Oh, I see." Grey smirked. "So, you're spoiled."

"No." I could see the menacing shadow of my father in the window; I imagined he was glaring out at us even as we spoke. I tried to ignore him.

"Thanks for coming to get me." I wrapped my arms around Grey's neck and smiled. "I had a really great time."

He nodded, and smirked, and bent down to kiss me. I loved the taste of his lips, every time seemed new, delicious. I never wanted to stop.

I hated to leave him, but I knew I had to. I sighed and pulled away.

"Bye."

"Good luck." He smirked. He held onto my hand as long as possible, dropping it as I slowly backed away from him. I turned regretfully and hurried across the quiet street, up the flagstone walkway lit by beaming little solar lights. The motorbike rumbled to life behind me. I heard it rev up and then peel away, and I knew that Grey was gone.

I was nervous. Not about getting in trouble, but about acting sober in front of my parents. I was totally ramped up, everything about me was accelerated. I hoped they wouldn't notice. I hoped they'd see my twitchiness as anger or frustration.

Dad had the door open before my foot hit the last stair. He glowered out at me, a silhouette in the light streaming through from inside. I bit my lip and slowed my gait, warily brushing by him on my way through the door. Dad followed me silently back into the house.

Mom was waiting, her arms crossed as she leaned against the wall in the entry. I was amazed by my parents' calmness, I had expected them to be yelling and screaming at me by now. It actually made me more nervous, this unforeseen serenity; it meant I was in more trouble than just a good old scream-fest was worth.

"Into the living room, please." Mom requested civilly. I stepped out of my flip-flops and placed my purse on the floor by the door. She led the way into the adjoining room, and then motioned for me to sit on one of the overstuffed, floral patterned sofas. She sat in the easy chair beside the couch, her legs crossed formally like this was a business meeting. Dad didn't sit at all. He just stood there, his arms across his chest like he was a bouncer or something. His face was hard and grim.

"So, Mackenzie." Mom started. I turned to face her, unconsciously chewing on my lower lip. My heart was hammering in my chest, how could they not hear it? I took a deep breath, focused on acting as calm as they appeared to be.

"First of all, do you mind telling us where you've been all evening?"

"Uh, yeah. I was with a friend, we were hanging out. No big deal." I shrugged. Dad breathed heavily.

"Do you not remember me specifically asking you to be home right after school?"

"Yeah, I remember." I admitted.

"So why didn't you?"

"I don't know. My friend has a bike and he asked me to go for a ride, and I just … I couldn't resist."

"You couldn't resist." Mom sighed. "Ugh, Mackenzie. What are we going to do with you?"

"The same thing you did before. Nothing." I suggested.

Mom scoffed. "That's the last thing that's going to happen, young lady. There are going to be some changes here. And like it or not, you will have to accept them. We are your parents, you are our child. We must enforce some boundaries for you."

"Really?" I threw my hands up in amazement. "Really, though? I'm seventeen years old, I graduate in two days. Don't you think it's a little late? Don't you think we should've had this conversation, I don't know, a few years ago, maybe?"

"We didn't need this conversation a few years ago," Mom shook her head, "I don't know what's come over you lately, but you're changing. Are you on weed?"

"Weed?" I looked at her like the very thought was insulting. "Mom."

"I'm sorry." She sighed and rubbed her hand across her forehead. I almost felt bad for her. Almost. "We just, we want to help. Can't you talk to us, tell us what's going on?"

"There's nothing to talk about." Not anymore, at least. There was a time that I was open to talk to my parents—a time when I actually wanted to talk to them. I could remember it clearly. But they were always too busy. Dad had to catch a plane; Mom had to get to bed so she could work all night. Marcy needed this, Marcy needed that. I'm sure they meant well, working hard to provide for us and everything, but really. How could they expect me to just open up now?

"Are you sure?" Mom prodded. "We're not the enemy, you know."

I shrugged silently. They weren't getting anything from me.

Mom sighed again. "Okay, I tried. Mitch," she waved her hand at him, like he was tagging in or something. "Go ahead."

Dad nodded. He had on his "insurance" face now, the one he used when he was determined to sell something. "You don't want to talk? Have it your way." He shrugged like it didn't matter. "From here on in, we're going to have the following rules in place, and like it or not, you're going to have to obey them."

I looked up at him, my eyes narrowing defiantly.

"One. No more staying out until all hours of the night. You're going to have a curfew like every other normal teenager, home by eleven during the week, midnight on the weekends."

"Dad." I glared. "You can't be serious. Midnight on the weekends?" I was incredulous. "You can't just start treating me like a little kid!"

"Then you should stop acting like one."

"What?"

"You heard me."

I stared at him a moment. Neither of us would back down, we were too similar in temperament. "Ugh, you know what? No." I stood up and shook my head at them. "No, this is bullshit. You've been home all of what—a week, and suddenly you get to judge me?"

"I'm only on rule one, kiddo. Shall I keep going?"

"No. No." My racing heartbeat was suddenly fuelled by more than cocaine. Anger pushed it even harder. I felt a surge of furious adrenaline shoot through my veins. My fingernails pressed into my clenched palms as I struggled to keep it together. Vaguely I remembered all the stories I'd heard of people totally freaking out when they were high on coke. I suddenly understood. My emotions were so intensified that I nearly saw red.

"I don't give a shit about your stupid rules." I concluded. "You can't just ignore me for years and then suddenly start trying to make decisions for me."

"We never ignored you." Mom looked appalled by the accusation.

"Really? For the last two years I've spent nearly every night by myself. I could've been doing anything, and no one would know. Does that classify as ignoring? But it never seemed to bother you, leaving me alone like that. You let me do whatever I wanted to for years."

"Did you ever think that maybe we trusted you?" Dad interjected.

"Trust? Yeah, right." I scoffed. "That had nothing to do with trust. You just didn't care about me. You had your friggin' golden child already."

"What?" Mom sat up in her chair. She stared at me for a long moment, as if trying to rationalize my words. They seemed to disturb her. "Mackenzie, is that really how you feel?"

I shrugged and stared hard at the red woven area rug beneath my feet. I could've proved my point, God knows I had enough material, but why should I bother? There was no way they'd sympathise. I'd just come off sounding immature and jealous and petty and then they'd have even another reason to like Marcy more than me.

"Well. I'm really sorry if you feel that way. Really sorry." Mom looked repentant; her eyebrows were knit in sincere apology. I had to remind myself to stay angry at her. "That was never our intention, of course it wasn't. We just felt that you were more … capable, I guess, to be alone. Marcy was always so dependent on us, on me. But you've always been braver than her. It was so different after she moved away, when you didn't need me as much. That's why I didn't start working fulltime until after she graduated."

I shrugged again. "Whatever." I sighed. I could feel myself softening but resolved not to let it happen. Mom wasn't going to talk her way out of the last few years of total indifference, no matter how sweet her words were now. I drudged up a memory to keep me focused on anger. The memory that worked every time.

It was back when I was chubby. I remember because my skirt wouldn't zip up all the way, I had a most unfortunate roll that did that to all my zippers. I had to safety pin most of them so they would stay up. On this occasion I was wearing a red and black plaid skirt with a white tucked-in blouse, and black Mary-Jane shoes atop knee-high white tights. My dark hair was done up properly in a French braid. I was in grade eight at the time, because it was my second year playing flute in Band. It was the night of our recital, and I was nervous because I had a solo in one of the songs. I had beat out the other five flutists to win that honour. Grade eight Mackenzie was a bit of an over-achiever.

We had four songs to play. The last song was my big moment. I spent nearly the entire first three songs looking out into the crowded gymnasium from the stage, searching for one of my parent's faces. See, Marcy also had a recital that night—she had taken ballet and jazz/tap for most of her young life. My parents hadn't decided yet who would go to which show, but one was going to watch Marcy dance and one was coming to watch me play.

Except neither of them were at my recital. I missed playing a good twelve bars during the third song in my desperation to see a familiar face in the crowd, but they were nowhere to be found. When the time came for my solo, I wanted to do good, I wanted to be perfect like always, but in my distress I totally screwed it up. I played an F instead of an E, and then became so flustered by my mistake that it was all downhill from there. I practically ran from the stage after, I was so embarrassed. I locked myself in a bathroom stall and cried for what felt like hours. Not just because I had messed up the solo and neither of my parents had been there, but because I had a sneaking suspicion where both of them had gone.

And I was right, in the end. When all three of them came to pick me up from the school, my parents apologized profusely for their "miscommunication." That would have been an okay excuse, except that both of them had stayed for Marcy's entire recital. They bought me an ice cream on the way home and kept wondering why I was so quiet, why I didn't tell them how it went at my concert. I think it was something in the way Marcy gloated—the little half smile she gave me as she flipped back her perfect shiny hair. That look said it all. Give it up before you totally humiliate yourself, Mackenzie. There's no way you can compete with me.

I dropped Band that year. And Advanced Science. And the Chess Club.

"Mackenzie?"

"What?" I came back to the present then, good and justifiably angry, just how I wanted to be. Mom could give me that damn sorry look all night, but there was no way I was giving in now. All I had to do was imagine that safety-pinned plaid skirt for the heat to start flowing.

"Did you hear me? I was just saying that we're willing to be flexible here, if you'll cooperate with us. We can work on a compromise and come up with some reasonable boundaries for you."

"I don't need boundaries, mom. Haven't you been listening to me, like at all?"

"No, Mackenzie. We've been too lax for too long." Dad decided firmly. "We're making some changes around here. Mom will switch her shifts if she has to, and I'm going to rearrange my schedule. From now on one of us will always be here with you."

I groaned loudly and slumped back against the couch cushions.

"Complain all you want, but this is how it's going to be."

I had to shut my eyes. I hated, hated the way he was talking to me, so smug and casually matter-of-fact. I'd show him. Suddenly it was all I could do not to pick up the crystal vase on the coffee table and smash it on the floor. I imagined the delicious shattering noise it would make and clenched my fists again to keep from actually doing it. A deep breath helped to calm me.

"No, dad, it's not."

"Excuse me?"

"I said, no, dad, it's not. It's not going to be this way. Look, you go ahead and make all the damn rules you want." I chuckled mirthlessly. "But I'm not going to follow them. I haven't had a curfew since I was like, twelve, and there's no way I'm going to start again now."

"Mackenzie, don't be so difficult." Mom frowned. I could tell she was trying to be the rational one among us. "It'll take some adjusting to, that's for sure, but it won't be all bad. We can come up with a living situation that works for all of us."

"Yes, you know what, I've got one." Dad's face was hard and angry, his calm façade nearly out the window. He stabbed at me in the air with his finger. "She moves out."

His icy words hung suspended a moment, totally unexpected. Both mom and I just stared at him for a second.

"Mitch!"

"What?"

"Quit being so irrational."

"Who's being irrational? There are rules here. If she doesn't like them, she can leave." He motioned to the front door. "We don't need to put up with this."

It took me a minute to fully comprehend his words. My dad wanted me to move out. I had to admit, it stung a little, as I imagine it always will whenever a child is told their parents' desirable life scenario doesn't involve them anymore. I just hadn't realized we'd reached the kicking-out stage yet. At first I was hurt, but the more I thought about it, the more I realized that moving out was exactly what I wanted. What I'd always wanted. If I was on my own I could do my own thing without having to put up with my parents anymore. There'd be no one to try and tell me what to do. No one to fight with and argue with about stupid shit that didn't matter. Then I could stay out all night, every night. I could be with Grey as much as I wanted to.

Never had my father ever had a better idea in his whole life.

I couldn't let on how excited I was by this unexpected turn of events, so I sat quietly on the sofa, acting every part the wounded party. Apparently my dad had failed to inform my mother of this new, impromptu plan. She was more upset than I was about it.

"Mitch, you're overreacting. Let's just sleep on it. Tomorrow we can talk again once we've cleared our heads. There's no need to do anything rash."

"No." I stood up then, hugging myself. "No. He wants me out, I can move out." I gave my mom a sad, brave smile. I avoided Dad all together.

"Mackenzie, you don't have to go …."

"Yes, she does." He insisted.

"Mitch, how could you do this—" Mom started in on him. I took this as the perfect opportunity to leave, sliding away as they began to argue and sneaking up the stairs to my room.

The first thing I did upon entering my bedroom was pick up the phone and call Charlie. It was just after ten, I hoped she'd be home from work by then. I sat on my mattress and scanned the room idly as the phone rang in my ear, picking out the things I would take with me and the stuff I would leave behind when it came time for me to go.

"Hello?"

"Hey, Charlie, it's me."

"Oh, hey baby! How's it going?"

"Good." I could barely make out Charlie's voice amid the noisy din in the background. I could hear a number of voices and loud, angry music. "What's going on over there?"

"Oh, not much. The guys are over; we're just drinking and hanging out."

"Oh, yeah?" I listened harder, frowning. I hated not being there with them, I hated missing out on anything. "That's cool."

"Can you come over?"

"I don't think so, not tonight anyway. But my last test is tomorrow, so after that I'll be free."

"Oh, great. I bet you're looking forward to that." She was exhaling her smoke; I could hear it over the phone.

"I am. And, you'll never believe this but … I think I just got kicked out of my house." I cradled the phone against my shoulder.

"What? Really?"

"Yeah, I think so. I mean, ultimately I guess the choice is mine, but there's no way I'm going to choose to live here with their gay-ass rules."

"No kidding. Wow, that's crazy. What—no, Mackenzie got kicked out of her house." She was speaking to someone there. "I think so, I don't know … hey, Mackenzie?"

"Yes?"

"Grey wants to know if you're okay."

I smiled. Pure happiness spread through my entire being. "Yes, I'm okay." I answered. I heard her relaying my message.

"Grey wants me to ask if he should come and pick you up."

I laughed. His concern made my whole night. "Tell him thanks, but that's probably not the best idea."

"So, what are you going to do? Where are you going to live?" Charlie wondered when she was back to me.

"I don't know, I've got to find a place, I guess. You don't know of anything, do you? I can't afford much …." I thought of my measly paychecks from the restaurant. "But I guess once school's done I can work full time or something."

"I don't know … I don't know of anything off hand, but, maybe I can figure out something. I'll let you know as soon as I do."

"Thanks Charlie. That's a big help, I don't even know where to start."

"No problem."

"I should let you go have fun." I decided wistfully. "I don't know if I'll be around tomorrow either, I think a bunch of family is coming out for my grad."

"Oh right, that's this Saturday, isn't it?"

"Yeah. Oh hey," I bit my lip, "I was actually going to ask about that. I forgot to get an appointment for my hair and stuff … do you think you could help me get ready?"

"For grad? I'd love to."

"Are you sure?"

"Of course I'm sure. Just come over Saturday, bring your dress and everything, we'll make sure you're all gussied up."

"Oh, thanks Charlie."

"Anytime. No problem. Hey, I've gotta go, it's time to hit the rails. See you Saturday?"

"Yeah, Saturday. Have a good night, do one of those for me."

"I already have." She giggled. "Night Mac."

"Night." I hung up the phone and sighed heavily. I tried not to think of all the fun they were having without me. It didn't work.

CHAPTER 26

Saturday morning dawned clear and bright. I lay in my bed, blinking at the sunlight and thinking about everything I had to do that day. Despite myself, I was actually a little bit excited. Having never graduated before, I wasn't sure what to expect. Our school didn't go all out or anything, there was a family reception followed by a formal ceremony and then the grad party that happened afterwards. It was basically just an excuse to dress up and celebrate the end of school and the beginning of the sweet, sweet freedom that I'd been looking forward to for so long.

I made myself get out of bed and get in the shower. I took extra care shaving my legs, careful not to knick my knees like I always did. I put on extra lotion afterwards so my skin would gleam. I didn't have to worry about my hair and make-up and clothes yet, Charlie would help take care of that. I put on my black lace underwear and matching bra, then my jeans and a t-shirt overtop. I let my long dark hair air-dry over my shoulders.

The house was bustling. My Aunt Linda and Uncle Paul had come the night before with my three rowdy little boy cousins; I could hear them running around downstairs. I got a kick out of them; they all still called me "Mac 'n Cheese" instead of Mackenzie, a nickname given to me by the oldest one when he was just learning to talk. Other than them, the only family coming to the graduation was my Grandma and my Uncle Pat, who lived in town. My other aunts and uncles and cousins either lived too far away to make the trip or they were all grown up with kids of their own, too busy to come so far for just the weekend. I didn't really mind, I wouldn't have a lot of time to spend with them anyway. I tried to ignore the fact that nearly every single one of them had been present when Marcy graduated.

I guess I couldn't blame them though. There would be no honours behind my name when I crossed the stage, no scholarships or awards, not like when Marcy graduated. I wasn't even sure I had passed my tests. No, my family would be seeing nothing that day but an unremarkable Mackenzie who had scraped by with the minimum of effort. And that was just how I wanted it.

I bounded down the stairs and into the kitchen. Aunt Linda was standing in front of the stove flipping pancakes. She was definitely my favourite Aunt, tons of fun, constantly laughing and joking. She was plumper, with curly red hair streaked with blonde and cut short. I leaned on the counter and watched her for a minute.

"Good morning, graduate." She smiled warmly at me. "I'm making your favourite for breakfast. Pancakes with whipped cream and maple syrup!"

"You spoil me." I grinned.

"As much as I can." She admitted. "You make sure you eat today. It's easy to get caught up in the excitement and wind up fainting because you're half-starved. You don't want that to happen when you're on that stage, do you?"

"No ma'am."

"That's right. Now sit yourself down and eat these before they get cold."

"Okay. Thank you." I grabbed the plate piled high with steaming pancakes, loaded them up with whipped cream and syrup and then sat down at the table to dig in. Dad came in as I was eating; he nodded at me and smiled at my Aunt as he got himself a coffee. We were still at an impasse, him and me, but since my Aunt and Uncle had arrived we'd all been acting like nothing had happened. Like he hadn't kicked me out and I wasn't leaving as soon as possible.

It was fairly amusing to me that we instinctively put on a show of being a happy, functional family around other people. At least we could agree on that.

We may have been acting civilly, but the tension was still there, right under the surface. I don't think my mom had forgiven my dad for kicking me out without consulting her first. Dad was clearly still pissed at me, as I was frustrated with him, but for the moment it simmered just below the surface, safe and out of sight. He had—to my horror of horrors—driven me straight to school the day before so I could write my last test. He picked me up afterwards as well. When I walked out the front doors his car had been there, idling, as if he expected me to make a run for it and was fully prepared to chase me down. We spent the drive, both there and back, in total heated silence.

Luckily we hadn't had to spend much time together since. He was preoccupied with my Aunt and Uncle and I was able to hole up in my room, painting my nails and making other important preparations for my big day. My dress was pressed and hung up in my room, my little clutch purse held all the necessities—cigarettes and a lighter, some clear nail polish and shiny lip-gloss.

"I'm so excited to see your dress." Aunt Linda exclaimed. She joined me at the table and took a sip of coffee. "Your mother was telling me about it, it sounds … neat."

I laughed. "I doubt my mom thought it was neat. But I think it's awesome. Just wait till you see it on."

"I can't wait! So, where are you getting your hair done?"

"Oh," I finished chewing and swallowed. "At my friend's house. She's really, really good, I'm trying to convince her to go to school for it."

"Fun! I can just imagine the giggling and the boy talk."

"Yeah, there's definitely some of that." I nodded. And hard drug use.

"So, tell me about it." She leaned in conspiratorially, checking to make sure that neither of my parents were around. Dad had gone into the den to watch TV with Uncle Paul. "Tell me about the boy."

"What boy?"

"The boy." She rolled her eyes at me. "Come on, Mackenzie. There's always a boy."

"Is there?" I giggled. "Yeah. There is." I smiled at the very thought of him.

"So, what's he like? Are you two serious?"

"Not, like super serious. But *I* really like him. Like, love him, like him."

"Really? Tell me more! Is he handsome?"

"Oh, yes, so handsome." I pictured Grey's dreamy face. "He's perfect. He sings in a rock band, and drives a motorcycle and he's just …." I sighed happily. "He's great."

"Will I get to meet him?"

"Oh … I don't know." I frowned thoughtfully. I hadn't actually told Grey about my grad or invited him or anything. I'm sure he had a trillion better things to do than come to a high school graduation. "Maybe, I'm not sure." I shrugged.

"Well, if he's there, you be sure to introduce me."

"You'll know him when you see him. He'll be the hottest guy around."

"I bet." She winked at me. "Oh, to be young. There's nothing like it, you know. You treasure these days, Mackenzie."

"I will." I smiled. "I'm going to."

My mom dropped me off at Charlie's house early that afternoon. I could tell she didn't like the look of the place—her nose did that flare thing it does when she's not impressed with something. But at least she didn't say anything about it. I could tell she was trying extra hard to get along with me.

"Do you need me to pick you up later?" Mom wondered as I got out of the car.

"No. Charlie can give me a ride."

"Are you sure?"

"Yes."

"Okay. Four o'clock, then, right?"

"Right. See you then." I shut the door and grabbed my stuff from the backseat, draping the dress over my arm as I started up the old, wobbly stairs. Charlie opened the front door when I was halfway there and gave my mom a little wave before her car sped away.

"Hey!" Charlie greeted me excitedly, a wide smile spread over her face. She looked gorgeous as usual—her blonde hair was straight and shiny, she wore black Capri's and a white button-up blouse. I didn't understand how she could wear white so much and never spill on it.

"Or should I say, hey, roomy!" She held out her hands to me.

"Hey … what?" I stopped on the top stair.

"I said hey, roomy." Charlie repeated with a giggle. "Welcome home."

"What …?" I was speechless with surprise. A smile broke over my face. "You want me to live with you? But what about Katrina?"

"What about Katrina?" She made a face. "I've been thinking of kicking her out for ages. She's never around anyway; it'll give her the perfect excuse to move in with that loser boyfriend she spends so much time with."

"Really? Are you sure?"

"Of course I'm sure! It makes perfect sense. Do you want to?"

"Are you kidding me?" I laughed excitedly. "That's the most … wow … it's just, so perfect."

"Then welcome to your new abode." She opened up the door for me with a flourish. "Katrina is such a pain in the ass; I can't wait until she's gone."

"Me either, now." I admitted. I looked around the small, tidy space of Charlie's home, appreciating it even more since it would soon be mine to share. I couldn't have imagined a better scenario. Living with Charlie was sure to be nothing but a good time. "I'm so excited." I gushed. "When do you think Katrina will move out?"

"Um, I'll probably give her until the end of the month. So a week or so, is that cool?"

"Absolutely, it'll give me time to pack. How much is the rent?"

Charlie flipped on her stereo. *Hanging by a Moment* by Lifehouse was playing. "It's six-hundred a month, so you'd pay three-hundred, and then half the power and utilities and stuff, and then groceries or whatever. But if you're working full time you shouldn't have any problem affording it."

"Awesome." I lit a smoke and smiled. "I should be able to get more hours at work, hey?"

"Oh, yeah. That shouldn't be a problem either. I'm really excited about this Mac, you have no idea." Charlie moved about her kitchen, plugging in a set of hot rollers and setting her make-up case on the counter. She pulled a baggie full of white powder out of a drawer and poured some onto a small square mirror, then took her credit card and started breaking up the chunks and crushing it fine. I giggled excitedly, watching her work with eager impatience.

"To celebrate your happy graduation and your new home," she passed me the straw, "and the beginning of the awesomest summer ever!"

"I'll snort to that." I joked. Long gone was any kind of pause or hesitation, I took the straw immediately and inhaled the blow expertly; an old pro by now, sniffing it back deep.

"Wooh." I could already feel it working, the happy numbing trembles that satisfied the things in me I hadn't known were lacking. It felt like I was complete again, like everything was right and good the moment the burn hit my sinuses. We did some lines for a while, laughing and giggling and snorting until we reached a near fever pitch of happiness and excitement. I was crazily, totally high. My teeth ground together with pent-up energy.

I sat on a chair in the kitchen as Charlie got to work. The room was wreathed in smoke and the music pumped loudly around us. She put my hair up in the rollers and started on my face. I found it hard to sit still; I had to concentrate to keep from fidgeting. We talked about her high school graduation and how lame it had been, about typical cheesy grad themes like, "the future looks bright," and "don't stop believing." I could vaguely remember Charlie in high school now that I thought about it; she had been a few grades ahead of me, pretty and popular.

"How come you didn't go to college?" I wondered. "Or school or something."

"College." Charlie made a face. "No thanks. I couldn't pick just one thing to do for the rest of my life, I've never been like, career driven. Obviously, I mean, look where I work. I don't know. I just, I want to learn it all. I want to see it all. I couldn't do the whole cookie cutter get a job and work at it for the next thirty years thing, you know."

"Yeah, I know." I agreed. We had a lot in common. "There's more to life than a good job to make money and have stuff."

"Exactly."

When she was satisfied with my make-up, she started on my hair. There was no mirror before me so I couldn't see what she was doing. I could feel her piling the dark tresses on top of my head, and though there was no way to tell what it looked like, I trusted her completely. She was truly a genius when it came to beauty.

"If you ever did go to school for something, it should be for this." I motioned to myself. "Seriously. I think you'd do amazing. And that'd be fun, right?"

Charlie shrugged. "Maybe. I mean, I've always liked doing it."

"You totally should. I'd come to you, every time."

"Thanks, Mac."

The afternoon sped away, accelerated by the drugs as we sat in the warm kitchen of Charlie's—soon to be our—house. It wasn't long until she was finished doing my hair. Then she helped me out of my clothes and into my dress. Excitement churned in my stomach as she zipped me up. I couldn't believe I was going to be graduating.

Charlie stepped in front and looked me over, head to toe.

"Oh, Mackenzie. You look …," she shook her head, "amazing."

"Yeah?"

"Yeah." She nodded. "Come on; let's look in the mirror in my room."

We giggled our way into the bedroom and I stood before the full-length mirror. Charlie had done it again. I did look amazing. My make-up was quite natural, nothing too bold or daring, but totally tasteful. I had cheekbones again; I had to find out how she did that. My dark eyes were large and wide, lined just right to make them seem bigger and softer. My wide lips were coloured a nice, deep red—they shone with just the right amount of gloss.

All of my hair was up, sleek and smooth in a voluminous glossy French twist, and my bangs were side-swept over my face. I looked at my hair in awe; I couldn't believe that Charlie had done it. It was amazing, an elegant style that perfectly suited my dress.

My dress. I was in love with my dress. I had found it at a vintage shop in the city, and the moment I saw it I had to have it. It was soft and black and strapless, with a snug fitting pencil skirt that came down just to my knees and a high, thick black belt that cinched tightly at the curve of my waist. It was very vintage sixties, very Audrey Hepburn. I looked totally different in it, totally grown up and mature.

I shook my head at the reflection in the mirror. "Thank you, Charlie. It's just … you're amazing." I gave my friend a hug.

"Wait, we're not done yet, just hold on a sec." She left the room; I could hear her rummaging around in the bathroom as I admired myself incredulously.

"Here." She came back triumphantly, holding up a necklace that she placed at the base of my throat. It was heavy; one necklace that looked like many, a silver rope of baubles—some delicate and shiny, some matte silver mixed with plain, silver chains. It went perfectly with the look, worked well with the neckline of my dress and added just a flash of sparkle.

I felt amazing, like a runway model or something. Since it was nearly time to go, I spent the few remaining minutes practicing to walk on the cracked linoleum in my black velvet peep-toe pumps. I wondered what my mom would say, for she had vetoed this dress from the very beginning, but maybe she'd change her mind when she saw me in it. She'd preferred a frosted pink crinoline princess gown that made me shudder the moment I saw it.

It was about quarter to four, but Charlie didn't seem in any rush. She cut a few more lines for us and I did mine fervently, careful not to get any blow on the soft black fabric of my dress. It gave me the extra boost of confidence I needed. I lit a smoke and exhaled shakily.

"Shouldn't we go now?" I wondered. I couldn't sit still, pent-up with the combination of cocaine and nervous expectation. I didn't even think to wonder or worry if my parents would know I was high. For the few minutes we saw each other, if they did notice anything, they'd probably think it was just nerves.

"Oh, yeah. We'll go soon." Charlie was putting lipstick on as I asked. She had dressed up as well and looked amazing, of course, in a frilly white dress and strappy little sandals that were perfect on her. She kept glancing at the clock like she was stalling or something.

"You don't have to come if you don't want. I imagine it'll be fairly boring."

"No, it'll be fun. Besides, nothing's boring when you're high enough."

I laughed. "True."

And then I heard it. It started as a deep rumbling somewhere off in the distance, and the noise grew gradually louder as it came nearer. Eventually, the rumbling stopped right outside Charlie's apartment, just sitting there, idling. My heart did a little flip as I recognized the sound. I looked over at Charlie in surprise.

"Right on time." She confirmed.

I couldn't believe it. The thought had never even occurred to me. I grabbed my clutch and gave Charlie a kiss on the cheek, nearly squealing with delight. She laughed.

"See you there, Mac." She called on my way out the door.

It seemed too good to be true, but it wasn't. There he was, astride his motorcycle, flashing a grin at me as I stepped into the bright afternoon sunshine. I smiled back at him, taking the stairs slowly, one at a time, until I was safely on the ground and walking confidently, ecstatically towards him.

Grey looked amazing. He wore dark jeans and black motorcycle boots with a crisp, white button-down shirt, tucked in and rolled up at the sleeves. Overtop his shirt he had a black wool sweater vest with distorted white graphics, edgy and cool. His dark hair, albeit messy, was still styled carefully, spiky with gel. I could see myself reflected back in his large, aviator sunglasses. My heart skipped a beat as I approached.

"Wow." I smiled, touched by how much effort he had clearly gone to on my behalf. The white motorcycle beneath him practically sparkled, it was so clean.

He took off his sunglasses and the startling blue of his eyes nearly took my breath away. A smirk curved his lips as he looked me over—again and again—until finally he shook his head at me, as if in disbelief. A low whistle escaped his lips.

I giggled and did a twirl. "You like?" I wondered.

Grey grasped my hand and pulled me near. "I like." He kissed me gently.

"You shaved." I cupped his smooth, tanned cheek in my hand. "How did you—" I shook my head in happy amazement. "How did you know about this?"

He shrugged. "Charlie."

"Charlie." That explained everything.

Grey looked doubtfully at my high heeled pumps. "Can you ride in those?" He chuckled, smiling at me as he put his sunglasses back on.

"Oh yeah." I smiled confidently, though really, I had no idea. I grasped his arms to get on the bike, but after a few stunted efforts to swing my leg over the seat, I threw my head back in laughter.

"It's not my shoes, it's my skirt. I can't get on, it's too tight!"

"I'd say it's just right." He laughed with me.

"Okay, here." I sat down on the bike seat sidesaddle style, so that both my feet were on the same side and my high heels rested precariously on the one little peg. I grasped Grey tightly around the waist.

"Now, just go slow, and we'll be good."

He chuckled at my ingenuity. "Are you okay?"

I settled myself behind him, my arms wound around his hard waist, the warm sun shining on us in the clear blue summer sky. All I could feel was excitement; it spread within me and filled the air around me. Everything was changing. School was done and I was moving out, moving on, about to start the new chapter of my life that I had always looked so forward to. I was about to embark on the world—one full of countless potential possibilities and new, wonderful experiences that were just waiting for me to come and enjoy. I would take full advantage, would take all they had to offer.

A shiver of utter thrill rushed through me. I smiled wildly.

"I've never been better."

CHAPTER 27

In the history of grad reception entrances, it had to be the coolest one ever. Grey drove up to the entrance of the Community Center where my classmates and their families were gathered in little groups, waiting for the reception to start. Everyone was dressed to the nines—all the guys were in dark suits and ties, most of the girls were in fluffy, frilly pastel coloured dresses.

We rumbled slowly in, drawing the attention of the crowd as everyone stopped to look up at us. If I hadn't been so high on coke I probably would have been blushing like mad, but as it was, I felt hot and glamorous and just … special. Out of the ordinary. I was nearly bursting with pride to be the one on Grey's motorcycle, to be the one with the gorgeously hot, mysterious older man that all the girls were gawking at.

The engine growled idly as he stopped the bike at the curb and I climbed lightly off, smoothing my dress back into place. I could feel everyone's eyes on us.

"Everyone's staring at us." I giggled.

Grey chuckled. "No. Everyone's staring at you. I can't say I blame them."

I smiled bashfully. "Yeah?"

"Come on. You know you're the prettiest one here."

"I am?"

"Oh yeah." He scoured the crowd for a moment and then nodded certainly at me. "Oh yeah. Without a doubt." He tilted my chin up with his finger and then we kissed. I hoped that everyone was still watching us, hoped the gawking girls would see that he was kissing me. I felt so amazing at that moment. It was surreal, like I was caught in a dream or something. A dream come true. I felt I might burst from happiness.

"Seven o'clock, right?" He smirked at me. "I'll see you then."

"Bye." I nodded, smiling as I stepped back from the bike. I gave Grey a little wave as he revved the engine once and then started smoothly off into the street.

With a happy sigh, I turned once he had gone, heading down the sidewalk towards the Community Center. My heels clipped upon the cement; I liked the noise. I scanned the crowds of people gathered as I strolled, looking idly for my family, suddenly wondering if they had seen my little entrance. Wickedly I hoped they had.

It was a perfect day, the sun was sailing warmly in the clear blue sky, a soft and gentle breeze stirred the branches of the large old poplar trees that lined the streets. The grass was deep green and fresh cut, filling the air with the delicious scent of summer. A buzz of nervous, excited energy came from the gathered groups of graduates and their families staggered among the wide lawn, waiting for the reception to begin. A smile curved my lips as I passed them all.

I walked by Brad and his friends without really looking his way, just enough to notice that he still wore the remnants of the absolute beat down he'd received—courtesy of Grey and Zack—upon his face. His eyes were still puffy and yellowy-blue with bruises. I smirked to myself and wondered how much trouble his mom had given him for fighting right before graduation. Served him right.

Ben and Toby and Jacob were off by themselves, so obviously stoned that I wondered how their parents didn't know. I giggled and waved at them as I passed. Toby gave me appraising thumbs up and Jacob whistled loudly. I awarded them with a smile and a quick twirl on the sidewalk, which was met by a smattering of applause from their little circle. With a laugh, I curtsied low at them—well, as low as I could in that tight of a skirt.

"Nice moves." Riley commented. Startled by the sudden voice behind me, I gave a little jump, and then my breath came out in a relieved gasp when I realized who it was.

"Riley, you scared me." I pressed a hand to my chest. Jacob and Toby and Ben laughed at me, they had seen the whole thing. I gave them a mock glare.

"Sorry." He apologized, but he didn't look sorry. He didn't look overly impressed at all—his eyebrows furrowed slightly and he was frowning.

But other than the tense expression, Riley looked good. Like, really good in his tux. He had gone with the traditional black and white three piece, a silver tie and shiny dress shoes. His dark hair had been cut quite short—almost a buzz, really. His dark eyes glowered out at me. He looked older, distinguished, almost … sexy. I barely recognized him.

"Wow. You clean up nice." I admitted.

"So do you." His dark eyes trailed over me, up and down, as if paying special attention to detail. "That's the dress you found that one time in the city, right?"

"Right." I shouldn't be surprised that he remembered; at one time we did mean something to each other. Still, I was touched by his thoughtfulness, and a little saddened. I shook my head and pushed any negative thoughts away, determined not to ruin my graduation with the same old Riley song and dance that didn't solve anything or get us anywhere.

"Well, you look amazing. Like a grown up or something."

"Yeah, you too."

We stood awkwardly for a moment. I scanned the crowd for my family again.

"Oh, they're over by the doors." Riley noticed my search and pointed towards the Center. "I saw them on the benches over there."

"Great, thanks. Where's your mom? I should say hello."

"She's there, with Emily and her mother." He pointed again, in the opposite direction. I tried to keep the frown from my face as I looked over and found Mrs. McIntyre in happy conversation with the Christian and her mother. The Christian was wearing a silver dress with long sleeves and a full-length skirt, I couldn't decide if I liked it. But obviously Riley did, since he had dressed to match her.

At least she was still chubby.

"Why don't you come over, say hello?" Riley invited.

"Oh, um … that's okay." I shook my head. "Maybe later, I should really get over to … uh … my family."

Riley saw right through me. "Yeah, right, okay." He chuckled. "Tell your mom hello."

"Yeah, you too …." I began to walk away, just in case he tried to pull me over or something. I loved Riley's mom, she had always been so cool to me, so accepting. I could talk to her more than I could my own parents. But it would be too painful to see her sharing that same kindness with this new girl, I just didn't want to witness that. I couldn't watch the entire McIntyre family move on without me so easily.

I turned my back and kept walking. I waved to a few of the people I was friendlier with—there weren't many though, mostly just from partying together. I found my family right where Riley said I would, congregated on some benches next to the Center entrance.

"So who's the guy on the motorcycle?" Dad demanded as soon as I was in earshot. "Is that your friend from the other night?"

"Yes. Boy-friend, actually." I admitted proudly. Dad raised his eyebrows.

"Will we get to meet this boyfriend?"

"Maybe." I shrugged.

Aunt Linda smiled at me, intervening. "Wow. You weren't kidding, Mac. He's gorgeous. But so are you, just look at you. You're an image. All grown up." She squealed.

"Thank you." I smiled sincerely at my favourite aunt.

"What are you, depressed or something?" Greg the dick asked, giving one of his snooty laughs. "What's with the black? You're not at a funeral."

I could feel the ire he inspired building up in me. I choked it down and smiled sweetly. "I'll wear it to your funeral." I promised.

"Come on Greg. Black is classy." Marcy stood up and smiled. She looked gorgeous, as usual, and I wondered if she were trying to upstage me. She wore a satin pink halter-top dress and white strappy sandals; her shining dark hair was perfectly curled. "You look great, Mac." She complimented. Just not as great as me, I imagined her thinking.

I muttered something in response. Mom got up then too, and gave me a kiss on the cheek. "I can't believe you're graduating. You look nice, honey, all grown up. I can just imagine how you would've looked in that pretty gown I liked so much."

I looked down at the ground, indignant. "Thanks mom."

Grandma smiled at me a moment, but instead of saying something, she began to complain about the heat of the sun. My uncles helped her up and escorted her into the cool shade of the building, giving me an acknowledging nod. Then, sudden yelling sent Aunt Linda scurrying to deal with my little cousins, who were running pell-mell around the wide green lawn before the center, screaming.

For an instant, I felt like joining in.

"Well, I guess …." Dad got up and began ushering everyone into the Community Center. "This'll start fairly soon. Let's go find our seats. Come on Mackenzie."

"Yeah, I'll be right in." I mumbled. He nodded and took my mother's elbow, heading up the stairs into the building with Marcy and Greg right behind them. I watched them go, deflated. It wasn't like I had expected them to gush and go on about how great I looked or to shower me with accolades or anything, but still—really? Was that all the attention I would get at my own graduation? Was that all I was worth?

The cocaine was wearing off. That was it. Suddenly I wasn't numb anymore. The disappointment was registering in my mind and the sweet, buzzing hum had faded from my vibrating nerves. I bit my lip. Luckily, I knew how to fix this. And I had to fix it.

In mere moments I was alone in the bathroom. Charlie, my saviour, had fixed me up with a little emergency coke for such a moment as this. I had apologized for wasting her entire vial over the week, but she let it go this time, making it my graduation present. I had paid for what I had now, just a little by comparison in the same silver vial.

Quickly I did some, my heart hammering eagerly, my tension melting away by the third inhale. Sighing happily, I braced my hand against the bathroom door and let the deliciousness flow through me. That was better. Now I felt good again, like I would make it, no matter what they said or did or didn't say or didn't do. I forced myself to screw the lid back on and put the vial back in my purse, to save the rest for later. What I had done would hopefully get me through the reception.

I flushed the toilet to make it seem like I had actually used it, then came out and washed my hands at the sink. I stared at my reflection for a minute, scrutinizing myself and my features. My dark eyes were wide and clear, a pleasant shimmer of color stained my cheeks and my lips were full and soft. They curved into a smile as I stared in the mirror. Maybe I wasn't as gorgeous and wonderful as Marcy always was, but Grey seemed to like what he saw. And that was all that mattered to me.

My family could just go and screw themselves.

With that happy monologue running through my head, I entered the reception hall in a much better mood. Everyone was filing in by then, the hall was noisy with the din of talk and laughter and the harsh sound of chairs scraping against the wooden floor as people found their seats. It smelt like buffet, like vegetables and chicken and coffee.

The evening passed in a blur. We graduates were called in one at a time to take our places at a long table stretching the length of the hall. We were served plates of food while our families went through the buffet. We ate, sat through some speeches, and then had to suffer through like a trillion pictures. I ended up making a few trips to the bathroom in between, as the coke didn't last near as long as I had hoped.

With the reception finally concluded, we crossed the park to the large auditorium where the ceremony was to take place. I was a bit nervous because I knew that Grey and Charlie would be there. This time, we had to enter the auditorium escorted by our parents. We lined up in alphabetical order down the hallway, waiting for the ceremony to begin, my mom on one side of me and my dad on the other.

"Are you getting a cold, Mackenzie?" Mom wondered at one point as I was rubbing my nose. "You keep sniffling."

"Maybe." I answered quickly and dropped my hand. "Yeah, that must be it."

"Well, remind me to get you some Echinacea later."

"Sure. Thanks." I nodded.

Eventually it was our turn to enter. We walked to the archway, where our picture was snapped, and then I headed across the front by myself and was taken up the steps to the stage by a guy from our class. I found my seat and sat down; relieved I hadn't tripped in my heels. The lights were hot. I couldn't believe how many people were there, I stared out in amazement at the sea of strange faces.

Our grad theme was "Shoot for the Moon." I hope Charlie appreciated that. I'm pretty sure it was from the quote, "Shoot for the moon—even if you miss, you'll end up among the stars," which was nice and all, but really, what did it even mean? I hoped whoever was singing had picked a nice moon-themed song to go along with it, but in the end she sang *Good Riddance*, by Green Day. I liked the song, it was a good choice.

I looked in vain for Grey and Charlie throughout, but they were impossible to discern in the dimly lit auditorium. Nevertheless, when my name was called to receive a diploma from the principle, I could hear them cheering even above the smattering of applause. I blushed and rose to shake the principle's hand, sure that what he gave me was just a blank rolled up piece of paper and not an actual diploma.

Some kids from our class got up afterwards and gave the traditional Most Famous For speech, singling us out one at a time and saying a few words about our most typical behaviours. There were a few predictable ones, like "staying home because of a bad hair day," "freaking out over exams," "having a new truck every year," that kind of stuff.

But then, it was Riley's turn.

"Riley McIntyre. Without a doubt, Riley McIntyre is most famous for … being with Mackenzie Taylor. Any year for as long as we can all remember, it doesn't matter when, if you're looking for Riley, you'll find him with Mackenzie …." My classmate was reading from her paper in a sweet for-the-crowd kind of voice, totally oblivious that she was breaking my heart a little more with every word she spoke. I bit my lip, wondering if Riley felt the same way as I did.

I dreaded my Famous For as soon as I heard Riley's—I just knew it would be similar. I braced myself for it.

"Mackenzie Taylor. Mackenzie Taylor is most famous for … being with Riley McIntyre. As you can see, they're completely inseparable, even when Mackenzie insists on skipping school as much as she does, he'll still be with her …."

Holy crap. Were they kidding? Really? I stared down at the floor and felt my face blush bright crimson, waiting out the awkward moment until the audience laughed and they moved on to the next student. The entire student body was either totally oblivious or that list had been made up months ago. Riley and I were anything but inseparable now, a grim reminder I certainly didn't need. I crossed my arms and hugged myself, wishing that the stupid kids would get off the stupid stage so this could be done already and I could go get high.

The worst was that the Christian knew. She knew that Riley's and my supposed inseparability simply wasn't the truth. I could practically feel her gloating from a few rows behind me. Just for the record, she was proclaimed the most famous for … "being sweet." Being "chubby" or "a Christian" must have already been taken, the only other two attributes I would've likened to her.

By the time the ceremony had come to a close and we headed, single file, down the stairs and up the aisle, I was in desperate need for some more blow. I ducked out of the line and into the bathroom before anyone could notice I was missing.

But someone noticed. Sure, when I wanted his attention, Riley was nowhere to be found, but when I was trying clandestinely to be alone and sneak away, he came looking for me. He was standing in the hall outside the bathroom when I re-emerged, his arms crossed as he leaned against the wall.

"You okay?" Riley surprised me by asking. He did look sincerely concerned.

"Yeah. Why wouldn't I be?" I played dumb.

"I don't know, I just, I saw you running to the bathroom, and I thought maybe you were upset, about what they said up there …."

"Oh. No, I mean, it was totally awkward, but … whatever." I shrugged, like it didn't matter. My nose burned, and I rubbed at it without thinking.

"Right." Riley eyed me suspiciously. "So … what were you doing in there, Mackenzie?"

"Um, going to the bathroom." I chuckled casually. "That's what people normally do in a bathroom."

"Yeah right." He scoffed angrily. "You're lit up, aren't you?"

"Ha!" I laughed again, good and high now. "Of course not."

"Don't. Don't lie to me. I can tell that you are." He shook his head, as if he were disappointed or something. "Sweet. So you're into the blow now, hey? Like, all the time? Nice. Good choice."

"Thanks." I shrugged. I didn't care for his judgement, but really, I was feeling too good to let it get to me. I shook my head at him. "So, are you and your Christian ready to head off into the sunset yet or what?"

"Ugh … why do you call her that?"

"That's what she is, isn't it?"

"Yes, but that's not all she is. Maybe if you got to know her—"

I scoffed. "That is not going to happen."

"You'd probably end up liking her. Would that be so bad?"

"Yes."

He shook his head. "Fine. Whatever. She's better than your supposed boyfriend, anyway."

"What?"

"You heard me."

I glared at him. "You have some friggin' nerve, Riley. Why would you … what even makes you say that?"

"Yeah, what could it be? I'll just pick one from the hundreds of reasons. He's totally irresponsible. Letting you ride on the back of his bike like that? What if you'd fallen off?"

"He wouldn't have let me fall." I defended. "It's no big deal Ry."

"Right. Right, I forgot. He can do no wrong, can he?" Riley stated wryly.

"It was my idea anyway."

"Okay, then, how about getting hooked on coke? Was that your idea too?"

"No!" My voice rose in frustration. I dropped my hands hopelessly. "No. I'm not hooked on coke. Riley … I can't … ugh … I can't do this with you anymore."

It was just too hard. It didn't seem to matter how many times we swore off our friendship, because we were still inevitably drawn to each other, even now, even when we both knew it would cause us nothing but pain and frustration. We couldn't sever the ties of our relationship no matter how doomed it was, and we seemed destined to act out the same argument time and time again, to live in a state of constant conflict with no reconciliation in sight. Because we were afraid. Afraid to really end it, to end us, even though that was exactly what we needed.

I had to get away from him. I turned and started walking, suddenly in desperate need of the cool night air on my skin. I felt heated to the very core, and mixing words and feelings with Riley was not helping, even despite the coke-buzz. I pushed my way through the crowded foyer and out the front doors. It was pleasantly calm and cool outside, dim with the dwindling light that remained from the sunset. I breathed deep the sweet evening air.

"Mac, wait up." Riley called to me through the mass. He caught up quickly. "I'm sorry. Please. I don't want to leave it this way with you."

"I don't think we have a choice, Riley." I realized grimly. "We can't even talk to each other without one of us getting upset. You should … you should just go."

"I know, I am," he grabbed my hand to stop me, "I'm going … we're going, tonight. We're going to the airport in half an hour."

This news was shocking to me. I had known he was leaving, but I hadn't anticipated so soon. I stared up at him, suddenly speechless. It was the answer to our problems, his leaving, but I wished it didn't have to be so. I would've given anything in that moment to make him stay, despite everything else.

"Riley—"

"I know. I know."

"But … will …" I bit my lip. "Will you be coming back?"

"I don't know. Probably. We'll come visit at holidays and stuff."

"Will I see you then?"

"Maybe." He relented. "If I know where you are … and if you're still alive by then."

"Of course I'll be alive." I rolled my eyes.

"We'll see." Riley frowned. His dark eyes focused on me seriously, like there was something else he wanted to say. He opened his mouth to speak. But then, from amongst the throng, I could hear someone calling his name. The Christian was calling him, beckoning him away from me.

It was time for Riley to leave.

"I don't want to say goodbye." He admitted. He looked torn.

"Just say it and get it over with." I demanded. The coke must have been wearing off, because I could feel again. And I didn't like what I felt, like my very heart was hurting, like it was throbbing with pain. I took a deep breath.

Riley wrapped me in a sudden, fierce hug. I couldn't believe the strength in his arms as he held me tightly to him. I snuggled into the chest of his tuxedo, fighting with all my might to keep from crying all over him. For that moment, I was safe again in my best friend's arms and everything was right between us. I clung to the moment. I clung to my friend.

"You be careful on that bike." Riley whispered in my ear. He kissed the top of my hair and then he let me go. He pulled away from me and I was all alone again, cold and exposed. I wrapped my arms around myself and gave him a weak smile, blinking furiously to keep from crying.

Riley walked away. Towards the Christian. I couldn't watch him go; I turned away and looked up at the calm, quiet night, seeking solace from my sudden emotional upheaval in its dim, dark stillness. It wasn't enough though. I needed something more, I needed the blissful numbness and complete tranquility that only more cocaine could bring to me.

"Hey, gorgeous." A different pair of strong arms suddenly wrapped around my waist and pulled me close. Despite everything, I found myself smiling and curving up against the warm strength behind me—less alone now, less exposed. Riley was gone, but I still had Grey.

He kissed my cheek. "You okay?" He wondered.

"Yeah." I decided quietly. At least, I would be. "Riley just left."

"I figured." He hugged me tightly.

"Grey?"

"Yeah?"

I sighed heavily. "Will you take me away from here?

"I'll take you anywhere you want to go."

CHAPTER 28

I met Grey and Charlie at her car. I had basically bypassed my family, finding them only to say goodbye so at least my relatives wouldn't be offended. My parents looked a bit put off by my abrupt departure, probably because I left before they could enforce their intended curfew. I walked as quickly as I could in my sky-high heels towards Charlie's sedan.

"Congratulations!" She smiled and wrapped me in a hug, which lasted a bit long for just a celebratory embrace. Grey must have told her about the whole Riley scene. "You okay?" She wondered quietly.

"Yeah, I'm good." I nodded, pushing the sadness away. I added a smile. "About to be even better."

"That's my girl." She laughed and opened the passenger door for me. Grey climbed in the back as Charlie got in to drive. We sat for a moment and all lit a smoke.

"So, what'd you think of our grad theme? Pretty cheesy, huh?" I giggled.

"Shoot for the moon. I'd say its green cheesy. " Charlie laughed. She put the car in reverse and backed out the parking lot. "Are you sure you don't want to stay for your grad party?"

"Are you kidding me? No thanks. I actually want to party tonight." I blew my smoke out the opened window, the warm wind washing in. "It's going to be this super lame dance where you can't even drink if you're not of age, which I'm not."

"Well, then, I'm afraid you're just going to have to party with us." Charlie winked at me. "We're going to Grey's house."

I giggled excitedly. "Shot for shot again, is it?" I challenged her.

"Baby, I could out drink you any day. Don't you remember last time?"

I laughed. "That wasn't fair. I hadn't eaten anything for like a week that night."

"Wait," Grey chuckled from the backseat. "Wasn't that the night I walked in and you were in nothing but your underwear?"

Charlie burst out laughing. I blushed. "Yeah."

"So … you guys should probably do it again." He decided innocently. "You know, just for curiosity's sake."

"Yeah right," I turned to face him in the backseat and giggled. "You just want to see me in my underwear."

A sexy smirk lit his perfect face. "Hell yeah I do."

I blushed an even deeper red.

There was already loud music pumping from Grey's house as we pulled up in front, cars were parked up and down the street. I was surprised. I had thought it'd just be the five of us like usual, I didn't realize they were having an actual party. I grinned enthusiastically as I stepped out of the car, fully prepared to have an awesome time. Grey took my hand and led me up the front walk while Charlie wasted no time rushing to the house for a lip-lock with Zack.

I laughed. "Is she already drunk or something?"

Grey stopped. He looked guilty. "Uh … yeah, a bit. We came here during your reception and kind of … got a head start."

"You did?" I looked up at him, noticing for the first time the slight blear of his beautiful blue eyes and the unsteadiness of his stance. I remembered also the exuberant cheering they had done for me at the reception. No wonder they'd been so enthused, since they were already so wasted.

"Are you mad?" Grey wondered.

I thought about it a moment and I couldn't really decide. I was a bit put out that they hadn't waited for me—I mean, it would have been only a few more hours and it was my graduation, after all. But as I looked up at Grey, into his perfect, impossibly handsome face, I decided that it didn't matter. I wanted to be the best girlfriend he ever had, I wanted him to brag about me to his friends about how awesome I was. I didn't want to be one of those whiny girls that got all naggy with her boyfriend when he did something without her.

I smiled. "Are you kidding me? Now I'll kick her ass at shots for sure."

Grey laughed with relief. He looked down at me happily as his hand cupped my cheek, his other turned up my chin so we could kiss. I tasted whiskey on his breath, but his lips were sweet and enticing.

"Are you sure you don't want to bypass this whole party thing and just go straight to my room?" He wondered, his voice thick.

"… No …." I smiled and wrapped my arms around his neck.

"Hey guys! It's you!" Alex flung the door open and stood leering in the doorway, dressed in nothing but a pair of long underwear. "Get in here! You get in here!" He demanded, a wild, crazy grin lighting his face. He couldn't even stand straight, he was so drunk.

I groaned and covered my eyes with a laugh. "Alex! Put some clothes on! I can see your junk!"

"Not until you get in here!"

"Okay, okay." I smiled up at Grey. He grinned and rolled his eyes at his friend.

"Alex, get in the house, man! You're scaring all the neighbours."

"Get in here, Grey. You especially. Get in here!"

"We're coming, we're coming." He chuckled. Sadly we disentangled ourselves, but Grey held tight to my hand.

"Later." He promised me. A shiver of anticipation tingled down my spine. I smiled as we walked up the front steps and through the door.

There were tons of people inside, many I had never met before. Most everyone said congratulations to me though, like they knew it was a party for my graduation. Grey introduced me to a bunch of them—all were older than me, some were even older than Grey. I smiled politely, but knew I'd never remember all their names.

Some people full on stared at me. Well, I don't think they were staring at me so much as they were me and Grey together. Apparently it was a sight to behold, Grey with a girlfriend. He held my hand the entire time as we mingled around, and I loved it—it felt amazing to know that I was the only girlfriend he'd ever had, even if I did get looks of doubt and surprise because of it. Like they were all thinking, why the hell would he choose her, of all people?

I ignored them and held tightly to Grey's warm, strong hand instead. I didn't know the answer to that myself, really. But he had chosen me. And that was all that mattered.

Lucas and Jimmy were there from the city and they had brought Natasha and Tracy with them. I tried to strike up a conversation with the two girls in an effort to ease the constant pout of sheer boredom on their faces. But after some tedious, one word replies, I gave up. There just wasn't any interest there at all.

"Mackenzie!" A voice called to me then, coming from the kitchen. "Get your ass in here!"

"Uh oh," I laughed to Grey, "that's Charlie. I think it's time for some shots." I smiled excitedly. I had some catching up to do, everyone else seemed pretty loaded already and I wanted to get as wasted as I possibly could.

"You go. I'll be right in." Grey promised, dropping my hand for the first time since we had arrived. I nodded and headed eagerly for the kitchen, my heels clipping on the linoleum floor. I was still clad in all my grad attire, but I had a good reason to be dressed up, so I didn't mind. I would never have come to a party in a dress if it weren't for my graduation.

"What's up?" I smiled on my way into the kitchen. Charlie flipped back her blonde hair and pointed to the center island, where two shot glasses and a bottle of Crown Royal were sitting. We were the only ones in the room—some kid came in to grab some ice once, but that was it. I looked longingly at the beer-can castle and wanted badly to knock it down.

"This is up, bitch." Charlie laughed and poured us each a shot. "Get up here."

"You're so on. And this time, Charlie, you're going down." I threatened, setting down my purse and climbing up onto the stool. Charlie sat down as well, facing me from the other side of the counter, smiling at my challenge.

"Then go." She dared me. I picked up my shot and swallowed it in one gulp.

"One." I declared. The whiskey burned all the way down my throat, hitting my empty stomach and spreading in lazy, pleasant warmth throughout my body.

"One." Charlie duplicated, after slamming back her shot.

"Two."

"Two."

"Three."

"Three."

"Four."

"Four." Charlie set down her shot and cheered. A crowd was gathering around us. Alex had come and was now sloppily taking bets on who would win. I couldn't stop laughing at the disparaging remarks that were being thrown around the room at our expense. First I was the lightweight, then Charlie, and then we were both lightweights, and then the bet changed from one of us winning to either of us even making it past five. I was ramped up with excitement and in the mood to prove them wrong—the mood I was in, I would last all night. I poured us another shot and flipped it back.

"Five." The crowd cheered.

"Five." They cheered again for Charlie. There didn't seem to be a favourite, as long as one of us was shooting back alcohol. I giggled and filled up the shots again, the bottle shaking in my unsteady hand.

"Six."

"Six."

Grey joined us then, in the now crowded kitchen. He came and stood behind me, resting his arm lazily around my shoulders. His touch was lingering, sending delicious shivers through me. The booze was starting to hit me and I stared up at him, drunk and smiling. He looked at me a moment and his beautiful blue eyes seemed pleased. He bent down and kissed me. The crowd cheered as he did so, and I was smiling gloriously as I took my next shot.

"Seven."

"Seven." Charlie wasn't backing down. She was talking and laughing and joking but could barely keep her eyes open, she was so drunk. She poured us the next shot, spilling whiskey all over the table as she did so.

"Eight."

"Eight." She hiccupped. I lit a cigarette, and my lips were numb as I blew the smoke out.

"Nine."

"Nine."

I knew I couldn't keep this up much longer, but I had to outlast Charlie. I stamped my smoke out in the ashtray and poured our next shot, since she didn't seem capable of doing it anymore. I swear she was asleep sitting up. Nearly everyone was in the kitchen, pressing in, loud and rowdy around us. Bets were changing rapidly as our motor skills deteriorated. I sat back a moment, a crazy perma-smile on my face. I just couldn't stop grinning.

"Go for ten." Grey whispered in my ear. "Come on, you got this."

Still smiling, I flipped back the shot and swallowed, gulping the strong, burning whiskey. I set the glass down and knew that I was done.

"Ten." My arms were heavy and my vision blurred. I stared across at Charlie as best I could and wondered what she would do.

Everyone was champing her name. Charlie was totally dishevelled, red-eyed and bleary, but still managed to look beautiful. She rested her head weakly on her hand, smiled a moment, and then slumped over. Zack caught her before she fell, but Charlie was definitely out. I had won.

"Winner!" I exclaimed, throwing my hands in the air. "Wooooooohhh! Winner!" Everyone was cheering for me. People were high-fiving me like crazy. I laughed and smiled and cheered along with them.

And then I fell off my chair.

One second I was upright and the next I had fallen. What happened in between there, I can't recall. Everything went black for a moment and then I was on the floor, face down in a pile of laughter, and there was a second of stunned silence while everyone waited to see if I was okay.

"Hey, you all right?" Grey bent over me carefully.

"Winner!" I exclaimed again, this time from my position on the floor. "Winner!"

Cheering and laughter erupted from around the room. I joined in, giggling like crazy. Grey was smiling, his blue eyes twinkling as he picked me up off the linoleum.

"Come on, winner." He cradled me in his arms. "I think you've had enough."

People were still giving me high-fives as Grey carried me out of the kitchen and down the hallway where it was quiet, away from the party.

"Did you hit your head?" He wondered, opening a door and flicking the light on.

"I don't think sooo." I sang. He chuckled and set me down. I nearly fell over, grasping the wall for support.

"Let's get these shoes off." Gently he lifted up my knees and pulled off my pumps, one at a time. "That should help your balance a bit, if anything will."

The difference in my height was staggering without my shoes on, and my feet felt strange flat on the floor after being arched all day long.

"Wait, Grey, is this your bedroom?"

"Yes."

"Wow." I looked around in awe. His walls were covered in posters; all of them were rock bands, most of them I had never heard of. Bands like Dream Theatre and Smile Empty Soul, Sepultura and Rage Against The Machine. There were many Tool posters, which I recognized, and Metallica and System of a Down and Sevendust and countless others I didn't know.

His room was fairly neat, cleaner than mine at home—his closet doors actually shut. A queen-size, unmade bed sat beneath a large, coverless window looking out into the backyard. I could see the stars through it, twinkling in the night sky. Music equipment, amps and cords and who knows what else were stacked up neatly along the wall. A large desk sat along the back, piled with paper and notebooks and loose-leaf pages, all covered in writing by Grey's inky scrawl. An acoustic guitar sat in its stand by the bed.

"Wow. You can tell a lot about a person from their room, you know." I walked slowly, swaying across the soft blue carpet to sit on the edge of Grey's bed.

"And what does my room tell you?" He wondered.

"Um ... I'd say that ... you love music. That's pretty obvious."

"True."

"And ... from the posters, I'd say that you're a fan of the metal."

"Also true. But classic rock is still sweet."

"Yeah." I agreed. My hazy gaze came to rest on the acoustic guitar. "Will you play me something?" I wondered suddenly.

"If you want." Grey shrugged complacently. He picked up the instrument and placed the strap over his shoulders, then sat back down on the bed with it. "What do you want me to play?" He asked, strumming idly, waiting for me to answer.

I drew a complete blank. I loved music of every kind, so long as it was passionate, but for some reason at that moment I couldn't think of a single song. I laughed and shook my head.

"Okay, then, how about this one." Grey bent over the guitar and began to play. He was impressive. I watched him intently—the way his hands seemed to dance over the strings; I was amazed at how quickly they moved. He didn't even need to look down.

I recognized the song almost immediately. It was *Good Riddance,* by Green Day. My grad song. I watched as Grey strummed the rhythm, his fingers deftly changing chords and picking the notes, playing the sweet, slow melody perfectly. I sat back on the bed, pulled my knees up to my chest and listened.

The song was sweetly sad, like graduating was supposed to be … but the haunting, reminiscent notes that came from the guitar made me feel hollow inside, totally lonely. It made me see how much I missed Riley, made me realize how much I was going to miss him. How a huge part of my life just wasn't there anymore.

At the very thought of his name, memories of Riley flooded my mind, like my life was flashing before my eyes, like in a car crash or something.

I saw Riley and me when we first met, when he had been shy and reserved, and I had grabbed his hand and forced him to come and play with me. The third grade when I had peed my pants and Riley leant me his gym shorts so no one would know. Climbing the big hill in our neighbourhood and eating plums at the top. Countless birthdays and Christmases and presents he'd given me. Getting his car stuck in the ditch a few winters ago, when he'd let me sit in the warm car while he shovelled and pushed us out. The hundreds of times we'd gotten wasted together. I remembered it all, just then, as the lyrics to the Green Day song played dimly in my mind.

"It's something unpredictable, but in the end it's right.
I hope you had the time of your life."

"Hey, Mackenzie, you okay?" Abruptly Grey stopped playing and he looked up at me with concern.

"What, yeah, I'm okay." It was hard to talk.

"You're crying." He took the guitar off and placed it back in its stand. I wiped the tears from my eyes; I hadn't even realized they were there.

"Come here." Grey pulled me to him, wrapping his strong arm around my back and cradling me against his chest. "What's wrong?"

"Nothing. That was beautiful … you play amazing." I sniffled. I hated that I was letting Riley ruin our time together. "It's stupid, I'm just … drunk. I'm sorry, Grey. Just forget about it."

His blue eyes were pensive for a moment, and then a sudden thought occurred to him. "You're thinking about Riley, aren't you?"

My silence was the same as a yes. Grey sighed heavily.

"Mackenzie … are you in love with this guy or something?"

"What? No." I sat up in earnest. "Of course not. Why would you think that?"

Grey shrugged. "You spend a lot of time being upset over him."

"I'm not upset over him, I just … he's like my brother, you know? And I'm, I'm drunk and that song made me nostalgic and …." I looked up at him. "I'm really sorry, Grey, honestly, you have nothing to be jealous of."

"I'm not jealous." He shook his head. "It's just … it's pretty obvious."

"Oh, Grey, no." I sat up on my knees and grasped his hands, looked up into his face, imploring him. "Please, don't think that way. You're on my mind, like, all the time. Riley's just my friend, I mean, he's not even my friend anymore, really …." I shook my head, angry at myself for letting this happen. Furiously I pushed any feelings and all thoughts and images of Riley from my mind, determined not to let them surface again, ever. We were over; we were done. I wouldn't let his very memory ruin things for me. I promised myself that I would never agonize over Riley McIntyre ever again.

Ever.

"Grey." I looked up into his deep blue eyes, into his perfect, tan face, darkened by just a hint of stubble. His lips were hard as he looked down at me, his face tense. I knew what I had to tell him, but the dim memory of how this information had last been received made me hesitate a moment. I shook the unpleasant image from my mind and took a deep breath, working up the courage.

"You don't have to worry, Grey, at all. Because I love you. *You*."

Inwardly, I braced myself for rejection. Outwardly, I was calm and hopeful, waiting for his reaction. I watched as Grey softened at my words, watched his jaw relax and his lips curve into a smile. He looked me over warmly for a moment.

"You're a bit dramatic, aren't you?" He chuckled.

"Why does everyone always say that—?"

My words were cut off then as he, smiling, swept me up in a kiss.

CHAPTER 29

I moved into Charlie's house on a Friday. Mom and Dad came to help, but I really didn't have much stuff—just my bed and my dresser and a few suitcases of clothes, a box of pots and pans and a set of dishes I was given for graduation. Dad put my bed frame together in Katrina's old room for me. We could hear him grumbling as Mom and I put my dishes away.

Charlie and I snuck excited smiles at each other, neither of us could wait for my parents to leave so we could get good and high. Mom didn't like the place, I could tell, but at least she approved of Charlie. From the look of her she was a sweet, well-dressed, pretty young lady, very proper; of course mom would like her. She never would have guessed that Charlie was my biggest source of illicit fun.

Finally everything was unpacked. My dad looked fairly unaffected but I could tell my mom was stalling, putting off saying goodbye to me for as long as she could. For the last week or so I think she'd been in denial that I was actually moving out. Amidst all my packing and planning, maybe she thought I'd change my mind. But I would never stay at home now, not when I'd realized how awesome it'd be on my own. Even if my parents renounced all their rules and their Nazi-ness, which they hadn't, I wouldn't even consider it.

My ultimate, total freedom was just minutes away from fruition. Mom was cleaning everything she could get her hands on in an attempt to prolong the inevitable goodbye, and I could tell my dad was getting impatient. The entire house was sparkling by the time they finally gathered their things to go.

Dad gave me a pat goodbye and his face was smug, like he expected me to come crawling back home once I discovered how tough it really was out on my own. I kissed his cheek, smirking to myself. I'd show him.

Mom had a tough time leaving. She wrung her hands, her expression pained.

"You be sure to call us, if you need anything."

"I'll call." I nodded.

"You can come home, you know, if you change your mind."

"Mom, I'm only ten minutes away." It was hard not to roll my eyes.

"I know, but it's not the same." She shook her head, her dark curls bouncing, and then pulled me into a sudden, fierce hug. "I can't believe I'm an empty-nester. It'll be so lonely at home without you there."

I grimaced. Welcome to the last two years of my life, I wanted to say. But when Mom pulled away from me, there were actual tears swimming in her sad eyes, so I bit my tongue and just smiled sympathetically instead.

"You remember the deal, right? You have to come home on Sundays for dinner."

I sighed. How I had ever agreed to that little clause was unbelievable. Mom must have cornered me at an especially weak moment or something. She'd been so nice to me all last week and when she asked me to come home every Sunday for supper, I just … gave in. I still don't know why. Dinner with Marcy and Greg was probably my most hated event of the whole week. I'd rather clean the men's bathroom at the Red Wheat than sit across the table from those two. But for some reason I had agreed to it, and from the look on Mom's face now, she'd be crushed if I didn't show.

"Yes, alright mom. I'll be there." I was getting impatient. All I wanted to do was get high and I hadn't realized my parents would be hanging around for so long. I thought it'd be more of a drop off my stuff and leave kind of thing, but they'd been there for hours now, sharpening my craving for cocaine by the long, drawn out anticipation.

"Come on, Deb." Dad nearly growled. "I've got to pack for tomorrow yet."

"Okay, Mitch. Okay." Mom sighed and nodded. "Goodbye Mackenzie." She kissed me on the cheek. "Don't be a stranger."

"I won't." I managed a tight smile. "I'll see you in two days, Mom."

"Right. Bye, honey."

"Bye." Eagerly I shut the door behind them and leaned against it for a moment. I sighed in relief. "Finally. I didn't think they'd ever leave."

"You're so dramatic. They're not that bad and they didn't stay that long." Charlie argued with a grin. She was already cutting up the coke for us. I listened as my parents' car pulled out from the curb and then drove on down the street. They were gone. Finally, we were alone. I was free.

I felt so light-hearted I was nearly giddy. I could do anything, everything I had ever wanted to do. I could go anywhere. I could stay up as late as I wanted. I could smoke in my house. I could do copious amounts of totally illegal drugs and there was nothing that anyone could do about it.

I giggled and lit a cigarette, then sniffed back a hard line, just to prove my point.

Charlie and I hung out by ourselves for a while, celebrating the start of our new beginning and the best summer ever. We got majorly high on cocaine. I loved that I didn't have to worry about trying to find a ride home and acting half-ass sober when I got there. I was home. I could get as wrecked as I possibly wanted and just head down the hallway to bed. This was freedom. Sheer, complete, irresponsibility.

The guys came over to help us celebrate. We drank and got high and partied late into the night. When finally I fell onto my bed, drunk and sleepy, I stared out at the dark, still night sky through my bedroom window. My life was really beginning, I could feel it. I grinned at the moon, white amidst the silver clouds. The stars were twinkling in the sky, the country lights bright and pretty on the horizon. The whole world spread out before me, and I could experience all its secrets now, everything it had been hiding, all the wonder it had been keeping from me. No longer would I be sheltered from what was out there.

I fell asleep with a smile on my face.

CHAPTER 30

I could hear them giggling on the other side of the door. Quickly and as silently as I could, I sniffed the coke up my nose and pinched my nostrils together. I stood a minute, motionless as the drugs hit my veins and spread throughout my system. Relief hit me and I let out a heavy, shaky breath.

"Mackenzie, I need the bathroom." Marcy knocked curtly on the door.

"Yep. Be right out." I shoved the drugs back into my purse and wiped at my nose, checking quickly in the mirror to make sure there was no evidence left. I opened the door and smiled at my sister as I passed by—much calmer now, much more in control of myself. She didn't look my way even once.

Marcy's wedding was in three weeks and we were at the dress shop for the final fittings of the wedding gown and our bridesmaids dresses. I could not imagine a more vivid portrayal of my personal hell on earth. Marcy's two snobby friends, Whitney and Marie—A.K.A the maid of honour and the other bridesmaid—were sipping champagne from their flutes, talking in hushed tones with their arms crossed and glancing my way every now and again. It was obvious they were talking about me, but I didn't care. They were both in college, so I think that made them feel horribly smart and very above me, especially given my current condition.

Of the two bridesmaids, I liked Marie best. Whitney was the prettier one and had obviously been uber popular in high school, as she still liked to act superior to everyone even though she had gained noticeable weight over the years. She was tall with long blonde hair and hazel eyes; she had a really pretty face. Marie was plainer, but she had a better personality, more humour. She could have been really pretty if she tried a bit more, like if she dyed her mousy brown hair and maybe waxed the uni-brow. She was thinner than Whitney, though shorter, and this seemed to put the two girls on even turf.

And they were both looking at me now like I was someone to be pitied.

I ignored them as best I could from where I sat slumped over silently in my chair, horribly sleep deprived and somewhere in between hung over and still drunk. I whiled away the unfortunate time lost in my own meandering thought, impatient for the day to be over so I could go back home and pick up where I left off the night before. My friends would already be partying, and I hated missing out.

The summer had been awesome so far, everything I hoped it would be. Every night after work Charlie and I came home and blew all of our tips on booze and cocaine and cigarettes and weed and whatever else we wanted to do that night. Most nights Grey and Zack and Alex would come over after band practice and party with us until the wee hours of the morning. We all got so drunk and high that most times we just passed out wherever we happened to be sitting.

Charlie and Grey and I all worked the evening shift full time at the restaurant. Work was a ton of fun with all three of us together, but even then I'd count down the hours until we were free to go home and start the party all over again. There seemed to be no end to my energy. I'd stay up every night until four or five in the morning, wake up about eleven, do some cocaine, get ready for work, work from about four until ten, and then get wasted the rest of the night. It was awesome—I couldn't get enough of it, I loved hanging out with my friends.

Those were just the weeknights. On the weekends, we went all out. Grey's band had a show nearly every Saturday, so Charlie and I would come watch them at the club, crazily high on E or drunk and high on cocaine or stoned on weed or mushrooms, whatever we had on hand, whatever would totally fuck us up. Those were the best nights, I so looked forward to Saturday, when I could watch my gorgeously hot, unbelievably talented boyfriend rock and sing and seduce me with his guitar. Afterward, we'd all meet up in the VIP room and do some more cocaine and drink more booze and party until the house lights went up and we all had to go home.

Sunday, as per the promise to my mother, I would drag my tired, bedraggled, sick, hung over ass to my parents' house for dinner. Most of the time I was still drunk and high from the night before, and I would sit at the table as I came down, pushing the food around on my plate as the substance leaked slowly from my system. I must've smelt terrible, and I certainly didn't add much to the conversation—grunting for most my answers and groaning for the others. I wondered if my mom regretted asking me to come over. I knew she didn't like how I was behaving—her nose did the flare and I could tell she was disappointed by my actions and my choices. But she still couldn't stop me, none of them could. Dad ignored me for the most part, and though Marcy and Greg acted shocked, they seemed to enjoy my total lack of propriety. I think it made them feel good to "tsk tsk" about me behind my back.

I didn't care what they thought, not in the least. I was having the best time of my life, just like I had hoped. We were having one of the hottest summers on record that year too, as if even Mother Nature was smiling on me. Nearly everyday was the same bright hot sun in the clear blue sky. Charlie and I spent every possible moment we could in skimpy little bikinis, sun tanning in the backyard and reading magazines and talking and laughing, stretched out on loungers and enjoying the heated quiet of the lazy summer afternoons, smelling the fresh cut grass from the gentle whir of neighbouring lawn mowers.

Amidst the utter perfection, there was only one thing in the whole world that could have made my summer even better. Something that I wanted desperately, but for some reason, hadn't happened.

Grey and I hadn't had sex yet.

I tried not to let it bother me. I mean, we made out practically every chance we got, so he must have wanted me, at least a little. But every time things got really hot and heavy, every time I began to think there might be a chance, he'd pull away and stop us. I just didn't understand it. I was living in a state of constant lust; I spent nearly as much money on fancy underwear as I did on blow. None of it worked. My total lack of experience mixed with just a dash of insecurity and made it nearly impossible for me to broach the subject with him. So I fretted to myself, wondering what I should do, what I could do to make him want me more. I loved him desperately; I wanted to share everything I could with him, to experience it all with him, to know every part of him. The secret fear that began to gnaw at my mind every time he stopped us was that he didn't feel the same way.

"Mac! Mackenzie!" Marcy's impatient voice jolted me from my wayward thoughts. I shook my head and returned to the present.

"Yes?"

"Are you even awake?" Her dark eyes glared at me. "I was talking to you."

I sat up and focused on my sister. "Sorry. I didn't hear you."

She shook her head in exasperation. "I was asking what you think."

"Oh," I noticed for the first time that Marcy was standing on the stage before tri-fold mirrors, each reflecting back a picture of total elegance and beauty. The dressmaker was pinning and pulling at the vast layers of gauzy white fabric as she hemmed up the bustle. The wedding gown Marcy wore was gorgeous; satin encrusted with jewels and embroidery in the typical princess cut, the skirt about four times wider than Marcy was, the train about four times longer.

Mom stood by, glaring at me with blatant disapproval. Her lips were thin, pursed so tightly that they matched the color of her face. That was another one of her signs, like the nose flare. She was not happy with me.

"Wow, Marce. You look great." I smiled woodenly and nodded. Mom shook her head at me, clearly not impressed with my response, but as she turned back to Marcy her face totally transformed. She smiled grandly at her eldest daughter, her face radiating pride as she oohed and aahed over the fit and the cut and the fabric. Marcy practically glowed with happiness at my mother's abundant compliments, her beautiful face beamed as she looked at herself in the mirror. Her dark eyes met my mother's and they shared a happy, teary smile

That was about the time I felt the need to excuse myself again.

When Marcy's alterations were finally finished, we bridesmaids were next. I stared at the dress hanging in the change room like it was my mortal enemy. It was pink—light, fluffy, cotton candy pink. Pretty much exactly what Mom had wanted for my grad. It was cut in the same style as Marcy's wedding dress, with a tight fitting bodice and a knee length, poufy skirt. If the skirt had been but a bit shorter, it would have looked exactly like a ballerina tutu.

I couldn't help but shudder as I stepped into the layers of crinoline. I zipped up as best I could on my own and then went to stand before the tri-fold mirror as well, surrendering myself to the mercy of the dressmaker and her fabric tomato full of pins.

She frowned at me, her face wrinkling. "You've lost weight since last time." She decided, pinching the fabric around my waist. I couldn't decide if she meant it as a compliment or not. "This'll have to be taken in." She frowned.

"Typical first year college student," Whitney laughed, stepping out of the change room behind me in her tutu. "They can't ever afford anything to eat."

Whitney was probably just jealous. Her ass hadn't seen this side of a size four in years. "I'm actually not going to school this year." I informed her.

"Not at all?"

"No." I shook my head.

"Are you kidding? That would cut into her constant drinking and partying, wouldn't it Mac?" Marcy raised an eyebrow at me, her arms crossed. "It's so cool to get wasted all the time, Whitney, didn't you know that?"

I looked up at my sister's face in the mirror. She was obviously pissed at me—her dark eyes were flashing and she wore the same look my mother had all day, her face frowning with impatience and irritation. I shrugged at her.

"I don't know what you're talking about."

"Right, sure." Marcy leaned back in her chair, glaring at me. It was silent for a moment, awkwardly so. Whitney and Marie looked at each other uncomfortably, like they didn't quite know what to do. I could practically feel their heated stares boring into me, but I ignored them, staring at myself in the mirror like I was completely oblivious.

My dress didn't fit right anymore. I had lost a size over the last few months. The dressmaker pinned the fabric tight to my skin and I was amazed by how much extra material there was. I hadn't realized I was losing weight. Really though, my diet was nothing but a hearty serving of drugs and alcohol, so I guess it made sense. I was just never really hungry—I mean, I still ate of course but it really took a backseat to other things. I liked my new size though, now I had really lost whatever might have been left of my baby fat.

I looked up at my face. My cheekbones were more pronounced too—attractively so, my cheeks sunk in slightly from the lost weight. It was like I was seeing myself for the first time, or through someone else's eyes or something. I saw long, slim legs; a firm butt and tiny waist; flat abs; a long, sleek torso; high, perky breasts and nicely toned arms. I gazed at myself with wonder. Maybe it was just the cocaine, but I felt beautiful. I looked beautiful. A surge of newfound confidence suddenly boosted my thoughts. I was beautiful. There was no way that Grey couldn't want me. All I needed was a little self-confidence.

Now, even more so, I couldn't wait to get home.

"So, how long do you think this will take?" I blurted foolishly, completely forgetting the plentiful resentment that already filled the room, emanating towards me from four pairs of narrowed, watchful eyes.

Marcy stood from her chair. "Oh, I'm sorry, Mackenzie," she spat, "am I cutting into your precious time? How thoughtless of me. I thought that maybe you could take a few minutes from yourself and focus on *my* wedding." She scoffed and rolled her eyes. "But apparently that's impossible. Don't worry, though, we'll have you home in plenty of time so you can go and *drink yourself into oblivion*!"

She yelled the last part at me—which was very un-Marcy like—and then stormed off down the hallway. I watched her go in the mirror. Whitney and Marie followed after her, but not before shooting daggers at me with their glares. I turned and stared after them, wide-eyed with surprise.

"What the hell is *their* problem?" I wondered. I couldn't think of anything I'd done to deserve all this anger. I hadn't made us late for the appointment or anything even though I'd only gotten like, three hours of sleep. And yes, maybe I was a little tired—and yes, maybe a little hung over—but really, weren't they totally overreacting?

"*You* are their problem." Mom declared through narrowed eyes, her expression scorching with disappointment. "I can't believe you. Seriously Mackenzie, what's going on?"

"What do you mean?"

"You know what I mean. I'm not an idiot, okay? You look terrible all the time, and you have this awful attitude every time I see you. Dammit, Mackenzie, you can't even sober up enough to be here for your sister. It's her wedding, for God's sake!"

"I'm right here, mom." My voice rose defensively as I turned to glare back at her. The dressmaker gave up all pretence of work and just sat back on her heels, listening to us, enjoying the drama as it ensued. I gave her a look.

"I know you're here, but you're not *here*." Mom scoffed. "I bet you're still drunk from last night."

"No I'm not. Mom, come on. You were young once, I'm sure you did a little partying. Why is everyone making such a big deal about this?"

"Partying on the weekends is one thing, but today is a Wednesday, and you knew we had this appointment." Mom sighed, closing her eyes and rubbing her forehead with her hand. "Mackenzie …," she shook her head, "maybe you should just go … sit in the car or something."

I blinked at her a moment, incredulous. "And why the hell should I do that?"

"Because," Mom was exasperated, her brown curls bouncing as she spoke. "You are doing your damndest to ruin this day for your sister."

"No I'm not—"

"Mackenzie! Just go!" She demanded. "I don't want you near me right now."

Her words shocked me. I stared at her defiantly a moment, but there was no apology in sight. "Fine." I turned back to the mirror, my fists clenching angrily. I glowered down at the dressmaker. "Can you get this off of me now?"

"Off?" She looked up at me in confusion.

"Yes, off, off!" I pulled at the dress is frustration and pins popped off everywhere. She put up her hands to help me but I pushed them away, stalking past her off the stage and back into the dressing room, slamming the door shut behind me. I sat down on the little bench inside and leaned my head back against the wall. My veins were thrumming, my blood pounding with coke-rage.

"I'm so sorry," I could hear my mother apologizing to the dressmaker, "I'm so embarrassed."

"No, no, it's fine …," the lady answered in her thick Russian accent. I rested my head in my hands and took a deep breath in, trying to calm myself. *She* was embarrassed? They were the ones that totally ganged up on me, like I was a total loser or something. I felt like crying; I just couldn't understand why everyone was being so mean. I hadn't done anything wrong. So I partied a little bit, so what? I wasn't hurting anybody. What was the matter with a little harmless fun?

It was none of their business anyway, I decided. They could go screw themselves. I stood up then and took the pink tutu off, careful not to jab myself with the remaining pins. Then I put my clothes back on, noticing as I pulled my black tank top over my head that it did smell pretty bad, but I really didn't care.

Once I put myself back together and gathered my things, I stepped out of the change room to face my mother again. Calmer, more in control of myself. Marcy still hadn't returned.

"Here." I handed the dressmaker my gown. "I'm sorry." I hoped I hadn't wrecked anything with my little fit.

She nodded and took the pile of fabric from me. "It's okay. I'll make do."

I turned to my mom. "Can I have the keys?" I demanded, completely avoiding all contact with her as I did so. If I had my way, I wouldn't have to speak to her ever again. She dropped the set into my outstretched hands and I turned to leave before she could say anything more. Grabbing my purse on the way out, I headed for the car and spent the rest of the day in exile.

CHAPTER 31

The day from hell was finally over. Mom dropped me off late in the evening after the quietest ride home in the history of the world. The tension in the car was almost tangible. The lights were on inside my house as we pulled up at the curb; loud music was pumping out, noisy laughter filtering through the open windows to meet us on the street. I was cheered by just the sight. Mom peered up at the apartment, a worried look on her face as I opened the door, totally prepared to leave her without even saying goodbye.

"Mackenzie," she stopped me just before I could. I didn't answer, but sighed, turning to show that she had my attention. I'd been waiting for her to apologize all night.

"Mackenzie," she started again, "I need to tell you something."

I nodded for her to continue.

"I talked to Marcy about it and she's still willing to have you as a bridesmaid, but you have to promise to be sober. If you honestly can't do that … then she'll … she'll find someone else."

My response was a blank stare. "Are you kidding me?"

Mom shook her head.

I could feel the anger building again. I let it escape in a hiss through my teeth. "You guys are unbelievable. When did I become this … this raging alcoholic to you? I party a little, yes, but I'm not a friggin' idiot."

"Marcy just doesn't want her wedding ruined—"

"Heaven for-fucking-fend that precious Marcy ever be disappointed." I got up out of the car. I felt so … betrayed by them, I couldn't help but swear. I could feel my hands trembling. "You really think I'm capable of ruining her wedding? Thanks mom. Thanks for thinking so highly of me."

I think she was shocked by my reaction. Her face looked crushed. "Mackenzie—" she started.

"Whatever." I slammed the door before she could continue. I couldn't stand to hear another word. Frantically I searched through my purse for my cigarettes, but my hands were shaking so badly that it proved impossible. Frustrated, I dumped the bag upside down and let its contents fall onto the withered grass clumped in our front yard.

The headlights from mom's car fell on the pack when she backed up and pulled out. I picked them up and lit a smoke as her taillights bumped down the road before disappearing from sight. I couldn't believe her. I couldn't believe them.

I toyed with the idea of backing out of the bridesmaid thing altogether, but somehow I knew I couldn't do it. I knew that sometime, maybe years from now, I'd regret missing out on my only sister's wedding. At the moment though, I was just mad enough that even the thought of standing Marcy up made me feel better.

I clawed through the grass until I found my cocaine, and sitting in the shadows of my front yard, brought the scoop to my nose, time and time again. In the cocaine-haze, mom and Marcy didn't exist, the wedding didn't exist, and being second didn't exist. It was like a fog of bliss, enveloping me, cutting me off from the rest of the total BS. I lit a smoke off my first one and gave into the superman-like qualities of the drugs.

With them, I could do anything, I could get through anything, survive anything. They were like my hero, my refuge. My saviour. I don't know what I would've done without them.

The urge to cry had been strong, so strong that my throat ached with the effort, but the cocaine swept it away, replacing it with the numbing, happy trembles that I had so grown to love. I let out a shaky sigh of relief and pure pleasure, and found that I was good again.

After gathering most of my things from the grass, I headed slowly up the creaky old stairs. I knew that seeing my friends would make me feel even better, knew their exuberance would be contagious. Alex and Grey and Charlie and Zack were gathered around the counter playing a loud, rowdy game of quarters as I opened the door.

"Hey, baby!" Charlie greeted me. "How was your day?"

"Oh, you have no idea." I managed a smile for her and set down my things. There was dead grass all over my jeans, I wiped at it absently. "Marcy's got me wearing a tutu. Like, an actual tutu."

"When, tonight?" Grey looked up hopefully. His blue eyes smiled at me. I grinned back; my first actual sincere smile of the day was for him. Just his voice buoyed me.

"No." I laughed. "For her wedding, three weeks from Saturday. Remember? You're coming with me."

"Oh, yeah. Right ...." Grey looked sheepish. He cleared his throat as a sudden silence descended over the room. Zack and Alex avoided my gaze.

"What's going on?" I wondered. "Can you not come?"

"Well ... our recording schedule just came in. We fly out this Sunday for the studio."

"This Sunday? Like, four days from now?"

"Yeah."

"Wow," I was incredulous. "That's exciting." It took me a minute to process, for this new information to register in my already exhausted frame of mind. I smiled at him again, but this time it was forced. Really, could this day get any worse? I mean, it was awesome that the guys were going to record their music. They had worked so hard, they were so talented, and they totally deserved it. Still, I was selfish enough to wish it wasn't happening at all. I didn't want Grey to leave me.

"How long will you be gone for?"

"I don't know. A few weeks probably, maybe a month. However long it takes to make the record." He shrugged.

"Really? A month?" My stomach sank at the thought. I was happy for him, I really was, but I couldn't help feeling deflated. That interminable amount of time stretched out in my mind, seeming like forever, feeling that way already. He was going to be gone for the rest of the summer. I was going to be alone for the rest of the summer.

"Hey, I'll be your date for the wedding." Charlie promised in an effort to lighten the mood. "I've even got a matching tutu I could wear."

"You do?" Zack grinned at her.

"Thanks Charlie." My voice was quiet, subdued, ignored over the sudden deafening cheers as Zack flipped his quarter expertly into the cup. It was Grey's turn to drink then. They carried on with their game, laughing and cheering, completely oblivious to me and my utter disappointment. I stood by a moment, vexed, my arms crossed impatiently as I watched and waited for something else—more of an explanation or maybe even an apology, but none came. It didn't help that everyone was half-cut while I felt completely sober; the cocaine seemed to have already worn off, which made me even angrier as I listened to their stupid, happy jabber. Finally, in frustration, I headed down the hallway to my room and shut the door behind me.

I flopped down on my bed, grumbling as I dug through the dead grass scattered inside my purse until I found the vial again. Eagerly I snorted back the blow, doing more and more, trying to drown out the happy laughter from the kitchen with the dim buzzing in my head. Finally spent, I lay back and stared up at the ceiling, nearly overwhelmed by the sheer volume of cocaine shooting through my veins. My hands were trembling.

I looked around my room, my eyes darting rapidly as I tried to catch my breath. It was a fairly tiny space, holding just my bed and my dresser. The walls were totally bare. It was already as messy as my room had been at home, and now I had to do my own laundry. Once in a while Charlie and I would load up her car with garbage bags of our clothes and do them all in one day at the local Laundromat, but for the most part they just lay wherever I threw them off at night until I was desperate for some clean ones.

I grabbed my stash of cigarettes from the nightstand and lit one. Even though I was super high now, I felt no urge to join my friends. I preferred to sit alone and feel sorry for myself, alert enough to think rationally about how much life sucked at the moment, but high enough now that it didn't really bother me. Even without feeling, I knew how badly I was going to miss Grey, how I couldn't imagine my life without him in it, even for a day. And he'd been so casual about it, so aloof—like it didn't even matter that we'd be spending a month of more apart, like it was no big deal.

There came a sudden knock on my door. I looked towards the noise, but didn't answer until the knocking came again.

"Mackenzie?" It was Grey.

"Yeah?"

The door opened to reveal him, and most of my anger melted away at just the sight. He would always have that affect on me, it really wasn't fair. Dressed in his dark jeans and a red Volcom t-shirt, his dark hair was hidden behind a well worn hat, his perfect lips curved into a cautious smile, his gorgeous blue eyes—though a bit bleary—looked at me hopefully.

"Can I come in?"

"Sure." I was twitching as I looked back up at the roof. The bed sunk as Grey lay down next to me; his weight caused the springs to groan. I smelt his delicious cologne and tried to breathe it in as deeply as I could while remaining as stiff beside him as possible.

"Your room's a mess." He noticed with a chuckle. "What are you doing in here? Aren't you going to come and join us?"

"No." I shook my head, my teeth grinding.

"Why not?"

I rubbed at my nose with a shaky hand, avoiding his gaze.

"You're mad about the recording thing, aren't you? 'Cause I'll be missing the wedding?" He asked.

"No." I managed to answer.

"Yes you are."

"No, I'm not." My heart was pounding in my chest and my skin shone with the cool sheen of sweat. Heat was pouring off of me. I sat up and looked at Grey. "I'm not mad, really," I panted, "I'm happy for you. I mean … I'm going to miss … I'm going to miss …."

"Hey, Mackenzie … are you okay?" He sat up and looked at me, his face concerned, his eyebrows furrowed. "You don't look so good."

"What … yeah, I just …." I pressed a hand to my chest. It felt like someone was sitting on it, or pushing against it or something, like I couldn't breathe. I wiped a hand over my damp face and got up off the bed, but the change made me feel dizzy and I staggered back against it. I fanned myself with my hand. "I just … I gotta …." What did I have to do? Wasn't there something I had to do?

"Mackenzie," Grey was suddenly before me. When did he get there? He was waving his hand before my face as if trying to get my attention. I felt the sudden urge to run, like I had to get away from the mounting panic balling in my stomach. My hands were tingling like they had fallen asleep. I stared blankly in front of me, trying to think, trying to get my mind right. There was something I had to do. Run. I wanted to run.

"Mackenzie!" Grey's face was close to mine—too close, he was stealing my breath. I couldn't breathe. His hands were on my arms, burning me, searing my skin. "Mackenzie, look at me!" He implored.

Then everything went blurry, like water poured on a painting, and there was a flash of white, blinding light that engulfed my entire being. I knew nothing more.

CHAPTER 32

"Mackenzie, Mackenzie, shit, wake up. Wake up!" Grey's voice was the first thing that registered in my mind. It sounded hoarse, like he had been screaming, like he was frantic with worry. I turned my head towards the sound, struggling to open my heavy eyelids. My throat was dry and sore as I swallowed sluggishly. My head was pounding.

"Grey?" I choked out, my voice cracking. I felt terrible, like every single cell in my body was sick, but at least I could breathe now. I inhaled deeply, which made me cough, and my entire body radiated with pain from the action. I opened my eyes.

Grey was leaning over me, his blue eyes looking me over, a mixture of worry and relief playing on his face. He let out a breath and dropped his head into his hands.

"Holy shit, Mackenzie. Don't you ever do that to me again."

"What happened?" I wondered slowly. I couldn't really remember anything past the overwhelming flash of white.

"You had a seizure." Grey shook his head at me in disbelief. "How much friggin' coke did you do today?"

"I don't know …." I swallowed thickly, trying to remember. "A bit."

"A bit." He repeated, his face grim. "You mean enough to make you O.D. Right?"

I didn't know what to say to that. I bit my lip and shut my eyes instead. My head was pounding fiercely. "My head hurts," I complained, trying to change the subject.

"Your whole body's going to hurt. You were thrashing into everything." Grey shook his head again, as if he were reliving the moment but trying to rid himself of the memory. "I couldn't stop you. I tried everything."

"Really?" I tried to imagine it. I couldn't believe what had happened, I felt so normal now, I just couldn't picture myself convulsing there on the floor like a fish flapping around out of water. The throbbing in my head and my arms and my legs proved it really happened though, that I'd really had a seizure, one that must have been terrifying to witness. I looked up at Grey and his face was hard, almost like the worry made him angry. His eyes didn't leave me for a second.

I gave him a shaky smile. "I'm sorry, Grey. I'm okay now, though. I mean, I feel okay, at least. Wow. Has this ... ever happened to you before?"

"Yeah, once." He admitted. "We'd been doing coke all day before a show. I just blacked out, and woke up with this huge gash across my chin. Everyone was amazed that I was still alive. I wound up getting stitches and had to do the show with this huge bandage."

"But you were okay after?"

"Yeah." Grey remembered. "I mean, I did end up going to the hospital, but it was more for the cut than the coke."

"Why does it happen?"

"It's like any overdose. Your body just shuts down, it can't handle it."

"Crazy."

"Yeah. Coke leaves your system pretty quickly though, so it doesn't take long to recover. Thankfully." Grey let out a shaky sigh. "Fuck, you scared me."

"I'm sorry, Grey." Weakly I sat up, wedged on the floor between the bed and the dresser. My arms trembled, barely able to support me.

"Here," Grey stood up and grasped me under the arms with his strong hands, lifting me up from the floor with ease. He set me down gently on the bed. I felt weak and achy and my limbs were quivering. I hugged him for a minute before he let me go, breathing in his scent, loving the feel of his warm arms around me. I was surprised to find that I wasn't even scared—though really, I could've died; who knows what would've happened if Grey hadn't been there. But Grey *was* there, and I knew everything would be all right. I knew he wouldn't let anything bad happen to me. I felt totally safe with him, all the time.

"Mackenzie." He pulled away from me, his dark face serious. "You've got to be more careful."

"I know," I realized. It had all happened so easily, too easily, I couldn't even believe it. "I will, I'm sorry. I just ... I had such a horrible day; I didn't even think about how much I was doing. I just kept going, to try and make it better. You know?"

"Yeah, but you gotta take it easy. You can't go so hard all the time. You could've really hurt yourself. If I hadn't been here …." He cringed at the thought. "I don't know. Maybe we should take you to the hospital."

"No, no, no." I shook my head. "I'm fine, I promise." I was achy and kind of nauseous, but I didn't feel like I was dying anymore. I still felt a bit buzzed actually, dizzy from all the coke. "I'll be fine. I won't do anymore for a while, okay?"

He hesitated "You promise?"

"Promise." I agreed quickly, almost too quickly. I wondered fleetingly how long we were talking about. I hoped hours and not days. Even now, after all I'd been through, after the sheer volume of cocaine I'd done that day, I still wanted more. I still craved the feeling that cocaine gave me … the superhero-ness of it all. I fumbled with a cigarette from my nightstand and lit it instead, hoping the nicotine would help to tide me over.

"You'll tell me if anything changes, right? Like if you suddenly can't breathe or you go numb or something, let me know, okay?"

"Of course." I nodded.

Grey sighed and rubbed a hand over his face, but he seemed convinced. He pulled himself back onto the bed and lay next to me, resting his arm around my waist. He seemed reluctant to let me go for even a second, but I didn't mind it at all. I welcomed his warm body beside me, smiling at his proximity.

"So, you wanna tell me what happened to make your day so terrible? You were just getting dresses, right, for the wedding?" He asked then, his voice low beside my ear.

"Yeah." I blew my smoke out in a hiss.

"And?"

"And … ugh, it's just my stupid family. They're so … I don't know. They were just like, super bitchy all day, and then my mom made me go and sit in the car, like I was a five-year old on a time out or something. And for like, no reason at all. It was so embarrassing."

"Why did she do that?"

"I don't know. They think I'm trying to ruin everything or something. Like, tonight, when my mom dropped me off, she basically threatened to kick me out of Marcy's wedding if I don't behave myself. As if I'd really want to ruin my sister's wedding. I'm not that horrible." I scoffed. "It's just so … it's so frustrating."

"Why would they think that?"

"I don't know." I shook my head and thought for a moment, blowing my smoke out, watching it dissipate in the air. Grey sat by patiently, waiting for me to continue. "My mom mentioned something about how I have this awful attitude, how she thinks I party too much. But so what? I'm young, I like to have fun. That doesn't mean I'm going to get all wasted at my sister's wedding and make a scene or something."

"Maybe she's just worried about you." Grey decided. I shot him a look.

"No." I scoffed. "That is definitely not it. If she's worried about anyone, it's my sister. She doesn't want me getting in the way of Marcy's happiness. Heaven forbid." I rolled my eyes.

"What makes you think that?" Grey asked, resting his head on his fist, watching me, his eyes narrowing as he listened. I glared at him again, but he held his hand up defensively. "Hey, I'm just trying to understand."

"Because, Grey. When it comes to Marcy, I don't count. I mean, you should see her. She's perfect, she's always been perfect. Everything any parent could ever want in a daughter, she's gorgeous and smart, and she's going to be a doctor … I just, I can't compete with her." I shook my head in frustration. "Look, I don't want to get into it, it'd take me all night. Just, trust me, okay?"

"Okay …," Grey wisely let the subject be, "… So … you came home, and you were already pissed, and then, when you heard we'd be leaving …."

"Yeah, that was kind of the breaking point." I sighed. "I'm sorry, that wasn't cool of me. Honestly, I hate that you're leaving. But I am happy for you." I looked up to show him that I meant it. I even smiled. "It's awesome that you're going to record your music, I just wish it wasn't for so long."

"Well, while we're being honest with each other," Grey smirked, "I gotta admit, I'm kind of relieved to be missing the wedding. I mean, it sucks to let you down, but I hate that shit. I really do. The suit, the speeches, everything."

I giggled at him. "So do I …." I groaned. "Maybe I should ruin it all. At least then it'd be over sooner."

"Did you say you were going to be a … ballerina, or something?"

I rolled my eyes. "Yes. Grey, honestly. We're wearing tutus. Like, they come to here …." I lifted my pant leg to show him, and as I did, I noticed for the first time the deep bruise covering most of my calf—it was purple in color and sore to the touch. "Oh shit," I spoke in amazement, fairly alarmed by the welt. "Did I really do that to myself?"

"I was afraid of that." Grey's handsome face was regretful as he inspected the wound. "I tried to stop it, but you were right between the dresser and the bed, and you bashed into them pretty hard."

"Oh, man," I lifted up the other pant leg to reveal more bruises and smaller welts. Morbidly curious, I unbuttoned my jeans and pulled them off, my limbs groaning at me in the process. My thighs weren't nearly as bad, there were some marks and a big bruise on my knee. I winced as Grey pressed lightly on it.

Gently, he took his hand and ran it softly up the length of my leg. A wicked gleam lit his blue eyes as he did so, a smirk curling his lips.

"We'd better get that shirt off too, just in case." He decided. I giggled, and held my arms up for him to gently tug the tank top off over my head. It looked like I had bruised my ribs a bit but it didn't hurt to breathe in, so Grey was satisfied for my health—but I could tell he wasn't happy about my wounds.

"I'm sorry. I should've pulled you out of the way or something, I wasn't even thinking." He shook his head. I looked up at him in amazement. His concern was so sweet, it surprised me. I couldn't believe he thought in any way that this was his fault. I gazed into his gorgeous face, at his brilliant blue eyes full of such care, and was nearly overcome by the love I felt for him. He was so perfect, so beyond me, and yet there he was, with me … and I was laying before him in nothing but my underwear.

I was suddenly very conscious of that fact. It became hard for me to breathe again, but it had nothing to do with the cocaine and everything to do with Grey. Pure heat shivered up my spine at just the slightest brush of his fingers. I remembered the newfound confidence that had swept over me earlier that afternoon, and determined now, I decided to do something about it.

It took him totally by surprise as I reached up for him, pulling his face to mine and kissing him as deeply as I could. My muscles throbbed at the action, but I didn't care. I wrapped my arms around him, pressing myself against his hard chest. He responded eagerly, his hands were warm on my bare skin, making me feel flushed all over. Almost frantically I pulled him down over me, crushing him against me, clutching him tightly with my legs.

"Wait, Mackenzie," he broke away from me suddenly. Both of us were breathless. "We shouldn't do this."

"Yes, we should." My heart was racing in my chest, but I didn't want to stop.

"No." He sat up, disentangling himself. "We shouldn't."

"What? Why?"

Grey shot me a look. "You know why."

"Grey, I'm fine, honest. I feel fine." I insisted.

"I'm sorry." He stated resolutely. "But we're not doing this."

I could see it took him obvious effort to exercise such restraint. Every time his eyes rested on my near naked form his resolve seemed to waver, his fists clenched as if willing them self-control. Finally he tore his eyes from me, and with a firm shake of his head Grey stood up from the bed, leaving me there lying all alone. I sighed theatrically and stared up at the roof, disappointed and frustrated—and cold now, without his warm body covering me.

Grey paced the tiny quarters of my room a minute, his arms stretched behind his head as he took a deep breath in. "You should really just get some sleep, Mackenzie." He decided, looking at the piles of clothing strewn messily upon the floor. "What do you wear at night?"

"Nothing." I answered slyly, my voice icy, my arms crossed before me. Grey shook his head at me and chuckled.

"Here, put this on." He threw me a ratty old Blondie t-shirt from my overflowing dresser drawer. I glared at him a moment, picked up the t-shirt and shoved my arms roughly through the sleeves in resigned aggravation. Deep down, I knew that Grey was doing the right thing, deep down I knew I should be in awe of his restraint—touched by it, really—since he'd put my wellbeing before his own needs. But it was so … frustrating. I was impatient, and curious and just … eager to experience sex. To experience everything. Everything with Grey.

I lay back against the pillows with a heavy sigh, watching as he took the duvet piled at the bottom of the bed and rested it gently on top of me.

Grey leaned down and kissed me lightly on the forehead.

"I'll call you in the morning." He promised.

"Wait, Grey," I grasped his arm, completely forgetting my irritation, panicked by the sudden thought of him leaving. We had so little time left together. I didn't need to have sex that night, I could wait. I just didn't want him to go. "Please don't leave. Won't you stay with me?"

He shook his head. "Mackenzie, no, I told you …."

"I know, but we don't have to do anything. Please? We'll just sleep. I'm sorry; I just want to … to have you with me. Will you stay?" I looked up at him, my dark eyes wide, pleading. I bit my lip. "Please?"

I was worried he'd be exasperated with me. But Grey gazed at me a moment, his blue eyes warm and soft, and then he relented, nodding; his smile … amused, almost. I grinned happily at his response and moved over in my bed, patting the pillow next to me.

"You'd better not snore." He threatened. I giggled, sneaking a peek at his tanned, muscular, glorious perfection of a body as he undressed. I had never been so attracted to someone before, it was beyond my very limited experience to want someone so badly. I wished I could take back my promise of just sleep as Grey crawled into my bed in nothing but his boxers, pulling the blanket over his taut form.

"I don't snore, but I am a kicker." I warned him with a sigh.

"In that case, I'd better keep you close to me." He grinned, and his strong arms wrapped around me, pulling me closely against his hard body. I couldn't help but smile as he held me tightly, his warmth and his smell enveloping me, making me feel warm and cozy and safe. I snuggled into him, lacing my fingers through his and kissing his hand.

"I haven't been to bed this early since I was eight." I laughed.

"Me either." Grey admitted from behind me. I didn't feel tired, but with his strong arms around me, I was perfectly content. With my free hand, I reached over and clicked off the lamp. Darkness blanketed the room, adding to my cocoon of total serenity.

"Goodnight, Grey." I whispered into the blackness.

"Goodnight, Mackenzie."

CHAPTER 33

The week went by way too quickly. I had to share Grey during the day, with work and his constant band practices, but at night he was all mine. We would hole up in my room and get high and just … be together. There were no distractions, no interruptions—just Grey and I, hanging out, having fun. With every moment I spent with him, I dreaded his leaving that much more.

I was happy when the guys decided to cancel their usual Saturday night gig at the Aurora that week, even happier when Grey chose to spend that free time at home with me. Don't get me wrong, I loved to party, nothing cheered me up faster than a night out on the town. But I loved being alone with Grey even more.

Presently he leaned across my bed, handing me the railed up mirror carefully. I bent over and snorted the blow, pulling back on my forehead as I sniffed in.

"That's good." I commented, sniffing the drugs deep into my sinuses. I could feel their effects almost immediately. I smiled shakily and took a drag of my cigarette, aware of Grey's eyes on me. Ever since the overdose, he'd been extra cautious when it came to my coke use … how much I did, how often I did it. I didn't mind though. The bruises covering my legs had just begun to heal, but they were still a little sore. If Grey's concern would keep me from having a seizure again, I was all for it.

"Your turn." I passed him the mirror and fidgeted with my smoke, crossing and re-crossing my legs, smiling at the warm energy that permeated my being. He took the mirror from me and sniffed back the lines of soft, chalky powder. I studied him closely, taking in his every feature and committing them to memory so I could easily recall his gorgeous face when he was gone. His cheeks were tan and covered in coarse, dark stubble; his eyes of the most beautiful blue, his lips full and curved into the usual smirk. His dark hair was short and messy, sticking out from under his ball cap. The shirt he wore was plain and black, he had leather-studded bracelets upon his right wrist; his arms were just as dark, just as tan as the rest of him, and they were muscular and strong.

"What?" He chuckled when he noticed me staring. I shook my head, biting my lip, pulling my fingers absently through the long, dark hair hanging loose around my shoulders.

"Nothing. I'm just going to miss you, that's all."

"It's only for a month … or so, but it'll go by faster than you can imagine."

"Yeah." I nodded, though I didn't believe him. I knew the time was going to drag by; at least, it would for me. I chewed my nails. "Promise you won't forget me?"

"You mean, while I'm off making myself famous?"

"*Rich* and famous." I corrected.

"Right. I forgot you were spoiled." Grey teased. "Can't forget rich."

"Shut up." I slapped him playfully. His fist clenched tightly around the offending wrist and pinned it back against the bed. I tried to fight him with the other hand, but it suffered the same fate as the first, trapped in an iron grip against the mattress. Laughing, I lay back, pinioned by him as he leaned overtop of me.

"Grey … Grey … stop …." I choked out between laughs. "… I'm serious …."

"If you're so serious, then why are you laughing?" His voice was suddenly thick, his eyes heady as they scanned my face. His face hung just inches from mine.

"I'm not." I whispered, the last traces of mirth disappearing from my voice. I smiled at him pleadingly. "Grey, promise me."

"Promise you what?" Grey bent and kissed my collarbone, just below my neck, sending a shiver of pure heat through me. Then his lips moved slowly, achingly down my breastbone, beyond my ribs, gliding across the smooth skin of my stomach. He let go of my wrists but I didn't move them. My heart was beating loudly in my throat; my breath was shaky, faster.

"Promise that you won't forget me." I pleaded.

"Forget you? I could never."

Grey stopped his trail of kisses just above the waistband of my jeans. His lips curved into a smile as he looked up at me, his blue eyes gleaming wickedly.

"What about you? Would you forget me?"

I shook my head, breathless.

"You won't after this."

We were still entwined the next morning when I awoke. It took me a few minutes to come too, a few minutes to assimilate the heavy weight of Grey's arm around my waist. Once I understood, a smile curved my lips and I snuggled against the hard form behind me.

We still hadn't had sex. I mean, we had done many other things … wonderful things … things that sent a quick blush of heat to my cheeks at just the thought of them. We'd spent the most amazing night together. But still, Grey had stopped us before we could go the final distance, and I just didn't understand it. I was actually starting to get a complex about the whole thing. I mean, we'd had plenty of opportunity, plenty of chances to do it, but we just … didn't. He didn't want to, for some reason. I couldn't help but think it had something to do with me.

Grey stirred. It was early in the morning, the sun was doing its damndest to sneak through the Venetian blinds on the window, peaking around the edges and filtering through the cracks. We'd been awakened by the sound of the radio coming through my alarm clock. I hated the noise; I knew it meant that Grey would be leaving me soon.

"Good morning." He whispered in my ear, his voice low, like velvet. His stubble rubbed against my cheek. My heart wanted to burst, I was so content. I tried to enjoy the moment as best I could while it lasted.

"Good morning." I brought his hand to my lips and kissed it. I thought quickly about doing some more cocaine, but pushed the thought from my mind. I had to save my rations; I'd need them after Grey left. "Do you want a smoke?" I asked instead.

"Sure." He answered. I had recently discovered the brilliance of smoking in bed. I grabbed my pack from the nightstand and lit two cigarettes, turning over and handing him one. We smoked in satisfied silence a moment.

The blankets were low on his torso, his tan chest naked on the bed, his head resting against his arms. I propped my head on my hand and slowly trailed my fingers over the hard contours of his pecks and his abs in open admiration. He was so perfect, so unbelievably beautiful. I sighed happily. I'd never been this intimate with someone before.

I'd never experienced what happened last night, to sleep wrapped up around someone wearing nothing at all, to wake up with them the next morning in a cocoon of total bliss and contentment. He'd held me all night long, and I'd never felt safer.

I couldn't help but wonder if anything would change once we did have sex. Would it be better? Would we be closer? I blew my smoke out thoughtfully, trying to imagine what it'd be like, how it would feel. The curiosity was driving me crazy. I knew he had to leave soon, I knew our time together was fleeting. I had to ask him, I had to know before he left.

"Grey?"

"What?" His voice was still raspy from sleep.

I could feel the heat in my face, and knew I was blushing. "Nothing, never mind." I changed my mind, I couldn't ask him. It was too embarrassing.

"What is it? Tell me." He chuckled. "You have to tell me now."

"No, it's stupid. Forget it."

"Mackenzie."

I shook my head. "No, it's …." I groaned and shut my eyes, forcing out the words. "I just, I've been wondering … I mean, don't get me wrong, last night was amazing … but I was just wondering … why we don't …" I couldn't say it.

"Why we don't have sex?" He finished for me.

I nodded shamefully. "Yeah."

"Well, you're a virgin, right?"

"Is it that obvious?" My blush deepened. Why did I bring this up? I was going to die of humiliation; I knew it.

"No, it's not obvious. Not in the way you're thinking. Not in a bad way." Grey smiled at me.

"Okay …."

"Look, Mackenzie." He sat up a bit, adjusting the blankets as he did so. He looked at me seriously, but his lips were still bent in a smile. "I'm not in any rush or anything. We can wait until you're ready."

"I'm ready." I stated certainly.

He chuckled. "I know you think that, but are you really? Maybe you just feel that way because you think I expect it. And I don't. I mean, I'd like to, yeah … hell yeah," he looked me over roguishly and smirked, "and it's definitely not easy. But I can wait."

I was stunned. And relieved. I had no idea Grey was so … thoughtful. That he cared enough to wait until I was truly ready, that he wanted to make sure I knew for certain when I was. I shook my head at him in utter disbelief.

"Wow. What makes you so … careful?"

"I don't know." Grey shrugged. He took a drag of his cigarette and blew out the smoke, avoiding my gaze, like he was the uncomfortable one now. "I don't know," he repeated. "I've had a shit life, Mackenzie. A total shit life. But I've got a chance now, to do something right for once. You know?" He met my eyes then, his burning blue. "I feel like if I do right by you, it's, I don't know, it's like a shot at redemption, or something. Does that make any sense?"

I nodded. "Yeah, I guess so. But … what do you need redemption for?" Though elated by his sentiment, my heart swelled with compassion for him. I hated hearing that he had a "shit life," I couldn't imagine what that meant. As much as I complained about my family and my parents, deep down I knew I had it pretty good. What Grey was alluding to, I had no real idea, only a feeling that it was bad. I looked up at him with concern.

"It's nothing. It doesn't matter." Grey chuckled and shrugged it off. "I just; I don't want to screw this up. That's all you need to know."

"How could you?" I lay my head down on his hard chest; my long, dark curls spreading over him. "I won't let you."

Grey's hand found my hair, stroking the soft tresses and running his fingers through them, sending little shivers through me. We lay together in comfortable silence for a while. I wondered what he was thinking about, if he were back reliving the memories of his youth that he so needed to be absolved of. I hoped that one day he would talk to me about it, but I wasn't going to push him or pry. Grey was always so cool, so casual, he would never convey even a hint of trauma or torment about him. I had a feeling that all of it was buried, somewhere deep and lost inside, hidden in a dark corner that no light could ever touch.

His life was a mystery to me; there was so much I had left to discover. It was odd growing up in a small town not to know absolutely everything about a person before you even meet. I loved it though; I loved the ambiguity of it all. I looked forward to learning everything there was to know about Grey. I had so many questions about the different chapters in his life, and could only hope that one day he would tell me the rest of the story, the parts edited for content, kept only to himself.

His heartbeat was loud in my ear. I smiled contentedly. When Grey was ready to talk, I would be there to listen.

Zack's car idled loudly against the curb as the guys loaded their luggage into the trunk. It was a gorgeous day, hot enough to "fry a cat on a sidewalk," as my Grandma would say. I stood back and waited, my arms crossed, watching as they packed their things. The guys were jovial and cheery, obviously excited as they prepared to embark on their adventure. But I couldn't say the same for me.

I hated this day. I couldn't even pretend to be happy about it. I wasn't going to cry though, I had promised myself that much. I could be strong; I was going to be strong. After Grey threw his last bag into the trunk of the car, he turned back to me and smiled. I forced myself to grin back at him. I was going to be strong.

He gathered me into his arms then, and I clung to the hard warmth of his body, breathing deeply for one last time his delicious scent. I could tell he was trying to hide his excitement, his perfect face seemed crestfallen as he looked down at me, but there was no mistaking the light apparent in his clear blue eyes. At least he had tried, for my sake.

"Have fun while I'm gone." Grey brushed the hair back from my face. "But not too much fun, okay?"

"Yeah." I nodded. "Same for you."

"Promise you'll be careful? I don't want to go crazy worrying about you."

"I promise." I smiled, despite myself, at his obvious concern.

Grey bent down and kissed me then, long and slowly, his lips lingering on mine. I wrapped my arms tightly around his neck. I wanted to beg him to stay.

"I love you." I whispered.

He smiled at me. "I'll call you."

I nodded as he pulled away. I forced myself to take a breath, to hold back the tears that were threatening. My throat was aching.

"Let's go boys!" Alex called—ever his loud, grinning self—cheering as he slammed the trunk shut. "It's time to make some music."

"You be good while I'm gone." Grey implored. I nodded again, unable to speak, and watched in agony while they all piled into the car. Charlie came and joined me after saying goodbye to Zack. She wrapped an arm around my shoulders and gave me a comforting squeeze. We waved forlornly as the vehicle pulled out onto the road, music cranking from the open windows as they drove away. We could still hear Alex cheering, even from afar.

I sighed heavily, crossing my arms.

"Well, Mac, it's just you and me now." Charlie stated.

"Yep."

"So …." She grinned at me. "You wanna get blitzed or what?"

CHAPTER 34

Charlie and I kept ourselves as high as we could for the rest of the day. It helped me forget how badly I already missed Grey, how my heart had begun aching for him the moment the car was out of sight. We ignored the creeping loneliness with cocaine and sun tanning and by watching Jim Carrey movies well into the night. It wasn't until I crawled beneath the covers of my too empty bed that I recognized the heartbreak of solitude. I wished for Grey's strong, warm arms around me; to have him whisper in my ear, to feel his lips on mine. I sighed and curled up into as tight a ball as I could. This was going to be a looong month.

Monday was the same. Cocaine was on the menu for breakfast and lunch and most of the afternoon. I was doing a bit more than I should've been, but I justified it easily. I needed it now, it wasn't just a want.

Work was pitiful. There was some strange guy behind the counter covering for Grey, but at times I'd forget he wasn't Grey and bend to look through the window, expecting his gorgeously handsome face to smile at me in return. The new guy must have thought I was crazy. He didn't deserve half the disappointed glares I threw his way.

I continued this mind-numbing routine for most of the week. I found it actually got easier as time went by, not harder like I had expected. The ache was still there, it hadn't gone away or anything, but I was learning to live with it. I began to feel like maybe I could do it—maybe I could get through the month without Grey and emerge with my sanity still intact.

That was before I started waiting for him to call. I let a few days pass without thinking anything of it; Grey was excited, he was getting settled, he was probably busy. I could understand that. I spent Friday night alone at home while Charlie went to the club, partly because I'd promised Grey to be good—and good was not something I was at the club—but mostly because I was sure he'd call me. Charlie rang numerous times to try and pry me off the couch, so I knew my phone wasn't broken or anything. But Grey never called. I did some cocaine by myself for awhile and then called it a night, trying to keep my spirits up.

Sunday morning came, and still no word. I looked out my bedroom window, laying in bed, smoking a joint and staring up at the perfect, cloudless sky. A myriad of possibilities flashed through my mind; reasons why Grey couldn't call. They ranged from a car accident to the studio burning down, or Grey locked in a room and forced to sing twenty-four hours a day. Maybe they'd signed a contract forbidding any outside communication until the record was complete. The higher I got the more ridiculous the explanations became. When I imagined Grey on a spaceship, playing his guitar for bright green alien creatures, I knew it was time for me to stop.

But then my phone rang. *"Leila! You got me on my knees, Leila …,"* It sang. I sat up, gasping, nearly falling out of bed in my rush to answer the cell phone that I kept on my nightstand, right next to my head so there was no way I'd miss it.

"Hello?" I was breathless with excitement; I couldn't wait to hear his voice again.

"Mac?" It was Charlie.

"… Yes?" I let out a sigh. "What's up?"

"Come in here and get high with me."

"What?" I laughed. "Where are you?"

"In my room. Let's smoke a bowl!"

"Did you seriously just call me from your room?"

"I'm comfy. Come on, I'm waiting."

"Okay, okay, I'll be right there." I hung up my phone, giggling. Thank God for Charlie. I didn't know what I'd do without her.

I jumped out of bed and ran down the hallway to her bedroom, my cell phone still clutched in my hand. Her room was bigger, but it was just as messy as mine. The only major difference were the posters and pictures that plastered her walls, making it feel homey and lived in, unlike my hospital/jail cell room. I made up my mind to put up some pictures or hang some art or something soon.

My favourite Tool song was playing on her stereo—*Sober*. Charlie laughed and moved over to make space for me in her bed, and I crawled eagerly under her covers.

"You do the honours, my dear." Charlie handed me a pipe packed with weed. I lit the lighter and pressed the flame to the bowl, sucking in the sweet, fragrant smoke. I held it in for a moment, passing the pipe to Charlie before I blew it out.

"What's with you and that thing?" Charlie wondered then, pointing at my cell phone as she tapped the bowl gently with her lighter. "Can you not be separated?"

"Apparently not." I coughed. "I've been expecting Grey to call."

"Ah, yes." She chuckled mirthlessly. "I gave up on that already."

"You did? Why? I'm sure Zack will call you."

"Well, I'm not holding my breath for it."

"Why not?"

"Because, Mac. I know what they're doing up there."

"Um … recording their album?"

"Yeah … maybe, during the day. But the rest of the time, they're getting as fucked up as they possibly can. Trust me, that is all Zack talked about. They have wicked friggin' clubs in that city, and they're going out every night and getting blotto'd. Totally shit-faced." Charlie looked at me pointedly. "Just like you should be. I can't believe you've ditched me two nights in a row so you can stay home just in case your phone rings."

"I know, I know …." I shrugged. "But I told Grey I'd be careful while he was gone. And I just really wanted to hear his voice again, you know?"

"I know, just, please don't turn into one of those girls who gets all crazy and depressed whenever her boyfriend leaves. I don't want to come home one night and see that you've, I don't know, dressed up a broomstick or something."

"I won't," I laughed, "I won't, I promise. I just miss him. I can't help it."

"Yeah," Charlie allowed. "I know how you feel. Trust me. It's impossible for me not to think about Zack, but then every time I do, I just picture him out partying and getting super wasted, and then I start thinking about him being with other girls and …." She shook her head, as if trying to clear the image. "It makes me crazy. It's not good for me."

"Really? Other girls?" I frowned. The thought hadn't even crossed my mind. Whenever I paused to think about Grey—wondering what he was doing, who he was doing it with—I just always assumed he'd be at the studio, working. Or at the hotel, sleeping. Now, I pictured the exact scenario Charlie had described.

I imagined Grey out with the guys, at some club, the music loud in the background, strobe lights flashing. They're being rowdy and loud, like always, and it's the five of them like usual. But then, some tall, leggy blonde dressed in some super skanky dress comes up and put her arms around Grey. I see him laughing and joking with her, see him giving her *my* favourite smirk. They flirt and drink and dance. Then I see—crystal clear and painfully real—the moment when they first start to kiss, his hands moving over her body and his lips pressing against hers.

I shook my head, my mind shying away from even the thought of such betrayal, my very being rejecting the possibility, refusing to accept it.

"No, no, no." I refuted stubbornly. "There's no way. Come on Charlie, just because they're gone doesn't mean they've just like … forgotten about us."

"I know, you're probably right." She sighed. "But, they're guys, you know? Guys do that kind of stuff all the time. And they stick together too. If Zack was cheating on me, I'd probably never find out. There's no way one of his 'bro's' would tell me."

I relented. "Yeah. That's true." She did have a point. We sat in silence for a minute as Charlie packed another bowl, both of us lost in aggravated thought. I bit my lip and contemplated. Grey had never given me any reason not to trust him. Just because he hadn't called didn't mean he was shacking up with some stranger. I didn't want to jump to the wrong conclusions, I wanted to give him the benefit of the doubt, I wanted to believe there was no way he could do that to me. No way that he would.

I sighed heavily and took the pipe eagerly from Charlie's hands. She gave me an apologetic smile and rubbed my arm soothingly.

"I'm sorry, I didn't mean to make you upset."

"No, it's okay." I gave her a brave smile. "I just, I couldn't picture anything worse, you know?"

"Yeah, I know. Trust me. But, Mackenzie, honestly, moping around the house and making yourself sick with worry isn't going to help anything. You should come out with me next time. It really helps to get your mind off things. I mean, Grey's out having fun, right? So why shouldn't you?"

"Yeah." I lit the bowl and sucked back the weed smoke deeply, until my lungs felt like they might burst. I could see her logic, but at the same time, I wanted to keep my promise to Grey. I didn't want him to be worried about me. I blew out the waft of smoke and winced, not just to keep from coughing, but from the new thought that just occurred.

How could Grey be worried, if he didn't even care enough to call?

Charlie and I stuck together over the next couple of days, even more than we normally did. It was kind of nice, actually, just to be with her when there were no guys around. She stayed home with me at night after work although I knew she'd rather be out at the clubs. I made it up to her with copious amounts of cocaine. We talked and painted each other's nails and watched mindless comedies we found totally hilarious in our drugged out state. Neither of us could even stomach the thought of watching some gushy romance. No need to rub salt in the wounds.

Needless to say, the guys had not called. Either of them. It was like the elephant in the room—we both knew about it, but chose not to talk about it. Really, there was nothing left to say. With every day that passed I was that much more thankful Charlie was my friend. I don't know what I would've done without her.

It was on one of those nights that I suddenly discovered a solution to my problem. I wanted to hear from Grey, but he wasn't calling. The answer was simple, really.

I was just going to have to call him.

I had to work up the nerve for some reason. I felt stupid, sneaking off to my room with my phone while Charlie was in the shower. I had a feeling she wouldn't approve, but I just had to do it. I was past the point of trying to play it cool, and I knew the moment I heard Grey's voice it would totally set my mind at ease. So I took a deep breath, shut my eyes, and dialled his number.

I lit a smoke as the phone rang in my ear, and the rush of nicotine helped me relax. It rang and rang, and I was just about to give up, disappointed—when finally he answered.

"Hello?" There it was—his lovely, velvety low voice.

"Hey," I greeted, almost giddily.

"Hello? I can't hear you."

"Grey? Hello, can you hear me?" I plugged my other ear. There was a great deal of noise on his end—the loud, pulsating beat of techno music and numerous voices jabbering away in the background, I couldn't tell who they were in the din.

"Are you there? Hello?"

"Grey? Grey, I'm here. Hello?" I walked towards the window. Maybe I was getting bad reception or something, but I could hear his end fine. He was muttering to himself, maybe trying to make his phone work, I didn't know. I was about to giggle at his muffled swearing, but then I heard it.

"Grey, baby," said a female voice, one I didn't recognize but instantly hated, "get off the phone. You promised to dance with me, remember?" She beckoned, giggling ditzily.

He laughed. "Yeah, okay. I'm coming."

I didn't hear anymore. I dropped the phone and it landed with a thud, bouncing across my carpeted floor. I stood, struck, like I had been slapped in the face or punched in the stomach. I was shell-shocked, stunned. I stared at the phone in horror and clutched at my chest, my stomach plummeting somewhere down towards my toes, my heart beating loudly in my ears.

"He's going to hurt you, Mackenzie." Suddenly Riley's voice invaded my mind, stabbing into my already wounded psyche. I hadn't thought about him in months, but there was no mistaking the unexpected sound in my memory. *"I know his type,"* he had said, *"I know what he's like. He'll hurt you, in the end."*

I didn't even allow myself to think about it. I couldn't. Frantically almost, trying to outrun the heartbreak striving to catch up with me, I threw on some different clothes and pulled my hair roughly into a ponytail.

"Charlie!" I yelled—my voice bordered screeching. "Put some clothes on. We're going out!"

I left my room without looking back, my cell phone abandoned on the floor.

CHAPTER 35

I can honestly say that I have almost no recollection of the weeks and days that followed. I wouldn't allow myself to be sober enough to let my mind work properly. At work I screwed up orders and dropped plates and walked around with glazed over eyes, but still I managed to make enough money to pay for my drug use. I learned some things from Charlie; she showed me how to dress to make the most tips. Since I needed the money, my skirts got shorter, my tops got lower, and my heels higher. At the end of every night, I would gather almost all my earnings and hand them over to her—my source—who would in turn procure whatever drug she felt I might like to try. I don't know where she went or how she got them, I preferred not to know. But I was more than eager to do whatever she brought home for me, whatever would get me fucked right out of my tree.

I tried meth and crack cocaine. We did PCP and Dilaudids, ecstasy and MDMA. I laced my cigarettes with cocaine. We'd go out to the club nearly every night, drink our faces off and dance and smoke up. Guys would hit on us, which felt good, but sometimes they would get too friendly, too persistent, and I'd barely remember myself in time before doing something totally regretful. I was so mind-breakingly stoned it was nearly impossible not to have a good time, nearly impossible not to forget. I was being stupid and dangerous, but I didn't care. Grey had wanted me to be careful, so I rebelled, giving him a physical "F-you," by being as reckless as I possibly could be. I almost wanted something bad to happen. Then, maybe he'd remember me.

Somehow, I survived the binge mostly unscathed, except for a majorly deflated wallet and some severely crippling hangovers. I only came too when Charlie reminded me, somewhat painfully one morning, that

Marcy's rehearsal dinner/wedding was happening that weekend and I had to sober up for it. I didn't want to, I craved the numbness I'd depended on and dreaded what would come once normal thoughts were allowed to form again. But Charlie forced me. She nearly dragged me into the shower, then sat me down afterwards and did my hair and my make-up. I was complacent for the most part, blinking stupidly in the mirror while she fixed me up—on the outside anyway. My insides were beyond her repair.

Charlie drove me into the city so I wouldn't be forced to ride with my parents. I thanked her profusely, over and over again, forgetting the initial irritation I'd felt towards her after she manhandled me all morning. I stared out the window as we drove, my eyes darting over the never-ending blanket of prairie fields stretching out towards the horizon. I began to feel more and more like myself and less and less like the fake, chemically diminished version of Mackenzie as I sobered up. But with that, just like I'd expected, came a world of hurt I wanted nothing to do with. With it came remembering that Grey had completely forgotten about me.

"Charlie?" My voice was faint.

"Yeah, sweetie?"

"Thank you for coming with me." I looked at my friend, her pretty blonde hair tumbling down her back, wide-lens sunglasses perched upon her nose. She blew her smoke out the opened window

"Don't mention it, Mac."

My parents had rented the entire private room of a restaurant in the city, La Grille it was called, some fancy kind of steak house, for Marcy's rehearsal dinner. My mom was simpering with pride; my dad was strutting around the place quite importantly. Marcy and Greg seemed to have their own personal spotlight on them at all times, they nearly shone from all the attention. She was wearing a sleek golden coloured dress with jewelled shoes; he was dapper in a dark suit and tie. For the most part, their friends and family closed in around them, oohing and aahing at their matching beauty and cracking clichéd, cheesy jokes about marriage that have been around since the stone age. Charlie and I sat at the private bar, our backs to the room, having a glass of wine. No one paid us any real attention, but I could still feel the cautious eyes of my parents and sister upon us, as if we were ticking time bombs that could explode at any minute.

We were just about to sneak away for a cigarette when a tall, fairly handsome, but obviously rich and snobby type came and stood next to me at the bar. He ordered a cognac—what the hell was that anyway—on the rocks.

"You must be Mackenzie." He turned to me then, his voice thick with I'm-wearing-a-thousand-dollar-suit arrogance. I smiled politely up at him.

"Yes. And you are …?"

"Smitten." He smirked, raising his eyebrows at me.

"Alright then." That was officially my cue. I grabbed my jacket off the chair and started for the exit, pulling a giggling Charlie along behind me. I looked back at him once from across the room and he was still standing there, watching me with the same stupid smirk set on his face. I rolled my eyes and headed out the door.

We found a picnic table in the alley of the restaurant, I think it was reserved for staff breaks, but I figured they wouldn't mind. I climbed on top of it and lit a smoke as Charlie leaned against the brick wall.

"Can you believe that guy?" I chuckled. "I can't believe those cheesy lines actually work on some women."

"He was pretty cute." She shrugged. "I bet he doesn't get denied very often."

"Are you kidding? I'm probably the first one who had the audacity."

"Probably," Charlie laughed.

"It's your fault he tried to pick me up, anyway. You're the one who insisted on making me all pretty." I decided, looking down at my tight, dark blue skinny jeans and high, black peep-toed shoes. I wore a black scooped back halter-top, my hair was in a high ponytail, and my dark curls cascaded elegantly down my back.

"Well, I'd tell you to go for him, but I don't want another Brad incident on my hands." Charlie admitted. "He is really cute though. And obviously rich."

I shook my head. "No way. I'd never go for someone like him. Even if Grey and I weren't …." I trailed off, my words hanging suspended in the air. I realized I didn't know how to finish my sentence. I didn't know what Grey and I were anymore. I sighed and blew out my smoke. "Anyway, I'd never go for someone like him."

"Yeah." Charlie nodded. "Once you go bad, you can never go back."

"Something like that." I stamped my cigarette out on the table and then dug through my purse until I found what I was looking for. What I needed desperately. I brought the scoop to my nose and did some cocaine, super quickly—I was such a pro now that it barely took any effort.

"Are you sure you should be doing that now, Mac?" Charlie wondered sceptically.

"Yes." I snorted deeply. "Want some?"

She shrugged and took the coke from my hand.

By the time we headed back into the party, it was time for us to eat. I took my place next to Whitney since we had to sit in wedding party order, and Charlie found a place at a table not far from mine. I felt pretty good, better now, I had a nice combo of wine and blow going for me. I actually smiled and talked a bit to the people around me.

The food was delicious; I took my time with a beautiful filet mignon done to a medium-rare perfection. It was the most I'd eaten in a long, long time. I finished it up with a large glass of wine, but no one seemed to care that I was underage.

Whitney and Marie were sizing up the groomsmen, trying to decide which one they'd be paired with at the wedding. I leaned forward curiously to look, I hadn't even thought about that awkwardness yet.

"Maybe I'll get Colin." Whitney whispered. "I hear he's going to be a surgeon."

"I think you will. I think Derek is my partner, the married one." Marie frowned.

"Who's mine?" I interrupted.

"Oh, um," Whitney glanced over. The other bridesmaids were still kind of awkward around me since the whole dress-day fiasco. "Oh, right. You're with Greg's brother, Craig."

"Greg's brother's name is Craig?" I giggled.

"Yeah. Why?"

"They rhyme. Like, Julia Gulia." I laughed. "Don't you find that funny?"

They just stared at me. I began to wonder if I was drunker than I thought. I cleared my throat. "So, which one is he?"

"That one, there. Next to Greg." Whitney pointed for me. "He's a stunner, huh? A total catch, he's in finance. Totally loaded."

Of course he was. I looked with disdain at Craig—A.K.A Smitten—Greg the dick's brother. I should've known he was related to Greg. His superior countenance should've given that away immediately.

"Great." I stated sourly.

"I'd trade with you in a heartbeat." Marie decided.

"Yeah, I'd take a piece." Whitney agreed. They giggled like girls at a school dance. I rolled my eyes at them. They could have him, as far as I was concerned.

The night drew on. There were a few speeches, but nothing overly dire. I left my table as soon as dinner was officially over so I could join Charlie back at the bar. She was going to stay the night with me at the hotel, but had to depart early the next morning to get back for work.

I tried to think of a good excuse for us to leave the shindig so we could go and actually party. The crowd was thinning out, and we probably could've gotten away with it, but then Greg cornered me.

"Hey there, little sister." He joined us at the bar, leaning heavily on the counter.

"Oh, hey, Greg." I forced a smile. He seemed pretty drunk, his eyes were bleary and a ridiculous smirk curved his lips. "This is my friend, Charlie." I introduced.

"Hey, Charlie, I'm getting married tomorrow." He announced.

"That you are." She lifted her glass to him.

"Woooh." He cheered, raising a limp hand upright in celebration.

"Woah. Don't over do it now." I smiled wryly. Charlie laughed behind me.

"Say, Mackenzie, have you met … my brother?" Greg was looking past me and beckoning him over. "He's in finance, you know."

"So I hear." I glanced over my shoulder as Smitten made his way towards us, swaggering in his finely tailored suit. I sighed.

"Craig, this is the beautiful Mackenzie. Marcy's little sister. Soon to be my little sister." Greg grinned. He actually pinched one of my cheeks. I slapped his hand away.

"Mackenzie." Craig held out his hand. I nodded and shook it.

"Craig. This is my friend Charlie." He shook her hand as well, but his eyes never left me. I tried to avoid them.

"Now, Mackenzie," Greg leaned in, like he was about to tell me a very important secret. "You be nice to young Craig, you see, because he's absolutely perfect for you."

"Is he?"

"Oh yes." Greg nodded.

I flipped my hair behind my shoulder. Even if Grey and I weren't together anymore, he would serve as the perfect excuse, for the moment. "Well, I already have a boyfriend, and I happen to think that *he's* perfect for me."

To my astonishment, the brothers laughed, like I had just told them a hilarious joke or something. I crossed my arms and glared at them.

"Right, right. The rock star, right? Motorbike, the whole shebang." Greg chortled. "He sounds like a real winner."

"If he actually even exists." Craig grinned.

"Oh, he exists."

"So, where is he then?" Craig held up his hands, looking around the room.

"He's in the studio, actually, with the band. They've got a record deal, and right now they're recording their album." I bragged.

"Oh, wow, an album, he's practically famous." Greg mocked. This made the two morons laugh harder, and they leaned against each other with mirth. I shook my head and began to gather my things from the bar. I was not in the mood for this bullshit.

"Come on, Mackenzie." Craig grasped my arm. "Think about it. He's obviously not that smart. If you were my girl, I'd lock you up; at least, I wouldn't let you out of my sight. You guys can't be that serious."

Wow. I really didn't need this. I could do without a play by play of my exact thoughts and fears, especially coming from this dickhead. I pulled my arm from his grasp.

"You don't know anything." Angrily I stepped down from the stool.

"Uh oh, you hit a nerve, brother. I think you're onto something." Greg grinned.

"I am, aren't I Mackenzie?" Craig persisted, smiling smugly. "Come on, are you guys even together?"

"Of course they're together." Charlie came to my defence then, her blue eyes flashing smartly at Craig. She put her arm around me. "They're inseparable."

"Oh yeah? Well, if they're so inseparable, where is this guy?"

"I told you. He's in the studio!" Fuming, I pushed roughly past the two men in their matching expensive cologne and disappeared through the dwindling crowd beyond. I didn't stop to talk to my mom or my dad or Marcy or anyone. I rushed out of the room and stormed through the exit, not stopping until I was out on the sidewalk. There, I paused to gather myself and wait for Charlie. The cool night air felt good against my heated cheeks, the general city noise helped somewhat to drown out the angry thoughts swirling through my head. The traffic rushed by on the busy street, horns were honking, a car alarm was sounding somewhere in the distance.

"Hey Mac," I heard Charlie's heels clipping on the sidewalk as she came to join me. "You okay?"

"Yeah." I lit a smoke. "Sorry. I just had to get out of there."

"I don't blame you. What a couple of dicks." She scoffed in disbelief.

I nodded. "Right? I mean … ugh … idiots." I crossed my arms and wordlessly we started walking down the sidewalk towards the hotel; it was only a few blocks away. I pulled my cell phone from my purse but the screen was blank—no messages, no nothing, just infuriatingly silent like always. I sighed.

"You know what the worst part is, Charlie?"

"What's that?

"They're right. Greg and his brother. About Grey and I." I looked up at the sky, but I couldn't see the stars from the bright city lights. "I don't know what I thought we had, Charlie. But I think, whatever it was, it must be over now."

Charlie didn't have anything to say to that. She slung a comforting arm around my shoulders and we walked in silence the rest of the way.

CHAPTER 36

I did my tenth line of the morning, grinning as soon as I felt the sweet burn, and leaned heavily against the bathroom counter. My heart was pounding furiously in my chest, hammering against my ribs—the blood was racing through my veins. I managed a shaky smile, invigorated by the spasms of happiness and pleasure the cocaine gave me. I needed this. There was no way I could act the chipper, ever-helpful bridesmaid all day without a little help.

I sucked in a quivering breath and stared at myself in the mirror a moment. This was actually happening. I was a full-blown ballerina. The hairdresser had done my hair up in a loose French knot, with curly tendrils falling down my shoulders and my back, as if I'd just finished dancing at an intense recital or something. I'm not sure if that's what she was going for, but that's what it looked like. There was actually a tiara in my hair, perched upon the crown of my head, glinting in the bathroom lights. My dress was on in all its pink, sequined, crinoline splendour; my shoes resembled real ballet slippers, tied up with pink ribbons and all. I didn't look bad, the beautician had done a great job on my make-up, giving me catty eyes in dark liner and bright red lips, so I actually looked really good. But still, I was a friggin' ballerina.

I put the drugs back in my pink bejewelled clutch—a bridesmaid's gift from Marcy, who had given each of us one—and snapped it shut. My eyes were still a little red and puffy from the previous night, it had been hard to stop the tears of despair once they'd finally forced their way through, once I finally felt the pain I'd tried for weeks to ignore.

I pushed the sadness away with a shake of my head and stepped out of the bathroom, eager to get this day done and over with so I could stop faking cheerfulness and revert back to my depressed state of mind. The cocaine gave me some much-needed energy. I ran around the room in shaky acceleration, taking care of last minute details, helping Whitney with her shoes, fixing Marie's hair that kept falling from its pins. When the bridesmaids were finally ready, we crossed the hall to Marcy's suite where she was getting dressed with my mother's eager, helpful hands. Dad was sitting in the living room area of the suite, dressed in a stiff dark blue suit, his hair neatly combed and gelled. He looked nervous, flicking randomly through the channels on TV. He ignored me.

Marcy was a sight. I stopped in my charged walking and just stared at her a moment, locked in a drug-induced stupor. There was a flush of nervous excitement in her cheeks and her eyes twinkled happily as she looked in the mirror. Her hair was dark and sleek, straightened in a perfect bob; a simple veil was pinned in her hair with tortoiseshell combs. Her dress fit to a tee, accenting her narrow waist and toned arms; a turquoise tear-dropped silver necklace emphasised the neckline of her gown and brought out the perfect evenness of her tan. The wedding dress cascaded around her frame in layers of silky white and sparkling embellishments, pleasing to the eye.

A few emotions flitted through me at that instant—happiness, jealousy, sadness. I stood there, resigned. Never in this lifetime could I ever compete with Marcy. I would always be second, no matter what.

"What do you think, Mac?" She asked me carefully. We hadn't really spoken since the big fight, and she was still guarded around me—actually they all were, like I could just fly off the handle at any moment.

I smiled quietly, reconciled to the fact. "Marcy … you're perfect."

I made it through the ceremony without tripping or fainting or anything else that might ruin a wedding. My bouquet of creamy white peonies shook violently while I made my way up the aisle, unaccustomed to all the eyes on me. The room was packed with people dressed in suits and gowns—at least three-hundred of them filled the wooden pews. The church was gorgeous and old, with stained glass windows and dark, impressively carved wood. Lit candelabras hung from the ceiling, giving the sanctuary a soft glow, a romantic feel. White flowers were everywhere, lining the aisle, overflowing the stage, hanging from the archways.

I avoided Craig's eyes as I made my way up the aisle, focusing on the Pastor, who smiled at me in a friendly way. I wondered randomly how terrible it was to be lit up in a church.

People may have been looking at me, but it didn't last for long. The moment Marcy stepped into the flower-strewn aisle, all eyes were on her. Mom was on one side of the blushing bride, looking regal and stately in a dark blue dress suit, her dark hair curled perfectly. Dad was on the other side of Marcy, absolutely beaming in his pride. The pianist was playing *Apachabelle's Canon* and the beautiful song floated softly in the air as they walked slowly towards Greg's love-soft face. I bit my lip and watched the perfect moment, deciding that when it came time for me to get married, it'd be at a chapel in Vegas or something. A rushed, drunken elopement complete with poker chips and cheap beer, followed by a hasty divorce once we finally sobered up.

I could do nothing but stand by and watch while Marcy married Greg the dick. It was a thankfully short ceremony. I couldn't stand all the love talk, the sickeningly sweet glances that Marcy and Greg were giving each other, the tears in my mother's eyes as she watched them kiss. When Marcy and Greg were officially man and wife, they ran back down the aisle to the thundering crash of jubilant applause. Stiffly I took Craig's extended elbow and allowed him to escort me down the steps after them. He smirked cockily at me, chuckling as if he found my abhorrence amusing. I bit my lip to keep from smacking the stupid grin off his handsome face.

All eight of us piled quickly into the stretch limo that waited at the entrance to avoid a receiving line. I had never been in a limo before; I took in the rich leather upholstery beneath the soft glow of pot lights. Craig sat next to me and I pointedly ignored him, talking instead to the other bridesmaids and groomsmen, who were lively and chatty with excitement. The limo crawled slowly through the crowded city streets, the driver honking the horn embarrassingly to announce the cause for celebration as Whitney popped open a bottle of champagne from the stocked bar inside. Marcy and Grey sat together in the back, holding hands and their flutes and kissing and giggling in their newlywed bliss. I chugged back my champagne and hurriedly held out my glass for more.

We drove to some gardens in the middle of the city for an excruciating bout of posed and candid photos. It was a perfect summer day, the sun blazing hot. I felt sorry for the guys in their sweltering tuxes. Well, all the guys but Greg and Craig. I smiled in wicked enjoyment at their discomfort, welcoming the stunted breeze that blew upon my bare legs and helped to cool me off.

There were group shots, bridal party shots, sister shots, bride and groom shots. Near the end we were all sweaty and tired and I was in desperate need of more cocaine. Craig always managed to be irritatingly close to me and he kept smiling my way, though I gave him no encouragement whatsoever. He didn't mention anything about Grey again; I think he figured that I too, had realized there was nothing there. He seemed to be waiting for my resolve to break, for me to give in to his utter perfection and finally accept his advances. The grin on his face told me he was certain of my eventual surrender to his arrogant charms. I did my best to ignore him.

We piled back into the limo, finally, the air conditioner cranked as Whitney passed around more champagne. I wasn't in the mood to join the rambunctious conversation this time, instead I stared pensively out my window as we drove, taking in the dim sights of the city through the dark tint. The car was heading to the reception site, and as we neared the five-star hotel, us girls checked and fixed our make-up as best we could in the rocking interior. Marie's needle straight dark hair refused to stay upswept but stubbornly I tried to pin it back for her. Eventually I got it somewhat how it was supposed to be. She smiled at me in thanks.

The limo slowed as we pulled up in front of The Windsor Hotel. A bellman opened the door for us; I could see my parents waiting eagerly outside. Whitney and Marie exited the car first with their escorts. Craig got out and then turned, pausing at the opened door with his hand outstretched, waiting for me. I sighed and placed my palm in his, avoiding his gaze by looking out at the front of the hotel as he helped me down.

There was a red carpet leading up to the grand glass front entrance. Huge golden letters were perched atop the awning, spelling out The Windsor in gilded extravagance. The building was made of impressive beige stone and stretched imposingly up sixty floors or more. I took in the sight with awe, but then as I looked, my eyes fell on something—or someone, rather—that I hadn't expected to see.

He was leaning against the granite wall off to the side of the entrance, looking uncomfortable as he smoked a cigarette, his arms crossed against a crisp black suit and tie.

I honestly had no idea how to react to him. Grey turned his head towards us, and his perfect lips curved into my favourite smirk when he saw me there. I just stared at him, stunned, stock-still with surprise. He looked at me a moment, and then his expression changed, his eyes narrowing like he was angry. I realized that Craig was still holding my hand. Abruptly, I ripped it from his grasp and hugged my arms around myself, taking a deep breath in as I went to meet Grey.

I approached him cautiously, nervous. After all of the doubt and suspicion and uncertainty, I didn't know what to do, how to feel. As I neared him, tears began to sting my eyes. God, I loved him. It'd been easier to ignore, easier to try and forget when he was far away and out of sight. But now he was standing before me, and the sheer force of the love I felt for that man was nearly overwhelming.

"Who was that?" Grey asked me when I was close enough, his voice accusing, his blue eyes suspicious. He was looking past me back at Craig, who was standing by the limo, watching us.

"He's no one." I shrugged.

"He was holding your hand."

"He was helping me out of the limo." I corrected icily. We stared at each other a moment. Grey looked so good in his suit. He was freshly shaved, his dark, messy hair was carefully gelled, and his blue eyes were piercing as he looked me over. His familiar, sweet, masculine cologne wafted over me, and my knees threatened to buckle at the very scent. I shut my eyes and tried to stay strong.

"You don't seem happy to see me." Grey realized.

"I don't know how to feel." I admitted with a shake of my head. "Grey ... what are you doing here?"

"What do you mean? I came here to surprise you." His handsome face turned hard. "Why, did I crash your date or something?"

"No, of course not." I bit my lip. It was all so confusing—his weeks of complete disregard, his sudden presence here. "You ... you came here to surprise me? Why?"

"Why?" He looked taken aback by the question. "Because ... because I ...." He ran a hand through his hair, struggling for words. "Because I missed you."

"You missed me?"

"Yeah, I missed you."

I didn't know what to say. I looked away from him, away from the startling blue of his eyes. My voice was thick with threatening tears. "Well," I scoffed, "you sure have some way of showing it."

Grey just looked at me, confused, contemplative. "What did I do?"

I shook my head at him. Where guys really that dense? Could he really not know? I thought back over the weeks of torment and utter heartache I had suffered at his total lack of concern. My chest burned with indignation.

"Grey, I haven't heard from you in weeks." I glared.

He shook his head. "I know … I'm sorry, we've just been … busy."

"I know you've been busy." I scoffed, my voice low and angry. "I heard her voice on the phone."

"What? Whose voice?" Grey's face fell as he considered my words. "What are you talking about?"

"Her voice. The girl. I called you one night, you were at a club or something, and I heard her, Grey. I heard her flirting with you, asking you to dance."

"That was you on the phone? Why didn't you call me back?"

"I'd already heard enough." I could see my parents out of the corner of my eye, watching from the entrance of the hotel. Mom had her arms crossed in disapproval, staring at us. I ignored her, turning my gaze back to Grey. I looked up into his gorgeous face and waited for his answer, his explanation. Our whole relationship hung on it.

"Mackenzie." His face softened with concern and he grasped me by the arms. His touch on my skin was enough to make me tremble, and I could feel all the pain and all the anger start melting away from me. I grasped at it, trying to remember, trying to hold on to the hurt and the anguish like I knew I should, though every bone in my body was screaming to forgive him. Aching to forgive him.

"Mackenzie," Grey repeated. "That was nothing. I promise you. We met one night after the studio, and we danced a couple times, and that's it. She's nobody. Please, look at me." He lifted my chin with his hand, forcing me to stare into his gorgeous blue eyes, deep and sincere. "Mackenzie, you have to believe me. I told you that I wouldn't screw this up. I would never … I could never …."

"I want to believe you." I admitted breathlessly, daring to hope. But I had no proof. Only his word. I stared up into his face—so honest, so innocent and concerned—and my eyes burned with fresh tears. I loved him enough that suddenly, none of it mattered. Grey's expression told me everything I needed to know, restored to me all the hope that had been lost. Maybe someone stronger, someone better than me would've held out, would've demanded some proof, more of an apology, a better explanation. But I just didn't care anymore. I wanted him too badly.

Wordlessly I stepped into his arms. The moment I felt them wrap around me, I knew I was exactly where I needed to be. He kissed my hair as I nuzzled my cheek against his hard chest, letting his warmth and his scent envelop me. I could hear his heartbeat through the soft fabric of his suit, and I just shut my eyes and listened to the sound.

"I'm sorry." He spoke softly in my ear.

"I missed you." I whispered. "So much."

"Ahem."

Regretfully, I opened my eyes. My father was standing near us, his arms crossed before his chest with impatience.

"The reception's about to start, young lady." His tone was thick with disapproval, but I just nodded at him. I didn't want to leave the strength and comfort of Grey's arms, for him or anybody.

It was Grey that pulled away from me, clearing his throat uncomfortably. "Hello, sir," he stretched out his hand to my father. "It's nice to finally meet you. I'm Grey Lewis."

"Grey." Gruffly Dad shook his hand. "We really need to get going."

Completely unaffected by my father's obvious displeasure, Grey and I followed him towards the entrance of the hotel and through the grand, marble foyer. His hand held mine, my fingers laced through his. Every now and then I'd just look up at him, cautiously, and smile like I couldn't believe he was there, like he was too good to be true. He'd smirk at me, just like I loved, and squeeze my hand as if he felt the same way. My pulse quickened in my chest; my heart warmed happily, melting away the icy cold grip of hurt and sadness that had held me in such sorrow.

It was with a happy, hopeful smile on my face that we approached the rest of the wedding party. They were gathered in the hallway outside the reception room, and I was completely oblivious to the heated stares they threw my way. I was too thrilled by the very presence of the man beside me to pay them any heed.

"So, that's the great Marcy, is it? The one in the white?" Grey wondered quietly to me as we walked.

"Yeah, how'd you guess?" I smiled. "Pretty gorgeous, huh?" I couldn't keep the sour note of jealousy from leaking into my voice.

To my utter amazement, Grey just shrugged. "I don't know. I guess so. I mean, she's definitely pretty, but she doesn't do it for me." He looked pointedly my way. "I don't think she even compares to some."

I looked up at him, surprised. "You don't mean that."

"The hell I don't." If it hadn't been for his eyes, smiling and sincere as they studied me fondly, I never would have believed him. I found myself beaming at his words, moved by his sentiment, by far the sweetest thing anyone had ever said to me.

"Mackenzie." My mother's sharp voice interrupted my bliss. "Where've you been? We've been waiting for you."

"Sorry." I shrugged. "Mom, this is Grey."

"Nice to meet you, Mrs. Taylor." Grey held out his hand. Mom stared at it a moment, as if it might bite her, and then hesitantly shook his hand.

"Nice to meet you." Her voice sounded like it was anything but. "You'll be joining us then? Come, I'll show you to the table." Her voice was brisk and clipped. "Mackenzie, they're waiting."

"Okay, Mom." I rolled my eyes at her. I flashed Grey an apologetic smile, trying to compensate for the obvious lack of welcome shown by my parents. "I'll see you in there." I promised. Grey nodded and turned to follow my mother, who was already rampaging ahead.

CHAPTER 37

The reception began with the typical embarrassing entrance, as the MC announced, "and now for the first time, Mr. and Mrs. Greg Donovan!" Marcy and Greg strolled into the lavish ballroom. Everyone stood from their chairs and clapped and cheered for the happy couple. We followed in pairs behind them, squeezing past the tables and guests to find our way to the front of the room, where the head table had been set up. We had to be introduced, but then finally, thankfully, were permitted to sit down.

The hall was decorated much the same way as the church had been. Everything dripped with fragrant white flowers and glowed with soft white candlelight. The table linens and chair covers were a brilliant white satin with silver bows wrapped around the backs. Delicate silver cases, in the shape of hearts, held favours for each place setting. The white, crisp napkins were folded into the shape of a flower, sitting prettily upon the clean white and silver china that adorned the round tables. Giant bouquets of white roses and peonies sat in tall, shapely vases as the centerpiece, surrounded by tea lights in crystal holders. It looked extravagant, and elegant, and expensive. I wondered how much my parents had spent. Obviously nothing was too good for their little girl.

I couldn't help but feel for Grey, trapped at a table with my parents who regarded him with nothing but obvious disdain. They weren't even giving him a chance. I'd never thought of my parents as snobby, but it was clear from their actions that they felt Grey beneath them, like he wasn't even worth the fifty-dollar a plate meal, like they resented his very presence. To earn my eternal gratefulness, Aunt Linda leaned over and spoke to him for a while from her table. I smiled at her while my parents frowned with disapproval.

When finally my mom did condescend to talk to Grey, it was with cool indifference, as if she were just trying to prove a point or something. I was sitting close enough to hear and kept my head down over my plate, pushing around the creamed baby potatoes in pretence of eating while I blatantly eavesdropped on their conversation.

"So, what do you do again?" Mom asked, following a polite compliment from Grey regarding the tenderness of the chicken.

"I'm a chef at the Red Wheat. That's where Mackenzie and I met." He explained.

"So you know a little about gourmet cooking, do you?"

"Not exactly." He laughed. "You obviously haven't eaten there before. It's a good restaurant, but it's not gourmet."

"I see."

"I don't think I'll be there too much longer though." Grey admitted.

"Oh?" This caught my dad's interest. "What will you do?"

"Well, I'm hoping that this record deal turns into something … more profitable."

"So, you're going to be a rock star then." Dad's tone was obviously mocking. If Grey was going to get a chance, I had a feeling that was it. I frowned at my baby vegetables, biting my lip.

"I hope so." Grey admitted shamelessly. "We're really pretty good. We're working on our first album now, actually."

"Hmmm." Mom pondered. "But isn't it awfully hard to become a famous musician? What if that doesn't work out?"

"I don't know. I haven't got that far yet."

"You know, Craig Donovan, that's Greg's brother …." Mom motioned to him.

"Wait—Greg's brothers name is Craig?"

"Yes."

Grey laughed in amusement. "Their names rhyme?" I smiled to myself at his observation, a giggle escaping my lips. I had thought the exact same thing.

"He's a solid young man, that Craig." Dad spoke up in his defence. "He's only twenty-years old, and already an up-and-comer at his firm."

"Really? What does he do?" Grey's voice was polite, but completely uninterested.

"He's in finance." My mom burst excitedly. "Very exciting. Everyone's talking about him."

"Yes, he's very successful, for someone so young. Maybe you could talk to him. He might have an opportunity for you, you know, maybe a more … reliable career." Dad offered.

I sat there, listening, remembering the day that Marcy first brought Greg home to meet my parents. They hadn't acted anything like this; they had practically rolled out the red carpet and placed a crown on his head. But now they couldn't treat Grey with even a little common courtesy. Why? Because he wasn't rich like Greg? Because he didn't have a six-figure trust fund waiting in the wings? That sucked. I dropped my fork—giving up the entire eating façade—and looked over at Grey, an open apology written on my face. He was just sitting there, calm and cool and gorgeously handsome like always. I was completely amazed at his total composure.

"Yeah, thanks. I'll remember that." Grey answered my father.

"Something to consider. Nothing wrong with respectable employment."

"No, sir." He agreed.

I couldn't take it anymore. I leaned over the table and caught Grey's eye, then motioned with my head for him to follow me. He smirked and nodded, and I got up from my seat and headed out of the room. It was during the time between the end of the meal and the beginning of the formal program, when the guests were chatting and mingling and getting up to use the washroom. I knew we wouldn't be missed.

He met me just outside the hallway. Giggling, I took his hand and led him out of the banquet hall and through the lavish lobby, my heels clipping on the gleaming polished floors. My eyes lit up when I found just what I was looking for—a vacant, single occupancy washroom just off the foyer.

Grey's face was curious as I pulled him clandestinely into the bathroom, shutting and locking the door behind.

"What are we doing?" He wondered suggestively. I set my purse down on the thick stone counter and rummaged through it.

"This." I held up my vial triumphantly.

His blue eyes lit up in surprise and amusement. He chuckled in amazement. "And why are we doing this?"

I smiled and scooped up the cocaine, rapidly inhaling it. I shut my eyes in relief and then handed the container to him with a shrug. "Because, fuck 'em. That's why."

"Fuck 'em." Grey agreed, sniffing some blow quickly and handing it back to me. I did some more, sucking it back as deeply as I could muster. The happy, buzzing trembles overwhelmed me once again, and I felt normal, like I could finally think straight. I let out a happy, shaky sigh as Grey took some more. It wasn't long before we were both thoroughly, impossibly, giddily stoned.

My heart was pounding, my teeth grinding, and I couldn't keep the smile from my face. I met his eyes and we laughed together at nothing.

"Now that I'm good and wrecked," he wiped at his nose, "your parents should really approve of me." Grey laughed.

"Ugh, trust me. With them, it's better to be stoned." I checked the mirror and wiped the white residue from my nose, then fixed my hair with a trembling hand. "Do I look okay?"

"Better than okay," he smirked, and his blue eyes narrowed lustily as they looked me over. He placed his hands around my waist and with a careful, wicked grin, lifted me up so I was sitting on the bathroom counter. It may have been the blow or the time we'd spent apart, but the warmth of his hands shot heat straight through my veins. I couldn't remember ever wanting Grey as badly as I did at that moment. I pressed my knees around him and grasped his tie, pulling him towards me, slowly, until our lips finally touched.

Sparks flew then. I forgot everything … Marcy … my parents … the wedding … everything but the feel of his lips pressed to mine and the hard strength of his hands on my body. In moments we were breathless, dishevelled, and desperate for each other. I couldn't stop; I didn't want to, everything within me was screaming go, go, go ….

A hard, sharp rap on the door jolted us both out of the moment. Only then did I remember where we were and what we were supposed to be doing. I couldn't believe the sheer lust that had come over us, the depth of the desire that still burned in my veins.

"Yes?" I tried to calm my frantic breathing.

"Mackenzie? Are you in there?" Mom demanded impatiently. I met Grey's eyes in shocked realization. He lifted his eyebrows in amusement.

"Yes." I answered.

"What are you doing? The speeches are about to start."

Holy crap. Had she followed us or something?

"Sorry … I'm not … feeling well," I lied quickly. "I'll be out in a minute."

"Are you okay?"

"Yeah, I just … I need a sec."

"Okay. Hurry up. They're waiting." Irritation was evident in her voice. I waited until I could hear her heels clipping briskly away from the door.

"Shit, Grey, what do we do?" I barely stifled a giggle. "We're so busted."

"I know. Here, you go first." He grinned, pulling the straps of my dress back in place. "I'll wait until you've gone in, and then I'll come later."

"Okay." I agreed to his hasty plan, smoothed my dress and took a breath to calm my frenzied pulse. I wondered if my cheeks were flushing as hotly as they felt. "Do I look high?"

He looked me over and shook his head. "I don't think so. Do I?"

Grey was gorgeous as usual. His eyes were a little glassy, but not noticeably so. I straightened his tie, my touch lingering on his chest. "No." I breathed.

"Go." He smirked, removing my hand. "Before you get in trouble."

"See you in there." I kissed him quickly, grabbed my purse and opened the door. He pulled it shut behind me so no one would see him. I hurried through the lobby and down the hallway into the reception room. I couldn't keep the smile from my face; I had to suppress the urge to giggle the entire time.

Marcy shot me a suspicious glare as I took my seat back at the head table. I ignored her and took a drink of wine to try and cool my blood. Grey came back in after awhile, giving no excuse for his absence as he sat back down at my parents' table. They pointedly ignored him. He winked at me, and I grinned right back.

The MC began the program then. There were speeches, and then more speeches, and then a slideshow. I sat through the entire ordeal, restless and fidgety and high, itching for the night to be over. After the thousandth picture of Greg and Marcy cuddling to the tune of *I Honestly Love You* by Olivia Newton John, the program was finally concluded, but not the reception. Just when I thought that Grey and I were free, that it was all over at last, the MC announced the start of yet another tradition.

It was time for the first dance. Marcy and Greg took their places on the dance floor; somehow she still managed to look as fresh as a daisy after the tiresome, weary day. She glowed with happiness. The newlyweds whirled around the parquet boards as a three-piece orchestra accompanied them with soft, gentle music. After a few moments of this, it was time for the bridal party to join in. This meant I had to dance with Craig.

I bit my lip as he bleared victoriously at me, obviously drunk. He approached me unsteadily, grasping my wrist a little rougher than intended and wrapping it around his back, then taking my other hand in his clammy palm. I stiffened at his touch and deliberately looked at anything but him as we moved about the dance floor.

"I don't know what's wrong with you." Craig spoke finally. His breath smelt like wine. He scoffed and glared in Grey's direction with total repugnance. "Why would you want someone like *him*? He's got nothing."

"Actually, he's got everything I want." I retorted.

"Yeah, he's got looks. Those don't last. I'm talking money."

"I don't care about money."

"You say that now, but, you'll change your mind, someday. By then, it'll be too late. You'll be kicking yourself for missing out on this opportunity."

I shook my head, determined to ignore him. We waltzed closer to my parents' table, where my mother took the opportunity to smile and snap pictures of us.

"Just look at them. Don't they look great together?" She was exclaiming, loud enough to be certain that Grey could hear her. I groaned and shot her a look. It was obvious what she was getting at, but Mom could keep right on dreaming. Craig and I were never going to happen.

"See? Even your mother approves of us." Craig smiled. "I heard them at dinner. They don't like your boyfriend, do they? Not as much as me."

"Like that matters." I rolled my eyes.

"Come on, Mackenzie. You know you could do better." His eyes were bleary, his grin stupid. His hand moved down the bodice of my dress, resting just against the crinoline on the back of my skirt. I moved it back up.

"No, Craig." I sighed. "Just drop it, will you?"

Craig chuckled, grinning at me in amusement. "I know what you're doing."

"You do, do you? And what is that?"

"You are playing hard to get. It surprised me, actually. But it works, okay? It works. I'm officially interested."

"That is not what I'm doing. Trust me."

"Oh yeah?"

"Yeah."

"Then explain this …." He caught me totally off guard. One moment we were the proper distance apart, and the next, his lips were mashed up against mine. A cry of surprise escaped my mouth, but before I could even think to push Craig away, he was already off of me. I staggered back in surprise, watching in stunned amazement as Grey's fist slammed into Craig's face and sent him sprawling backwards across the dance floor.

There was a collective gasp from the reception guests as Craig landed on the ground in an undignified heap of Armani, I think a few people even shrieked at the sight. I couldn't believe my eyes; I couldn't stop the giggle that bubbled from my throat as he struggled to collect himself, his cheek swollen and puffy with the beginnings of a handsome shiner.

Greg stepped forward to avenge his brother, his face taut with anger, but Marcy grasped his arm and held him back with a quick shake of her head. My mother was absolutely livid; her face flushed deep red as she glanced around in apologetic embarrassment at the appalled wedding guests. Dad merely stood, his mouth hung open with shock and dismay that quickly turned to full on outrage. The veins stood out on his forehead as he turned his eyes to my boyfriend.

"Are you okay?" Grey was indifferent to the hushed murmurs of the horrified guests and the heated stares from my humiliated parents. His blue eyes were concerned, edged with residual anger as he turned them to me, his handsome face still tense with aggression.

"Yeah, I'm okay." I couldn't help but smile at him. All eyes were on us, everyone had stopped in their tracks—even the musicians stopped playing to see what would happen next, but I didn't care if they all caught me smiling. I loved that Grey had punched out that arrogant jerk on my behalf. Craig had it coming.

"Mitch, do something." I heard my mother hiss as she glared up at my father expectantly. "Get him out of here!"

Dad's eyes narrowed at Grey as he cleared his throat and pointed his finger menacingly towards the door. "Son, I think it's time you leave." He threatened.

"What? Why?" I stepped between them, indignant. "For stopping that creep—"

"No, Mackenzie." Grey placed his hand on my arm, and his touch was gentle, even though his face was furious. "Don't .... It's okay. I'll go." He shook his head. "I'll see you later."

His warm hand slid down my arm, and then, under the watchful eyes of my parents, he turned to go. The guests made a path for him like he was a pariah. My mom crossed her arms, her eyes flashing triumphantly, and dad shook his head at me in disgust. My eyes glittered angrily as I glared right back at them.

I didn't stop to think, I only knew that I was going with Grey. There was no way I'd stay there—not with them, not after this. I rushed back to my chair to gather my things, and once my mother saw what I was doing, she pounced on me.

"What are you doing? Mackenzie, you are not going with him." She whispered harshly.

"The hell I'm not." I grabbed my jacket off the back of the chair and took my purse from its safe spot on the floor. She stood in front of me as if to block the way, but I stepped easily around her.

"Mackenzie Anne. Stop this, right now!" Mom insisted. Her protests fell on deaf ears. I completely ignored her. I paused only long enough to stop before Marcy, whose arms were crossed in fury, her dark eyes glittering with angry tears—and I was shocked to realize that maybe I'd ruined her wedding after all. I was sorry for it. I really hadn't meant to.

"I'm sorry, Marcy." I didn't have time for anything else. I had to catch Grey before he was gone.

"Just go." She demanded. I knew, without a shadow of a doubt, that I wasn't welcome there anymore. But I didn't care. I turned and fled down the same path Grey had taken, and no one tried to stop me.

I didn't look back.

CHAPTER 38

The wind sailed over us as we raced down the highway on his motorcycle. I clung to Grey, clad in his large black jacket, feeling just like Allison from my favourite movie *Cry-Baby* after Wade Walker picks her up from the charm school. My large crinoline skirt blew haphazardly in the breeze; I had to try and pin it down with my hands as best I could while still maintaining my grip on Grey's muscular waist. He wore only his white dress shirt with the sleeves rolled up and I wondered how he wasn't freezing. We'd been riding for a half an hour solid but there was still plenty of highway to go until we reached our little Podunk town. I snuggled down into his warm jacket and hugged Grey closer.

When I caught up to him back in the lobby at the hotel, his fists were clenched with anger, the tension obvious in his stiff gait as he stalked across the polished floors.

"Grey!" I had called, running to meet him. "Wait."

He half turned to me, his eyes lighting up with surprise, but then shook his head. "I'm really sorry, Mackenzie." He walked on. "But I have to go."

"I know." I panted, keeping pace with him. "I'm coming with you."

That stopped him in his tracks. He whirled to face me. "What?"

"I said I'm coming with you."

"But … the wedding … your family … they're going to be pissed at you."

"I don't care."

Grey had stared at me a moment, hesitating. For a brief moment the scowl set upon his lips was replaced by the smirk I loved so much.

He shrugged out of his jacket and handed it to me, the internal debate resolved.

"Then you're going to need this." He stated, grasping my hand. "Come on."

Now I wrapped my arms tightly around his waist; my fingers could feel the taut, warm muscle of his abdomen beneath his thin white shirt. I felt so alive at that moment, clinging to Grey's hard form, escaping from those that would come between us to ride off into the sunset. It was a warm summer night; the sun had just sunk below the horizon, bathing the sky in deep blues and purple, vibrant orange and pinks. I was exactly where I wanted to be at that moment, I would go wherever he would drive me, I'd be happy so long as we were together.

There was something in the air. Something thrilling, I could feel it. Like the fire from our earlier stolen moments had been banked, and now the wind was feeding the flames, igniting them to burn hotter and hotter as we inched nearer to his empty house. The air was charged almost, thick with anticipation, like watching a lightning storm approach from the distance. I wondered if Grey could feel it too, the current of electricity pulsing between us. He was pushing the motorcycle unnecessarily fast, as if trying to cool the unbearable heat with the rushing, freezing wind. I was calm but breathless, excited—my racing pulse had nothing to do with the exhilaration of the wind in my face as its fingers twisted through my hair and breezed over my skin until my very nerves stood on end, and had everything to do with Grey.

When at long last we finally pulled up before his house, it was totally dark outside. Anticipation tingled through me and I bit my lip in frenzied excitement, climbing slowly off the bike, my heart thrumming in my chest.

"You're shaking." Grey noticed as he grasped my hand.

I just shook my head, unable to speak. I wasn't trembling from the cold. If anything, I felt overheated from his proximity as we walked together towards the front door. It was cool and stuffy and smelt of stale cigarette smoke inside the darkened house. Grey went ahead of me, flipping on the lights and opening some windows as I stepped out of my ballerina high heels and shrugged out of his coat. The night air felt cool against my heated, dewy skin, but brought no relief to the glowing warmth within me.

I couldn't take it any longer. Grey stood with his back to me, his white shirt sleeves rolled up against the hard, dark muscles of his arm, completely sexy and totally irresistible even at that angle. He took some bottles of beer from the fridge and set them on the counter to open.

"There's not much for food here. Are you hungry?" He asked casually.

"No." Not for food, anyway. I gulped and took a shaky breath, biting my lip.

"Hey," Grey smirked, "you okay? You look kinda flushed."

"No." My voice was barely audible. Then, with some nerve I didn't know existed, I kept his eyes locked in my gaze, and with a trembling hand I slowly undid the zipper on the back of my dress. Grey watched me, stunned, his blue eyes burning as the gown fell to my feet—crinoline, sequins and all. I saw his fists clench, his jaw tense. I stood before him in nothing but my black strapless bra and lace underwear, letting him take me in; his gaze languid, savouring. Then, with one last brazen shred of daring, I reached up and pulled the pins from my hair until the black curls were tumbling wild and free, cascading around my shoulders.

"Mackenzie …." His voice was low, throaty and uneven. He seemed to be hesitating, but even then, he couldn't rip his eyes away. Grey stared at me in awe, his fists clenching tighter as if to keep from reaching for me. "… Are you … sure?"

"Yes." I declared breathlessly. "Yes, Grey … please …."

In a matter of moments I was in his strong, warm arms, his lips furious—feverish against mine as he crushed me to him. I kissed him back with just as much fervour, my hands in his hair; cupping his face, pulling open the buttons of his shirt … I couldn't get enough of him. I couldn't be close enough to him. My heart sailed with happiness; my lips smiled as I kissed him everywhere that I could reach.

"I love you, Grey, I want you …," I whispered into his ear. I wrapped my legs around his waist as he lifted me up against him, and staggering with passion, he carried me down the hallway and into his bedroom.

I was no longer a virgin. The thought made me smile, like now I was part of some exclusive, special club, like Grey and I had this great secret to share. I had never imagined being so intimate with someone, so totally … naked in every sense of the word. I loved it. It was everything I'd ever wanted, and more. Thrilling, pleasing … just … satisfying. I sighed contentedly and blew the smoke from my mouth, thankful I'd waited all those years and finally done it with someone I actually loved.

I'd felt so safe the entire time, Grey made sure I felt that way. Even in the heat of the moment, in the throes of utter lust and passion he'd held back, forcing himself to stop until he knew for sure that this was what I wanted. His eyes had been so brilliantly blue, so full of care and concern for me when he asked that I would've said yes anyway, even if I hadn't been one-hundred percent certain.

He was relaxed now, his face was peaceful, satisfied as he lay back against his bent arms and smoked. I cuddled up against his chest, my arm thrown over him, my fingers trailing lightly down his taut skin. It was dark in his room; his bedside lamp cast dim light upon us and threw long shadows across the band posters covering the walls. The moon was almost full; it shone brightly in the summer night sky, glowing in through the uncovered window to rest gently upon our bare skin.

"When do you have to go back to the city?" My voice was faint; I was already saddened by just the thought of his departure. Now that we'd started exploring these unchartered waters, it seemed a total shame to drop anchor for the next few weeks. I was eager to discover the unknown, impatient to continue the adventure. Like everything I'd every experienced with Grey, once I got a taste, I only wanted more.

"My flight leaves Monday morning, early. It was the first I could get …. The guys will probably be pissed at me for not being back sooner."

"Monday?" I was elated by the news. "Really? That's awesome." That meant I got Grey to myself for another whole day. I shivered excitedly and smiled. "I'm sorry about the guys, though. Were they mad that you left?"

"Yeah. Well … more like … they didn't understand it." Grey chuckled wryly. "I didn't understand it either, really."

"Didn't understand what?" I turned my head to look up at his face.

"Well …," he avoided my gaze, like he always did when struggling for words. "I mean … there I was … in the studio, doing the only thing I've ever wanted to do … and I couldn't stop thinking … about you."

"About me?" I couldn't believe it.

"Yes. You." He cleared his throat. I nestled back against his hard chest.

"Then … why didn't you call?" I wondered. It just didn't make any sense to me. "I wanted to hear from you so badly."

"I know …." He rubbed my arm. "I'm sorry. It was stupid. I guess I just … I'm not used to … needing people, you know? I've always just kind of been on my own; I've never really needed anyone else. But then, when

I was gone … when I realized how badly I missed you … it scared me. I tried to deny it; I didn't want to admit how badly I … need you. But I do." He stroked his hand through my hair, sending little shivers through me. I listened intently. "I thought it would get easier, but it didn't. I just had to accept it. And once I did, I knew I had to see you. I couldn't really take it anymore. I wanted to call you then, but I wanted to see you more, and I knew the moment I heard your voice, I'd give it all away. It was hard, but I wanted you to be surprised."

I smiled, touched by his admission. I loved that he needed me just as badly as I needed him, the thought made me happy. "Well, I was surprised. You have no idea."

"Good." Grey smirked. His lips spread into a grin, and then he chuckled. "But not as surprised as Craig Donovan was."

"No." I laughed with him, remembering the way Craig had flailed across the dance floor, picturing the look of total shock on his face when Grey punched him.

"I don't know, maybe it was stupid of me. But it felt really, really good to hit that guy." Grey mused. "Just listening to your parents rant and rave about him all night, I mean, it's obvious that they'd prefer you with someone like him." Apparently Grey hadn't been as impervious to their little comments as I thought. "And then seeing him kiss you … I just … I guess I lost it." His fists clenched unconsciously at the memory.

"I'm glad you did. He deserved it." I sighed. "And, Grey … I'm sorry about my parents. I had no idea they'd be so … horrible."

Grey shrugged. "Whatever, it's fine. I didn't expect them to welcome me with open arms or anything."

"Why not?" I frowned. "You deserve that much."

"Because Mackenzie," Grey smirked at me again, like I was missing something obvious. "Look at me. I've got nothing. I'm a twenty-one year old cook; I've got no house, no education … nothing but my guitar and some lyrics and this crazy hope of making it big. I'm not exactly the guy parents dream about for their daughter."

"But that's not fair." My frown deepened. "To just judge the outside stuff, the stuff that doesn't even matter … it's so stupid. If they gave you an actual chance and really got to know you, I know they'd love you … just as much as I do."

"I doubt that." He shook his head. "You're blind, Mackenzie. I mean, you think I'm this amazing guy, but I'm really not. I'm a loser, a total screw-up. Everyone can see it but you."

"Grey," I was appalled. "You are not a loser. I will never forgive them for making you feel that way."

"Everyone in that room was thinking the exact same thing when they saw us together. Even I've been thinking it." He looked down at me then, his smirk fading seriously. "You could do better, you know."

"Better?" I repeated, as if trying to make sense of the word. "How could I do better?" I sat up slightly so he could see the sincerity in my expression. "Who else would leave the studio … their dream … just to be with me for a weekend? You … you take care of me; tonight you gave me your coat and went without, just so I wouldn't get cold. And you cared enough to wait for sex until I was really, truly ready. Who else would do that?" My voice was soft, earnest. "Grey, trust me, there is no one better for me than you."

His arms tightened around me, his blue eyes were soft and tender as he looked down into my face. "I'll try. I'll try to be the best for you." He promised. "It's hard though … sometimes … I mean, you are so trusting, and you look at me with such … pride, like I'm this dream come true or something. I know it's only a matter of time before I do screw up, before I do something to really hurt you … and I can't … I can't bear the thought. You think too highly of me, and I'm only going to disappoint you."

I didn't know what to say. I couldn't picture any situation that would make me love Grey any less. Even if he had cheated on me, I would be hurt, yes; I'd be heartbroken, yes; but I wouldn't love him any less. I didn't know how to convince him that he could never disappoint me, no matter what, that I would love him no matter what. Silently I stroked my fingers slowly down his chest.

He sighed. "Maybe I don't have to worry. One day you're going to figure out how beautiful you are, and then I'll be out of the picture for good." Grey shrugged. "It'll be better that way. I'm too selfish to let you go."

I wanted to argue with him, I sat up to protest, but he stopped me with a shake of his head. A smirk bent his lips as he looked at me, and his blue eyes began to gleam wickedly.

"Until then …," he pulled me up to him, his strong arms wrapping around me and holding me close. "I'm going to enjoy every minute."

My smile was glorious as he kissed me.

CHAPTER 39

We awoke the next morning wrapped up in each other and stayed that way for the remainder of the day. The rest of the house was dark and quiet and empty, but in Grey's room the lights were on, the music blaring, a party taking place on his bed. We didn't leave it for anything but to answer the door for food delivery. We smoked and got high and did coke and laughed and talked and kissed and made love between the rumpled sheets. It was going down in history as one of the happiest days of my life.

I wore his white button-down shirt, I'd always seen women do it in the movies and now I could see the attraction. It smelt delicious and I loved having something he wore so close to my own skin. Grey lounged in just his boxers, allowing my eyes to feast on his perfect muscular body as we lazed around.

We talked about everything. Simple things like our favourite color and food, TV shows and movies and bands … every new tidbit of information we learned seemed more interesting than the last. Hours went by, our tongues fuelled by cocaine, driven by sheer curiosity and utter fascination. I couldn't get enough of him, I couldn't learn enough—I hung on his every word, asking question after question.

He told me things about his childhood that I hadn't known before. I learned a little about the friends he'd lost touch with and the crazy BMX jumps they used to make, how he broke the same arm on three separate occasions taking those very same jumps. He was an only child and they had lived in the poorer end of the city. He got a paper route and saved up the money he made to purchase his very own Yamaha acoustic guitar from the Sears magazine when he was only seven.

"So, what about your parents?" I wondered carefully. He always failed to mention them; their names hadn't come up once in all his tales, so I could tell it was a sensitive subject. "What do they do?"

I was sitting cross-legged on the bed, leaning up against the wall, Grey's white shirt draped over my petite frame as he lay on his side, facing me, his legs tangled up in the blankets. He avoided my gaze a moment, taking a drag of his cigarette and blowing the smoke slowly from his mouth.

"I don't know where my parents are." He admitted reluctantly, with a shrug.

"Not at all?" My dark eyes were wide with wonder.

"No. I've never known my dad; I don't think he was ever around. My mom left when I was young. I haven't heard from her since."

I bit my lip in empathy, surprised by this new information. "Where did you go … when she left?"

"I stayed with my Grandma," Grey sighed heavily, like the topic weighed on him. "She was fifty-eight when she took me in, but a far better mother than my mom ever was, from what I can remember."

"Is your grandma still in the city?" I smiled in an effort to lighten the conversation.

"No." He grimaced. "She died when I was sixteen."

"Oh." I didn't know what to say. "I'm so sorry, Grey. That's awful."

Grey shrugged again. "I didn't have any other family to live with, so I bounced around the system for awhile. I never stayed in a foster home for more than a few months. I dropped out of high school about the same time, and as soon as I was old enough I moved out here with Alex."

"But, you didn't have anyone, at all?" I was horrified by the thought. My family sucked most of the time, but at least I knew they were there. If I did happen to lose my mom and dad, there was always an Auntie Linda and an Uncle Paul, and an Uncle Pat, and a Marcy … I always knew I'd be taken care of by someone. Grey had been so young when he lost his only family, he must have felt so … utterly scared, and alone. My heart broke for him at the thought, stirred by compassion.

"I did okay. It wasn't that bad." His coolness almost had me convinced. If I didn't know him as well as I did, I would've missed the slight sadness in his eyes, the tightness in his voice. He was more affected by the past than he let on, but I was willing to let the issue go, for now. He'd already told me so much, and I could tell it'd been hard for him to do so.

I smiled shrewdly and looked for a subject change. "So … what are all those?" I asked then, pointing randomly towards the stacks of crumpled loose-leaf piled and littered upon the desk in the corner of the room. Grey looked up at me in surprise, relieved by the sudden change in topic.

"Paper." Grey smirked, and I could see him relaxing. "No. It's music."

"Music?"

"Yes. Music." He sighed fondly at me. "Some lyrics, some melody lines, just stuff I've written as it comes to me."

"You wrote all that?" I was amazed. "Can I read them?"

"Uhhhh …," Grey hesitated, "… I don't know."

"Why not? I won't laugh, I promise."

"I know you won't, but …." He ran a hand through his messy dark hair. "See, I find it hard to … express … myself sometimes. Maybe you've noticed." He chuckled. I nodded; I knew exactly what he was talking about. "But, it's different with music." He explained. "It's like the one place that I can just … be free, you know? I write anything that comes to my head. And some of it's … pretty embarrassing."

"Now I want to read them even more." I pouted.

"Maybe another time, okay?" It was his turn to change the subject. "So, speaking of music … what's your favourite song, Mackenzie?"

I relented begrudgingly. "Like … ever in the world?"

"Yeah."

"Um …." I giggled. "My all time favourite song is probably … *Name*, by the Goo Goo Dolls." I shrugged sheepishly.

Grey just grinned at me a moment. "You're serious?" His smile widened.

"Yes!" I laughed in defence. "And there is nothing wrong with that song. It's beautiful."

"Of all the songs in the world, your favourite is *Name,* by the Goo Goo Dolls."

"Yes."

"I don't believe it." Grey chuckled, and then he picked up his acoustic guitar. I watched in disbelief as moments later, the sweet, haunting chords of my favourite song were floating in the air, his fingers deftly strumming the notes. He sang to me with his beautiful voice.

"And even though the moment passed me by
I still can't turn away
'Cause all the dreams you never thought you'd lose
Got tossed along the way.
Letters that you never meant to send
Get lost or thrown away.

And now we're grown up orphans that never knew their names
We don't belong to no one that's a shame.
But if you could hide beside me, maybe for a while
And I won't tell no one you're name …,
And I won't tell 'em your name …."

I blinked back sudden, happy tears as Grey sang the song, his voice soft and raspy, touching my very heart. His blue eyes smiled at me as he played, seeming to enjoy my reaction to his tune. I couldn't even help myself … he just … moved me.

"This is one of the first songs I ever learned." He explained over the music.

"You play so beautifully." I shook my head in admiration. I had never met anyone so talented in all my life. His dreams of making it big weren't crazy; they were inevitable. Grey finished the song, strumming out the last note so that it rang in the air.

"I love you." It was nearly bursting out of me; I just had to say it.

"What can I say?" he smirked. "The Goo Goo Dolls, they do it every time."

I didn't want to sleep that night. I knew we had only a few precious hours left before he had to leave, and I didn't want to waste them with unconsciousness. Grey chuckled at me, cuddled up together beneath the blankets, his lips to my ear.

"Go to sleep, Mackenzie." He nuzzled, his voice low and drowsy.

"I can't … sleep …." My eyelids were so heavy; I struggled to keep them open. "It's like the Aerosmith song … I don't want to close … my eyes … 'cause I don't … want to … miss a thing …."

When I awoke, it was dark outside but the moon was bright, flooding his bedroom with silvery light filtering through the large window beside the bed. It took me a moment before I realized I was all alone. I stretched my arm out for Grey, but my hand touched empty mattress. My eyes flew open and I sat up, instantly panicked that he had left for the airport already, that I had missed his goodbye and Grey was gone.

"Hey." His voice calmed me. I turned over and found him sitting in a chair beside the bed. He was dressed and ready to go, but his acoustic guitar sat on his lap. I smiled, bemused, and sat up in the sheets. His gorgeous face was barely visible in the moonlight, but I could see that he was smiling at me.

"I've gotta go, but I just … I wanted to play you something first."

I smiled my answer, and waited.

He started strumming the guitar then, and the rhythm was gentle—not quite a ballad, but not upbeat either. After the sweet, softly picked intro, Grey began to sing.

"Sitting here in the dark, Mackenzie's next to me.
She's lying in the moonlight shining silver in the sheets.
And though it pains me so, it's time for me to go.
I've got to leave Mackenzie lying all alone."

The chords changed, the strumming got stronger as he entered the chorus.

"Mackenzie, I hope you miss me
When I'm gone, when I'm gone.
I gotta go now, but you need to know how
Much you're loved, how much you're loved …."

His voice was beautiful, silky and rough. I sat on the bed, watching and listening to him in utter disbelief. Grey had written me a song, and that would've been enough to cause the happy tears that sprang to my eyes, even if he hadn't said he loved me. Those affectionate words rang in my head and echoed in my heart, swollen with happiness. I smiled at him through my tears.

"That's all I have so far." He shrugged, and his smile was bashful.

"That was the most beautiful …." I shook my head, at a loss for words. I gave up speaking and crawled over the bed to him. I placed my hands gently on his face, looking up into his eyes shining silvery blue in the moonlight. Beautiful. "I will miss you, so much. Every minute." I whispered. I moved my lips up to his. "I love you."

He wrapped his arms around me, tight and warm, pulling me close. And his guitar, unheeded, slid to the floor with a noisy lurch.

CHAPTER 40

Grey was gone again. The days resumed themselves much the same as they had before—Charlie and I got as high as we could, went to work, came home, got high, and then went to bed to start it all over again the next morning. The only difference was now I took it much easier, I didn't go nearly as hard, and I didn't go out anymore. Grey called me every day. Sometimes he was busy and would just say hi, sometimes he'd have time and we'd spend nearly all night talking on the phone together. It wasn't a perfect scenario, but it was the best it could be, given the circumstances.

The cocaine helped the time pass, but even that wasn't as rewarding as it used to be. I still loved it, it still felt amazing, but I noticed I had to do more and more of the drug to get as high as I once did. Also the buzz wasn't lasting near as long. All of my tips now went towards my drug habit so I could chase down the high I was craving, but it just wasn't as … satisfying as it used to be.

Before I knew it, the month of August was passing by, the summer heat waning as the days ticked nearer to the end. The leaves on the trees were slowly starting to turn colors, and there was a bite to the wind that one could only associate with the coming of fall. In the blink of an eye, it seemed, the summer had passed, but it had been everything I'd hoped for. Memorable, amazing, fun, exciting and new. I looked forward to September, not only did it mean that Grey would be back, but I would be celebrating my eighteenth birthday in only a matter of weeks. It was so exciting; I was going to party my ass off, I couldn't wait.

I realized then, when thinking of my birthday, that a day had come and gone without me even noticing it. It was strange to me, since for the last two some odd years I had set this day as a pivotal landmark in the journey of my life, and my … I should say our … entire future had been centered on it.

I'd missed Riley's birthday.

It had been a big deal for us, it meant that he'd be able to score us booze and cigarettes whenever we wanted … really, nothing is more depressing that not being of age. Nothing is more humbling that begging anybody older than eighteen, mostly strangers, to boot smokes for you. I'd really hit the jackpot with all my older friends now, it was no problem to get hooked up with anything I wanted, but at the time, back then, Riley turning eighteen was a huge climb up the ladder of our social lives.

I hadn't really thought about Riley since the night his voice had abruptly entered my mind. Sometimes it was inevitable, if we were driving past his house or if I saw something that reminded me of him, his face would flash before my eyes. But I wouldn't let myself dwell on him; I'd push the image away, ignoring it as best I could. Now, carefully, I allowed myself a brief instant to wonder what Riley was doing, who he was doing it with, if he were really happy, and if he'd found what he'd been looking for.

I wondered if he ever thought of me. Or if he'd forgotten all about me.

The sadness bubbled up in me again, like Riley had just left, the pain fresh and raw. I remembered then why I was forbidden to think about him. I couldn't let my guard down, even a little bit, or I'd be crippled by the gnawing ache. I missed him. As much as I wanted to deny it, as badly as I wanted those feelings to go away, to just disappear, I missed Riley with all of my being. And there was nothing I could do but push it away, bury it down deep, and pretend it didn't exist.

Just like I was doing with my parents. I hadn't seen or spoken to them since Marcy's wedding. I wouldn't even dream of heading over there for Sunday supper, though I wasn't sure the invitation still stood. I had a feeling I wasn't exactly welcome over there anymore, at least, not for a while. Mom had left a message on my phone about picking up the stuff I'd left at the hotel, but remembering the furious looks on the faces of my family members when I left the wedding, I figured I'd just leave it for now. I wasn't in the mood for a lecture, but knew I had one coming.

It was nice to be free of them. About this time last year they'd been bugging me about school supplies and class registrations and college applications. As happy as I was that they were off my back now, it felt strange not to be preparing for the start of school. The first few days back had always been a bit exciting, seeing everyone you missed over the summer, catching up with them, showing off how much weight you'd lost and how much you'd matured in the few months spent apart. That feeling of excitement was still in the air, I could sense it—I think it had something to do with the changing of the seasons. But it was all the more exciting to me knowing I didn't have to go back.

Somehow—I don't know, a miracle from heaven maybe—I had actually graduated high school. My real diploma came in the mail one day, and my transcripts showed that I had passed every class, though just barely. I hung the paper happily on the fridge, my ticket to freedom, the approval I needed to keep enjoying my life just the way it was.

And it was awesome. I loved being on my own, doing my own thing, taking care of myself. I loved my new friends and my boyfriend and partying with them and just living for a good time. I was young, and invincible, and there wasn't anything I was going to miss out on. The summer may've been gone, but the rest of my life stretched on before me, limitless in its potential, budding with possibilities.

I had only to seize them, to make them happen.

CHAPTER 41

My birthday was in less than a week. I was sorting through the mail, looking for the card that my Grandma sent me every year. I knew there'd be a twenty-five dollar check inside, which I could put to good use, right up my nose. I found the large, square envelope covered in shaky, light cursive and held it up triumphantly. Happy birthday to me. I ripped open the envelope and briefly scanned the rhyming poem inside the card. My Grandma continued to pick out birthday cards meant for little girls, covered with balloons and puppies and dolls, but I didn't mind. I set the card on the counter, displaying it proudly, and pocketed the check from inside.

Then I spotted another envelope addressed to me, one I didn't recognize at all. It was thick and plain white. Curiously I ripped it open.

Inside there was a narrow blue folder covered in pictures and a single piece of folded paper. I opened up the sheet, instantly recognizing Grey's inky scrawl spread across the page. Hastily I read his written words.

Hey, happy birthday. I know it's early, but I wanted to give you your present now. Your flight leaves Friday at 4:00PM and I'll be there to pick you up. You'd better be ready for the best weekend of your life. See you soon.

Love, Grey.

I read and reread the letter over and over again, my lips curving into a smile. Grey and the guys were still at the studio, they'd hoped to be done already, but hit a snag when some of the songs were erased or something. Last time we spoke, he had broken the news that they wouldn't be back in time for my birthday. I was disappointed—it was hard not to be, but I tried not to let it bother me. Even though it wouldn't be the same, we could celebrate whenever he got back.

Apparently, that hadn't been good enough for him. I nearly squealed with excitement as I pored over the ticket he'd given me, memorizing my flight times and gate numbers. This was by far the best birthday present I had ever received. I couldn't wait to call him, to say thank you.

But Charlie came into the kitchen then, still in her pyjamas, obviously hung over from the night before. I smiled at her cautiously. Things had been tense between us lately. I think she secretly hated that Grey and I had reconciled—that he'd been out to see me, that he called me everyday. The moment she'd heard about the weekend we'd spent together and the song he wrote for me, her entire attitude towards me changed, like she resented me now or something. I didn't go to the clubs with her anymore, I really didn't want to, I was content enough to stay at home and do some coke and wait for Grey to call. But Charlie went out every night after work and got super wasted, and sometimes she didn't even come home. I was worried about her, but every time I asked what or how she was doing, I almost got my head bit off.

"Hey, how you doing?" I wondered politely, causally. Charlie glared at me; her blue eyes glazed beneath her heavy lids, and opened up the refrigerator. I tried not to mind her resentment towards me, even though I really didn't deserve it. For the most part, I just tiptoed around her and tried to be understanding and patient. The drugs helped.

"Where'd you go last night?" I set her pile of mail on the counter next to her. She drank some orange juice straight from the container and then wiped her lips on the sleeve of her housecoat.

"Out." She replied. She briefly glanced at her mail and took another swig.

"Was it fun?"

"Loads."

"Cool."

That seemed like the extent of our conversation, but it was actually an improvement. We stood in silence for a moment as I opened the rest of my mail, mostly bills. They were the one downside to living on my own.

"Oh, how sweet," Charlie's voice was sarcastic as she picked up the birthday card I'd gotten from my Grandma. "Does this mean you're going to come out with me this weekend? To celebrate your eighteenth?" She seemed to brighten at the thought.

"Um … no," I avoided her hopeful gaze. "I'm sorry, I can't. Uh … Grey sent me a plane ticket; so I'm going to fly up there for the weekend." I braced myself for her reaction; I knew it wasn't going to be pretty. I didn't want to lie to her though.

Her face fell, her blue eyes narrowing at me. "Oh."

"But … you could come with me? I'm sure between the two of us, we can afford another ticket."

Charlie chuckled darkly. "Thanks for the pity invite, Mac. I'd love to come and be your third wheel for the weekend." She scoffed. "Please. I'm not that pathetic."

"I don't think you're pathetic at all."

"Whatever. I can't come anyway, I've got plans."

"Charlie, come on. You don't have plans. Come with me. I don't like to think of you sitting here alone, all by yourself for the whole weekend."

"You worry about me?" She raised an eyebrow, like she didn't believe it.

"Yes, I do." I admitted.

Charlie scoffed. "Yeah, right. Do me a favour, Mac. Cut the bullshit, and just worry about yourself." She put the juice back in the fridge and slammed the door shut. The noise made me jump. "Besides, I'm not going to be alone." She smiled at me, wickedly, and then stalked out of the kitchen.

I wanted to ask her what she meant. I wanted to beg her not to do anything stupid. But she slammed her bedroom door on my face, just like she had done in our friendship, effectively keeping me out of it.

CHAPTER 42

"Can I have a rye and Coke please?" The man next to me requested. I watched as the flight attendant gave him a little bottle of Crown Royal and a Coca Cola. Excitement surged in my stomach. In less than twenty-four hours, I would legally be able to do the same thing.

I sighed and leaned back against my seat. The plane jostled and my stomach lurched with it. I had never flown before and I wasn't used to the sudden bumping and dropping of the aircraft, which I found especially nerve-racking at twenty some odd thousand feet in the air. No one else seemed concerned though, so I tried to just relax and enjoy. It was hard to sit still since I was nearly bursting with excitement. I fidgeted, crossing and re-crossing my legs, pulling out my book and putting it away, sighing and staring out the window at the black nothingness outside. I'm sure I was driving the gentleman beside me crazy, but I couldn't help it. Every minute that passed brought me closer to Grey and my fantastic birthday weekend. My very stomach was tingling.

It wasn't long before the landing gear was skidding across the pavement, the plane decelerating so noisily I could barely hear the pilot announcing the current time and temperature. I had made it. Grey was only minutes away. Waiting for the seats to clear ahead of me was almost torture, I bit my lip with impatience as the other passengers took their sweet-ass time collecting their luggage and moseying off down the aisle. Once in the jet way I motored past them and down the hallway.

I took a few precious seconds to find a washroom and give myself a quick once-over. I wasn't as put together as I would've liked since I didn't dare ask Charlie for help, but I had picked some things up from her. My hair was up in a messy, punky ponytail; my eye make-up dark and smoky.

I was wearing jeans and heels and a tight black turtleneck for the cooler weather, it was a classy outfit. I fixed my make-up where it had smudged and sprayed just a touch more perfume on, then reapplied my lip-gloss. I looked good, grown up, like the adult I was going to be tomorrow. I grinned on my way out the door.

My heart was pounding excitedly in my chest as I turned the corner at the arrivals gate, searching the terminal for Grey. I spotted him easily; he was even more gorgeous than the last time I saw him. Grey smirked as I approached, his blue eyes taking me in, looking me over with blatant admiration. His dark, messy hair was beneath a hat, he was dressed warmly in a snowboarding jacket and dark blue jeans, and he looked so good. I didn't want to do the whole embarrassing run-up-to-him-scene, but I couldn't help myself. He was so close. I couldn't wait even the time it would take to approach all cool and casually.

I squealed with pent-up excitement and leapt into his arms, and he chuckled, hugging me to him. I snuggled up against his hard chest and breathed deep his delicious smell, a glorious smile on my face. He'd been gone for weeks, but already it felt like we'd never been apart, like we were picking up right where we left off.

"I'm so happy to see you." I exclaimed.

"Happy Birthday." Grey smiled and kissed me. "Did you have a good flight?"

"I guess so. I've never flown before so I have nothing to compare it too."

"You've never flown before?" He laughed and took my bag, slinging it over his shoulder, and then grasped my hand tightly in his. "How did Little Miss Rich Girl make it to eighteen without flying before?"

I slapped him playfully for the Rich Girl comment as he led me towards the exit. "I don't know. My parents were always too busy working and studying and shit to take us anywhere." I explained.

"Ahh," he nodded and held the door open for me. We stepped out into the night. It was cooler outside, but not cold. The wind was brisk, cooling my flushed cheeks as we walked to the rental car—a sleek black Grand Prix that was parked alongside the curb.

"Nice car," I admired, getting into the passenger seat. Grey threw my bag in the trunk and then climbed in behind the wheel.

"Yeah, we're pretty much high-rollers now," he shrugged. We laughed together for a moment, and then he turned to me, and his blue eyes were warm as he studied my face.

"Now that we're alone," he smirked wickedly, "I should welcome you properly."

I giggled as he leaned across the seat, his hand reaching up to cradle my cheek as he gently kissed my lips. He tasted so good, I had almost forgotten how good. I wrapped my arms around his neck and pulled him closer; it wasn't long before my blood became heated, impassioned by his touch. He kissed me deeper, and the warmth of his hands sank through my clothes until I wished again that I weren't wearing anything at all.

Grey seemed to share the sentiment. Regretfully he broke away from me, but his breathing was shallow, his eyes narrowed lustily. He sat up and started the engine.

"We should go."

"Where are we going?" I wondered shakily, trying to catch my breath.

"You and I," he smirked at me as he pulled into traffic, "are going back to my hotel room."

Heat washed through me, anticipation, excitement. "Yes, we are." I smiled.

Grey drove the car much like his bicycle—revving the engine, switching lanes, tearing through the city streets. I was thankful for his frenzied driving. I couldn't wait to be alone with him; it'd been way too long.

He put on a Rage against the Machine CD and the music came blaring through the speakers, loud and rowdy. I lit a smoke and sat back, letting the music rev me up, getting me in the mood to party, in the mood to go wild. I couldn't wait.

"So, where are we going tomorrow night?" I wondered, yelling to be heard.

"Uh, there's this club we like not far from the hotel," Grey yelled back, "everyone's going to meet us there," he laughed, "and I hope you're in the mood to get fucked up."

"Why's that?" I smiled.

"Well, I may have … talked you up a little. All the guys from the studio want to meet you … I kind of bragged about how much you can drink. They really want to prove me wrong. You may be in for some trouble."

"I can handle it," I declared confidently.

"I don't know. I think its gong to be crazy." Grey laughed again.

"Don't worry baby," I smiled and blew out my smoke, "I'll make you proud."

He grinned at me. "I know you will."

We pulled up at the hotel not long afterwards. It wasn't a Best Western or any other moderately priced hotel like the kind I'd imagined. This was a swimming pool, penthouse suite kind of hotel. I glanced around in surprise, waiting as Grey hurriedly grabbed my bag from the trunk and tossed a Valet his car keys.

"This way." He took my hand again and led me into the lobby. The girls at the reception desk greeted him warmly—maybe a little too warmly—and they threw me a glare as we passed by. I wanted to stick my tongue out at them, but instead I wrapped my arm around Grey's waist as we walked through the foyer, tucking my hand into his back pocket. I hoped that would get my point across. We got into the elevator, alone, and Grey pressed floor twenty-three. Slowly we lurched upwards.

"Those girls totally want you." I pointed out.

"Do they?" He shrugged innocently. "I hadn't noticed."

"Yeah, right." I rolled my eyes. "Come on, I'm sure girls have been throwing themselves at you this whole time." I tried not to think of the distinctly female voice I'd heard over the phone that once. "You can't tell me you don't notice."

Grey just shrugged again, but his eyes were gleaming mischievously.

"Are you ever tempted? Even a little bit?"

He looked down at me, a smirk on his lips, and shook his head. "No."

"Why not?"

"Because. None of them are you."

I smiled bashfully at his answer. The elevator opened onto our floor with a quiet ding, and Grey took my hand in his and squeezed it. I followed him happily down the hallway, pausing as he unlocked the door to his room and then ushered me inside. It was bigger than average, not quite a suite, with two queen-sized beds and a little living area and kitchenette all done in the typical hotel neutrals. The bathroom held both a shower and a Jacuzzi tub. As Grey set my bag down and took his coat off, I looked around, opening the blinds and staring out at the city lights below us, twinkling prettily against the inky night sky.

I could see Grey in the reflection of the window. He strode up behind me, and smirked, wrapping his arms around my waist and pulling me tightly against him. The room became charged, almost buzzing with the instant electricity that flowed between us, electricity neither one of us could resist. I arched against him as he bent and kissed my neck.

In moments we were wrapped around each other, frenzied and frantic, and it was all I could do to keep from ruining his clothes, I couldn't rip them off fast enough. He pushed me back against the bed, pressing me against it, crushing me to him. We flung the rest of our clothes off, quickly, roughly, until there was nothing left between us but skin. My heart sang in my chest the entire time, this was all still so new to me, but it felt so right there was no denying how good it was.

No denying how good we were, together.

CHAPTER 43

The moment I awoke the next morning, my eyes flew open and a wide, ecstatic smile spread across my face. It was my birthday. I was eighteen! I'd been looking forward to this day for years and now it was finally here. Legally, I was an adult. There was no bar that could deny me, no liquor store off limits, no cigarettes that ever had to be booted again. I was finally eighteen!

I turned over and wrapped my arm around Grey's slumbering form, pressing kisses along his shoulder and his neck. I was excited and eager to share my happiness with him, ready to start what was sure to be one of the best days of my life.

"Good morning," I whispered in his ear. Even my voice was smiling. Grey groaned into the pillow, trying to ignore me, but the corner of his mouth lifted in amusement. I knew he probably wasn't used to such exuberance first thing in the morning, but I couldn't help myself. I was too excited to just let him sleep.

"Grey," I gave him a little shake. "Grey, wake up."

His blue eyes were bleary as he slowly blinked them open, and he looked up at me with affectionate tolerance. "… Why? Is the building on fire?"

"No." I shook my head.

"Is Zakk Wylde on the phone for me?"

"Uh … no." Who the hell was Zakk Wylde anyway?

"Then why do I have to get up? There's nothing the least bit exciting going on today." He resisted, nestling back into the pillow. "Shut the blinds, could you?"

"Grey!" I slapped him playfully. His blue eyes opened abruptly.

"Ouch. What was that for?"

"You know what it was for."

"Oh, okay, you're right." He nodded. "I did forget something important."

I waited, blinking at him expectantly.

"The fight is on tonight. It's a good thing there's nothing going on. I really want to watch it …."

Grey couldn't finish. I attacked him gleefully, trying my best to pin his arms down against the bed. We wrestled around for a moment, laughing, but he was way too strong for me. In a matter of seconds, our roles were reversed and he flipped me over, holding me back easily against the mattress.

"Grey," I protested, breathless with giggling. It wasn't fair that he was so strong.

"What? Was there something else?" His handsome face leaned over me, his blue eyes light with amusement, his lips smirking innocently. "Oh, wait. Now I remember." He bent down and kissed me. "Happy Birthday Mackenzie."

"Thanks." I smiled up at him, wondrously, gloriously happy.

"So what do you want to do?"

"I don't know." I shrugged. I wanted to get wasted, that much I knew, but it was a little early for that. There was something else though, something I really, really wanted to do, something I'd wanted to do for ages. The thought made me giggle with embarrassment. "Okay, there is one thing, but you're going to laugh at me."

"Me? Never." Grey smiled.

"I want to go buy some cigarettes."

He looked confused. "Oh, are you out? I've got some here … somewhere."

"No, I've got some, but … I want to go buy some. Grey, I can buy them now!" I nearly squealed with excitement.

Grey shook his head at me, laughing incredibly. "Wow. It doesn't take much to make you happy, does it?"

"No. Not when I'm with you."

"Oh yeah?" His blue eyes gleamed.

"Yeah."

Grey pulled me towards him and kissed me, gently, his lips lingering. "Do you think you could wait for your cigarettes … just a bit longer?" He wondered, his breathing uneven as his lips moved slowly down my neck.

"Uh, yeah." I bit my lip and arched into him, shutting my eyes as the heat rushed through me. "I think I can manage that."

"I'll take a pack of Export A Gold regular, please." I asked politely. The store clerk just looked at me, completely uninterested, like he didn't realize this was a pivotal moment for me or something.

"Can I see some I.D?"

"Sure!" I exclaimed proudly. Grey chuckled behind me. I pulled my wallet out of my purse and flipped it open excitedly.

And then my heart stopped.

My license was missing. Frowning, I quickly thumbed through the rest of the cards in my wallet, but it wasn't there. Hastily I patted my pockets, and then rummaged frantically through my purse, but to no avail. I looked up at Grey, panicked, stricken.

"I don't have it." I admitted, my cheeks flushing red with heat. The clerk raised a doubtful eyebrow at me, as if to say, "nice try, minor."

"You don't have it? Check again. You probably just missed it." Grey assured me. He stepped forward and flashed his I.D at the clerk, who, satisfied, proceeded with the transaction.

I stepped back, calmed myself from full fledged panic, took a breath, and slowly looked through the slots of my wallet and then again through my purse, my hands shaking with near desperation. It wasn't there. This wasn't happening. This couldn't be happening. I had checked and rechecked my wallet before leaving the house, making sure I had my ID with me, knowing how badly it would suck to leave it behind. Without my license, there was no way I'd get into any clubs. No way I'd celebrate my eighteenth birthday. The whole weekends plans came crashing down around me, all of them weighing on that one stupid, plastic card with my birth date plastered officially across the front. The exact card I was missing.

"Any luck?" Grey asked casually, handing me the pack of cigarettes.

"No." I shook my head in humiliated stupor as we left the store. I went over each and every one of my actions during the past twenty-four hours, trying to remember if I'd taken my license out for any reason or left my wallet somewhere by accident. But that was the thing. I was so paranoid about losing my ID that I'd kept my purse with me nearly every second. Except for the two minutes I'd left it in Charlie's car when I ran in to use the bathroom at the gas station on the way ….

I gasped out loud, covering my mouth with my hand. A sudden thought occurred to me, but it was so horrible, I didn't even want to entertain it.

"What?" Grey wondered. "Did you leave it somewhere?"

"No, Grey." I turned my dark, wide eyes up to him. "I think Charlie took it."

"Charlie?" He looked sceptical. "Why would she do that?"

"Because. Because, she's been … choked at me lately, because you and I are … and she and Zack … aren't."

"So you think she'd ruin your whole weekend because of that?"

"I don't know." I sighed. "I can't think of any other explanation. Grey, I made sure it was in there. I know for a fact I had it with me." I blinked back exasperated tears. This was so unfair, so brutally stupid.

"Hey, its okay, Mackenzie." Grey took my hand and smiled at me hopefully. "Maybe it's back at the hotel. We'll go and check."

I nodded glumly and let him lead me down the city streets, totally miserable. The day was cloudy and cold, threatening with icy rain. People bustled around us and the traffic sped by noisily. I wrapped my arms around myself and frowned.

My license wasn't at the hotel either, but deep down, I knew it wouldn't be. I just knew that Charlie had taken it. I hated to think she could be capable of such spite, but with the way she'd been acting lately, it really wasn't that surprising. Even still, it hurt to think my friend harboured such malice towards me, that she would sabotage all my plans just because she was jealous of my relationship with Grey. I didn't deserve her anger; it wasn't my fault that her boyfriend was a total dick.

"So, what's going on with Zack, anyway?" I asked Grey as we searched; perturbed that Zack's idiocy had ended up ruining my weekend.

"What do you mean?" He wondered innocently.

"You know what I mean. Charlie, remember her? He hasn't even called her."

"Oh, right. That." Grey shrugged and continued looking through my purse.

"Yes, that." I stopped what I was doing and looked up at him. "So?"

"So …." Grey sighed. "Mackenzie, it's none of our business."

"Um, yeah, it wasn't my business until my friggin' license was stolen." I insisted. "But it sure the hell is now."

"Fine. Zack is seeing somebody else. Okay? Happy?"

"What! He is? Here?" I froze in disbelief. I thought of my friend at home, pining for a boyfriend who was totally cheating on her, and felt a little less anger towards her. But only a little. "Are you sure? How do you know?"

"Because, normally I share this room with Zack. He was nice enough to stay with Alex for the weekend. But trust me. I know."

I cast a wary glance at the other bed. "Then …. Why didn't you tell me?"

"Because you would tell Charlie."

"Of course I would."

"You ever heard of the phrase, 'shoot the messenger'?"

I stared back at him in amazement, "Yes, but don't you think she deserves to know?"

"Yeah. But I think that Zack should be the one to tell her."

"But he hasn't, Grey." My voice rose defensively. "And she's totally heartbroken because of it. You should see her."

"It's none of our business." Grey stated again.

"Well, I'm telling her." I decided. He just shrugged, like he didn't really care.

"Suit yourself." He answered noncommittally. "Just keep me out of it."

"I will." I shook my head and bent down to rifle through my suitcase again, riddled with disbelief. I had always feared the worst as far as Zack was concerned, but it was still shocking to learn the truth.

After our search proved fruitless, I flopped down on the bed, defeated.

"Ugh, this sucks." I covered my face with my hands. I wanted to punch something, to hit something really, really hard until all my anger and frustration were released. Better yet, I wanted to get high. I wanted to get wasted, even more so that I had that morning, but now, ironically, without my ID the Club was out of the question.

"This ruins everything, doesn't it?" I spoke through clenched teeth, staring up at the ceiling in aggravation.

"Man, you're dramatic." Grey chuckled, and his blue eyes were amused as he looked down at my despondent form lying crushed across the bed. "Nothing is ruined. So the plans change a bit. No big deal."

"No big deal?" I looked up at him incredibly.

"Yeah." He shrugged. "We'll find something else to do."

"Like what? Watch the UFC?" I suggested sourly.

"Maybe." He grinned. "Just leave it up to me, Mackenzie. License or no, I promise you an eighteenth birthday that you'll never forget."

I sighed. It wasn't that I doubted him, but I couldn't see how anything would top the Club, especially after I'd had my heart set on it for so long. But Grey's handsome face was so hopeful, so eager, I couldn't help but have my spirits lifted. It sucked that my birthday was ruined, it was a huge disappointment, but at least I got to spend it with him. Softly, I returned his smile.

"Promise?"

"Promise. Just let me make a couple calls."

"Grey." I grasped his hand as he moved from the bed, and smiled my gratitude up at him. "Thank you. I'm sorry if I ruined your weekend."

"Mackenzie," he smirked, "my weekend was made the moment you got off the plane."

Grey left shortly afterwards. I had no idea where he was going or what he was doing, but he promised not to be long and gave me a wicked grin before heading out the door. Fervently I hoped he was going to get some cocaine or something, I hadn't been able to bring my own stash onto the plane with me and was beginning to get antsy from the lack, especially given the mood I was in. With a heavy sigh, I picked up the remote control and idly flipped through the channels on TV, trying not to feel too sorry for myself.

I was smoking and mindlessly staring at an old episode of *Family Guy* when my cell phone rang. *"Leila … you got me on my knees …."* Absently I fished through my purse and answered it, nodding my head in time with the song.

"Hello?" I blew my smoke out.

"Hello? Mackenzie?"

"Oh … hi … Mom." I muted the TV and sat up, totally surprised to hear my mother's voice on the other end of the phone.

"I just wanted to call and wish you happy birthday." She was saying.

"Oh … thanks."

"Have you had a good day so far?"

"Uh … yeah, it's been great." I lied.

"That's good." Mom's voice was overly chipper; like last time we spoke was just the other day and not ages ago, when I was storming out of my sister's wedding after my boyfriend punched the groomsman in the face.

I shouldn't have been surprised though, this was typically the way things went with my parents. It was easier for them to ignore the issues than to deal with them properly, to let them fester just below the surface—always present, but never talked about. I shrugged to myself. They could act like nothing happened all they wanted, but I still hadn't forgotten how badly they treated Grey. And I hadn't forgiven them for it either.

"So, your dad and I were thinking about throwing you a little birthday party." Mom continued hopefully. "Not much … just family. I think Marcy and Greg are coming over, we could have a little dinner, some birthday cake … what do you say?"

"I don't know." I hesitated, grinning wickedly at a sudden idea. "Maybe … if Grey can come."

I caught her off guard. "Oh, um …," she stammered, her careful composure shattered by my question. "Uh … well, do you think that'd be a … good idea?"

"Yes." I answered immediately. I knew there was no way Grey could make it; he had to stay in the city for at least another week. I just wanted to see what she'd say.

"Well … it's your party." She agreed finally, but her voice sounded strained, like it had taken a lot for her to say. "So, we'll see you tonight, then?"

"Oh, no. Not tonight. I won't be back in town until tomorrow."

"Oh, really? You're not in town?"

"No. I'm with Grey for the weekend. We're staying together at a hotel." I goaded.

"Are you?" Mom's nose was flaring; I could tell.

"Yeah. 'Cause they're in the studio right now, remember?"

"Oh, right. I remember him mentioning that."

I rolled my eyes doubtfully. "Anyway, mom, I'm not sure what time our flight gets in tomorrow. It might be late."

"Well … do you need a ride home from the airport?" Her voice seemed buoyed by the thought. "We could come pick you up. Maybe go to dinner in the city?"

Ugh. I had walked right into this one. The worst part was I did need a ride. If Charlie hadn't begrudgingly given me a lift to the airport on Friday I would've been totally S.O.L, but I wouldn't have lost my license either. What I really needed was a car. I shut my eyes and took a breath, resigned to my automobiley-challenged fate. "Yeah, sure mom." I sighed. "I'll find out what time our flight gets in."

"Great. I'll tell your father."

"Okay."

"See you tomorrow, honey."

"Bye." I flipped my phone shut and leaned back against the bed for a moment. This was going to be interesting. But it was only dinner. And a ride home. Surely I could live through that.

Not two seconds after hanging up my phone, it rang again. Mom must have forgotten something. I rolled my eyes and answered abruptly.

"What is it?"

"… Mackenzie?"

I sat up again, stock-still. Holy crap. "… Riley?" My entire being was startled by the unexpected sound of his voice—so unmistakable, so familiar in my ear. It was such a shock; I couldn't decide how I felt about it. "Wow. Is that really you?"

"Yeah, it's me." He chuckled. "And is that how you answer your phone now?"

"No, I just didn't expect it to be … you."

"I know, it's been awhile. I probably shouldn't have called, but I wanted to wish you happy birthday …."

"No, no. I'm glad you called." The moment I spoke the words, I realized they were true. There was no denying the instant, explicit joy that had surged within me at merely the sound of his voice. It just felt … right. "And thanks. I'm sorry, I just, I can't get over … I mean, I can't believe it's really you."

"Don't I sound the same?" He wondered.

"Yeah." I answered thoughtfully, "but no at the same time. You sound older or something. Different."

"Hmmm."

"How about me?" I giggled nervously. I lit a smoke to help my nerves and leaned back against the pillows, amazed by how flustered I was. This was Riley, one of my oldest friends, one of my best friends. And yet my heart was pounding in my chest. "Do I sound the same?"

"Yes, you do. Exactly the same." He spoke wistfully. "Just really far away."

"Yeah, well, I am far away."

"I know." Riley chuckled mirthlessly. "So, anyway … what's up? What's new with you?"

"Oh, not much." I shrugged. "Uh … Marcy got married a few weeks ago."

"Oh, right. I forgot. How was that?"

"It was alright. I can't really stand her husband though. I don't know what she sees in him."

"Yeah, well, you can't help who you love."

"No, I guess not." I relented, wondering fleetingly if he were referring to the Christian with that statement. I tried to shake the thought from my mind. "So anyway, what's new with you? Are you liking it up there?"

"Yeah, it's alright. I spent the summer tree planting. Can you believe it? My whole summer."

"Tree planting?" I squinched my nose. "Why?"

"I don't know. It was this youth thing. I made some good money though."

"That's good." I giggled. "But that doesn't really sound like you. You spent like, all last summer in bed during the day. Remember?"

"Yeah, well, I had to build up my strength to party at night." He chuckled. "Wow. That seems like a lifetime ago. I can't believe we did that."

"I know." I laughed with him. It felt really, really good to talk to him again, like actually talk, instead of just argue. It felt like old times again. I smiled into the phone.

"So, what about school?" I wondered. "I thought you were looking into one."

"Yeah, I did. That's what I needed to make the money for."

"Oh. So you are in school?"

"Yeah."

"Which one?"

Riley hesitated. "Uhh … well …."

"What? You're not becoming an acrobat or something, are you?"

"No. Not an acrobat." He chuckled.

"What then?"

"Mackenzie," he sighed.

"What? Just tell me. I won't laugh or anything. Let me guess, a figure skater? Is that what you're going to school for?"

"No. It's a Bible school."

"A Bible school?"

"Yes. Both Emily and I are enrolled, and we live in the dorms here."

"Together?"

"No, separate."

"Oh." I breathed with relief. The thought of him living with the Christian was too much to bear. "So … you're in a Bible school." I couldn't keep the surprise out of my tone, though I honestly did try. Never in a million years would I have placed Riley there. Of all places. I mean, I knew his views on certain things had changed, I just hadn't realized how much. I tried to be supportive though. "Do you … like it?"

"Yeah, I do, so far." He seemed relieved. "It's actually really, really good."

"But what do you … do?"

"What you normally do at any school. Learn."

"But what do you learn about?"

"The Bible." He teased. "It's not rocket science, Mac."

"Shut up." I giggled. "I didn't know."

"Are you sure you don't want to rethink the whole higher-education thing?"

"Shut up Riley!" I laughed. "Be nice."

"Okay, okay." He chuckled. "Sorry. I forgot how much fun you were to bug."

"Did you?"

"No." Riley admitted. "I could never …," he cleared his throat. "Um … anyway, what are your big birthday plans for tonight? Grey taking you somewhere nice so you can throw up everywhere, or are you just staying in?"

I rolled my eyes, and sighed theatrically. "Yeah, I guess you're right. This was going too well, wasn't it?"

"What do you mean?"

"You know what I mean, Riley. This will only lead to an argument."

"No, no argument." He argued. "Don't get mad. I just want to know that you'll be careful tonight. That's all."

"You didn't call after all this time just to lecture me, did you?"

"No. I'm not lecturing. But I do want you to take it easy, Mac; I know what you're like."

"You do? And how is that?"

He chuckled. "Come on. You know how you are. There's no middle ground with you. It's either all or nothing, go hard or go home. Right?"

"I don't know." I shrugged.

"Yeah you do." He chuckled. "Remember back in … um, grade five or six I think, when we had that UPC contest?"

"Kind of."

"The school was doing that big recycling campaign. Whoever brought in the most UPC codes from milk cartons and stuff won a bike. You remember."

I did remember. "Yeah." I relented. The bike was beautiful, a cherry red two wheel with spoke-clickers, fluorescent yellow streamers and a wire basket on the front. It was my dream bike. I just had to make it mine.

"All the other kids brought in maybe thirty, or forty UPC's. I think there was one that had a hundred or something. But then you came with ... what was it, seven-hundred and thirty nine?"

"Yeah!" I laughed out loud; I couldn't keep the smile from my lips at the memory. I had terrorized my neighbours out of their garbage for weeks, unable to rest until I knew that shiny red bike was mine for certain. "But I won, didn't I?" I giggled.

"Yes, you did. That's what I mean. When you get your head wrapped around something, you don't quit. You know? That's what worries me."

"What?"

"I don't even know. It's not like turning eighteen really changes things for you, does it? You've been clubbing this whole time."

"Yeah."

"I don't know how to explain it. I've just had this ... this nagging feeling of, of dread for you lately. I know that sounds lame, but I do."

"You're really that worried?"

"Yeah. I don't try to be, but I just can't help it."

"Riley, I can take care of myself." I rolled my eyes. "Honestly. I'm fine."

"I know, I just .... Just promise me that you'll be careful, okay? It would set my mind at ease, just knowing that you'll try."

"Okay, fine." I sighed. "I promise I'll be careful. Okay?"

"Okay." Riley still sounded doubtful. I didn't know what else to do for him, how else to alleviate this totally unfounded concern. He sighed heavily, like he was unsatisfied, like my promise really hadn't eased his mind like he thought it would.

"Well, I should go. I'm supposed to be meeting Emily."

"Okay."

"But it was nice to talk to you."

"Yeah, you too. Hey, Riley?"

"Yeah?"

"I could never forget about you, either."

I could hear the smile in his voice. "Bye, Mac."

"Bye."

When I hung up the phone, I was happy. I sighed contentedly, lay back against the pillows and lit another cigarette, going over our conversation in my mind. But the longer I sat by myself in the dimly lit hotel room, thinking of it, thinking of Riley—the lonelier I became. His warm, familiar voice faded from my ears, leaving me empty, hollow, alone. Suddenly I felt all the hurt and heartsickness I'd managed to avoid all summer, the throbbing pain of missing Riley that I could no longer ignore.

It was like the emotion was intensified from all my months of pretending it didn't exist, like it had strengthened itself, somehow, pushed away in the farthest places of my mind. I wrapped my arms around myself, trying to fill the empty void within me, and it felt like I couldn't breathe. I missed Riley so much, it physically hurt.

I had to see him. That was it, all there was to it. I knew I wouldn't feel better until I was with him again. I got up off the bed and paced, frantically shoving things into my bag, all the while making hasty plans in my head. I would get a taxi to the nearest airport, and catch the soonest flight and then call when I got there and then … and then ….

And then what? I forced myself to stop, to take a breath and think somewhat rationally. What would I do? Hang out with Riley and (shudder) Emily? What would it change? It wouldn't be the same, not like it had been, just because I missed him. Riley had Emily. They were together. There was no room in his life for me, not now.

I was being ridiculous. There was no way I could leave. I sat on the bed, resigned. I had Grey now, there was no reason I should feel such loneliness. And yet, it seemed like I was eight again and away at camp, homesick and sad, lonely and aching for home. The feeling was unsettling, unnerving.

I ran my hands up into my hair in frustration. All the walls I had managed to build to save myself from this pain had been torn down by Riley's phone call. The realization angered me. Why did Riley have to call at all? Why couldn't he just leave me alone, leave me in the relative peace that I had cultivated for myself? Why did he have to call and drudge up all the old feelings again?

I needed to stick with my original plan. I needed to forget about Riley McIntyre. And for that, I needed drugs. I left my half-packed suitcase on the bed and began to scrounge desperately, opening drawers and banging shut the cabinets, searching for something, anything to help and numb the pain. I found chalky mirrors and rolling papers and all the paraphernalia associated with them, but there were no actual drugs to help me. At that point, I would've taken anything, Nyquil, Tylenol Three … something, anything to take the edge off, to ease the frantic pounding of my broken heart.

It was as if he read my mind. The door to the hotel room opened and Grey swept in, his handsome face brilliant as he smirked at me, his blue eyes alight with excitement. The entire room seemed to brighten as soon as he entered it, just his presence helped alleviate my sadness, and I smiled back at him, relieved.

"I'm so glad you're back." I threw my arms around him as soon as I was near enough. Grey hugged me and chuckled into my hair.

"Me too." He kissed my forehead. "And, I have a surprise for you."

"You do?" Desperately I hoped it was some kind of drug. "What is it?"

"You have to shut your eyes." He instructed. "Here, sit down."

I did as I was told; keeping my eyes shut even when I felt Grey's weight sinking onto the bed next to me. He put something into my hand then, something small and plastic.

"Okay, you can open them."

I blinked for a minute, staring down at the little baggie sitting in my palm. It was full of whitish-brown powdery crystals, like dirty snow or beach sand. I smiled excitedly. "Is this some kind of cocaine?" I wondered eagerly.

"No. This stuff is called China White."

"China White?" I had never heard of it before.

"Yeah. Heroin." Grey stated casually. I looked up at him in surprise, and he just smiled back at me, like it was no big deal.

"Heroin?" My eyes lit up with curiosity. "Like, real heroin?"

"Yeah."

"Have you done it before?"

"Yeah, a few times. The guys at the studio do it now and then, they hooked us up." He grinned. "It's good, Mackenzie. You'll like it."

"What does it feel like?"

Grey's blue eyes gleamed fondly. "It's like … I don't know … it just feels so good. I don't even know how to describe it. Like warm, and totally relaxed, and just … heavy. I don't know, I'm not doing it justice, but trust me, after this, you won't care that your license is missing. You won't have a care in the world."

I grinned eagerly, and nodded. It sounded perfect, just what I needed. Something that would take it all away. "Okay." I handed him the baggie back and my stomach churned in anticipation, sending thrilling tingles throughout me.

"The good thing about this stuff," Grey explained as he pulled out a mirror from the bedside table. "Is that you don't have to inject it. You can sniff it, just like coke."

"You *have* to inject the other stuff?" I asked with horror, subconsciously covering my elbow pit with my hand. I made a face.

Grey chuckled at me. "Yeah. Why? Don't tell me you're afraid of needles."

"Afraid doesn't begin to describe it. Petrified, maybe. Terrified, even."

"This coming from a girl who can do a shot of Appleton rum with barely a grimace." He looked up at me fondly, amused. "Wonders never cease."

I shrugged, watching as Grey divided the dirty powder into two lines for us. I lit a smoke and tapped my hands against my jeans, anxious and eager. I honestly didn't know enough about heroin to even think of the consequences like I usually did. It had always been some far off legend, something people did in the city—apart from us, removed. Even if I had known more about it, more than just how good it seemed, the drugs were too alluring, the high too enticing for me to even consider not doing it. There was no turning back now. Soon, the pain I felt for Riley would be only a distant memory. I couldn't wait.

"You have to be careful with this shit." Grey was saying. "You can't do too much. It's really easy to OD, even easier than coke. Just take a little to start, and see how you handle it."

"Okay." I nodded excitedly.

"This one's for you." He pointed to the smaller of the two lines on the mirror and then handed me a straw. I grabbed it from his hand and took a deep breath. "Okay." I repeated.

"Mackenzie?"

"Yes?"

"Happy birthday." Grey smirked. I giggled at him, nearly giddy, and leaned towards him over the mirror so we could share a brief, happy kiss. Then, tremulous and excited, unable to wait for another second, I bent down over the glass with the straw gripped tightly within my shaky fingers.

As I did so, there was a brief flash in my mind. I saw Riley's face, and he was shaking his head at me, as if willing me, pleading for me not to do this. I heard his voice again. "*... Promise me that you'll be careful, okay? Please?*"

I shook the image away and bent down to my task, even more determined now.

Screw you, Riley. You never should have left me.

I chased the line quickly, impatiently almost. The heroin shot up my nose, smoother than the cocaine—like it was softer, somehow. I felt it hit my nostrils, felt the sweet burn radiate from deep within my sinuses.

And nothing was ever the same.

CHAPTER 44

I was actually disappointed at first, like I'd been expecting my brain to explode from a mind-ravaging high or something. Grey did his line and then we lit a smoke, leaned back against the headboard and just … waited for it to hit. Grey flipped on the TV, and we laughed together as the UFC slowly warmed into view. I still didn't feel anything. I thought maybe the line Grey made for me had been too small. But then, I began to notice it.

It started small; I could feel it creeping up on me—slowly, building in intensity. I reached down for Grey's hand and laced my fingers through his, glad that he was with me, happy to be sharing this with him. He turned over towards me and propped his head on his hand, studying my face, his blue eyes eager as they swept me over.

"I want to watch" He smirked. "I want to know the moment you feel it."

I nodded, but I suddenly found it hard to speak. Wave after wave of warmth was crashing over me—blissful heat, the perfect temperature, pouring all over my body—loosening my muscles until they felt weak and heavy, beyond the point of relaxed. I couldn't pinpoint the exact moment it hit me, I just knew I felt it, and it seemed like I'd been feeling that way forever. I melted back against the bed, unbelievably tranquil, overwhelmingly comfortable, like I was snuggled on a cloud of the softest, warmest air. Nothing mattered then, just like he'd said. Not Riley, not the pain. Nothing but how good I felt.

Grey was kissing me, his lips brushing over my face. I tried to smile for him.

"It's good, isn't it?" His voice was low in my ear.

"Yes." I couldn't raise my voice above a whisper. I nodded weakly. "Yes ...."

Time passed. I had no idea how much time, but it felt like ages. We didn't talk much. There wasn't much to say. I was perfectly content just to lay there, to let the warmth have its way, to shut my eyes and let my body soften, like butter, against the mattress in total, euphoric apathy. I didn't have a care in the world. There wasn't one thought that could interfere, not one emotion that could penetrate the heroin's silky embrace, the velvety soft blanket that was draped over me. It was like heaven.

But then I felt something else. I felt sick. My eyes fluttered open as my stomach twisted with a sudden surge of nausea, and I knew I was going to throw up.

"Grey?" I forced myself out of the bed, amazed I even had the strength to stand. I clutched my stomach as it lurched and hurried towards the bathroom.

"It's okay," Grey called to me from the bed. He could barely open his eyes. "You'll feel better ... after ...."

I barely made it to the toilet. My body heaved as I retched, trying to purge the poison from my system, emptying my insides over and over again. Even the vomiting felt good though, in its own way. When the tremors finally receded I collapsed on the cold tile of the bathroom floor, sweaty, shivering from the effort as the racking nausea faded at last.

"Hey, Mackenzie, you okay?" Grey leaned heavily against the door.

I nodded in response, but couldn't bring myself to move. He came and helped me up off the floor. I was weak and shaky, but I still felt amazing—not as high as I had been, but weighty and sedated, heavy and warm. We crawled back into the bed. Everything felt so right again, so perfect ... the temperature of the room, the soft mattress beneath me. The sickness was completely forgotten. I lit a cigarette and smoked it slowly, then lit another, and another. Perfectly happy. Perfectly content.

Cocaine didn't last me fifteen minutes. This high lasted for hours, like a long, languid bath that never ended; full of warm, fragrant water that never cooled.

Heroin was it. A contented smile curved my lips. This was what I'd been looking for, all along, the secret I knew the world had been keeping from me. I turned to Grey, who was nodding off beside me, nearly overcome by the euphoric surge of love I felt for him, the total gratitude for sharing with me this pleasure, this secret. He had found for me something I didn't know was missing.

And suddenly couldn't live without.

When I awoke the next morning, my first thought was of heroin. The depth that I longed for it actually kind of scared me. Logically, the sheer intensity of my craving should've been enough to keep me from ever doing it again. I needed more though. I could feel the loneliness again, creeping on the edges of my mind. Once we awoke, groggy and irritable from the lack of sleep and the night spent tossing and turning in an itchy, uncomfortably hot slumber, Grey made some more lines from the dope left over and I snorted it back without a second thought.

This time it hit me in the elevator. Grey was taking me somewhere, I didn't know where, but we were up and dressed and out the door when I felt the creeping waves descending and smiled knowingly at Grey, shutting my eyes and letting them have me. He led me, blissfully numb and euphoric, through the lobby of the hotel and into the awaiting cab. Everything after that was a perfect, hazy blur. I can remember how good Grey's warm hand felt in mine … how the grey, dismal colors over the dreary, rainy city were beautiful to my eye … how the cold, brisk breeze couldn't touch me, how … how amazing it felt to be so content, so utterly satisfied and comfortable.

Grey took me to the studio. I was pleasantly surprised when we pulled up in front of the red brick building, even more so when I discovered that all the guys were there, the whole band, recording away. It was really good to see them after so long. I sat on one of the black leather couches that stretched the length of the room and nodded in and out of the conversation, a soft, joyous smile on my face as the guys talked and laughed and filled the room with a happy buzzing din—the perfect background noise to accompany the peaceful quiet of my mind. It didn't escape my notice that some of my friends were nodding off as well, on heroin—and I felt so united with them, so in tune, closer to them that I've ever felt before. The only person I couldn't have cared less about was Zack, but he proved easy to ignore. Most of the time he was up in the sound booth, wailing away on his guitar.

Everyone took a turn recording their individual instruments to the same song. I had no idea that's how records were made. I thought they all played as a band, at once, together. After Zack, Alex got up and played on his drums. The two guys working the soundboard were Steve and Mike, and though I had just met them, they were my new best friends as far as

I was concerned. They tried to show me some things but I was really too high to pay much attention.

But then Grey got up to sing. The moment his beautiful, husky low voice hit my ears I sat up, totally aware, and then stood so I could watch him. Grey smirked when he noticed me, his blue eyes intent—he didn't seem to care at all that I was watching him. His voice draped over me as he sang, melting my heart, making my breath catch in my throat, stealing my very soul with the impossible beauty and the glorious sweetness of his voice.

I bit my lip and let the radiating love I felt for him fill me to the point of tears. I mouthed it to him through the glass. I love you, Grey. I love you.

It was over all too soon. Before I knew it, before it seemed possible, we had to leave so I would make my flight back home. I held Grey's hand as tight as I could, reluctant to let him go for even a second, knowing we'd be separated by hundreds of miles in just a few short, precious hours. We went back to the hotel first and I packed my things quickly so as not to waste a moment. Grey sat back on the bed and watched while I ran around the room, collecting my clothes and make-up and jewellery and hurriedly shoving them into my bag, which was already half-haphazardly packed from my Riley panic the night before.

When I was done, he pulled me down onto his lap, wrapping his strong, warm arms around me. I melted against him, shutting my eyes and breathing deeply the delicious smell that emanated from the warm base of his throat.

"So, Mackenzie," his voice was low in my ear, sending shivers down my spine. "Did you have a good birthday?"

"mmm … only the best." I nodded. "Thank you, Grey. This was the greatest present ever."

"I can agree with that." He smirked and bent down to kiss me. I wove my fingers through his short, messy dark hair and kissed him like it was our last.

"I don't want to go." I admitted, as he pulled away. "I don't want to leave you."

"Yeah, but if all goes well, it'll only be another week. Maybe two, tops."

I nodded glumly. "Yeah."

We sat together in silence for a moment. I could practically hear the seconds ticking down to the inevitable moment when I would have to leave him. I sighed miserably. The heroin high was all but over ... the warmth had faded away and a heavy weariness was settling in my bones, a dull achiness replacing the blissful heat that had inhabited my muscles, a pang of sudden loneliness taking place of the contented happiness I'd felt all day.

"Hey, don't be sad." Grey brushed the hair back from my face. As if reading my mind, his eyes gleamed down at me as he pulled a little baggie out of his pocket. "How about a hit for the road? It'll make this whole parting thing easier."

"You know me too well," I grinned, "I'm going to need all the help I can get."

"Well, you're not the only one." He smiled. "But no more after this. This shit is way too easy to get hooked on to do every day."

"But, we can still do it like, every once in awhile, can't we?"

Grey nodded. "I think so. On special occasions and stuff." He shrugged. "I don't see why not, as long as we're smart about it."

"Yeah." I nodded eagerly, ready to agree to anything as long as it got me more heroin now. I looked forward to the dense warmth and blissful apathy that would accompany me on the plane ride home, the warm nothingness that would fall on me like a blanket of utter contentment, covering the pain that would come from leaving Grey behind.

I watched as he cut the lines. I did mine quickly—he gave me a little more this time—and then he sniffed his back. We sat for a moment, smiling widely at each other, the air thick with the thrill of anticipation as we waited for the high to settle into our bones.

The airport was busy, and noisy, full of the typical chaos of people coming and going and greeting and saying their farewells. I stood with my ticket in hand, my luggage already loaded, outside the gate where Grey and I had to say our goodbye. I knew if it weren't for the warmth of the heroin already creeping up my body, I would be intensely sad. But at the moment, I couldn't keep the smile from my face.

"I'll let you know what's happening, when we're coming home." Grey was saying. His eyes were barely open.

"Yeah." I nodded slowly.

He pulled me into his arms, and their strength was the only thing that could compare with the goodness of the numbing heat stealing through my veins. I savoured my time spent in them; I never wanted to let him go.

"I love you, Grey." I whispered in his ear. He paused a moment then, his mouth open, but frozen, as if he were struggling for words that just wouldn't come.

"Have a good flight." He smiled finally. He kissed me and I held onto him, but as my final boarding call was announced, ringing through the noisy din surrounding us, I knew I couldn't put the inevitable off any longer. I had to go.

"Goodbye, Grey."

"Goodbye." He answered. I forced myself to turn away from him, to rip myself away from those gorgeous blue eyes I could surely lose myself in. I walked towards the gate, leaving him behind.

"Wait, Mackenzie." Grey called suddenly. He came up behind me, grabbed my hand and spun me around to meet him.

"Yes?"

He stared at me moment, his face soft as he looked me over, warm with obvious affection. "I love you." Grey stated lowly. "I love you, and I'm sorry I never tell you that. I feel bad, because you say it to me … all the time. But it's hard for me … I don't know why … just, just know I love you, okay? Even if I can't say it."

I blinked at him a moment, and a smile spread across my face as I savoured his words. It was so good to hear him say it. I knew he loved me—I did—because that was the thing about Grey, the thing I had come to understand. He spoke with his actions more than his words, and his love was evident in all the little things. Like the way he wrote me a song and how he carried my bag for me, or the way he turned and grasped my hand whenever we were walking. Even in the lengths he had gone to try and cheer me up after our weekend was ruined.

"I do know." I nodded softly. "Grey, you tell me you love me all the time."

CHAPTER 45

When the plane touched down, I blinked awake, but I had never really been sleeping—just nodding as the warmth drowsed me deliciously, totally carefree in my seat, completely oblivious to the people around me. I forced myself to get up and move as the other passengers made their way through the cabin, grasping my purse and following slowly behind them.

I knew my family would be waiting for me, but I didn't mind. Not even they could ruin the numbness, not even they would be able to penetrate the silky embrace of the drugs. There would probably be a lecture involved, from Marcy if no one else, since I had somewhat managed to ruin at least a portion of her wedding. With that, I knew there'd be some judgemental staring and frowning, but I really didn't care. Inside I laughed, hoping they would try to get in, to get under my skin somehow.

I smiled, knowing they would never be able to. They couldn't touch me now.

Sure enough, the first couple I recognized at the arrivals gate was my mom and dad. Mom smiled and waved enthusiastically, but Dad didn't look too happy to see me, even after he noticed that Grey hadn't come and they both relaxed in a painfully obvious manner.

"Hey guys." I greeted.

"Hey, sweetie. Happy birthday!" Mom exclaimed, wrapping me in a hug.

"Happy birthday, Mackenzie." Dad nodded gruffly, a frown creasing his forehead.

"Thanks."

We made our way through the airport as mom prattled on and on in her excitement, her brown curls shaking in her enthusiasm. I trailed along with a half smile on my face, nodding at the right moments and pretending to listen the rest of the time. By the time we made it to the Parkade my ears were practically ringing. I got in the back of the car and slumped against the seat.

"You okay honey? You look sleepy."

"Yeah, I'm a little tired." I admitted. I imagined myself telling her, "no mom, I'm not sleepy. Just high on dope. You should try it. It's amazing."

"You can have some coffee once we get to the restaurant. Greg and Marcy are meeting us there. Have you ever eaten at The Fern? I hear it's fantastic."

"No." I shook my head. My favourite restaurant was Earls—I was a fan of the Bigger Better Bacon Cheddar Burger and I'd told my mom that thousands of times. But apparently that didn't matter. The Fern it was.

Dad drove us silently through the city streets, grown quieter now as evening approached. I stared out the window at the people walking by and the cars driving around us, watching the sun slowly sinking through the ripped shreds of clouds that clung to the heavy grey sky. I missed Grey already. I tried to imagine what he was doing.

Mom droned on.

The Fern was a fancier restaurant, I felt way underdressed in my hoodie and jeans, and mom wondered why I hadn't brought a nice skirt to put on. I rolled my eyes and wished for a cigarette. The lovely warmth was still buzzing throughout me, luckily. I couldn't imagine what state I'd be in if it weren't.

We made our way inside, through the maze of dimly lit tables and patrons dressed in business suits and skirts. I spotted Marcy and Greg at a table near the back, and there beside them sat Craig Donovan.

I stopped in my tracks, speechless, and a waiter nearly ran into me. I muttered an apology and stepped out of his way, totally baffled.

"What's the matter, Mackenzie?" Mom wondered.

"Craig is here."

"He wanted to help you celebrate. Come on, now, don't be difficult. We'll have a nice supper, and we'll talk about it after."

She grasped me by the arm and I let her lead me back to the table. At least this explained some of her avid excitement. I knew I should be mad at them—fuming even—and knew I would be later. But at the moment, I didn't care. I couldn't care less that Craig was sitting there with a smug, arrogant grin on his face, watching as we approached. I felt too good to be bothered by the fact that my family was clearly trying to set me up with that dick-weed, even after everything that happened. I slid into the booth beside him and smiled sweetly.

"Hey Craig. Wow, that shiner healed nicely." I commented innocently.

He cleared his throat. "Uh … yeah, thanks."

Marcy and Greg were just as impressed with my observation as Craig had been. Greg leaned back with disapproval and Marcy glared at me. I smiled right back at her. She looked gorgeous, as usual; her hair curled perfectly around her jaw, her beautiful face impeccably radiant. But this time, as I compared myself to her, there was no feeling of inferiority like there always had been before. All I felt was amazing, contented and serene. I felt beautiful. My grin widened at this discovery, I actually almost laughed. Marcy may have been perfect on the outside, but right then, I was perfect on the inside.

To my surprise, no one took the opportunity to launch into a lecture about what happened at the wedding. Things were tense around the table, I could feel it, and I was probably the only one completely relaxed and at ease. But it didn't bother me. I wasn't really hungry but I scoured the menu, ordering the closest thing I could find to a cheeseburger, some fancy pasta with Bolognese and feta cheese. After the waitress took our order, Marcy looked pointedly at me.

"So, Mac, how was the big birthday? Did you get totally wasted? End up in the hospital, anything like that?"

"I had a good time." I answered, unperturbed.

"So what'd you do?"

"Just … hung out." Actually Marce, I tried heroin for the first time. It was awesome!

"Still with that boyfriend of yours then?" Craig interjected, giving Greg a glance that made him chuckle cockily.

"Yeah. He was going to come tonight, but they're still in the studio."

"Too bad he didn't come." Greg decided. "I'd like to have a word with him."

"Oh yeah?" I smiled. "Why? Because he punched your brother out for kissing me? Or were you going to talk music or something?"

"Mackenzie." Dad warned, like the fourth thing he'd said to me all night. His eyebrows were furrowed my direction.

"What Dad?" I turned to him. "Did you not know that? This gentleman here," I pointed my thumb in Craig's direction, "isn't as gallant as you think."

"Still, Grey didn't have to punch him." Marcy came to her brother-in-law's defence, crossing her arms. "Talk about overreacting."

"And he didn't punch me out." Craig insisted. "He just caught me by surprise. I think the correct term is, 'sucker-punch'? Isn't that right Greg?"

"Yeah, I think that's what they call it. Not how a real man fights, anyway." Greg smirked at me so arrogantly that if I hadn't been so high, I would've taken him by the crisply ironed shirt collar and slammed him up against the wall. Or I would've wanted to, anyway. But as it was, I just smiled at him and shrugged.

"Call it what you want. Craig got what he deserved."

Mom frowned. I think she could see her little scheme of setting us up go flying through the window, but honestly, I don't know what she'd been thinking even attempting such a stupid ploy. Like I'd magically fall in love with Craig just because Grey wasn't around or something. How perfect it would be for them if I'd just behave and follow their cleverly ordained little plan. Then they'd have both daughters married off to super rich husbands, and just think of what their friends would say.

Our meal continued, fairly awkwardly, but I knew it would be. Conversations ensued around me, but they had nothing to do with me … actually I was basically ignored for the rest of the meal. There was a lot of talk about Craig's job that I barely paid attention to—my parents subtly mentioned his various successes slyly for my benefit as I tried to keep from rolling my eyes at them. I could feel the heroin wane, the bliss fading slowly from my veins, and hoped our evening would be coming to a close soon. I really didn't want to be around my family when it totally wore off.

Finally—thankfully—it was over. Dad paid the bill and we all went our separate ways; Marcy and Greg took Craig home and I was forced to pile in the car with mom and dad. I realized climbing into the backseat that not one person besides my parents had even said happy birthday to me. There'd been no singing, no presents … not even a cake. Whatever, it would all be over soon. I just had to make it home.

I sat back to try and enjoy the ride. I'd always liked driving in the city at night, looking out over the twinkling lights beneath the huge dark sky, the streetlights flooding the cab with a pale, warm glow; the gentle braking and accelerating of the car. It felt cozy to me, quiet.

"So, Mackenzie, was that really necessary?" Mom posed, turning in her seat to look at me, though it was pretty much pitch black inside the car.

So much for my quiet. "What mom?"

"Why'd you have to bring it up? Why'd you have to act that way to Craig?"

"Um … because he's a total dick. And for some reason, no one cares that he kissed me. Grey had every right to punch him, but for some reason, *he's* the bad guy. It's so stupid."

"Mackenzie." Mom sighed. "Really. Look, I know you like this … Grey fellow, and he's a … he's a nice boy, but can you really see yourself settling down with someone like him?"

"Mom, who the hell is talking about settling down? I just turned eighteen."

"I know, but, why waste your time? Craig is mature, and responsible, he's a—"

"Okay, stop right there." My patience was thinning as the heroin ebbed. "Get it out of your mind that I'll ever be with Craig Donovan, okay? Forget it. And I'm not wasting my time with Grey. He's amazing, for your information, though you don't know that because you won't even give him the time of day, for some stupid reason."

"I just think you could do better."

"Well, I don't. And luckily for me, I'm the one that gets to live my life, not you. So just butt out, alright?"

There was a moment's silence. "Alright." Mom finally answered, her words clipped, her voice terse. Dad sat silently in his seat, his eyes on the road.

We rode the rest of the way in silence.

CHAPTER 46

There was nothing on TV. I sighed and flipped absently through the channels, bored and lonely. I leaned quickly over the coffee table and did another line, then sat back on the couch and let the cocaine race through my veins. A shaky smile bent my lips as I lit a cigarette.

It was Thursday. Somehow, I'd managed to get through the week without doing any more heroin. Not because Grey had mentioned how addictive it was, not because we were supposed to save it for special occasions, but simply because I had absolutely no means of getting any. As badly as I wanted it, I had no hope of finding some in a town as small as ours. Sometimes I would just sit and think fondly back to my blur of a weekend, trying to remember how good heroin felt, trying to relive the delicious, warm nothingness. I did copious amounts of cocaine to try and fill the void, but nothing could satisfy, nothing could compare with what I really wanted.

Grey was coming home that Friday. I was so excited; I couldn't wait to have him here with me again, for good this time. Just one more day and I wouldn't be alone anymore, not like I had been all that week. I had no idea where Charlie was or what she'd been doing—she didn't come home and she didn't show up to work and she didn't answer her cell. I was to the point that I wasn't even mad at her anymore, at all—I just wanted to know that she was okay, that she was safe and alive. I had played with the idea of calling the police, but in the end decided against it. If Charlie were just off binging somewhere it would do more harm than good for the police to find her. She'd probably never speak to me again if I got her in any sort of trouble.

My worries were put to rest though, when after an old rerun of *The Simpson's*, I heard sudden footsteps hurrying up our stairs. My heart leapt with relief as the door swung open and Charlie swept in, her blonde hair curled and her make-up on, dressed up like she was about to go clubbing.

"Oh, hey." She smiled at me—but it was more like a sneer—and threw something my direction. I knew what it was without having to look. "You left this in my car." She snickered, breezing by me on the way to her bedroom.

I blinked a moment in amazement, and then sat up to retrieve my license card from where it had landed on the floor. I looked down at it—at the little photo of the young girl I'd been then, smiling widely as the picture snapped, just given the key to new freedom. I remembered that day, how exciting it had been to finally be allowed to drive, how Riley and I had celebrated by getting stoned and then cruising around town. I'd hit a parked car pulling out of my parking spot, and Riley had screamed "Go, go, go!" and I'd peeled out, terrified, laughing uproariously with my friend as we stole away from the scene of the crime.

No, no, no. I shook the thought of Riley firmly out of my head, knowing if I didn't that I'd never be able to keep the sadness at bay. Forgetting him proved harder than I expected this time. I'd tried all week—with copious amounts of cocaine—to shelve him back to the farthest corners of my mind. But he seemed impossible to ignore. My thoughts skittered to him constantly; memories of him long forgotten would suddenly pop into my head. His face even invaded my dreams at night. I was holding onto my sanity by a tenuous thread and counting down the days to Grey's arrival, knowing full well that only his gloriously handsome face would help distract me entirely.

Charlie waltzed back into the kitchen then, interrupting my musings, and opened the fridge. "I'm not staying, Courtney's in the car. I just had to grab some things." She explained. I looked up at her, puzzled. Who the hell was Courtney? I frowned to myself. A new best friend? How easily everyone replaced me.

"How was your weekend, anyway?" Charlie wondered. "It must have sucked not being able to go out." Her voice was insincere, gloating almost.

I stared at her evenly. "Zack is cheating on you." I blurted. It wasn't the most tactful way to tell her, I could admit, but I figured she was still getting off easy.

That was enough to wipe the smirk from her face. She froze in her steps, her head whipping up to glare at me. "What did you say?"

"Zack's cheating on you."

Charlie swayed. She grasped the edge of the counter for support and teetered a moment as the full weight of my words crashed down on her. She let out a little gasp, almost like a sob, and then sat weakly down in a little faded armchair.

"Really?" Gone was the sardonic grimace that had distorted Charlie's beautiful face to me for so long. It was like something had broken in her, like the walls of resentment she felt towards me had come crumbling down with an explosion of humility. She gazed up at me now, her blue eyes wide and sad—repentant. "Are you sure, Mac?"

I sighed. "Yeah." Already I could feel the air clearing between us. I forgave her easily, for everything, feeling nothing but compassion for her now. "I'm so sorry, Charlie."

"I mean, I'd always feared … the worst, but I never actually thought …." She shook her head and dropped her face into her hands. "I never really thought he'd do it."

Wordlessly, I crossed the living room and joined her on the chair, wrapping my arm around my friend and drawing her near. She wasn't actually crying, but her petite frame was shaking with pent-up emotion.

"Hey, you can do better." I encouraged. "You can do so much better than that asshole, Charlie. He doesn't deserve you."

"Yeah." She sniffed doubtfully.

"No, I mean it. You are way too beautiful to waste tears on a loser like him."

Charlie smiled weakly, her blue eyes full of emotion as she cast them up at me. "Why are you being so nice to me, Mac? I've been terrible to you."

"Because you're my friend." I shrugged. "And I love you."

Charlie scoffed and sniffled loudly. She looked down at her hands, twisting in her lap. "So this is what it feels like to have your heart broken."

"I'm sorry." I repeated. I didn't know what else to say. She leaned her head against my shoulder and we sat silently for a moment. Despite Charlie's sorrow, I couldn't help but be happy that we were friends again. Now I wanted nothing more than to help relieve her pain, to help her forget everything, to help her forget all about Zack ….

A wicked, horribly tempting idea crossed my mind then. I sat up, excitement coursing through my veins at just the thought, and glanced down at Charlie, beaming impishly.

"Charlie, I have the perfect thing, something I know will cheer you up."

"Oh yeah?" She replied doubtfully. "What's that?"

"Heroin."

"Heroin?" That sparked some interest in her dull blue eyes. "What? Where'd that come from?"

"I did some on the weekend." I remembered fondly. "Trust me, nothing on earth will ever make you feel better. It feels so friggin' good. I can't even describe it."

That intrigued her, I could tell. "Really? But … where would we get some?"

"I don't know. I was hoping you might know somebody."

"I don't." She frowned a moment, but then her eyes lit up with an idea. "But I bet Courtney would. Come on, let's go ask her."

"Okay." I smiled eagerly.

It felt like old times again as Charlie and I—swept away with anticipation and the age old desire to get as wrecked as we possibly could—hurriedly readied ourselves and then trounced out down the old wooden steps, giggling as we headed for Courtney's idling car.

CHAPTER 47

Courtney was really pretty. Not Charlie pretty, but pretty in her own punky, perky way. She had dark short hair, straightened, with bold chunks of blonde and red throughout. Her wide almond eyes were lined heavily with black liner, her lips smiled with blood-red lipstick. She was a waitress at the Aurora; I knew I recognized her from somewhere. She had this experienced, bored aura about her, like she had seen everything and been everywhere and tried everything at least once. Just from looking at her I could tell she was bad. It made her mysterious to me, I couldn't help but wonder what wild, crazy things she'd been a part of before.

Courtney barely batted an eye when we asked for heroin, just threw her car into gear and started driving, tearing through the streets, chain-smoking and swearing a lot. She knew someone in town that could hook us up and was taking us straight there. I was amazed and surprised by the fact. I figured our little town too small, too innocent for anything like heroin.

We stopped before a small, decrepit old house; the saggy entryway lit by one dim, failing bulb. Charlie and I eyed the exterior nervously as Courtney got out of the car.

"I'll go talk to him, and if he's cool with it, you can come inside." She explained. I nodded silently, my eyes wide. I wasn't usually involved with dealers and I didn't really want to be now. But I didn't want to argue with her, either.

Charlie and I watched as Courtney ambled up the crumbling sidewalk and paused upon the entry, the dim light casting over her little figure. It took a few seconds before she was let in—a single hand pushed the door open and then she was swallowed up inside. Charlie and I glanced at each other silently. I bit my lip. I didn't know what it was about the situation that made me feel so sketchy, but it seemed to have the word "danger" written all over it.

But then Courtney reappeared in the doorway and waved us in. I really didn't want to go, but as Charlie clicked her seatbelt off and opened the car door, I found myself following her. We ushered silently into the little house, hit by a wave of heat and stranger smell as we trailed behind Courtney into a tiny living room off the main entrance.

I was nervous. Part of me wanted to get away, to run right out the door and keep on running until I felt safe again. My heart was beating loudly in my chest. But the other part of me—the part that wanted the heroin—was more than willing to stay, to sit with the sweaty, shifty eyed men that occupied the dim, hot little room as we waited for one of them to get us our stuff. I didn't look at them, I didn't look at anything but my sweaty hands in my lap, I didn't want any recollection of that place and how dirty it made me feel. Thankfully Charlie was beside me. She seemed calm, anyway, though neither of us was brave enough to speak to the other. Courtney was the only one that seemed totally unaffected—she smiled and swore and joked with the guys around us like they were her closest friends. For all I knew, they were. I could feel the sweat trickling down my back, but I was too afraid to even wipe my hands down the legs of my jeans, too frightened to bring any kind of attention to myself by moving. I wished fervently that Grey was with me. I just wanted to get the dope and get out of there.

"Okay, ladies." The man who introduced himself as Jack strode back into the room. He was good looking enough, with longer blonde hair and a huge, built body. He was just as sweaty as everybody else. I could understand the need for privacy, for the thick curtains hanging in the windows that would block out every ounce of light and all the neighbours prying eyes, but really, couldn't they open a window or something?

"Here you go." Jack handed Courtney a little ball, it looked like a balloon or something, full of black sticky stuff.

"Uh …." My craving overcame my terror and stupidly, I spoke. "The kind I had was like, powder. Do you have any of that? China White, I think? You can sniff it."

"No." Jack looked at me from the side of his eye, like it angered him that I had opened my mouth. I clamped it shut. "Mexican black tar is all we serve here. Like it or leave it." The way he said it sounded like a threat.

"No, no, this is good." Courtney gave me a quick glare, like, shut up and quit being an idiot. "But I don't think she knows how to do it this way. Can you show her?"

I wanted to intercede, to tell them I really had no interest doing it any other way—but at the moment I was too petrified to argue, terrified of angering this lumbering hulk of a drug dealer any further. My tongue seemed swollen, dry, stuck to the roof of my mouth. I didn't know what to do. And I wanted the heroin.

"Well, why didn't you say so?" Jack smiled at me, creepily, like he enjoyed teaching new users how to inject. "Let old Jacky here show you how it goes."

He sat down on the beat-up, old reclining chair beside the loveseat we were occupying. Pulling out a kit from beside his chair, he proceeded to take out a spoon, a lighter, a cotton ball, some water, and two clean syringes that he set on the coffee table before him.

My heart began to pound furiously in my chest at the sight of the needles. I hated needles with such a passion. In school they had to wrap me up in a sheet to immunize me, and the only way I could get my belly button ring was with Riley standing between me and the needle, holding my hand. My mouth went horribly dry, like the cotton ball on the coffee table. The part of me that was scared before nearly got up off the chair and bolted, but I knew I couldn't go now; I was trapped there, feeble, helpless. I tried to calm myself down, to focus on the heroin and how good it had felt, how good it was going to feel. How all of this would be worth it, in the end. But it didn't work. The same, panicky sentence repeated itself over and over in my mind, "… not safe, not safe, not safe, not safe …." I nearly wanted to cry. I wished for Grey, prayed for Grey. For Riley. For anyone to come and get me out of there.

I watched anxiously as Jack took a chunk of dark, sticky heroin from our balloon and put it on the spoon. He added a splash of water and then expertly flicked the lighter and began to heat up the concoction. I watched the heroin dissolve, turning the liquid an oily, browny-black. Then, using a little piece of cotton as a filter, he sucked it up into a syringe.

"Ready?" He wondered wickedly. I shook my head as he held the needle menacingly towards me.

"N-No, I think I'm good." I stammered thickly, trying to be cool.

"Yeah, you will be, in a moment." Jack promised, ignoring my request. He grasped my arm and quickly tied one of those rubber band things they use at the hospital around it, the kind that pinch the skin with their tightness.

I tried to pry my arm free, but he had it locked in his hand. My heart hammered wildly as I watched the veins sticking up in my arm.

"No! D-Don't!" I blurted, tears of terror stinging my eyes. I couldn't get my arm free. What had I done? What had I gotten myself into? Jack held the syringe just above my elbow. He gave me a wicked upwards glance and re-gripped my arm like a vice. I struggled against him as then, with a grin, he plunged the needle into my arm.

It was instant. It was intense. It was wonderful, beautiful, magical. All the fear was gone, all the tension, all the anxiety. I've never felt so good in my entire life, I've never known that kind of euphoria—not in all my drug use had I even been so overcome with such overwhelming bliss. I couldn't speak, I couldn't do anything but relax against the couch cushions, my mouth open in awe, a tear slipping down my cheek. I was awash in utter joy, I could feel the heroin dancing in my veins, spreading and peaking and making me tremble with uncontrollable pleasure.

Charlie went next. At least, I think she did. I couldn't really concentrate, but suddenly she was next to me on the couch, slack and motionless, her eyes shut and a peaceful, ecstatic smile on her face. I don't know how long we lay there for. I forgot everything, my fear of the sweaty men, the dirty junkiness of the house, the unbearable heat. I couldn't even feel the heat. It couldn't even affect me.

When I "came too," basically, when I was aware enough again to take in my surroundings, we were back in Courtney's car. Charlie was slumped over in the front seat; Courtney was driving us around the darkened town, smoking, humming quietly along with the intro to the Rolling Stones song, *Gimme Shelter*. I'd always found that part creepy and haunting, but right now it seemed to fit.

"How you feeling?" Courtney chuckled, eyeing me in the rear view.

I didn't know how to put it into words, the warm nothingness that consumed me, the peaceful lethargy I felt, the emanating bliss that wound its way through my entire being.

"… Good …." I answered simply, my head nodding with pleasure.

Her blood-red lips smiled at me in the mirror.

"What time is it?"

"I don't know." Charlie groaned. Her beautiful blonde curls were a tangled mess around her face, her make-up smudged beneath her eyes. She peeled her cheek from the carpeted floor. "Morning?"

"It's too bright to be morning." I argued, laying my arm over my eyes to keep out the blinding rays from the window. My throat was parched, it hurt to swallow. I tried to sit up but my stomach muscles still ached from all the heaving and vomiting I'd done, a blur in my distant memory. "Can't you see the clock?"

"No."

"What time did we get to bed last night?" I wondered.

"I don't know."

I couldn't really remember either. I knew it had been very, very late when Courtney finally dropped us off at home and Charlie had insisted we shoot up again. I'd been just high enough from the last batch that I hadn't minded the needle so much that time, but I made Charlie do it for me—I couldn't even look as the cold steel penetrated my skin. She was sloppier than Jack had been, but the results had been the same, and we'd spent the rest of the night nodding off in the living room, apathetic and perfectly, wonderfully happy.

Aside from the odd bout of crippling nausea, of course.

"So, was I right, or what?" I wondered, risking the light to look over at my friend. "Did you like it? Wasn't it great?"

"Better than great." Charlie admitted. "So good. Do we have any left?"

"I don't know. You cooked up our last one. Did you use it all?"

"I don't think so."

I rubbed my face with my hand, already craving more. "What time is it?"

Charlie laughed at me. "I still don't know."

"I've got to work tonight, and Grey's getting in …." I started, stopping myself as Charlie's face fell. I realized my mistake too late. If Grey was getting in, that meant Zack was getting in as well. She closed her eyes and frowned at my reminder.

"Sorry, Charlie." I grimaced.

"It's okay." She shrugged. "Let's do some more." Her blue eyes lit up at the prospect. "Jack gave me some more needles, they're clean."

"He did?" I couldn't keep the eagerness out of my voice. With much effort, I sat up and peered at the clock. If I had even an hour to spare before work, I was going to do some more with her. I stared at the timepiece, puzzled by what I read there.

"What is it?" Charlie wondered.

"The clock says its 5:17." I frowned. "It can't be five in the morning, can it? I feel like I've slept all day."

Charlie just shrugged. Confused, I flipped on the TV and changed the channel to the cable guide. The channels scrolled down the screen, some twangy country music playing in the background. And then I realized why it felt like I had slept all day. Because I had. It was 5:17. PM.

"Oh, shit." I looked at Charlie, aghast. "I'm like, over an hour late for work."

Charlie grinned up at me wickedly. "I guess that means you're not going."

I bit my lip, lit a smoke and debated for a moment. I needed my job. I needed the money I made to support all of my habits, to keep living on my own. Surely, going in an hour late was at least better than not showing up at all. They'd probably forgive me.

But Charlie was already getting out the supplies to whip us up another batch. At the very prospect of more heroin, all my responsible deliberating went right out the window. All I could think about was how good it felt, how in mere moments, I wouldn't even care about missing work. And then my decision was made.

CHAPTER 48

It was like I was moving in slow motion. Everything took me about three times as long as normal. In the shower I just stood beneath the hot spray, amazed at how good it felt, how the warm, beating water seemed to soak directly into my skin. And when the water turned cold from my lengthy stay, it still felt good, invigorating almost. I had to take the time to appreciate the softness of the towel as I dried myself, the smell of the laundry soap. Slowly I picked out something to wear, amazed at the sheer beauty and variance of the colours in my closet. I settled on a tight turquoise sweater dress and some black skinny jeans. Then, like old times, Charlie sat me down before her and did my hair and make-up. This too, took way longer than intended, like we both lacked the energy to put any speed into our movements, savouring each moment instead.

I was so happy to be friends with Charlie again; I had missed her very badly. Not just for her beauty expertise. We chatted now and then as she worked. Our thoughts were slow and profound, but I'd never felt more connected to her, I'd never been closer to her. We were on such the same level that words didn't even seem necessary.

Grey was going to be home soon. The very thought sent tingles up my spine. That was the reason for all the fuss, Grey's homecoming. I was touched when Charlie had offered to make me up, knowing how hard it must have been for her to see me so excited. I wondered what it was going to be like now that Zack and Charlie had split up, I wondered if we'd all hang out again like before.

"So, what are you going to do?" I asked her carefully.

"About Zack?" She shrugged, but his name didn't seem to ruin her mood any. "I don't know. I wonder if he was even going to tell me, or if he thinks we can just pick up where we left off."

"Would you?"

"I don't know." She shrugged again. "I mean, there goes all hope of us having like, a real relationship, you know? But, I don't see why we can't still be … friends."

"You'd want to be friends?"

"Yeah, I would. I don't know how to explain it Mac. He's like … he's like, the only one for me. I've never known anyone so … perfect. I don't know." She looked up at me sheepishly. "Does that make me pathetic?"

"No." I decided resolutely. If Grey had cheated on me, I'd feel the same way. "I know exactly what you mean. Are you going to tell him though, that you know?"

"I guess we'll see if he tells me or not." Charlie sighed. "And maybe this is weak of me, but if he asks me for another chance, if he asks me to forgive him, I already know that I will. Even knowing that he's cheated on me doesn't change how I feel about him. It just hurts more."

"Yeah. Well, you deserve to be happy, Charlie. Whatever that entails."

"Thanks Mac. And you look beautiful, if I do say so myself." She smiled at me. "Go look in the mirror."

I did look beautiful. Maybe it was just my heroin-induced haze, but Charlie had worked her magic, yet again. My long dark hair hung in shimmering waves to tumble around the teal shoulders of my sweater that hugged down my torso and flared slightly at my hips. The jeans I wore could have been painted on, they were so tight, emphasizing my long, lean legs. My eyes were smouldering, dark and lined with black—my lips a natural, shimmery red that went well with the sweater.

Charlie was packing up her things as I went back to thank her. She grinned at me.

"No problem Mac. I owe you that much, for being such a jerk to you for so long."

"Don't worry about it." I brushed it off. "I totally understand."

She smiled at me and looked down at her watch. "Well, Grey's going to be here soon. I'm going to go out, give you guys the place to yourselves. I think Courtney and I might swing by Jack's again, should I get some more … stuff … for you?"

"Mmm, yes, please." I found my purse and dug through it, pulling out almost the last of my tip money from the week. "Here. But you don't have to leave just because Grey's coming over."

"Yes. I do." She took my cash and gathered her things. "Have fun tonight."

"Thank you." I gave her a quick hug. "And tell Courtney hi."

Charlie nodded on her way out the door. I heard her limber footsteps trailing off down the old wooden stairs, and then she was gone.

I had nothing to do then but wait. I lit a smoke and sat down gingerly on the couch, careful not to muss anything. I was itching a bit as the heroin slowly faded from my system, but it was bearable. Secretly I hoped that Grey was bringing some China White with him, thinking that surely, this was as special an occasion as any. I still cringed at just the thought of using a needle—though shooting up was faster and more satisfying, seemingly snorting lasted longer.

My heart jumped when finally I heard the crunch of car tires pulling up into the drive. I flicked the TV off and hurried to the front door. Grey was getting out of Zack's car, saying his goodbyes. I couldn't see much more than his outline. My breath hung in the cool fall air, panting; excited as I raced down the front steps. The car was still backing out of the driveway by the time I was in Grey's arms again, crushing him close to me, a wide, glorious smile upon my lips.

Grey chuckled. "Hey." His arms were warm around me, hugging me to him, nestling his face against my neck. His stubble tickled my skin.

"I'm so happy you're back!" I squeezed. I didn't want to let him go, not even just to get inside. He pulled away from me and his blue eyes were warm, shining with happiness. A smirk curved his lips.

"It's good to be back." He admitted. I knew what he was really trying to say. With a happy giggle, I took his hand in mine and led him up the steps.

"What are the guys up to?" I wondered idly, though I didn't really care what they were doing. I was just thankful to have Grey all to myself.

"They're just going to head home and unpack and stuff. They figured we'd want to have some … time, to ourselves."

"Well, they figured right." I smiled slyly and opened up the door for us. Grey set down his bag and took off his heavy coat and shoes. I stood just inside the entry, waiting for him, my pulse racing with anticipation, my flesh nearly aching to touch him, to have him close to me, to feel his body against mine and his lips on my skin again. If it were possible, he had grown more gorgeous in just the week we'd been apart. His dark hair was in its usual perma-mess—I couldn't wait to run my fingers through it—and his cheeks were darkened with stubble. His skin was still dark and tan though summer was long over; it intensified the brilliant blue of his eyes as they finally rested on me—smouldering, cloudy already with the charge of sheer lust that thickened the air.

His eyes raked me over, up and down, so slowly that I nearly couldn't bear it. With agonizing exaggeration, he crossed over to me. All was silent but the sound of my breathing, fast and shallow. Grey rested his hands on my waist, holding them there until I could feel the heat through my sweater. I traced my hands slowly up his arms, thick with muscle, and then down his chest … feeling every contour of his definition beneath my fingertips. I met his eyes—hazy, eager. Without another word he grasped me to him, up in his arms, and then carried me down the hall to my bedroom.

"I love your hair. Have I ever told you that?" Grey wondered, his fingers trailing through my dark silky tresses. It felt amazing, sending shivers up my spine. I smiled.

"No, you haven't."

"Hmm. I guess there's a lot I haven't told you."

"Is there?"

He shrugged. "It's not all easy for me to say." He brought a handful of my hair to his nose and breathed deeply. "You smell so good."

"That's a new one, too." I smiled at him, sprawled upon my stomach on the bed, half-covered by blankets. He was curled up next to me, tracing his fingers down my naked back and arms. It was so serene, such a wonderful, happy moment. I sighed contentedly.

"The first time we met, at the club, I saw you first." Grey admitted then. "And then when I saw Riley, it was the perfect excuse to come over."

"Really?"

"Yeah. And the whole time I told myself, 'Grey, don't do it. Don't do it Grey.' But … I couldn't stop. You just … you stood out."

"I did?"

"Yeah."

I shook my head, fondly remembering that first night. "I think I fell in love with you the moment I saw you on that stage." I giggled. "I felt like an idiot all night, trailing you around like a lost puppy."

"Nah. You were cute." He chuckled. I made a face at the word.

He smirked. "You were adorable."

I slapped him playfully. Grey grinned, seeming to remember something.

"Kiddo."

"Don't call me that!" I twisted around and tried unsuccessfully to wrestle him down against the bed. His hands wrapped around my arms like a vice and pinned me back down, his blue eyes laughing. I giggled as we play fought until unwittingly, mid-wrestle, Grey grasped me by the elbow.

"Ow!" Abruptly I cried out, all trace of humour gone. He stopped immediately, regretful as he looked down at my arm.

"Oh, sorry." He frowned down at the yellowish-purple bruise staining my forearm, the bruise he had just accidentally grasped. His brow furrowed. "What happened here?"

"Oh," I struggled a moment, trying to decide how to tell him. I chose to play it casual; shrugging like it was no big deal. "I took Charlie out the other night, you know, to cheer her up about Zack, but they didn't have any of the China White stuff, like you had, so we shot up instead."

I watched as Grey took in all this information. His eyes narrowed; his dark brow creasing. "Okay, wait a minute. You went out the other night, to get heroin?"

"Yeah." I nodded. "I wanted to cheer Charlie up."

He considered this a moment. "Where did you go?"

"I don't know. We went with Charlie's friend Courtney, maybe you know her, she works at the Aurora. Anyway, we went to this Jack guy's house …."

"Stop." Grey's face was suddenly hard, his body tense. He glared at me intensely. "Jack? As in, Jack Turcotte?"

"I don't know his last name." Instinctively I cringed back from Grey's heated stare. I had a distinct feeling that I was in trouble. Big trouble.

"Big guy? Blonde?"

I nodded.

"Fuck. Are you serious? Oh my …." Grey cursed. He dropped his head into his hands and shook it back and forth in vexation. His entire form was rigid. I sat up in the bed, pulling the blankets over myself and watching him anxiously.

"What is it?" I wondered, biting my lip. "What's the matter?"

"You went to Jack's house, alone?"

"No, not alone. I was with Courtney and Charlie."

At this Grey scoffed, rolling his eyes—but I continued, stupidly, wanting to be honest with him. "I didn't really want to shoot up, I was scared of the needle, but then Jack did it for me. I think I bruised because I was trying to pull away from him."

Grey just stared at me a moment, his expression blank. The only thing that gave away the true fury of his anger was the clenching of his jaw, the hardness of his eyes as they bored into me.

"You mean Jack Turcotte did that to you?" He pointed accusingly at the bruise on my arm. "Even though you didn't want to? He forced you?"

"No, well, yeah," I wasn't sure what to say, what might incur more anger, "but, I mean, I wanted to get high … I was just being a chicken about the needle …."

Grey was silent a long moment. His breath escaped in a long, drawn out sigh, and his hands clenched into fists. "I'm going over there."

"What?" I got up on my knees. "Why?"

"To kick that guy's ass!" Agitated, Grey stood up and started dressing, hastily throwing on his boxers and searching for the rest of his clothes among the piles of dirty laundry that inhabited my floor.

"No, no, Grey don't." I blanched at the thought. "It's no big deal. He's not worth it."

"Really?" Grey spat. "Do you have any idea what could have happened to you over there?"

I shook my head, my dark eyes wide.

"Ugh. I don't even want to tell you. I don't even want to picture it."

I gulped. "That bad?"

"Yes, that bad." Grey glared at me again, like I wasn't taking him seriously enough. "You are never to go over there again. Promise me!"

"I promise." I answered quickly.

"If you want more heroin, you ask me, you get it from me and you do it with me. Okay? You don't know how easy it is to … all it takes is some fuckup trying to be funny …." He trailed off, closing his eyes, his entire countenance tense with anger. "You know what guys like that … do you know what they do to girls when they're … like that? Do you?"

I shook my head again. The thought honestly hadn't even occurred to me, and I wasn't even a hundred percent sure just what he was referring to. Something bad enough to make him react this way.

"I'm sorry, Grey." I stammered shakily, alarmed by this new information. "Please don't go. It's my fault. I didn't know."

He stared hard at me a moment, his shirt in his hands.

"Of course you didn't know." He sighed. He ran a hand through his dark hair. "I'm sorry. I didn't mean to freak you out. It just … it makes me crazy to think of someone … taking advantage of you. I mean …." He looked up at me again, and there was some warmth back in his blue eyes. "You're so …."

"Stupid?" I offered. I felt like a total idiot.

"No … no. You're innocent." He shrugged. "Trusting."

"Like … naïve."

"No. Well … maybe. But I like it, the way you are. I don't even really know how to describe it … kind of … the opposite of jaded. Just … fresh." He shook his head. "You don't belong in the drug world, Mackenzie. You're too … pure."

I frowned. Pure wasn't that far off from kiddo. "Grey, I belong in whatever world you're in."

"No." He shook his head. "You don't."

"Yes I do." I sat up and grasped his hand, pulling him back to the bed. "I love this world. I love every part of it."

"That doesn't mean you belong."

I rolled my eyes. "Whatever." It annoyed me when he talked this way, like he wasn't good enough for me … like what we had wasn't right. It was ridiculous. He was my dream come true. Before he could even think to continue, I stopped him with a wicked smile.

"You think I'm pure, Grey? I'll show you pure."

This time, when I pushed him down against the bed, he didn't resist me.

It was later … much, much later when, wrapped up in the blankets beneath a haze of smoke, we heard Charlie return. Secretly, I was relieved. I knew she'd been at Jack's house and given what I knew about the man now, I couldn't help but worry for her. It wasn't enough for me to tell Grey about it though, as horrible as that was … I couldn't stand the thought of him going over there and getting in a fight. Not that I doubted Grey, I was certain he could take Jack. But how would he fare against Jack and all the other sweaty, shifty eyed men that also resided there? I knew it wouldn't be a fair fight. And I didn't want Grey getting on the wrong side of such dangerous people. Not for me.

Charlie's arrival had also given me an idea. I knew what she now had in her possession, something I was suddenly desperate to do. I didn't know how to broach the topic with Grey though; I wasn't sure how he'd react. I propped myself up on my elbow and looked at him as sweetly as I could.

"Grey?"

"Hmm …?" he opened one eye quizzically, a smile upon his lips.

"I was just wondering … I mean, do you think that …." I hesitated, biting my lip. "… would this be considered a special occasion? Your homecoming?"

He knew instantly what I was referring to, but Grey shook his head, seemingly amused by my question. "I think it's pretty special."

"Me too." I cleared my throat. "But that wasn't really … what I was getting at."

"Oh, really? What were you getting at?" He teased.

I rolled my eyes at him. He was going to make me say it, I could tell. "Well, I know Charlie picked up some … stuff, and I was wondering if we could do some."

"Hmm." Grey paused thoughtfully. His blue eyes opened eagerly. "Yeah, I think that'd be okay."

"I'll go get it." I offered excitedly, sitting up in the bed and searching for my clothes.

"Mackenzie?"

"Yeah?"

"That's not really necessary."

"What isn't?"

"You getting dressed." His eyes, lazy and shining blue, raked up my naked form.

"But … I thought you said …."

"I know. I've got some in my bag." Grey chuckled sheepishly. "Apparently, you weren't the only one who couldn't hold out."

"Oh." I grinned. "Anything to keep me naked, huh?"

"Hell yeah." He laughed.

Excitement raced down my spine. I had to stifle my glee. "Do you have the sniffing kind?" I wondered hopefully. Grey shook his head.

"No. It's the needle kind. Is that enough to deter you?"

"No." I answered quickly. "I mean, not if you'll do it for me. Will you?"

Grey grinned. "Of course."

"Okay."

He grabbed the stuff and heated us up a batch, taking some supplies from his suitcase and mixing it all in one of my spoons. I watched him, my hands sweating in anticipation, knowing that in only moments I would be free as a bird, riding a wave of sheer bliss that would crest and crash down on me. I couldn't wait.

"Mackenzie."

"Yes?" I lifted my eyes from Grey's hands and met his sober gaze.

"Do you remember me telling you how addictive this stuff can be?"

"Yeah." I nodded. "But I thought we decided this was a special occasion."

"We did. It is." He smiled. "But do you think that you could … not do this with anybody else? Even Charlie? I mean, unless I'm around?"

"How come?" I wondered lightly.

"I don't know. This stuff's so volatile. I just … it would make me feel better if I knew … when you were doing it … and how much you were doing, you know?" He shook his head. "I know I sound like an asshole. But it would keep me from worrying."

I grinned. His concern touched me. "You don't sound like an asshole, Grey. Besides, as much as I can help it, I'm going to be with you anyway." I leaned over and kissed his shoulder, smiling up at him. "So it shouldn't be a problem."

"That sounds good to me." He smirked and kissed me softly on the lips. "Thanks."

He turned then to fill the syringe with the dark, tar coloured drugs.

"Okay. Make a fist." He instructed. I did as I was told, holding out my arm to him and tightening my muscles. Slowly the veins in my arm stood out, not as much as with the elastic, but enough to make it work. Even knowing how good the heroin would feel, I couldn't help but cower at the sight of the needle in his capable hand.

"Its okay, Mackenzie." Grey's voice was low and melodic, soothing. I kept my gaze on his, refusing to look down. "You'll barely notice."

Even so, I shut my eyes. Slowly and gently, he grasped my arm in his warm hands. I held my breath. I felt a tiny prick, the slightest of pinches in my elbow pit.

"It's in. Look, Mackenzie. Watch this."

The power Grey had over me was phenomenal. I actually opened my eyes and stared down at the needle breaking through my skin, the sharp steel cold against my flesh. I watched as Grey retracted the plunger, as my blood filled the syringe, mixing with the heroin, bright red blood dancing with the dark drugs, curling and twisting around each other. I was still staring, transfixed, as Grey shot the drugs straight into my veins.

It was even better than I remembered, even better than even hours before. I gasped shakily as it took me, the sheer pleasure rocketing through my body until I couldn't take it anymore, and slackened back against the bed with the most sincere of smiles spread wide across my face. I still don't know how to properly describe it. On the movie *Trainspotting*, Renton says, "Take the best orgasm you ever had, multiply it by a thousand and you're still nowhere near it."

He was right. That kind of pleasure isn't something one can just imagine or compare it to. Unless you've done heroin, there's no way you can know how good it feels. There aren't words to describe the bliss, the euphoria, the utter … nothingness.

Grey shot up beside me but I was barely aware of it. He fell back against the bed, his face deep with pleasure, close enough to mine that I could stare right into it. His beautiful, gorgeous, perfect face. For me, it didn't get any better than that. Life was perfect. Everything I could ever ask for. Everything I'd been searching for.

I smiled as the waves crashed over me.

CHAPTER 49

"Where do you think you're going?" Strong hands wrapped around my waist. I smiled at Grey in the mirror, looking over my shoulder, his blue eyes watching me as his lips pressed against my neck.

I groaned and leaned back against him. "I have to go to work." I sighed. "Not all of us can be rock stars, you know."

"Yeah." He chuckled. "Some rock star. I doubt there's ever been a rock star in history as broke-ass as I am right now."

"Maybe not." I shrugged encouragingly. "But you won't be for long."

"Yeah." Grey mumbled, bending to kiss me again. I felt his pain. I was seriously strapped for cash. All our money had gone to the weekend ... the perfect, blissfully high weekend that had gone by all too fast and managed to eat up the rest of my tip money and whatever savings Grey had left in the bank. I didn't want to go to work, not at all, but I had to make some tips or we'd be SOL for the evening's habits. Grey insisted that we slow down the heroin use now, since that was basically all we'd done for the last forty-eight odd hours. I was settling for cocaine, but it was way more expensive than heroin, and would probably take up whatever tips I made that night. I bit my lip in thought. I really needed more money. My rent was coming up soon as well, but I didn't want to think about that.

"You look really pretty." He pushed my dark hair back from my face and smirked at me in the mirror. "Isn't this skirt a little ... short, though?"

Teasingly, I rolled my eyes. Grey hadn't been around to witness the gradual shrinking of my wardrobe—my necklines getting lower, my skirts shorter, my heels higher. Presently, I wore a tiny lace miniskirt and a tight white sweater with a plunging v-neck. I chose it so the long sleeves would hide the sickly yellow bruise that stained my arm.

"You'll see when I get home tonight, the difference this look makes tip wise."

"I bet." He frowned slightly. "But I don't know if I should let you out of the house like this. I don't like the thought of other guys looking at you."

I smiled and turned around in his arms, so I was looking up into his gorgeous face. I shrugged. "So what if they look. You're the only one that gets to touch." I promised. This brought the smile back to his eyes. He smirked again and then pulled me up to him, crushing me against his lips.

It was in this sweet embrace that Charlie found us. She cleared her throat impatiently and rapped on my opened bedroom door.

"Comin' Mac? We're going to be late."

"Yeah." Regretfully, I pulled myself away from him. "I'll see you later."

"I'll be over at my house. Come by when you're done."

"Okay." I kissed him again, I couldn't help myself. "Bye."

"Bye."

"So, how was your weekend?" I asked my friend once we were seated in her car, smoking with the windows cracked only slightly. It was already cold out and the days were getting colder. I shivered, and realized that I was not looking forward to winter.

"It was alright." Charlie shrugged. "Courtney and I hung out. Did some H. You?"

"About the same." I downplayed how awesome it had really been, flicking my cigarette, trying not to ash on myself. "You really like heroin, don't you?"

"I do." She admitted.

"Me too." I exhaled a big waft of smoke. "I just wish it weren't so, you know … addictive. Grey says we can't do anymore for awhile, that we should save it for special occasions."

"That's probably smart." Charlie nodded begrudgingly. "But I don't know if it's really that bad. I mean, I'm definitely not addicted yet."

"Me either." I agreed, but I wondered if that were really true. I didn't tell Charlie that heroin had been my first thought upon waking up, how all morning I'd nearly paced with craving, nervous because I knew I wasn't going to get anymore for awhile. I tried to talk myself out of it though, out of the desperation, and having Grey around helped a ton. Just his presence was like a drug for me.

I shook the topic from my mind. Just the thought of it was enough to bring back the craving. "So, did you see Zack at all this weekend?"

Charlie turned a corner too fast. "No." She shook her head. "He never came around."

"Are you going to see him?"

She looked at me. "Do you think I should?"

"I have no idea."

"Me either." Charlie sighed. "I'd like to say I won't. I'd like to pretend I'm strong enough not to go over there. But just the thought that he's in town, that he's so close …." She took a deep drag of her cigarette and then tossed the butt out the window. "Whatever. We'll see."

We made it to the restaurant in record time. I was a bit apprehensive about work; I wondered what kind of reception I'd get after ditching last Friday. Charlie had skipped all last week but apparently she'd called in sick with Mark, so she was probably off the hook. We strode into the quiet restaurant, still with the calm before the inevitable rush, and went to hang up our coats in the waitress station. But there were already purses and jackets hanging there, taking up the hooks.

We eyed each other curiously, and just then Stacy and Mallory—two part-time girls—came floating in from the top section, laughing and joking as they made their way back to the station. Stacy had a bucket full of creamers in her hand and Mallory carried an empty tray. They looked like they were getting ready to work our shift.

"What are you girls doing here?" Charlie wondered. "Did the schedule change?"

Stacy shrugged, looking as surprised to see us as we were to see her. "I don't know. Ralph just called me and asked me to work."

"Yeah, me too." Mallory nodded. "Why, were you guys supposed to?"

"Uh, yeah. We always do." Charlie's voice was a little snippy. I bit my lip, not sure what was going on, but pretty certain it wasn't something good. Especially if Ralph was involved.

The girls just stared at us, as someone younger does when they've angered someone they look up to—repentantly. Charlie sighed and shook her head at them, flipping her blonde curls behind her shoulder.

"Whatever. We'll go talk to someone and get this straightened out."

The squeak of the swinging door on its hinges made us all look up with curiosity. Ralph came through it from the kitchen, his arms crossed against his burly chest, his red eyebrows raised with disapproval as he looked over at Charlie and me with indignation written across his face.

"Ralph." Charlie greeted coolly, trying to hide her surprise. "I think there's been a mix up."

He only nodded. "Yes. Can I have a word, girls, if you don't mind?" He opened the swinging door and motioned us forward. I gulped. Charlie let me walk in front of her through the kitchen and into the back, which I was thankful for. I didn't like to think about where Ralph's eyes would be if he were walking right behind me.

We filed into the office—it was cluttered with papers and orders and large silver canisters of Pepsi refills. There was an ashtray overflowing with butts on the desk and many plastic cups coated in sticky pop syrup. It smelt vaguely like beer as we stood, waiting as Ralph closed the door behind him and walked through the clutter to sit at his desk. I had a very sinking suspicion that we were in trouble. Big trouble.

"So, I'm sure you've probably already figured this out, but both of you are fired." He stared at us evenly, his voice totally calm and at ease ... like he'd just told us what sections we were covering instead of terminating our employment. My mouth dropped in surprise. I looked up at Charlie in horror, following her lead, not knowing what to do or say to get us out of the situation.

She looked at Ralph a moment, her brow furrowing. "And why is that?"

Ralph scoffed, like the answer was glaringly obvious. "Do you really want me to start? You're late, you drop things, and you're completely negligent. Both of you. The customers have been complaining. And the way you're dressing lately, I mean, not that I mind, but this is a family restaurant."

"Couldn't you just like, give us a warning or something?" Charlie negotiated.

"Maybe I would've. If you hadn't cut work all last week, and if you ...," he looked straight at me, making me gulp again, his beady little green eyes angry and intolerant, "... hadn't blown off your shift on Friday."

"I was sick!" Charlie insisted. "So was she!"

"Yeah right, with what? Cocaine?" Ralph scoffed again, his pudgy face leering. "I'm not an idiot, Charlene. I know what you girls do around here.

And I know that you were out at the Aurora almost every night last week. Sick? That's insulting."

Oh no. I bit my lip, closing my eyes as the situation really sank in. This wasn't happening. I had enough money troubles already without losing my job. No, I needed my job. I needed the tips, I needed the money. I needed to get high tonight, as soon as work was over. I needed cigarettes and alcohol and I needed to pay my rent. If Charlie and I were to get evicted, I'd be forced to move back in with my parents. I cringed at just the thought. No, I couldn't lose my job. I made too much money at it. There was nothing else I knew of in a town this small that could compare.

"Please, Ralph." My voice seemed quiet and shaky after Charlie's confidence. I cleared my throat and forced the words out. "What if we promised to be better? I mean, things kind of got out of control, but we're good at what we do. I mean, we were, I guess. But we can be again. You know how well we work together, how good we can be. Most of the customers like us. Please? I can't lose this job."

Something about my statement sparked an idea in Ralph's mind. He sat for a moment and then he sighed, considering my words. His chair groaned as he leaned back in it. When finally he looked up at Charlie and me again, there was a strange glint in his green eyes, like an evil thought had just occurred there.

"You're desperate to keep your job, then?"

"I'd like to, yes." I admitted.

"Yes." Charlie agreed.

"Okay, fine. You can both keep your jobs."

A smile spread across Charlie's face. She looked over at me with happy surprise.

"Oh, thanks Ralph. That's great—"

"On one condition." He continued, interrupting her. Charlie stopped mid-sentence and waited, glancing at me again, cautiously this time.

"What is that?"

Ralph's smile was sardonic. "Lock the door." He ordered.

"What? Why?"

"I take care of you ...," he shrugged, "... you take care of me."

He jingled his belt buckle.

It took me a moment to realize what he meant by that. I actually gasped. Charlie got it faster than I did. Her face froze in anger and disgust.

"Fuck you." She spat. "Never."

"It's your job." Ralph turned to me repugnantly. "Mackenzie?"

I was at a loss. I needed my job; I needed it badly. What was I going to do without any money? The panic rose in my chest again as I realized that tonight we'd have to go without—no heroin, no cocaine, no weed even. No nothing. I bit my lip. Maybe … maybe it wouldn't be so bad. Maybe it would be quick. And besides, if I had the money, I could get the drugs, and if I had the drugs, I could forget about … it … later.

"Mackenzie!" Charlie glared at me in horror. "We are leaving. Now!" She grasped my arm and slammed the door open, pulling me from Ralph's office and out the back door so fast I couldn't even resist. My cheeks flushed scarlet, the blood was pounding in my head.

"What the fuck was that?" Charlie demanded angrily, wrapping her arms around herself against the cold as we stumbled to her car. "Were you actually considering it!?"

"No! No!" I lied, shaking my head—furious, desperate. I couldn't believe what had happened. I couldn't believe I actually considered it, even for a moment. So much for being pure. By the time we reached her car, my tears were blinding me. I felt so ashamed of myself.

"Fuck Charlie!" I screamed. People on the street turned to stare at me, but I didn't care. I slammed my fist into the hood of her car. "I can't believe I just lost my job!"

She was wide-eyed, watching me. "It's okay Mac. You'll get another one."

"Ugh!" My breath was frosty in the dimming light. "Yeah, maybe tomorrow, or next week even. What do I do now? I need money now!"

Charlie shook her head. "Get in the car, Mackenzie."

I obeyed, only because the cold was starting to numb my fingertips. It felt like it could snow any moment. I rubbed my hands together to warm them as Charlie started the car. We sat in silence for a moment, letting the engine warm up. I reached for a cigarette, vexed when I realized my pack was almost empty. I had no money for more.

"Fuck!" I exclaimed again.

"Okay, Mac. Calm down."

I breathed for a moment, shutting my eyes, trying not to panic. "What am I going to do?"

"How much do you need?"

"I don't know. Enough for the week. And for rent and stuff, next week."

"You mean, you don't have anything?"

"No." I muttered sheepishly. "I spent almost all of it last weekend."

"What about Grey?"

"Nothing. Not until they start doing gigs again." I shrugged.

"Well … what about your parents?"

I cringed, instantly rejecting the thought. "No, Charlie. I can't ask them."

"Why not?"

"Because." I shut my eyes, shaking my head. I didn't feel like getting into it with her. I could picture the faces of my parents as I asked for money. I knew my dad would gloat. "See, I knew you couldn't do it on your own," his face would say.

I shook my head again, resolved. "I just can't ask them."

"Oh, okay. So you almost went down on that guy because you were so desperate for money, but you can't ask your parents for some?"

I glared at her. "I did not almost—"

"Whatever. Mackenzie, just don't be an idiot. Ask your parents."

I sighed. Loud and long. I did need money. I became more desperate for it as the agitated minutes passed by. "Fine." I relented—angry, irritated. "Fine, I'll ask them. Will you drive me there?"

"Sure." Charlie threw the car in reverse and backed out of the stall. "I'm sure they'll understand."

My answer was a grumble.

When Charlie pulled up at my parents' house it was empty, vacant—I could already tell. It had a hollow, dark feel to it … something I was all too familiar with. Something I'd come home to regularly. No one inside. No one expected anytime soon.

"They're not even home." I sighed.

"Well, you can call them later." Charlie suggested. "I'll drive you again."

"Thanks Charlie."

Just as she was about to pull away, I stopped her.

"Wait." My parents still had my things from Marcy's wedding. I kept putting off picking them up, unwilling to face my parents again until they apologized for the whole Craig Donovan stunt. But since they weren't home, I figured it was the perfect time. "I'll be right back."

I ran up the drive, pounded my code into the keypad and opened the door. It had been months since I'd been home, but I didn't waste any time looking around. The bag full of my stuff was in the front entry, where it had probably sat since mom called me weeks ago to come and pick it up. As I slung the bag over my shoulder, something else caught my eye.

It was my mom's purse. Just one of many. It was hanging over the deacons bench perched against the wall, and the flap had come open, the contents inside bulging out. I didn't even think twice. There wasn't even a whisper from my conscience that what I was doing was bad. Unthinkable until now. I opened up her purse and took what I knew would be inside. A neat green roll of twenties. There were a few red fifties tucked in as well. Why my mom always insisted on carrying so much cash was beyond me, but at the moment, I was thankful for her odd little habit. I stuffed the money into my pocket—there must have been at least three-hundred dollars there—and felt instantly better.

I ran back to the car after locking up the house, a broad smile of relief upon my face. Charlie noticed the change in my attitude immediately.

"Find what you were looking for?" She wondered curiously.

"You could say that." I grinned.

CHAPTER 50

I was dying. I tried to swallow and my poor parched throat scraped in protest. Unwillingly I opened my bleary eyes, desperate enough for water that I forced my weary muscles to work and get me out of my bed. It was cold away from Grey's slumbering form. I leaned on the wall for support and made my way painfully to the kitchen, trying to hurry, knowing that the faster I made it there the faster I could get back in bed.

It was quiet in the house, still early. I padded to the sink, clad in nothing but Grey's black Iron Maiden t-shirt and my underwear, and filled up the closest cup I could find with sweet, cold water. I chugged it back, my throat sorely struggling to swallow down the liquid, easing as the cool wet relieved the tightness there. I sighed, my eyes barely open, and poured myself another cup.

As I drank, I noticed the door to Charlie's room was wide open, her bedding rumpled, her bed unmade—but clearly not being slept in. I frowned with concern and my heart went out to my friend, knowing the state she was in and the reason she was in it. Zack. I bit my lip as I remembered the harsh reception Charlie had received from her once-boyfriend the night before at Grey's house. I had convinced her to come in after our brief stop at my parents', knowing how badly she wanted to see Zack and hoping the two of them could be reconciled. But Zack had barely given her a glance when she entered, just a small impertinent nod that was easily translated into a dismissal. That was it. No words, no apologies, no explanations. Like Charlie wasn't even worth the effort.

I had watched as a spasm of pain quickly shadowed Charlie's beautiful face, but she composed herself before anyone else could see and then wordlessly left the room, slamming the door on her way out of the house. I followed her, my heart breaking for her, into the cold, wintry evening.

"Charlie, I'm so sorry." I called. I hadn't time to put on a jacket, and wrapped my arms around myself for warmth. "Forget about Zack, he's nothing."

"Whatever." She made a noise—like a half-laugh, half-sob—and continued storming towards her car.

"Wait, Charlie, don't go, please? Wait for me, I'll get some stuff, we can go back to our house …."

"No thanks. Don't waste a second away from Grey. Not for me."

That brought me up short. My breath hung icy in the cold air. "But what are you going to do?"

"I don't know. Go find Courtney, go to Jack's house."

"No, Charlie." I followed her out to the car, lowering my voice so the neighbours couldn't hear. "Please, don't go to Jack's. Grey says it's not safe."

She made another noise—a half-sob, half-scoff—and shook her head at me.

"Perfect."

"Charlie …."

She sighed. "Go, Mackenzie. I'll be all right. I'm not mad at you. I just … I need to be … away. Okay. I'll see you later." She got into the car then and slammed the door. I stepped out of the way, backing onto the sidewalk as she peeled out into the street, watching in worry as the red taillights slowly bobbed off into the night.

Grey met me at the door with our jackets, stopping me before I could get back inside and really let Zack have it. I was seething, partly from the horrible, hideous day I'd already been through but mostly out of worry and anger for my friend. If anything bad happened to Charlie, anything at all, I was going to place every ounce of the blame on Zack.

"Come on, sugar. Don't worry about it. He doesn't deserve her, she's better off." Grey had convinced me, with the warmth of his arms, to let it go. I relented and leaned against him, but my tension didn't ease any. I knew what I needed to make me feel better, to help me get over the stress of the day. To help me forget that I had lost my job and stolen from my mother, to help me forget the leer on Ralph's face as he jingled his belt buckle. To make me forget what I had almost done ….

"Don't be upset Mackenzie. Please?" Grey misread the look on my face, thinking it was worry for Charlie. His blue eyes were pleading. "How can I make it better?"

Grey hated to see me upset, ever. He would do anything to make me happy again. At this thought an idea occurred to me, something I never would have considered before. But I was desperate, and I had discovered a weakness in Grey that could be easily manipulated. Me.

I shut my eyes and leaned against him, letting a sob-like shudder run through me. He felt it and his arms reacted, pulling me close. His hand stroked my hair, reassuringly, and he kissed my cheek just below my ear.

"What's the matter, Mackenzie? Tell me."

I shook my head and sighed. When I spoke, my voice was hoarse, like I was holding back tears. "It's nothing." I choked out. "I've just had such a terrible day."

"Don't cry. Please? Do you want to … should we push off? Would that help?"

"Maybe." I whispered.

"Wait here. I'll be right back." He kissed my forehead and headed quickly back inside. I stood out in the cold, relieved and amazed by how easily Grey had caved … but there was no joy in my victory. If anything, I was saddened by what I had done; what I was capable of. For the second time that day, I felt ashamed of myself.

But I knew it wouldn't take long until I forgot all about it.

I shook myself back to the present and poured the rest of my drink into the sink. I hoped fervently that Charlie was okay, that she was safe somewhere. I hated to think of her at Jack's house, the thought made me agitated and nervous. With a sigh, I headed back to my bedroom. There was one sure way to forget about it all.

I eyed the nightstand eagerly as I crawled back into bed, satisfied when I saw there was more than enough heroin in the little blue balloon to get us through the rest of the day. Though it beyond sucked that I lost my job, there were upsides to it. I didn't have to go to work. I was free to hang out with Grey all day long, to get high all day long—nothing could make me leave my bedroom if I didn't want to. I lit a smoke and smiled with anticipation. It was like the most perfect kind of holiday.

And I knew what I was going to do for money. I'd keep looking for a job, for sure, but in the meantime … well, my parents were loaded. And they were never home. Surely they wouldn't mind providing a little just to help us out, until Grey started gigging again and I found a job, at least.

They probably wouldn't even notice. It didn't even occur to me to feel guilty about robbing from my parents, it was all easily justified. They'd given Marcy a car when she graduated. What was a few hundred dollars for me?

By the time Grey stirred I had already mixed us a batch. I lay behind him, kissing his back and his shoulders and his neck until he was fully awake, his blue eyes gazing up at me lustily. Then I handed him the needle and held out my arm.

"Please?" I smiled. He pulled me down until I was lying beneath him and kissed me furiously, passionately, his warm hands all over my body until I was at a frenzy, nearly frantic for him. Just when I was on the brink of sheer pleasure, Grey paused a moment, a smirk curving his lips as he placed the cold steel to my skin.

And it was like nothing I'd ever known before. Nothing I'd ever thought possible. I thought I might die from the euphoria. And all the while Grey's arms were wrapped around me, and he was kissing me, and he was whispering in my ear how much he loved me. And I loved him, though I couldn't speak it at the time, my heart was nearly bursting with how much I loved him. I'd never been happier.

CHAPTER 51

Grey liked heroin just as much as I did. I'd been banking on it, actually, knowing that he'd cave that much more if he wanted the H as badly as I did. It was all too easy for us to go from balloon to balloon, justifying every one, calling each one our last and then finding some reason to go and get another. It was lovely, my holiday—spent almost entirely in my room with the man that I adored, smiling smiles of pure, relentless joy and forgetting all about the world surrounding us.

Charlie came and went. Every now and then I'd hear a door close or her hairdryer from the bathroom. She was spending more and more time with Courtney. At times a female voice—not Charlie's but still recognizable—would float to me from beyond my bliss and I'd know that it was Courtney, that she was over at our house. But nothing could coax me from my room, the ultimate zenith of my happiness. Nothing but the need for more heroin.

Once in awhile when our supply was getting low, I'd rise from my sloth-like existence and force myself into a shower, throw on some clothes and go out into the world. My parents were never home. I'd go through purses and jean pockets and bowls of change, always finding enough to fuel our habit for another week. At times I'd try to picture the conclusion my parents would come too when they found their money missing. Would they suspect me? Or would they blame it on their forgetfulness—just another side effect of the life-consuming careers they had chosen? It didn't matter. Sometimes I wondered if they knew how badly I needed the money. The more I stole from them, the more there seemed to be an overabundance of cash just lying around their house next time I went. I'd shrug it off though, chalking it up to mere coincidence so I wouldn't have to feel guilty for taking advantage of them.

When I got back home, it was Grey's turn. He'd dress and shower and take the money I'd procured and leave the house. Sometimes this meant just a simple trip to his house, where either Alex or Zack would be holding and generous enough to sell us some. Other times it meant a trip to the city, and the three of them would be gone for hours while I waited at home, edgy and impatient for my next fix. I'd take the time to straighten up my room and tidy up the house somewhat … washing the week old food from the plates piling up, shaking out my bedding, emptying the overflowing ashtrays, disposing of the countless needles covering every flat surface in my bedroom …. Basically, getting everything in order for our next binge.

I knew this couldn't last indefinitely. I mean, this wasn't really a way of life. It was just a time out, an extended break before we re-entered normal society again. It had been ages since I'd last been to a club; months, it seemed, since I'd hung out with all of my friends. And I needed to get a job soon. I couldn't steal from my parents forever. All this I knew, but the actual date to start my new life again kept getting pushed back, further and further. It loomed on the horizon, something I knew I needed to get back to—to do—but it was so easy to procrastinate, so easy to justify the next balloon of sticky black drugs.

Even so, when Grey returned home after a trip to the city one weekend and held only one rubber pouch in his hand, I was shocked, disappointed. I gazed up at him in alarm.

"Are you heading back again to the city this weekend? For more?" I wondered hopefully.

"No." He was hesitant to begin. I knew he wouldn't want to upset me, but at the same time, he knew he had to be firm. "No, Mackenzie. This is it. We've booked the Aurora again and we start playing next week. I have to get serious; I can't be strung out all the time. I can't even remember the last time I practiced my guitar." He held his hand out in front of him and stretched out his stiff fingers. "One last weekend, okay? And then we quit, for good."

I nodded. I knew the truth in his words, but still I was sad, afraid for my holiday to be over. I didn't want it to be over. I wanted to argue with him, but I had no argument. I tried to rationalize, to talk some sense into my brain. This wasn't living. This wasn't life. I needed to get straight too.

When was the last time I'd talked to Charlie? The last time I'd socialized with anyone? The last time I'd eaten?

"You're right." I admitted begrudgingly. "We need to quit."

"One last weekend." Grey smirked at me. He set the supplies down on my nightstand and began rolling up his shirtsleeve, revealing the dark, hard muscle of his arm. "Let's make it count."

Monday morning came too soon. Grey and I woke up about the same time, uncomfortable and sweaty. He grabbed my hand, lacing his fingers through mine, and kissed me encouragingly.

"We're done." He proclaimed. "We're done with heroin."

I nodded. "Yes." I agreed. I tried not to be sad, I tried to be excited for a fresh start. We're done, we're done with heroin, I repeated to myself, over and over again. But even though that thought was running foremost in my mind, nothing could prepare me for what we were in for.

At first I was merely … achy. Like I was coming down with the flu or something, like my bones were sore in their very marrow. It was unpleasant, but bearable. Grey and I lay back on my bed, smoking as our sweat dampened the sheets beneath us, trying to talk to each other and keep our minds from the withdrawal.

"The CD's almost finished." He informed me. "It's just being mastered now, and then it will be ready for distribution."

"So it'll be in music stores and stuff?" I wondered, amazed. My stomach churned within me. I tried to ignore it.

"Uh … I think so. I think it'll be more for having at our concerts, for fans to buy." A wave of pain contorted his handsome features for a split second, but he recovered quickly. "But Tom's going to try and get us some radio play."

"What? That's awesome!" I started to smile, but a blistering stab of heat bore into my guts. I panted around it. "Your songs are going to be on the radio?"

"Yeah." Grey wiped his brow. "Cool huh?"

"Yeah." I tried smiling again. "I'm so proud of you. I can't wait to just turn on the radio in the car and hear your voice." I imagined it then—anything to take my mind off the churning—and beamed at him through my sweat.

"It'll be a trip, that's for sure." He chuckled. "And … I didn't want to tell you until I knew more about it … but, there's been talk of a summer festival tour as well. Like with famous bands, like Green Day and Moist …." Grey put an arm around his stomach and winced. "It's like a ten-city tour."

"Grey!" I exclaimed. "That's amazing. When do you find out?"

"Soon. Tom's been setting stuff up for us, like, more than the Aurora. I think we may play a few times in the city. We're going to have a meeting soon and figure it all out."

"Wow, I can't believe it. I'm so happy for you. You're going to be so famous."

"I hope so." He tried to smile, but it was more like a grimace. I wondered if he were subconsciously trying to talk himself out of wanting the heroin. Like if telling me about all of his concerts was also a way to list the reasons for staying clean. The pros. Because I could tell it was getting harder for him—as it was for me—to ignore the symptoms anymore. Pain was lashing through my stomach, making me pant and lay weakly on my side. I drew my knees up to my chest.

"You okay?" Grey wondered, placing a sweaty hand on my slick arm.

"Yeah." I lied. Another spasm clutched me. "You?"

"Yeah." He lay back and shut his eyes though, his lips a hard, tight line.

"Grey?"

"Yes?"

"Keep talking to me, okay? It helps."

It seemed like he tried to laugh, but the sound never made it to his lips. "What do you want to hear?"

"Anything. Something about you, something I don't know about."

"Something you don't know … hmmm …." He inhaled sharply, and then his face relaxed. "Well, this isn't … the first time that I've had to get off … heroin."

"It's not?" I couldn't hide my surprise. "When did you?"

"When I was younger. Like, fifteen, sixteen."

"Really? I had no idea." I couldn't form a tight enough ball to keep the pain at bay. I grit my teeth and felt the sweat pouring from my brow. "Was it hard to quit?"

"Nah." He shook his head. "I barely got into it. We smoked it then, you know, tin foil, plastic pen tube. I was such a punk kid, into all kinds of shit."

I listened quietly, shutting my eyes and focusing on Grey's low, velvet voice instead of the gnawing in my stomach. "Things were bad before."

He explained. "I dropped out of school. We were stealing stereos and stuff to pay for drugs. One of my friends nearly got beat to death by a dealer." He paused for a moment, talking a breath. "I saw some messed up things go down. When I tried heroin … it was such freedom. I didn't have to think about my past and my parents, or my present and all the shit I'd seen and done, the little shit-hole apartment that was my home, my frail old grandma who was waiting for me there."

I nodded encouragingly. I loved it when Grey opened up like this to me. Most of his emotions he expressed in his songs—I had to listen to them, read the lyrics there to really understand what he'd been through, what was going through his head. He had my attention now, my rapt attention, overshadowing the sick, achy blood racing through my body. I would listen to whatever he had to say.

His eyes were shut, in remembrance or in pain, I couldn't tell. His voice shook ever so slightly. "It was my grandma that made me change. I could see her, wasting away, her hands worn with worry in her lap. I was leaving, it was late one night, and I needed a fix. She refused to let me leave. She begged me not to go, but I wouldn't listen. Finally, she lost it on me. I can still see her eyes, they were so wide, so furious. 'Go ahead and die then, and see if anyone cares! You're just like your parents, Grey Lewis. You're a loser! A screw up!'"

"That's the last thing she ever said to me. Of course I didn't listen to her, I needed to get high. And when I came back the next morning, she was dead."

"Oh, Grey." I gasped. I tried to sit up, to comfort him, but I was too weak. "That's horrible! I'm so sorry."

He cringed. "It was enough to clean me up. I had to prove her wrong, you know, to show her that I wasn't a screw up. To maybe make her proud of me … some day. She was all the family I had in the world, and I just …." He shook his head.

"How did you do it though? If it'd been me, I would've seen that as an excuse to do more, you know, to forget it all. How did you quit?"

"It was tempting to keep going, don't get me wrong. But that would have been … too easy. I would've been lost. I had to show her … I owed it to her to make something of myself. She gave me everything. So I threw myself into music, it became my drug, my heroin. Through it, I found some measure … of … peace …."

I grasped his hand; I didn't know what else to say. The pain was rocketing through me now, quickly tearing through my muscles. I moaned and pressed my face against the pillow.

"I'm sorry, Mackenzie. I'm sorry I let this get so far." The pain was evident in Grey's face as he watched me suffering. He blue eyes burned. "It wasn't like this before, I didn't realize … I mean, I felt vaguely nauseous … but it was nothing like this …."

"It's not your fault." I shook my head. It was mine; I had manipulated him into it, pulled him down deeper into the addiction with me. I choked back the guilt and squeezed his fingers. "I'm fine. I'll be fine. I'm with you."

"I love you." He panted. "I'd do anything for you."

"I know."

It was agony. I've never felt so sick in my entire life. Just when I thought I'd reached the pinnacle, that things couldn't get any worse, they did. I shook and trembled. I was violently ill. Every noise grated in my ears, the slightest breath of breeze from the window felt like razor blades against my weeping skin. The pain in my stomach doubled, tripled—until I was bent in half, crippled in torture. I tried to stay quiet, tried to keep my suffering to the panting horror of my breath. But I felt like screaming.

It was too much to bear. I swallowed thickly, keeping the bile at bay.

"Grey," my voice was unrecognisable, harsh and choking in my ears, "Grey, please … I can't do this … I can't …." I wept, tears of anguish disappearing into the beads of sweat upon my cheeks. "Please …."

He turned over to me; I knew it hurt for him to do so. Every movement hurt. He was in just as much agony as I was.

"It'll get better. I promise."

"No, it won't. It can't. I'm sick, Grey. I'm so sick."

"I know." He reached for my hand and brought it to his lips. "Please, just be strong. For me, be strong …."

Hours passed. It didn't get better. I was writhing, flipping in pain, groaning and gritting my teeth, my body pulsing with sweat and nausea. I was dying. That was all there was to it. I was going to die.

Grey voiced my exact thought. "I'm fucking dying here." He groaned. I'd never heard his voice so full of agony; I'd never seen him so weak. He sat up on the edge of the bed and dropped his head into his hands. "I can't do this. I can't do this."

"Grey …," I reached for him, but he was gone. "No, Grey, don't leave me, please. Don't leave me alone." I meant to yell for him, but my voice was no stronger than a strangled whisper. I collapsed back onto the bed, too weak for anything else, all my energy pent-up in my racking sickness. Crying, sobbing, shaking, trembling, I pulled myself into a ball and waited for death.

A voice came to me from beyond the pain, the voice of an angel.

"Mackenzie." Grey was calm again, in control of himself. I pried my eyes open, cringing as the light assailed them.

"Grey." I cried. "Please. Make it stop. Please."

His face was before me, tortured, his blue eyes desperate and sad. I barely felt him grip my arm, barely registered the sharp sting of the needle ....

And then everything was good again. The sickness receded, falling back, surrendering to the sweet heat of the drugs sweeping through my veins that killed off every ill feeling, every ounce of pain that had plagued my body. I could breathe again, breathe easily. My muscles relaxed, my body slackened against the bed. A few moments more and I found myself actually smiling, something I didn't think I'd ever do again.

"Thank you," I sighed. "Thank you."

Grey was playing his music. It came to me from somewhere beyond my dreams, making me smile in my sleep. When I opened my eyes, he was sitting on the edge of the bed, quietly strumming his guitar. Even without the practice he didn't make one mistake, and the notes weaved in and around me in a beautiful melody. I sighed happily.

"Grey?" I sat up.

"Hey," Grey turned back to me, "how you feeling?"

"Good." I realized with surprise. "Better. You?"

"Better." He nodded, looking back at his guitar. He seemed resigned ... relaxed, almost. I wasn't sure what I expected, but I thought he'd be more upset about our failure to get off the drugs. We'd given up; we hadn't been able to last. He smirked at me sheepishly.

"I'm sorry."

"For what?"

"Making you go through that. If I'd known it was going to be so hard to quit, I never would have started again in the first place. I never would have let you do it. It was stupid of me, I didn't realize ...."

"No, of course you couldn't." I stopped him short. "Don't worry about me, Grey. I'm totally fine."

"Yeah, you are now." He grimaced. "But you didn't look fine a few hours ago."

"It felt like I was going to die." I admitted, shuddering in remembrance. "But I didn't."

"No."

"So, what do we do now?"

"I don't know." Grey frowned and strummed idly. "Cut back, I guess, so next time it's not so hard."

"That makes sense." I nodded. I couldn't help but be relieved—this statement meant there was going to be more heroin in my near future. Again, Grey's attitude surprised me. It made me wonder if he'd been hoping this would happen. I knew how much he loved the drugs, almost as much as I did. We may have found it too hard to quit, but at least now we could say we tried.

"We do need to cut back though," he insisted, as if trying to convince himself, "like seriously. We have to get clean."

"Yeah." I agreed. But they were just words. Empty, meaningless words said with no real conviction. I loved heroin. I didn't really want to quit, and I knew Grey didn't want to either.

"I think you should at least get a job." His blue eyes smiled at me. "It'll help, knowing you have to go out and work. It'll keep us from getting high all day."

I stuck my tongue out at him and flopped back on the bed dramatically. "Grey, come on. Can't you just support all my habits?" I teased. Well, half-teased. I really never wanted this holiday to end.

"Not yet, sugar. Maybe one day." He smirked at me.

I huffed. "I need a shower."

"Don't change the subject. Seriously. Where are you going to look?"

"I don't know. The lumberyard? They must be hiring, now that Zack and Alex are done there."

"The lumberyard? You wouldn't last five minutes."

I glared at him. "Could too."

He chuckled. "Could not."

"Really?" I pushed the sleeve of my shirt up and flexed my bicep—impressively, I thought. "Now tell me I couldn't."

Grey burst into laughter. He pulled his guitar off over his head and set it gingerly against the bed, then wrapped his hand almost completely around the hard muscle of my arm.

"Wow, that is impressive." He snorted. "I take it back. Maybe you'd last seven minutes."

I knew it was futile, but I attacked him, trying to pin him back to the bed … apparently the only wrestling move I knew. He let me win again, falling back easily and chuckling as I used all of my one-hundred and ten pounds to keep him there.

"Mackenzie?"

"Yeah?" I gloated from above him.

"You're right."

"I am?"

"Yes. You do need a shower."

I attacked him again, gleefully, but he wasn't having it this time. In seconds I was pinned to my side, and we wrestled, and he tickled me, and the sounds of our happy, youthful laughter floated down the hallway.

CHAPTER 52

I couldn't find Charlie anywhere. I pressed my way through the throng of people—it still felt strange to be up and out of the house and around others after so long, even stranger to have put actual make-up on and done something with myself. It was Saturday night and I was at the Aurora, where the guys were slated to start playing any minute. The place was packed; apparently Serpentine's infamy had only grown from their time spent away at the studio. The club was busier now than I'd ever seen it.

I hoped Charlie would be there. I mean, I knew she didn't really have a reason to be there now—at least not like before, when she was with Zack—but still I hoped. Courtney worked at the Aurora; I had caught sight of her through the crowd, and thought maybe Charlie would be there as well. I hadn't seen her in what felt like ages, and I hadn't been lucid enough to have an actual conversation with her for even longer.

"Excuse me, miss?" A familiar voice chuckled behind me. "Can I get you a drink?"

I turned around, recognizing her instantly. "Charlie!"

"You know it, baby." She twirled for me, clad in an Aurora uniform, a little black skirt and a tank top with bright pink letters across the front. She carried a tray and wore a little waitress apron so full of cash that she jangled when she walked. I smiled at her in amazement.

"Wow! You work here!"

"Yeah. I just started, last week."

I felt terrible. I lived with the girl, and I had no idea. "That's so great Charlie! Wow. I'm sorry I've been so out of it lately. I got a bit … you know …."

"It's all good." She smiled, her lovely blonde curls shaking around her face. "I knew you were alive. I figured you'd snap out of it eventually."

We had to yell to talk. I knew this wasn't the time or place for the kind of conversation I wanted to have with her, which was a good heart to heart, like before. So I kept it light.

"Do you like it here?" I wondered.

"Yeah, I do. It's great. The tips are fantastic. And ...," she leaned in closer to me, her blue eyes delighted. "They're still hiring. I could put a good word in for you, if you want."

"What? Really?"

"Yeah, Mac, come on! Think about it. What other place would you get paid to party?"

"You get to party?"

"Hell yeah! I mean, you can't get like, sloshed or anything, you have to be able to function, but you can drink and shit. Come on, do it so we can work together again. It'd be great."

"What are your hours like?"

"I work from like seven till two or three. Seriously, Mac. It's awesome."

It sounded awesome. I smiled, and nodded. So far, I hadn't been able to get hired by the lumberyard. "I'd love to work with you. Do you think they'll hire me?"

"Come on." Charlie yanked on my hand. "Let's go see."

She made her way through the bustling crowd, which was definitely a skill I would have to attain if I were to work there, especially with a tray full of drinks. As she pulled me along behind her I had to admit that it scared me a little, the prospect of serving such an unruly, drunken mob. At the same time though, I was excited by the challenge.

I followed Charlie eagerly, happy that I'd actually put some effort into myself since it seemed I was going to an impromptu job interview. My dark hair was piled up in curls on top of my head, messy and punky; I wore black heels and tight black jeans with a deep red v-neck belted shirt. I looked pretty good—not Charlie good, but still very pretty.

We went through the staff entrance down a long, tiled hallway. The noise from the bass pumping on the dance floor could still be heard faintly, muted as it was by the walls in between. The general offices were tucked around the corner, and Charlie rapped on the dark wooden door, pushing it open after only waiting a moment.

"Hello?"

There was a man at the desk in the small cluttered office. He had dark short hair and wore glasses, his desk was covered in cash-out sheets and order forms. He motioned for us to come in and we waited quietly as he finished up his phone conversation.

"Hey Charlie, what can I do for you?" He finally said, acknowledging us as he flipped his cell phone shut.

"Hey Walter. You're still looking for waitresses, right?"

"Yeah." Walter smiled hopefully and looked me over. "Okay. You're hired. When can you start?"

I started to giggle, but then I realized he was serious. "Uhhh … I can start … whenever you want me to."

"Tonight?"

I stammered, taken aback. "Ye-yeah. Sure."

"Great. Charlie, you'll show her around, won't you?"

"Of course." She answered happily.

"Great, thank you. Oh, and hey," Walter smiled at me again, "maybe I should get your name."

"It's Mackenzie." I grinned, holding out my hand for him.

"Walter. Lovely to meet you." He shook it, and then motioned to the door. "I'll have to get your actual information sometime for payroll. But for now, off you go."

Charlie and I giggled to each other on the way out the door.

"Wow. Did that really just happen? That was so abrupt." I couldn't believe I just got a job; it was such a relief to me. And I got to work with Charlie again. I beamed ecstatically as we walked down the hallway, unable to believe my luck.

Charlie chuckled. "Yeah. That was Walter. We're a little desperate here, if you hadn't noticed." She pulled me through another door into a grungy little staff room. Old, peeling, black and white checked linoleum covered the floor, and dated vinyl booths took up a good portion of the wall. Charlie led me past these, over to an older metal storage locker scrawled with ink from years and years of graffiti. "Here, these should be your size." She rummaged around a moment and then held up a skirt and a tank top taken from the communal closet.

"Holy crap, Mackenzie. Do you eat anymore?" Charlie frowned, looking between my tiny frame and the size of the clothes in her hand.

I laughed. "Of course I eat." Just not very much.

She shook her head doubtfully and found me a size smaller. "Here. We each get a locker for our shit; you can have this one beside mine. Go change into your uniform, and then I'll show you the rest."

"Okay." Ecstatically I headed into the washroom and changed my clothes as quickly as I could. The only shoes I had with me were heels, and though they weren't exactly practical, they would have to do. The uniform skirt was short, showing ample leg; the tank top tight across my chest. Knowing what I did now about the skin to tip ratio, I figured I was going to have a good night.

Charlie looked me over once I was finished. "Hmm … don't worry about those," she pointed, "it's so dark in the club, no one will notice them."

"What do you mean?" I followed her gaze, confused. She was looking down at my arms, at the various track marks that were marring my skin.

"Wow. I didn't realize they were so … noticeable."

"It's bright in here. Anyway, don't worry about it. Besides that, you look awesome." She threw me an apron after I piled my clothes in the locker. "You should always carry about twenty-dollars change in this apron for a float. I'll lend you some until the end of the night, okay?" She instructed, pouring some coins into one of the pockets. "Ready?"

"Ready." I nodded. But then, Charlie smiled slyly at me.

"Not quite ready." She pulled something clandestinely from the bag in her locker and handed it over to me. "Here. Take some, for old times sake."

I giggled and quickly unscrewed the vial, snorting the beautiful cocaine powder up into my sinuses. I had missed this too, a lot. I took a few more and then handed it back to Charlie, who did one quickly and then replaced it in her bag.

"Okay, good. Come with me." She smiled.

The place was thrumming. Grey's band was on by the time we made it back out, and they were about partway through the first song of their set. It was nearly impossible to get through the avid crowd cheering before the stage. Charlie had to throw some elbows. I stared up at Grey as he sang, just as entranced as ever, like it was my first time seeing him up there. He was so gorgeous. I loved the way he spread his legs, the way his jeans were tight on his thighs, the way his muscular arms held his guitar and demanded such beautiful, screaming music of it. I loved how his blue eyes scanned the crowd, how a slight dimple graced his stubbled cheek as he smirked, how his perfect lips crooned the lyrics with his husky, perfect voice. And he was mine. That was the absolute best part. Grey was mine.

Charlie managed to lead me to the main bar. The pace wasn't too frantic while everyone's attention was diverted by the band. I did my best to listen and learn as Charlie dragged me around the place, talking a mile a minute about drink orders and computer systems and everything else. It was all a little overwhelming at first, but I knew I would get the hang of it eventually.

I worked mostly at clearing tables for the rest of the night, which was a relief, something I could handle. I didn't feel capable enough to try and run the computer system just yet. And the place was a mess. I could see now why the floor was always sticky and how the vinyl booths became ripped; why cigarette butts lined the floor. Drunk people were ridiculous. I wasn't used to being around them so sober. They were actually kind of … annoying. Every once in awhile though, Charlie would pull me aside and we'd do a shot at the bar. Once I had a good, happy buzz going I didn't mind the idiots spilling their drinks and stumbling overtop of me. It was actually kind of fun, like Charlie had said.

But there was one down side to working there that I hadn't foreseen.

When Grey's band finished, they went back to the VIP section, just like usual. But this time, I couldn't go with him. There were designated staff assigned especially for that section, and I'd have to work my way up the totem pole to ever be given such a position. I sighed, watching as pretty young girls filed into the VIP room, biting back the jealousy that flared within me. I knew I could trust Grey, without a doubt, but I also knew I couldn't trust any of those other girls.

I was busy working away, cleaning up the sticky, disgusting mess of tables, when I felt a sudden hand on my waist. I smiled at the touch—I knew without a doubt who it was standing behind me. And all my worries melted away.

"Excuse me, sir." I turned around, playfully slapping his hand away. "I have a boyfriend, and he wouldn't like you touching me."

"Well," he smirked, his voice low, "I have a girlfriend, too, but you're so damn pretty, I couldn't help myself."

"Hmm …." I smiled. "You're not so bad yourself." Gorgeous, more like.

"This boyfriend, is he a big guy?"

"Yeah. Huge." I raised my eyebrows.

"Well. That is a problem." Grey wrapped his hands around my waist. "I guess I'll have to take my chances."

I smiled as he pulled me to him and in seconds we were kissing. Lost in the sea of people, I knew no one would ever notice. Still, I made myself pull away from him before we got too hot and heavy. I was at work, after all.

"You guys sounded great." I wiped my lipstick from his lips. "Amazing turn out, hey?"

"Yeah, it was good." He shook his head. "I almost forgot my lines though, when I looked out and saw you … in this," he motioned to my scanty uniform. "Damn you're hot. Do you think this boyfriend will mind if I take you home tonight?"

"Who cares?" I shrugged happily.

He grinned. "So you're really working here now?"

"Yeah, I guess so. This guy just gave me a job, like, on the spot. And Charlie said she makes great tips. I think it'll be okay."

"Good." He kissed me again. "Well, I'll be in the VIP. Come get me when you're done. I'm taking you home with me tonight, boyfriend be damned."

I giggled as he left me and was shortly swallowed up by the crowd. I could still spot him, though I couldn't see him. I just had to watch for all the females craning their necks for a better look.

CHAPTER 53

The days passed, falling into a pattern of sorts, one that I took up quickly and happily. Whenever Grey and I woke up, either at his house or mine, we'd shoot up almost immediately. It wasn't even so much as a want anymore—it was a need, for the all too familiar sickness was always at bay, waiting to strike if we went without for too long. The rest of the day would pass in total, utter bliss, a blur of happiness and contentment. The thought of quitting heroin didn't even occur to us anymore, not if we could manage to function as we did. We forced ourselves to function, determined to have the best of both worlds. If I had to work, I'd start doing cocaine towards the evening to get ready for my shift. It gave me the energy I needed, the spunk required to make it through the long, sometimes tiring shift.

The tips were even better at the Aurora then they had been at the Red Wheat, on the weekends anyway, so I could manage to support all my drug habits and pay my rent. Grey's band played there a lot—some weekends, some weekdays—so I was essentially getting paid to watch nearly all of their shows, and he in turn was getting paid to play them. It was the perfect scenario. I'd stay just high enough on cocaine and drunk enough on alcohol during the evening to placate my constant craving for more heroin, but as soon as my shift was over I'd hurry to meet Grey at home, where he'd be waiting for me with a fresh batch all prepared, and then we'd shoot ourselves into oblivion once again. It was a fine balance, one that was always teetering towards the loss of control. But somehow we were able to make it work. We had to make it work.

Charlie was trying desperately to get over Zack. The evidence was obvious. If Grey and I stayed at my house overnight, it was inevitable the next morning to see or hear some strange guy heading out the door. Grey didn't really like it, he didn't like the thought of strange men coming and going at all hours of the night. We started spending more nights at his house because of it, which I thought was a bit of an overreaction, but one I didn't mind a bit. I was worried about Charlie but she seemed happy—she seemed to be doing much better than she had been, anyway. So I just let it go.

Courtney was now a constant in our lives. She and Charlie were nearly inseparable. I always felt a pang of jealously when I saw them laughing and joking and talking together. They always had private jokes. It reminded me of how Charlie and I used to be, before all the unpleasantness. Even though we'd managed to patch up our relationship, we were never as close as we had been, and I feared we never would be again. That's why—though it did hurt my feelings—I wasn't really surprised when Charlie asked me if Courtney could move in with us.

"But, where will she stay?" I wondered.

"She can sleep in my room." Charlie suggested. "Or … if, I mean, since you're at Grey's house all the time anyway … maybe she could stay …."

I didn't let her finish. "I'll talk to Grey." I interrupted.

He was amazingly receptive to the idea. I was surprised; I thought guys weren't into that kind of thing, not until they were ready to "settle down," anyway. But Grey just smirked at me.

"You should move in. You're here all the time anyway." He shrugged.

"Are you sure you're not just saying that?" I argued. "If I hadn't asked, would you have asked?"

"Yeah, sure. I just didn't think about it."

"Really?" I wondered doubtfully.

"Yes." He rolled his eyes at me. "Would it help if I said it?"

"Yes."

"Mackenzie, would you move in with me? Please?"

"Why, Grey," I exclaimed. "I thought you'd never ask."

By the end of November, I was officially living with Grey. It really was no different than before, since I'd spent almost all my time there anyway. I was sad to move out though, every excited giggle on Courtney's lips hurt me just a little more, shoved the knife in just a little deeper. She was always hanging around on the edges, watching as we loaded up my things, impatiently waiting for me to get the hell out of there. Charlie hugged me at least when I left for the last time.

"I'll miss you Mac. And this doesn't change anything, you know."

"Yeah." I nodded glumly. She punched me playfully in the arm.

"Don't be like that. You know you'll be happier over there."

"Maybe. But I'll miss you."

"Don't be silly. You'll see me all the time." She promised.

I knew I'd see her at work—I'd see both of them at work—but I also knew it wouldn't be the same. That it would never be the same. I forced myself to smile at her as I left, heading down the old rickety stairs, leaving my first apartment behind me. I tried not to remember how excited Charlie had been when I first moved in, how eager we'd been to get high, how we'd spent that whole first night giggling ecstatically. Suddenly I sympathised with Katrina or whatever the hell her name had been—Charlie's first roommate. I wondered if, like me, the door had been shut on her before her first foot hit the ground.

Grey tried to comfort me. He cooked up an extra shot that night just to raise my spirits. It worked too. I lay back on his bed with his warm arms around me, and suddenly I didn't care about Courtney and Charlie anymore. Suddenly, they just didn't matter. I was with the man of my dreams—like, I was actually living with the man of my dreams. I couldn't believe it. I propped myself up on my arm and just stared at him, amazed.

"What?" Grey asked me casually, suddenly aware of my scrutiny.

"I can't believe I found you." I said with awe. "How am I so lucky?"

He smirked at me, his blue eyes shining, and tucked an errant strand of dark hair behind my ear. "I wonder the same thing every time I look at you."

That night was a memorable one.

But they all were really. I'd never known such contentment … sleeping in Grey's arms every night, waking up to his gorgeous face every morning, spending every minute we possibly could together in a state of constant happiness. His room grew much messier after I moved in, my clothes were all over the place, underfoot, strewn across his chair and his bed. My make-up took up a dominant spot on the bathroom counter, my shampoo and conditioner and body wash left "slippery shit" all over the bottom of the tub, and my shoes practically overflowed the entryway. But for all this, Alex and Zack complained more than Grey did, and even that was done in jest.

Though I do wish someone besides me could've seen the look on Alex's face the first time he discovered my box of tampons under the sink.

Living with three guys was surprisingly easy. They may have been messier than girls in most respects, but they were also painfully easy going. And if they had a problem with something, they'd say it to my face instead of talking behind my back. We settled into a nice, harmonious arrangement. I'd even managed to forgive Zack for breaking my best friend's heart. We never talked about it or brought it up or anything, we just … agreed to disagree. And I had always loved Alex. He was just too sweet; he was too much fun not to fall in love with, with his lank brown hair and his winning smile. The only disagreement we ever had was whether or not I should be allowed to knock down the beer-can castle, which had grown larger over the months, now dominating the little dining room. I voted strongly in favour of the action, but he had yet to be swayed.

Winter hit with full force. Its icy claws clung to the windows, glazed up the sidewalks and frosted over the stubble fields surrounding our little frozen town. But I was oblivious to it. I was up above the clouds, sailing beneath an eternal summer sun, anchored to the earth by nothing more than Grey's strong arms around me. Heroin was like a beach in a needle. It was the only vacation I needed.

At times, when we were more lucid, Grey would take out his guitar and work on his music. That was my absolute favourite. I could sit on the bed and just watch him for hours as he practiced and composed, leaning over his guitar and deftly forcing notes from the strings. Grey would sing to me until I cried, overcome. He'd work on lyrics too, curled up with me on the bed with a pen in his hand. He could write the most beautiful poetry, I was in awe. He tried, unsuccessfully, to teach me how to do it, how to create.

"Just write what you're feeling." He encouraged. "It doesn't have to rhyme. Just make it … flow."

I took the notebook from him, chewing on the end of the pen for a moment.

"Write what I'm feeling?" I asked again.

"Yeah." He nodded.

Immediately, I put the pen to the paper, scrawling out one single word.

Happy.

And I was. Things had never been more perfect. Day after day of wondrous, contented bliss passed us by. Everything I'd ever wanted. And with every one, I loved Grey just that much more. He was my world, my everything. I wished I had the capacity to write it all down, like he did. I wished I could express my feelings for him properly. Just the way his blue eyes lit up when I came home from work, or the way his arm would find me sometime in the dark reaches of the night and pull me close to him was enough to fill my heart with delight, to make me sigh with such happiness that I never thought possible.

Poor Grey. He'd have to be satisfied with me showing him.

The only real interruption to our comfortable little pattern was the coming of the holidays. I dreaded them, knowing I'd have to go and pretend the whole big-happy-family scenario at my parents' house. I hadn't spoken to any of them since my birthday. Not once. There'd been no invitations to dinner, no phone calls to check in, no unexpected visits. I wondered if they knew how much I'd stolen from them. Maybe they were so disgusted that they didn't want anything to do with me now. I clung to the hope that somehow, someway, I'd be able to avoid them this Christmas.

Of course it was only a fool's hope. Eventually my phone rang—as I knew it would—and my mother's overly happy, chipper-to-compensate voice was buzzing in my ear, eager to find out what my work schedule was like and how long I'd be able to stay with them over the holidays. I gave her Christmas Eve and Christmas Day, knowing that if I stayed any longer Christmas would turn into a negative experience for all of us. She was satisfied with my agenda—though Marcy and Greg were going to be staying longer than I was, she'd take what she could.

Grey actually laughed at me as I was packing. I shot him a glare and stuffed a sweater into my overnight bag.

"You could come too, you know." I threatened.

"I wouldn't dream of it. I don't want to interrupt your happy family time."

"Please?"

"Sorry sugar." He shook his head. "But the boys and I have plans."

"You do? What plans?" I frowned.

"*Die Hard*. They always have a marathon on Christmas day."

"Well, I wouldn't want to wreck that for you." I scoffed. I really wasn't upset that he didn't want to hang out with my family. I couldn't blame him, and in truth, it would bring down the awkwardness level by far if he weren't around. But I was going to miss Grey, and miss him badly. I hadn't spent one night away from him for months.

I frowned again as he put my favourite pair of pyjamas in the bag for me. He smiled at my glum expression.

"Hey, don't be like that. It's only for two days. We've done weeks at a time before, remember?"

"Yeah, and I almost went crazy."

He chuckled. "Mackenzie, I'll be right here, in town. I'm five minutes away. If it gets too bad, you can escape them and come see me."

"Yeah." I relented. It was nearly time for me to go. I zipped up the suitcase and sat back on the bed, eager now, and excited, but for a different reason than seeing my family. I pushed the sleeve of my sweater up and glanced meaningfully at Grey. "Can we do some more now? Before I go?" I'd been waiting for this for hours, ever since we shot up the last time.

"Sure." He agreed, smirking casually. But I knew he was just as eager as I was. And then, a sudden thought occurred to me.

"Oh shit, Grey. What am I going to do tomorrow?"

"Open presents?"

I giggled. "No, I mean … for heroin. I'll have to do some. It won't be a very Merry Christmas for anyone if I turn green and start convulsing on the floor."

I meant it as a joke, but Grey frowned at my predicament. "Well … is there any way you could leave? You could come here quick and I could … fix you up."

"But how would I explain that?" I wondered. "Maybe I should just take some with me. Then I can do it myself, I can just slip to the bathroom or something." I looked down at my forearm riddled with little red, tiny dots. It couldn't be that hard.

He raised an eyebrow at me. "Will you be able to?"

"Maybe. I've seen you do it like, a trillion times."

"Yeah, but I'm not deathly afraid of needles." Grey frowned. "Here. Why don't you try doing this one, then? See how you do."

"Okay." I picked up the supplies and began, taking a small chunk of the dark, sticky, tar-like heroin and placing it on the spoon. I added a splash of water and then heated it all with my lighter until the mixture was a dull, oily brown. Taking a tiny piece of cotton, I placed it in the spoon and then, grasping the needle shakily, sucked it up into the syringe. This part I'd done a hundred times before, but I still looked up at Grey for reassurance.

"How was that?" I wondered. Grey nodded thoughtfully.

"You did good. Take a bit less though, if it's just you. Just to be careful."

"Okay." I breathed nervously and made a fist with my left arm, holding the needle in my right hand. I waited until a vein was apparent, glowing bluely beneath the translucent veil of my skin. I took a deep breath. I couldn't believe what I was doing, that I could actually be capable of sticking a needle into myself. But I had to. Slowly, trying to keep my hand steady, I sunk the sharp steel through my skin, hitting the vein with ease.

Carefully I retracted the plunger, watching as my blood splurted up into the syringe. Then, at Grey's nod, I shot the drugs into my veins.

It felt good, almost better than usual, because this time it came with an odd sense of power. I was able to do it myself. I could get myself high. I felt so independent, so … in control. I slumped over, a heavy smile on my face, and looked up at Grey.

"How'd I do?" I wondered breathily.

"You're a champion." Grey chuckled. He took a tiny chunk of the heroin and wrapped it up in a separate balloon for me, hiding everything else I'd need in the bottom of my bag. "Be careful, Mackenzie, and don't let your parents catch you with this stuff." He warned. "There's only one conclusion they'll jump to, and it'll be the right one this time."

"Okay." I nodded slowly. I watched, overcome by waves of bliss, as Grey got out some supplies for himself. He was so quick, such a pro, it took him seconds to inject rather than the minutes it took me. When he was done he fell back heavily, putting his arm around my shoulders and drawing me near to him.

"Merry Christmas, Mackenzie." He smiled drowsily, kissing my cheek.

"Merry Christmas, Grey."

CHAPTER 54

Christmas. So. This was it. I sat on the leather couch in my parents' house, wrapped in a cozy blanket and watching the scene play out before me. I was happy. I had just shot up not ten minutes earlier, and I was in my happy place. A smile lit my lips as I watched my father pass out the presents in joviality. A fire crackled on the hearth. My mom had out the camcorder and every few minutes she'd scan the room, though nothing had a chance to change from last time. Marcy and Greg were snuggled up on the other couch; Greg was actually wearing a striped two-piece pyjama set with matching robe and slippers. That guy was sixty if he was a day, and every time I looked at him, I laughed.

But Christmas did seem to hold some kind of special power, besides goodwill and peace and all that. Maybe the magic was all in the drugs, maybe my attitude had changed because I was too blissed out to resent everyone like I normally did. But it was like I'd been totally forgiven for the last six or seven months of what I knew had been less than desirable behaviour. My mom, my dad, my sister, her husband … no one seemed to harbour any ill will towards me, not like the last time I'd seen them. When I'd finally made it in the door last night, winded from the cold walk, my dad had actually hugged me. Mom was beside herself with excitement. Marcy offered me a drink, and Greg put his arm around me like it was a natural place for it to be.

I couldn't help but be touched. My family was brutal, they drove me crazy in thirty different ways, but it was hard to resent them when they were being so … nice, so accepting of me. It was like they'd had a meeting and unanimously voted to make me feel like I was loved, instead of the usual constant judgement passing and dirty, intolerant looks. I was surprised.

Baffled even—and wary at first, just in case this was some kind of trick. After awhile though, I settled in comfortably. I couldn't help myself. It felt good. For the first time in a long time, it felt like I belonged again.

No one mentioned Craig. No one mentioned the wedding. No one mentioned my birthday dinner. Someone did mention Grey. It was my mother, her face totally devoid of any agenda or intent, asking if Grey were coming over for dinner. I was flabbergasted by the question.

"No ... no, I think he has plans." I answered quickly, suspicious.

"Oh, well. Maybe next time." She had said. And it looked like she meant it.

I couldn't believe it. It was like aliens had come and taken my old family away, replacing them with identical twins—nice identical twins. As the time passed—harmoniously, for once—I felt all the anger I had towards them slowly fading away. Their treatment of Grey at the wedding, how they'd tried to set me up with Craig ... it was easy to forgive them for all of it. Maybe it was the months spent apart that had cooled my jets. Or maybe it was a sign; maybe I was growing up or something. Maturing.

Or maybe it was the drugs.

Either way, I was still happy. Dad exclaimed over the putting machine I'd given him—which had been Grey's idea, he said every executive needed one. Mom loved her pink Cashmere sweater, Marcy her silver earrings, and Greg his pipe. I had to get him a pipe, come on, look at the guy. But he liked it. Apparently, it reminded him of his grandfather. I was glad now that I'd scraped up enough money to actually buy them all presents, though at the time, I'd really wanted to save it for dope instead.

Marcy gave me a diary, it was beautiful—leather bound with brown and blue embellishments. Greg gave me a chess set which I was actually afraid of, it seemed way over my head. But he promised to teach me. My present from mom and dad was small, it fit into a little tiny box that they gave to me last, after all the other presents were opened.

"What's this?" I wondered. My parents became noticeably more animated as I held the box in my hands. "It's not going to explode, is it?"

"No! Open it!" Mom could barely contain herself.

I grinned and unwrapped the gift as slowly as I could, just to make her go crazy, until even I couldn't handle the suspense anymore. I ripped the paper away and tore the lid off the box. Inside sat a set of keys.

"Is this ...." My eyes were wide as I looked down at them. "Did you get me ... a car?"

"Yes!" Mom clapped, jumping up and down. "It's in the garage."

"An actual car?" I couldn't believe it. I was stunned, shocked into a stupor. I was terrible. I was a horrible, horrible child. I looked up at my parents, into their happy, shining faces—and was overcome with guilt. All consuming guilt.

"I don't deserve this." I decided, tears welling up in my eyes.

Dad shook his head. "Sure you do. Come on, don't you want to see it?"

I nodded briefly. I couldn't believe what they had done for me, after everything I'd done to them … so much they didn't even know about. I tried not to remember how much I had stolen from them; I tried to push the guilt from my mind. I couldn't tell them about it, not now. It would only give them reason to hate me again. But I could be good now, couldn't I? I could try to be someone worthy … I could try ….

"Thank you daddy." I whispered, reaching up to kiss his cheek.

"Thanks mom." I squeezed her into a hug. I think they were both surprised by my affection, but I couldn't blame them. They'd had months and months of nothing from me. Marcy and Greg sat nearby on the couch, smiling at the scene without a trace of jealousy or resentment on their faces. I hugged them too—just because I could—and though it took them by surprise as well, they seemed content—happy that I was happy.

My car was a thing of beauty. It wasn't fancy or rare or expensive, which I loved. It was an old Ford Thunderbird, light blue, made in the late eighties. It made my entire day. The seats were cushy with soft blue upholstery. It was necessarily an automatic and had a large, roomy back seat with plenty of space in the trunk. I couldn't stop thanking my parents; I thanked them over and over again. They were overcome with my happiness. I actually saw tears in my mother's eyes.

Dinner was a festive affair. I had only one glass of wine, which was a big restraint on my part. Even though my family wasn't watching me like a hawk—which again surprised me—I didn't want to wreck the evening. The whole day had been so lovely. We talked around the table, and ate until we were stuffed—which didn't take much for me—but then we lingered around our dessert plates, chatting and drinking coffee. Had I known such a relationship was possible with my family, I would have come over a lot more often. It boggled my mind; I kept trying to put my finger on what had changed, why we were suddenly able to get along. But there was no real explanation for it.

After supper we all took our drinks into the living room, sitting before the crackling fire and the soft glow of the Christmas tree lights. Everyone was relaxed and happy. I was excited too; I knew that soon, I'd get to do some more heroin. It was so easy to just sneak away and take care of myself, and then come back and continue on with total bliss and happiness. My family didn't even seem to notice. It was perfect.

Just when I thought the evening couldn't get any better, the doorbell rang.

My heart leapt into my throat at the noise. I had been hoping … it'd be just like him to … I jumped up and ran to the door before anyone else could even think to open it. Sure enough, there, standing in the cold with a smirk upon his face, stood Grey.

I jumped into his arms. He was by far the best Christmas present I could ever have received. I kissed his face, every spot I could reach.

"Thank you, thank you, thank you …." I repeated in a whisper. He laughed at my exuberance, wrapping his arms around me and twirling me around.

"Merry Christmas." He spoke into my ear.

"Uh … hey … come on you two, come out of the cold," my dad, having come to see who was at the door, forced pleasantness into his voice and motioned us back into the house. I grasped Grey's hand and pulled him forward as Dad shut out the cold winter breeze behind us. I took his coat and hung it up in the hall closet.

It suddenly felt very stiff in the living room; the change was almost tangible compared to the relaxed atmosphere I had left it in. Marcy and Greg sat up, wary, and my mom didn't seem to know what to do. Dad sat down by the fireplace, his expression blank, and he too seemed at a loss for words.

Grey cleared his throat. He looked gorgeous in a black collared shirt and dark blue jeans, but was obviously uncomfortable as well. I seemed to be the only one still completely at ease. Grey had come over to my parents', just for me, even knowing how awkward it would be … and it meant the world. But I didn't want it to be awkward. I was suddenly determined to make this one of the best evenings ever, for everyone involved. I knew my family could love Grey if they'd only give him a chance, and it seemed tonight—for whatever reason—would be the best time to try.

"You have a lovely home, Mrs. Taylor." Grey acknowledged.

"Thank you, Grey." Her answering smile was tight.

"Hey, Mackenzie, uh … why don't you go show Grey your present?" Dad suggested then, to the concealed relief of everybody else. While we were out of the room, they could have a few moments to compose themselves, to get a handle on the situation. And hopefully think of some topics of conversation.

"Yeah, sure. Come see." Still holding Grey's hand, I smiled and pulled him through the house, into the garage. It was better when we were alone. We were both able to breathe again, to act naturally.

"You got a car?" He was as incredulous as I had been, stepping into the three-car garage, obvious surprised written on his face.

"Yeah … what do you think?" I smiled, sweeping my hand over the auto in a motion very akin to Vanna White. "Pretty, hey?"

"Nice ride." Grey smiled and leaned in closer to inspect it. "Does it have a radio?"

"Yeah, why?"

"No reason. Just get in."

"Okay." I grinned with curiosity and got into the driver's side. Grey sat down in the passenger seat and looked down at his watch a moment, then started playing with the radio dials while I turned the key back to accessory.

"Wow. Thank you so much for coming." I smiled up at him as he fiddled, completely ecstatic. "You made my whole day."

"Well, Bruce Willis had already saved the day, a few times, actually … and, I wanted to give you your Christmas present." He winked slyly.

"But I thought we agreed not to get things for each other." I protested.

"It's just something little."

"Okay …?"

"Just listen." He turned up the volume dial. After a few minutes of DJ prattle, suddenly I recognized Grey's velvet voice, along with the rest of the band, coming to me in crystal clear audio from over the radio waves.

"Oh, Grey! That's you, on the radio! Wow!" I hugged him. "How does it feel?"

"Awesome." Grey frowned. His expression didn't match his answer.

"It doesn't look too awesome." I giggled.

He sighed. "They're playing the wrong song."

"Oh." I listened for a moment, but I didn't see what the big deal was. Who cared what song was playing? "Come on, Grey. This is you, on the radio. This is huge!"

"I know, but, I wanted them to play … I thought the first single was going to be … your song."

"Oh." It took me a moment to realize what he was saying. "Wait … do you mean … you recorded my song?"

His blue eyes shone at me. "Yeah. That's why we were at the studio for the extra week."

"Really?" Happy tears stung my eyes. I stared up at Grey, amazed, completely overwhelmed by his gift. "I still can't believe you even wrote me a song," I smiled gloriously at him. "… and then to record it …. Thank you."

"It's just the first of many." Grey shrugged. "And, if you can't hear it on the radio, I guess you'll just have to listen to … this." He pulled something from his pocket then; it was square and flat and had a picture of … him. And Zack, and Alex … and there was Lucas and Jimmy … and cover art ….

"Your CD." I grabbed it from his hands. "They're out now? Grey, this is awesome. That's you right there. Are there more pictures? Does it have the lyrics …?"

Grey laughed at my enthusiasm. He pulled me across the console and into his lap, kissing my smiling lips. "You, Mackenzie, are one of a kind."

"No, I'm not. You are." I replied seriously, gazing up at him. I placed my hands on his dark, stubbled cheeks so he would understand the sincerity of my words. "I'm so proud of you. Really."

Grey smiled, his cheeks reddening ever so slightly—but I could tell my words made him happy. He ripped the plastic off the CD case.

"Do you want to listen?"

"Of course." I nodded enthusiastically. Grey peered at the dashboard of my car a moment, and then he chuckled to himself.

"What?" I wondered.

"I think CD's were a little before your car's time." He tapped the cassette deck in the dash face and smirked.

"Oh." I hadn't realized my car was that old. "Sorry."

"It's okay. We can get you one of those adapters. But I guess this will have to wait." He put the CD back in its case and then snapped it shut. "For later."

"No it won't. Come on, I have the best idea." Eagerly, I turned the key off and opened up the door. "My parents have a stereo. Let's go blow their minds."

Grey followed hesitantly, unsure. "Um … somehow I doubt that our music is your parents' style. It's a bit … heavy, don't you think?"

"Oh, I'm sure they can handle some shaking up." I smiled and grasped his hand again. "Seriously, they've been … really cool today. I don't even know how to explain it … but I think … I have a feeling that they're going to love your music. Like really love it too, not just pretend."

"You think so?" He seemed sceptical, but there was no denying the hopefulness there, apparent in his face. Despite everything, he really wanted my family to like him. I could tell.

"I'd bet money on it."

"Okay then. You're on."

I held up Grey's CD triumphantly as we rejoined my family in the living room. He watched me, hanging back, unsure of the spotlight as I turned on the stereo and put the disc in the tray.

"What's this Mackenzie?" Mom wondered.

"Grey's CD. It's finally done." I showed them all the case.

"Can I see that?" Marcy asked, holding out her hands. I threw the jewel case expertly into her clutch and she opened it up, flipping through the booklet inside.

"So, what type of music do you play?" Dad asked Grey.

"Uh … it's hard rock … I guess you could say. It's not exactly seasonal."

I giggled at his description and then hit play. We sat back and listened as the first song came on—chugging heavy guitars and screaming, thrashing vocals. I looked over at Grey from the corner of my eye, and smiled. He tried to keep his mouth straight, his features composed, but as Zack wailed into a screaming guitar solo the laughter burst out of him. I couldn't help myself; I had to laugh as well.

It didn't take long before everyone was laughing, whether we were all in on the same joke or not, I couldn't tell. But it helped to ease the tension in the room.

"It's okay; we don't have to listen to it." Grey offered. "It's a bit heavy."

"No, I like it." Dad insisted. "I used to know a thing or two about rock and roll. Just ask Deb here."

"Yeah, you were a regular Paul McCartney." Mom rolled her eyes, which set us off laughing again. There was no way I could picture my dad—with his straight-laced suits and ties—liking anything that resembled actual rock and roll. He was a Simon and Garfunkel fan, through and through. But it was nice that he was trying.

"We can't stop listening until you hear the best part." I grinned. Grey cleared his throat as I flipped to the last song on the CD. He crossed his arms and leaned against the wall.

The music started slowly, quiet, with just the gentle plunking of a piano and the soft strumming of his guitar. As Grey's warm, velvet voice sounded through the speakers, I melted back into my chair, closing my eyes and letting the sweet sounds of his voice and the words of his lips sink deep into my heart.

"Sitting here in the dark, Mackenzie's next to me.
She's lying in the moonlight, shining silver in the sheets.
And though it pains me so, I know I have to go.
I have to leave Mackenzie lying all alone.

Mackenzie, I hope you miss me
When I'm gone, when I'm gone.
I gotta go now, but you need to know how
Much you're loved, how much you're loved ….

In the dark alone, now there's only me.
I'm staring at the moonlight shining silver in the streets.
The city lights are twinkling, glowing like her eyes.
No matter where I go, she's always on my mind.

Mackenzie, I hope you miss me,
When I'm gone, when I'm gone.
I'm away now, but you need to know how
Much you're loved, how much you're loved …."

The room was struck with silence as the song slowly ebbed, the beautiful notes fading softly away.

"Wow." Marcy was the first to speak, her voice awed, no louder than a whisper. "That was really good."

Mom's eyes had actual tears in them. She smiled at Grey. "That was beautiful." She nodded. "Really. Beautiful."

I glanced over at Grey. He accepted my family's compliments with great aplomb, but his blue eyes didn't leave my face for a second—like my opinion was the only one that mattered, the only one he really needed to hear.

There was nothing I could say to do it justice. Completely oblivious to the family members surrounding us, I crossed the room and threw my arms around his neck.

"Thank you." I whispered in his ear. "I love it." And then, because that wasn't enough either, I kissed him deep and long, my hands around his neck, my fingers twirling through his dark hair.

We stayed that way, oblivious, until Greg cleared his throat uncomfortably. The noise was enough to jolt us back to the present. I had totally forgotten our surroundings, had totally forgotten everything but Grey's lips on mine. We broke away, sheepish, but no one seemed appalled or annoyed by our affection. They looked at Grey, and then they looked at me, and whatever they saw there made them actually smile. Maybe it was the simple happiness that I could feel radiating from me, shining like the lights on the Christmas tree. Whatever it was, they seemed to approve. And then I knew, without a doubt, that Grey had won over my parents. Grey had won over my family, just like I knew he would. All he needed was a chance.

Nothing could have made me happier. It was all so easy after that. Grey spotted my as of yet unopened chess set and challenged Greg to a game. I opened my mouth to stop him—Grey was setting himself up for a slaughtering—but I held my tongue. Greg smiled at the challenge and helped Grey set up the board on the coffee table.

I sat by Marcy, who looked stunning in a white cowl neck sweater and the dangly silver earrings I'd given her, and we watched our men play chess. I didn't understand a thing; I made up my mind to give Grey the chess set as soon as we got home, because he seemed to be holding his own against Greg—of all people—which was impressive to me. Mom and Dad sat nearby, dad had an arm slung loosely over mom's shoulders and they looked very cozy, and happy, watching the game and laughing whenever someone made a joke. It was very peaceful.

But I knew one thing what would make it even better.

The first symptoms of withdrawal were already hitting me. I'd been distracted, with Grey's arrival and the car and the CD and everything, I hadn't really noticed the severity of my craving. It had my full attention now. I couldn't ignore the sweat that broke through my skin, the sudden weakness in my limbs. I couldn't wait, I didn't want to wait. I wrapped an arm around myself, fidgeting and uncomfortable. I needed to do some more heroin. And I needed to do it now.

"Mackenzie, are you okay?" Grey eyed me cautiously, instantly aware. He gave me a knowing look.

"Oh, yeah, I'm fine." I sat up, shakily. "I think I just ate too much."

"Do you need anything, honey?" Mom wondered.

"No, I'm okay. I'll … I'll be right back." I hurried from the living room and up the stairs to my old bedroom, where all the supplies were stashed in my overnight bag. I took them all into the nearest bathroom and shut the door. Quickly, my blood pounding in my ears, I fought back the nausea and started a batch. The sickness made my hands shake and it took me way longer than normal to get the heroin into the syringe.

I squeezed my hand shut. I felt better knowing that relief was near, that soon the bliss would find me and have its way. My veins were slow to pop. I clenched and re-clenched my fist until one was near enough to the surface. Then, slowly, compensating for the shakiness of my hands, I plunged the needle into my skin.

"You okay honey? I've got some Gravol here if you …." The door began to open. I realized with horror that in my haste, I had forgotten to lock the door.

"No, Mom! No, get out!" I screamed. But it was too late. The door was open. Mom looked confused at first when she found me leaning over the sink, my supplies scattered around me. And then comprehension hit when she saw the needle sticking out of my arm. Her blue eyes opened in fright, her mouth dropped but no words came. She pointed at me in terror.

"What are you doing?" Her voice, whisper thin at first, gradually gained back its strength. "Mackenzie, what are you doing to yourself?"

I didn't know what to say. I had no excuse, no lie to tell. I stared at her, my dark eyes wide, like a deer caught in the headlights. I must have looked just as afraid as she did.

"Answer me, young lady! *What are you doing to yourself*?"

"Everything okay, Deb?" Dad's voice floated up the hall, tight with concern.

"No, no, everything is not okay." Mom's voice started to shake; I recognized the noise. She was on the verge of tears.

"Mom, mom, its okay." I don't know why I was saying that. I knew it wasn't okay; I just wanted her to calm down.

"Get that thing out of your arm!" She demanded, grasping the needle from my numb fingertips and chucking it at the garbage. Her eyes were wild with despair as she looked at me, like she had never really seen me before. "Let me see you. Let me look at you."

"Mom, don't!" I tried to pry my arm from her grasp but her grip was surprisingly strong. She pushed the sleeve of my sweater up until all the skin was exposed. Her face went bone-white at the sight, at the clusters of tiny red dots that covered my skin. I felt the heat in my cheeks, the warm blush of shame that spread across my face. I looked down at the floor.

"Mitch. Mitch, look. Just look at what she's doing to herself." Mom's voice held horror now, and I understood that my dad was there as well, taking in the awful sight. I dared to look up at his face.

It was hard. Rigid, even. Colorless. He looked at me just as my mom had, like he'd never seen me before. Not before now. Now that they knew my terrible secret. I was addicted to heroin. Yes, I knew it then. There was no more denying it, no justifying it, no excusing it. I was a heroin addict. And I couldn't hide it anymore.

All the happiness from earlier slunk slowly from my being. Because all of it had been a lie. All of it. It wasn't me. It wasn't me feeling happiness, acceptance. I couldn't feel happiness, not real happiness.

I couldn't feel anything. Not anymore.

"This is what you've been doing with yourself?" Dad's voice was weak; there was no strength within it, none of its usual gusto. I nodded. His features hardened even further, as if he was steeling himself for what he had to do next. He shut his eyes.

"Get out of my house."

It took me a second. "… What?"

"Get out of my house. Do you hear me? I won't have this …," he didn't even know what to call it, "I won't have it in my house, Mackenzie."

"Dad, I'm sorry, I have to … I get sick if I don't."

"I had no idea." Mom gasped at my admission. "Oh, my baby … my baby …." She stood nearby, wringing her hands, tears in her eyes.

Dad's jaw clenched. "*Get out of my house!*" He boomed suddenly. The harshness of his voice surprised me out of my stupor of shame, jolted me into action.

"I'm going!" I shouted back. Tears filled my eyes, blinding me, but somehow I managed to collect my stuff, throwing my supplies into my bag and hastily zipping it up. I brushed past him and down the stairs, my arms around my stomach as it churned violently within me.

Grey was as pale as a ghost as I came back into the living room. I was out and out sobbing by then, tears streaming down my face. Nausea clutched at my stomach.

"Holy shit, Mackenzie, are you okay?" He stood and came before me, looking into my face. "Are you all right?"

I wondered what I must look like. Grey seemed really alarmed. "We've gotta go." I answered through my tears. Marcy and Greg just stared, frozen in place, their eyes wide with confusion as they watched us. I wasn't going to explain anything to them. They'd know soon enough. I grabbed the key to my car and the journal Marcy had given me. Grey found his coat in the hall closet and was back to me in an instant. He put an arm around my shoulders and helped me walk to the garage through the crippling pain.

"It's okay, sugar. We'll be home in no time." His voice was oddly panicked as he hit the garage door opener and helped me into the passenger seat of my car, then ran swiftly to the driver's side and starting the engine. I curled up into a ball in my seat, tighter than the fetal position, wrapping my arms around my knees and sobbing as if my very heart were broken.

Because it had been, in a way. I didn't know how to describe it, I still don't know how exactly, but it was just like … complete betrayal. I'd been lying to myself the entire time. It was the closest I'd ever come to actually experiencing the whole big-happy-family scenario. But all of it had been a lie. All the love, all the acceptance, all of it had been broken by my secret. I hadn't really been happy. I couldn't be happy. I wasn't capable of being happy. Not without the drugs.

Through it all, my craving growled in protest, famished, flaring with need. Screaming in my ear. More important than the rest. More important than anything.

"Its okay, Mackenzie." Grey was nearly desperate, listening to me sob. "We're almost home. They'll forgive you, they will."

"They won't," I cried. "They won't. And it's my fault. It's all my fault …."

CHAPTER 55

By the time we made it back to our room, I was calmer. My breath still hitched in my throat, but it was nothing like the racking, heart wrenching sobs that had broken from my body. I watched Grey, sniffling and trying to catch my breath as he hurriedly broke open a red rubber balloon and took a large chunk from the tarry substance inside. I was desperate for the heroin. Sick and getting sicker by the minute. Grey's features were tense as he worked, determined. I noticed he took enough for both of us.

"Are you okay, Mackenzie?" He asked worriedly, looking up from his actions just long enough to assess my expression. I knew I must've looked terrible, I probably had mascara running all the way to my chin, but he seemed relieved by whatever he saw there.

"Yeah," my voice was still hoarse from crying. I held my arms around myself to try and keep the nausea at bay. "I'm okay."

"That was pretty intense." He let out a breath, as if he'd been holding it this whole time. "What do you think your parents will do now?"

Inwardly, I cringed. I didn't want to think about them. Every time I shut my eyes, I saw again the look of utter revulsion on my dad's face … the deep, aching disappointment in my mom's gaze. I shook my head free from the vision.

"I don't know." I shrugged. "They'll probably do what they always do. Nothing."

"They wouldn't like, call the cops on you, would they?"

"No." I adamantly refused the idea. "No. Are you kidding? Think of what their friends would say. No, with my parents, its more … lets just pretend this didn't happen. Let's just sweep this under the rug."

Grey nodded. "I thought it might be something like that."

"Yeah." I didn't want to think about them anymore. I tried not to remember how good our day together had been, how loved and accepted I'd felt, before …. We sat in silence a moment as Grey struck the lighter beneath the spoon. I watched him eagerly. I knew that none of this would matter in a few seconds, that the whole scene would seem like a far off, distant nightmare. One that held no threat, one I could think about again without it scaring me anymore.

"I'm sorry I lost it." I apologized, biting my lip. Sweat was beading on my brow. "I don't know what came over me. Talk about dramatic." I tried to smile at my ridiculousness, tried to seem light-hearted for him. It came out as a grimace.

"It's okay. I mean, you freaked me out a little … but I understand." Grey looked up at me with avid concern, his blue eyes penetrating my gaze. "Are you sure you're okay?"

"I am. I am okay." I assured him. "Seriously. I just need to get high."

"Yeah, I know, but …." He sighed again, "… maybe we should think about getting off the drugs. For real this time."

"Yeah." I agreed easily. "Sure." But the words held no threat to me. That's all they were, just words, and we both knew it. Just more empty promises. We couldn't have quit the heroin then, even if we wanted to. I couldn't anyway. I needed it. I needed it because I was afraid to be sober, afraid to face everything that had happened and what I had become.

I needed it to cover up the little piece of me that died the moment my mother opened up the bathroom door. It was my problem. It was my solution.

Wordlessly, Grey seemed to understand.

Once the needle plunged into my vein everything was good again, just like I knew it would be. Then I was on my back, floating on a sea of sweetness, where nothing could touch me but the strong, warm sun on my face. I knew I should be upset; I knew I should feel sad, but with the heroin fresh in my veins, racing through them, erasing all the negativity, it was all too easy to forget.

Maybe Grey needed it too. He never left me once to shoot up alone, and whenever I'd sober up enough to hold my arm out for more, it wasn't long before he joined me again. We lived in a slackened state of total peace upon his bed.

We stayed that way for a long, long time.

"Mackenzie?" There was a soft rap on the door. "Hey, Mac, are you up?"

"Hmmm …." I moaned into the mattress. "What?" I croaked, opening my bleary eyes and squinting at the door. It was Alex, looking apologetic. His voice dropped to a whisper.

"There's someone here to see you. Some Riley guy?"

Riley? *Riley?* Riley was here …? Oh, right. It was the holidays. Riley would be on his vacation right now, he would have come home to see his mom, just like the good son that he was. Vaguely I remembered our graduation—it seemed like ages ago when Riley promised to come and visit me whenever he was back in town. And if I was still alive, he had joked. Was I still alive? I wondered, a wry smile on my lips. Not really. I was too deadened to even register surprise that he had come to see me, and my answer didn't require any thought. There was no way I could see Riley, not now. I sunk my face back into the mattress, relieved when all I felt was … nothing. I felt nothing—no sadness, no loneliness, no regret. I hadn't even thought of Riley in months. I shut my eyes again, at peace with my decision.

"I don't want to see him, Alex. Tell him to go away."

"You're the boss." He saluted me, and that was that.

But Riley didn't go quietly. He came to see me the next day as well. Grey was just about to ease the needle into my arm when Zack knocked on our door this time, interrupting us.

"There's a Riley at the door." He motioned with his thumb.

I shook my head adamantly, refusing to even entertain the idea. "No. I don't want to see him, Zack. Tell him I'm sleeping or something."

Grey eyed me quizzically, but I think my response secretly pleased him. He raised an eyebrow at me.

"We can wait, Mackenzie, if you want to go see him."

"No, we can't wait. And I don't want to see him."

"Okay. I'll get rid of the guy." Zack promised. Grey frowned at me as soon as the door had shut behind him.

"Not that I mind … but what was that about?"

"What?" I asked impatiently. I was antsy—eyeing the needle in Grey's hand, wishing it was in my arm.

"You haven't seen Riley in months. Why don't you want to now?"

"I don't know. I've got nothing to say to him." I lied. I couldn't tell Grey the truth. I couldn't tell him how hard it would be, to see Riley, to have him laugh and smile and talk to me before he ultimately left me and then went back to his real life. I had no coping skills for that. I had no coping skills at all.

Nothing but the needle.

But the next day when Riley came, I was all alone. Zack and Alex and Grey had gone into the city to get some more dope. I was actually up and out of bed, shakily standing in the kitchen in plaid pyjama pants and my Blondie t-shirt, forcing down some Honeycombs. The cereal made me nauseous, but I knew I had to eat something. I couldn't remember the last time anything had been chewed by my teeth and swallowed by my throat. Lately they'd only been used for vomiting.

As I stood there idly, I caught a reflection of myself in the microwave. The sight actually staggered me. I stopped. I nearly dropped my bowl of cereal. I gasped and took a step closer to the reflection, raising my hand to my cheekbone and touching it gingerly. It looked sunken into my face. Clumps of my dark hair were matted around my head—dreaded, tangled. The skin under my eyes was dark and purplish; my lips were pale and dry. I looked like a ghost. Like I should be haunting people. I stared at myself for a long moment, horrified. How long had I been binging for? How long had I looked like this?

And that was when Riley knocked on the door.

I crumpled to the floor, hiding myself from his view behind the kitchen island. I sat a moment, my eyes wide, listening and waiting—hoping, praying that Riley would just give up, that he'd just go away. It made me angry, his determination.

And then he knocked again.

"Mackenzie." Riley called. He voice rocked through me, with warmth and familiarity and comfort and a long lost feeling of ... security ... almost. His voice felt like home. And at that instant I was pained—heartbroken that he was so close, just on the other side of the door, but there was no way I could see him. Not now. He just couldn't see me like this, I wouldn't let him. I leaned my head back against the cabinet and steeled myself against the tears that threatened.

He knocked again. With sudden horror, it occurred to me that the front door might not be locked. And if it wasn't, there was nothing to stop him from just walking into the house. Walking in and discovering me there on the floor, looking like road kill. For a moment, I wondered if I could play dead. I looked like I was dead. Maybe it'd be enough for him to leave me alone.

I pushed the thought from my mind, bit my lip and slowly crawled across the kitchen floor, as stealthily as I could. Luckily, the blinds were down on the window and he couldn't see me as I slowly sidled up to the door. Crouching there, I lifted my arm and deliberately turned the knob on the padlock.

It clicked just a little too loudly. Riley started.

"Mackenzie?" He rapped again. "Mackenzie, I know you're in there. I know you can hear me. Open the door!"

I shook my head in silence, dropping my head into my hands. He was so close to me; only literal inches of metal separated us. I could hear his feet shuffling on the front step, could hear the hesitation in them.

"Mackenzie." His voice sounded choked. "Mackenzie, please?"

Tears smarted in my eyes again at the sincere concern deeply apparent in his all too familiar voice. I pressed my palm against the door, as if I could steal some of his comfort through the cold metal, and shook my head again. I can't, I mouthed in silence. I can't Riley. Just go away. Go away. Forget about me. Have a good life.

He sighed. I could hear him rubbing his hands in the cold. Then, after a few tense, silent moments, finally I heard the sound of his boots slowly crunching away on the snow. His step was heavy, defeated. I didn't relax until I heard his car start and pull out onto the road. I got up then, woodenly, and walked straight into the bathroom.

I got in the shower and washed my hair. I was numb, physically and mentally devoid of any kind of feeling. I let the hot spray pound in my face. I washed my hair again, using extra conditioner to try and detangle the clumpy, knotty mess. I felt blank, empty. I began to shave my legs. Swiping the razor too quickly, I nicked my knee, starting at the quick burst of pain and watching as the watery blood trickled down into the tub. But I felt it. And it felt … good. Inspired, I took the razor firmly in my grasp, sucked my breath in, and dragged it slowly across the forearm of my left hand. It hurt. Blood flowed down my wrist. But it made me smile. The pain was sweet. I shut my eyes with pleasure, letting out a shaky breath of relief. Here was the release I needed, the release I'd been craving. I felt something again.

I opened my eyes, and now they were gleaming.

CHAPTER 56

"Do you have to go?" I looked up at Grey hopefully. Damn, he was so gorgeous. It was impossible not to feel good, at the moment, with the liquid heroin dancing deep within my blood stream. I couldn't help but feel content.

He chuckled at me, rubbing remnants from the cocaine he'd just done across his gums. "Sorry, sugar. We have to play tonight, and I haven't practiced in …," he flexed his stiff fingers, "way too long."

"Ohhh …," I moaned. We both had to work that night. The Aurora was re-opening after the Christmas break with its annual New Years Eve party. Apparently it was a huge event, bringing in crowds of people every year. Grey's band was slated to play and I was going to be stationed in the bar. Walter had trained me to work there himself, as quickly and abruptly as he did everything else—but I actually found that I liked it. It was easier to bartend than to try and squeeze through the drunken throng, carrying a tray and trying not to get stepped on. It was harried and chaotic behind the bar, remembering recipes and shooter mixes and trying to keep up with the orders being screamed at me. But I always liked a challenge.

The biggest challenge yet was going to be just getting out of our bed. I didn't want to leave the room; I didn't really want to face the world. But Grey insisted it would be good for me to get up and out of the house. I think he was worried. Because of the heroin. We hadn't just slipped from the precipice of control, we'd jumped headfirst off of it, and now we had to try and regain some measure of the life we'd left behind on the cliff.

But I didn't know if I could. I didn't really want to. I could've spent the rest of my life with Grey in our room, his arms wrapped around me, drugs in our systems, staring out the big picture window at the twinkling stars, the bright face of the moon peeking out over the soft silver clouds. Just like we'd done on so many nights. Happy. Together.

He smirked at the play of sadness on my face as I watched him get ready to go. How rapidly this man had become my whole entire life. Even an afternoon without him was like total agony. If I could've felt sad at that moment, I would've.

"It's only for the afternoon, Mackenzie. I'll see you tonight, at the club." He chided.

"I know you will. But I miss you already." I pouted. "I love you, you know."

Grey laughed at my dramatics. "I love you too." It was easy for him to say now, but I never tired of hearing it. I gave him a glorious smile as he bent to kiss me goodbye, taking advantage of his nearness and grasping his hands to pull him closer yet.

"Will you play my song tonight?" I wondered in his ear.

"Hmmm … maybe. It's not exactly to the tune of *Auld Lang Synge* though, is it?"

I giggled. "I guess not. I just want everyone to know."

"Know what?" His blue eyes shone at me.

"That I'm yours."

"Mackenzie," he smirked, "that's never been a question."

And though he left me then, he left me on a good note. My lips were still tingling from his kisses as I fell back onto our bed with a sigh, dreading the long hours until we would be together again. I hated when Grey was gone, I hated being alone. I sat on our bed, tracing a finger down the red scabby lines that crossed my arm, lines I'd somehow managed to hide from him. I knew I shouldn't push off; I knew I had to be sober enough to concentrate on work in only a few hours. But I just couldn't handle the quiet. When the heroin began to fade, when there was no one else around, the thoughts began to seep in. Thoughts of sorrow and despair. Of utter hopelessness.

Thoughts I couldn't handle.

I cooked myself up a batch and shot it quickly. I was a pro by now; the needle didn't bother me at all. I still let Grey do it for me most of the time, but that was mostly because he liked to do it for me. He wanted to be the one to give me pleasure, of any kind. And I didn't mind that a bit.

I was still lying back against the bed, slack and motionless, when my cell phone started to ring. I stared at it a moment, debating, until it fell silent. Time passed. My cell phone rang again, and this time when it did, I sighed and rolled over to answer it.

"Hello?"

"Hey bitch! Where the hell are you?" Charlie giggled over the phone.

"Huh? What do you mean?"

"You're supposed to come over today, remember? To get ready for tonight."

"Oh, yeah. Shit." I sat up. "What time is it?"

"Like four. Grab your stuff and get over here."

"I like, just woke up." I lied. "I haven't showered or anything."

"Do it over here. Come on, Mac. I've got your uniform for tonight. It's sexy."

"Is it?" I bit my lip. I didn't want to face reality, not yet.

"Mac!"

"Okay, okay, I'll be right over."

"Hurry up!" She was laughing again as she hung up the phone. I groaned and flipped my cell shut. I forced myself off the bed, stumbling around my room and gathering some things—my heels, my bra, some undies, some jewellery. I shoved it all into my purse and then threw on some jeans, a t-shirt, my skate shoes and my old winter jacket. I didn't even look at myself in the mirror. Grabbing my car keys from the counter, I headed out of the house for the first time in a week.

I was totally unprepared for the cold. Somehow I had forgotten about winter. It hit me with all its force, the brunt of the icy wind shuddering down my back and stiffening my muscles. I cringed my head down into the collar of my jacket and headed blindly into the snow, climbing into my frozen car for the first time since … since Christmas. I tried not to think about that, shivering as I turned the key. To my utter amazement, the car chugged to life. I smiled at my good fortune and pulled into the icy streets, the engine whining in protest.

The vents were still blowing cold by the time I got to Charlie's house. I ran up the old familiar stairs—even more treacherous now that they were covered in snow and ice—and headed into the house without even bothering to knock.

Charlie and Courtney were sitting at the counter. Their heads turned in surprise as I burst into the room, letting a draft of cold, frozen air in with me. They stared at me as I took my shoes off.

"What?" I wondered.

"Fuck Mac," Charlie raised her eyebrows. "You look like shit."

"Yeah dude." Courtney agreed with surprise.

"I told you, I just woke up." I took off my coat and shuddered from the cold. "I haven't had a chance to do anything with myself yet."

"Right." Charlie was sceptical, I could tell. The smile fell from her face. "Well, go get a shower then. It looks like I have my work cut out for me tonight."

I made a face at her and breezed past them down the hallway. They were oddly silent, watching me walk by. I didn't like their scrutiny, so I hurried into the bathroom as quickly as I could and shut the door.

Evidence of my replacement was all around me. I took it all in as I caught my breath. It hurt a little to see Courtney's blow dryer on the sink, her toothbrush in the holder, her towels hanging up on the hook. The two of them were giggling now; I could hear them from the kitchen. I wondered fleetingly if they were laughing at me. I tried to ignore their happy laughter, avoiding the bathroom mirror—which was a natural instinct now, something I automatically shunned away from. My reflection was just another grim reminder of what I'd let myself become.

I stepped into the shower, letting the hot spray sink into my skin. Charlie's razor was balancing haphazardly on the ledge, and without thinking, I picked it up. As I gripped the handle, I remembered the sweet pain that came when I cut myself. The relief that came with actually feeling something again. Slowly, I dragged the razor sideways across my arm, shutting my eyes and shuddering as the blade ripped through my skin. Mmmm … the blood ran down my hand, and I smiled with delight.

"Mac, lets go! We don't have a lot of time!" Charlie called, knocking on the door. Then under her breath, more for Courtney than for me to hear, she muttered, "Not with the way you look, anyway."

I shut the water off immediately.

Charlie sat me down in a chair in the kitchen when I was ready, dragging up her seat before me so she could get to work on my face. Courtney sat on a stool at the island snorting cocaine. Black Eyed Peas was blaring out of the stereo. I noticed all of this out of my periphery. It held no interest to me anymore. I just sat, glum and despondent, as Charlie got to work.

"So, Mac," she sighed. "Tell me not to be worried about you." Her blue eyes held mine locked in her gaze, and the concern she felt was evident. She motioned her head to the cuts on my arm, some older and scabby, one obviously freshly done. It was still bleeding faintly. "What's going on with you, huh?"

"Nothing." I shrugged. "I'm fine."

"Yeah. I bet. You don't look fine."

"It's nothing. I haven't been getting a lot of sleep lately." I lied.

She made a noise at that, a scoff of disbelief. "You can talk to me, you know."

"I know." I replied. I just wasn't going to.

Charlie shook her head in obvious frustration, but she didn't press me. We sat in silence. It felt nice actually—the coolness of her fingers as she applied my make-up, the deftness of her hands as she worked with my hair. It kind of reminded me of old times. When I had actually cared about my appearance.

"There. All done." She proclaimed finally. "We should get dressed. We're supposed to get there early to get ready and stuff."

I nodded woodenly. The three of us went into Charlie's room, where she handed out our special uniforms for the night. They were actually kind of cool. They were made to resemble a man's tuxedo, with short dark skirts and white sleeveless blouses with ruffles down the front. A cute little bow tie went around the neck. Charlie and Courtney giggled as they got ready, talking about guys I didn't know, how hot they were, hoping they'd be there. I went through the motions of having fun, but I wasn't there in spirit. I needed to get high, but I knew I couldn't. Not when I had to work.

"Woooh! We look hot!" Charlie exclaimed with her usual exuberance. She and Courtney were standing before the floor-length mirror, their arms around each other. "Come on Mac, aren't you going to look?"

I bit my lip in hesitation before joining them. I wanted so badly to be able to enjoy what they were enjoying, to laugh with them, to be light-hearted. I stood awkwardly beside Charlie, who grasped me around the waist, and then looked into the mirror.

I didn't look as bad as I thought I might. Charlie was truly the worker of miracles. Where before my cheeks had been sallow, they now held the soft bloom of pink blush. My eyes were too big, overwhelming my skinny face, but they were lined with dark and silver, metallic and smoky. My lips were as deep red as Courtney's always were. My hair was up in a ponytail, curly and voluminous, but it seemed to have lost its shine.

I may have looked okay, but I was still barely recognizable. I gazed down at my arms instead. "But what about these?" I choked out. Neither of the other girls had deep red marks and cuts on their arms. For some reason, this made me want to cry.

"Don't worry about that, Mac." Charlie soothed. "I've got just the thing." She rummaged around in her room for a moment, producing a pair of white cuff bracelets that seemed to be made just for this occasion. She put the bracelets around my forearms. They managed to hide the majority of the marks on my arms. When she was done, she squeezed my hands and looked deep into my eyes.

"It's going to be okay, Mac." She promised me with a hopeful smile. "Just relax."

I nodded dumbly. Courtney got out some more cocaine and made some rails for us. I took mine without feeling, like I was a robot on automatic pilot or something. But it helped. It gave me some energy, some gusto. It made me think that maybe Charlie was right. Maybe everything would be okay. A slight smile graced my lips.

And then it was gone.

CHAPTER 57

I relied heavily on cocaine for the rest of the night, to keep me going. It was amazingly easy to just bend down behind the counter and sniff some back without anyone noticing. The place was packed almost instantly, full of rowdy people. Everyone was there for a good time. It was New Years Eve. Champagne was flowing. Every now and then I'd look out at the sea of people in their bright party hats, laughing and dancing like they didn't have a care in the world, and I'd imagine I was them. Before things had gotten so out of control, I was one of them. There for a good time. Careless. Happy.

Grey would come to visit me at the bar when the band wasn't playing. They had five different sets planned that they were dispersing throughout the evening. The only time I'd smile, like really smile, was when he was with me.

"Do you get to bring that uniform home?" He wondered clandestinely, leaning over the bar to speak the words so I'd hear him over the deafening crowd.

"I think that could be arranged." I promised slyly. I couldn't believe he still found me beautiful. I knew what I looked like. Did he actually even see me anymore? Couldn't he see what I'd become?

"Mmm …." His blue eyes were wicked as they looked me over. "How much longer will this stupid party go for?"

"At least midnight," I giggled. It was so easy with him, to be happy. Even despite everything else. "I think that's the tradition, anyway."

"Right." He grinned.

"Will you come find me at midnight? So I can kiss you?"

"Like I'd ever be able to turn that down." He smirked. But apparently he couldn't wait until midnight. He set his drink down and kissed me before he left to start another set. I smiled at his handsome face.

Even his voice helped. I could hear him singing as I worked, hear his glorious, velvet voice rasping away over the speakers, and it buoyed my spirits. I did some more cocaine, and I almost felt jovial, letting the happy little trembles erase the feeling of despair that nagged at me. And when the set ended, going out on a high note of wailing guitars and screaming fans, my spirits rose even further. Grey would be with me again soon. A wide smile spread across my face. Charlie noticed as she came into the bar, her beautiful face light and happy, her blue eyes sparkling. She grabbed my hands and spun me around in a little dance. Our patrons cheered for us, and I was actually giggling when she finally let me go.

I stopped twirling right before his face.

"Mackenzie." Riley was the only one in the entire crowd completely serious. I stopped short, surprised to find him there. He looked … had he always been this good looking? His dark hair was buzzed short; his face—so wonderfully familiar—looked older, wiser almost. He had filled out too, no longer was he lean and lank. He looked … he looked like a man. I cleared my throat.

"Hello, sir." I tried to play it casual. "What can I get you? On the house."

But Riley didn't answer me. He just stared. He stared and stared. His warm chocolate eyes didn't leave my face for a second. It made me uncomfortable; I wanted to cringe away from his gaze, because I knew that Riley would see too much. Didn't he always? Didn't he always just … know, somehow?

The club was full of people, but suddenly there was only me and him. And all he did was stare. His expression revealed nothing, I couldn't tell what was going through his mind, what he was thinking.

But then Grey strode up.

He was smirking as he pushed through the people to come and meet me. I looked away from Riley and watched him come, my dark eyes wide, anxious. Finally, finally Riley tore his gaze from me, turning them instead to glower at the man who was slowly coming to join us.

"Riley …." I warned. But it was too late.

If before Riley had been a locked box, now he was an open book. His brow furrowed with anger, his eyes glared with fury, his entire body tensed as Grey slowly sauntered over. He noticed Riley, its impossible not to notice when someone's uttering death threats with their eyes, but it didn't seem to bother him. He just came up and smiled at me, his blue eyes confident, casual. Only then did he turn to him.

"Hey man, how's it going—?"

"What have you done to her?" Riley interrupted him, his voice low, controlled.

"What?" Grey looked honestly confused.

"*What have you done to her*?" Riley bellowed, loud enough that the people surrounding them noticed. They began to spread out, to give them room, the tension in the crowd turning to excitement as they began to anticipate a fight.

"What are you talking about?" Grey glanced at me once and then back to Riley, like he really didn't get it. I bit my lip. I wanted Riley to stop. I needed Riley to stop. For whatever reason, Grey still found me beautiful. I didn't want him to see me … I didn't want him to look at me differently ….

"Stop it Riley!" I demanded. I was powerless behind the bar; they were too far out of my reach. Panicked, I pushed through my co-workers and then burst out onto the floor. "Stop it!"

Riley grasped me by the wrist and hauled me over. It hurt; he was grabbing the exact place I had cut myself earlier. I winced.

"Get your hands off of her!" Grey warned. I'd never heard him sound so … threatening. I looked up into his face, his handsome features hard and deadly serious, and felt actual fear for Riley. I tried to pull my hand free from his vice-like grip.

"Stop it Riley! Please!" I pleaded.

Grey's jaw clenched. "I mean it, asshole. Let her go."

"*Look at her*!" Riley shouted again. It all happened quickly then. Grey lunged for Riley, at the same time pulling me free of his grasp. But Riley's hand had been so tightly clenched around my wrist that he tore the white bracelet from my arm. Before the ripped shreds had a chance to hit the floor, the fight had come to a standstill.

"Mackenzie?" Grey paused in horror. He saw. He was looking at my arm, at the jagged marks the razor had made when it sliced through my skin. His blue eyes narrowed with confusion, with denial, with sorrow. "… What … what happened …?"

Tears swam in my eyes. I choked them back. I could have killed Riley at that moment, but instead I turned my back on him. I needed Grey to hear me. I needed him to understand.

"Grey … look, its nothing. It's okay." I insisted. I couldn't tell if he could hear me or not, it seemed like he was in shock. His blue eyes stared at nothing. His mouth was open with dread, as if he were struggling to process it all. And then it happened.

His jaw tensed, and he looked at me. His eyes traced over me, from my head to my toes, and they filled with anguish. With the worst kind of suffering. He took in the gaunt fragility of my shoulder blades, the boniness of my face, the scrawny legs sticking out from my skirt. At the cuts on my arms, the tracks in my elbows. He looked at me with horror. It hurt to see. The gorgeous blue eyes that before had only gazed at me full of adoration, now were wide as the stared at me with total dismay.

They were still gaping at me as Riley's fist slammed into his face.

That shocked me out of my stupor. "Riley, no! What are you doing?" I lunged in between them, expecting the worst. But Grey didn't fight back. Riley got up and shook his fist in pain, furiously staring down at my boyfriend levelled on the floor. I pushed him back as hard as I could, but I barely managed to move him an inch.

"Get out of here Riley!" I shouted, furious. "Get out of here!"

"You're coming with me." He decided, grasping my arm again. "Its okay, Mac. I'm going to get you out of here."

"*No*!" I panicked again. I couldn't leave Grey now. He had to see … he needed to see that I was really okay. "No!"

The bouncers were quick to step in. They were always around, blending into the shadows, waiting for a fight caused by some cocky jerk getting rowdy. They grabbed Riley and hauled him away from me. The moment I was free I ran to Grey's side. He was standing again, a welt across his cheekbone where Riley had punched him. But he wouldn't look at me. He was like I had been earlier, a robot, on automatic pilot as he turned and pushed through the crowd.

"Grey?" I ran to catch up with him. "What's the matter?" It was a stupid question. I knew the answer. But I wanted him to speak to me, to acknowledge I was there.

"Everything." His voice was devoid of any emotion.

A sob caught in my throat. "Am I really that hideous?"

"No." He stopped in his tracks, shaking his head. His eyes burned at me with sincerity. "You are beautiful."

"Then what—"

"This is my fault. It's all my fault." He started walking again, and I had no choice but to follow him. I didn't know where he was going until he headed up the stairs that lead to the back of the stage. The other guys were there, completely oblivious to our drama, prepping for their next set.

Grey was like a sleepwalker. He sat down on a stool and started tuning his guitar, staring down at his pedal like he was deep in concentration. I was beside myself. I had never seen him like this before … it actually scared me. I couldn't imagine what thoughts were going on in his mind that could keep him so … paralyzed.

"Grey, talk to me!" I demanded. I couldn't take it any longer. "Please, say something."

"She was right." He looked at me. "She was right. I am a screw up. A total loser."

"Stop that." I shook my head at him. "You are not a loser."

"No, I am. I am." His voice was so … lifeless. "I did the same thing to her, you know. I just sat back and watched while she slowly wasted away."

"Grey, stop it."

"I didn't do anything then. But I can do something now. I can do something." He didn't even seem to notice I was standing there. He was talking to himself and I wasn't meant to be a part of this conversation. "I can make it right …."

"Grey, please?" Tears stung my eyes. My heart plummeted somewhere deep inside my chest, strangling the breath from my lungs. "Please?"

But then he looked straight at me. "Mackenzie, we shouldn't be together." His blue eyes bored into mine, and only from knowing him could I tell how much this cost. The pain was evident in his eyes, the heartbreak apparent on his face. I shook my head wildly, refusing the words.

"Grey, don't do this. Don't do this."

"I can't. I can't do this to you anymore."

"No. No, Grey." The tears started flowing then, I was powerless to stop them. "We'll … we'll figure something out … we'll get clean … I'll go to rehab … something, anything …. Grey, we have to be together."

"I'm not strong enough."

"You are. You can be. We can be together."

"No. No Mackenzie." His voice found some power again, some life. "Can't you see? I'm killing you. I'm killing you!"

"You're not." I grasped his hand, desperate, and raised it to my cheek. "Grey, look at me. I love you. I won't let you leave me. You won't. You can't." I sobbed. "You love me too. I know you do."

"Of course I do." His eyes were wild with pain. His voice was like a whisper now, harsh and choking. "But I don't have a choice."

"Grey—"

"Grey, man." It was Zack. He seemed hesitant to interrupt us, but everyone was already on stage. It was time for them to play. "Come on, we're on."

Grey stood up, like he was on automatic pilot again, and picked up his guitar. He didn't even glance back at me as he took the stage, the screams deafening as he stood before the mike. Hopelessly I collapsed on the floor, watching him. When he started to sing I committed the sound to memory, every melodic pitch, every word his smooth voice rumbled over. I listened to him through my tears and thought back, trying to figure out where we went wrong and how everything had fallen apart. After everything we'd done, everything we'd gone through, how we could put it back together again? Back to the way it used to be?

The rest of the night dragged on, every second worse than the second before. I went back to the bar; I didn't know what else to do. I felt like everyone was staring at me out of the corner of their eyes, I felt like everyone was talking about me behind my back. Every breath was a shudder as I attempted to hold back my sobs. All around me, people were revelling, happy, joyful, celebrating. I hated them all.

Just before midnight, Serpentine played a wicked, hard rock version of *Auld Lang Syne*. The crowd went crazy for them. I was so proud of Grey up on the stage, in his tight jeans and his black t-shirt, with the studded leather bracelets on his wrists, the cherry red guitar held in his deft, capable hands. His dark messy hair, his gorgeous blue eyes, his cocky smirk. I loved Grey more than I could possibly love anybody. He was the only one for me, and suddenly, I was determined to make it work.

I would do anything I'd have to. I'd give up heroin. I'd start today, start right now, if that's what he needed. Anything.

The lights dimmed when the band stopped playing, and the countdown began. The club erupted with the deafening noise.

"Ten … nine … eight … seven … six … five … four …."

And then I was safe. Safe in Grey's arms again. I don't even know where he came from, but suddenly I was swept up into his warm, strong embrace, and he crushed me to him. I clung to him just as tightly, my hands in his hair, cupping his face. I smelt deeply his delicious cologne and pressed my lips against his neck.

"You're right, you know. There's no one for me but you." He whispered.

"I know." I giggled shakily. "I know. Grey, we can make this work." I stared up into his eyes, trying to read them, trying to convince him.

"I'm going to make this right." He pressed his forehead to mine, speaking with vehemence.

"I know. I know."

The clock struck twelve.

"Happy New Year, Mackenzie." He smirked.

"Happy New Year, Grey." I whispered back, through my happy tears. We smiled at each other, for just a moment, as the crowd started screaming and cheering and clapping for the stroke of midnight.

And as Grey bent to kiss me, a smile still on his lips, it seemed like they were cheering for us.

CHAPTER 58

I couldn't wait to go home. Grey and the guys had left the bar just shortly after midnight, and I knew exactly what they were going home to do. My craving for heroin pounded in my bones, reminding me—and I realized I couldn't wait to be done with it all. I couldn't wait to feel … healthy again. I knew it would hurt, I knew I'd be sick, I knew it would downright suck, but I wanted to get off the heroin. So Grey and I could be together, so it could be pure and real, just like it once was.

The rest of my shift I tried to picture our new life together. It seemed right that it was New Years, a time for new beginnings, a time to leave behind the old and start afresh. As people screamed their drink orders at me and I worked in a frenzy to fill them, all I could envision was Grey and I, our future together, sober and happy. We could do it, I knew we could. I felt hope again, it surged throughout me.

When the party finally came to a close; when I finally made it home—shivering from the cold—I bounded into the house. I couldn't help myself. I felt optimistic. Positive. More so than I had in a long time. Even though I could feel the start of the sickness pressing in, I gave Alex and Zack a happy smile as I burst into the living room. They both sat slumped over on the couch, nodding off in front of the TV.

Not even the beading cold sweat could dampen my mood.

"Hey guys, great show tonight!" I practically sang. It took a moment before either of them could respond.

"Oh, thanks Mac." Alex smiled drowsily. "It was … really … good …."

I giggled at him. "Is Grey in our room?"

"Yeah …."

I nearly ran down the hall to our bedroom, my eyes adjusting to the dim light within. The bedside lamp was on and I could see Grey's form lying on the bed. Our supplies were scattered in front of him. I grinned understandably. I couldn't begrudge him one last hit, one last time before we started our new life, our clean life. Maybe I'd have one too—just one more to tide over the sickness until he awoke, and then we could do it together, could go through it together. And I meant it this time, they weren't just words. We were going to get clean.

I crawled into the bed behind him, gazing down at his handsome face, slack and peaceful, utterly gorgeous. I wrapped an arm around his chest and hugged him to me, kissing his neck and breathing deep. With my fingers I slowly trailed down the hard muscle of his arm, expecting him to shiver … but he just lay there, still. Wow, he must really be out of it. I grinned, my lips following the pattern my fingers had taken down his arm. He still had the needle clutched in his hand, and gently I pried it loose from his grip.

"Grey." I whispered, nudging him slightly. "Grey, will you do one for me?"

He didn't respond. I giggled softly in his ear, reaching my hand beneath his t-shirt and skimming it over the smooth, hard muscle of his abdomen. I pressed my palm against his chest, trying to coax a reaction from him. "Grey?"

But he was still. He was too still … something was wrong. Frowning, I pressed my hand harder yet against his chest. But it didn't move. It just stayed flat and hard, without rising or falling ….

"Grey? Grey?" I rolled him over so he was flat on his back. His slack form was completely yielding, his head lolling on the pillow. His lips were blue.

My heart stopped beating

"No, no, no, no, no, no, no …." I was frozen. Terrified by my discovery. Part of my brain tried to jolt me into action, tried to tell me to get up, to run, to go and get help. But I couldn't, I was shaking too badly. And I didn't want to leave him; I didn't want to leave him alone.

Part of me shut down. I was only barely aware as I got up off the bed, my footsteps staggering in utter horror. I had to use the wall for support. It was like I was outside myself, like a spectator at a play, watching some horrible drama ensue. I rooted for the girl I could see, I hoped for her. Yes, go get help, I told her. Go get Alex and Zack ….

I wobbled, teetering down the hallway. My muscles wouldn't move, like I was in a nightmare or something, paralysed with fear.

"*Zack!*" I barked. "*Alex!*"

There was no movement from the couches.

Damn, stupid junkies. "*Zack! Alex! Help me!*" My voice was so shrill, so high pitched—like the fear had frozen my voice box and all it could make now was this strangled, harsh soprano.

They must have heard the sheer panic of my scream. Both of them shook awake, staring up at me in confusion for a moment. Alex was the first to move.

"What's wrong, Mac?" He came to me in the hallway, helped me stand straight, his eyes hazy with concern.

"Grey … it's Grey …." I panted. "Oh god … it's Grey … please … please …."

He left me there. Zack brushed past me an instant later. I clutched the wall for support; my limbs were shaking so badly that my teeth nearly chattered. I couldn't see straight. I couldn't watch. I shut my eyes and listened as Zack and Alex ran into our room, hoping I had made some terrible mistake—that Grey would be up and sitting in bed, wondering what the hell all the noise was about.

"Shit! Shit! Grey … Grey buddy … wake up man …."

I could hear someone slapping him. It was true then, it was real. A sob escaped my throat and I slid down the wall, my legs refusing to hold my weight up anymore.

"Come on man … come on … come on buddy …."

Sirens. Paramedics. Red, flashing lights. A stretcher. A body on the stretcher. CPR. Shouting. White lights. Sterile. Emergency room. Beeping machines. IV.

My mom.

She came up out of nowhere. Of course she was working tonight. Wasn't she always working? Isn't that why I had always been alone?

I had never felt more alone than I did at that instant.

She scanned the limp body on the stretcher for a half a second, assessing the situation, and then sprang into action. I'd never seen my mom at work before, she was commanding—everyone hurried to follow her orders.

"I need 10cc's! Lori, start the Defibrillator …." She pulled on a pair of white gloves and hurried to the front of the bed. At that moment, she saw me. Her blue eyes filled with anguish for just a second.

"Get her out of here!" She shouted. Someone grabbed me, but I fought them. I couldn't leave Grey. I'd been in a total trance until then, just blinking at the nurses and paramedics surrounding him as they worked frantically—pushing needles into his skin, shouting orders at each other. His handsome face was covered by an oxygen mask. He wasn't breathing, he couldn't breathe. I wanted to be near him until he did; I needed to feel the warmth of his hand, to know that he was going to be okay. He had to be okay ….

"Mom! Please!" I shouted desperately. "Help him! Please, help him!"

"Get her out of here!" She boomed. The grip on my arms tightened and then I was being hauled away, beyond the swinging doors, out into the waiting room.

"*No! No! Grey!*" I was screaming, fighting them. They didn't understand. They couldn't understand how badly I needed to be beside him. It would help him, my closeness. It would give him a reason to open his eyes again.

Someone held my writhing body. I couldn't look at them; I looked past them, straining for a glimpse inside the ER. "Let me go!" I shouted. "Let me go!"

And then, I was calmer. I didn't want to be; I knew there was a reason for me to keep fighting. But then my head got cloudy and my muscles relaxed without my bidding. I hadn't even felt the needle until I saw the orderly holding it in his hand. They'd given me something to calm down. Valium, probably. He set me on a chair then, and they left me all alone.

It was too quiet in the waiting room. The change was tangible after the frantic chaos of the ER. I had no choice but to just sit there; I had no energy to move my limbs. I was thankful for the Valium, it wouldn't let me think straight. It wouldn't let me gnaw the ends of my fingertips off with worry. But it was also making me sleepy. I fought with my eyelids as they drooped heavily. I knew there was something I should stay awake for, but I was losing the battle. Despite my best efforts I dropped my head, slumped in the chair, and gave in to the relative comfort of sleep.

My mom shook me awake. I stared up at her a moment, bleary eyed. How could it be time to get up for school already? It felt like I had just gone to sleep ….

"Mackenzie?" Her eyes were full of sorrow, her face tense, like she was stressed about something. She was in her white Doctor's coat. Didn't she usually leave that at work?

And then it all came rushing back to me, in a tidal wave of dread. All of it. Grey's still chest. The ambulance. The nurses, the machines, the tubes. The beeping. His limp, motionless body. I sat up rigidly, already reaching for the doors to the emergency room.

"Grey!"

"Mackenzie." Mom stopped me, her hand firm on my arm.

"Can I see him? Can I see him mom?"

Tears began to swim in her eyes.

"Mom?" My whisper was choked, desperate. "Mom, can I see him?"

"I don't think so, honey."

I swallowed heavily. "… Why not?"

"Because. Sweetie, Grey … Grey didn't make it. He overdosed, Mackenzie. It was too late; there was too much heroin in his system …."

"No. What? No." Slowly I shook my head. No. No. Liar. She was lying. Grey couldn't be dead. I knew what this was; I knew what she was doing. They were trying to keep us apart. When I was drugged, she'd hatched up some plot. She'd give Grey something … money maybe, if he promised to stay away from me. And then she'd tell me he was dead. They never wanted us to be together. Ha. The joke was on her. No amount of money could keep Grey from me. He'd find me, he would.

"I'm so sorry, baby." My mom was crying now, like it hurt her deeply to tell me the news. I hadn't realized she was such a good actress before. Was this the part where I was supposed to believe her? I scoffed. I'd show her. I wasn't going to fall for her little ploy.

I ripped my arm from her grasp.

"Mackenzie! Mackenzie! Where are you going? Come back!"

But I was already gone, running down the hallway, searching for the exit. I'd go and find Grey before he got away. Then, together, we'd take the money and go live on an island somewhere, away from all of this. We'd sit on a porch swing at sunset and laugh about how we overcame all the odds, how we'd finally made it, despite everything.

I burst through the front doors and into the staggering cold. Yes, we'd definitely have to find an island somewhere. I hated winter. Grenada, maybe—I'd heard great things about Grenada. I searched frantically for my car; I couldn't really remember driving it, I couldn't remember following the ambulance to the hospital. The red lights had been blinding, the sirens ear splitting.

But the lot was small, so it didn't take long before I was in the driver's seat, starting the engine. I just had to make it home. Then I'd be able to forget everything. As my car wheezed slowly down the street, I dreamed of the beach. I dreamed of grass and sunshine and an eternity of summer. I thought of waves pounding on the shore, the wet sand between my toes, the far off call of the gulls. I kept this vision in my head until I pulled up before the house. I ran inside, out of the cold, towards the only possible thing that would give me any measure of comfort.

"Mackenzie!" Alex stopped me. His face was ashen with worry. "How is he?"

I shook my head and ran down the hall to my bedroom. They want us to believe he's dead, Alex. But we'll show them. Don't worry. We'll show them.

I grabbed the needle that I had pried from Grey's fingers only hours ago. My hands were shaking as I cooked up the batch, a little stronger than usual. I knew I would need it. I always hated it when Grey was gone.

The needle hit my vein with the telltale sign of spurting blood, and then I slammed the drugs into myself. They nearly knocked me down, they were so potent. But it was nice. I could breathe again. The horror that had gripped my heart all night finally eased. I lay back against the bed and shut my eyes.

Don't worry Grey. I just needed one more shot. We're still going to get clean. We're still going to start our new life. Don't worry. I just needed one more shot ….

CHAPTER 59

When I woke up, or rather "came too," my first thought was of happy endings. I had to conjure the thought quickly before anything else could get in, before the pressing, nagging feeling rimmed in dread could break through my denial and reveal itself. I focused intently as I quickly mixed the heroin in my spoon. I thought of Cinderella and Snow White and Sleeping Beauty and all those other bitches who were rescued by their prince and got their happy endings. I was determined to get mine.

I shot up quickly, my eyes rolling back into my head with a pure spasm of pleasure. I let out a shaky breath and slowly pulled the needle from my arm. That was the thing about heroin, the thing I loved. Instant gratification. One second you're losing it, and the next you're better than you've ever been in your whole life. Like each syringe contained it's very own special, happy ending. A weak smile lifted my lips. And she lived happily ever after ....

When the intensity faded, when I was able to think more coherently, I realized that I was missing one vital portion to my happy ending. The Prince. He had yet to come back. But he was going to come back for me, of that I was certain. And when he did, I was going to be pretty for him. I was going to look like a Princess. Shakily, I got to my feet, buoyed by the idea. It would give me something to do while I waited; it would help me pass the time until Grey came back. And I wanted to look good for him. I wanted him to see that I was healthy again—pretty—so he wouldn't have to worry about me anymore.

It was quiet as I stepped a hesitant foot out of my bedroom. It didn't sound like anyone was home. Relieved, I tiptoed down the hallway and into the bathroom. I hadn't really done my make-up in so long, I wondered if I'd still be able to do it. But it was like riding a bike, right? Bike … mmm. It'd been so long since Grey and I had ridden on his bike. As soon as it was warm enough, I'd make him take me. Maybe he could teach me how to drive it ….

Was I being crazy? I stared into the mirror a moment—at my wide, bloodshot eyes, the purple shadows beneath them, the messy, stringy hair about my face. For some reason, I couldn't stop thinking about the funny old lady from *Ace Ventura*, the one who's like, "when Ray gets back and starts kicking again …," totally delusional. And then when the husband's talking about her, he says, "See, the engine's running, but nobody's behind the wheel."

That was such a funny movie. Grey and I would have to watch it when he got back. "Nobody's behind the wheel." I shook my head in amusement and grabbed my make-up kit from the counter. What a funny thing to say.

I pulled my hair up, piling it on top of my head. It felt like straw in my fingers, the dark strands were dry and lifeless. Then I started on my eyes, drawing dark, thick black lines around them. I layered copious amounts of grey eye shadow overtop the liner and then coated my eyelashes with mascara. After this came blush, and I swept the dark peach powder over my cheekbones with a flourish. Remembering how pretty Courtney looked with her deep red lips, I pulled out a lipstick in a similar color and filled in my mouth, lining the rim of my lips and painting the rest until they shone like blood.

I stood back and looked at my reflection. I looked like a clown. I stared at myself a moment, taking in the garish, disturbing image reflected back in the mirror. The sight made me laugh; I didn't know what else to do. I pointed at myself and cackled, and in a brief, fleeting second of clarity, realized I was acting like a lunatic.

"Mackenzie? What are you doing?"

Alex's sudden appearance made me jump. I held a hand to my chest and willed my heart to slow down.

"Oh, Alex. You scared me." I laughed.

He cleared his throat, his light eyes wide, and damp. He looked sad.

"You okay Mac?"

"Yeah." I nodded casually. "You?"

"No. No, I'm not okay." Alex's voice was hoarse. "What are you doing?"

"Making myself pretty." I shrugged, fluffing my hair in the mirror. "For when Grey comes back. I want to look good for him."

Alex's chin quivered, only slightly. He took a breath before he spoke, and when he did, his words were a whisper. "But Mackenzie, Grey's not coming back."

I shook my head, adamantly refusing the possibility. "He *is* coming back, Alex." I insisted. I didn't feel like explaining the whole situation to him, how my parents were trying to keep us apart. He'd probably think I was crazy. But I'd show him, we both would. Nothing could keep us apart. Nothing.

Alex swallowed heavily, his eyes falling to the floor, like he couldn't bear to look at me anymore.

It hit me sometime in the night. I rolled over in bed and reached out for Grey—a familiar motion, something I'd done a million times before. But this time, he wasn't there.

He's not there. I bolted upright in bed. Finally, the thoughts emerged; the horrendous, gut wrenching truth I'd been so fervently denying came screaming into the light. *He's not there! He's not there because he's dead! He's gone! Grey's gone!*

No. No. It couldn't be true. Desperately, I clung to my delusion like a branch hanging over a waterfall, the one lifeline that could keep me from the horrible, drowning pain that threatened to engulf me. Grey was coming for me. He was. He had to be ....

But the truth would not be quieted, not now that it was out. It hit me like a kick in the guts, doubling me over, making me clutch my chest in pain as a long, shuddering, soundless sob tore through my body. *Grey was gone. He was gone. Forever. He'd never be back. He was never coming for me. He had left me all alone. Forever. He was never coming back ....*

I had never known the echoing emptiness of total loss before. It tore through me now in a heart-sickening wave. I fell from the bed and hit the floor, crawling, trying to catch my breath. Grey was all around me, but he was gone. Our room seemed too still without him there, like it was holding its breath—expectant—waiting for Grey to come sauntering through the door with his gorgeous face smirking, his blue eyes gleaming. His amps were lined up against the wall, the pages of his lyrics piled on the desk, his scent clinging to his pillow, his guitar in its stand beside the bed. His clothes hung neatly on their hangers, clinging to the closet rod as if in fear of my chaotic, haphazard piles of laundry.

I took all this in, my eyes wild, my mind reeling. How could everybody say that death was natural? How was it natural for someone to be here one moment and then be gone the next? Forever? In the deepest pit of my heart I missed him. It had only been a matter of hours—maybe a day since I had last seen him, touched him, kissed him. Knowing I'd never be able to do so again, that he'd never smirk at me again, that he'd never whisper in my ear or sing to me with his beautiful voice, ever again … it was too much to bear.

Sobs ravaged through me, quiet sobs that shook my entire body, coming from somewhere deep inside, rattling my core with agony and torment. I grabbed the closest thing I could find, some remnant of Grey, anything he had once touched with his warm, strong hands. I cuddled myself around his amplifier. This was all that I had left, his things. Never him. Ever again.

I couldn't take it. My mind was too fragile, too weak to cope with the depth of such sorrow. I felt it tearing my soul apart, threatening to break me. It was unbearable, it was excruciating. There was only one thing that would help me escape, one thing that would enable me to survive such anguish. With tears flooding my eyes, gasping, I reached for my supplies.

Things were much better after. I found I could breathe again when I wasn't being crushed with the weight of total despair. I curled up in a ball on the bed, wrapping my arms around my legs, and buried my face into Grey's pillow. It smelt like him, like the delicious, masculine scent of his cologne.

I lay emotionless, slack with relief, blinking slowly, staring at nothing.

CHAPTER 60

At some point, Charlie came. I honestly had no idea how much time had lapsed since Grey's death. It could have been hours, it could have been days. But it felt like eternity. I hadn't moved much, maintaining a near zombie-like existence on our bed, clutching Grey's pillow to my breast. As soon as I came down enough for the thoughts to permeate the velvet veil of self-medicated fog, I'd shoot up again. This was how Charlie found me, in a state somewhere between living and dying. Numb.

It was dim in the room, which I was thankful for. I couldn't imagine what I looked like, especially now with the bright, clown like make-up smeared all over my face; the black trails of mascara that surely stained my cheeks. But Charlie didn't say anything about it. She just climbed into the bed behind and wrapped her arms around me.

"I'm so sorry sweetie. I'm so sorry …," she crooned, like I was a little child, smoothing my hair back from my brow. I couldn't respond; I didn't have anything to say. I just blinked and continued existing.

When I next woke up Charlie was still there. She was sitting at the end of the bed now, my feet tucked in her lap. Zack was with her, sitting in the chair beside, his head bowed in his hands. They were talking in low, hushed voices. I didn't want to disturb them, but I needed to shoot up again. I propped myself up on an elbow and went about my business. The talking stopped, and I could feel them both staring at me.

"Mac?" Charlie had tears in her throat, I could hear them. "You okay?"

I gave her a sidelong glance and shook my head once, curtly. No.

"Do you want to talk?" she encouraged.

I shook my head again. No.

"I'm sorry Mackenzie." Now it was Zack's turn. "I'm so sorry .... If I'd known ... I could've .... If I only would have checked on him, once ...."

I shrugged. Tears pricked my eyes, but I choked them back. I didn't want to think about it, I didn't want to dwell. I shook my head, fighting for control, just long enough to feel the needle slice into my skin. I pushed down the plunger and collapsed back onto the bed, relieved.

More time passed in much the same way. Sometimes I slept, sometimes I dreamt, sometimes I just lay there, staring at nothing. The light streaming through the open window would fade and I'd know another day had passed. This was my life now, the only way I could possibly live without Grey. It was bleak, it was grim. But it was better than the alternative.

There was talk of a Wake, but I refused to go. I didn't want to see Grey that way—pudgy from the embalming fluid, swollen in death. I didn't want to remember him as anything but totally alive. He was beautiful in life. He was so beautiful to me ....

Why! Through the haze, I suddenly pounded the pillow with my fist, overcome with emotion. *Why! Why did he have to die? He was always so careful. How could he have overdosed?*

Tears pushed through. I let them come, now, when I was all alone, when no one else could see. *Grey; please ... please don't be dead. Please, come back to me ....*

I love you ....

More time passed. More time of lying like a dead thing across the bed, oblivious to anyone and everything except the needle, curled up in a ball and clutching Grey's pillow. People would come and check on me, try to talk to me; try to shake some life back into me ... but to no avail. I waited as they spoke their words of comfort, blinking at them until they were done their spiel, ignoring the concern in their eyes, the hopeful tenor ringing in their voices—the encouragement. I wanted them to give up, just like I had. Because there was no point anymore. Not without him.

But Charlie forced me out of bed one morning, waiting until after I'd shot up so I was in no state to fight her. She dragged me to the bathroom and into an awaiting bath, the water hot and deep, sudsy with bubbles. I let her wash my hair. Neither of us spoke, not once the entire time. Even afterwards—first when she was doing my make-up, then later when she straightened my long, dark curls with her hot iron—we did so in silence. I sat willingly enough under her capable hands. I was too out of it, too numb to really pay much attention, too anaesthetized to care about what she was doing.

Until it was time to get dressed. Charlie pulled out an old familiar dress from the closet and laid it on the bed for me to wear. I stared at it a moment, lifting my weary eyes to her beautiful face, barely curious enough to ask.

"Where are we going Charlie?" My voice was dull, lifeless.

She answered softly. "To the funeral."

"The funeral?" I whispered.

"Yeah." She nodded. She tried to help me out of my housecoat so I could get changed, but I shook my head and pushed her weakly away.

"You want to do this on your own?" Charlie wondered.

I nodded. The drugs were waning; the thoughts were starting to emerge. I needed to shoot up again and I just wanted a moment alone, away from all the watchfulness, away from all the concern.

"Okay." Charlie gave me a squeeze and then left me to change, shutting the door on her way out. I sighed, lifting a hand to finger the soft black fabric of my graduation dress, the dress I had wore on one of the happiest days of my life. It was impossible not to remember my graduation then, impossible to fight the sudden memories that flooded my mind. They were bright—Technicolor, compared to all my dull, drear thoughts of late. I swallowed heavily, shut my eyes, and let them come.

I heard it first. The sound of Grey's rumbling motorcycle as it tore up the street. I remembered the surprise, and then the overwhelming joy I felt when I ripped open the front door and saw him there along the curb, straddling his bike, waiting for me. I saw him smirk, saw my own reflection in his shiny aviator glasses, saw my smile. I heard the sound of our distant laughter, coming from somewhere removed, somewhere far off. It felt so good to climb onto the seat behind him, the sun warm on my shoulders, my heart nearly bursting with happiness. How free and promising and full of possibility the world had seemed to me then ....

And then I was hunched over, reeling, gasping with the force of the pent-up sorrow breaking its way out of me. Grey. I missed him so much. I couldn't bear it without him; I couldn't live without him. It hurt. It hurt so badly.

Blindly I staggered my way over to the nightstand, seeking the refuge of the needle, the comfort of the heroin, the numbness of the drugs. They were the only thing that could make it all go away. The only answer to all my soundless pleading.

Within moments of the delicious steel piercing its way through my flesh, the memories had faded from my mind, the pain had receded, my breathing had calmed. I was back where I belonged, in a world without feeling, in a place of total indifference; of essential, embracing apathy. In a place where I didn't care, where I didn't have to pretend that I was okay. Because I wasn't. And I never would be again.

After a few moments, I put my dress on. Not a thought crossed my mind as I shrugged into the silky black gown and pulled it down around my body. Where before the dress had fit me perfectly, now it was loose and baggy, hanging unflatteringly upon my frail frame like a potato sack on a stick. I stared at myself in the mirror. Despite Charlie's beauty expertise my face was gaunt and tired looking. My eyes had lost their sparkle. I let them roam down—down my body—over the ribs protruding through my chest, along the long lean arms hanging from my sleeves, over the bony wrists and my long, skeletal hands.

I smirked mirthlessly at myself. I felt dead. I looked dead.

Why fight it?

Slowly I sunk back down onto the bed, traced a finger down the ragged bloody scabs that were slashed across my wrist … and realized that I wanted to die. There was nothing left for me here. Death would end it all; end all the pain, all the hopelessness. The thought actually gave me hope in a crazy, desperate sort of way. Knowing that I had an out, that I wouldn't be forced to suffer through this agony forever, it … relieved me. It almost made the day … bearable. I would go to the funeral. I would endure. And if it got too bad ….

I had a plan.

Before Charlie or any of my other guardians could see, I shoved everything I'd need—all my supplies, the balloon full of drugs, the needle, the spoon—roughly into my purse. I held it there on my lap a moment, and for just a brief second, I felt less helpless. I smiled a bit. This was something I could do, some way to take control again.

His funeral. Grey's funeral. I was so determined not to remember anything and so strung out that it mostly became a blur. A sickening blur interrupted by sudden moments of utter clarity. Like I wasn't permitted to just sit and observe the whole thing—like a cold, detached bystander—like I'd hoped. I was being forced to feel, to live through these horrible, devastating moments of lucidity before the blur would come again, would swallow me up and help protect me from the torment.

My parents were there. They hugged me the moment we pulled up at the church. I was ready to blame them, to call them out for their actions, to see if they were happy now that Grey was dead. But then they hugged me and I didn't know what to do. I let them wrap their arms around me, let myself feel their warmth, let myself hear how sorry they were, how much they professed to love me. My resolve crumbled. I let them lead us through the foyer and into a back room where we could hide until the service began.

The church reminded me of Marcy's wedding. Candles glowed softly and flowers were everywhere, but this time they weren't white. They were black. Black calla lilies on graceful green stems, placed artfully in cut glass vases. They were perfect. Grey would've loved them.

I whispered lowly in Charlie's ear. "… Who? Who did all this?" I wondered. Grey didn't have any family. I was his family. And I doubted that Tom and the band ….

"Your parents did it." She answered back. "They've done everything … they've been so great, Mackenzie. They paid for it all."

"What?" For a moment, I was shocked with disbelief. "But they hate Grey."

"No." Charlie shook her head. "They don't."

I bit my lip. Tears warmed my eyes. Marcy got a wedding, I got a funeral.

It was fitting, almost.

When the service finally started, Charlie gripped me tightly by the hand and helped me walk down the long aisle, past the countless pairs of sympathetic eyes to a pew at the front of the church. I was amazed by the amount of people present to honour Grey's memory, people I'd never seen before, people I'd never met. I should have expected it though. Grey had that affect on people—he touched them, he warmed his way into their hearts without them even knowing. He was popular, he was loved.

He was gone.

Alex, Zack, Tom, and the rest of the band filed into the pew beside us. We were considered Grey's family. The Minister started speaking, but I couldn't listen. I couldn't do anything but stare at the large, gleaming oak casket that dominated the stage of the church, holding the body of the man that I loved. He was in there, he was inside. I raised a shaky hand to my mouth in an attempt to quiet the sudden sob that burst through my lips. He was so near to me, but he was so far away, forever removed. A large picture sat next to the coffin upon an easel; Grey's happy, smiling face in life—his blue eyes shining, his smirk dimpling his stubbled cheek. I stared at his picture as the tears flooded my eyes, as they fell cascading down my cheeks. No amount of heroin could have prevented this hurt.

I felt it in the deepest pit of my soul, felt the terrible yearning for someone forever lost to me, the desperate longing for something I would never know again.

What I would give to have you hold my hand. What I would pay to feel your breath on my face. I love you Grey, I love you with all my heart.

Why did you have to die?

We drove out to the cemetery. I couldn't find my parents, but I just knew they were there. I could feel them there. And Riley. Somewhere, deep inside me, I knew Riley was there as well. He was keeping his distance, which I could understand. But he wouldn't have left me to do this alone. I suppose the thought should have comforted me. But at the moment, I was beyond comforting.

Before Grey's coffin was lowered into the ground, I set a rose upon the shining lid. I pressed my hand against the silky lacquered wood and held it there a moment—the tears pouring freely—and in that instant my mind was made up.

I couldn't do it. I couldn't do it without him. It was too hard. Even with the drugs, it was unbearable. There was no point living. Not without him.

I didn't say goodbye to Grey then. More like … see you soon.

I cried the hardest as we pulled away from the cemetery. It didn't feel right to just leave him there, alone. Wouldn't he get cold? What if he was afraid?

It was a long drive to my parents' house. They were hosting a luncheon, which touched me, deeply—but was something I wanted no part of. The house was packed, but I didn't want to socialize, I didn't want to accept condolences. I stole one of my father's super thick, heavy winter coats and escaped outside, leaning against the house and chain smoking. I could feel the nausea hitting, my stomach churning, the craving pulsing within me. This was the longest I'd gone without heroin in weeks. I knew I couldn't hold out much longer.

Nor did I want to. I was exhausted, weary, ready for everything to be over. I clutched my purse against my chest and threw my cigarette butt into the snow. Everything felt strangely clear—sharpened, almost—as I walked back into the house and hung my dad's coat back up in the closet. My steps had purpose for the first time in what felt like eternity. I'd been so lost for so long. It felt good to have direction again.

I slipped through the crowd of mourners in their dark dresses and suits, up the stairs and into the bathroom. I set my supplies out on the counter, slowly and methodically. I wouldn't allow myself to think of my family, my parents, my sister, Greg—the sixty-year-old man stuck in the twenty-something body—my friends. I wouldn't let myself picture Charlie or Alex or Zack, or Toby and Ben. Or Riley. I refused to think of Riley. They'd all just have to understand. It was way too hard.

It was kind of poetic, in a way, going out the same way Grey had. At least it would be peaceful. And quick. I put as much heroin on the spoon as it would hold, diluting it just enough to make it liquid. The mix was dark—darker than normal—much, much stronger than normal. I heated it all, sucking up the lethal combination until the syringe was nearly full.

I kept Grey's face before my eyes. My hand shook as I gripped the needle. I didn't want to lose courage, not now, not when I was so close. *I'm coming, Grey.* I promised. *Soon, we'll be together forever. Nothing will keep us apart.*

A smile bent my lips as I pressed the needle against my skin. It was like I could already feel the sweet relief of death, like I could taste its promise. The needle slid in easily, found my vein effortlessly, sucked my blood fluidly up into the chamber. I sat down on the toilet seat, ready; gripping the needle, shutting my eyes in sweet anticipation.

I love you Grey ....

I pressed the plunger down, slowly, prolonging the moment. I smiled as the drugs took hold of my system. And then they just kept coming, rushing through my blood stream, taking my breath away with the sheer force of them—my heart pounding harder and harder as they slammed through my swollen veins. Taking over me. Surrounding me. Drowning me. I didn't fight them; I let them have their way, giving up, giving in to the sweet surrender of blackness that loomed on the very edge of my being.

I fell over, slowly—it seemed to take forever. Everything was in slow motion. *Was this how it felt, Grey?* I wondered. *Did you feel this way when you died?*

I fell, slumped over between the toilet and the wall, and knew no more.

CHAPTER 61

There was a banging noise. Like a fist on a door. Muffled voices were coming from somewhere far, far away. I was removed from the noises; apart from the chaos unfolding. It was peaceful where I was. Tranquil. Heavenly.

"How long has she been in there?" Riley's voice, frantic with worry.

"I don't know. I didn't even see her come up here!" Charlie wailed.

Ah. I understood what was happening now. They were outside the bathroom door, trying to get in. They were about to find my body, cold and dead on the floor. It's too late, I wanted to tell them. You're too late. I'm dead.

"Mackenzie! Answer me!" Riley tried the knob again. "Please?"

I can't. I'm dead.

"Get out of the way, Charlie. Move!"

"What are you—?"

Bang! The noise jerked me in surprise. *Bang!* It sounded like Riley was hurtling himself at the door, throwing his weight against it, kicking it with as much strength as he could muster.

There was a sudden splintering sound, like breaking wood and wrecking metal. I listened faintly, curious as they burst through the broken door. What were they going to do now? What were they going to do when they discovered they were too late?

"Mackenzie!" Charlie screamed in horror. The shrillness startled me. Warm, strong hands were suddenly on my arms, on my shoulders, turning me over, propping me up ....

You're too late ....

"Mackenzie." Riley's voice was close now, in my ears, gasping, pleading with me. "Please. Open your eyes. Please be okay." He shook me; he slapped me, lightly. "Mackenzie!"

I turned my face from the sting of his slap. It was more annoying than anything.

"Is she okay? Is she breathing?"

"Yeah, she's breathing." Riley's voice oozed relief. "She just needs to wake up."

His touch was lighter now.

"Mackenzie, Mackenzie, can you hear me?"

No … oh, wait. Yes, I can hear you. Why can I hear you?

I frowned. No, this wasn't right. Something had gone wrong. Why could I hear him? Why could I feel him? Slowly, I tried to open my eyes.

"Is she waking up?"

"I think so. Mackenzie?" Riley's face was close, so close to mine. I blinked up at him, confused by the warm, chocolate eyes that gazed down at me. They were filled with tears, with agony. Why could I see him? And why the hell was *he* crying? I was the one who was supposed to be dead.

He picked me up in his arms, gingerly; as if I were fragile, easily breakable. I let him; I had no energy to fight him at all. It was warmer in his arms than it had been on the floor. We left the bathroom and started down the hall, rushing, Charlie close behind us.

I tried to pay attention to the chaos that ensued once we reached the main floor and my parents learned about my state—the frantic, dramatic worry of their voices mingling together, a cacophony of concern surrounding me. But I was still too overcome by the sweet waves of bliss to care, too out of it to really hear them. The heroin that burned through my swollen veins was intense, it was good—I hadn't been that high in ages. Warm and comfortable and safe in Riley's arms, I gave into the numbing heat, nodding in drowsy pleasure. I shut my eyes and leaned against his hard chest and succumbed, more content, more peaceful than I had been for days.

Wearily, I opened my eyes. Just a bit at first, and I didn't understand a thing. Stupidly I blinked into the dark, trying to place myself, trying to remember. The last thing I could really recall were Riley's dark brown eyes hovering over me, filled with tears. I turned my head, relived to see he was still with me—his face a dim silhouette against the dashboard lights, his eyebrows furrowed as he focused on the road before him. We were in a car. My car, I realized. I sat up a bit, my neck aching in protest from the odd position I'd been resting in. It made me groan.

Riley looked over at me sharply. I glanced back at him, achy and uncomfortable.

"You're awake." He observed.

"So it would seem." I admitted reluctantly.

"How are you feeling?"

"Terrible."

"You had me worried there for a minute."

I shrugged. I didn't want to be awake; I didn't want to be aware. I leaned back against the seat, staring out the window at the dark beyond while Riley navigated us over the icy roads. It was quiet, and warm. I'd always liked driving at night; it had always been so calm, so peaceful. Lulling. But now, it was too quiet. The precious drugs were leaving me. Even now I could feel them slipping away, could feel the warmth evaporate, the peace fading. I sat up and switched on the radio, eager for some background noise, for something else to focus on besides the utter gloom and depression of the thoughts now penetrating my flimsy veil of protection.

The DJ from the local station was prattling on in his low, monotonous tenor. I crossed my arms and leaned back against the seat, listening. Riley stared at the road ahead; he didn't seem to know what else to say, but I wasn't really up for talking at the moment anyway. I shut my eyes and hoped for sleep.

"And this one goes out to all those Serpentine fans grieving the loss of lead singer Grey Lewis, who passed away New Years Day." The DJ was saying. "Funeral services were held today for the guitar wielding local hero, and their debut CD, Seize the Day, has been selling out of stores ever since the late singers tragic death. Here's the latest single from the album. Enjoy. This one's for you, Grey."

I stared straight ahead, shocked. Every muscle in my body tensed as the all too familiar intro began—the beautiful streaming guitar and the melodic piano blending together into the world's most perfect song. Tears warmed my eyes. I realized that I was holding my breath, waiting in agonizing anticipation for the bittersweet moment when I would hear his voice again, when it would come to me from beyond the grave.

I shut my eyes, like a masochist, and focused on nothing but his raspy, velvet sound. A sound I loved with all my heart. A sound I lived to hear.

"Sitting here in the dark, Mackenzie's next to me.
She's lying in the moonlight, shining silver in the sheets.
And though it pains me so, I know I have to go.
I have to leave Mackenzie lying all alone.

Mackenzie, I hope you miss me
When I'm gone, when I'm gone.
I gotta go now, but you need to know how
Much you're loved, how much you're loved ....

Mackenzie ...."

His voice—Grey's beautiful, unmistakable voice—ripped through my mind and tore through my soul, leaving a wake of burning fire smouldering in my wounds. The pain was all the more potent for the meaning behind his words, words I couldn't fathom. Grey loved me. I was precious to him; the song was about me. He loved me. So why did he leave me? Why? The sound of his voice was the only thing in the entire world that I wished to hear. But I wanted it from him. I wanted his lips to move, I wanted his mouth to speak. And he never would again.

"Stop the car, Riley." I ordered. My breath was coming in gasps.

"What?"

"Stop the car!" I shouted. *"Stop the fucking car!"*

The brakes locked, the wheels skidded across the icy highway. By the time we slowed to a stop, I was already out of the car.

Damn, it was freezing. The icy wind whipped around my legs, my hair, taking my breath away. Traffic whizzed by. I ran to the side of the road. I didn't know what I was doing, I just knew I had to get out of there. I couldn't handle it. I couldn't bear it. It was too much to take. I ran frenzied hands up into my hair, trying to yank it out by the roots, trying to distract myself from the uncontrollable pain tearing my heart in two. *It wasn't fair! It wasn't fair! How could you, Grey! How could you leave me? Why?*

I was so mad. I was so furious. I screamed into the wind—shrill, crazy. I took off my shoes and threw them as far as I could, oblivious to the crusty frozen snow stabbing into my bare feet.

"No! I won't miss you!" I shouted. *"I won't! I hate you! I hate you!"* Liar. Liar. You love him.

I sunk to my knees, defeated, sobbing as the pain gripped my heart, its clutch as icy as the freezing wind. "I love you, Grey. I love you so much. Why did you leave me?"

"Mackenzie," Riley grasped me by the elbow. I hadn't even noticed him approaching. "Come on. Let's get back in the car."

I tried to shrug him off. "Just leave me here, Riley." I sobbed. Just leave me here to die. Please.

"Come on." He pulled me up, out of the snow. "It's freezing."

"I don't care."

He sighed a moment and then, like I was two, bent and scooped me out of the snow. With his warm arms around me, I cried against his shoulder, and he carried me back to the car.

How could anybody live through such agony? How could I be expected to go on, to lead a normal, happy life? I would never recover from this, there was no way—the pain was too great. Too constant. There was only one way for me to escape, one way for me to forget everything. I needed a hit. I needed one soon. I needed one badly.

"Riley." I sniffled as he buckled me into the seat. It hadn't occurred to me to ask before; I hadn't really cared. But now I needed to know how much time stood between me and my next hit. "Where are we going?"

"Are your feet okay?" He ignored my question, bending to inspect my toes.

"Fuck my feet, Riley." I snapped. "Where are we going?"

He smiled at me. "Watch your hand." He ordered, slamming my door shut. I wiped furiously at the tears on my cheeks as he walked around the car and got into the driver's seat. It was freezing out, and he took a minute to warm his hands before the vents. I glared at him.

"Riley, answer me. Where are we going?" I demanded.

He ignored me again. He didn't even look at me, slowly pulling back onto the road and accelerating over the icy pavement. He waited until we reached highway speed, until we were going too fast for me to jump out of the moving car. Then, Riley turned to me.

"I'm taking you to rehab."

"You're … what?" I glared at him incredulously.

"You need help, Mac. I'm going to get you help."

"But I …." I froze with horror, realizing fully what he meant. I couldn't go to rehab. Not without Grey. I needed heroin, now more than ever. I wouldn't survive without it. What would I do when the pain got too bad? The very thought made my blood run cold with fear.

"I can't go to rehab." I shook my head resolutely. "Riley, I can't."

"Yes, you can Mackenzie. You have to."

"No, I don't. I'll … I'll do it on my own, Riley. I'll cut back; I'll get clean on my own …."

"No."

"You could help me, Ry, we can go somewhere, we can be alone and you can help me and I'll quit, I really will …."

"No."

"Please? Please Riley, I need a hit, you don't know what it's like." Desperate, my eyes filled with tears again. I looked over at him, pleading. "Please, Ry. Please? It hurts so badly, I can't go through it. Not alone, not now. It's too soon. Please?"

"No, Mackenzie." His jaw clenched, but he was resolved. "No."

"You can't make me go!" Panicked, I screamed at him. My craving flared within me. I needed heroin. I needed more, now. "You can't force me!"

"You're right. I can't force you."

I sighed with relief. "Good. Take me home."

"But I don't think you're going to like the other option."

"What other option?"

He avoided my scorching gaze. "Jail."

"Jail." I scoffed angrily. "Yeah, right."

"Seriously, Mackenzie. It won't be that hard. The Constable wanted to bring you in already. Your parents had to use every personal favour they had just to keep them from searching your house. And what would they have found there, Mac? Enough to keep you in jail for a long, long time, I'll bet. You and all your friends."

I was speechless, dumfounded. I opened my mouth to argue, but no words came.

"You think that cops in a town as small as ours will just allow heroin to go unnoticed? We have your stash Mac, all your stuff, it was in the bathroom. We just have to show them."

I blinked back tears—angry, frustrated tears—because I knew that Riley was right. "You would send me to jail?" I whispered. "You would do that to me?"

"Yes, I would. If I knew that it would help you."

I shook my head, dropping it into my hands and sobbing with defeat. This wasn't fair. None of it was fair. Why was this happening to me? I didn't want to go to rehab. I didn't want to get clean, not without Grey. I didn't want Grey to be dead.

"Why are you doing this to me?" I cried.

Riley turned his tortured gaze to me before looking back at the road. "Because, Mac. Look at you. I'm not just going to sit here and let you die. You are too important to me. I'm going to do what's best for you, even if you don't like it."

"You care about me." I scoffed disdainfully.

"You know that I do."

I shook my head and wailed into my hands, curling up into a ball on the seat. If he cared about me at all, he'd understand why I couldn't go to rehab. Only vaguely did I remember the last time I tried to get clean and the racking pain from the withdrawal. Just the memory of the sickness was enough to make me shudder. I had no motivation to stop using, not now. I wanted to die. Why wouldn't he just let me die?

The car slowed and Riley turned into a brightly lit parking lot. I hadn't realized we'd made it to the city; I'd been too upset about the thought of rehab to pay any attention. I looked around wildly now, taking in my surroundings—my suitcase sitting in the backseat, the intimidating brick building we were pulling up to. A large, scripted sign hung over the front door, "Second Chances," it was called. Riley stopped the car before the entrance and put it in park.

"Please, Riley." I tried again, furtively pleading. I grasped his arm and forced him to look at me. "Please, don't do this to me."

"It's rehab or jail, Mackenzie. You choose."

Upon noticing our arrival, a man and a lady dressed heavily in winter coats came out the front door and strode up towards the car. I thought about running, about making a break for it. My hand grasped the door handle.

"You can't run, Mackenzie." Riley grabbed my arm. "You've been running for too long. You have to face it."

I sobbed in defeat, sinking back against the seat. He put an arm around me and tried to hug me, but I pushed him off with a sudden burst of rage. I'd never been so angry in my whole entire life. He knew I hated things being pushed on me; he knew I hated being told what to do. And now I had no choice. I had to go to rehab.

"I hate you Riley. I hate you!" I spat through my tears. "How could you do this to me? How? I hate you! I never want to see you again!" I shouted. I pushed his hand away again and then burst out of the car, taking the man and the lady by surprise in their approach. The lady put an arm around me and started pulling me inside, out of the cold. I had to go with her, but first I turned to yell one last disparaging remark at my old, former friend.

The words never made it past my lips. Upon turning around, I saw Riley crumple in his seat, saw him bury his head in his hands, saw his shoulders silently shaking.

Wordlessly, I turned my back on him, no choice left but the one before me.

CHAPTER 62

Detox. Hell. They were synonymous.

I've never felt so sick in all my life. So wretched. So desperate for death. Like I was being punished for every moment of happiness the drugs had ever given me, they left my system with five times as much agony. I shook and vomited and convulsed and sweat. I cried and cried, sobbing for relief, for help, but no one answered. No one came. I was trapped, all alone in a tiny little room with a single cot bed. I was crazy, delirious, overcome. I was too sick to think straight. Fervently I wished for Grey. I wished we were doing this together, that he'd be there with me at the end and all of this would just seem like some terrible nightmare. At times I swore he was holding my hand. At times I swore I could hear him humming the tune to my song. It was loud in my ears. But when I opened my eyes, no one was there.

I wanted to scream, but it wouldn't do any good. No one would come. Doctors and nurses would check up on me from time to time, but they offered no solace, no comfort. They'd check my vitals and then, apparently satisfied, they'd leave me alone again. They gave me no drugs, nothing at all to numb the pain. I had no choice but to endure it; to live through the burning, ripping hurt and gut wrenching, freezing sickness that strained every muscle in my body until I was weak and sore from the effort. There seemed to be no end in sight, no end to the vile torture. I grit my teeth and bit my lip until it bled, but still the sickness ravaged on. I couldn't sleep. I couldn't eat. I couldn't do anything but be sick. Disgustingly ill. I couldn't do anything but moan for death. And itch. I don't know how else to describe it, but my very blood felt itchy. I scratched and scratched until my skin broke. I lived breath by torturous breath.

"Don't focus on how lousy you feel. Focus on how much closer you are to getting healthy …." They had said before locking me up. That sentence ran over and over again in my mind. "Don't focus on how lousy you feel …."

And then, there came a morning when I awoke without sweat. Without nausea. I found I could swallow again, that I was warm again. My body still ached like I had run a marathon; my muscles were stiff and sore. But I knew the worst was over. And I was glad. I was so relieved, at first.

But it didn't take long before I realized I was actually sober. Like, stone cold sober. Without the sickness to focus on, I was now capable of coherent thought. Competent. I hadn't been that way in ages.

And then the real pain crashed around me, like cymbals during a crescendo.

It actually took my breath away. There was nothing I could do, nowhere I could hide, no escape from the mind-ravaging hurt and sorrow. At that moment, I would've chosen withdrawal over this. Anything but this. I clutched my arms around my stomach and gasped, my fingers running through my limp hair as I sobbed into my empty hands.

Grey was gone. Grey was gone and I was all alone.

"Please, Grey. Please don't be dead …." I pleaded with the quiet. I shut my eyes and pictured him, hanging on the memory. I imagined him—his gorgeous, handsome face coming through the door into my room, smirking with his cocky grin and shaking his head at me, his blue eyes shining.

"You did it, Mackenzie." He'd say, his voice velvet in my ears. "I'm so proud of you. You did it, you're clean …."

I opened my eyes, but there was no one there but me. There was nothing in the bare, sterile little room but me and my sweaty cot bed.

Then the door opened. I sat up abruptly, daring to hope, my heart pounding a mile-a-minute with delusional optimism. But it was just the nurse. Giselle was her name, and she was looking at her clipboard as she came in to check on me. She was a bigger lady, with beautiful chocolate skin and big, pretty warm eyes. Her hair was back in a simple ponytail and she wore the traditional pastel patterned nurse's garb.

"Well, you're looking better." She observed. My breath hitched in my throat, I could feel how red and swollen my eyes must be. My hospital gown was wrinkled and plastered to my dewy skin. I couldn't even imagine how I smelt. And this was better?

"How are you feeling?" Giselle asked me.

I shrugged, sniffing. "Better, I guess."

"I'd say you're over the worst, anyway." She slapped her clipboard shut.

I scoffed and wiped the tears from my eyes. Doubtful. Really doubtful.

"Don't cry, honey." She patted my arm. "I know it was hard, but you did it. All by yourself. Doesn't that make you proud?"

I shook my head. "Giselle?"

"Yes, sugar?"

I flinched. Sugar. Grey had called me sugar. Fresh tears started, filling my eyes until everything around me was a blur. I tried to blink them away.

"Can I have a cigarette?" I cried.

"Sure thing, hon." She pulled a pack from her pocket and gave me one. "You've got your whole life ahead of you now. Don't worry. You'll feel even better after a nice hot shower." She gave me a pleasant smile. I tried to smile in return, but I couldn't. Her brave words of encouragement did nothing to ease the ache in my heart.

I took a deep drag of my cigarette, letting the sweet smoke burn down my throat and into my lungs. The moment Giselle was out of the room, the heavy weight of gloom pressed down upon me again. I hugged my knees to my chest and tried not to think about Grey. Even still, I couldn't help shedding a few tears. It just felt so empty without him.

I was moved from the detox center into the rehabilitation wing that day, into what was going to be my room for the next three long months. I had to share it with another girl, some stranger I had never met. I trudged along after the orderlies because I had to. I felt no excitement, no enthusiasm about the move. No part of me wanted to be there, even with the hard part over.

I sighed as I stepped into the space. It was a cross between a hotel and a hospital room. Plain, beige, mass-quantity type furnishings adorned the space with no personality at all. There were two twin beds, two dressers, two nightstands. A little bathroom adjoined it. The one solitary window on the boringly painted, beige brick wall faced the courtyard; giving me a dismal view of the grey, frozen wasteland beyond, crusted in ice.

The orderly set my suitcase on the bed closest to me, gave me a polite smile, and then left me all alone.

I sank down on the bed and shut my eyes. So this was sober living. So far, it sucked.

Since there was nothing else to do, I opened up my suitcase and started unpacking my things. Two packs of cigarettes sat on the top—a gift from Charlie, no doubt. I couldn't help but feel grateful as I tore into them. I missed her. I missed everybody.

I missed Grey.

With a shaky sigh, I moved on to the rest of my belongings. The familiarity of them brought me some comfort, but brought me sadness as well. Every one of my possessions had a memory attached to them. I picked up my favourite jeans first; they were old and threadbare and comfortable. Grey had doodled on them with a ballpoint pen one day when we were laying in bed and he was working on his lyrics.

That was hard to see. I stroked my finger over the ink preciously, biting my lip as the all too familiar tears flooded my eyes. I pressed my face against the denim and cried for a little while, but the tears gave me no relief. There was nothing that would fill the emptiness inside me. I was being forced to quit the one thing that could.

Quickly I unpacked the rest of my stuff, shoving my clothes roughly into drawers, looking at them as little as possible. My diary—the one Marcy had given me for Christmas—was in the bag as well. I tossed it into the nightstand, threw my suitcase beneath the bed, grabbed my bag of toiletries, and headed into the bathroom for a long, hot shower.

It felt better to be clean. The pressure wasn't much, but the water was hot, and I stayed beneath it for as long as I could. The whole time I thought about heroin. There may not have been any left in my system, but that didn't stop me from craving it. I remembered the feeling, the rush of euphoria it gave me—the numbness, the apathy, the delicious … nothingness. I shut my eyes and pictured myself mixing a batch, sucking it into the needle, feeling the sharp sting as I injected it into my body ….

I could leave. I could leave here; I could run out the front doors and catch a cab. Did I have any money? There had to be some around. I could hitchhike home, or just somewhere, anywhere in the city. Some dark back alley. There was sure to be heroin there. In less than an hour, I could get my fix. Riley wouldn't have to know, he'd never find me again; I'd never have to go to jail. Everything would be good again ….

The water ran cold, freezing. I shook my head and shut it off, almost breathless with excitement. Quickly I towelled off and got dressed in some old clothes that were too big for me, then ran a brush through my tangled, messy, wet hair. I didn't want to be here. I didn't want to be clean. Nothing mattered to me now, nothing but the heroin.

I rushed quickly out of the bathroom, my cheeks flushed nervously. It shouldn't be too hard to run away. I'd throw on a few sweaters; go for a causal walk down the hallway. I'd sprint out the front doors before anyone even noticed. I hadn't seen a huge amount of security; it'd probably be hours before anyone even realized I was missing. And by that time, I'd already have a needle in my vein ….

"You're thinking of running, aren't you?"

I whipped around in surprise, slamming my drawer shut as I did so, my cheeks blushing guiltily.

"N-No." I lied.

The girl lying on the other bed in the room, the one near the window, scoffed at me. "Trust me; it's not going to happen."

"I wasn't going to run." Amazed and embarrassed by this stranger's perception, I sat down hard on my bed, the springs squeaking in protest. I grabbed my pack of smokes and lit one.

"You're Mackenzie, right?" She wondered.

I looked back at her and nodded. "Yeah."

"Allison."

"Nice to meet you." I blew my smoke out in a waft.

"Do you want to know why it wouldn't work? Running?"

"Whatever."

"Cameras." She pointed up at a corner of the room. "In the hallways too. And the front doors are locked from the inside."

"What is this, a mental institution?" I frowned. "Why the lock down?"

Allison shrugged. "It's like *Hotel California*. You can check out anytime you like, but you can never leave." She laughed.

I lay back on the bed, sighing heavily. "How many times did you try?"

"Twice."

"Stubborn."

"That's me." She grinned. Alison was pretty, in a hard kind of way, though kind of intimidating. She was the first person I'd ever met—besides Jack Turcotte—who actually looked like a heroin addict. Her short, pixie-cut blonde hair framed glittering blue eyes lined by thick, dark eyeliner—she kind of reminded me of that singer, Pink. Both her arms sported full sleeves of colourful tattoos. She grinned at me wickedly, and had I met her in different circumstances, I knew without a doubt that we would've had a ton of fun together. I wouldn't want to meet her in a dark alley or something though.

"I was going to run." I admitted.

"I know. You had that look about you."

"I still might try it."

"I wouldn't. Seriously. Unless you want to endure a few hours of bullshit lectures, you know, living your life in the now and all that crap."

I stared up at the ceiling, chuckling mirthlessly. "No thanks."

"I know. I can barely stand it. Therapy every day …,"she sighed, rolling her eyes. "Please. I have an addiction, right? Like, tell me something I don't know."

"We have to do therapy every day?"

"Yeah, like, group therapy. Ooh, and then once a week, you get a real treat, one-on-one therapy. Ugh, it's such a bore."

"Great. Wow, this place couldn't get any better." I shook my head.

"So, this wasn't a voluntary check in, I presume."

"Uh, no. This was a rehab or jail check in." I looked up at her. "You?"

"Yeah, about the same. You know, rehab or no place to live, no money, no car, no friends. I chose rehab, but only barely."

"How long have you been here?"

"Three weeks, two days and six … no, seventeen hours. Not that I'm counting." She sat up on the bed and stretched her arms, revealing the light blue, dead-happy-face Nirvana t-shirt she was wearing. "But the moment I get out of here, I'm getting high. That's the only thing that keeps me from totally freaking out, knowing that. I hear that it's better too, after going without for so long. Rinse cycle."

"Oh yeah?"

"Yeah." She stood up then and smiled at me. "Come on, let's go eat."

"Eat?" I frowned and looked up at the clock. "What time is it?"

"It's five. Come on, I don't want to be late. This is the best part of my day."

"The food's that good here?" I wondered, raising an eyebrow.

"No, it's not." She laughed again. "That's how shitty the rest of the day is."

"Oh." Reluctantly, I got up off the bed to follow her.

"And Mackenzie?" Allison stopped at the doorway, eyeing me knowingly.

"Yeah?"

"I'd just eat if I were you. I've never actually seen them do it, but I've heard them threaten the tube on the other girls. It doesn't sound pleasant."

I stared at her a moment, blinking in confusion.

"Well … I mean … you're anorexic, right?"

"What? No."

"You're not? Come on, you must weigh, like, eighty pounds."

"I'm not anorexic." I declared defensively. "I just … I don't really eat."

"No offence, but isn't that, like, exactly what anorexics do? Or don't do, I guess."

"I don't know. I'm not purposely starving myself, it just …." I shrugged. "It never occurs to me, you know, I'm just not … hungry."

"Well, you will be here. Trust me." She smiled again, opened up our door and led me down the hallway. It wasn't very busy; there were a few people here and there, coming and going. It was an odd atmosphere. Sort of like summer camp gone horribly, horribly awry. Most of the time, when this many different people were together, it was for some kind of fun. But here the air seemed gloomy, thick with struggle, almost. Everyone I saw was fighting some kind of battle with addiction; they all had their own story, their own set of circumstances. Fleetingly I wondered how many of them would actually conquer the monkey on their back. And if I would, as well, by the end.

Not that I wanted to.

Allison led me into the cafeteria-style dining room. Plastic tables, plastic chairs, plastic trays, buffet line. I raised my eyebrows at her as she handed me a tray.

"Man, if this is the highlight, your day must be really shitty." I quipped.

"You have no idea." She laughed.

After supper, Allison took me on a short tour of the facility. I liked her, almost immediately. She was a wonderful distraction from the constant burning pain in the pit of my soul, and I welcomed her mindless chatter and her quirky, jaded energy. She showed me to the therapy rooms and the TV/games room. There was ping-pong and pool and shuffleboard and a huge flat screen TV surrounded by faded old couches. It wasn't bad, actually. After that she took me to a huge old gym at the back of the building, for playing volleyball and basketball and all the other sports I'd effectively avoided for the duration of my high school career.

I let her do most of the talking. Slowly we made our way back to our room, and as we walked Allison told me how she found herself on the dark road to addiction.

"We were at some party, you know, the usual. But there was this guy there, and he had these pills, Oxy's or something. Of course we tried some. I was only fifteen, and when you're fifteen, shit can't touch you. I did one, and it was so good. So relaxing, so … ugh, I can't even tell you how much I loved that first one. So me and my friend, we start doing them, first just on the weekend, then maybe like, once during the week, you know … the whole, downward spiral thing." She lifted an eyebrow at me. "It wasn't long before we were doing them every day. But these pills, they cost like eighty-dollars each. We were stealing car stereos, like, anything we could get our hands on just to afford them, but it was getting really hard. It was only a matter of time before we got busted. And that's when we heard about heroin."

I nodded for her to continue.

"Heroin, the poor man's Oxy. It does pretty much the same thing, right, but for like, fifteen-dollars. We started sniffing it, and it was good. Really, damn good. Then we started injecting." Allison sighed fondly. "And never looked back."

"How old are you?" I wondered. I was desperate for her to keep talking. We made it back to our room and she sprawled out on her bed, cuddling the pillow. I sat on my saggy old mattress, my back against the wall, and looked at her expectantly.

"Nineteen."

"You're only a year older than I am."

"Yeah?" She looked at me a moment, her blue eyes narrowing. "What's the deal with you, Mackenzie? When I first saw you, I was like, no, they've got the wrong girl. I'd never place you for a heroin addict, not in a million years. You're too … pure looking."

Ah … that hurt. Grey had said that about me once … it seemed like ages ago. I pressed a hand against the sudden stab of hurt in my chest, hugging myself around the burning wound, blinking back tears. I turned my face to the wall so Allison wouldn't notice.

"So what's your story?" She asked.

"It's not very interesting." I lit a cigarette, taking a deep drag of delicious smoke, letting it relax me. "I just liked to party. I really liked to party."

"Go on." Her blue eyes sparked with interest.

"It started out harmless enough. Weed, ecstasy, whatever anyone had that weekend. Mushrooms. I did Quaaludes once too. Booze, you know. Typical teenager." I shrugged. "When I tried cocaine, I thought I'd found the answer. But then heroin came along. And it was … it was like … what I'd been searching for. " I shut my eyes and remembered that first time. Sitting with Grey in the hotel bed, waiting for the waves to crash over us. I remembered holding his hand, resting my head on his chest, being with him.

I shook my head. This was a one-way ticket to a meltdown, one I wasn't eager for Allison to witness.

"It was so good. At first we tried to be … responsible with it, I guess. But I loved it too much. As soon as I did it, I thought about the next time. If we ran out, I obsessed with getting more. As soon as I had more, I wouldn't rest until I'd done it." I looked down at myself. "It was perfect. I'd do heroin when I wanted to relax, cocaine when I wanted some energy. I didn't realize things were getting so out of control."

"Yeah. You always feel like you're on top of it all, don't you? Like, it's no big deal, you're just having fun, you can quit when you want." Allison sighed heavily and stared up at the ceiling. "Right now, I'd give anything for some tar."

"Yeah." I lit another smoke, but it didn't help to quench the craving inside of me, coming from somewhere in the very pit of my stomach, demanding to be fed. I bit my lip and tried to ignore it.

"Well." Allison yawned. "Looks like story time is over." She pointed to the clock. "Lights out at ten o'clock."

"Lights out?" I grinned wryly. "Are you serious?"

"Unfortunately." She rolled her eyes. "*Hotel California*."

I grimaced as Allison got up and started getting ready for bed. For some reason the thought of bedtime made me anxious. It felt like summer camp all over again. I was one of those children who'd suffered from near crippling homesickness, but my parents still insisted I spend at least two weeks of the year at this camp a few hours away from home. I think they did it so they wouldn't have to feel guilty about leaving us all alone for the entire summer, even after every year when I begged and pleaded not to be sent back. I'd always be fine during the day, when crafts and canoe rides would distract me … but at night, in the dark, with the quiet pressing in, I'd always been plagued with the heaviest kind of loneliness.

I felt that way again. I went through the motions normally enough, putting on my pyjamas, brushing my teeth. I crawled under the unfamiliar covers, tried to get comfortable on the old, lumpy mattress. Allison got into her bed and then reached over to flick the lamp off.

"Goodnight Mackenzie."

There was a sudden lump in my throat as the room was blanketed in darkness.

"Goodnight." I managed.

"Hey, can I tell you something?"

"Sure."

"I'm glad you're my roommate. I thought maybe I'd get stuck with some … I don't know, some lame-o that just wanted to read books all day or something."

"Are there many book-worm heroin addicts here?"

"No." Allison laughed. "I guess not."

I managed a slight smile into the darkness. Allison rolled over.

"Goodnight."

"Goodnight." And then it was quiet.

I tried to talk myself out of it. I was tired. I could've slept. But the moment there was nothing else to distract me, my mind started racing, like it needed to go over everything I'd been avoiding all day, to make sure I didn't miss what it was trying to communicate. As soon as I shut my eyes, I saw his face. Grey's gorgeous, handsome face, dark and tan; his stubbled cheeks; his perfect lips curved into the constant smirk. His blue eyes shining happily at me; his messy, dark hair. I bit my lip to stifle a sob. *Grey, Grey, Grey …. I wish you were here with me. I wish we were together.*

I wouldn't feel lonely if he were here, holding me in his warm, strong arms. I'd never be sad again. I would hold his face in my hands, and tell him in a hundred different ways just how much I loved him. How I needed him, how I couldn't be without him.

He'd smirk and he'd kiss me, and then maybe, he'd sing me to sleep. His voice a raspy whisper, low and melodic, breathy in my ear. I'd hold onto every note like a precious gift from heaven, every fan of his breath against my cheek like the rarest treasure on earth.

It's hard to stay completely quiet when crying, but somehow I managed it. I didn't make one noise as the tears streamed from my eyes—my swollen, broken heart pouring out all the overflowing anguish, all the aching hurt, all the injustice. The utter loneliness pulsed through me with every beat. The dark pressed in—the quiet, the strange noises in the unfamiliar blackness, the groaning of the old pipes, Allison stirring quietly in her slumber. Please, let me go to sleep, I beseeched my tortured mind. Let this all be some terrible nightmare. Let me wake up, safe in Grey's arms. Please.

The night dragged on.

Finally, the first rays of gloomy dawn began to lighten the weary bedroom. It was a relief to me—the light—and my mind rested enough to allow me a few hours of fitful, restless sleep. But I found when I awoke—staring up at the strange ceiling with swollen, puffy eyes—that this was real. It wasn't just some nightmare. This was my life now. Grey was gone. He was never coming back. My life was empty, meaningless, hollow.

And for the third time in only a matter of days, I wished for death.

I fell quickly into a drear, monotonous pattern over the next little while. I had no enthusiasm for anything; I just went with the flow, not talking much, not contributing. Just existing. In the morning we'd get up and go for breakfast. Shortly after that came group therapy. Allison was in my group, which I was grateful for. It was nice to have someone I knew there, even though most of the time I'd just stare off into space, not really paying attention. I'd give one-word answers if ever asked a question. It was frustrating, I could see the therapist trying to draw me out more and more every day, but stubbornly I refused to participate. I wasn't interested in getting better. I wasn't interested in anything but getting the hell out of there.

Next came lunch. Allison and I would always sit together; sometimes we were joined by other girls but I didn't bother to even learn their names. What was the point? In three months we'd all go our separate ways and I'd never hear from them again. I just sat silently and ate as much as I could so people would stop thinking I was anorexic.

After that we had some free time. There were usually scheduled group activities, like cards or games or something, which I went to but wouldn't get in on—just being there was enough to distract me. Once a week I had to suffer through an hour or two of one-on-one time with my therapist. This guy was like sixty years old, he reminded me of Greg. I was even more closed up with him than I was at group. Seriously though, how could a greybeard like him expect to relate to me? Back in his day, the hardest thing they had around the place was firewater. He was smug though—I could tell he kept trying to crack me, like I was a challenge to him or something.

After supper we'd usually go hang out in front of the big screen. I liked watching TV, it was mindless, a good distraction. But then, when the time started winding down, when people started leaving and it was time to go back to our rooms, the anxiety would start. I knew what awaited me in the dark reaches of the night—the longing, the sorrow. I dragged my feet the entire way back to our room, trying to prolong the inevitable.

But it caught up to me as it always did, and I spent nearly every night sleepless, sobbing silently into my pillow, hoping for an end. I knew I couldn't last like this. It was only a matter of time before I went really insane. My sleepless nights were beginning to affect me. If it were possible, I became even more zombie-like, walking around in a trance with heavy purple shadows beneath my eyes.

And always through it all, the craving for heroin nagged at me, like a beast—starving, demanding to be fed. Pictures would pop into my head, a syringe full of the dark promise of heroin, blood squirting into the needle. I'd shut my eyes and try to remember what it was like. What it felt like. I was counting down the days until my freedom, when I would leave this place and find a hit as soon as I could. I dreamed about it. It kept me going. Just seventy more days, I'd tell myself.

Seventy more days, and it'll be mine again.

CHAPTER 63

It was just another ordinary, painstakingly boring day in the hellhole otherwise known as sober living. I was curled up on my side on my bed, staring at nothing, and Allison was lying on her stomach writing in her journal. Journaling was something they recommended we do while we were here, to try and get our thoughts down on paper. I had my diary, but it was still in my nightstand, completely untouched. If I were to write anything down right now, it'd be three single letters. F.M.L. (Fuck my life.)

I brought my cigarette to my lips and took a slow, mindless drag.

There was a knock on our door. Allison looked up, but I didn't care enough to even turn my head.

"Mackenzie?" It was one of the administrators ... Janet I think her name was. I recognized her voice. She was a petite, friendly little woman.

"Yes." I answered without moving.

"You have a visitor."

"A visitor?" Allison frowned and looked at me suspiciously. "But we aren't allowed visitors."

Janet shrugged. "Apparently they've made an exception. Mackenzie?"

"Who is it?"

"I have no idea. I was just sent to give you the message. Come on, dear."

Rolling my eyes, I slumped wearily off the bed.

"See you later." I waved absently at Allison.

"Yeah. Later." She watched me go, her blue eyes confused.

Janet led the way down the hallway. She pulled me closer to her as we walked so we could talk more discreetly.

"Mackenzie," she looped her arm through mine, which was kind of funny because I was at least a half a foot taller than her. She patted my hand. "It's true; we don't usually allow visitors here. But we've been informed about your … situation. Your boyfriend died shortly before you were admitted, is that correct?"

I nodded.

"I'm sorry. But we've noticed that … that you're not … doing the best here. Treatment is pointless if you don't want to get better. We thought that maybe it'd be beneficial for you to have a friend, someone to talk to … since you don't seem to want to talk to our resident therapist." She gave me a knowing look, smiling wryly. "We're all on your side here, Mackenzie, remember that. We want you to get better. But *you* need to want to get better too. Okay?"

I shrugged. "Sure."

She took me down a long hallway with several doors on either side, stopping before the second one of the left. The door had a square window inset. Janet pushed me gently towards it.

"Go ahead. You've got an hour."

I nodded dumbly as she headed back down the hall, her heels clipping on the beige, industrial linoleum. I watched her go a moment. Then, I strode ahead and took a hesitant glance in the window.

It was Riley. Of course it was. I sighed and shook my head. He looked uncomfortable—nervous, even—sitting on the edge of his chair, fidgeting with something in his hands. He was dressed simply in blue jeans and a long sleeved blue shirt, but I was amazed again at just how much older he looked. Grown up, almost. His dark hair was growing out of his buzz cut; it was short and shaggy now. But he was Riley. My Riley. My old friend, my best friend.

I hesitated a moment outside the door, torn. Part of me—no, most of me—was still furious at him, at his betrayal. I was in here because of him. I was sober because of him. Against my will, he'd ripped me away from my only semblance of life. I still hadn't forgiven him for it. It felt like I'd never really be able to.

I pressed my hand to the glass window and shut my eyes. The other part of me was so … lost. So … flailing. So alone. The other part of me needed him, like I always had, like I always would. I was too weak to care about the anger. Too broken. My hand moved to the knob then, seemingly of its own volition, and slowly opened the door.

I don't know what Riley saw, but I could feel the strain of anguish written in my expression. He stared at me for a moment as I entered, and the smile that had started in greeting slowly fell from his face.

"Oh, Mackenzie." Was all he said.

And then I was in his arms. Safe, warm, comfortable arms. Weakly I hugged him back, burying my face into his shoulder, doing my absolute damndest to try and keep from crying. But he held me so tightly and with his old familiar voice he whispered, "its okay, its okay," in my ear, and before I knew it I was sobbing, the combination of utter exhaustion and total heartbreak pouring from me in noiseless, racking shudders. I was so tired. So sad. None of it was fair, and it was all happening to me.

Wordlessly, Riley took me over to one of the couches that dominated the little room, pulling me down onto his lap like I was a child, holding me and letting me cry on his shoulder. His hands stroked my hair so soothingly. I didn't let it last long, my breakdown, I hated being this way. I hated letting him see me this way. Somehow I managed to pull myself together, biting my lip in an effort to stop the tears, my breath hitching in my throat. When I was somewhat calm again, I pulled myself away from Riley's shoulder and looked up into his dark chocolate eyes.

"If only I'd known this was all it took for you to come back," I scoffed sarcastically, my voice wobbling, "I'd have gone to rehab sooner."

"Are you still mad at me for this? For the whole rehab thing?" He wondered, his expression hopeful, though I could see the sadness in his eyes.

"Yes." I sniffled. He nodded slowly.

"Well, I'm mad at you too."

I smiled dully. "Ha. What else is new?"

"I mean it. You're the one that did this to yourself. You're the one who needed rehab, I mean, how could you let it come to this? How could you let it get so bad?"

I just shook my head. I didn't know what to say to that.

Riley made a noise of frustration. "Are you even trying to get better?"

"No."

"Why? Why not?"

I looked away. He wasn't going to like the answer to this question.

"Mackenzie, please. Why won't you even try?"

"Because, Riley. I don't want to get better! I don't want to live!" I wailed.

Riley took my by surprise then. He grabbed me by the arms, fiercely, forcing me to look at him. His hands were like a vice. "Don't say that!" He demanded, giving me a shake, his face rigid with anger. "Don't ever say that! How could you?"

"I can't do this, Riley. It's too hard!"

"Bullshit." He spat. "It's not too hard. You're too selfish. There are people in your life who love you, Mac. What about Marcy, or your parents? Charlie and your other friends? What about me? Do you know what it would do to me if you died? Do you even care?"

I shook my head, dropping my face in my hands, my dark hair tumbling around me. "You don't know what it's like."

Riley sighed. His grip lightened, his hands loosening until they were warm again, comforting on my arms. He rubbed them soothingly a moment and when he spoke again, his voice was softer. "Talk to me then." He implored. "Tell me about it."

"It's …." I took a deep breath. "I just … I miss him, you know? So badly. It hurts … like, all the time, and it's not getting better. I miss us. I miss what we had."

Riley listened and nodded silently, but there was a sudden hardness in his face that I instantly recognized. Like my words had made him … angry, somehow. I frowned up at him, puzzled.

"What?"

"Nothing."

"What is it, Riley? Tell me."

He paused a moment, thoughtful. "I just … I guess I don't get how you could … miss … what you had." He confessed.

His statement brought me up short. "What?"

"Mackenzie, your entire relationship was based on partying. On drugs. It wasn't healthy at all … it got you into this situation. It turned you into a heroin addict. *He* turned you into a heroin addict." Riley shook his head at me. "How can you miss that?"

It took me a moment to realize what he was saying. I couldn't speak, I was so flustered, so offended by his careless words.

"… How could I miss that?" I managed finally, my voice riddled with disbelief. "How … could you? You have no idea what we had, what we shared. It was amazing. I mean, yes, maybe we did some drugs—and yes, maybe we liked to party, but we loved each other. We really loved each other." I glared fiercely, daring him to disagree. "You don't know anything about it."

Riley was undeterred, raising his eyebrows in doubt. "I know you wouldn't be in here if not for him." He stated bluntly.

"That's not true!"

"Really? Well, when I left town, you weren't anything like—"

"Yeah, exactly. When you left." I interrupted. "You left me Riley; you totally abandoned me. And Grey was there. He was there for me when you weren't. He … he … took care of me … he …." I shook my head, unable to continue.

He loved me.

My anger was rapidly dissolving, the all too familiar tears of heartache burning just below the surface … the sadness, the aching. I wrapped my arms around the fearsome blazing in my chest and swallowed heavily.

"You know what Riley?" I managed, trying to breathe through the surging pain. "I think you should leave now."

"Mac, come on—"

"No. I mean it. Please." I blinked back my tears, avoiding his gaze. "Just go."

"Why? You think you're the only one that's suffering? You think this isn't hard for me too?" Riley sat stubbornly. "To see you like this, to put you in here? Grey did this to you, Mackenzie, but still he can do no wrong. Don't you see it? Do you know how frustrating that is for me?"

I shook my head vehemently, my entire being rejecting his words, refusing to hear them. "Just go." I pleaded desperately. "Please. Just go."

Riley fell silent. The air was tense between us; I could feel his eyes on me but couldn't bring myself to meet his gaze. I didn't want to know it; I didn't want to see the concern there, the sincerity sure to be in his expression—the truth. I wiped the tears hastily from my eyes and stared down at the floor, wishing he would leave. After a long moment of my silent defiance, Riley sighed heavily and got up off the couch, rubbing his face with his hands in defeat. He grabbed his jacket from the chair and headed for the door. I listened, distraught, as it opened up behind me.

"Look … I'm sorry, Mackenzie. I really am. Just … forget what I said, okay? I'm an idiot." Riley admitted lowly. "I'm staying at my mom's, and I'm just a phone call away. If you want me to, I'll come back anytime you want, anytime you need to talk." He paused, as if waiting for a response, but I gave him nothing, not even a nod. Resigned, he spoke again, but now his voice was soft. Sad. "I know you're hurting … I know you're going through hell. But it doesn't have to be this way forever. You have so much to live for, Mac. But you have to stop feeling sorry for yourself first."

I let out a heavy breath. I didn't want to hear it, but somewhere deep inside me, I knew Riley was right. The reason I wasn't getting any better was because I didn't want to. Life sucked, but it was up to me to change that. If I could. If I wanted to.

The door shut quietly, and then Riley was gone.

That evening we headed back to our room after an uneventful night of TV watching. I'd spent almost the entire time since Riley's departure pensive with anger, with confusion, with sadness and denial—too distracted by the severity of his words to feign an interest in anything we'd been doing. Now, I flopped down on my bed and pulled my diary from the night table instead of getting ready for sleep like Allison was.

Riley wanted me to try, I was going to try. I was going to write down all my thoughts and all my feelings and all the different ways I knew he was wrong. How Grey and I had been good together, how what we had was special—right—something I would never, ever regret. How it had been real, how it had been true in every way.

I flipped quickly through the first few pages of my diary I had written on, my pathetic attempts at composing lyrics that Grey had encouraged me to do. But I could never write like he did. He was so brilliant, so gifted and talented. My thoughts were stunted, immature. His poetry was so deep, so meaningful ....

I flipped another page and found—to my surprise—Grey's messy scrawl. I frowned, and for a moment, tears stung my eyes as I looked down at his familiar writing. And then I was curious. As far as I knew, he had never written anything in my diary. But there, at the bottom of the page, were four lines of simple prose:

"If I have the strength to leave,
It'd be the greatest gift that I could give.
The greatest gift that I can give,
I want you to truly live."

And then, at the end, "I love you. Forgive me."

My frown deepened. Confused, I read and re-read his lines, my fingers passing delicately over his words. "If I have the strength to leave ... the greatest gift that I could give ... I want you to truly live ...." And then, abruptly, I understood.

The diary fell from my trembling fingers, and I looked up, seeing nothing, blankly staring. These words weren't just an idle poem or a song or a lyric. They were a message to me.

"If I have the strength to leave …."

It was a suicide note.

No, it couldn't be. But it was. The horrible truth crashed down on me, and for a moment I couldn't breathe. The fact that Grey had overdosed never really made sense to me, not when he was always so careful, so cautious about the amount we did, ever wary about the possibility of OD'ing.

I'd always wondered how he could've made such a fatal mistake. I knew the answer now. I shut my eyes, dropping my head into my hands, my throat aching with tears. Grey hadn't made a mistake. He had deliberately taken too big a dose, just as I had. Only unlike mine, his dose had been lethal. Grey had killed himself on purpose.

Why? Why?

My horrid, terrible musings were interrupted as Allison strolled out from the bathroom, drying her short blonde hair idly with a towel. Quickly I wiped at my eyes and tried to pull myself together before she could notice.

"Bathroom's all yours, if you want." She offered politely.

"Yeah … thanks …," I mumbled. Leaving my diary where it lay upside down in the mess of blankets, I stood up and got ready for bed, my motions automatic—wooden, like I was on autopilot again. Grey had killed himself, and my whole world was changed by this realization. It hadn't been an act of chance or fate or God. It had been a decision. Grey had chosen death. He had purposely taken himself away from this world. Away from everything. Away from me.

Grey, what have you done? Why? Why did you do it?

I got into my bed and instantly rolled over, facing the wall. Allison shut off the light, and even in the pitch black, my eyes stayed open wide—stunned, like a deer in the headlights. My heart was pounding fearfully hard in my chest. Grey had opted for death. Grey had killed himself. Why? I ran over and over the words of his slight poem. I wished he'd given me more, I wished I knew his motive.

In my mind, I pictured our last night together, the New Years Eve party at the Aurora. He'd been so upset to see that I had cut myself and he'd finally realized just how sickly and grotesque I had become. But I thought I'd convinced him that we could change our lives—that we could get clean together and live sober and happy. Hadn't I?

"I'm going to make this right," Grey had said, just before the stroke of midnight, when our kiss had seemed like a promise. Was that what he meant? By killing himself? But how did that make it right … how did that make anything right? He was my life, my whole life. He knew how badly I needed him, how badly we needed each other ….

I gasped as a sudden thought occurred to me. Maybe that was it, though. Maybe Grey knew how … dependent we were on each other. That we were addicted to each other as much as we were to the heroin, and together, we'd never be able to kick the drugs. He knew we couldn't be apart, but if he stuck around, I'd never get clean. I'd just keep dying the same, slow, drawn-out death that was so apparent in my features. But he couldn't bear to just leave me, either. He couldn't bear to *live* without me ….

This new realization sunk deep, deep down into my soul. Riley was right.

Our relationship hadn't been healthy, as good as it was. We were too much the same, Grey and I—too eager for a good time, too willing to pursue the next high at the expense of our bodies. We were slowly destroying each other. And Grey realized that, in the end. So he took himself out of the picture. Gave me a chance … a chance at life.

"I want you to truly live …."

" … *Forgive me* …."

"Grey …." I whispered into the darkness, "There's nothing to forgive. It's not your fault … it was never your fault …."

Maybe our relationship hadn't been healthy, but Grey had truly loved me.

He loved me the only way he knew how.

I missed that love. The great, vast emptiness in my soul suddenly flared to life, throbbing, pounding with hurt. I'd never felt so alone. The hollowness was echoing. The dark was pressing in. Every time I shut my eyes I pictured Grey alone in his room that night. Had he been scared? Had he cried? Or had he steeled himself to that final decision? I saw him in my mind, his handsome brow furrowed with determination as he mixed his last lethal dose of heroin. I saw the drugs on the spoon, as dark as blackness. Poor Grey, so alone ….

Allison was already sleeping, I could tell from her slow, even breaths. So fretfully, I pushed back my covers and ran to the door. I couldn't take it anymore. I needed … I needed someone—someone I knew—someone who could comfort me with just the sound of his voice.

I wiped frantically at the tears that continued to stream down my cheeks, allowing myself a breathy sob in the relative privacy of the hallway. I snuck down the darkened corridor as lithely as I could, aiming for the shadows of the communal phone booth by the game room. Everything was so hushed, so quiet. I was afraid to make even the slightest noise.

I reached the phone and pounded in the number. I didn't need to see to know which buttons to push; I had used them almost every day for the last fourteen years or so. I didn't know how late it was, I didn't know how many hours I had lay in my bed tormented with such sorrowful thought. I hoped he'd answer, and not his mom. I knew Mrs. McIntyre was up every morning at five-thirty for work at the meatpacking plant.

The first time around, there was no response. It must have been really late, but I didn't care. I hung up the phone and dialled again, my broken heart pounding with anxiety. This time, on the fifth ring, he answered.

"Hello?" His voice was deep, raspy from sleep.

"Riley?"

"Mackenzie? What's up, are you okay?" His voice sharpened with concern.

"I don't know Ry," I couldn't keep the tears out of my voice, "I can't sleep."

"How come?"

"… It's too dark …." I whispered. I couldn't tell him the real reason. I made up my mind at that moment never to tell anyone the real reason for Grey's death. It'd be our secret. Forever. I wrapped the phone cord through my fingers, holding back a sob. Grey wanted me to live. He gave up his life so I would. And I could do it, for him. I could live.

"Riley?" I sniffed.

"Yeah?"

"Will you come visit me tomorrow?"

CHAPTER 64

The room was the same—same bland wallpaper, same beige furniture crammed into the same nondescript tiny space—but today the atmosphere was different. For the first time in a long, long time, I felt … something. Motivation, maybe. A kind of drive. Like more than just the sheer unwillingness of my body to die was keeping me alive. Like my life had a purpose again. All night after my phone call to Riley, I had thought about the things I could do if I got better. Once upon a time, back in my straight "A" days, I had wanted to be something. A doctor, like Marcy and my Mom, or a lawyer even … just someone … important. Those dreams were lost now, but never really suited me anyway—having been born from an ill-conceived attempt to try and impress my parents. I could do anything, though. And I was determined to. I was going to make Grey proud.

If Riley noticed my sudden change of heart, he didn't say anything. He sat across the table from me, drinking lukewarm coffee from a Styrofoam cup. We actually had a few moments of normal, light conversation without the heavy burden of utter heartbreak and despair. Neither of us mentioned anything about his visit the previous day. He knew he was forgiven—mostly—but he shuffled a bit in his seat, a telltale sign he was still anxious about something.

"What is it Riley?" I wondered impatiently. It came from knowing him so well, being able to tell exactly what he was thinking just from his body movements. I looked up at him expectantly.

"Well, I brought you something." He admitted, his warm, dark eyes on my face. "But I don't know how you're going to react to it. Well, I do know how you'll react, but I want you to keep an open mind."

"Just give it to me, and then we'll see."

"Okay." He bent down and pulled something from a bag beneath his seat. I peered over the edge of the table curiously. And then, he set a book down on the table in front of me. "Here." He offered.

The book was thick and heavy. I picked up the soft leather cover and inspected the front. Holy Bible was imprinted in thick gold letters. I put the book down.

"What the hell is this?" I scoffed.

"The Bible." He answered imperviously.

"I know it's a Bible. Why are you giving it to me?"

"Well … you said it was dark, right? Last night, when you were trying to sleep?"

"Yes." He had no idea how dark. "So?"

"Maybe this will help." Riley shrugged.

"How? Does it come with a nightlight?" I smirked and lit a cigarette, blowing the smoke up over his head.

"No." He shook his head at my joke. "But it's been a great source of comfort for me. Maybe it will help you, too."

I raised my eyebrows. It was always staggering how much Riley had changed. It never ceased to shock me. But he really did seem … peaceful. Content, almost. I crossed my arms thoughtfully and sat back in my chair.

"How does it comfort you?"

"Well … it's just … it's God, right? He's what was missing in my life … and he's what's missing in yours."

"Okay …." I chuckled wryly. "If you say so."

"Mackenzie, just bear with me here. Why do you think you got addicted to drugs in the first place?"

I shrugged. "I don't know … 'cause they're awesome? 'Cause they made me feel really, really good … and when I did them … I don't know … everything was okay."

"But you were just medicating yourself … don't you see? You're covering up what's really missing inside of you, all the emptiness inside. Everyone is born with this … this God shaped hole inside them. And we rush around, trying to fill that hole with anything we can, anything that satisfies us, however temporarily. But God is the only thing that will fit there, that will fit and stay and truly satisfy you—like nothing you've ever known before. His peace … it passes all understanding."

"So … drug addicts are really just searching for God?"

"Not just drug addicts, everyone. The good people that go about their good lives without harming anyone and only trying to do what's right … even they have a hunger inside of them for God. But they don't know it. They worship music instead, or video games, or sports—movies, money, clothes, people … cooking, even. Whatever they choose to live their life for. But every single one of us, no matter how good or bad, is in desperate need of God."

I smirked again as a thought occurred to me. "Even Marcy?"

"Especially Marcy." Riley smiled at me. He pushed the Bible across the table. "Just, try reading it. See if anything speaks to you. It's amazing you know, once you discover him. You won't understand how you've been able to live without him for so long."

I put my hand on the soft leather cover and looked up at Riley. I didn't know if God was real or not, but if he was, he'd probably want nothing to do with me. Not when I was so horrible, not when I was such a miserable mess. Not after I'd pushed my boyfriend, the love of my life, to kill himself in an attempt to save me. I was selfish and brutal and … wrong. It felt like every part of me was wrong. But I had decided to try ….

"You're going to be okay, Mackenzie." Riley placed his warm hand on top of mine. "I really believe that, you know."

I stared down at our hands for a moment. He stroked mine delicately with his thumb, and for some reason, it made me uncomfortable. His dark eyes gazed down at me with such tenderness, such affection … it was unsettling. Undeserved. As causally as I could, I moved my hand from his and tried to change the subject.

"So, what's Emily think of you being here?" I wondered.

"Oh, she understands." He answered flippantly. "She hopes you get better."

"She does? Where is she, at your mom's?"

"No, she's back at school. The semester started last week."

"Wait, your semester started already?" I blinked in surprise. "So what are you still doing here?"

Riley scoffed. "What, you think I'd just put you in here and then go back to school like nothing ever happened? Give me a little credit."

"You're missing your school?" I frowned. For some reason, this upset me. "Don't wreck your life for me Riley, I'm not worth it."

"I'm not wrecking my life. Man, you're dramatic." He laughed. "I can just pick up where I left off next semester. No big deal."

"Yeah, but, you've worked so hard, and you really like it, I can tell—"

"Mackenzie, just stop." Riley shook his head at me. "All that matters to me right now is that you get better. I'm not going anywhere, okay? So just drop it."

I stared at him a moment. "Fine." I wouldn't ever admit it to him, but the selfish part of me was nearly drunk with relief that he had chosen to stay. For me. I honestly couldn't imagine my life without him again, without the subconscious comfort of knowing he was so close, only a phone call away. How quickly I had come to rely on him. I needed him now, even more than I had before.

We just looked at each other for a moment. I stared into his deep, dark eyes as he gazed at me. I wanted to thank him for everything—for putting up with me, for trying to help me—but the words wouldn't reach my lips. The air felt tense, heavy.

"I guess I should be going." Riley decided suddenly, ripping his eyes from mine and looking up at the clock, breaking the spell.

I cleared my throat. What the hell was that? "Well … I think we were fairly successful today." I offered casually.

"Oh yeah?" He chuckled. "Are you cured?"

"Uh … not yet …." For an instant, the picture of a needle flashed into my mind, and with it, the intense craving for heroin knotted my stomach with need. I breathed through it, trying to shake the image from my head. "I mean, this visit didn't end in a fight. That's a pretty big deal, don't you think? For us?"

Riley stared at me a moment, his lips curled in amusement. "Yeah, I guess it is."

"So you'll come back tomorrow, right?"

"I'll be here every day." He promised.

CHAPTER 65

The days and weeks passed, as they often do. I had bad days and good days—mostly bad, with a few good sprinkled in. The fact that I could have any good days at all was amazing to me. But they came. I don't know what brought them about, but I'd wake up in the morning after a fitful, tenuous sleep, and I'd feel some hope. Some strength. Like I could get through it all. Like I was going to make it.

And then came the bad days.

Those days I didn't even want to get out of bed. Those days my heart ached as if it were on fire, my thoughts knew no peace, my mind no rest. Those days I missed Grey abominably. Overwhelmed with guilt and sorrow and loss I'd plod on through the day, sullen, arms crossed defensively, snapping at those around me. Snapping at Riley. Poor Riley always suffered the brunt of my emotion, especially during my bad days. But it didn't seem to faze him. He apparently had a never-ending supply of patience at his disposal, for all he put up with—my moroseness, my bitter gloom, my cruel remarks. He seemed to understand that it wasn't about him, but of course, he wasn't shy about telling me when to shut up, either.

Riley continued to talk to me about God, and for some reason every time he did, it made me want to cry. I tried fitfully to read the Bible he had given me. The first few chapters were enjoyable, the whole Adam and Eve story and Noah and all that. Of course I had heard those stories before, but it was kind of neat to read them in their original context. I found it hard to believe they really happened—like nursery rhymes or fairy tales—and I asked Riley a trillion questions, most he couldn't answer. Like, did Noah take mosquitoes with him on the ark? If he did, why? He could have saved us a whole bunch of trouble, not to mention a bunch of diseases, if he'd just left those pests behind. And Adam and Eve. If they were the first two people on earth, who did their sons marry? Their sisters?

I couldn't help myself. It was easier to make light of the situation, to keep things casual, shallow. I didn't want to tell Riley about it, but whenever he got into the real stuff, the heart stuff ... it made me teary. Teary and uncomfortable. I just couldn't explain it, like there was this ... voice inside of me, one I was trying fervently to deny. One I didn't want to have. One I didn't want to need.

But still I struggled through. Until I reached Deuteronomy, that is.

"There's an awful lot of begotting in that book." I admitted sourly to Riley one particularly ugly day.

He laughed outright at me, more heartily than I had heard him laugh for a long, long time. I waited, seething, until he was finished. I didn't see what was so funny about it.

"I'm sorry." He managed between chuckles. "I've just never heard it put that way before."

"Well," I defended stiffly, "maybe I just won't read any more, if what I think is so amusing to you."

"Wow. Touchy." He smiled at me, his dark eyes warming. "No. Don't stop reading it. I'm glad you are. Just ... maybe try something, a little closer to the middle. Like the Psalms, or the New Testament. I think you'll like that."

"I don't know, Riley." I shook my head in frustration. "I just don't think I get it. You know? It's just ... words. I don't get any ... it's all kind of ... meaningless, to me. I don't understand any of it."

"Try asking God to show you," he suggested, "he'd love to speak to you, you know. He wants to speak to you."

Tears pricked my eyes. I couldn't explain them, I blinked them away.

"Yeah." Whatever.

"You're going to get through this," Riley grasped my hand and gave it a squeeze. "Just take it one day at a time. Ask him for help."

I nodded and stared silently at the floor. Sometimes it felt like my sorrow was engulfing me—that it was all I had left, that I had lost every part of me to it. I missed Grey so much. I blamed myself for his death. I couldn't bear to look at myself in the mirror, to face what I had become—everything I had done. I was wasted. Broken. Lost.

Miserable.

"I know you're hurting right now, Mackenzie." Riley's voice reached my ears, low, serious, as if he'd been reading my mind. "But you need to hurt. You need to hurt if ever you're going to change."

"But you changed." I realized glumly. "You totally changed, and you didn't feel any hurt. Not like this."

Riley hesitated, his dark eyes scanning the drab interior of the room as he thought out his reply. He took a sip of coffee. "Maybe I didn't hurt like you do now. But I hurt, Mac. More than you know."

"How?"

"It … it hurt to know what a … what a piece of shit I had become. Even when I look back now, when I think about the way I acted, the way I was. So selfish, you know? So … destructive. It hurt to think about what I was doing to my mom. I'm all she has in the whole world. And what I was doing to all those kids, kids younger than me, giving them drugs, taking their money …." He paused thoughtfully, hesitating as he met my eyes across the table. "… It … it hurt for me to think about what I'd done to you, too. I mean, if it weren't for me … we probably never would've gotten high that first time. I felt guilty … responsible … just … wretched. I hurt. But it helped me. It made me see that I had to change."

I listened to him, wide-eyed, totally able to empathise. I knew what he meant about the guilt, the misery … the hopelessness that came with realizing how terrible I actually was, in every single way. How nearly every one of my actions for the last few years had been entirely selfish, entirely wrong.

I didn't deserve happiness. Not after what I'd done.

"So … you changed … and now, everything is good?" I wondered.

"… Yes … and no." Riley shrugged. "Just because I've got … God now, doesn't mean my life is just a total cake walk. I mean, sure, I'm not doing those bad things anymore, but truthfully, I'm still a piece of shit. Everyone is, Mac. Compared to God's goodness, every single person you meet, no matter how 'good' they may seem … they're disgusting. We're all disgusting. None of us deserve him, it doesn't matter what we do."

"That seems pretty grim," I realized despondently. "So what's the point then?"

"The point is … He doesn't see us that way. We are precious to him. He knows how brutally terrible we all are, but he loves us anyway. And he forgives us. All we have to do is ask, and he'll forgive us, for everything. See? We need him in such a desperate way."

I bit my lip doubtfully. "But how does it …?"

Riley sat up, leaning forward towards me. "Okay. You know the Christmas story, right? How Jesus was born in a manger and everything?"

"Yeah." I nodded. More fairy tales.

"Jesus is God's son, right? He walked this earth, like physically walked the earth. He went through every trial and experience that we could ever face, but he did it perfectly. Without sin. His entire life, he didn't sin once. Not even once." Riley scoffed. "I can't even go five minutes without some kind of sin."

"Go on." I insisted impatiently.

"So, though he's God's son, though he's utterly blameless, he ends up getting arrested. And in the end, he gets put to death. They beat him, and whipped him, and completely shredded his body. They tortured him, Mac. They made him carry his own cross, and then they nailed his hands and his feet to it, and hung him there until he died."

I hadn't realized I was holding my breath until Riley paused. I let it out, hanging on his words. "And …?"

"He died for us, Mac. The only person alive who's ever lived without sinning. But it was all a part of God's plan; it was the only way he could save us from *our* sin. He became sin. He became what is killing us. And then he died, so that we could be free of it. And then he rose again, so that we could live with him. Truly live Mac, free. Totally free. Jesus is alive today, Mac, he's alive in you. And you are his desire."

I raised my eyebrows at the story. "I'm sorry … Ry, I still don't really … get it. I mean … its great and all … but doesn't it seem kind of … fictitious?"

"Of course it does." Riley smiled, like he knew some great secret. After a moment he sat up again, leaning forward conspiratorially. His voice dropped lowly. "'Cause you know what really saves you, Mac?"

"What?"

"Faith. Faith in the impossible. Faith that Jesus did die for you, as crazy as it may seem. Believing in God, believing that he exists, believing that Jesus is as alive today as he was back then. Faith. Like that of a child. Ignoring all the voices that tell you none of it could be real, that none of it could actually happen. Just … believing. Believe everything. Believe him."

"Believe it?"

"Yes." Riley stared at me a moment. "Believe that Jesus willingly died for you, to save you. He knew how sinful you'd be, he knew how terrible all of us would be. We're sinful from birth, it's in our very nature, but still, he loved us enough to die for us. He chose to sacrifice himself to give us life."

"He did?"

"Think about it, Mackenzie. He's the son of God. He preformed countless miracles here on earth, he turned water into wine, he fed five thousand people with a few loaves of bread. He healed the sick; he *raised* people from the dead! Do you think a few measly nails could've held him to that cross?"

"No?"

"No. Of course not." Riley smiled at me. "Only his love for you could do that."

Riley had given me a lot to think about. I still didn't know how I felt about God … it all seemed so … crazy. All of it. Something I'd never really needed before, and wasn't sure I needed now. I sat pensively, quiet at the cafeteria table while the girls around me laughed and joked with each other. They had given up trying to extricate me from my shell. For the most part, I was invisible to them, but I didn't really mind. Idly, I brought my fork to my mouth and chewed a bite full of lukewarm, sticky macaroni. Another month and a half and I'd be going home.

I wondered fleetingly what Charlie was doing. What Alex and Zack were up to. My mind scanned quickly over my parents and my sister, trying to picture them going through the daily routine of life, trying to imagine where they were. Mom would be at work at the hospital, Dad would be on a plane somewhere. Marcy was probably studying.

Hopefully, Greg was smoking a pipe somewhere with his bedroom slippers on. I smiled to myself at the image. It was so strange to think that outside of rehab, normal life was continuing just like it had before. To me it seemed like everyone's life should be on hold, just as mine was.

I wondered if they worried about me at all, my family, or if they had shipped me off without a thought, chalking me up as a "goner," hopeless that I'd ever get better. I wouldn't have blamed them. But secretly, I hoped they were rooting for me. I hoped they wanted me to take part in their lives again—soberly, a new version of the old Mackenzie before the drugs had taken her away. I wondered what the new Mackenzie would be like. I wondered who she was.

I put my fork down and sighed, taking a sip from my Coke. As gross as the cafeteria food might've been, it was doing its job. My pants fit again—they weren't straining by any means, but they weren't sagging off my protruding hipbones anymore either. And the few times I allowed myself to glance into a mirror, I noticed the new fullness of my face. Slowly I was losing the sallow, gaunt cheekbones; the more weight I gained the softer my appearance became. A slight blush of color was returning to my skin, so I looked less and less like death and more and more alive with every passing day. I was looking healthy again. On the outside, anyway.

After supper was finished, we headed down the bland old hallway towards the TV room. I trailed behind the other girls, my fingers dragging absently down the wall. There was something kind of off about how I was feeling. Introspective, definitely—but with that came … anxiety. A new kind of anxiety, distantly related to how I felt when the lights went off at night. But more … panicky. Like, stressful. And I didn't know what was causing it.

Maybe it was Allison. I bit my lip and looked up at the back of my roommate as she led the way towards the TV room. Her blonde hair was in messy spikes around her head, her ripped jeans tucked loosely into large black boots. She'd been distant with me lately; I think she was resentful of all the "special" visits I was getting from Riley. What's more, she hated the fact that I was actually trying. Well, trying to try. Paying attention in group therapy now, journaling, opening up a little more with my ancient one-on-one therapist—though that was extremely hard to want to do. I knew that all the resentment would stop if I told her about Grey and the overdose, but I just couldn't bring myself to do it. Deep down, I think it was more than that.

From the moment I'd arrived, we'd had sort of an unspoken agreement between us, a willingness to fail, a suffer-through-until-we're-out-and-can-get-a-hit kind of mentality. Now that I wanted to get better, not only did we disagree, but she refused to try and understand how I felt … my sudden desire to … live again.

I sighed. That wasn't what was making me anxious though. I considered Allison a friend but really—I barely knew her, she only had weeks left of her stay, and it was doubtful we'd ever see each other again after rehab. It sucked that she was perma-mad at me, but that wouldn't be enough to make me feel so … unsettled. Troubled. Like I'd forgotten something—something important—but couldn't figure out what it was. Just relative … unease. Tension. Apprehension.

I tried to ignore it, tried to push it away and focus on the mindless chatter coming from the TV for the rest of the evening.

But by the time we made it back to our room, despite all my efforts to the contrary, the disquiet within me had reached a near fever pitch. This new unexplained restlessness—combined with my usual angst once the lights were shut off—threatened to make me nearly crazy. The darkness in the room pressed against my open eyes. My heart hammered wildly in my chest. For a terrible instant, I felt like I couldn't breathe. I sat up in bed and took a few deep breaths, trying to calm myself down. I didn't really know what to do; I'd never experienced a panic attack before. What I needed was light. As quietly as I could, I took the little pencil flashlight that Riley had smuggled in for me one week from the bedside drawer. As a second thought, I grabbed the Bible he'd given me as well. Then, my heart still racing, I ducked under my covers and turned the flashlight on. If Allison was aware of my activities she didn't say anything. Her slow, even breaths told me she was enjoying that rare skill she possessed for falling asleep instantly.

I flipped impatiently through my Bible. I wasn't even sure what I was searching for, some answer that would make all the craziness stop. Riley had suggested I read somewhere closer to the middle. I flipped and flipped and flipped, and then stopped. I read the first chapter my eyes rested on. It was a Psalm. Psalm 107.

"Oh, thank God - he's so good! His love never runs out. All of you set free by God, tell the world! Tell how he freed you from oppression, then rounded you up from all over the place, from the four winds, from the seven seas. Some of you wandered for years in the desert, looking but not finding a good place to live, half-starved and parched with thirst, staggering and stumbling, on the brink of exhaustion. Then, in your desperate condition, you called out to God. He got you out in the nick of time; he put your feet on a wonderful road that took you straight to a good place to live. So thank God for his marvellous love, for his miracle mercy to the children he loves. He poured great draughts of water down parched throats; the starved and hungry got plenty to eat.

Some of you were locked in a dark cell, cruelly confined behind bars, punished for defying God's Word, for turning your back on the High God's counsel - a hard sentence, and your hearts so heavy, and not a soul in sight to help. Then you called out to God in your desperate condition; he got you out in the nick of time. He led you out of your dark, dark cell, broke open the jail and led you out. So thank God for his marvellous love, for his miracle mercy to the children he loves; he shattered the heavy jailhouse doors, he snapped the prison bars like matchsticks!

Some of you were sick because you'd lived a bad life, your bodies feeling the effects of your sin; you couldn't stand the sight of food, so miserable you thought you'd be better off dead. Then you called out to God in your desperate condition; he got you out in the nick of time. He spoke the word that healed you, that pulled you back from the brink of death. So thank God for his marvellous love, for his miracle mercy to the children he loves; Offer thanksgiving sacrifices, tell the world what he's done - sing it out!

Some of you set sail in big ships; you put to sea to do business in faraway ports. Out at sea you saw God in action, saw his breathtaking ways with the ocean: with a word he called up the wind - an ocean storm, towering waves! You shot high in the sky, then the bottom dropped out; your hearts were stuck in your throats. You were spun like a top, you reeled like a drunk, you didn't know which end was up. Then you called out to God in your desperate condition; he got you out in the nick of time. He quieted the wind down to a whisper, put a muzzle on all the big waves. And you were so glad when the storm died down, and he led you safely back to harbour. So thank God for his marvellous love, for his miracle mercy to the children he loves. Lift high your praises when the people assemble, shout Hallelujah when the elders meet!

God turned rivers into wasteland, springs of water into sun baked mud; luscious orchards became alkali flats because of the evil of the people who lived there. Then he changed wasteland into fresh pools of water, arid earth into springs of water, brought in the hungry and settled them there; they moved in - what a great place to live! They sowed the fields, they planted vineyards, they reaped a bountiful harvest. He blessed them and they prospered greatly; their herds of cattle never decreased. But abuse and evil and trouble declined as he heaped scorn on princes and sent them away. He gave the poor a safe place to live, treated their clans like well-cared-for sheep. Good people see this and are glad; bad people are speechless, stopped in their tracks.

If you are really wise, you'll think this over - it's time you appreciated God's deep love."

I read it a few times, my eyes wide as saucers in my face. I was surprised. So much of it spoke to me … like actually spoke to me. "Your heart so heavy; and not a soul to help." That was exactly how I felt. "You couldn't stand the sight of food, so miserable you thought you'd be better off dead."

Hadn't I felt that very thing? Hadn't I actually tried to kill myself? But why didn't I die? I had taken more than enough heroin to overdose—way more than enough. Yet here I was, living, breathing. Fine. "He spoke the word that healed you, that pulled you back from the brink of death." Could it be true? Could what Riley said be true? Did God have a plan for me? Did he … love me, despite my horridness? Did he love me enough to save me?

There was one line in that chapter that had been repeated over and over. "Then you called out to God in your desperate condition; he got you out in the nick of time."

Did I believe? Did I believe that God would save me if I asked him to? Could I take that leap, that leap of faith? I had to try. I couldn't take this for much longer—the heaviness of my heart, the despair in my soul, the wretchedness that permeated my entire being. Just one night of peace, that's all I wanted. One night where I could shut my eyes and sleep, and know no hurt, no pain, no discontent. I had to try.

I laid my Bible down on my chest and shut off the flashlight. I felt silly. I had never done this before. I laid there for a minute, silent, staring up into the dark—into the utter blackness. My heart was pounding. After a few, deep breaths, I began.

"God, please," I begged silently into the night, "please, if you're there … help me. I … I need you. Please, if you're real, show me. Help me to believe. Help me, God. I'm calling to you in a desperate condition, I can't take much more. Get me out in the nick of time, God … please; please … I beg you … help me …."

I'm not sure when the tears started, but I felt them wet and heavy on my cheeks. I don't know what I expected—some whisper in the dark perhaps, or a hand heavy on my shoulder—but there was nothing, just dark and the quiet surrounding me, unchanging.

But then, there was something. I don't know how to describe it … it was so subtle. There weren't any fireworks exploding within me or anything, it was more like something just … clicked. Like whatever had been missing before was suddenly found. Like the last piece of the puzzle was finally in place. That's not even it though; it was even more delicate than that. Suddenly, I just knew that God was real. That everything the

Bible said was true. That my heart was beating for a purpose, and that purpose was God.

Peace flooded over me. More peace than I had ever known. I couldn't explain it. It was better than any high I'd ever had. More potent than heroin, and … cleaner feeling. Like this peace was the right kind of peace. Like a soft, warm blanket it enveloped me. I felt safer than I ever had, more love than I had ever known. All my agony was gone, all my sadness, all my guilt and despair. After a few moments of nothing but amazing light-heartedness, all I could do was utter silent thoughts of deep, sincere thankfulness. And sometime in the midst of thanking God, I fell fast asleep, and stayed that way until morning.

"He led you out of your dark, dark cell, broke open the jail and led you out. So thank God for his marvellous love, for his miracle mercy to the children he loves …."

Allison had to shake me awake. "Mackenzie!" She called. "You're going to be late for breakfast."

I stretched in my bed, and yawned. I hadn't slept so wonderfully in ages and ages—I hadn't felt such peace in my entire life. The moment I opened my eyes I expected it all to come crashing down on me again—the heaviness, the sorrow. And while I did still feel the pain that came from losing Grey … it was more bearable than it had ever been. And the peace … it remained. I couldn't explain it … it was just there. I smiled at Allison—like actually smiled, I felt so hopeful. All this time my life had felt like the beginning of night; dark, fretful and weary, with no end in sight. Now, I felt the first light of dawn slowly creeping over the horizon of my world, chasing the darkness and the shadows away, holding real hope in its warmth. Like today was the beginning. Like nothing before today even mattered.

My smile surprised Allison so much that she actually frowned at me. I had broken another unwritten rule between us, smiling upon waking apparently was not allowed, not when in rehab. Part of me wanted to share with her what I had experienced, what I had found in the dark reaches of the night. But I knew that Allison wouldn't appreciate it, and this was all too new to me to have it sullied by someone who didn't understand. So, as much as the words were nearly bursting out of me, just dying to be told, I bit my tongue. There was only one person I was ready to tell. One person who would really understand.

I nearly raced to the meeting room that afternoon when it was time. Riley was there, like usual, sitting behind the table and waiting for me. I paused outside the door and just looked at him a moment. His dark hair was still growing out from his buzz cut; it was thicker now, nearly to his ears. He wore a burnt orange long sleeved t-shirt, tight against his broad shoulders; and dark blue jeans that accentuated his newfound muscular physic. His dark eyes were staring down at the coffee cup he was gripping with both hands, as if he were still chilled from the arctic-like weather we'd been having.

He was the same. He was different. I felt like I really knew him now, now that I understood. I felt more connected to him than I had in a really, really long time. With a smile on my face, I opened the door.

Riley was nearly as shocked as Allison had been by the sincere expression of happiness upon my face. He looked taken aback; he just stared and stared at me a moment. The look on his face made me want to laugh aloud, but I held back, giggling instead into my hand.

"I can't believe I'm laughing, Riley." I shook my head. "I never thought I'd laugh again."

I didn't have to say it, but just from that sentence, Riley understood. The smile he gave me then was unlike any smile he'd ever given me before. His dark eyes were shining with tears as he came around the table and wrapped me up in a tremendous hug.

"I'm so happy, Mac." He spoke into my ear. "You have no idea, how long I've … I've been praying and praying." He held me tightly. His arms were so warm, so safe. I pressed my face against his chest and muffled my laughter into his shirt.

"He's real, Ry. He's really real."

"I know. I know he is."

"I'm so …." I shook my head. How to describe it? "I feel so … light … so … happy. I can't believe it." I looked up at my friend, worriedly. "Is it wrong? Is it wrong to feel this good?"

"No." Riley held my arms in his warm, strong hands and answered me sincerely. "No, it's not wrong. As hard as it may be to believe, you do deserve happiness, Mac."

"But … will he understand?" I wondered hopefully.

"Of course he will." Riley hugged me tightly against him. "Grey wants you to be happy too."

I pressed myself against Riley's hard chest and shut my eyes, knowing his words to be true. I imagined Grey's perfect face, his blue eyes shining, his lips smirking as he whispered in my ear.

"Live. Be happy."

I will be happy, Grey, someday.

But I'll never stop loving you.

CHAPTER 66

I tore into my rehabilitation with such fervour that I took even myself by surprise. I surprised everyone but Riley. He knew once I made up my mind there'd be no stopping me. And he was right. Now, instead of rolling my eyes at the twelve-step program, I deliberately and wholeheartedly went through each one, embracing them as necessary for my healing. I opened up with my personal therapist, allowing him to recognize my utter lack of coping skills—how my answer to stress or hurt or anger was to push it all away, choosing drugs and alcohol instead of actually dealing with my troubles. Together, he took me through healthy coping strategies, showing me how to deal with my problems instead of ignoring them completely. Digging at the root of my issues, he told me how my feelings of inferiority with Marcy were completely unfounded. How we were two totally different people—special and unique and gifted in our own way—and that our parents loved us both, equally and as individuals.

I was still working on that one.

But I was truly becoming transformed. And all because of God. Riley was right again. Now that I knew him, I couldn't fathom having ever lived without him. I still had my bad days; I still had days when I missed Grey so badly it felt like I couldn't breathe. Sometimes—like a masochist—I'd lie on my bed and just think about him, dredging up all our memories together, remembering the velvet perfection of his voice and the handsomeness of his face until my pillow was soaked with tears. But Jesus was there through it all—helping me along—there for me in every possible way. Lending me his strength so that I never gave up hope. I wanted to get through it all and I wanted to do it right. I wanted to feel the pain, to change as Riley had. I wanted to do it all for him, I wanted to truly live for him. When things got too much, when my craving for heroin was gnawing away at my insides, I'd stop and pray and beg and plead for God to help me. And somehow, it got easier. The craving would pass without agony, without much torment and torture until suddenly, I'd realize it was gone.

And I slept. At night I slept like a baby, and awoke nearly every morning feeling totally rested. I read my Bible whenever I got a spare minute and wrote in my journal the new revelations I was discovering, each and every day. Riley was a constant help, guiding me, trying to answer my constant flood of questions, eagerly and happily trying to teach me about this amazing God that I had only just discovered. The time seemed to fly by, each and every day faster than the one before it, easier from my newfound strength. With it I felt like I could take on the world.

Other times I was terrified of that very thing.

Allison was leaving me. Her three months were up, and I sat on my bed, worriedly watching her pack. She was whistling, her blue eyes gleaming excitedly as she quickly folded her clothes into the suitcase.

I was concerned for her. I knew exactly what she was going to do the moment she set foot out the doors, and I knew where that decision would lead her. I could almost see her future spiralling away. How long would it take before she was circling the drain again? Before she ended up hurt or sick or … worse? What if she ended up dead?

I knew there was nothing I could do to make her change her mind.

But I had to try.

"You don't have to do it, you know." I blurted suddenly. She paused for a moment and stopped whistling, looking up to frown at me.

"I don't have to do what?"

"It." I sat up and stamped my cigarette out in the ashtray. "Heroin. You don't have to use again, Allison. You can start your life again, fresh. Sober."

"Yeah, I guess I could." She chuckled. "Except I don't want to."

"You've gone ninety days without. Allison, that's huge. You should be proud of yourself."

She rolled her eyes at me.

"What about your friends and your family … what about them?"

"What about them?" Allison asked icily, her blue eyes narrowing at me. "They threw me in here so they wouldn't have to deal with me anymore. That's fine. I don't need them. I'll be just fine on my own."

"I think they put you in here because they love you."

"You don't know the first thing about it." She threw the last of her shirts into the suitcase and angrily zipped up the bag.

I shrugged. "It just … it seems to me like you're looking for excuses to start again, and you don't have to do it. I know you've been planning on … it … but you can change—"

"Shut up, Mackenzie, okay?" Allison shook her head at me. "Just shut up. Man, I liked you a lot better when you didn't give a damn. Just, don't get all high and mighty on me. I'm leaving, and there's nothing you can do to stop me."

"I know that, trust me. No one can stop you. No one but yourself. But Allison, you can do it. I know you can."

"Fuck off." She wavered.

But I was unwavering. "I know it's too late for the motivational speech. All I can do now is ask." I put my hand on her shoulder, my dark eyes pleading with her. "Please don't use, Allison. Please, will you just try? I do care about you, and I want you to get better. I want you to stay better."

Her blue eyes met mine for a moment, softened by my words. But then I saw the exact moment when they hardened again, when her resolve was strengthened, when her decision was made. She cackled mockingly and pulled her arm from my grasp.

"Save it, Mac. I'm gone." She declared, and brushed by me out the door.

That was the last I ever saw of her.

CHAPTER 67

Metallica was blasting through the stereo. Groups of rowdy kids were taking up absolutely every single space available. Some were belting out the words to the song—it drifted towards me, harsh and out of key ....

"What I felt, what I've known,
Turn the pages turn the stone,
Behind the door
Should I open it for you ...."

I looked idly around the room, taking in the scene—my vision foggy, my glance hazy. The red plastic cup in my hand was heavy, the cigarette in my fingers wreathing my face with smoke. A smile contorted my lips as I walked forward with leaden feet. There was something I had to do, something I'd wanted to do for a long time, and this propelled my steps—stumbling and unbalanced—towards the stairs.

Suddenly I wasn't holding my drink, but someone's hand. I was pulling someone up the stairs with me. The image shifted then, the camera angle changed. I saw the stairs as we took them, slowly. I could hear myself laughing, could feel the giddiness in my stomach. I watched my feet as they reached the landing and stumbled into the nearest bedroom. I heard the silence once the door shut behind me. I turned, and the whole world spun, reeling wildly.

"I can't believe this is happening ...."

I woke with a start, blinking into the dark, momentarily confused until I realized it had all been a dream. Yet it had all seemed so familiar.

The faded brown carpet, the chipped yellow walls. I knew I had seen them before, somewhere.

Allison was gone and I was all alone in our room, but the loneliness didn't taunt me like it once had. I knew I was never really truly alone, not anymore. I breathed peacefully and turned my thoughts back to the dream. The dream that had seemed almost like déjà vu, like I had lived through it before. Especially the voice at the end. I knew that voice, even through the haze, the distortion. It was Riley.

I frowned into the dark now, searching, straining my mind to come up with the memory. I just couldn't place it. We'd been to hundreds of house parties over the course of the years, almost one a weekend. It was impossible to decipher where this one had taken place. And why remember it now, anyway? What was the significance of remembering another crazy old drunken night of debauchery?

I focused on Riley's voice. *"I can't believe this is happening."* He'd said. What was happening? I had pulled him up the stairs; we'd gone into a bedroom. He'd shut the door behind us ….

Oh! I sat straight up in bed, my eyes wide, my hand over my mouth as I gasped in vivid remembrance. I could feel the heat staining my cheeks as the memory suddenly invaded my head. The vision was crystal clear—which was baffling to me. I thought I blacked out that night. But now, I remembered everything. I saw it all. I filled in the blanks of my dream.

I'd been feeling woozy from the Quaaludes—but good, confident. Riley and I had been kidding around, joking and laughing, when suddenly I'd lost my balance and fallen into him. I remembered landing against the solid width of his chest, how the abruptness of it had shocked me, how good it felt to be so close to him.

I'd never really wanted him like that before—though I'd always been curious—so at that moment, I went for it. He was still laughing when I looked up at him, amazed, and silenced his mouth with my lips.

I can't believe I'd ever forgotten this. Now I could remember everything … the taste of his mouth, the feel of it against mine. I think I'd taken him by surprise, but after he recovered Riley returned my kiss just as eagerly.

It'd been my idea to go upstairs. Of course it had been, wasn't everything always my idea? Once the door to the bedroom was shut we'd made out in frenzy, fuelled by the cheap beer and the good drugs coursing through our veins, the years of pent-up curiosity, the sudden culmination of all our hidden feelings. It had been … amazing. Hot. Better than I ever could have expected. Riley and I had drunkenly tripped our way over to the bed … and then … and then ….

I frowned. I couldn't remember anymore, my memories just stopped. They vanished.

I flicked the light on—rules be damned—and grabbed a cigarette from my nightstand. I couldn't believe this had actually transpired. What the hell was I supposed to do with this now? I took a deep drag in thought. How far had we gone? And did Riley know, did he remember? If he did, why didn't he say anything? Why had nothing happened between us afterwards?

Had I wanted something to happen? Would I have, had I known?

I took a deep drag of my smoke and slowly blew it out, staring up at ceiling, trying to sort out my twisted, roiling emotions. I had no idea how to answer those questions. This revelation turned my entire world upside down—one I'd barely established as somewhat stable—and I had absolutely no idea how to feel about it. Everything was still so new, so different, I hadn't even figured out who I really was yet.

And Riley was my oldest friend in the world. He was my best friend. I couldn't even think about him that way … could I? I rejected the thought automatically, shying away from the possibility. What Riley and I had was true, it was exasperating at times but it was just … timeless. How could either one of us dare to ruin it like that? I knew I couldn't. I cared too much about him to take such a terrible chance.

I pictured the dark, warm eyes of my friend as he gazed at me so often, with so much tenderness and affection. I thought of the deep bond between us, the impossible camaraderie we shared that enabled us to be totally honest and frank with each other. So what had prompted him to keep this of all secrets from me? Was it just embarrassment? Or was it something more?

What if … what if Riley loved me, like really loved me, more than a friend?

I shook my head, scoffing at the sheer ridiculousness of such a thought. I was agonizing over nothing. Riley didn't love me; there was no way he could, so there was nothing to worry about. I was just his friend—his best friend maybe, but only a friend. I mean, not two weeks after our one secret, stolen night—a night he hadn't even bothered enough to tell me about—Riley had found Emily, and now they were in love.

And then of course there was the biggest reason, the reason I couldn't seem to forget, or really forgive. Riley had left me. I blew out a drag of my smoke, relieved by that fact for the first time since it happened. Riley had left me behind so easily. Too easily. There was no way he could love me.

Was there?

For as long as I'd known him, I had never been so nervous to see my friend.

I was early. This time, I was the one waiting for him. I sat at the table in the little room, my legs crossed, my foot shaking restlessly. I lit yet another cigarette and looked up at the clock for the umpteenth time. He was late. I hoped nothing had happened. The roads were slick with ice this time of year and the snow falling lightly now could easily have hampered his vision. I prayed fervently that Riley hadn't been in an accident or something. I needed answers.

He finally arrived, whistling as he pushed his way through the door. He coughed in mock exaggeration and waved the smoke out of the air, a smile on his face.

"Smoke much?" Riley laughed, pausing in his stride to open the window a touch. The smoke wafted away and the cool, fresh air felt good on my heated cheeks.

"Yeah, I guess." I chuckled nervously. I waited while Riley hung up his coat and made himself a coffee. He sat down across the table and eyed me suspiciously.

"You okay?" He wondered, taking a sip from his cup. "You look pretty ramped up today."

"Do I?" I wiped my sweaty hands on the legs of my jeans and tried unsuccessfully to sound casual. "Huh."

"What's up Mac? You nervous about getting out? Only a few days left."

Oh, right. Five days until D-day. I had totally forgotten about it, my mind had been thoroughly occupied with … other things. But actually, I was nervous about getting out of rehab. I was afraid of having a choice. I was afraid I'd choose wrong.

"Yeah, I'm nervous." I admitted.

"Don't be." Riley shook his head. "The sober-living facility is supposed to be great. You'll be housed with other recovering addicts, people who understand where you're coming from. You'll be supported every step of the way."

"Yeah." I nodded. I tried to imagine my future living in the city, away from my family, away from Charlie and all my other friends. I'd have to get a job, I'd have to pay rent, and I'd have to … live again, for real. Sober. It all seemed fairly overwhelming. Especially since Riley wasn't going to be with me. That was the hardest part.

"How about you?" I asked him. "Are you excited to get back to school?"

"Yeah." He answered, but shrugged noncommittally. "I guess."

It seemed neither of us was eager to leave the other. I thought about that a moment, lighting another cigarette and biting my lip. I couldn't put it off any longer; I needed to talk to him about my dream. I needed some answers.

"So, I had this crazy dream last night." I started.

"Oh yeah? What about?"

"Uh … I don't know. We were at this party … I don't know where, but we were all totally loaded."

"Uh huh." Riley smirked. "That all seems plausible."

"Yeah, that part does, but then … man, this is crazy. You and I, we went upstairs—" I paused, watching as Riley stiffened, his dark eyes boring into mine, his hands suddenly tense around the coffee cup, " … and we … we like, made out." I finished.

The room was totally silent for a moment. I stared at my friend, and he stared back at me.

"Riley … this actually happened, didn't it?" I whispered, like I was afraid to say it out loud. Riley gazed up at me, his face totally blank. Then his head nodded ever so slightly. Yes.

I didn't really know what to say. I took a drag of my smoke. "I can't believe I didn't remember this until right now."

"You said you blacked out. From the Quaaludes." He answered evenly.

"I know. I think I did. But for some reason, now I remember almost everything." I shook my head in amazement. "This is huge, Riley. Why didn't you say anything to me?"

"I tried." He looked down at his hands. "But I was a coward. I wanted to talk to you about it, but you had no recollection. You seemed so happy that way, not knowing … though I always wondered if maybe you did remember, but pretended not to so we wouldn't have to deal with it." He shrugged. "I was afraid it'd ruin our friendship. I was afraid … I was afraid of a lot of things."

"Riley … did we …?" I bit my lip. I couldn't say the words. "Did we …?"

"No." He shook his head. "No. We were maybe about to ... but once we hit the bed, you passed out."

"Oh." My cheeks flushed red. "So I did pass out. That explains why I can't remember."

"Yeah."

"Well, you still could've told me about it."

"I wanted to ... but I didn't know what to do. You were so in love with Grey, and I knew I'd just ruin everything by telling you."

"Wait—" Suddenly I remembered that night at the Aurora, the first time I ever laid eyes on Grey and instantly fell in love with him. I remembered Riley wanting to tell me something; trying desperately to tell me something. "That night, at the concert. You were trying to tell me then, weren't you?"

"Yes." He admitted. "But I couldn't."

"I can't believe you." I sat back, fuming. "We kissed. We made out. This is huge, Riley. Were you ever going to tell me about it?"

"I don't know. Probably not."

"What? Why not?"

"Because. I mean, I feel bad enough that you don't remember. I didn't know you were on 'ludes at the time ...." He paused. "But honestly Mackenzie ... it was amazing. It was probably the most amazing night of my life, until you passed out." He met my gaze, his dark eyes smiling fondly. "I'm glad it happened, and I didn't want you to ... not be."

"What do you mean?" Oh why did I ask him that? I met Riley's gaze, terrified of what was coming next, just knowing somehow what he was about to say ....

"I mean ...." Riley took a deep breath, as if willing himself some courage. He looked me straight in the eyes. "What I mean is ... I'm in love with you Mackenzie." He admitted, rushing his words. "I've been in love with you for as long as I can remember. Being apart from you this year was torture for me, you'll never know how bad it was. And I know I may regret telling you this, and I know I might just be wrecking everything, and I know this is probably horribly inappropriate since your boyfriend died only three months ago, but I love you. There. I said it."

I stared at him. I blinked stupidly. My mind rejected his words automatically. I couldn't bear to hear them. I didn't want to hear them. They would ruin everything, they threatened our entire relationship.

I swallowed heavily. "What about Emily?"

Riley shook his head. "Emily's great. But you're the only one for me." He smiled and let out a breath of relief. "I've wanted to tell you this for so long."

I didn't know what to do, how to respond. I stared into space, trying to fathom what Riley was saying to me, trying to decide how to react. This was impossible. It couldn't be true. This was going to change everything.

"You don't love me Riley." I shook my head in vehement denial. "I mean, we kissed, we could've … become something. But then you just left. You left me. Maybe you feel some … some misplaced guilt for what's happened to me, or some sense of responsibility or something, but it's not love."

"Listen to me, Mackenzie." Seriously Riley took my hands in his, forcing me to look into his eyes, deep and sincere. "I will never forgive myself for leaving you. Ever. I can't say it was a mistake, because I had to do it … I guess I just wish it could've happened differently. I'm not asking you to understand. But believe me when I say this. I do love you. I love you." Riley squeezed my hand in his. It felt nice, like an anchor for my swirling emotions. I didn't know how to deal with them. I didn't know how to deal with this.

"I know it's a lot to take in, and I know it's not really fair for me to ask you this. Don't feel like you have to answer right away …."

"Riley don't—"

"I have to know, Mac. Now that it's out there, I have to know. Do you ever think—maybe not now, but one day—that you will ever feel the same way for me?" The words were rushed, like he had to get them out before he lost his nerve.

"Could you love me?"

I pulled my hand away from him, overcome. Tears filled my eyes. "Stop it, Riley. How can you expect me to answer that? I'm still in love with Grey!"

"I know. I know." He groaned, dropping his head into his hands.

"How could you do this to me?" I cried. "I need you so badly. So badly, you have no idea. Things will never be the same after this." The realization shook me to the core. Abruptly I got up to my feet. "I have to go."

"No, stay Mackenzie. Let's talk this out …."

"I can't." I shook my head, ripping my hands from his grasp and running for the door. By the time I made it to the hallway I was in a full sprint. I took off so Riley couldn't catch up—so he wouldn't be able to stop me—and I didn't pause until I was safe in my bedroom, breathless, the door shut on those terrible words and the threat they represented.

CHAPTER 68

At first I was mad at him. Angry, furious, livid. Red cheeked, I paced the meagre space of my little apartment in heated agitation. Why did Riley have to feel this way about me? Why did he have to tell me about it? Didn't he know this was going to ruin everything? That we'd never be the same again after this?

But as time went on my terrified anger slowly faded away, gradually surrendering itself to genuine compassion for my friend. I sat down on the edge of my bed, willing myself to breathe—to breathe and think rationally. Deep down I knew Riley couldn't help it, that he didn't want to wreck things between us. "*We can't help the ones we love, Mac*," he said over the phone that one time, when he'd called to wish me happy birthday. I thought he'd been referring to the Christian with that statement. But now I realized, in surprise, he must have been talking about me.

I shook my head and lit another cigarette, reluctantly impressed by the power of Riley's restraint. In awe of it, even. If he felt for me even an iota like I'd felt for Grey, it was amazing he'd held out this long. I remembered how recklessly, how impetuously I'd confessed my feelings for Grey, so moved by his charm and his talent that I couldn't even hold the words in. But not Riley. He'd kept the secret for years.

I sighed. That was classic Riley though. Always putting my feelings first. He saw how happy I was with Grey, so he denied himself; he suffered in silence for months so he wouldn't interfere with my delight, with my contentment, my happiness. Completely selfless. It was the true epitome of love.

It was touching. Flattering, even. But I didn't know if I could return that love. I didn't know if I could … feel that way about Riley. I mean, he was my world—my whole world at the moment—and I honestly couldn't say where I'd be without him. Dead in a back alley somewhere; or maybe like Allison, eagerly counting down the days until my next hit. Riley had cared enough to put me in rehab. He'd known enough to teach me about God. He'd loved me enough to try and save my life.

But he'd also left me. Maybe it was juvenile, but I couldn't get past that one harsh reality. Riley had left me. Just like that, we'd become like strangers to each other. I couldn't understand it, and for some reason, I couldn't forgive him for it either. How could he have done that to me? How could he claim to love me, and then just leave me like that?

I rested my head in my hands and blinked down at the floor for a moment, trying to get a handle on my thoughts and my feelings. I shut my eyes and prayed, hoping for some divine wisdom, some insight that would help us through this delicate situation with our relationship still intact.

Because I needed Riley dreadfully. That much I knew for certain. I just wanted to cling to him. For a terrible, tempting moment, I actually considered just ... pretending. Pretending to love him, pretending to feel the same way for him. If I did and he believed it ... then maybe he wouldn't leave. Maybe he'd stay with me, and then I'd never have to be alone. We'd never have to be apart ....

No, no, no. I shook the idea quickly from my mind, appalled by the notion, ashamed by the sheer depth of my selfishness. Riley truly loved me and there I was, thinking of ways to manipulate him to stay. I chuckled at myself in total disbelief, amazed that after all this time, I could still be so awful. Rehab hadn't changed that. Being sober hadn't changed that. Even God hadn't changed that, not yet. I was still selfish, still wrong. The only difference was now, I felt convicted by it.

It hurt. The guilt was actually painful. But like Riley said, it made me want to change. With a sigh, I walked over to the window and stared glumly out at the icy landscape beyond. Maybe for once in my life I could try to do something right. I could try to be good. I could try, for Riley. Shutting my eyes, I leaned against the cool brick wall and forced myself to think of him, pushing all my wants and needs and feelings to the side for once. What would be best for him? What would make him happiest, in the long run?

And in an instant, I knew I had the answer. I had to let Riley go.

It was the only thing left, the only thing that made sense. Until I knew for certain how I felt, until I knew if I could love him like he deserved, I had to let him go. But the prospect was daunting. I bit my lip, blinking back tears, my throat aching with every beat of my quaking heart. I knew it was the right thing to do. Something I had to do.

And the one thing I'd never been able to, no matter how hard I tried.

Last summer when Riley left me, the pain had been devastating. And this time, there'd be no Grey to cushion the blow of his absence. There'd be no drugs for me to use to hide from the hurt, to help push the tormenting thoughts and memories of Riley away. I'd have to live with it; I'd have to deal with it. Healthily, this time.

But I could do it for him. Couldn't I? Didn't I owe him that much? I may not have Grey to soothe me and I wouldn't have the drugs to ease the hurt … but I had God now. And I knew that borrowing his strength—somehow, someway—I would get through it. I knew that he would help me. And I knew that my friend, my best friend in the whole world, deserved whatever happiness I could afford him. After everything he'd done for me, I knew that Riley was worth it.

I loved him enough to let him go. I had to.

I kept this statement running through my head the next afternoon, as I forced myself—with heavy heart and dragging feet—down the hallway to the meeting room. I wasn't sure what to expect. I was nervous, anticipating inevitable awkwardness between us, afraid of what I was going to do. It felt so unnatural to be selfless, like a vegetarian suddenly having to down a t-bone. Against the grain. Wrong.

But somewhere deep, deep down, I knew it was right, too.

Riley gave me a hesitant smile as I came through the door. I studied his face a moment, grown so handsome over our time apart, so much older and mature—and felt the first icy stab of loneliness pierce into my soul. I tried to keep my expression blank and tried to calm my heart—overwrought with expectation of the pain—from hammering its way out of my ribs. With a shaky breath I sat down across from him, steeling my resolve, hardening my will.

"So." Riley cleared his throat a moment, shifting uncomfortably in his chair. He looked just as nervous as I was, but his dark eyes were still warm, gazing at me fondly.

"So." I repeated quietly. I had no idea how to start.

He smiled at me tentatively. "Mac, I owe you an apology."

I blinked. "You do?"

"Yeah." Riley cleared his throat.

"For what?"

"For yesterday. For our conversation." He let out a heavy breath. "Don't get me wrong. I don't regret telling you. I'm glad it's out there now. But I do regret … asking you … how you feel …."

"Riley—"

"No." He held up a hand, stopping me. "Please, don't say a word. Really. The whole drive home yesterday and all last night I just … thought about it. And I realized how … how cruel it was of me to ask you that question. So insensitive."

"Insensitive?" I frowned.

"Yes." Fervently Riley shook his head. "I mean, some friend I am. You have enough on your plate right now; you have enough to worry about without having to … agonize over us … over the state of our relationship. You know?" His dark eyes warmed to mine, his expression sheepish. "Mac, you don't have to answer that question. Not now. Not ever, if you don't want. Not until you're really ready."

He was silent for a long moment, waiting for me to look up at him. I gulped and worked up the nerve to meet those dark eyes—so familiar, so full of affection for me.

"Mackenzie, yesterday I told you I love you, and I meant every word." Riley continued. "And I'm going to be here for you, Mac. Anything you need, however you need me to be, whatever that entails. If you need a shoulder to cry on, or a friend, a best friend … or more …." He shrugged. "I'll be that for you. Just know that I'm … that I'm here, okay? That I'll always be here for you, no matter what."

There was definitely something wrong with me. Certainly any other girl in the world would have had their heart melted by this moving speech, but all I could feel was relief. I was nearly giddy with it. Things didn't have to change between us; things didn't have to be ruined. We could go back the way we were before his confession, before he asked me that terrible question. Like nothing ever happened. Gratefully, I looked up into the fathomless gaze of my best friend, meaning to thank him. But suddenly I couldn't speak.

He was looking at me so fondly, so sincerely … I almost couldn't bear to see it, the genuine love reflected in his deep, dark eyes. And I knew then with a sinking heart—no matter what happened or what Riley said to the contrary—that we could never go back. We could never be just friends again. Because he loved me. He really loved me.

Even now, as I furiously tried to blink back the tears, he was holding my hand and speaking such words of comfort—alleviating my every fear, putting to rest any doubt and uncertainty his confession may have caused.

"And, also …," he was saying, "I think you'll like this. I've decided to put off school until after the summer." He announced with a smile. "So I can come see you every day … maybe I can find a place in the city or something. I'll get a job while you're in sober-living, and then when you're out, I'll help you get settled …."

I couldn't listen anymore, I just couldn't. Not when he was promising me everything I'd ever wanted, speaking those words that—just like him—were too good to be true. The selfish part of me was heady with relief, warming instantly to the idea, straining for me to agree. It'd be so easy to give in, to say yes and let Riley put his life on hold for me. But I knew I couldn't let him. I knew it wouldn't be fair. He was doing this because he loved me. Truly loved me. And I … I ….

I had to let him go.

My eyes were burning with tears as I opened them, trying to strengthen my flimsy resolve. "Riley, no. Don't be crazy." I forced the words out. "You need to go back to school."

He stared at me, momentarily stunned. "… Why?"

"Because. You've put off your life for too long already."

"Mac, we've gone over this and over this." Riley rolled his eyes at me. "I told you already, that doesn't matter to me. I'm here for you."

"I know." God, this was hard. Harder than I'd ever imagined. I was torn. Half of me wanted to grab onto him, to hold on tight, to never let go. The other half … the other half just watched. Determined, strengthened somehow, her eyes shining with tears as she told her best friend to leave her. "I know you're here for me, and I'll never be able to thank you for everything you've done. But Riley … just … just trust me, okay? I've let this go on far too long already." I bit my lip. "You should go back to school."

He eyed me darkly. "Why? You don't need me anymore?"

"No," I shook my head vehemently. "No, that's not it, at all. I just … I want to do what's best for you, for once. You know? I mean, you've been so amazing to me. I want to return the favour."

"Really?" Riley chuckled, raising his eyebrows at me. "That doesn't sound like you."

"I know, right?" I laughed mirthlessly. "But I have to start somewhere."

"What if it's not your decision to make though? What if I want to stay?"

"No. You can't, Riley." I implored him. "Please. I mean, you're my best friend in the whole world, and the last thing I want to do is hurt you." I gazed up at him, my eyes wide and soft. "Can you just trust me? Trust me when I say … its better that you … go. I need you to go, Riley. Please?"

Riley just stared at me, defiant as he mulled over my words, like he wanted to argue with them. But then he stopped. I don't know what he saw in my gaze, I don't know what he read there. But then—like some terrible conclusion had taken place in his mind—he suddenly deflated, slumping down in his seat, casting his eyes down to the floor. My heart beat profusely in my chest as I watched him, wanting desperately to reassure him. I wanted to tell him how hard this was for me, how every single bone in my body was screaming for him to stay … but I knew I couldn't. There'd be no convincing him to go if he knew how much this hurt.

"Go back to school." My throat ached with the unshed tears burning down my throat, but I tried to smile for him. "Trust me Ry," I stated softly then, "I'm doing you a favour here."

"Yeah." Riley scoffed. "Sure." He muttered. And as he lifted his eyes back to mine, soft with hurt but still warm with affection, I knew he believed anything but.

The day had finally come. That morning, when I opened my eyes, I couldn't believe it. I couldn't believe it was all over. That day I was free. Rehab was done. I was going home.

Slowly I prepared myself in the bathroom—washing my face, combing my hair, applying my make-up, brushing my teeth. It took all my effort all morning to try and remain calm. I concentrated all my energies on the most mundane tasks, anything that would keep me from thinking about what was coming next. Finally I stood back, let out a shaky breath, and stared at myself in the mirror. I was done. I was finished.

But I was nowhere near ready.

My heart was pounding in my chest, and not with excitement. I should've been like Allison, jumping off the walls excited at the prospect of going home. I think most people usually were. But I wasn't. I was anything but excited. Terrified, more like. When once these walls had seemed stifling and claustrophobic, now I would've given anything to stay within the safety of their confines, away from the world waiting at the doorstep.

It wasn't to be though. Riley was coming to take me home, back to my parents. I was anxious about seeing them again too, I didn't know what to expect, how to act, who to be around them now. But nothing could make me so nervous as just the thought of being out on my own. A pit of anxiety gnawed at my stomach. As if taunting me, the craving for heroin flared up inside, like it knew we'd taste fresh air again soon; like it knew that nothing but my own willpower would stop me from finding some dope and injecting it straight into my veins. It was testing my strength, trying to make me cave. I prayed fervently that somehow, somewhere, I'd find the will not to give in.

"Hey," there was a gentle rapping on my door. "Are you decent?"

"Oh, hey Ry." I grabbed my make-up off the counter and headed back into my bedroom. The instant I saw him, I smiled. I couldn't help myself; he just had that affect on me. His very presence was comforting. Already I could feel myself relaxing, could feel myself strengthened, could feel the tension ease.

But things had still been understandably … different between us lately. I had given it a lot of thought over the last few days, a lot more than I expected to. I found it was nice to realize—just in the middle of whatever I was doing—that Riley loved me. I'd stop, and I'd remember, and the thought would make me smile. I mean, who wouldn't want to be loved? It didn't mean anything; it was just really nice to … know.

That was the pro of the situation. The con was the sudden awkwardness that would spring up between us, the constant elephant in the room. With every word we spoke to each other, there was no forgetting what he'd said and what I'd said and what had happened—like a white noise in the background, there no matter how we tried to ignore it. Every look, every moment of silence spoke volumes.

Riley loves Mackenzie, but she's making him leave.

And I was. Riley was going—he was getting on a plane that very night, heading back to school. In my deepest heart I knew it would be better that way. He'd forget me soon enough. Maybe … maybe he and Emily would even get married. I frowned darkly at the thought, shuddering, deciding instantly that I hated the idea.

"Mac?"

I shook my head and gave him a smile. "Sorry … I was just …."

"Stressing?" He smiled knowingly at me. I felt my cheeks blush crimson and nodded guiltily.

"Yeah. Stupid, right?"

"Not at all. A little fear is good. It shows you want the right things."

"Does it?"

"I don't know." Riley smiled. "Just trying to sound wise."

"Oh." I tried to laugh, but it sounded strained. I threw some last minute things into the suitcase lying open on my bed and then zipped it up. It reminded me vaguely of my birthday, when Riley had called me out of the blue and then I decided—in a panic—that I had to see him. How I'd been desperate to see him. Until I remembered Emily.

"You look really pretty today, Mac." Riley stated suddenly, interrupting my hateful thoughts his warm, familiar voice. I could feel his eyes on me.

His words were flustering. I felt my cheeks blush even redder, but secretly I was glad he noticed. It was sick actually … it was really wrong of me, but I couldn't help it. Riley had professed to love me, and though I couldn't return the sentiment—though I knew it wasn't really fair—for some reason, I didn't want him to stop loving me, either. The two opposing sides of me were constantly warring with each other. But today—knowing that my time with Riley was dwindling—I'd given in to the selfish side. I'd actually put some real effort into myself, mostly because I needed something to preoccupy my thoughts, but also because I wanted to look … good for him.

My make-up was all done and my hair hung in curls around my shoulders. My clothes were still a little baggy, but not as loose as they had been. I wore blue jeans, my old black skater shoes, my blue Three Stones fireball shirt and a grey zip-up hoodie overtop. It seemed right—comfortable and fitting, an outfit I used to wear all the time before Charlie took me under her wing and totally glammed me up. It was more … me.

"You mean, I don't look as scared as I feel?" I asked in an attempt to act causal. Riley picked up my suitcases and flashed me a grin.

"I didn't say that."

I laughed and followed him to the doorway. There, I turned and cast one long, last look at my old room—at my old life, over now. I sighed and flicked off the light, and then shut the door behind me.

I said all my goodbyes to the staff and to some of the other girls, to my group leader and my old, decrepit therapist. They all wished me the best and gave me many words of encouragement, approving my decision to move into a sober-living facility before totally striking out on my own.

It was the best chance I had for staying sober. I had to take it. I needed all the help I could get.

So then—armed with a deep, exciting and newfound love for God, the various coping skills I'd been taught and ninety days of sober living under my belt—I was released back into society. It was the beginning of April. I breathed deeply the air outside; softer now that the harsh crust of winter was spent. It was still cold out, but the sun's rays held some warmth. I could feel the promise of spring in the air as Riley loaded my bag into the back of his car. The promise of life. Of renewal.

"Ready for this?" He asked me with a grin. At once, I felt a familiar pang of regret as he looked at me. Dressed now for the weather, Riley wore a dark red toque and wide black sunglasses. When he smiled at me I barely recognized him; he was just so … handsome, so grown up. I dropped my gaze before he could see the sudden sadness in my expression. If only I felt something for him, this would all be so much easier.

"Yeah." I lied, forcing a smile. "So ready."

I didn't realize how uptight I was until Riley pointed out my clenched fists in the car. I looked down at my lap and relaxed my hands, giggling nervously. We were only about ten minutes from my parents' house, and each mile made my heart thud that much harder. I was so afraid to be home, afraid to be back in town, afraid of the familiarity that could bring back much of my heartbreak. Afraid of the sights and sounds and smells that would make me want to use again. Even though I was only going to be back home for a night—until my room at the SLF was ready—the interminable hours stretched before me, overwhelming with the opportunities they presented.

Riley pulled the car up at the curb in front of my house. My home was the same as always, but it still looked … different, somehow. Marcy and Greg's black Jag was in the driveway. The snow was melting off the roof, dripping down the eavestrough. The sky above was still grey, but the wind had turned warm in classic Chinook form.

"It looks like it might rain." I noticed, staring up at the sky, attempting to act casual—normal—although my heart was hammering away in my ribs. I wiped my sweaty palms against my jeans and let out a shaky breath.

"Yeah, it does. Better than snow, anyway." Riley looked up at the sky as well, playing along with me. I stared at him a moment, suddenly overtaken by just how badly I was going to miss him.

"I wish you didn't have to go." I blurted foolishly.

His dark eyes were serious on my face. "I don't have to, you know."

"No. You do. You do." Furiously, I blinked back my tears. "I'm sorry, I shouldn't have said …." I couldn't finish my sentence.

Riley looked down at the steering wheel, his jaw clenching. "Don't cry Mac, please?"

"I'm sorry." I sniffed. "I just … I wouldn't have made it without you … you know?"

"Yeah … well, you stay sober, and we're even." He smiled then, trying to lighten the mood. "Deal?"

I nodded, biting my lip to try and hold back the tears. This was still fairly new to me, having to deal with the pain. Before, whenever I hurt—for whatever reason—I would go and get high and therefore solve all my problems. But now, I felt the full scorch of the pain burning my lungs, throbbing in my chest. There was nothing I could do but feel it. It hurt. It was deep, aching. Hollow.

"I don't want to say goodbye to you." I admitted.

Riley was silent a moment. "Come on, Mac. Your family's waiting."

Somehow, I managed to get out of the car. I felt like I didn't have the strength to stand, my heart was pounding so profusely, aching so abominably. I stood by helplessly as Riley grabbed my suitcase from the trunk. Sensing my hesitation and always caring for me more than himself—always putting my feelings above his own, Riley took my hand in his and led me up the walkway.

"You can do this Mac. I believe in you." He squeezed my hand.

"Yeah …" But there was no confidence in my voice. I focused on his hand around mine, trying to draw some strength from him, holding on to everything I could until the terrible moment when he left.

We stopped before the door and Riley set my bag down on the stoop. I gazed up at him, into the eyes of my best and oldest friend, and the pain was so bad I felt like I couldn't breathe. I held on to my resolve by a tenuous thread. It'd be so easy to ask him to stay ….

"Goodbye, Mackenzie." He managed a smile, but I could see that he was hurting too, that this goodbye was just as hard for him. He loved me, after all.

"Goodbye, Riley." I choked out. The tears were coming, I couldn't stop them.

Tenderly, he stroked my cheek, and I leaned my face against the warmth of his palm. With my eyes locked in his dark gaze, Riley bent towards me agonizingly slow, and then gently, he kissed me. It was light, and his touch was soft, and his sweet breath on my tongue was warm and familiar. But with it came … something else. Something totally unexpected. Like a quick jolt of electricity that barrelled through me. A spark. No—bigger than a spark. A current. When Riley pulled away from me I couldn't fathom it. I just stood there, stunned into a stupor, blinking before me, reeling from the new sensation.

And then I realized that he was gone. I looked for him, gasping, watching his broad back as he made his way down the flagstone steps and back towards his car. What the hell was that? I didn't know what to do. I felt like I should stop him, but I didn't know why. I didn't know what to say. I didn't have time to decide.

I took a step towards him, my limbs trembling with uncertainty. He was at the car now. All I had to do was call for him; all I had to do was shout for him to stop. I opened my mouth but no words came, no sound. I was frozen, rooted in place by the sheer depth of my indecision, grounded by my hesitation … like I was in a nightmare or something.

I heard the door open behind me. "Mackenzie?"

I gulped, tearing my eyes from Riley's form, sparing a terrible moment to turn around and find my mother's smiling face, beaming in her exuberance when she spotted me there on the step.

"You're home." She smiled through her tears, swept me up into her arms and hugged me as tightly as she could. I hugged her back, resting my face against her soft, warm shoulder; holding back my tears, trying to find some solace in her embrace from the sudden turmoil of my emotions. I just didn't know what to do. I was so confused, so … unsure.

Then, with a sinking heart, I heard Riley start the car behind us. I heard him put it in drive, heard him pull out onto the street; heard the sound of his engine slowly fading away into the distance. And I knew that he was gone. I knew that Riley had left me, again, but for good this time.

Mom smiled at me through her tears. "Honey, I'm so proud of you." Gently, she stroked my hair back from my face, her eyes shining with sincerity. "I've missed you so much." And instinctively I knew that she didn't just mean the last three months.

I'd been gone for years.

Mom put an arm around me and led me into the house. I followed eagerly, welcoming any distraction from the utter upheaval of my emotions, no matter how awkward it might be. I tried to sniff back my sadness as I entered, my distress. All along I'd known how hard it would be when

Riley actually left, but I had anticipated some … victory, some relief in it as well. Like peace—knowing I had done something selfless for once, something right.

All I felt now was panic. I had to fight the urge to turn and run out the front door, to run straight to Riley's house and take it all back. To do or say anything to make him cancel his flight and stay.

Why is it so hard Riley? Why is it so hard to let you go?

I forced myself to ignore it, forced a smile on my face; forced myself to focus on the rest of my family, waiting in the living room beneath a "Welcome Home Mackenzie!" banner that hung across the mantle of the fireplace. Marcy was there, and Greg, and my dad—and from the moment we walked in the door, they were all beaming at me.

Dad came right over and hugged us both, kissing my hair, tears shining in his eyes. He passed me over to Marcy, who whispered in my ear how impressed she was by what I'd done. And even Greg—in an awkward, brother-in-law kind of way—hugged me to him with great sincerity and told me that I'd been missed.

I couldn't have asked for a better reception. It reminded me of Christmas—before my parents had caught me using in their bathroom. I felt like I was accepted again, like I was truly loved. For real this time. I sat down on the couch and we caught up on the last three months. I did most of the talking, but my family hung on every word, like they'd never expected to hear me speak again, like every sentence was a special gift. I wasn't used to such attention; it was … touching. Nothing was really said about Grey, but it didn't have to be. I knew they were all truly, deeply sorry for my loss. I knew now that they wanted nothing but my happiness.

I had much to say to them. In treatment, I had made it to step six and seven, and now it was time to make my amends. Tearfully, I apologized for everything I'd ever done. For lying and sneaking out, for my terrible attitude, for stealing their money, for ruining Marcy's wedding … for everything. I wouldn't let myself stop until every guilty thought within my heart was brought into the light. And when I was done, I knew I was forgiven. I knew that we could start again with a clean slate. I knew I had a family that loved me, a family I felt lucky to be a part of.

It was such a weight off my shoulders. When we sat down to dinner, the conversation around me was light and happy, like I should've been. My confessions had been difficult, but they were over, and I should have been relieved. I sat back and tried to join in the talk around the table, tried to revel in the aura of celebration around me. But I couldn't. I'd been bothered all afternoon, nagged at by a dreadful knot of worry gnawing away at my stomach. One I just couldn't ignore, no matter how I tried.

I couldn't stop thinking about Riley.

"So, where's Riley?" Mom wondered suddenly, as if reading my mind. "I thought I'd see him here for dinner."

I stared at her a moment, my forkful of pot-roast halfway to my mouth. I raised my eyebrows. "Uh ... you did?"

"Yes." She smiled warmly at me. "I know he's been visiting you. He comes here almost every day after seeing you, to let us know how you're doing."

I couldn't contain my surprise. "He doesn't."

"Yes, he does. And I invited him for supper tonight too ... but I guess he had plans?"

"Yeah ... he's ... he's heading back to school tonight." I mumbled.

Mom nodded, and then looked down at her plate, seemingly embarrassed. "I actually have an apology to make, too, Mackenzie. I'm sorry. I was wrong about Riley." She looked up again, meeting my eyes. "He's a fine young man. And I really need to call his mother." She added as an afterthought.

I looked despairingly at Marcy. "Seriously? Where's my real mom?"

"I know." Marcy laughed. "But trust me, that's her."

"Riley really came here every day?" I asked in amazement, intrigued. "What did you talk about? What did he say?"

"He just told us how you were doing. Some days not so good, other days really good, most days, in between." Mom winked at Marcy. "But almost everyday, he said you were more beautiful than ever."

"He didn't." My instant reaction was to deny it all.

"No, Mac, he did." Marcy nodded at me with a smile. "Seriously."

I looked down at my baked potato and speared at it uneasily with my fork. I could feel my cheeks betraying me, could feel the crimson blush staining my skin. Mom and Marcy exchanged a secret, knowing glance, like they thought Riley's sweetness was to blame for my sudden discomfit. I mean, it was—but not only that ... it was just ... everything. The sudden sinking feeling deep in my soul that told me I had done the wrong thing by making Riley leave. The fearful, nagging voice in my head that insisted it was the only way. And then on top of everything else, the kiss I couldn't seem to stop thinking about. The crazy, unexpected spark that had erupted between us and totally blew my mind, totally threw my whole being off its well-intended course.

Anxiously, I bit my lip and let my fork fall with a clatter on my near empty plate. My heart was pounding and a panicked sweat ran cold over my tensed limbs. I just didn't know what to do, and time was running out. I needed to talk to someone about it, someone who knew me, someone who'd understand, who'd really get the situation.

The person I needed was Riley. But he was out of the question, and without him, there was no one left. No one left to talk to, no one left to turn to ….

No. That wasn't true. My eyes widened as a sudden thought occurred to me—a horribly dangerous, wonderfully appealing idea. Of course. Charlie. I had Charlie. She knew me, she'd understand. Once upon a time, we had told each other everything. And suddenly, I was desperate to see my old friend again. To talk to her, to laugh with her, to let her know how badly she'd been missed. To hear from her lips the answer to my problems.

And she was so close now ….

"Mom, do you mind if I go out for a bit?" I asked abruptly. "There's something I need to do."

Everyone around the table stopped and looked at me cautiously. I chuckled to myself. "I'm not going to get high." I reassured them. "I just need to go … see someone."

Mom tried really hard not to offend me. "Who, sweetie?" She asked warily.

"Riley." I answered quickly the first name that came to my head, the only name I could say without arousing further suspicion. It wasn't really a lie … I was going to go see someone *about* Riley. It was basically the same thing.

"Oh." Mom nodded, smiling knowingly, even managing a wink towards my older sister. Everyone around the table relaxed. Everyone but me. I bit my lip restlessly.

"Do you want to take your car, hon?" Dad asked. "The keys are next to the door."

"No, it's okay. I think I'll walk." I got up and grabbed my jacket, quickly shrugging into it. "It's still pretty nice outside."

"Okay."

"Don't be too long, honey." Mom admonished.

"I won't." I promised. With a quick wave, I headed out the door.

I lit a smoke as I walked. Charlie lived down by Riley, by the trailer park, so I had a way to go. The cool air helped clear my head, helped calm my racing heart. But I still felt oddly … frantic. Like I needed to hurry, like I needed to get to Charlie's house before I realized just how stupid I was being, hurtling recklessly towards the exact situation that I'd feared—the people, the substance … the temptation. But my mind was made up. Charlie could help me; I knew it. I couldn't go back now. I quickened my steps and tried to distract myself—tried to ignore the quiet, urging voice of reason within me—focusing instead on the streets I passed by, taking in the sights of my old, familiar town.

A wave of nostalgia hit me as I walked. I realized wistfully that although I had grown up here, although I had lived my entire life here, already it didn't feel like home to me. Everything looked the same, but it was all … different now. Like something had changed in the last three months I'd been away … something I couldn't name, but definitely couldn't ignore.

I threw my smoke into the street, put my head down, and hurried on.

CHAPTER 69

My heart was pounding nervously as I finally approached Charlie's apartment. I knew that Riley wouldn't approve of what I was doing. I knew that my sponsor would be having a shit-fit. But I needed to see my friend. I just wanted to talk to her, that's all. I wasn't going to get high, I wouldn't even smoke weed or have a drink. I just wanted to talk.

I trudged up the old, icy, treacherous stairs, bombarded by memories as I knocked on the door. How many times had I fled up these steps, drunk, high … a bit of both. I bit my lip uncertainly as I heard slow, sluggish footsteps coming to the entry.

"Holy shit! It's Mackenzie!" Charlie exclaimed with as much enthusiasm as she could muster, her beautiful face lighting up at the sight of me. I expected to feel the same happiness in seeing her, but the moment the door opened I felt stricken—felt my heart sinking heavily in my chest. I managed a smile though, and stepped inside the apartment, accepting Charlie's exuberant hug.

"Baby, you look good." She decided, giving me a once over. "Rehab has done wonders, hey?" Charlie giggled. "Hey guys, look who it is!"

Charlie was high, I could tell. I looked over into the living room. Alex was there—wasted—with Courtney leaning drowsily over his lap. Were they together now? And Zack was sprawled across the couch. He looked up at me and smiled hazily.

"Mac, how've you been?" Zack was the only one capable of speech.

I couldn't answer. I looked wildly around the room. Once it had been homey and comforting, but now it seemed dirty … dark, depressing. Needles were scattered across the coffee table. Beer bottles were upturned on every surface. The entire room bespoke of gloom, of oppression and just

… desperation. Even Charlie—as beautiful as she was—I saw in a different light. Her blue eyes were glazed over, her tiny frame sunken in. My spirit squirmed within me, my soul revolted, and it took everything I had not to run straight out of the room. I couldn't be there. I loved Charlie, I loved Alex and Zack, but I couldn't be there. The air was thick with despair; I could feel it in every breath I took, choking me with its heaviness, with its misery.

Now that I had seen the light, the darkness was blinding.

My craving roared to life within me, like gas thrown on a fire, but now there was no power in its demand. Because I knew, that I knew, that I just couldn't do it. That it wasn't for me, not anymore. It was terrifying—empowering—but for the first time in my life, I knew what was right. I knew which way to go, which direction to choose, which course would bring me life. And all of them lead me away from there. Far, far away from there.

"I'm so glad you're back, man, I've missed you." Charlie smiled. "Here, let me take your coat."

"No." I shrunk away from her. "No … I've gotta go."

"What?" She blinked at me. "But you just got back."

"I know." I didn't know how to explain it to her. I didn't want to hurt her. "I'm sorry Charlie, but I have to go. I can't stay here."

Her eyebrows creased together. "What do you mean, you can't stay here? What are you, too good for us now?" She seemed genuinely offended.

"No. No. Charlie, I love you." I insisted. "I just have to go."

"Fine. Go then." She scoffed, crossing her arms. "What's stopping you?"

Nothing. Nothing was stopping me. I hugged her abruptly—she was stiff with anger in my arms—and then I hastened for the door. I felt terrible for doing this to them, to her, but I couldn't explain it. As badly as I wanted to be their friend, as badly as I would miss them, I knew that past was forever off limits to me now.

It was then I realized what had irrevocably changed over the last three months.

Me.

My steps were heavy as I made my way down the rickety old stairs, saddened by my discovery, resigned to it. I knew it was inevitable—necessary, even—but still I wished it could be different. I wished I could be friends with them and live my new life as well. It was impossible though, they just weren't for me anymore—none of it was. I knew that now.

With a sigh, I sat down on the bottom step and lit a cigarette, just as the first drops of rain began to fall, pattering around me. And suddenly, like the rain, it hit me. Suddenly, I understood. Why Riley had left me all those months ago, how he could've left me, even though he loved me. It was the same as Charlie and I. I wanted to stay with her, I loved her, but I couldn't. I just couldn't ….

"Holy shit!" I exclaimed in surprise, abruptly getting to my feet, gasping at the realization that shook my entire world. It hit me like a ton of bricks, like a kick in the guts. Riley had left me; he left me because he had to. But then he came back. He came back because he loved me.

And I loved him. I loved him.

It took mere seconds before I was running down the street, as fast as I could—desperate, fighting the ice slick with rain, fighting the clock. How could I not have realized? How could I have ignored it for so long? Of course I loved Riley. Hadn't I always loved Riley? I'd loved him forever, but I'd been fighting it this whole time. Blocking it all out on purpose, for fear that it would ruin the best thing I'd ever known. That it would wreck us permanently.

But now, a new fear fuelled my aching muscles; pushed them to keep moving. I was panicked, terrified by my actions, afraid that I had made the biggest mistake of my life telling Riley to leave. I loved him—I knew that now, and I would love him with everything that remained of my broken, selfish heart. It was all I had, but it was all for him, and he needed to know that. He had to know that before he got on the plane.

I turned the corner of his block, slowing in tangible relief when I saw his car was still there, parked in the drive. It was idling noisily, ready to go—I had barely made it. But there was still time. Time for me to say what I had to say, time for him to hear what he had to hear. My heart was hammering in my chest as I approached, my lungs burning from the effort. But I had made it.

I was soaked but I didn't feel the cold. My dark hair hung damp around my shoulders, curly from the rain. My face was pelted with the icy drops. My jeans were wet up to the knees from the frantic puddles I had jumped through. But it was worth it. I ran up to Riley just as he loaded his suitcase into the trunk.

"Mackenzie?" He looked up at me in surprise and slammed the trunk shut. "What the hell are you doing here?"

I stopped before him, panting, totally winded, and took a moment to catch my breath. I braced my hands on my knees.

"I need to stop smoking." I wheezed.

"Yeah, I'll say." Riley chuckled. "What's going on?"

I wiped the rain from my face. "I just … I need to tell you something. Can we …?" I motioned to his car. "Can we talk?"

"Sure." He looked confused; his dark eyes gazed over me with concern. "Is everything okay?"

"No." I answered, opening the passenger door of his car. "It's not okay."

We climbed into the car and shut the doors. The rain pattered lightly on the windshield, tinny on the roof. We sat in silence for a moment. I could feel Riley's eyes on me, but I couldn't start, not yet. Instead, I studied the familiar interior of his car—the purple velour upholstery, the cracked, broken dashboard. I rubbed my hand over it, smiling wistfully. All the hours we'd spent in this vehicle together, cruising aimlessly, getting high, laughing, talking, fighting, arguing. It felt right that it should happen here, the culmination of our relationship. It was poetic, almost.

"Mac, come on." Riley shook his head in exasperation. "You're killing me here."

I blurted it shamelessly. "I went over to Charlie's house."

"You did what?"

I knew he'd be pissed. It made me smile, knowing him so well.

"Why the hell did you do that? After all you've been through … after all your work? That was so stupid." He shook his head in avid disappointment. "I can't believe you. I can't believe you'd just throw it all away like that."

I rolled my eyes. "Will you calm down? I didn't get high or anything. I just wanted to see her again, you know? I missed her. I missed them."

"Oh." Riley relaxed in his seat, letting out a breath of relief. "Well, it was still stupid of you. You knew what they'd be doing. You knew what they'd have there."

"I know." I relented. "I know it was stupid. And the moment I walked in the door … I felt it. Such … unease. I could feel how … how wrong it was. The entire atmosphere of that room was so, heavy. Like, life sucking. Suffocating. I don't know. I don't really know how to describe it." I shook my head, blinking back to the present. "I just knew I couldn't be there anymore. I knew that life wasn't for me anymore."

"Yeah?"

"Yeah." I took a deep breath. This was the hard part. I bit my lip and looked over at my friend, at my best friend, at the man who knew me in every single way. He'd seen me at my best; he'd seen me at my worst. And still, somehow—he loved me.

"I get it now, Riley. I get why you couldn't be with me, why you had to leave me last summer. But it hurt me, deeply, and I've held it against you ever since."

"I'm sorry, Mac, I—"

"No. Let me finish." I stopped him, gathering my courage. "I know now that you couldn't help it. I know that you … that you still loved me, even though you had to leave."

Riley nodded silently.

"And I know why it hurt me so badly. Why I couldn't take the pain … why I've been so … unreasonably angry with you about it."

"You do?"

"Yeah." I nodded, and took a breath. "I love you, Ry."

Riley stopped. He just stared at me, stunned into silence.

So I continued.

"Every part of me loves you." I admitted. "I think I have forever, I don't know, but I just realized it now. It's not like Grey … it's not more than Grey, it's not less than Grey … I can't even compare the two of you. It's just different. But it's the same, too. It's … it's … deeper, because I know you so well … and you know me …." I gazed up into his warm, dark eyes—eyes I'd never been able to live without. "You know me better than anyone." I grasped his hand. "You're my … my breath. Riley, you saved my fucking life."

He didn't speak. He didn't answer. He just smiled and pulled me to him, into his warm, strong arms, and then he kissed me like our lives depended on it. It felt so right, so natural. And the spark from before ignited like I never thought possible, like I never could have imagined until—even despite being soaked from the rain—it felt like we might both start on fire. The feel of his lips, the taste of them … I couldn't get enough.

When at last he released me, I smiled up at him, staring breathlessly into his handsome face. As happy as I was, I felt I had to say it.

"You know there are a million reasons why this won't work out, don't you?"

"Really." He smiled, humouring me. "Name one."

"We fight, like, constantly."

"Hmm …." He kissed me again, lightly. "That just means we're communicating."

I lost my concentration for a moment. I couldn't believe that Riley could have such an effect on me. I couldn't be close enough to him. I took my hand and weaved it into his, lacing our fingers together. "And, I don't want to be the one to tell you this," I grinned, "but you are *really* bossy."

"Only because you're so stubborn."

"Plus, really, you're kind of a square now. What are we going to do for fun? I mean, you don't even swear anymore. When was the last time you dropped the F-bomb, huh?"

"Mackenzie?"

"Yeah?"

"Shut up." Riley smiled, and he looked down at me then like I was his greatest wish come true. His look said it all; his look took my breath away. When he kissed me, I smiled. I knew that none of it mattered. There may've been reasons why we wouldn't work, but I knew why we would. Because we were Riley and Mackenzie.

Because we belonged together.

"I love you so much." I whispered. Every time I said it, the realization shook me. I ran my hands through his hair and stroked his smooth cheek and revelled in the warmth of his arms around me. Mine to discover. Mine forever.

"Let's go inside. Get you some dry clothes." He grinned, kissing my hand, holding my gaze as he took the key out of the ignition. The engine shuddered into silence.

"But, aren't you going to miss your plane?" I eyed the clock warily, instantly saddened by the thought. I was the one who told him to go; who forced him to leave. I knew I had no right to ask, but I just couldn't help myself. I wanted him too badly.

"Please don't go Riley." I blurted pleadingly. "Please stay with me."

Riley chuckled fondly then, and tucked a lock of long, wet hair behind my ear, his fingers lightly brushing my cheek. "Mackenzie, I've waited years for you to say you love me." He grinned wickedly. "If you think I could leave you now, you're fucking insane."

And for that, I had no argument.

THE END

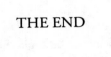

EPILOUGE

People say that God doesn't work miracles anymore. They long for the Bible days, desperate to witness the hand of God moving in obvious ways like he did back then. Holding the sun in the sky, turning water to wine, raising people from the dead. But I know better. I know God works miracles. He worked one in me.

Once upon a time, I was lost. Lost; but blind to my aimlessness. Searching desperately, seeking always for something to satisfy my soul, for something to fill me up. Looking and striving and toiling in vain for the answer.

Who knew I would find what I was looking for, the second I stopped searching.

I've never been worth saving. I'll never be worth saving. I thank God every day for his grace, for stretching out his hand and pulling me from the mire of my life, the mess I had created, and saving me.

Sometimes I can't fathom it, but luckily for me, he doesn't feel that way. He loves me like no other, like no other love I've ever found. Like the sky, stretching far off into distant space, ever reaching, never stopping … that's like his love for me. It's incomprehensible. How? Why? How could someone so unworthy be worth saving, worth loving? From the mountaintops I want to shout out all the great things he's done for me.

I'll write them down instead.

I wish that there were words to fully describe it … I hope you know what I'm speaking of. He is it. The purpose for everything. The reason. Like a great treasure, far off in the distance, beaming brightly, drawing you near. More than gold and silver and all the riches of the earth. When you find him, you find peace. Joy. Salvation. And for the rest of your life, you rejoice in your treasure. You thank the Lord for drawing your feet down the path that lead you to him. The moment he speaks to you, your life will change completely. The moment you reach out for him, you'll never be the same.

I don't know how else to explain it. It's nothing wild and hyper-spiritual or odd or crazy. It's just God. Believing in God. Believing in Jesus. Believing that I'm saved.

I'm going to be battling this addiction for the rest of my life. I know that. I've accepted it. God doesn't magically take away all your problems. But he helps you deal. He can help you with anything. All you have to do is ask.

All day long, I see people struggling. Succumbing to their sickness, defeated by their weakness, helpless in their obsessions. Addicted. So I tell them my story, in hopes that it will save them, somehow. It's the only way I know.

God saved me in a real way, and I know He can save them too.

And he can save you, if you'll let him.